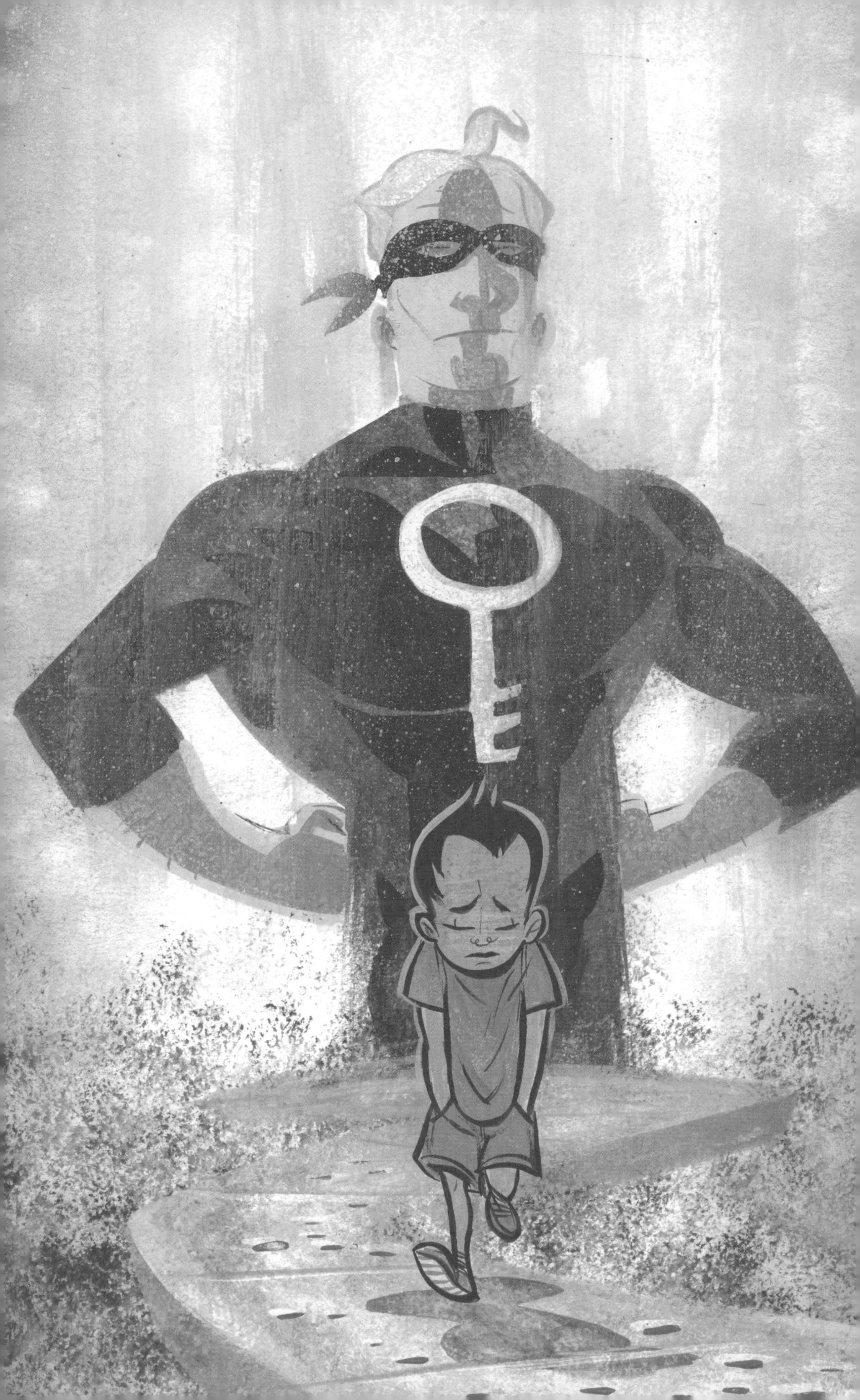

# MICHAEL CHABON'S

# The ESCAPIST™

## AMAZING ADVENTURES

### *Writers & Artists*

KYLE BAKER   EDUARDO BARRETO   DAN BRERETON
MICHAEL CHABON   HOWARD CHAYKIN   GENE COLAN
STEVE CONLEY   ALEM ĆURIN   ALEX DE CAMPI
JED DOUGHERTY   MICHAEL T. GILBERT   GLEN DAVID GOLD
DEAN HASPIEL   PAUL HORNSCHEMEIER   KEN KRISTENSEN
TONY LEONARD   STEVE LIEBER   VAL MAYERIK
KEVIN MCCARTHY   STUART MOORE   C. SCOTT MORSE
JAMES PEATY   HARVEY PEKAR   M.K. PERKER
ROGER PETERSON   BILL SIENKIEWICZ   JIM STARLIN
BRIAN K. VAUGHAN   ERIC WIGHT   PHIL WINSLADE

### *Cover Artists*

EDUARDO BARRETO   JOHN CASSADAY
ROGER PETERSON   DEAN HASPIEL

INSPIRED BY
*THE AMAZING ADVENTURES OF KAVALIER & CLAY*
BY MICHAEL CHABON

**DARK HORSE BOOKS**

*President & Publisher*
**MIKE RICHARDSON**

*Series Editor*
**DIANA SCHUTZ**

*Series Assistant and Associate Editors*
**KATIE MOODY, AARON WALKER**

*Collection Editor*
**FREDDYE MILLER**

*Collection Assistant Editors*
**KEVIN BURKHALTER, BRETT ISRAEL**

*Collection Designer*
**PATRICK SATTERFIELD**

*Digital Art Technician*
**ADAM PRUETT**

MICHAEL CHABON'S THE ESCAPIST™: AMAZING ADVENTURES

This volume collects stories and prose from the Dark Horse comic book series *The Amazing Adventures of The Escapist*, originally published 2004 through 2005, as well as additional previously unpublished stories and prose pieces.

Published by Dark Horse Books
A division of Dark Horse Comics, Inc.
10956 SE Main Street
Milwaukie, OR 97222

DarkHorse.com

To find a comics shop in your area, visit: comicshoplocator.com

International Licensing: 503-905-2377

First edition: January 2018
ISBN 978-1-50670-405-0

10 9 8 7 6 5 4 3 2 1
PRINTED IN CHINA

NEIL HANKERSON EXECUTIVE VICE PRESIDENT TOM WEDDLE CHIEF FINANCIAL OFFICER RANDY STRADLEY VICE PRESIDENT OF PUBLISHING NICK McWHORTER CHIEF BUSINESS DEVELOPMENT OFFICER MATT PARKINSON VICE PRESIDENT OF MARKETING DAVID SCROGGY VICE PRESIDENT OF PRODUCT DEVELOPMENT DALE LaFOUNTAIN VICE PRESIDENT OF INFORMATION TECHNOLOGY CARA NIECE VICE PRESIDENT OF PRODUCTION AND SCHEDULING MARK BERNARDI VICE PRESIDENT OF BOOK TRADE AND DIGITAL SALES KEN LIZZI GENERAL COUNSEL DAVE MARSHALL EDITOR IN CHIEF DAVEY ESTRADA EDITORIAL DIRECTOR SCOTT ALLIE EXECUTIVE SENIOR EDITOR CHRIS WARNER SENIOR BOOKS EDITOR CARY GRAZZINI DIRECTOR OF SPECIALTY PROJECTS LIA RIBACCHI ART DIRECTOR VANESSA TODD DIRECTOR OF PRINT PURCHASING MATT DRYER DIRECTOR OF DIGITAL ART AND PREPRESS MICHAEL GOMBOS DIRECTOR OF INTERNATIONAL PUBLISHING AND LICENSING

# CONTENTS

# CONTENTS

# INTRODUCTION

## BY MICHAEL CHABON

I STILL REMEMBER THE FIRST ESCAPIST COMIC I EVER CAME ACROSS. It appears to have been one of the later Fab Comics issues, from 1968, though I did not discover it until four or five years later, at the bottom of a box of old comics passed along to me by my cousin Arthur when he went off to college. It contained a story in which the Escapist fell prey to a villain named the Junkman, who employed an "atom spike" to administer a dose of "superjunk" that first plunged the Escapist into a deep coma and then subjected him to a string of unbearable nightmares. All I can really remember about the story—but I have never forgotten it—is a single, stunning panel (possibly drawn by Neal Adams). It depicted the Escapist, in his simple blue costume, in the disturbing, inspiring, and surrealistic act of *escaping from his own head*.

That single panel, it seems to me, perfectly expresses the appeal not only of the Escapist, Master of Elusion, but of the entire genre of comic books from which, as from a great dreaming forehead, he sprang. Escape and escapism, in art and literature, have received a bad name. It was given to them, I believe, by the very people who forged the locks and barred the windows in the first place.

Twenty years would pass before I encountered the Escapist again. By then—at the end of 1995—I had begun actively to research the novel that would become *The Amazing Adventures of Kavalier & Clay*. As I made my way through the literature—from the Steranko *History of Comics* to Bob Harvey's *The Art of the Comic Book*—I was intrigued by hints and references, here and there, to "the great lost superhero of the Golden Age," and in time I decided to make that character, and his youthful creators, the subject of my fictional history.

The Golden Age Escapist, as published from 1940 to 1954 by Sheldon Anapol's Empire Comics, turned out to be the easiest to track down. After Sheldon Anapol settled the famous lawsuit with DC Comics, and ceased publication of his flagship title, the history of the Escapist grew Byzantine and sketchy. During the Golden Age, the Escapist and his Kavalier & Clay-created cohorts were ubiquitous in the druggists' and candy stores of America; after 1954 the Escapist began a fugitive and phantom career, surfacing, disappearing, reappearing, the Sasquatch of comics, often stumbled upon, never quite caught on film. I can't tell you how many people have described, after hearing about my cousin Artie's box of comics, their own chance, not-to-be-repeated encounters with an *Escapist* comic book over the years; how they came across a tattered book featuring the Score Comics or Hi-Tone Comics or Fab Comics version of the character, loved it, and were never able to locate another.

Now, thanks to the determination of the dedicated archivists and Dark Horse Comics, the generosity of the Kavalier and Clay estates, and the implacable scholarship of Kevin McCarthy, widely acknowledged to be the world's leading expert in "Escapistry," the entire patchwork epic of the Escapist is being reassembled for your reading pleasure. This volume and others feature stories culled from every epoch of the Escapist's strange and checkered history, as well as the best of the secondary Kavalier & Clay characters—Luna Moth, Kid Vixen, Mr. Machine Gun among them—and samples of the later comics work done, separately and together, by Sam Clay and Joe Kavalier. I hope that they bring all the reading pleasure that bad luck and good lawyers have so long conspired to deny you.

---

Michael Chabon is the bestselling and Pulitzer Prize–winning author of *The Amazing Adventures of Kavalier & Clay*, one volume among a varied and growing list of novels and short stories. He lives in Berkeley, California.

# THE PASSING OF THE KEY

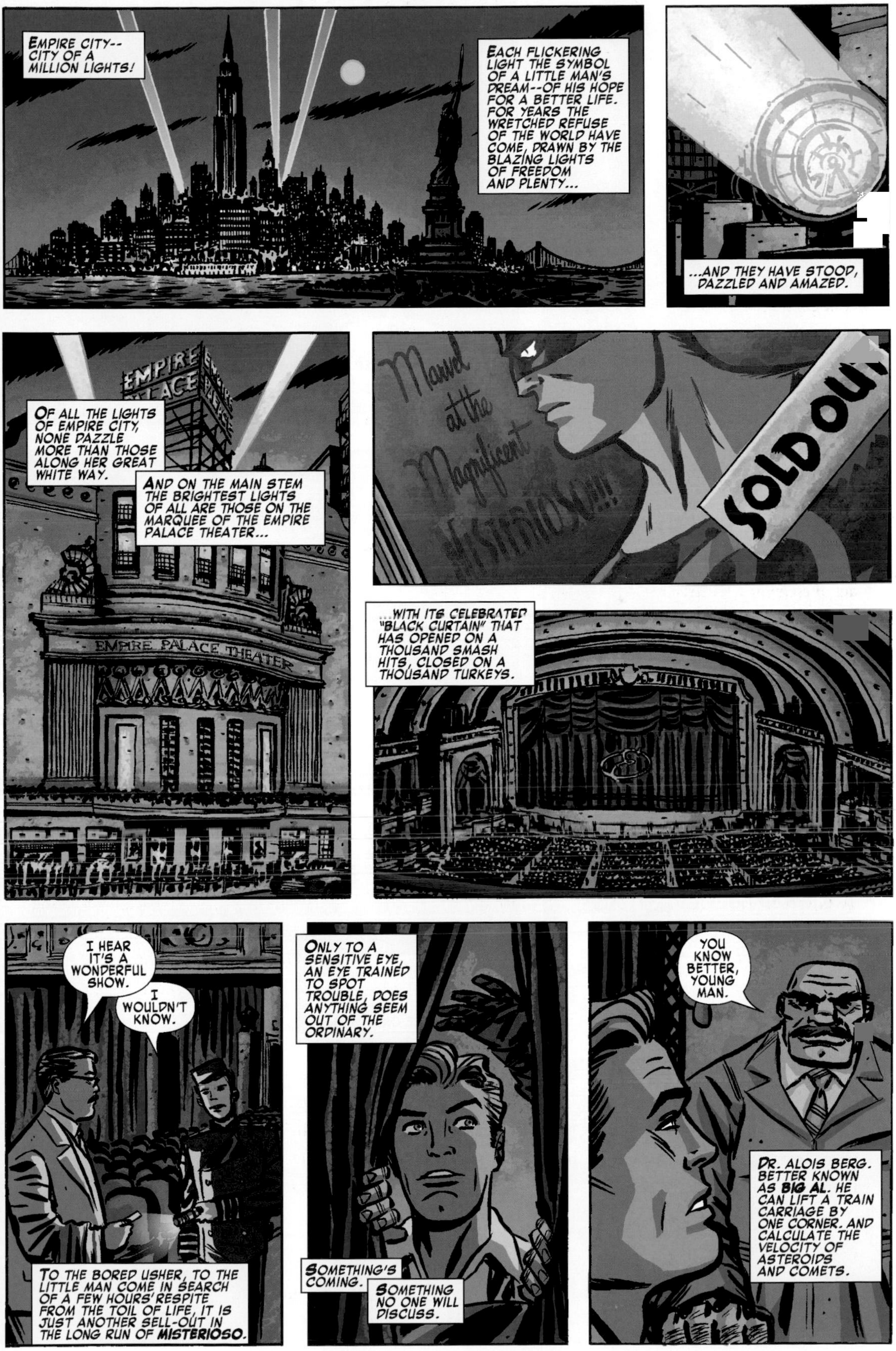
EMPIRE CITY--CITY OF A MILLION LIGHTS!
EACH FLICKERING LIGHT THE SYMBOL OF A LITTLE MAN'S DREAM--OF HIS HOPE FOR A BETTER LIFE. FOR YEARS THE WRETCHED REFUSE OF THE WORLD HAVE COME, DRAWN BY THE BLAZING LIGHTS OF FREEDOM AND PLENTY...
...AND THEY HAVE STOOD, DAZZLED AND AMAZED.
EMPIRE PALACE
OF ALL THE LIGHTS OF EMPIRE CITY, NONE DAZZLE MORE THAN THOSE ALONG HER GREAT WHITE WAY.
AND ON THE MAIN STEM THE BRIGHTEST LIGHTS OF ALL ARE THOSE ON THE MARQUEE OF THE EMPIRE PALACE THEATER...
EMPIRE PALACE THEATER
Marvel at the Magnificent
SOLD OU
...WITH ITS CELEBRATED "BLACK CURTAIN" THAT HAS OPENED ON A THOUSAND SMASH HITS, CLOSED ON A THOUSAND TURKEYS.
I HEAR IT'S A WONDERFUL SHOW.
I WOULDN'T KNOW.
TO THE BORED USHER, TO THE LITTLE MAN COME IN SEARCH OF A FEW HOURS' RESPITE FROM THE TOIL OF LIFE, IT IS JUST ANOTHER SELL-OUT IN THE LONG RUN OF MISTERIOSO.
ONLY TO A SENSITIVE EYE, AN EYE TRAINED TO SPOT TROUBLE, DOES ANYTHING SEEM OUT OF THE ORDINARY.
SOMETHING'S COMING.
SOMETHING NO ONE WILL DISCUSS.
YOU KNOW BETTER, YOUNG MAN.
DR. ALOIS BERG. BETTER KNOWN AS BIG AL. HE CAN LIFT A TRAIN CARRIAGE BY ONE CORNER. AND CALCULATE THE VELOCITY OF ASTEROIDS AND COMETS.

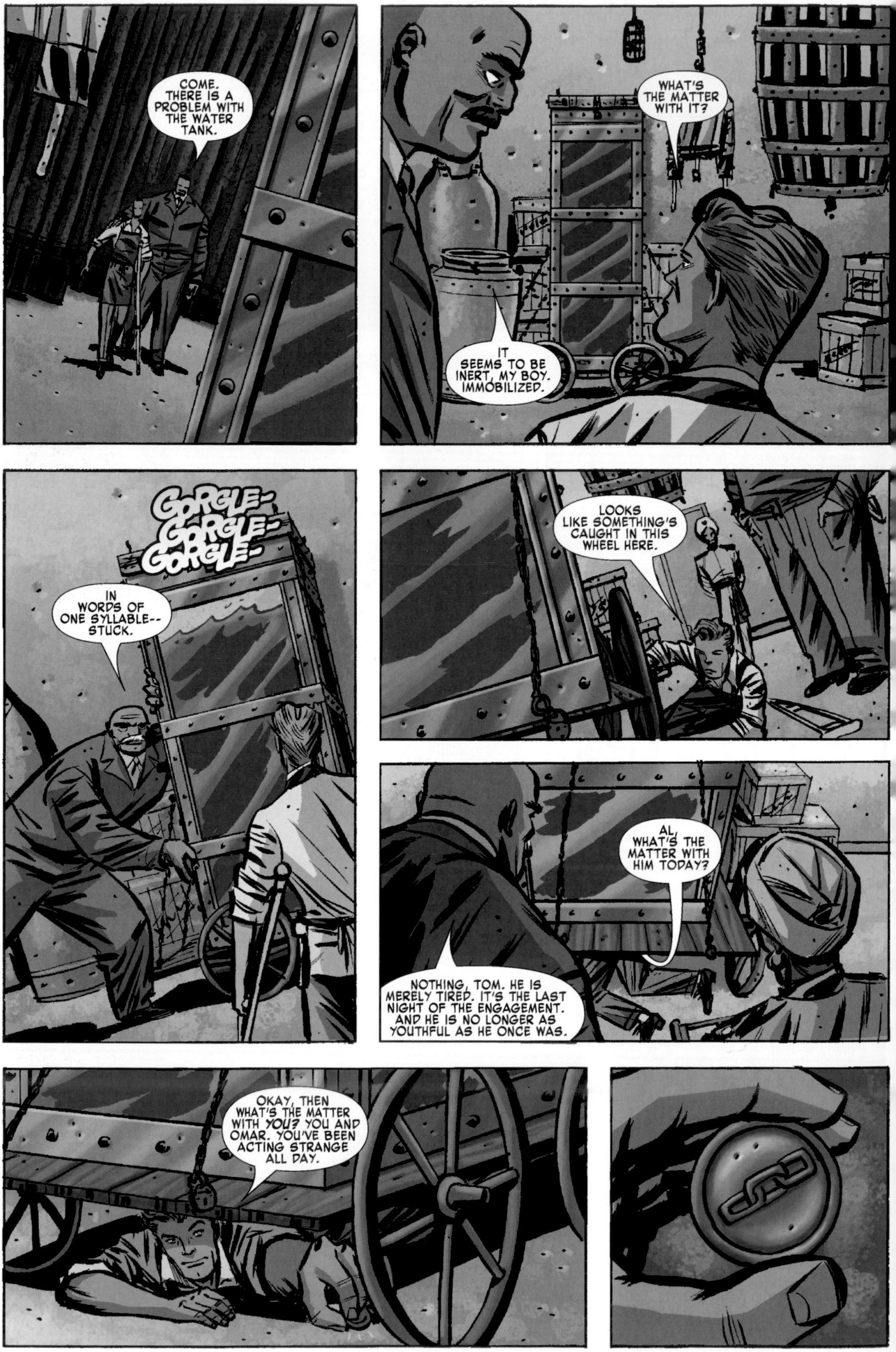
COME. THERE IS A PROBLEM WITH THE WATER TANK.
WHAT'S THE MATTER WITH IT?
IT SEEMS TO BE INERT, MY BOY. IMMOBILIZED.
GORGLE-GORGLE-GORGLE-
IN WORDS OF ONE SYLLABLE--STUCK.
LOOKS LIKE SOMETHING'S CAUGHT IN THIS WHEEL HERE.
AL, WHAT'S THE MATTER WITH HIM TODAY?
NOTHING, TOM. HE IS MERELY TIRED. IT'S THE LAST NIGHT OF THE ENGAGEMENT. AND HE IS NO LONGER AS YOUTHFUL AS HE ONCE WAS.
OKAY, THEN WHAT'S THE MATTER WITH *YOU?* YOU AND OMAR. YOU'VE BEEN ACTING STRANGE ALL DAY.

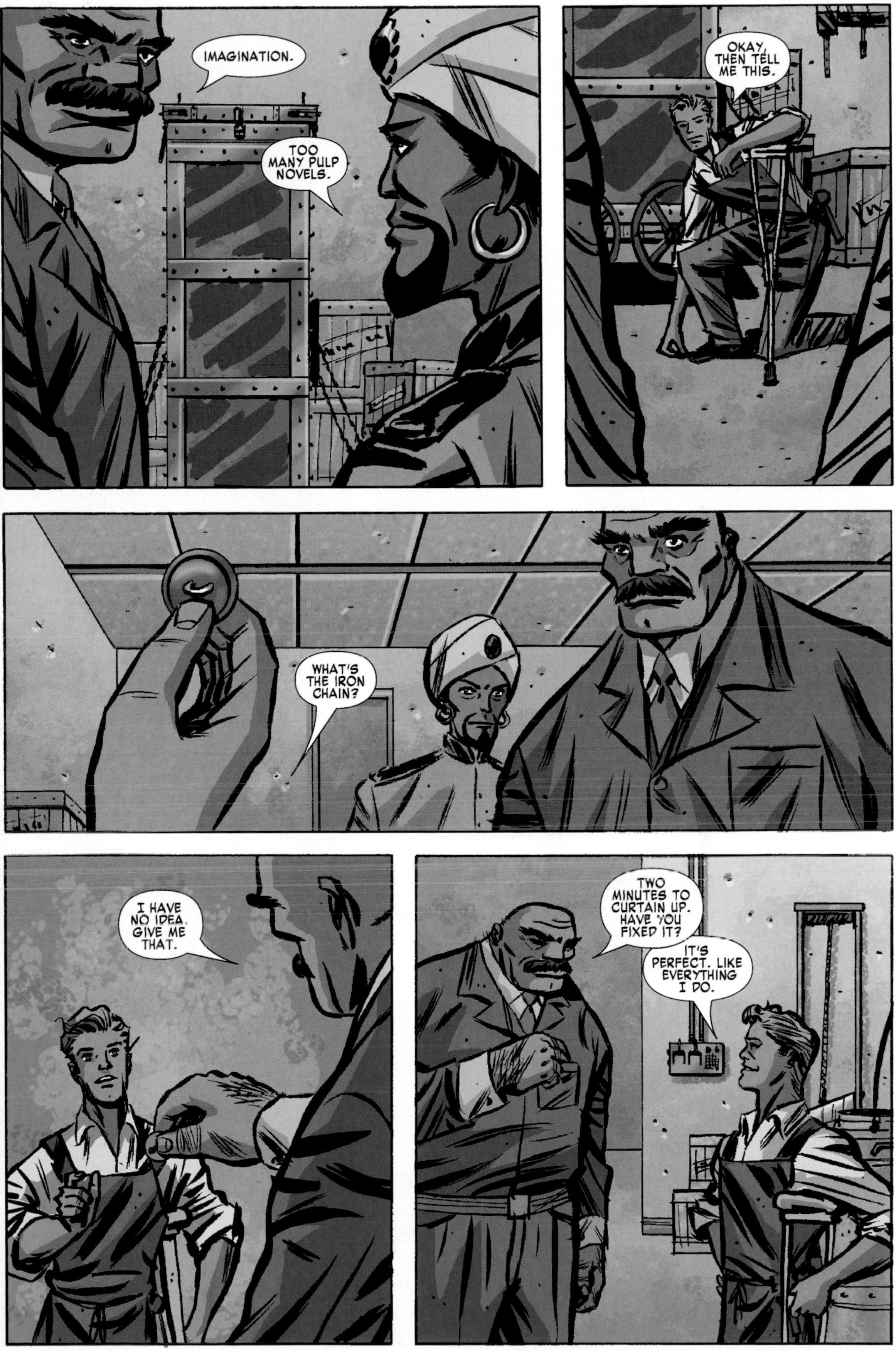
IMAGINATION.
TOO MANY PULP NOVELS.
OKAY, THEN TELL ME THIS.
WHAT'S THE IRON CHAIN?
I HAVE NO IDEA. GIVE ME THAT.
TWO MINUTES TO CURTAIN UP. HAVE YOU FIXED IT?
IT'S PERFECT. LIKE EVERYTHING I DO.

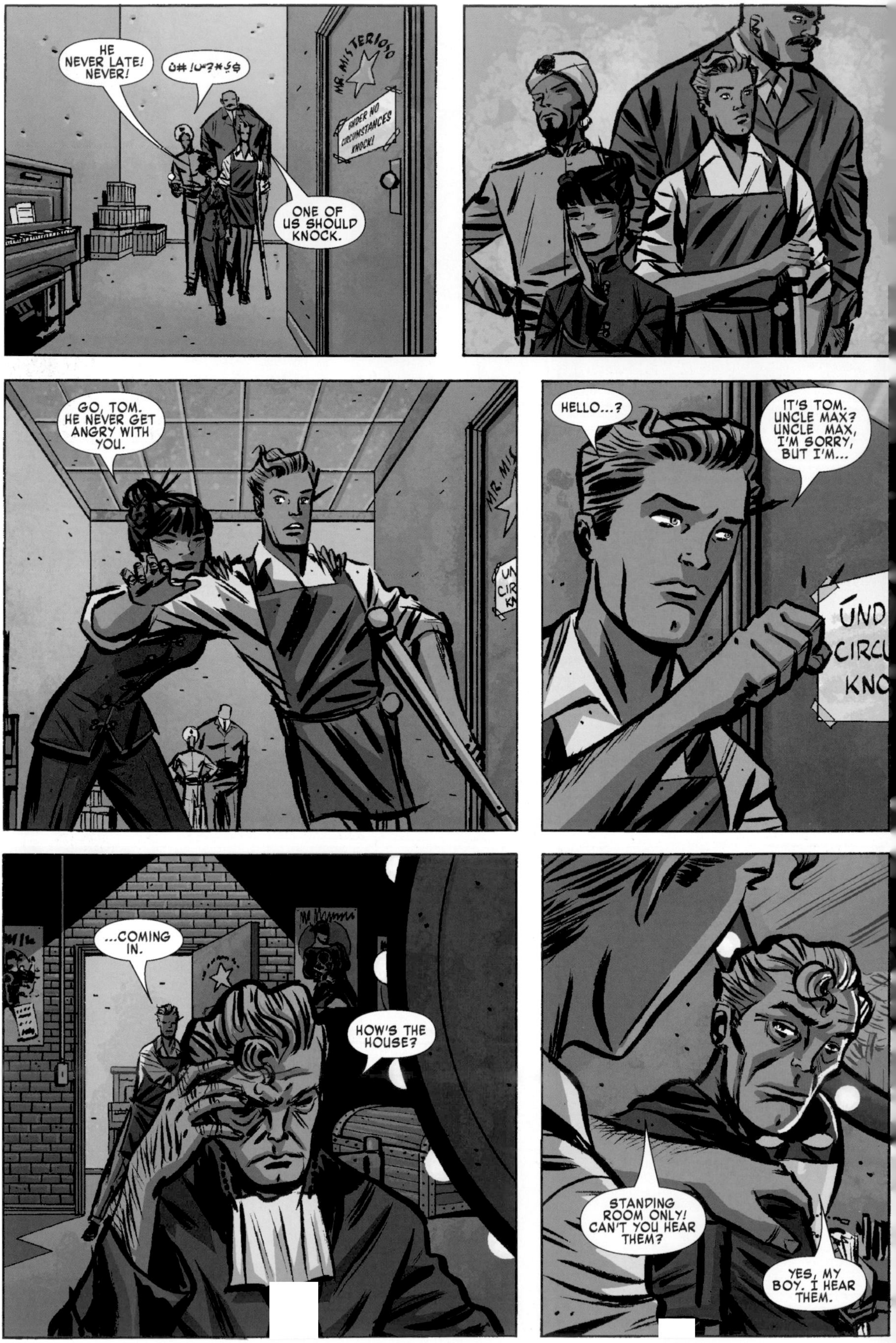
HE NEVER LATE! NEVER!
MR. MISTERIOSO
UNDER NO CIRCUMSTANCES KNOCK!
ONE OF US SHOULD KNOCK.
GO, TOM. HE NEVER GET ANGRY WITH YOU.
HELLO...?
IT'S TOM. UNCLE MAX? UNCLE MAX, I'M SORRY, BUT I'M...
...COMING IN.
HOW'S THE HOUSE?
STANDING ROOM ONLY! CAN'T YOU HEAR THEM?
YES, MY BOY. I HEAR THEM.

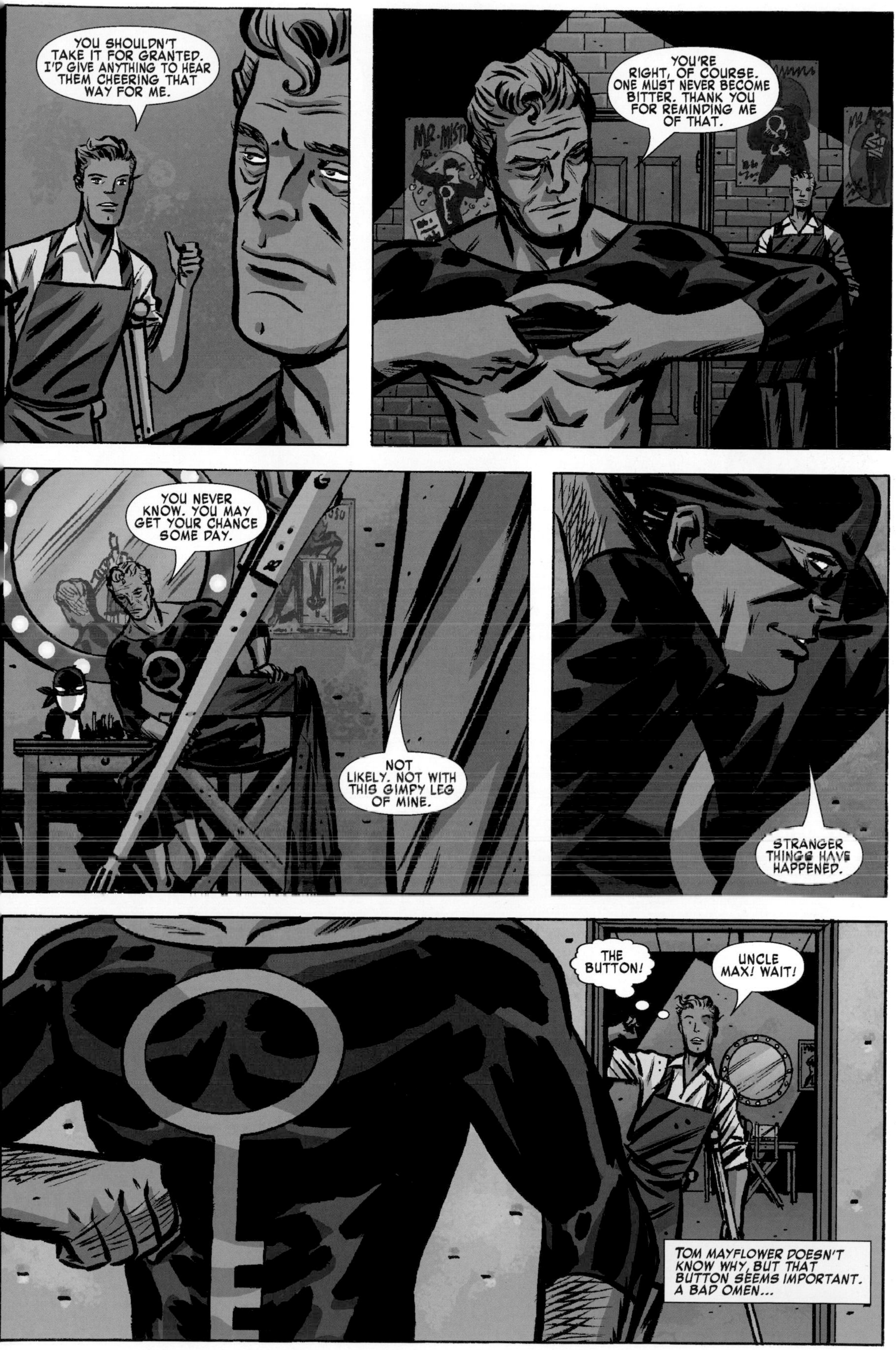
YOU SHOULDN'T TAKE IT FOR GRANTED. I'D GIVE ANYTHING TO HEAR THEM CHEERING THAT WAY FOR ME.
YOU'RE RIGHT, OF COURSE. ONE MUST NEVER BECOME BITTER. THANK YOU FOR REMINDING ME OF THAT.
YOU NEVER KNOW. YOU MAY GET YOUR CHANCE SOME DAY.
NOT LIKELY. NOT WITH THIS GIMPY LEG OF MINE.
STRANGER THINGS HAVE HAPPENED.
THE BUTTON!
UNCLE MAX! WAIT!
TOM MAYFLOWER DOESN'T KNOW WHY, BUT THAT BUTTON SEEMS IMPORTANT. A BAD OMEN...

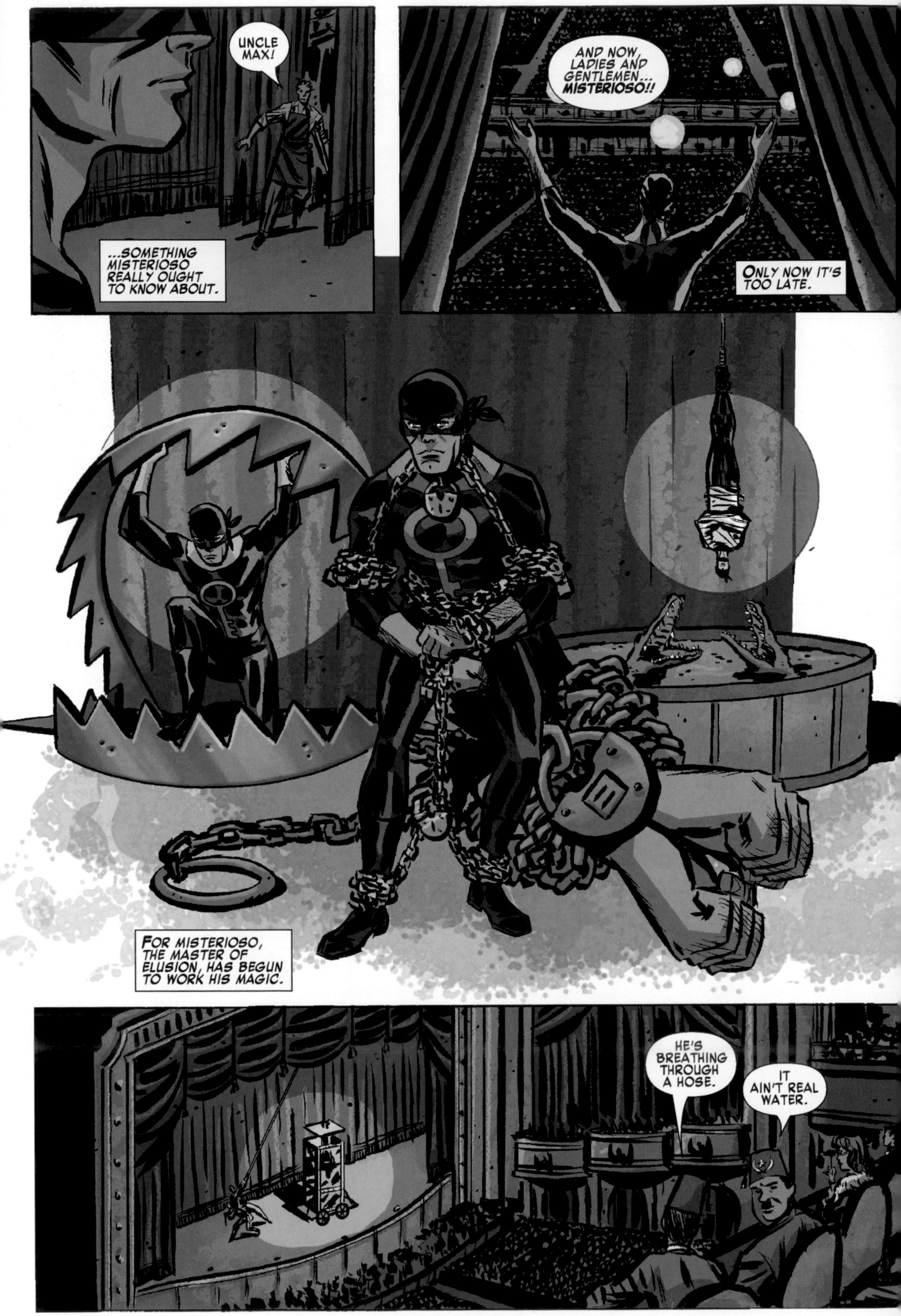
UNCLE MAX!
...SOMETHING MISTERIOSO REALLY OUGHT TO KNOW ABOUT.
AND NOW, LADIES AND GENTLEMEN... MISTERIOSO!!
ONLY NOW IT'S TOO LATE.
FOR MISTERIOSO, THE MASTER OF ELUSION, HAS BEGUN TO WORK HIS MAGIC.
HE'S BREATHING THROUGH A HOSE.
IT AIN'T REAL WATER.

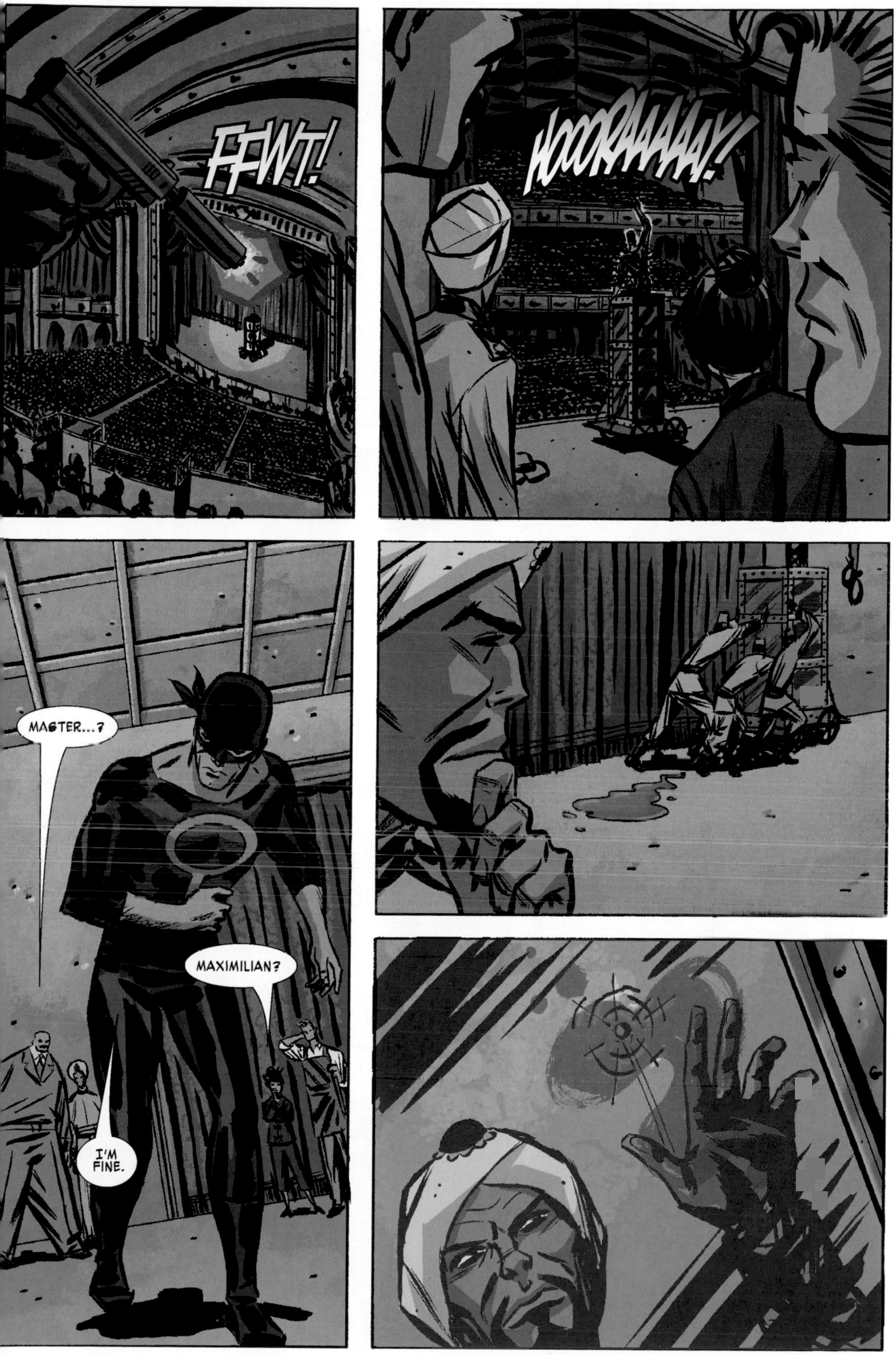
FFWT!
HOOORAAAAAY!
MASTER...?
MAXIMILIAN?
I'M FINE.

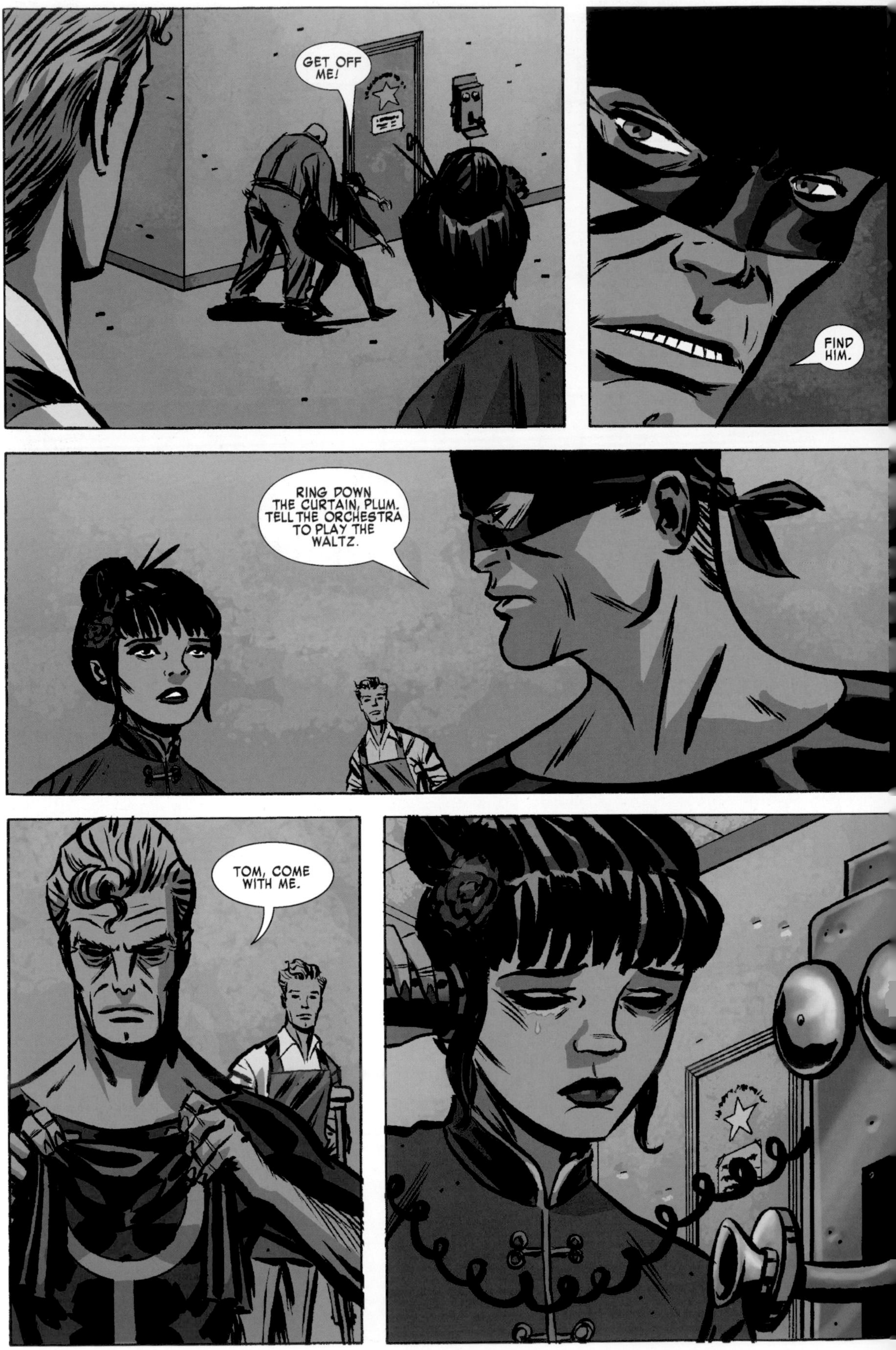
GET OFF ME!
FIND HIM.
RING DOWN THE CURTAIN, PLUM. TELL THE ORCHESTRA TO PLAY THE WALTZ.
TOM, COME WITH ME.

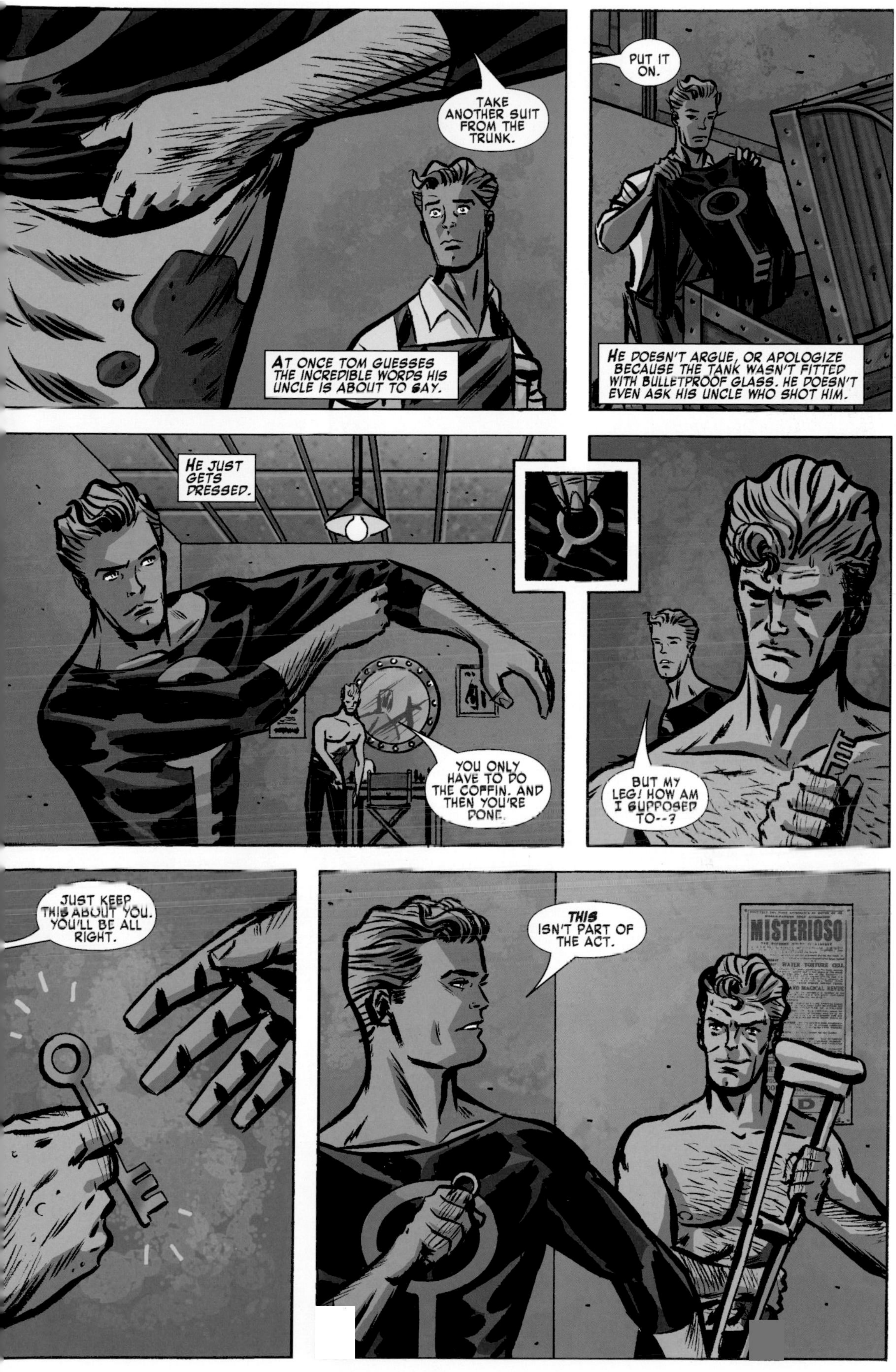
TAKE ANOTHER SUIT FROM THE TRUNK.
AT ONCE TOM GUESSES THE INCREDIBLE WORDS HIS UNCLE IS ABOUT TO SAY.
PUT IT ON.
HE DOESN'T ARGUE, OR APOLOGIZE BECAUSE THE TANK WASN'T FITTED WITH BULLETPROOF GLASS. HE DOESN'T EVEN ASK HIS UNCLE WHO SHOT HIM.
HE JUST GETS DRESSED.
YOU ONLY HAVE TO DO THE COFFIN. AND THEN YOU'RE DONE.
BUT MY LEG! HOW AM I SUPPOSED TO--?
JUST KEEP THIS ABOUT YOU. YOU'LL BE ALL RIGHT.
*THIS* ISN'T PART OF THE ACT.
MISTERIOSO
WATER TORTURE CELL

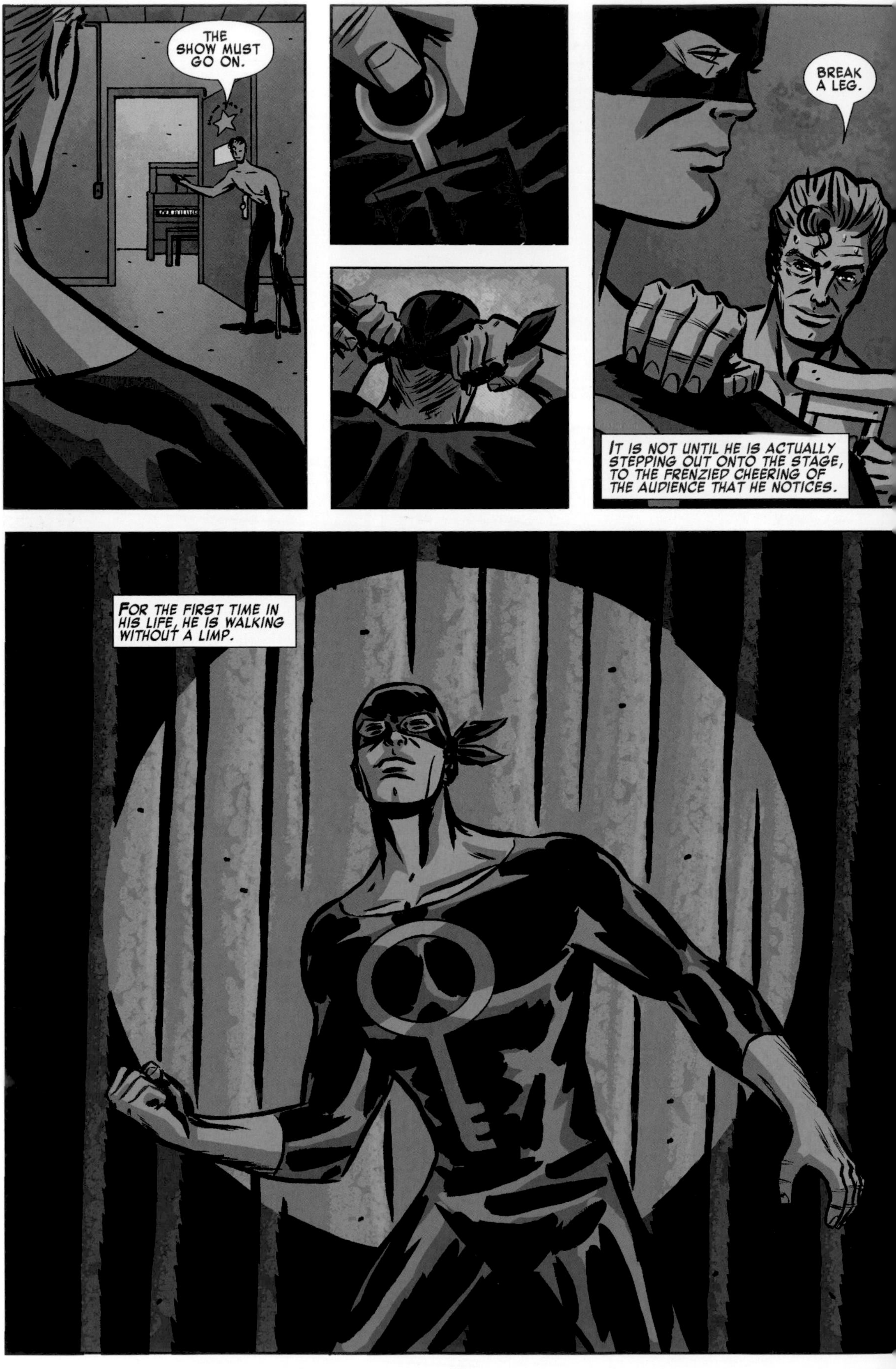
THE SHOW MUST GO ON.
BREAK A LEG.
IT IS NOT UNTIL HE IS ACTUALLY STEPPING OUT ONTO THE STAGE, TO THE FRENZIED CHEERING OF THE AUDIENCE THAT HE NOTICES.
FOR THE FIRST TIME IN HIS LIFE, HE IS WALKING WITHOUT A LIMP.

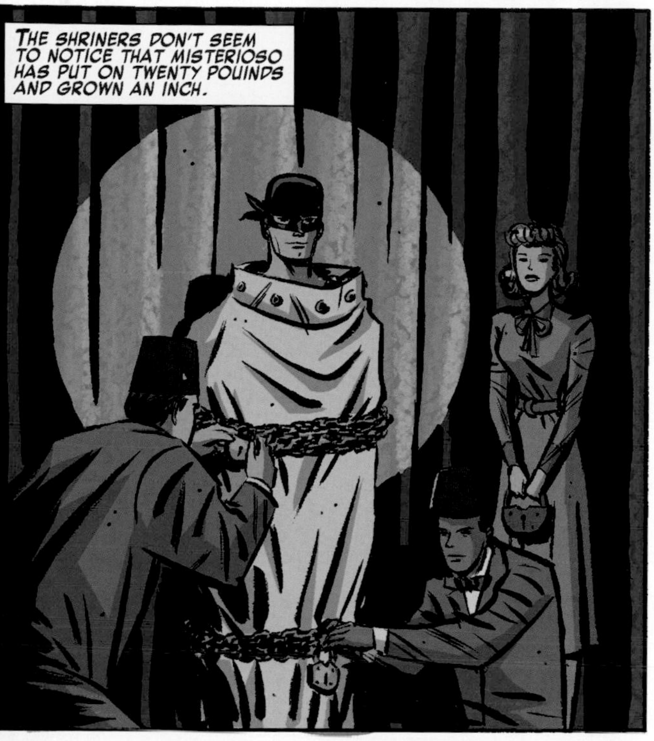
THE SHRINERS DON'T SEEM TO NOTICE THAT MISTERIOSO HAS PUT ON TWENTY POUNDS AND GROWN AN INCH.
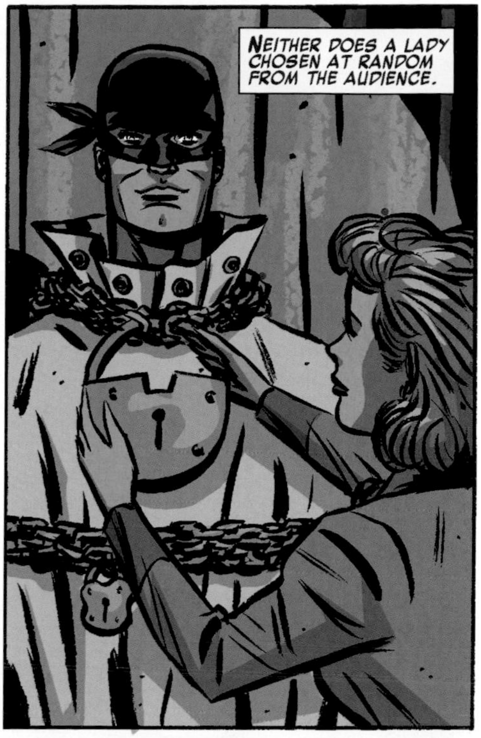
NEITHER DOES A LADY CHOSEN AT RANDOM FROM THE AUDIENCE.
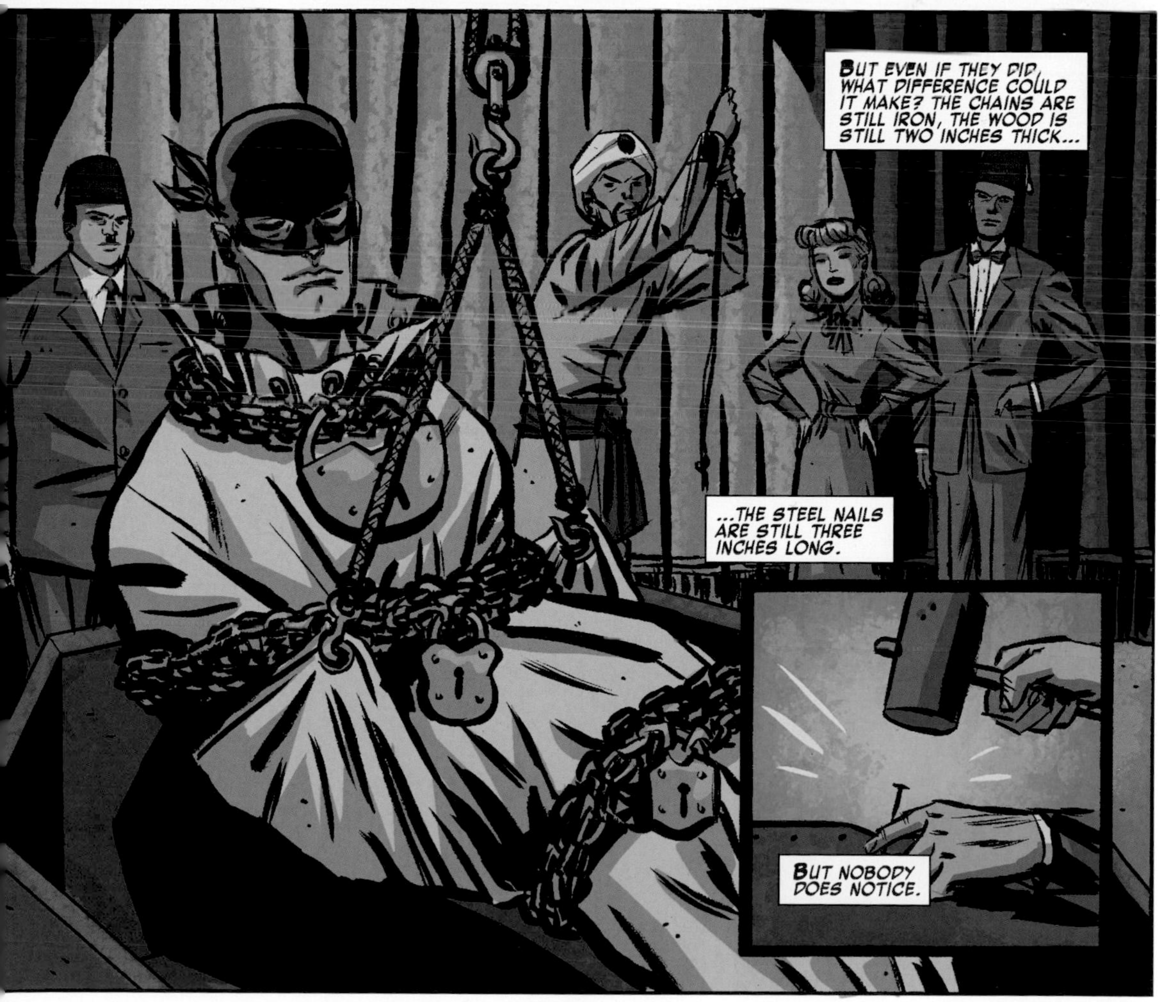
BUT EVEN IF THEY DID, WHAT DIFFERENCE COULD IT MAKE? THE CHAINS ARE STILL IRON, THE WOOD IS STILL TWO INCHES THICK...
...THE STEEL NAILS ARE STILL THREE INCHES LONG.
BUT NOBODY DOES NOTICE.

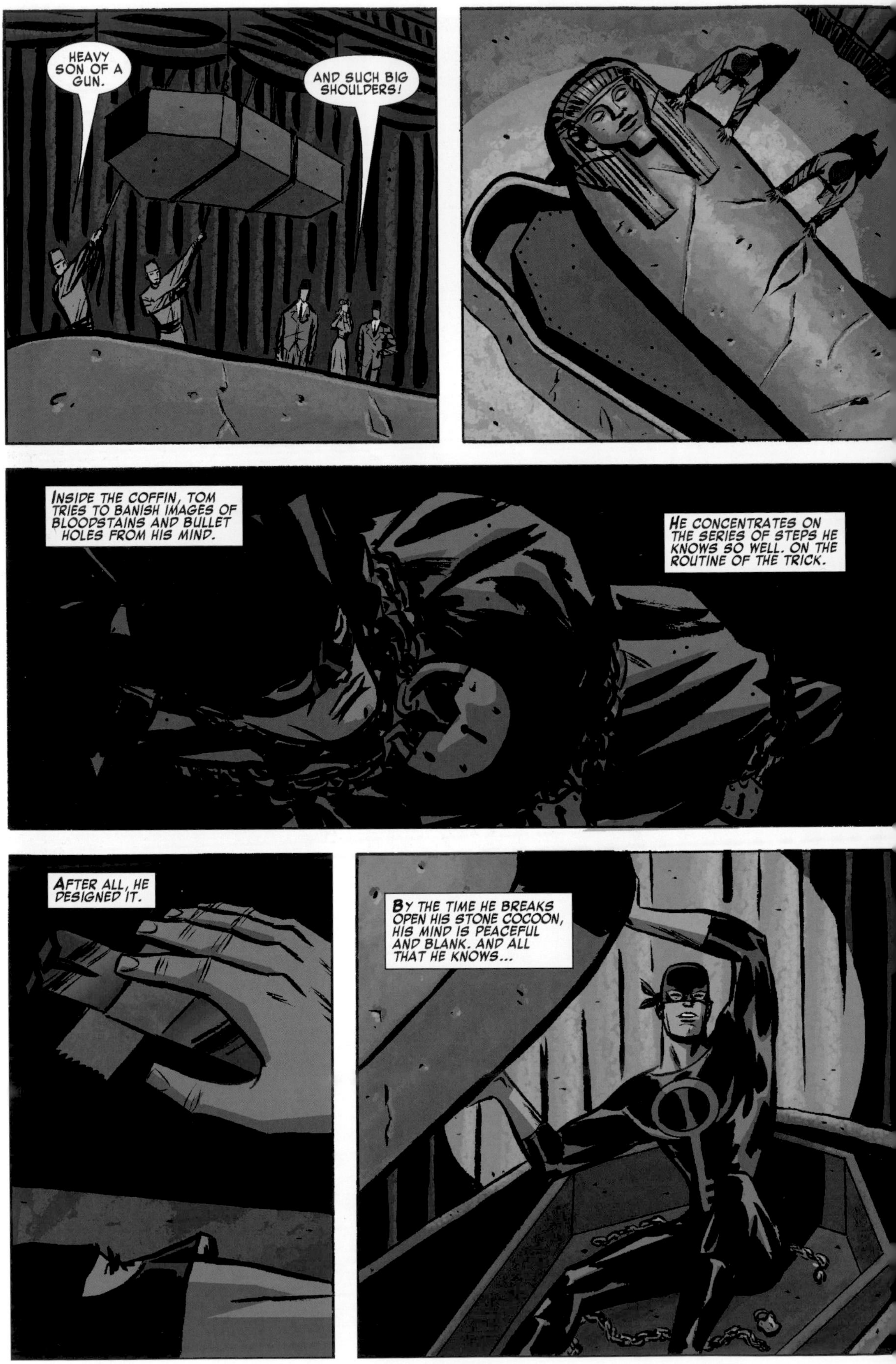
HEAVY SON OF A GUN.
AND SUCH BIG SHOULDERS!
INSIDE THE COFFIN, TOM TRIES TO BANISH IMAGES OF BLOODSTAINS AND BULLET HOLES FROM HIS MIND.
HE CONCENTRATES ON THE SERIES OF STEPS HE KNOWS SO WELL. ON THE ROUTINE OF THE TRICK.
AFTER ALL, HE DESIGNED IT.
BY THE TIME HE BREAKS OPEN HIS STONE COCOON, HIS MIND IS PEACEFUL AND BLANK. AND ALL THAT HE KNOWS...

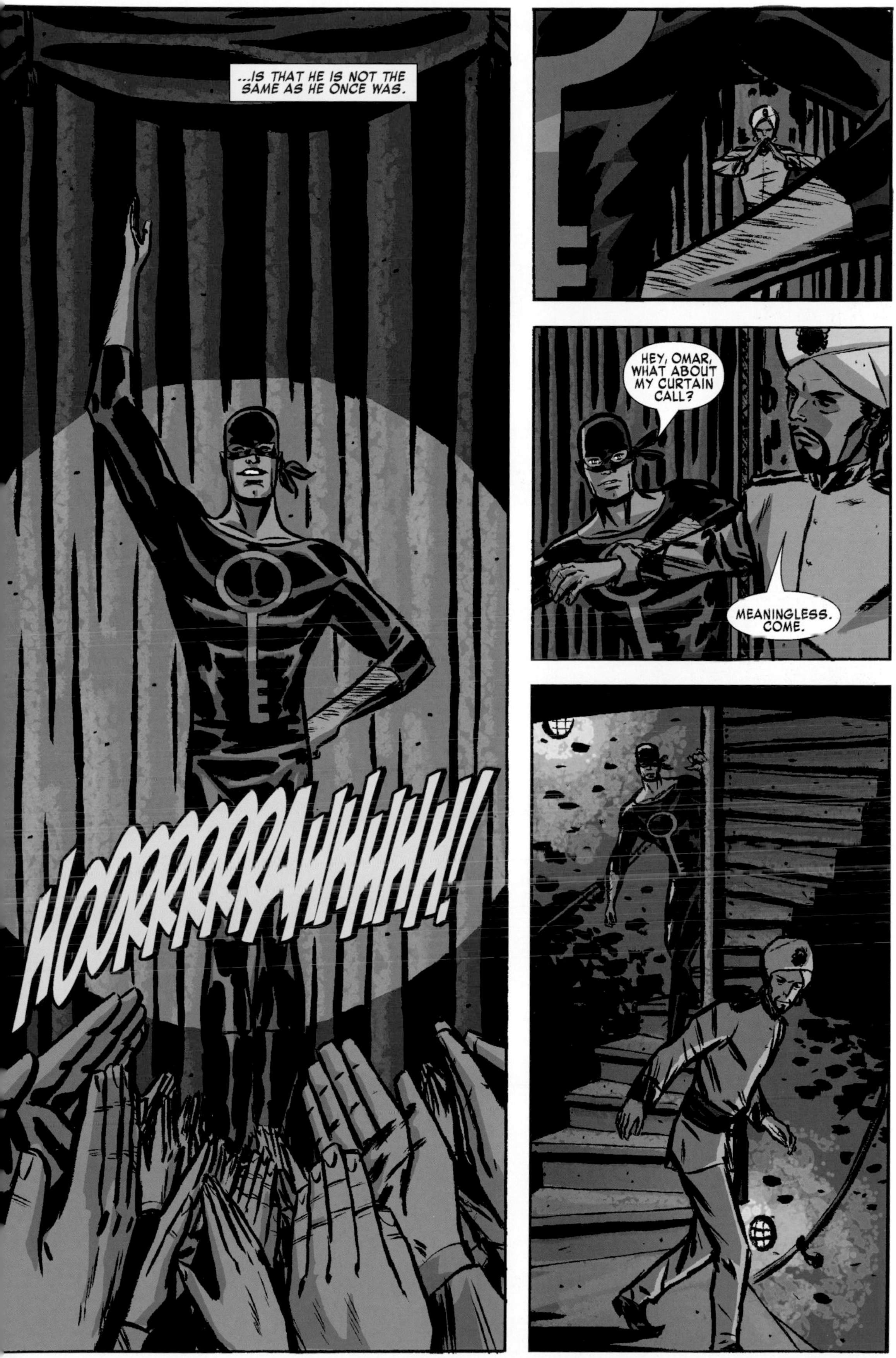
...IS THAT HE IS NOT THE SAME AS HE ONCE WAS.
HOORRRRRAHHHHHH!
HEY, OMAR, WHAT ABOUT MY CURTAIN CALL?
MEANINGLESS. COME.

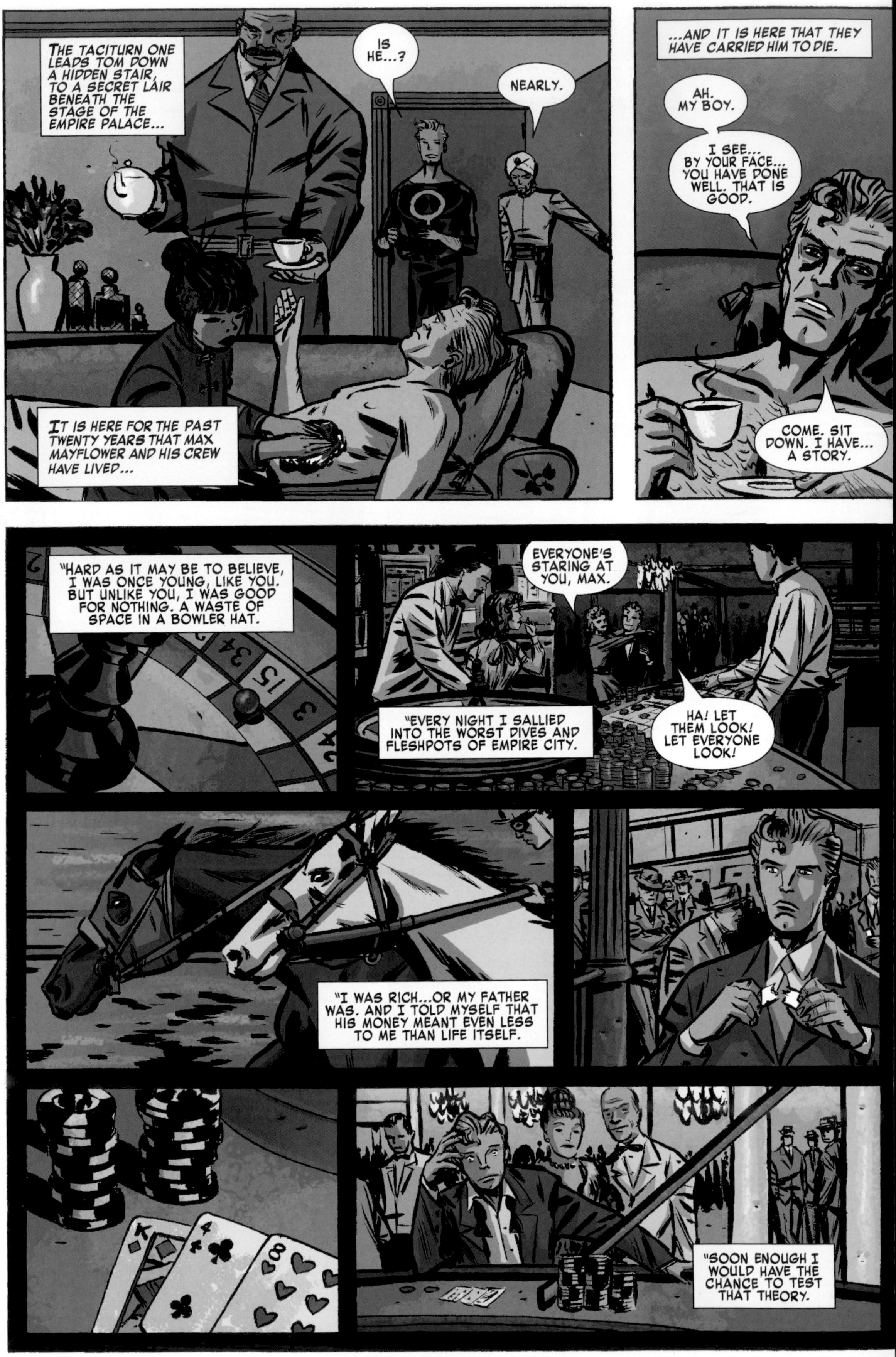
THE TACITURN ONE LEADS TOM DOWN A HIDDEN STAIR, TO A SECRET LAIR BENEATH THE STAGE OF THE EMPIRE PALACE...
IS HE...?
NEARLY.
IT IS HERE FOR THE PAST TWENTY YEARS THAT MAX MAYFLOWER AND HIS CREW HAVE LIVED...
...AND IT IS HERE THAT THEY HAVE CARRIED HIM TO DIE.
AH. MY BOY.
I SEE... BY YOUR FACE... YOU HAVE DONE WELL. THAT IS GOOD.
COME. SIT DOWN. I HAVE... A STORY.
"HARD AS IT MAY BE TO BELIEVE, I WAS ONCE YOUNG, LIKE YOU. BUT UNLIKE YOU, I WAS GOOD FOR NOTHING. A WASTE OF SPACE IN A BOWLER HAT.
EVERYONE'S STARING AT YOU, MAX.
"EVERY NIGHT I SALLIED INTO THE WORST DIVES AND FLESHPOTS OF EMPIRE CITY.
HA! LET THEM LOOK! LET EVERYONE LOOK!
"I WAS RICH...OR MY FATHER WAS. AND I TOLD MYSELF THAT HIS MONEY MEANT EVEN LESS TO ME THAN LIFE ITSELF.
"SOON ENOUGH I WOULD HAVE THE CHANCE TO TEST THAT THEORY.

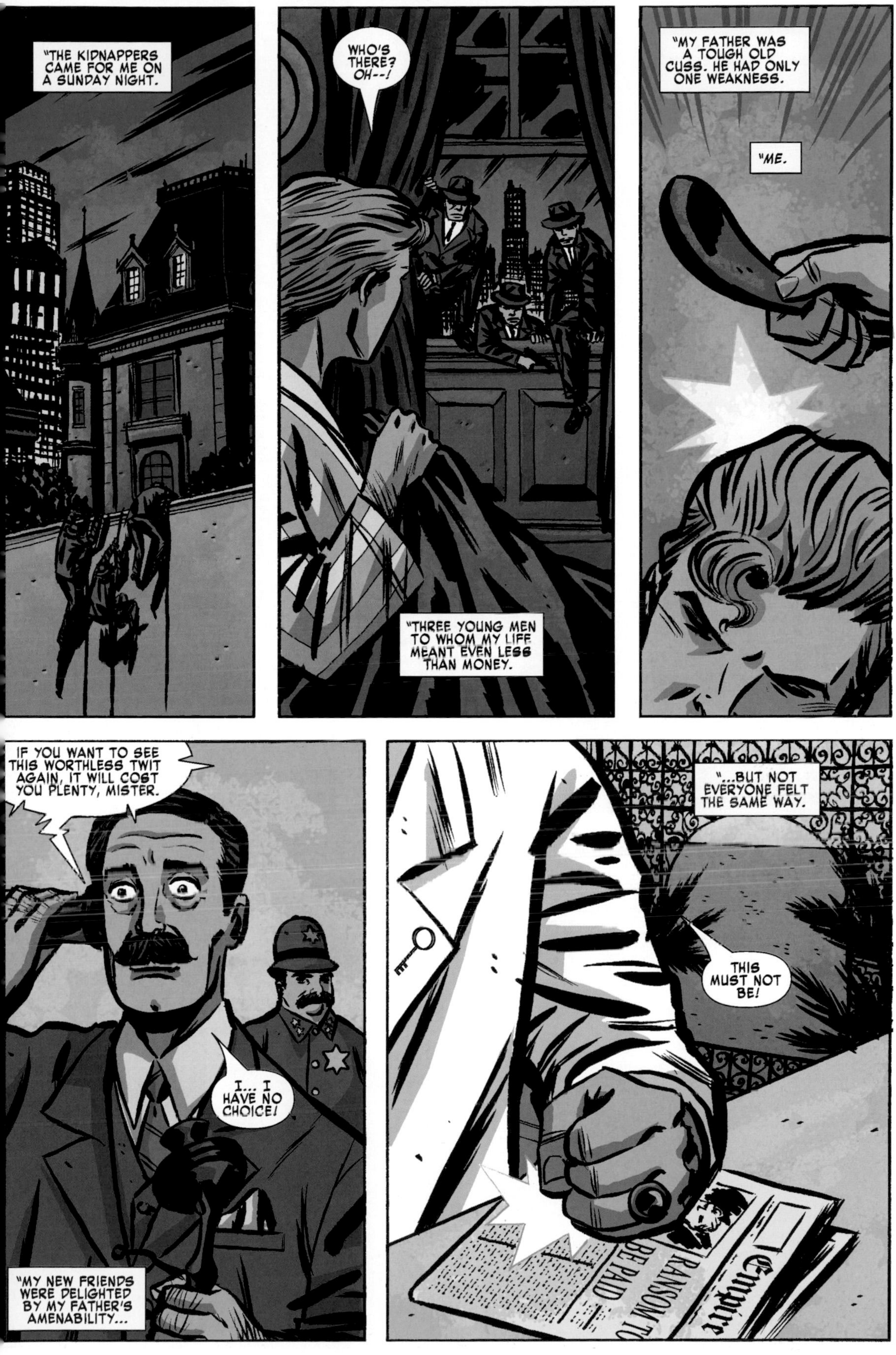
"THE KIDNAPPERS CAME FOR ME ON A SUNDAY NIGHT.
WHO'S THERE? OH--!
"THREE YOUNG MEN TO WHOM MY LIFE MEANT EVEN LESS THAN MONEY.
"MY FATHER WAS A TOUGH OLD CUSS. HE HAD ONLY ONE WEAKNESS.
"ME.
IF YOU WANT TO SEE THIS WORTHLESS TWIT AGAIN, IT WILL COST YOU PLENTY, MISTER.
I... I HAVE NO CHOICE!
"MY NEW FRIENDS WERE DELIGHTED BY MY FATHER'S AMENABILITY...
"...BUT NOT EVERYONE FELT THE SAME WAY.
THIS MUST NOT BE!
Empire
RANSOM TO
BE PAID

"THE NEXT DAY I WAS WAKENED FROM GRAY DREAMS BY A STRANGER'S VOICE.

GET UP, YOUNG MAN.

HOW DID YOU GET IN HERE?

LOCKS MEAN NOTHING TO US.

US?

"HE MADE SHORT WORK OF MY BONDS.

NOW, FLEE THIS PLACE! BUT DON'T FORGET:

FREEDOM IS A DEBT WHICH CAN ONLY BE REPAID BY PURCHASING THE FREEDOM OF OTHERS!

"AT THAT MOMENT, THE BOSS KIDNAPPER CAME BACK WITH THE DAY'S NEWSPAPER.

HEY, BLACKIE. GET A LOAD OF--WHAT'S THIS? WHY, YOU BIG OX!

HUH?

THAT'LL TEACH YOU TO SLEEP ON THE JOB! EH?

WHAT'S THAT? VOICES...

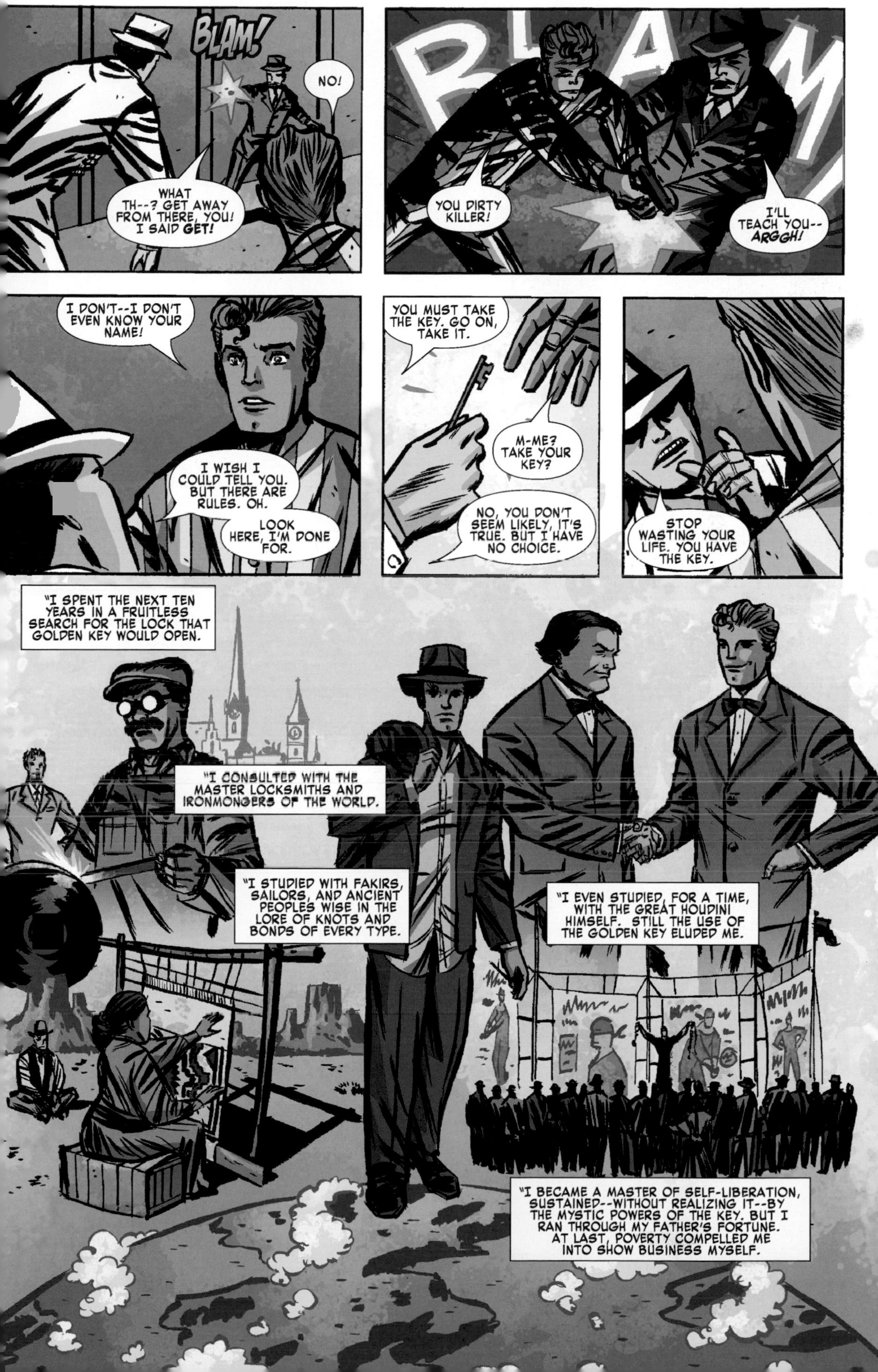
BLAM!
NO!
WHAT TH--? GET AWAY FROM THERE, YOU! I SAID GET!
BLAM!
YOU DIRTY KILLER!
I'LL TEACH YOU-- ARGGH!
I DON'T--I DON'T EVEN KNOW YOUR NAME!
I WISH I COULD TELL YOU. BUT THERE ARE RULES. OH.
LOOK HERE, I'M DONE FOR.
YOU MUST TAKE THE KEY. GO ON, TAKE IT.
M-ME? TAKE YOUR KEY?
NO, YOU DON'T SEEM LIKELY, IT'S TRUE. BUT I HAVE NO CHOICE.
STOP WASTING YOUR LIFE. YOU HAVE THE KEY.
"I SPENT THE NEXT TEN YEARS IN A FRUITLESS SEARCH FOR THE LOCK THAT GOLDEN KEY WOULD OPEN.
"I CONSULTED WITH THE MASTER LOCKSMITHS AND IRONMONGERS OF THE WORLD.
"I STUDIED WITH FAKIRS, SAILORS, AND ANCIENT PEOPLES WISE IN THE LORE OF KNOTS AND BONDS OF EVERY TYPE.
"I EVEN STUDIED, FOR A TIME, WITH THE GREAT HOUDINI HIMSELF. STILL THE USE OF THE GOLDEN KEY ELUDED ME.
"I BECAME A MASTER OF SELF-LIBERATION, SUSTAINED--WITHOUT REALIZING IT--BY THE MYSTIC POWERS OF THE KEY. BUT I RAN THROUGH MY FATHER'S FORTUNE. AT LAST, POVERTY COMPELLED ME INTO SHOW BUSINESS MYSELF.

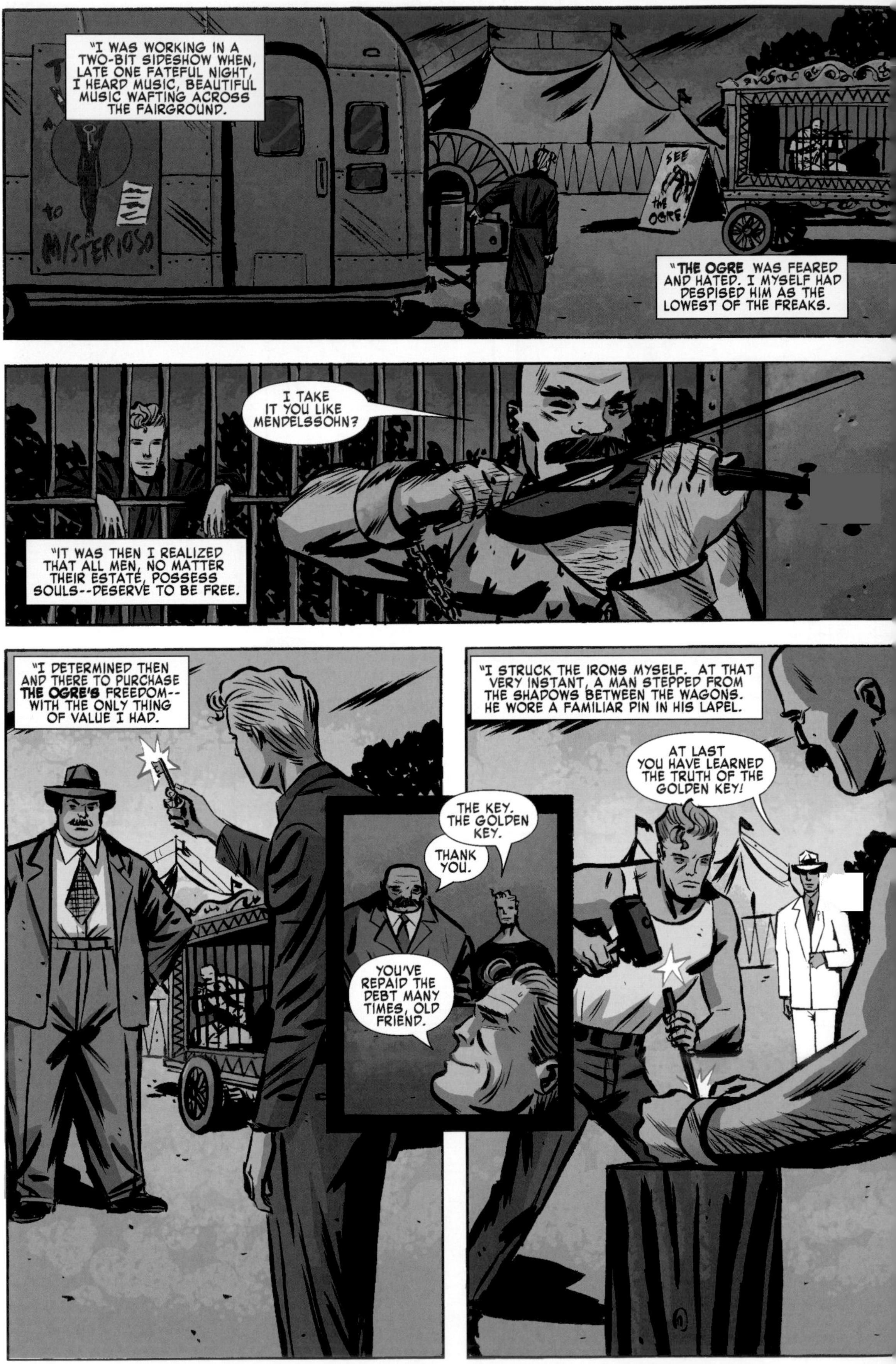

"I WAS WORKING IN A TWO-BIT SIDESHOW WHEN, LATE ONE FATEFUL NIGHT, I HEARD MUSIC, BEAUTIFUL MUSIC WAFTING ACROSS THE FAIRGROUND.
MISTERIOSO
SEE THE OGRE
"THE OGRE WAS FEARED AND HATED. I MYSELF HAD DESPISED HIM AS THE LOWEST OF THE FREAKS.
I TAKE IT YOU LIKE MENDELSSOHN?
"IT WAS THEN I REALIZED THAT ALL MEN, NO MATTER THEIR ESTATE, POSSESS SOULS--DESERVE TO BE FREE.
"I DETERMINED THEN AND THERE TO PURCHASE THE OGRE'S FREEDOM--WITH THE ONLY THING OF VALUE I HAD.
THE KEY. THE GOLDEN KEY.
THANK YOU.
YOU'VE REPAID THE DEBT MANY TIMES, OLD FRIEND.
"I STRUCK THE IRONS MYSELF. AT THAT VERY INSTANT, A MAN STEPPED FROM THE SHADOWS BETWEEN THE WAGONS. HE WORE A FAMILIAR PIN IN HIS LAPEL.
AT LAST YOU HAVE LEARNED THE TRUTH OF THE GOLDEN KEY!

HE EXPLAINED... HE AND THE MAN WHO SAVED ME...BELONGED TO AN ANCIENT SECRET SOCIETY...THE LEAGUE OF THE GOLDEN KEY...ROAMED THE WORLD...FREEING CAPTIVES... SLAVES--VICTIMS...

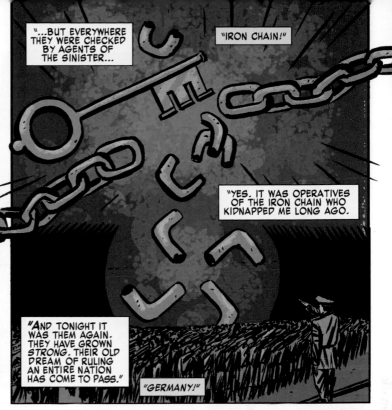

"...BUT EVERYWHERE THEY WERE CHECKED BY AGENTS OF THE SINISTER...

"IRON CHAIN!"

"YES. IT WAS OPERATIVES OF THE IRON CHAIN WHO KIDNAPPED ME LONG AGO."

"AND TONIGHT IT WAS THEM AGAIN. THEY HAVE GROWN STRONG. THEIR OLD DREAM OF RULING AN ENTIRE NATION HAS COME TO PASS."

"GERMANY!"

YES. ALL THE MORE REASON... WE MUST KEEP UP THE STRUGGLE. AS WE HAVE ALL THESE YEARS. AS WHEN I FREED YOU FROM THAT SWEATSHOP IN OLD MACAU, EH, PLUM? OR YOU, OMAR...

...WHEN I FOUND YOU A SLAVE OF THE SULTAN OF KHURVISTAN?

AND ME? WHAT ABOUT ME?

WE FOUND YOU-- IN AN ORPHANAGE, IN CENTRAL EUROPE. THAT WAS A CRUEL PLACE.

BLAM! BLAM!

"I REGRET I HAD TIME TO SAVE ONLY ONE OF YOU."

27

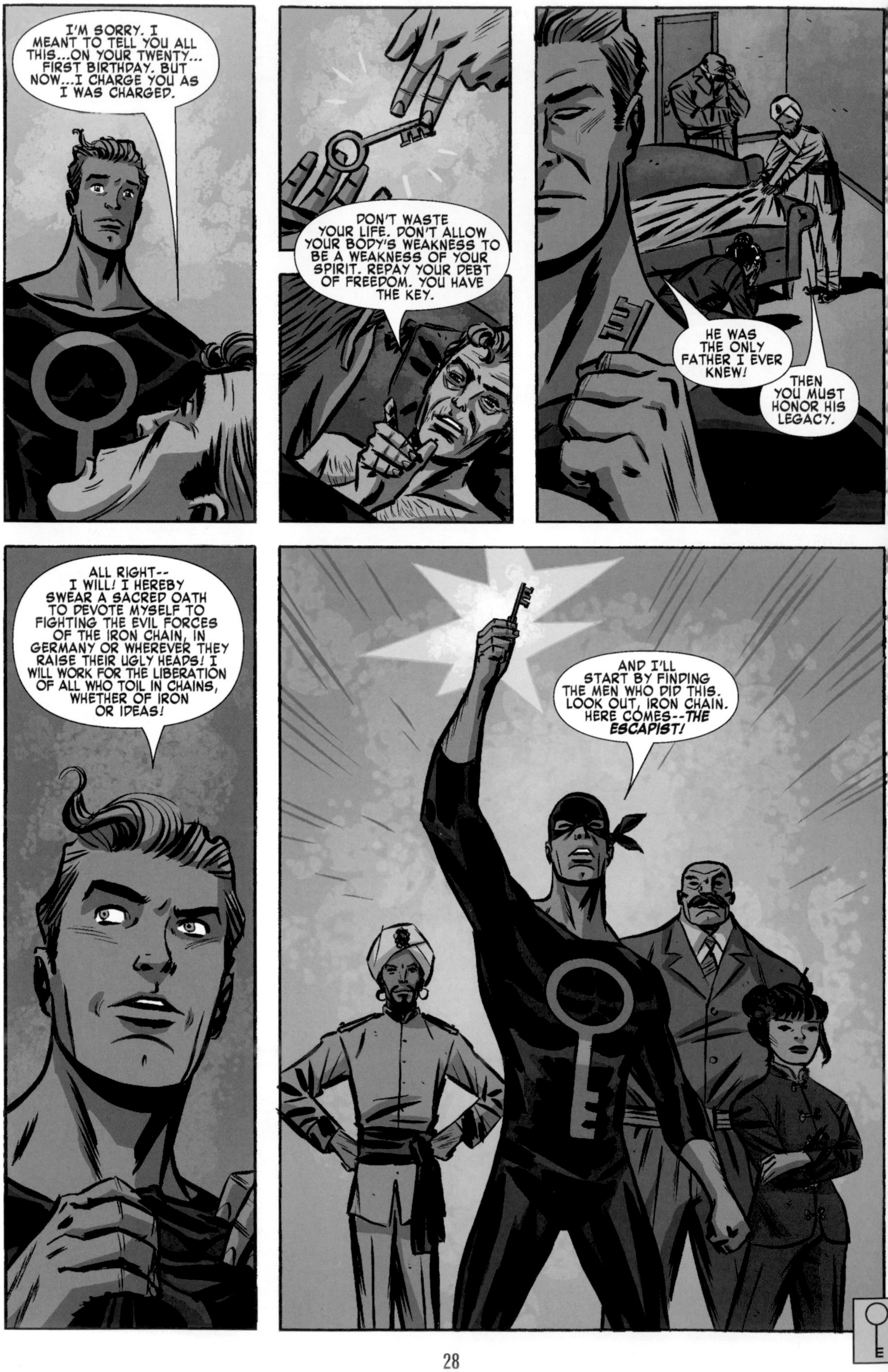

I'M SORRY. I MEANT TO TELL YOU ALL THIS...ON YOUR TWENTY... FIRST BIRTHDAY. BUT NOW...I CHARGE YOU AS I WAS CHARGED.
DON'T WASTE YOUR LIFE. DON'T ALLOW YOUR BODY'S WEAKNESS TO BE A WEAKNESS OF YOUR SPIRIT. REPAY YOUR DEBT OF FREEDOM. YOU HAVE THE KEY.
HE WAS THE ONLY FATHER I EVER KNEW!
THEN YOU MUST HONOR HIS LEGACY.
ALL RIGHT-- I WILL! I HEREBY SWEAR A SACRED OATH TO DEVOTE MYSELF TO FIGHTING THE EVIL FORCES OF THE IRON CHAIN, IN GERMANY OR WHEREVER THEY RAISE THEIR UGLY HEADS! I WILL WORK FOR THE LIBERATION OF ALL WHO TOIL IN CHAINS, WHETHER OF IRON OR IDEAS!
AND I'LL START BY FINDING THE MEN WHO DID THIS. LOOK OUT, IRON CHAIN. HERE COMES--*THE ESCAPIST!*

# ESCAPISM 101

*The tangled and glorious history of one of the comics' greatest characters.*

## BY MALACHI B. COHEN

**Reprinted from the pages of *The Comics Journal*,**
**with the kind permission of Messrs. Gary Groth and Kim Thompson, proprietors.**

*"To all those who toil in the bonds of slavery and the shackles of oppression, he offers the hope of liberation and the promise of freedom! Armed with superb physical and mental training, a crack team of assistants, and ancient wisdom, he roams the globe, performing amazing feats and coming to the aid of those who languish in tyranny's chains! He is — the Escapist!"*

WITH THESE STIRRING WORDS, rippling in a banner across the splash page of the first issue of *Amazing Midget Radio Comics* (January 1940), was launched one of the longest and most checkered careers in comics. Over the next sixty years, the man who made cheating death both an art and a mission would find himself repeatedly trapped in the figurative lockbox of oblivion, bound in the ropes of legal machinations and buffeted by the whims of the marketplace, only to leap free, time and time again, reborn, renewed, and ready to wow another generation of admiring fans.

The author of the present monograph has attempted to trace the thorny, at times wildly ramifying path of that career, taking note not merely of the shifts and dodges of the Escapist's legal fortunes but also of the way the character has changed, evolved, at times regressed, along with the medium of comics itself. In doing so, extensive use has been made of court documents and interviews, as well as of secondary materials, in particular Michael Chabon's detailed if somewhat hyperbolic and unreliable documentation of the period, *The Amazing Adventures of Kavalier & Clay*.

The history of the Escapist divides, more or less neatly, into five eras, beginning near the very dawn of comic book superhero history, with:

### I
### The Empire Comics Era
*January 1940 – April 1954*

Empire Comics was founded in October 1939, when Mr. Sheldon Anapol merged his Empire Novelties, Inc., the nation's seventh-largest wholesaler and retailer of cheap novelties, with Racy Publications,

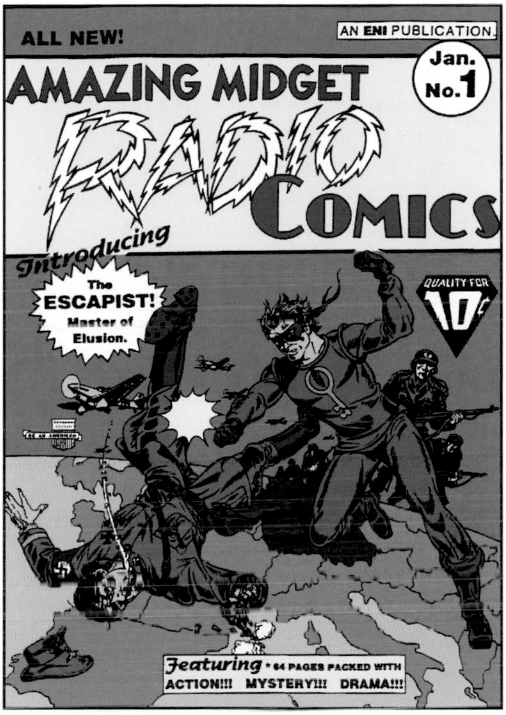

ALL NEW!
AN ENI PUBLICATION
Jan. No.1
AMAZING MIDGET
RADIO
COMICS
Introducing
The ESCAPIST! Master of Elusion.
QUALITY FOR 10¢
Featuring • 64 PAGES PACKED WITH
ACTION!!! MYSTERY!!! DRAMA!!!


The now classic cover of *Amazing Midget Radio Comics* #1. Art by Joe Kavalier. On loan from the Herb Trimpe collection.

Inc., a third- or perhaps fourth-rate publisher of pulp magazines owned by Mr. Jack Ashkenazy, Anapol's brother-in-law. Initially they published only one title, *Amazing Midget Radio Comics*, later shortened to *Radio Comics*. Eventually they expanded to some forty-seven titles, including, at the peak, around 1946, eight titles featuring the adventures of the Escapist and allied characters.

In 1946, Ashkenazy sold his interest in Empire to his brother-in-law and founded Pharaoh House, a third- or perhaps fourth-rate publisher of comic books.

The Empire Era can itself be usefully broken down into three distinct periods:

### The First Empire:

*January 1940 – April 1942*

This period covers the classic run of stories by the artist/writer team of Kavalier & Clay, beginning with the origin story in *Amazing Midget Radio Comics* #1. [See "The Passing of the Key" in this volume.] Chabon argues strongly that the work of this period, in particular after issue number 19 of *Radio Comics*, was heavily influenced by Kavalier & Clay's repeated self-exposure to that revolutionary work of cinema genius, *Citizen Kane*. As he puts it:

CUT!

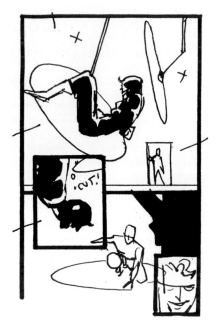

One of Kavalier's inventive thumbnail breakdowns. From the collection of Shawn Martinbrough.

> The sudden small efflorescence of art, minor but genuine, in the tawdry product line of what was then the fifth- or sixth-largest comic book company in America has usually been attributed to the potent spell of Citizen Kane acting on the renascent aspirations of Joe Kavalier. But without the thematic ban imposed by Sheldon Anapol at the behest of Parnassus Pictures—the censorship of all storylines having to do with Nazis (Japs, too), warfare, saboteurs, fifth columnists, and so on—which forced Sammy and Joe to a drastic reconsideration of the raw materials of their stories, the magical run of issues that commenced with *Radio Comics* #19 and finished when Pearl Harbor caught up to the two-month Empire lead time in the twenty-first issue of *Triumph Comics* (February 1942) looks pretty unlikely. In eight issues apiece of *Radio, Triumph, All Doll*, and the now-monthly *Escapist Adventures*, the emphasis is laid, for the first time, not only on the superpowered characters—normally so enveloped in their inevitable shrouds of bullets, torpedoes, poison gases, hurricane winds, evil spells, and so forth, that the lineaments of their personalities, if not of their deltoids and quadriceps, could hardly be discerned—but also, almost radically for the comic book of the time, on the ordinary people around them, whose own exploits, by the time hostilities with Germany were formally engaged in the early months of 1942, had advanced so far into the foreground of each story that such emphasis itself, on the everyday heroics of the "powerless," may be seen to constitute, at least in hindsight, a kind of secret, and hence probably ineffectual, propaganda. There were stories that dealt with the minutiae of what Mr. Machine Gun, at home in the pages of *Triumph*, liked to call "the hero biz," told not only from the point of view of the heroes but from those of various butlers, girlfriends, assistants, shoe-shine boys, doctors, and even the criminals. There was a story that followed the course of a handgun through the mean streets of Empire City, in which the Escapist appeared on only *two pages*. Another celebrated story told the tale of Luna Moth's girlhood, and filled in gaps in her biography, through a complicated series of flashbacks narrated by a group of unemployed witches' familiars, talking rats and cats and reptilian whatsits, in a "dark little hangout outside of Phantomville." And there was "Kane Street," focusing for sixty-four pages on one little street in Empire City, as its denizens, hearing the terrible news that the Escapist lies near death in the hospital, recall in turn the way he has touched

their lives and the lives of everyone in town (only to have it all turn out, in the end, as a cruel hoax perpetrated by the evil Crooked Man).

All of these forays into chopping up the elements of narrative, in mixing and isolating odd points of view, in stretching, as far as was possible in those days, under the constraints of a jaded editor and of publishers who cared chiefly for safe profit, the limits of comic book storytelling, all these exercises were, without question, raised far beyond the level of mere exercise by the unleashed inventiveness of Joe Kavalier's pencil. Joe, too, made a survey of the tools at hand, and found them more useful and interesting than he ever had before. But the daring use of perspective and shading, the radical placement of word balloons and captions, and above all the integration of narrative and picture by means of artfully disarranged, dislocated panels that stretched, shrank, opened into circles, spread across two full pages, marched diagonally toward one corner of a page, unreeled themselves like the frames of a film—all these were made possible only by the full collaboration of writer and artist together.

### The Second Empire
*May 1942 – May 1943*

For a year following Joe Kavalier's enlistment in the Navy and the subsequent exhaustion of the stockpile of Kavalier & Clay stories, Sam Clay continued to script all of the Escapist stories. Though some have noted a slight flagging in invention after Kavalier's departure, the level of storytelling remains high, and the artwork, though scattershot, benefits from the talents of a number of talented journeymen, including Bill Everett and Sam Glanzman.

### The Third Empire
*May 1944 – May 1954*

In this third and longest period, following Sam Clay's avowedly permanent but effectively rather brief departure from the comics business, literally dozens of different writers and artists handled the character. Careful research and interviews by the

author have revealed that among those working at Empire over this decade, many of whom may have or almost certainly did work on the Escapist books, were the aforementioned Everett and Glanzman, Mac Raboy, Mort Meskin, and John Severin.

Chabon characterizes this period in the history of the character as follows:

> In later years, in other hands, the Escapist was played for laughs. Tastes changed, and writers grew bored, and all the straight plots had been pretty well exhausted. Later writers and artists, with the connivance of George Deasey, turned the strip into a peculiar kind of inverted parody of the whole genre of the costumed hero. His chin grew larger and more emphatically dimpled, and his muscles hypertrophied until he bulged, as his post-war arch-foe Dr. Magma memorably expressed it, "like a sack full of cats." Miss Plum Blossom's ever-ready needle was pressed into providing the Escapist with a Liberacean array of specialized crime-fighting togs, and Omar and Big Al began to grumble openly about the bills their boss piled up by his extravagant expenditures on supervehicles, superplanes, and even a "handcarved ivory crutch" for Tom Mayflower to use on big date nights. The Escapist was quite vain; readers sometimes caught him stopping, on his way to fight evil, to check his reflection and comb his hair in a window

A jaunty and rather dapper Tom Mayflower, circa 1946. Courtesy of the Eric Wight archives.

or the mirror of a drugstore scale. In between acts of saving the earth from the evil Omnivores, in one of the late issues, #130 (March 1953), the Escapist works himself into quite a little lather as he attempts, with the help of a lisping decorator, to redo the Keyhole, the secret sanctum under the boards of the Empire Palace. While he continued to defend the weak and champion the helpless as reliably as ever, the Escapist never seemed to take his adventures very seriously. He took vacations in Cuba, Hawaii, and Las Vegas, where he shared a stage at the Sands Hotel with none other than Wladziu Liberace himself. Sometimes, if he was in no particular hurry to get anywhere, he let Big Al take over the controls of the Keyjet and picked up a movie magazine that had his picture on its cover. The so-called "Rube Goldberg plots," in which the Escapist, as bored as anyone by the dull routine of crimebusting, deliberately introduced obstacles and handicaps into his own efforts to thwart the large but finite variety of megalomaniacs, fiends, and rank hoodlums he fought in the years after the war, in order to make things more interesting for himself, became a trademark of the character: he would agree with himself beforehand, say, to dispatch some particular gang of criminal "barehanded," and only to use his by now vastly augmented physical strength if one of them uttered some random phrase like "ice water," and then, just after he was almost licked and the weather too cold for anyone ever to ask for a glass of ice water, the Escapist would hit on a way to arrange things so that inexorably the gang ended up in the back of a truck full of onions. He was a superpowerful, muscle-bound clown.

The Third Empire came to an abrupt end in April 1954. Nervous about the plummeting sales of the Escapist titles (and of superhero comics in general), troubled by his (correct) premonition of an impending loss in *DC v. Empire*, and fearing fallout from *Seduction of the Innocent* and the Kefauver hearings, Sheldon Anapol killed the three surviving Escapist titles. The next day, the New York Court of Appeals

The Hypertrophied muscle-bound, circa 1954. From the Kyle Baker collection.

handed down its ruling in favor of DC Comics. Soon after, Joe Kavalier purchased Empire Comics from Sheldon Anapol, but not before Anapol, in a characteristic move, had sold the rights to the entire Empire superhero stable, including the Escapist and Luna Moth, to DC. Kavalier continued to publish under the Empire Comics name, with an entirely new line of "Adult Interest" comics.

## II
## The Score Comics Era
*June 1954 – November 1959*

Shortly after DC acquired the rights to the Escapist and the rest of the Empire superheroes, one of Harry Donenfeld's nieces announced her impending marriage. Her intended was Marvin "Lucky" Lemberg, a man of no great ability or intelligence, and very little in the way of luck. It was felt in the family that suitable employment ought to be found for Lemberg, and when he evinced an interest in comic books (especially those drawn by Matt Baker) it was proposed and arranged that the old Empire stable be "spun off" and established at a new company, partially controlled by DC, which the new publisher, Mr. Lemberg, fatally named Score Comics.

Production problems, distribution problems, personnel problems, and, above all, Mr. Lemberg's own long-standing problems with alcohol, gambling, and the former Miss Donenfeld hampered Score from the start. His artists, working to suit Lemberg's own taste, constantly fell afoul of the new Comics Code Authority. In a little over five years Mr. Lemberg had so encumbered Score with entanglements, lawsuits, and creditors (some with rumored ties to the Profaci and Gambino crime families) that DC found it expedient to divest itself of all its holdings in the company, and its copyrights, lest its own sterling empire be tarnished by association. Lucky Lemberg's publishing career met an inglorious and unfortunate end with a five-year term at Sing Sing, and the Escapist and his costumed cohorts lapsed into a gray-lit realm of uncertain ownership, competing publishers, and general lack of interest.

Nonetheless, during this period some excellent stories appeared, written and drawn by a number of interesting people, some DC veterans or future DC stalwarts, among them Murphy Anderson, Jack Cole, Frank Frazetta, Bob Powell, Robert Kanigher, Edmond Hamilton, Otto Binder, Jerry Siegel, Ramona Fradon, Joe Maneely, Dick Ayers, and, some have argued, Steve Ditko.

The stories during the Score Era tend, roughly, to fall into three categories:

1) "Tough Guy" stories, often emphasizing a) the workings and operations of the entire Escapist team, generally in a noirish world of lowlifes and gangsters, and b) the breasts of Miss Plum Blossom.

2) "Puzzler" stories, Houdini-esque variations on the locked-room mystery, in which a seemingly impossible escape is effected by ingenious means which have been carefully laid out beforehand, and just as carefully concealed, from the reader. This type of story was a favorite of the great Hamilton, who wrote nearly two dozen of them.

3) Weird stories emphasizing the occult connections of the Escapist and the world of magic in which the League of the Golden Key operates. The Escapist featured in these stories is often pointed to as a precursor of Marvel's Doctor Strange.

### III
### The Wild Years
*Roughly 1960 – 1968*

During this woolly and fascinating period, with the copyright on the Escapist thrown into confusion, five separate publishers brought out competing versions of the character.

These varied wildly in tone, quality, approach, and personnel, with occasional bright spots, in particular the Fab Comics run of late '65–'68, with the fledgling Steranko and Neal Adams and a top-of-his-game post-Marvel Ditko taking interesting whacks at the character.

Fab Comics pursued an approach to the character centered around show-stopping artwork, while the battered remnant of Score Comics churned out poorly printed, badly lettered, juvenile (but withal entertaining) crap. Big Top Comics and Hi-Tone Comics (some have argued they were in fact the same entity operating under separate names) purveyed barely recognizable, in-name-only versions of the character, intended chiefly to capitalize on all the confusion.

The most interesting incarnation of the Escapist during this wide-open period, perhaps, was the short-lived version produced by Conquaire Comics, publishing arm of Conquaire Grooming Products, manufacturers of hair-care and skin-care products for African-Americans, and somehow or other

The 1974 re-design of The Escapist, by Howard Chaykin. Courtesy of the artist.

another of Lucky Lemberg's many creditors. For an all too brief run of five issues, the first of which predated Marvel's Black Panther (who debuted in *Fantastic Four* #52, July 1966) by a month, the streets of Empire City were prowled by a black Escapist whose unique, historically based twist on the theme of enslavement and liberation remains a personal favorite of the author's.

This chaos, however, could not continue, and in 1968, the greeting-card and poster publisher Gerald Sunshine, Lemberg's largest single creditor, succeeded in securing copyright to the Escapist and the other old Empire characters (by this point completely neglected and abandoned). Having won this victory, the owner and founder of Sunshine Cards celebrated by immediately ceasing production of all Escapist comic books while he pursued ambitious but illusory television, film, and theme park concepts, all of which in the end failed to pan out (though rumors persist of an hour-long pilot Escapist TV show, shot for ABC for the fall of 1970).

## IV
### The Sunshine Comics Years
*1972 – 1976*

In 1972, Gerald Sunshine died, and control of Sunshine Media Group passed to his son Danny. Danny Sonnenschein, then 21, was a lifelong fan of the Escapist and a protegé of Sam Clay's, and seized the opportunity to revive and restore the character to some of its former glory. A product of his era, Danny Sonnenschein also hoped to make the character of the Escapist "relevant" and expressive of the "nitty gritty."

This venture lasted for three and a half years. Production budgets were tight; Sonnenschein experimented heavily with black-and-white and magazine-format books. And while the Sunshine distribution network was extensive, it proved difficult to sell "gritty" comic books through suburban greeting card stores. Nonetheless some of the top early-'70s talent, including Gerber, Englehart, O'Neil, Rogers, Wrightson, Kaluta,

Chaykin, etc., worked for Sunshine. In 1976, Sunshine Media Group was acquired by the giant Omnigrip Corporation, its staff fired, and its operations shut down. For the Escapist, apart from one reprinting, by a tiny press, of classic Kavalier & Clay material, a period of nearly eight years of total obscurity followed.

## V
### The Escapist Comics Era
*1984 – Present*

In 1984, seeking to make itself more attractive to merger partners, Omnigrip sold off a number of its small, unproductive, or irrelevant holdings. These included, of course, the by now tattered and forgotten line of costumed superhero characters, most of them the brainchildren of Joe Kavalier and Sammy Clay, their glory days far behind them.

One person, however, had not forgotten the Escapist and his band: Danny Sonnenschein. After the collapse of the Sunshine Comics venture he had dabbled in a number of activities, one of which proved lucrative enough to enable him, when the opportunity arose, to repurchase the old Empire characters from Omnigrip, at a bargain price. With the balance of his personal fortune he set about acquiring the rights to all the prior versions and incarnations of the character. Reconstituting himself as publisher of Escapist Books in 1985, he initially intended only to create a kind of grand archive of the Escapist, and his series of hardbound, high-quality reproductions from that era, though difficult to find now, are considered definitive.

With the birth of the independent comics scene in the late '80s, Sonnenschein saw the opportunity to revive the characters he loved, and in 1991, under the imprint of Escapist Comics, he launched the first issue of *New Adventures of the Escapist*, updating the character and his cohorts, raising the quality of the writing and the level of realism in the treatment both of the world of performing magic and the nature of evil, and exploring the ambiguous nature of the League of the Golden Key itself.

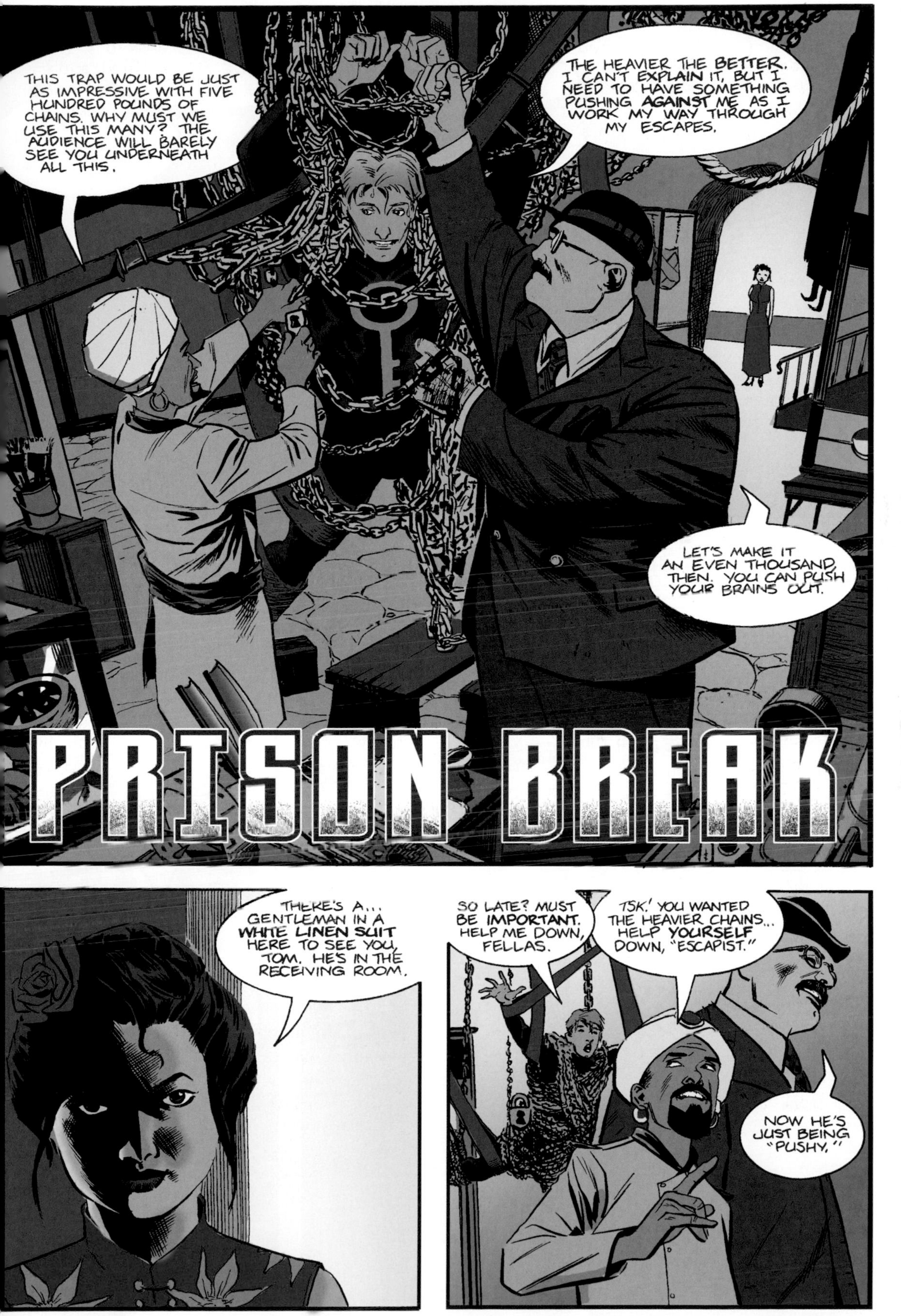
THIS TRAP WOULD BE JUST AS IMPRESSIVE WITH FIVE HUNDRED POUNDS OF CHAINS. WHY MUST WE USE THIS MANY? THE AUDIENCE WILL BARELY SEE YOU UNDERNEATH ALL THIS.
THE HEAVIER THE **BETTER**. I CAN'T **EXPLAIN** IT, BUT I NEED TO HAVE SOMETHING PUSHING **AGAINST** ME AS I WORK MY WAY THROUGH MY ESCAPES.
LET'S MAKE IT AN EVEN THOUSAND, THEN. YOU CAN PUSH YOUR BRAINS OUT.
PRISON BREAK
THERE'S A... GENTLEMAN IN A **WHITE LINEN SUIT** HERE TO SEE YOU, TOM. HE'S IN THE RECEIVING ROOM.
SO LATE? MUST BE **IMPORTANT**. HELP ME DOWN, FELLAS.
*TSK!* YOU WANTED THE HEAVIER CHAINS... HELP **YOURSELF** DOWN, "ESCAPIST."
NOW HE'S JUST BEING "PUSHY."

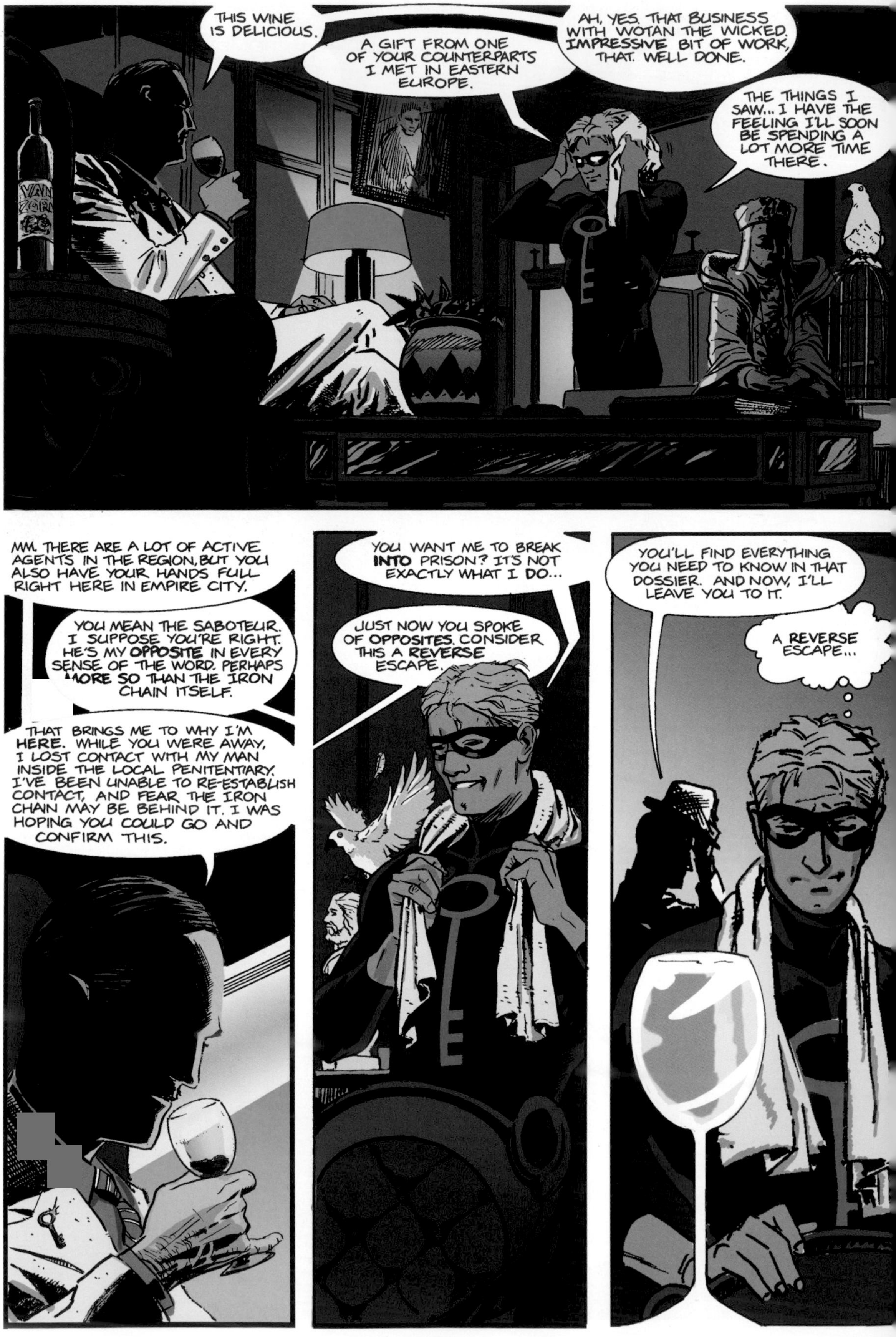

THIS WINE IS DELICIOUS.
A GIFT FROM ONE OF YOUR COUNTERPARTS I MET IN EASTERN EUROPE.
AH, YES. THAT BUSINESS WITH WOTAN THE WICKED. IMPRESSIVE BIT OF WORK, THAT. WELL DONE.
THE THINGS I SAW... I HAVE THE FEELING I'LL SOON BE SPENDING A LOT MORE TIME THERE.
MM. THERE ARE A LOT OF ACTIVE AGENTS IN THE REGION, BUT YOU ALSO HAVE YOUR HANDS FULL RIGHT HERE IN EMPIRE CITY.
YOU MEAN THE SABOTEUR. I SUPPOSE YOU'RE RIGHT. HE'S MY OPPOSITE IN EVERY SENSE OF THE WORD. PERHAPS MORE SO THAN THE IRON CHAIN ITSELF.
THAT BRINGS ME TO WHY I'M HERE. WHILE YOU WERE AWAY, I LOST CONTACT WITH MY MAN INSIDE THE LOCAL PENITENTIARY. I'VE BEEN UNABLE TO RE-ESTABLISH CONTACT, AND FEAR THE IRON CHAIN MAY BE BEHIND IT. I WAS HOPING YOU COULD GO AND CONFIRM THIS.
YOU WANT ME TO BREAK INTO PRISON? IT'S NOT EXACTLY WHAT I DO...
JUST NOW YOU SPOKE OF OPPOSITES. CONSIDER THIS A REVERSE ESCAPE.
YOU'LL FIND EVERYTHING YOU NEED TO KNOW IN THAT DOSSIER. AND NOW, I'LL LEAVE YOU TO IT.
A REVERSE ESCAPE...

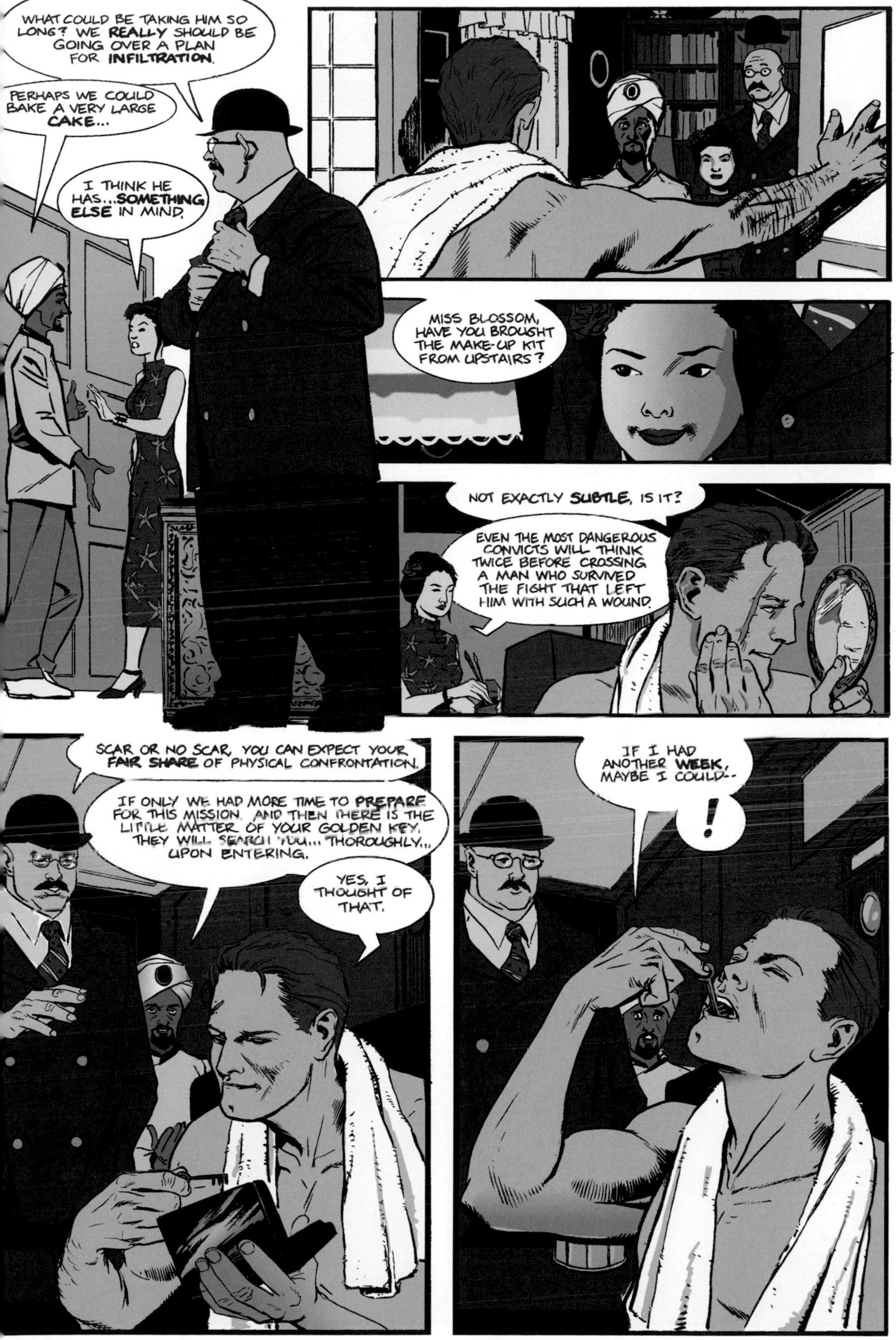
WHAT COULD BE TAKING HIM SO LONG? WE REALLY SHOULD BE GOING OVER A PLAN FOR INFILTRATION.
PERHAPS WE COULD BAKE A VERY LARGE CAKE...
I THINK HE HAS...SOMETHING ELSE IN MIND.
MISS BLOSSOM, HAVE YOU BROUGHT THE MAKE-UP KIT FROM UPSTAIRS?
NOT EXACTLY SUBTLE, IS IT?
EVEN THE MOST DANGEROUS CONVICTS WILL THINK TWICE BEFORE CROSSING A MAN WHO SURVIVED THE FIGHT THAT LEFT HIM WITH SUCH A WOUND.
SCAR OR NO SCAR, YOU CAN EXPECT YOUR FAIR SHARE OF PHYSICAL CONFRONTATION.
IF ONLY WE HAD MORE TIME TO PREPARE FOR THIS MISSION. AND THEN THERE IS THE LITTLE MATTER OF YOUR GOLDEN KEY. THEY WILL SEARCH YOU... THOROUGHLY... UPON ENTERING.
YES, I THOUGHT OF THAT.
IF I HAD ANOTHER WEEK, MAYBE I COULD--
!

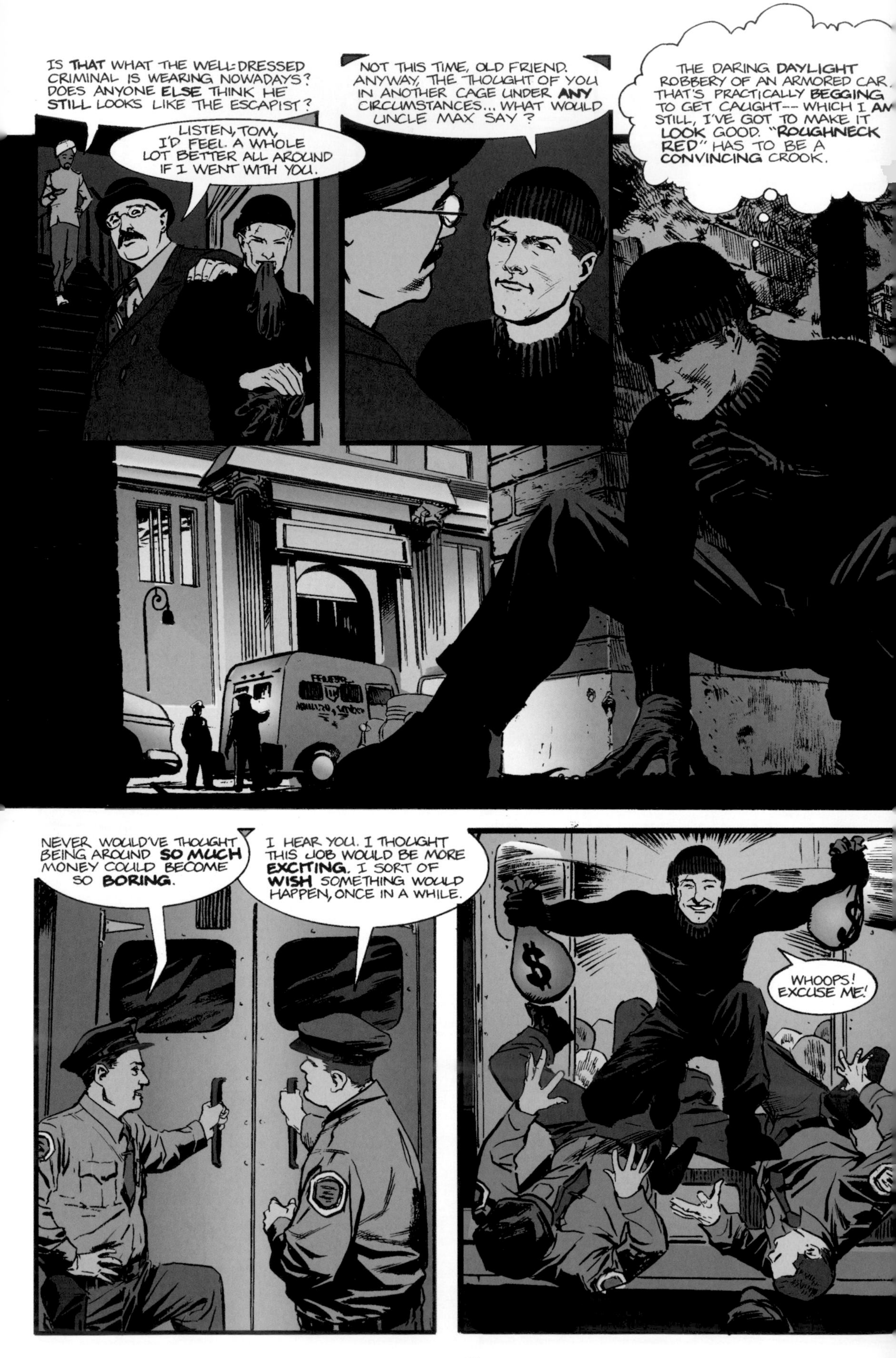

IS THAT WHAT THE WELL-DRESSED CRIMINAL IS WEARING NOWADAYS? DOES ANYONE ELSE THINK HE STILL LOOKS LIKE THE ESCAPIST?
LISTEN, TOM, I'D FEEL A WHOLE LOT BETTER ALL AROUND IF I WENT WITH YOU.
NOT THIS TIME, OLD FRIEND. ANYWAY, THE THOUGHT OF YOU IN ANOTHER CAGE UNDER ANY CIRCUMSTANCES... WHAT WOULD UNCLE MAX SAY?
THE DARING DAYLIGHT ROBBERY OF AN ARMORED CAR THAT'S PRACTICALLY BEGGING TO GET CAUGHT-- WHICH I AM. STILL, I'VE GOT TO MAKE IT LOOK GOOD. "ROUGHNECK RED" HAS TO BE A CONVINCING CROOK.
NEVER WOULD'VE THOUGHT BEING AROUND SO MUCH MONEY COULD BECOME SO BORING.
I HEAR YOU. I THOUGHT THIS JOB WOULD BE MORE EXCITING. I SORT OF WISH SOMETHING WOULD HAPPEN, ONCE IN A WHILE.
$
WHOOPS! EXCUSE ME!

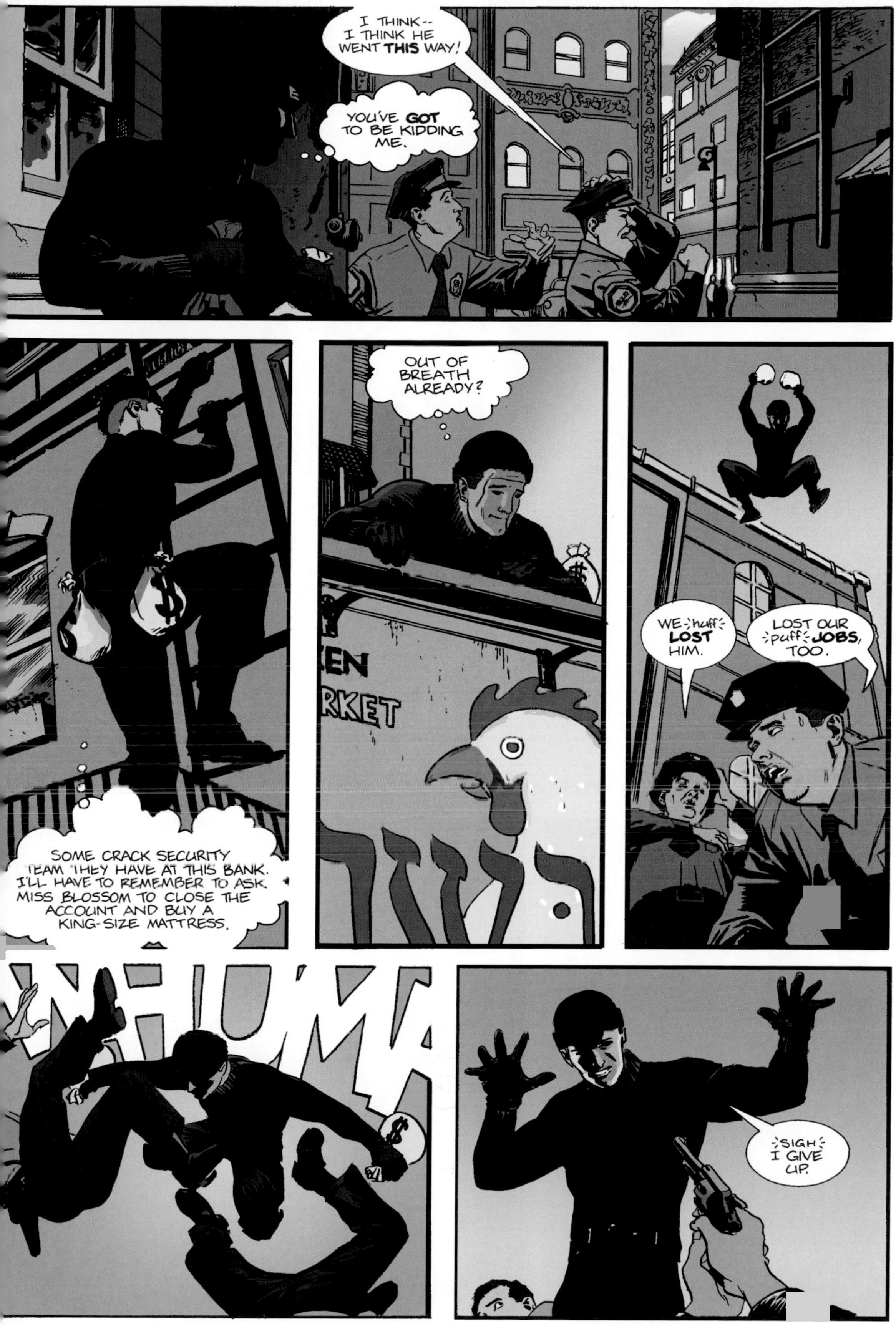
I THINK-- I THINK HE WENT **THIS** WAY!
YOU'VE **GOT** TO BE KIDDING ME.
SOME CRACK SECURITY TEAM THEY HAVE AT THIS BANK. I'LL HAVE TO REMEMBER TO ASK MISS BLOSSOM TO CLOSE THE ACCOUNT AND BUY A KING-SIZE MATTRESS.
OUT OF BREATH ALREADY?
WE -huff- **LOST** HIM.
LOST OUR -puff- **JOBS**, TOO.
-SIGH- I GIVE UP.

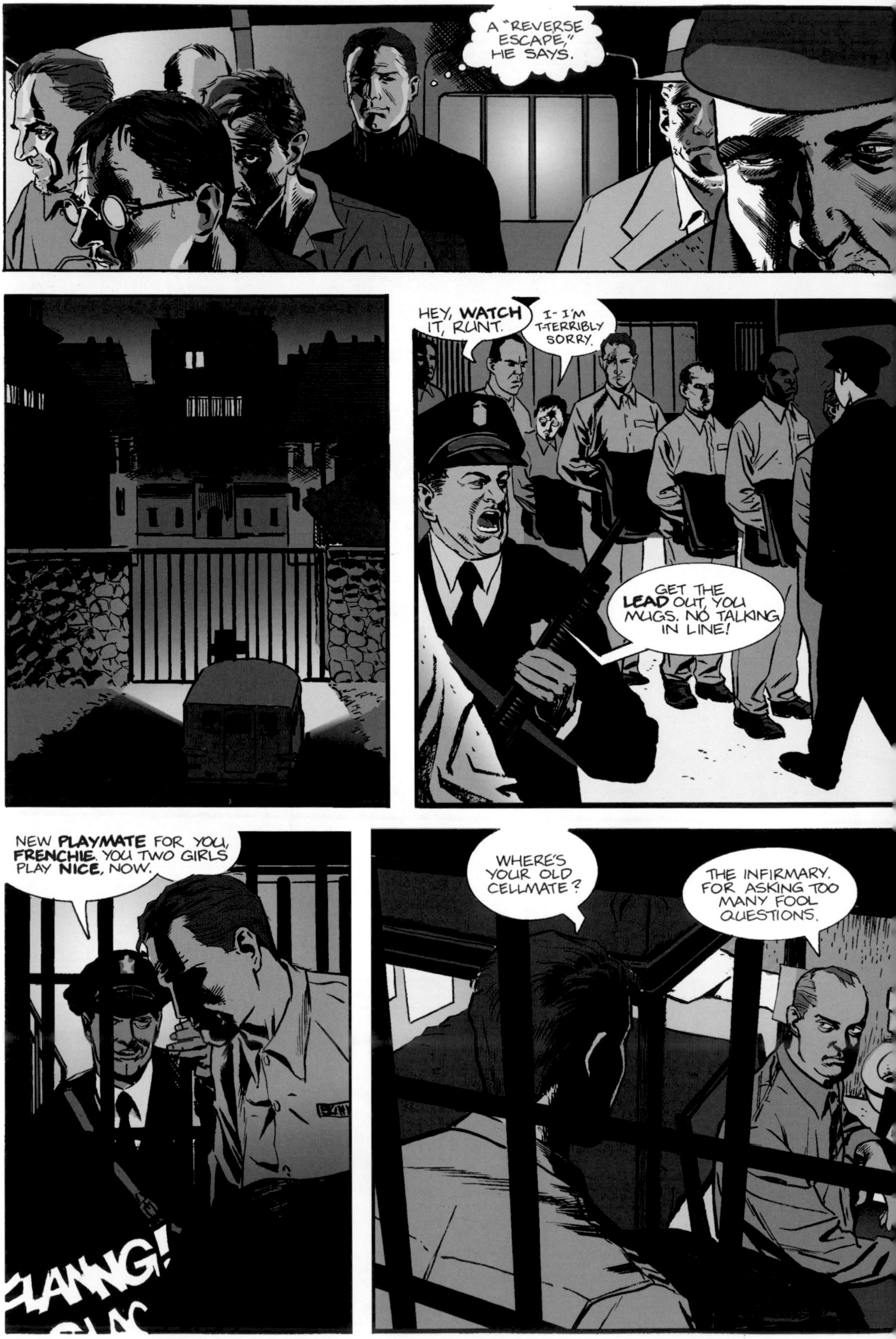
A "REVERSE ESCAPE," HE SAYS.
HEY, **WATCH** IT, RUNT.
I- I'M T-TERRIBLY SORRY.
GET THE **LEAD** OUT, YOU MUGS. NO TALKING IN LINE!
NEW **PLAYMATE** FOR YOU, **FRENCHIE**. YOU TWO GIRLS PLAY **NICE**, NOW.
CLANNG!
WHERE'S YOUR OLD CELLMATE?
THE INFIRMARY. FOR ASKING TOO MANY FOOL QUESTIONS.

WHAT'S HOLDING UP THAT LAST SHIPMENT OF GUNS? WE'RE ALREADY WAY **BEHIND** SCHEDULE. WHAT HAVE YOU **GOT** THERE?

THE FILES ON ALL OUR "GUESTS" WHO ARRIVED TODAY. I'M MAKING SURE WE DIDN'T LET ANY **RATS** SLIP IN.

YOU MEAN **MOLES**? LIKE **YOU** USED TO BE, TURNKEY, BEFORE YOU **TURNED RAT** AND JOINED UP WITH THE GOOD GUYS?

THE GOOD GUYS, WARDEN? HARDLY. OVERTAKING A PRISON IN AN EFFORT TO RECRUIT AND ARM CONVICTS FOR AN INVASION OF EMPIRE CITY? THIS IS THE WORK OF EVIL MEN. I **USED** TO BE ONE OF THE GOOD GUYS, BUT NO LONGER.

THE **TURNCOAT** TURNKEY. NOT THAT I'M **COMPLAINING.** YOU'VE GIVEN US VALUABLE **INSIGHT** INTO HOW THE LEAGUE OPERATES... BUT WHY'D YOU **DO** IT?

I DON'T KNOW THAT IT WAS ANY **ONE** THING. MAYBE TOO MUCH TIME AS A **PLANT** IN THIS PRISON AND A DOZEN LIKE IT RUBBED OFF ON ME, UNTIL IT BECAME SECOND NATURE TO BETRAY THE **TRUST** OF OTHERS.

MAYBE I FELT UNAPPRECIATED-- ABANDONED--BY THOSE WHITE-SUITED HYPOCRITES. WHO CAN SAY?

ALL I KNOW IS: I WON'T BE HAPPY UNTIL THIS WHOLE **CITY** BECOMES A PRISON. THEN EVERYONE WILL KNOW HOW IT FEELS.

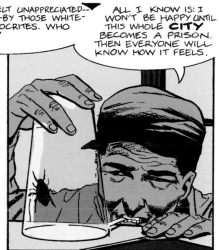

THAT TRAY LOOKS **HEAVY**, RUNT. I'LL CARRY IT FOR YOU.

NOW **BEAT** IT, BEFORE I PUSH YOUR **FACE** IN.

N-NO, THIS IS **MINE**! YOU **GOT** YOURS!

GIVING ME **LIP**, EH? I'LL GIVE YOU **YOURS** ALL RIGHT!

LEAVE HIM BE.

STAY OUT OF THIS, FRANKENS—

*UNGK!*

FRANKENSTEIN WAS **THE DOCTOR**, STUPID. IF YOU'RE GOING TO MAKE FUN OF MY SCAR, DO IT **RIGHT**.

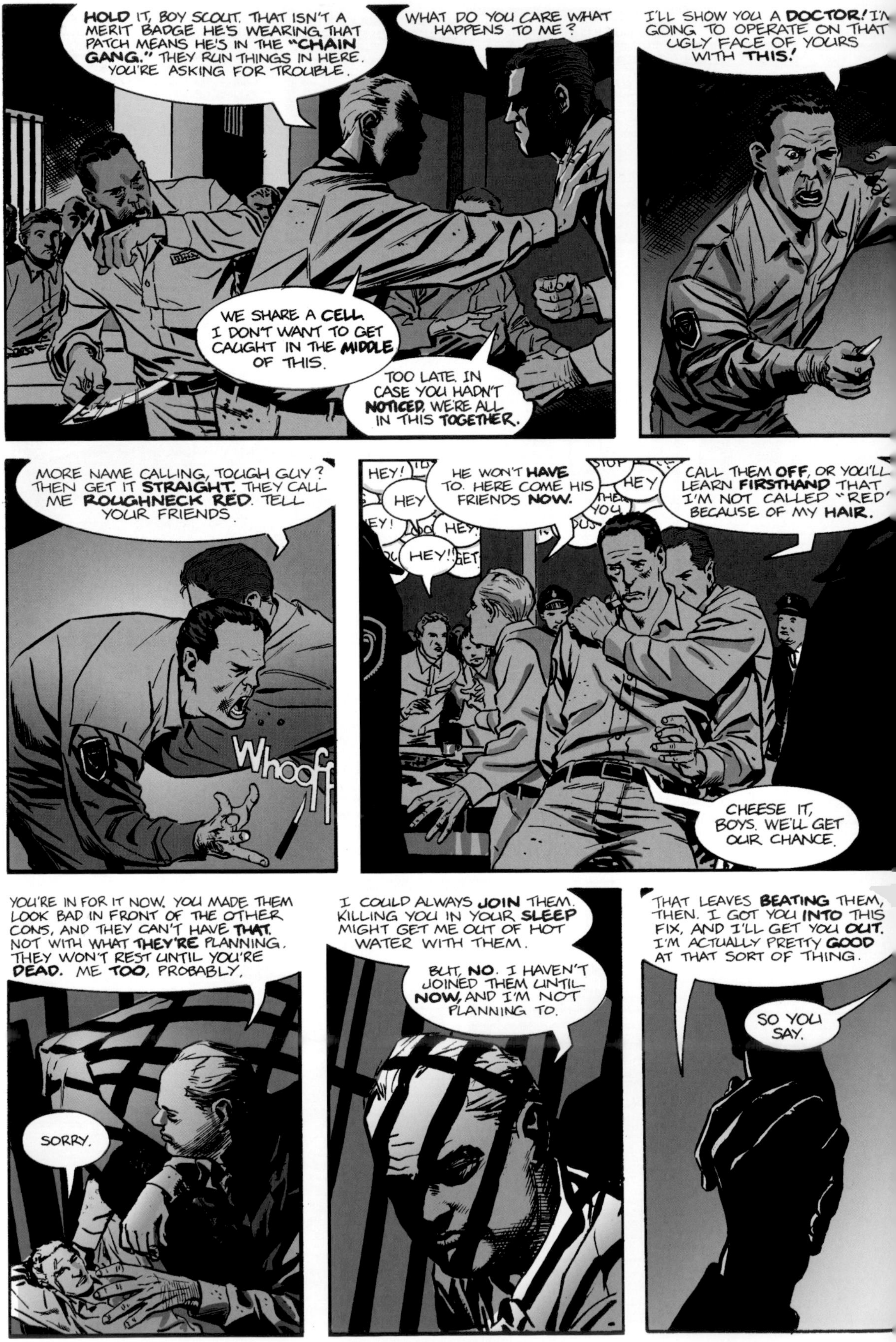
HOLD IT, BOY SCOUT. THAT ISN'T A MERIT BADGE HE'S WEARING. THAT PATCH MEANS HE'S IN THE "CHAIN GANG." THEY RUN THINGS IN HERE. YOU'RE ASKING FOR TROUBLE.
WHAT DO YOU CARE WHAT HAPPENS TO ME?
WE SHARE A CELL. I DON'T WANT TO GET CAUGHT IN THE MIDDLE OF THIS.
TOO LATE. IN CASE YOU HADN'T NOTICED, WE'RE ALL IN THIS TOGETHER.
I'LL SHOW YOU A DOCTOR! I'M GOING TO OPERATE ON THAT UGLY FACE OF YOURS WITH THIS!
MORE NAME CALLING, TOUGH GUY? THEN GET IT STRAIGHT. THEY CALL ME ROUGHNECK RED. TELL YOUR FRIENDS.
Whoofff
HEY!
HEY
HEY!!
HEY
HE WON'T HAVE TO. HERE COME HIS FRIENDS NOW.
CALL THEM OFF, OR YOU'LL LEARN FIRSTHAND THAT I'M NOT CALLED "RED" BECAUSE OF MY HAIR.
CHEESE IT, BOYS. WE'LL GET OUR CHANCE.
YOU'RE IN FOR IT NOW. YOU MADE THEM LOOK BAD IN FRONT OF THE OTHER CONS, AND THEY CAN'T HAVE THAT. NOT WITH WHAT THEY'RE PLANNING. THEY WON'T REST UNTIL YOU'RE DEAD. ME TOO, PROBABLY.
SORRY.
I COULD ALWAYS JOIN THEM. KILLING YOU IN YOUR SLEEP MIGHT GET ME OUT OF HOT WATER WITH THEM.
BUT, NO. I HAVEN'T JOINED THEM UNTIL NOW, AND I'M NOT PLANNING TO.
THAT LEAVES BEATING THEM, THEN. I GOT YOU INTO THIS FIX, AND I'LL GET YOU OUT. I'M ACTUALLY PRETTY GOOD AT THAT SORT OF THING.
SO YOU SAY.

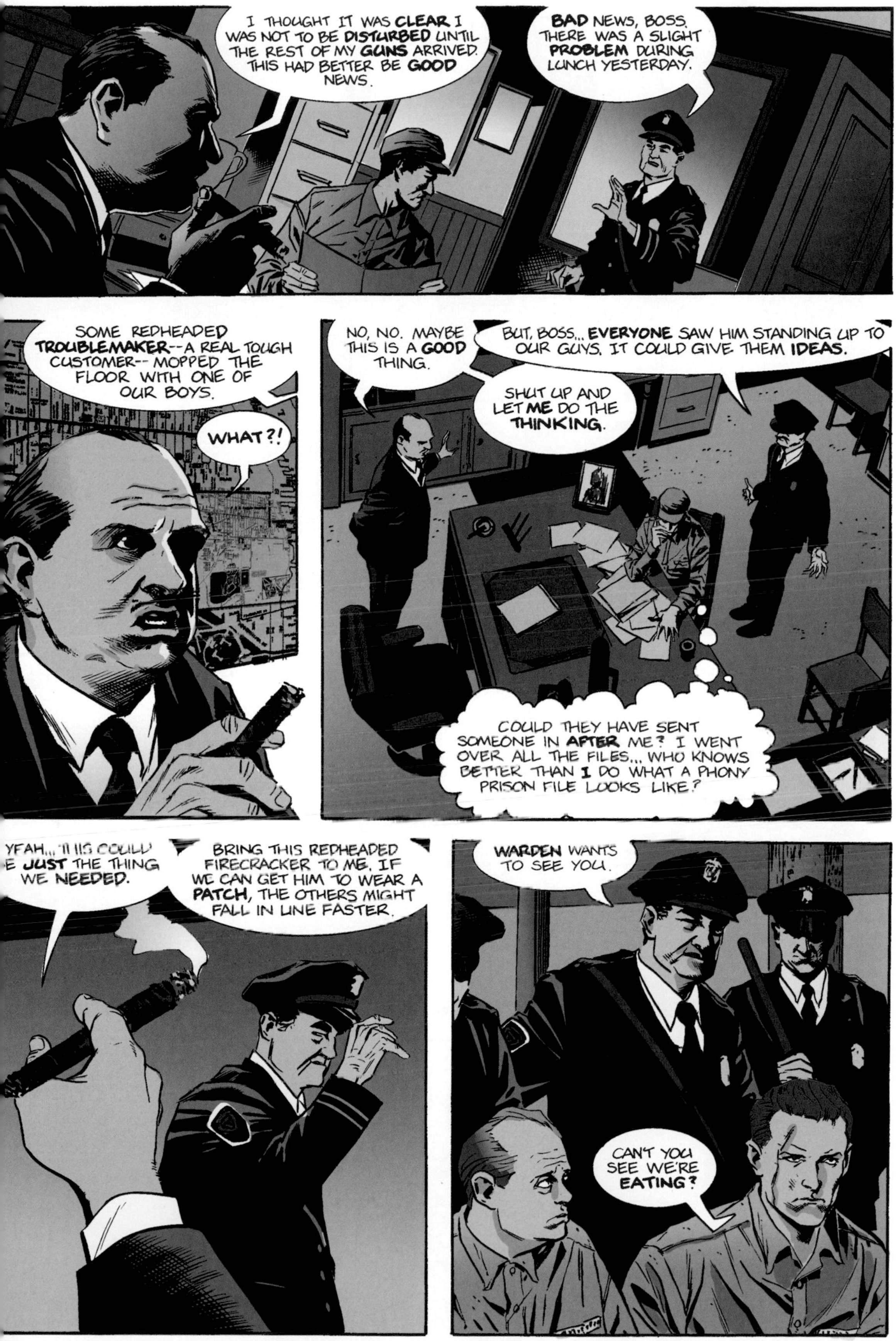
I THOUGHT IT WAS CLEAR I WAS NOT TO BE DISTURBED UNTIL THE REST OF MY GUNS ARRIVED. THIS HAD BETTER BE GOOD NEWS.
BAD NEWS, BOSS. THERE WAS A SLIGHT PROBLEM DURING LUNCH YESTERDAY.
SOME REDHEADED TROUBLEMAKER--A REAL TOUGH CUSTOMER--MOPPED THE FLOOR WITH ONE OF OUR BOYS.
WHAT?!
NO, NO. MAYBE THIS IS A GOOD THING.
BUT, BOSS... EVERYONE SAW HIM STANDING UP TO OUR GUYS. IT COULD GIVE THEM IDEAS.
SHUT UP AND LET ME DO THE THINKING.
COULD THEY HAVE SENT SOMEONE IN AFTER ME? I WENT OVER ALL THE FILES... WHO KNOWS BETTER THAN I DO WHAT A PHONY PRISON FILE LOOKS LIKE?
YEAH... THIS COULD E JUST THE THING WE NEEDED.
BRING THIS REDHEADED FIRECRACKER TO ME. IF WE CAN GET HIM TO WEAR A PATCH, THE OTHERS MIGHT FALL IN LINE FASTER.
WARDEN WANTS TO SEE YOU.
CAN'T YOU SEE WE'RE EATING?

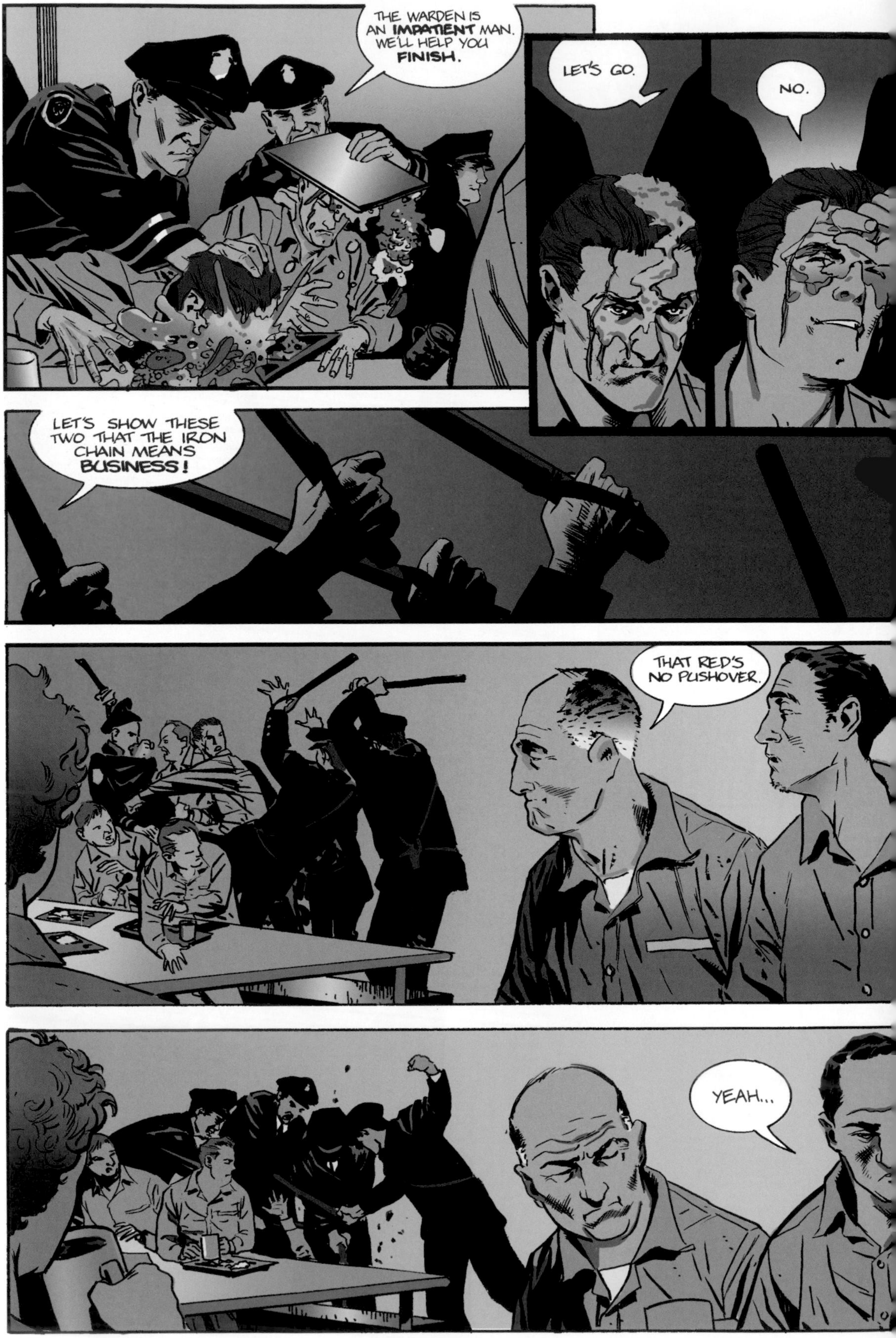
THE WARDEN IS AN **IMPATIENT** MAN. WE'LL HELP YOU **FINISH**.
LET'S GO.
NO.
LET'S SHOW THESE TWO THAT THE IRON CHAIN MEANS **BUSINESS!**
THAT RED'S NO PUSHOVER.
YEAH...

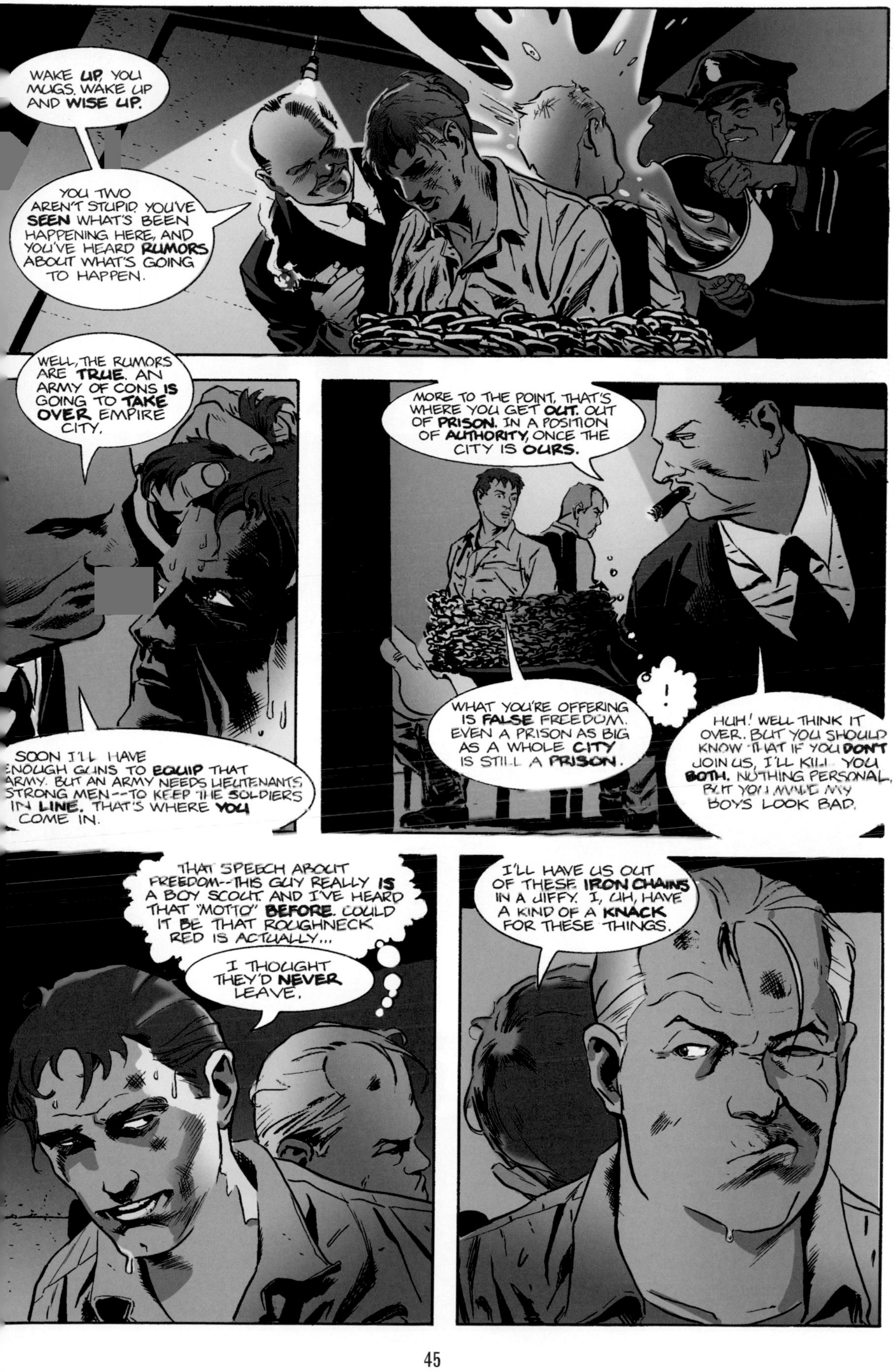

WAKE UP, YOU MUGS. WAKE UP AND WISE UP.
YOU TWO AREN'T STUPID. YOU'VE SEEN WHAT'S BEEN HAPPENING HERE, AND YOU'VE HEARD RUMORS ABOUT WHAT'S GOING TO HAPPEN.
WELL, THE RUMORS ARE TRUE. AN ARMY OF CONS IS GOING TO TAKE OVER EMPIRE CITY.
SOON I'LL HAVE ENOUGH GUNS TO EQUIP THAT ARMY. BUT AN ARMY NEEDS LIEUTENANTS, STRONG MEN--TO KEEP THE SOLDIERS IN LINE. THAT'S WHERE YOU COME IN.
MORE TO THE POINT, THAT'S WHERE YOU GET OUT. OUT OF PRISON. IN A POSITION OF AUTHORITY, ONCE THE CITY IS OURS.
WHAT YOU'RE OFFERING IS FALSE FREEDOM. EVEN A PRISON AS BIG AS A WHOLE CITY IS STILL A PRISON.
!
HUH! WELL THINK IT OVER. BUT YOU SHOULD KNOW THAT IF YOU DON'T JOIN US, I'LL KILL YOU BOTH. NOTHING PERSONAL, BUT YOU MADE MY BOYS LOOK BAD.
THAT SPEECH ABOUT FREEDOM--THIS GUY REALLY IS A BOY SCOUT. AND I'VE HEARD THAT "MOTTO" BEFORE. COULD IT BE THAT ROUGHNECK RED IS ACTUALLY...
I THOUGHT THEY'D NEVER LEAVE.
I'LL HAVE US OUT OF THESE IRON CHAINS IN A JIFFY. I, UH, HAVE A KIND OF A KNACK FOR THESE THINGS.

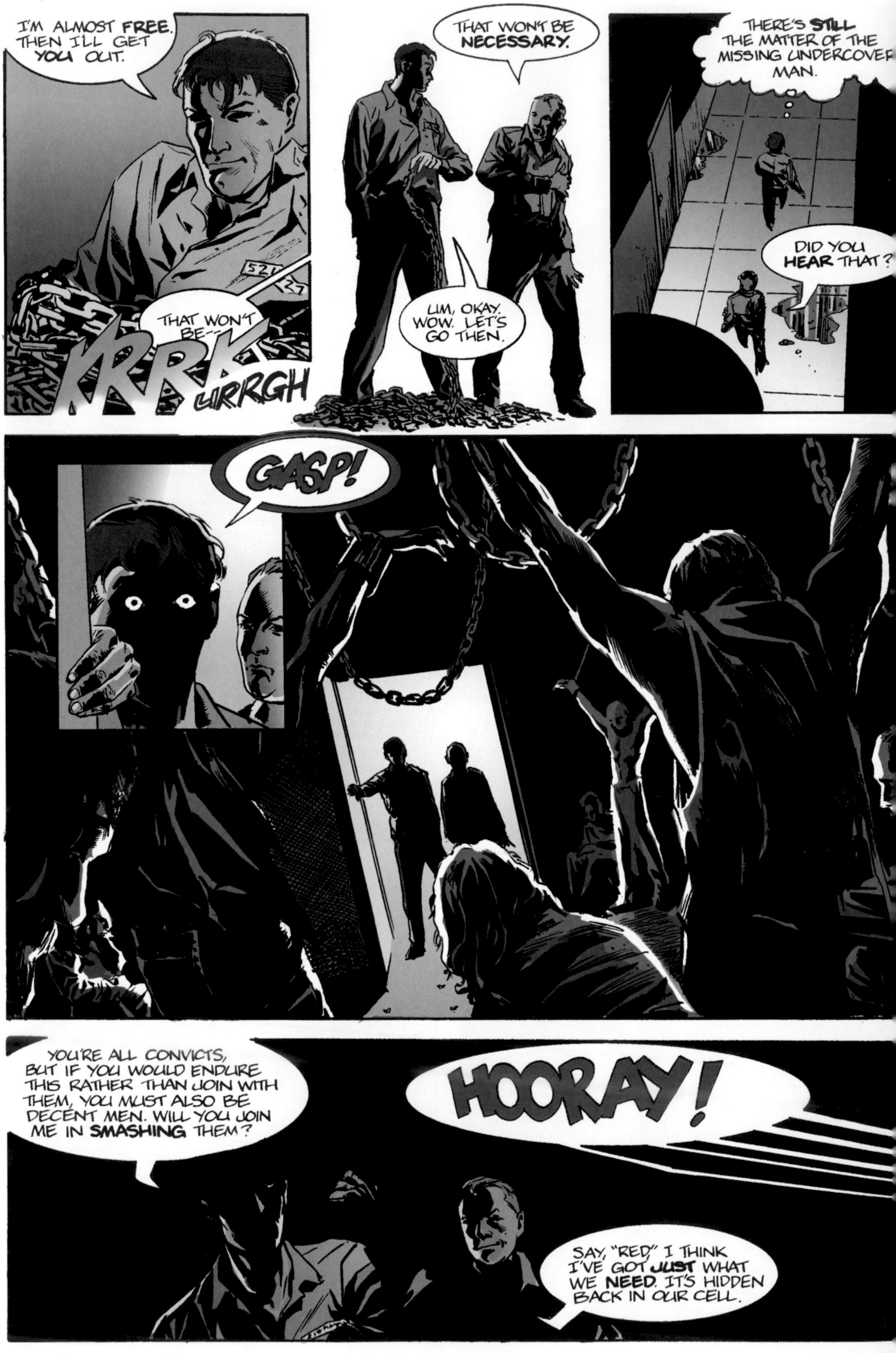
I'M ALMOST **FREE**. THEN I'LL GET **YOU** OUT.
THAT WON'T BE--
KRRK
URRGH
THAT WON'T BE **NECESSARY**.
UM, OKAY. WOW. LET'S GO THEN.
THERE'S **STILL** THE MATTER OF THE MISSING UNDERCOVER MAN.
DID YOU **HEAR** THAT?
GASP!
YOU'RE ALL CONVICTS, BUT IF YOU WOULD ENDURE THIS RATHER THAN JOIN WITH THEM, YOU MUST ALSO BE DECENT MEN. WILL YOU JOIN ME IN **SMASHING** THEM?
HOORAY!
SAY, "RED," I THINK I'VE GOT **JUST** WHAT WE **NEED**. IT'S HIDDEN BACK IN OUR CELL.

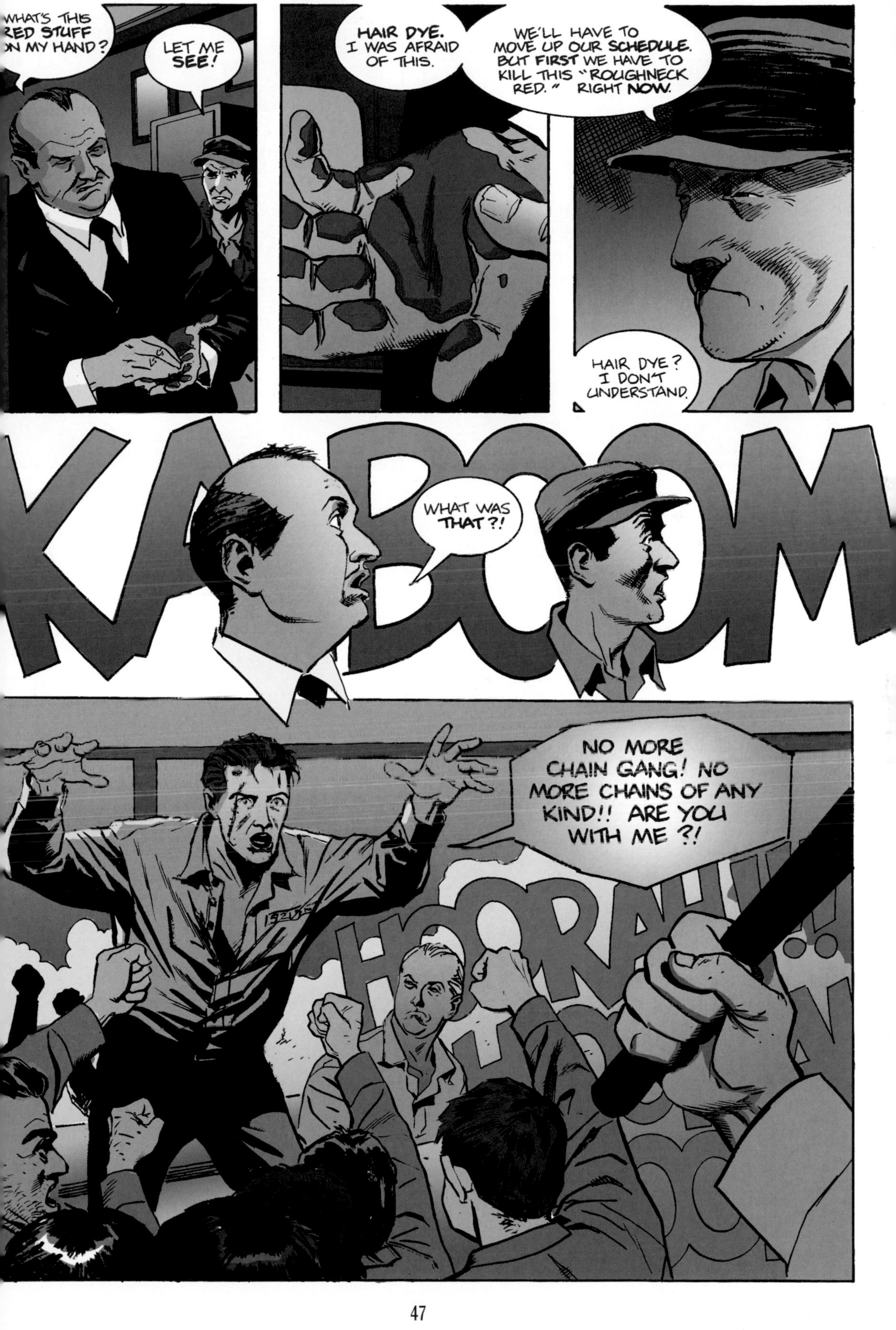

WHAT'S THIS RED STUFF ON MY HAND?
LET ME SEE!
HAIR DYE. I WAS AFRAID OF THIS.
WE'LL HAVE TO MOVE UP OUR SCHEDULE. BUT FIRST WE HAVE TO KILL THIS "ROUGHNECK RED." RIGHT NOW.
HAIR DYE? I DON'T UNDERSTAND.
KABOOM
WHAT WAS THAT?!
NO MORE CHAIN GANG! NO MORE CHAINS OF ANY KIND!! ARE YOU WITH ME?!
HOORAH!!

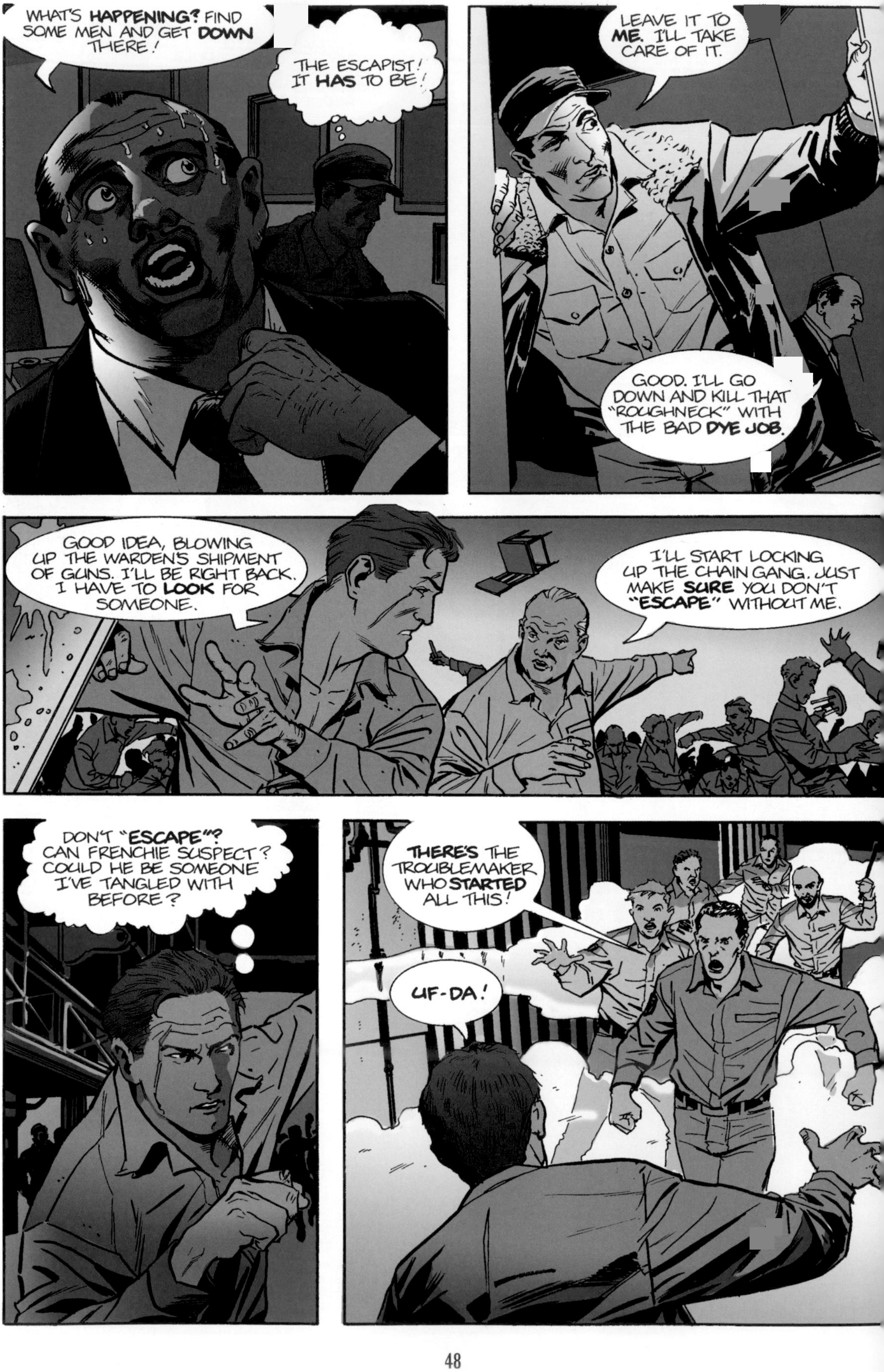
WHAT'S HAPPENING? FIND SOME MEN AND GET DOWN THERE!
THE ESCAPIST! IT HAS TO BE!
LEAVE IT TO ME. I'LL TAKE CARE OF IT.
GOOD. I'LL GO DOWN AND KILL THAT "ROUGHNECK" WITH THE BAD DYE JOB.
GOOD IDEA, BLOWING UP THE WARDEN'S SHIPMENT OF GUNS. I'LL BE RIGHT BACK. I HAVE TO LOOK FOR SOMEONE.
I'LL START LOCKING UP THE CHAIN GANG. JUST MAKE SURE YOU DON'T "ESCAPE" WITHOUT ME.
DON'T "ESCAPE"? CAN FRENCHIE SUSPECT? COULD HE BE SOMEONE I'VE TANGLED WITH BEFORE?
THERE'S THE TROUBLEMAKER WHO STARTED ALL THIS!
UF-DA!

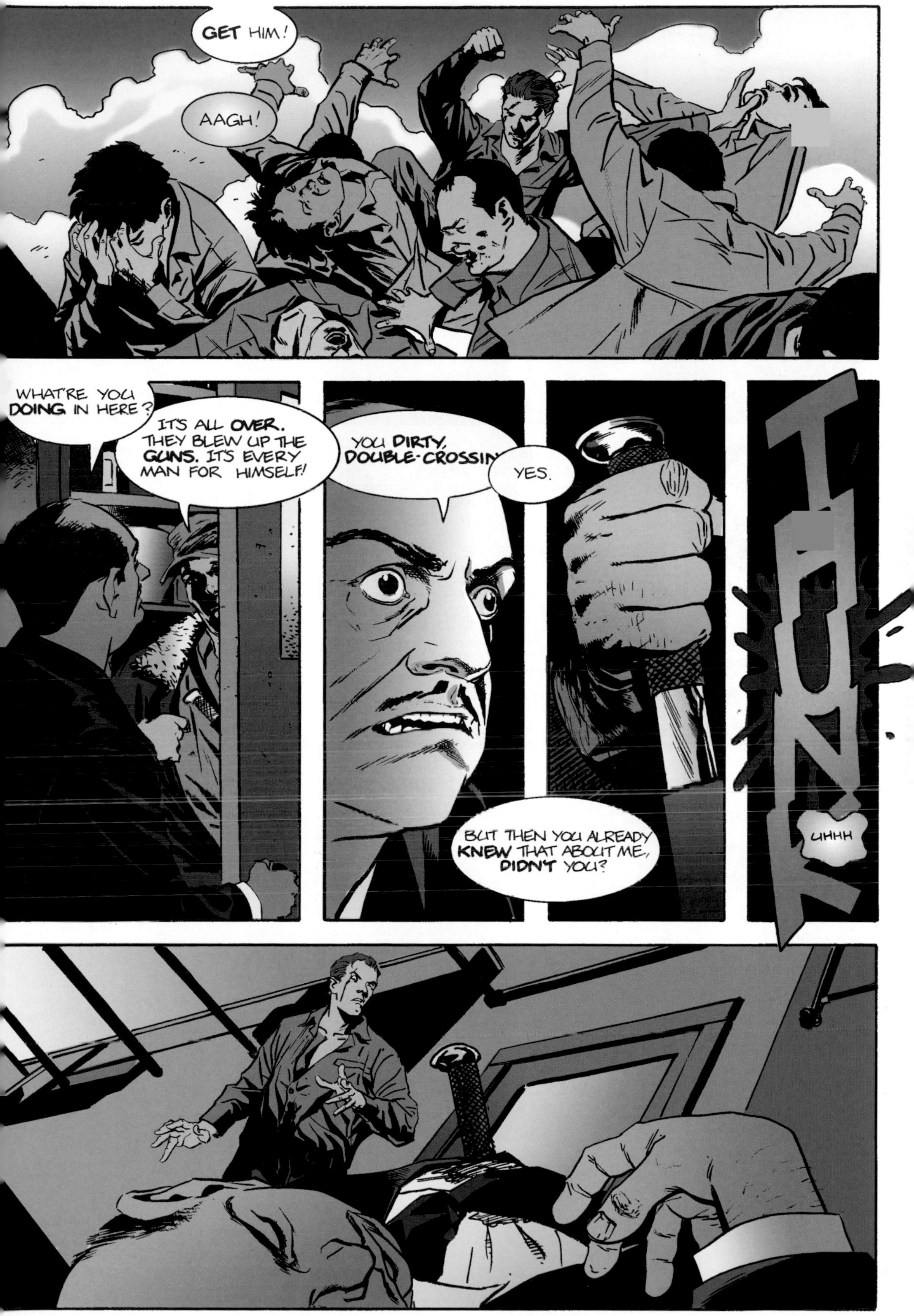
GET HIM!
AAGH!
WHAT'RE YOU DOING IN HERE?
IT'S ALL OVER. THEY BLEW UP THE GUNS. IT'S EVERY MAN FOR HIMSELF!
YOU DIRTY, DOUBLE-CROSSIN
YES.
BUT THEN YOU ALREADY KNEW THAT ABOUT ME, DIDN'T YOU?
UHHH

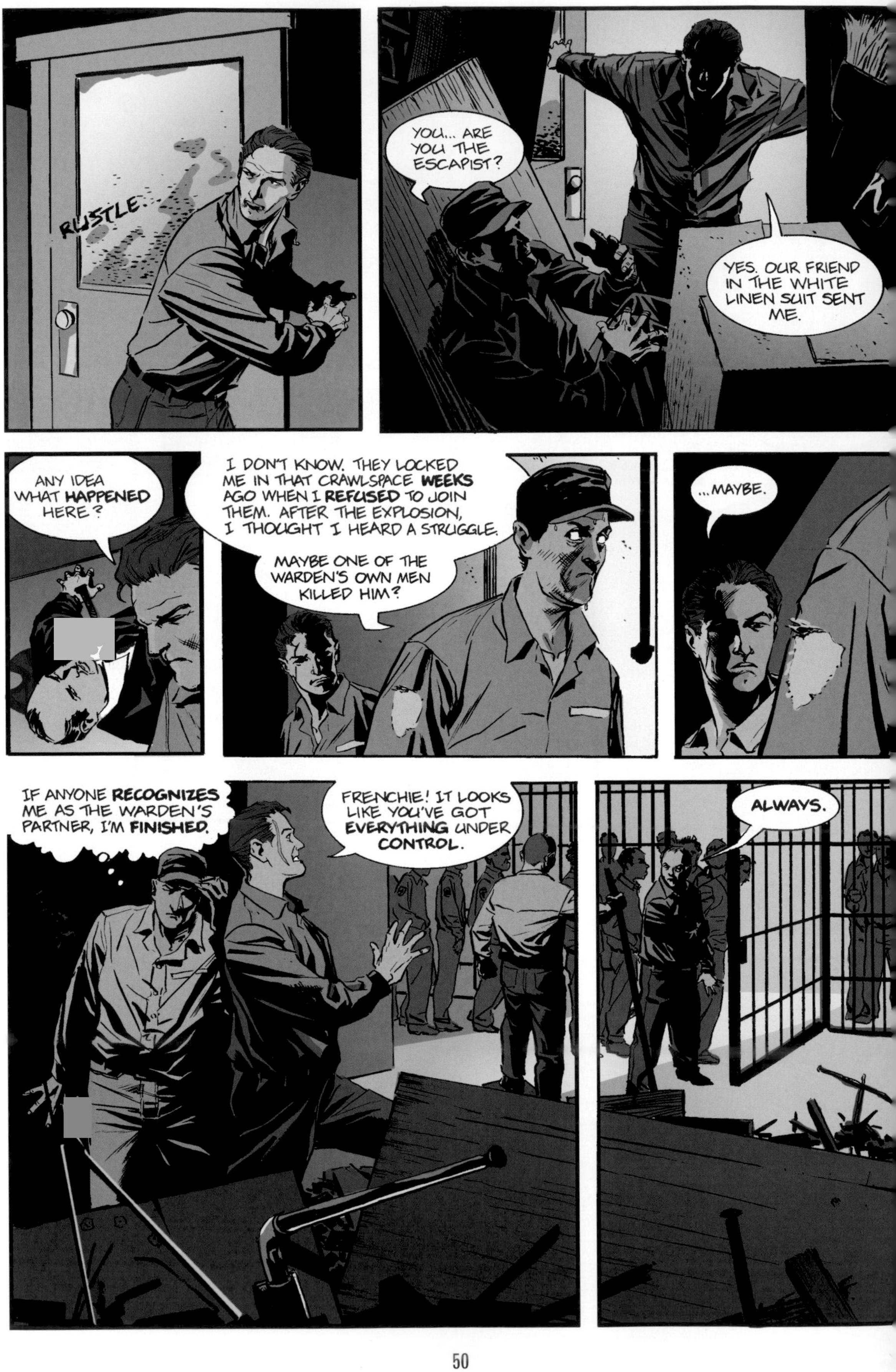
RUSTLE
YOU... ARE YOU THE ESCAPIST?
YES. OUR FRIEND IN THE WHITE LINEN SUIT SENT ME.
ANY IDEA WHAT **HAPPENED** HERE?
I DON'T KNOW. THEY LOCKED ME IN THAT CRAWLSPACE **WEEKS** AGO WHEN I **REFUSED** TO JOIN THEM. AFTER THE EXPLOSION, I THOUGHT I HEARD A STRUGGLE.
MAYBE ONE OF THE WARDEN'S OWN MEN KILLED HIM?
...MAYBE.
IF ANYONE **RECOGNIZES** ME AS THE WARDEN'S PARTNER, I'M **FINISHED**.
FRENCHIE! IT LOOKS LIKE YOU'VE GOT **EVERYTHING** UNDER **CONTROL**.
**ALWAYS.**

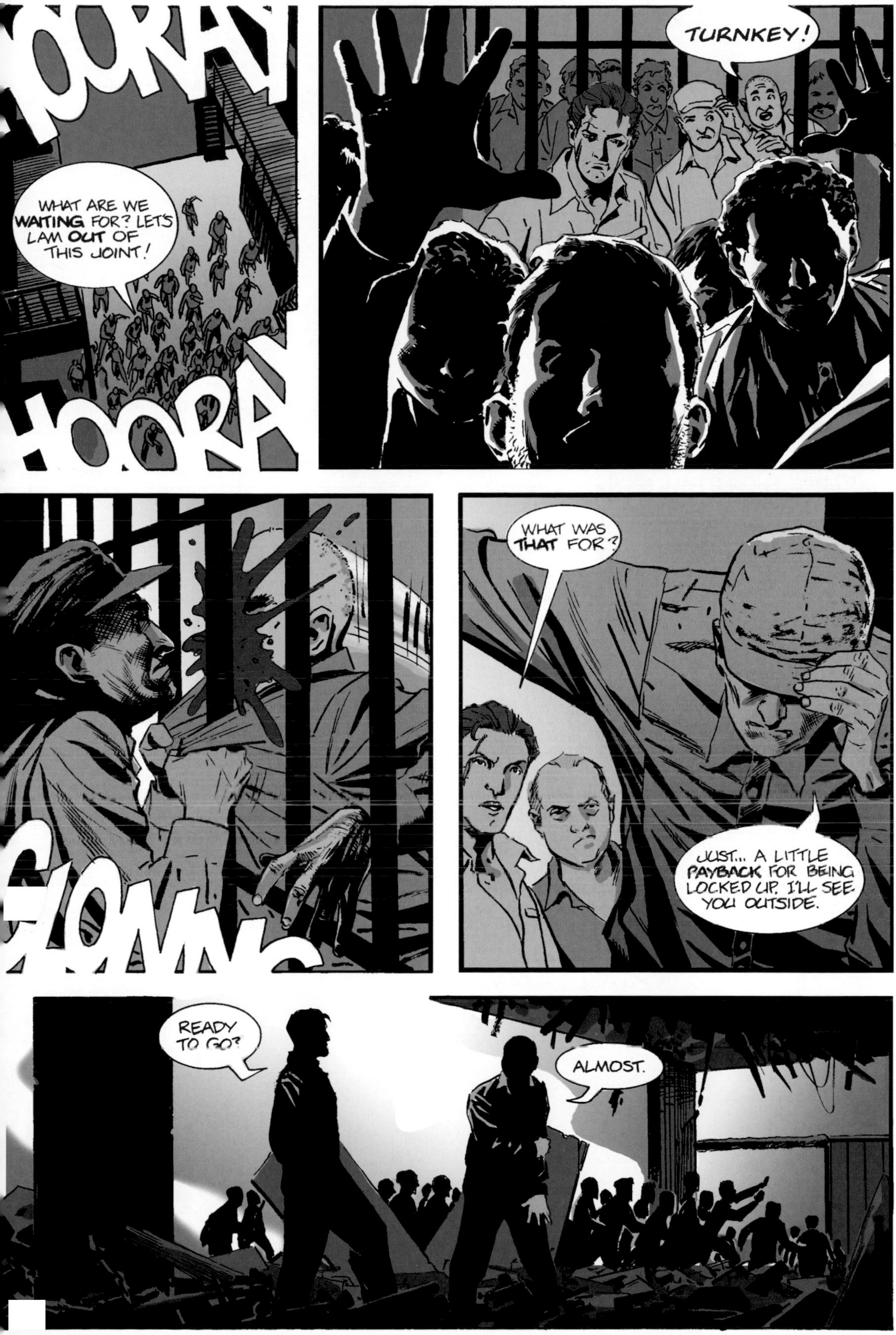
WHAT ARE WE **WAITING** FOR? LET'S LAM **OUT** OF THIS JOINT!
TURNKEY!
WHAT WAS **THAT** FOR?
JUST... A LITTLE **PAYBACK** FOR BEING LOCKED UP. I'LL SEE YOU OUTSIDE.
READY TO GO?
ALMOST.

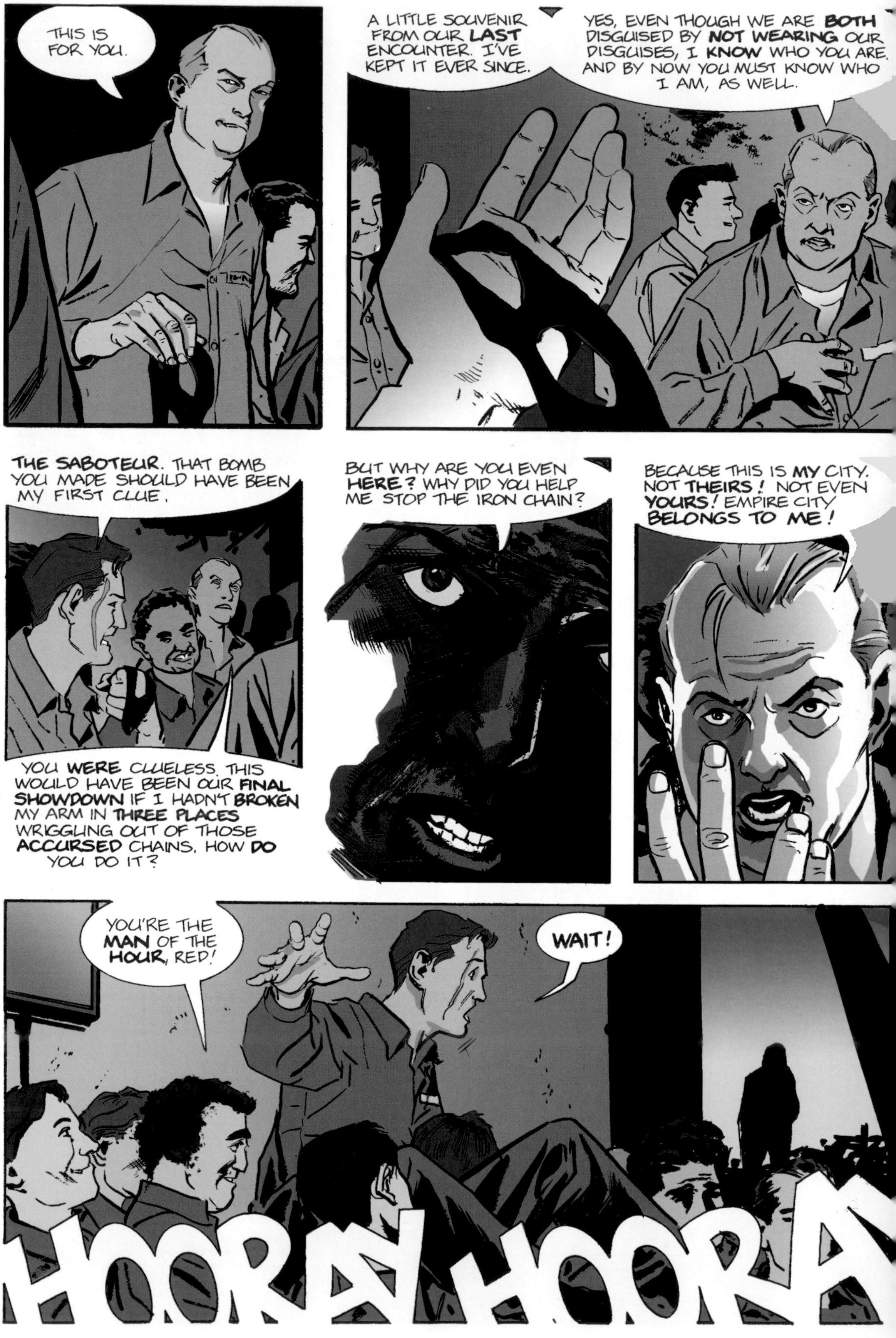
THIS IS FOR YOU.
A LITTLE SOUVENIR FROM OUR LAST ENCOUNTER. I'VE KEPT IT EVER SINCE.
YES, EVEN THOUGH WE ARE BOTH DISGUISED BY NOT WEARING OUR DISGUISES, I KNOW WHO YOU ARE. AND BY NOW YOU MUST KNOW WHO I AM, AS WELL.
THE SABOTEUR. THAT BOMB YOU MADE SHOULD HAVE BEEN MY FIRST CLUE.
YOU WERE CLUELESS. THIS WOULD HAVE BEEN OUR FINAL SHOWDOWN IF I HADN'T BROKEN MY ARM IN THREE PLACES WRIGGLING OUT OF THOSE ACCURSED CHAINS. HOW DO YOU DO IT?
BUT WHY ARE YOU EVEN HERE? WHY DID YOU HELP ME STOP THE IRON CHAIN?
BECAUSE THIS IS MY CITY. NOT THEIRS! NOT EVEN YOURS! EMPIRE CITY BELONGS TO ME!
YOU'RE THE MAN OF THE HOUR, RED!
WAIT!
HOORAY HOORA

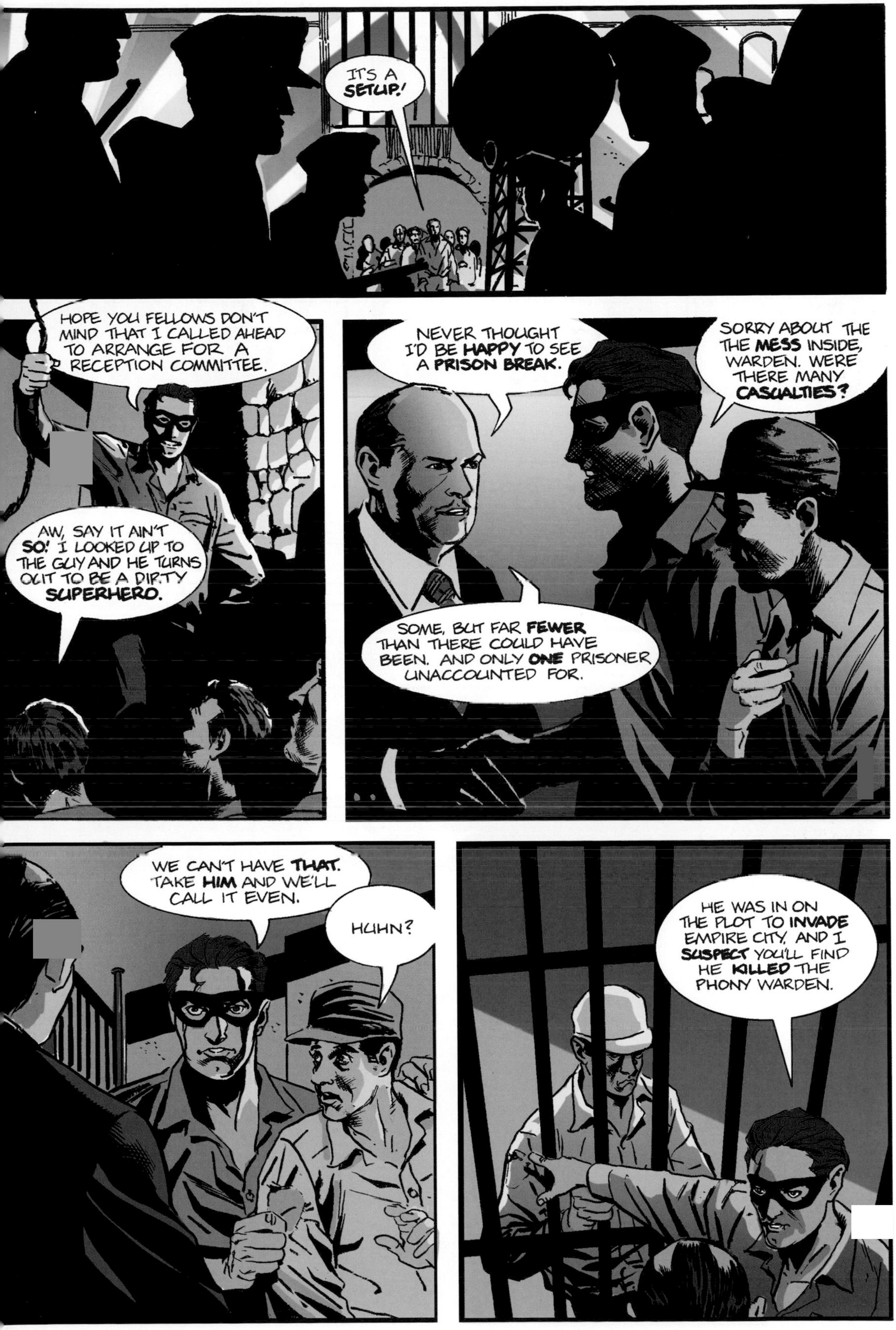
IT'S A SETUP!
HOPE YOU FELLOWS DON'T MIND THAT I CALLED AHEAD TO ARRANGE FOR A RECEPTION COMMITTEE.
AW, SAY IT AIN'T SO! I LOOKED UP TO THE GUY AND HE TURNS OUT TO BE A DIRTY SUPERHERO.
NEVER THOUGHT I'D BE HAPPY TO SEE A PRISON BREAK.
SORRY ABOUT THE THE MESS INSIDE, WARDEN. WERE THERE MANY CASUALTIES?
SOME, BUT FAR FEWER THAN THERE COULD HAVE BEEN. AND ONLY ONE PRISONER UNACCOUNTED FOR.
WE CAN'T HAVE THAT. TAKE HIM AND WE'LL CALL IT EVEN.
HUHN?
HE WAS IN ON THE PLOT TO INVADE EMPIRE CITY, AND I SUSPECT YOU'LL FIND HE KILLED THE PHONY WARDEN.

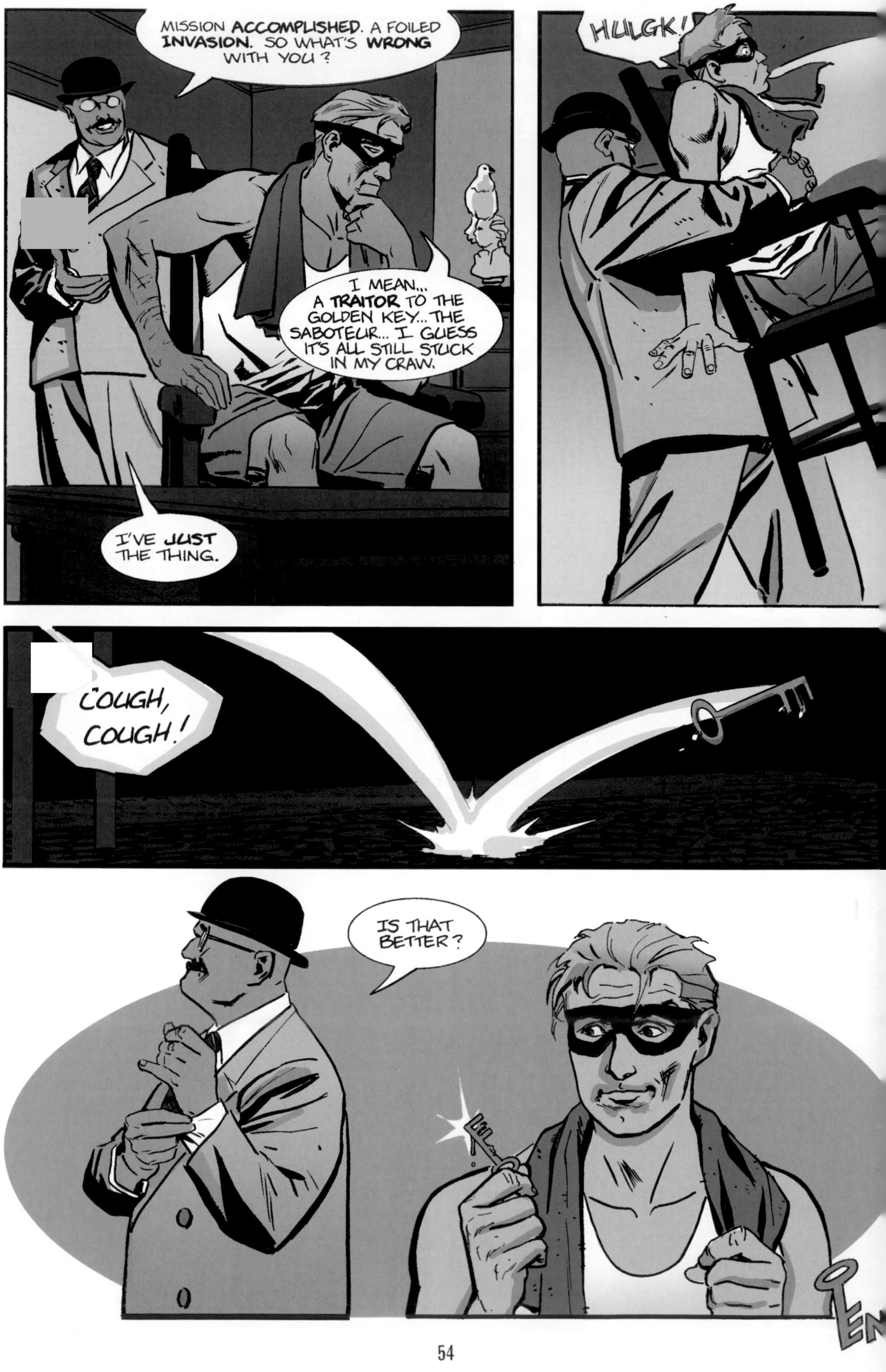
MISSION ACCOMPLISHED. A FOILED INVASION. SO WHAT'S WRONG WITH YOU?
I MEAN... A TRAITOR TO THE GOLDEN KEY... THE SABOTEUR... I GUESS IT'S ALL STILL STUCK IN MY CRAW.
I'VE JUST THE THING.
HULGK!
COUGH, COUGH!
IS THAT BETTER?

# "ARE YOU NOW OR HAVE YOU EVER BEEN..."

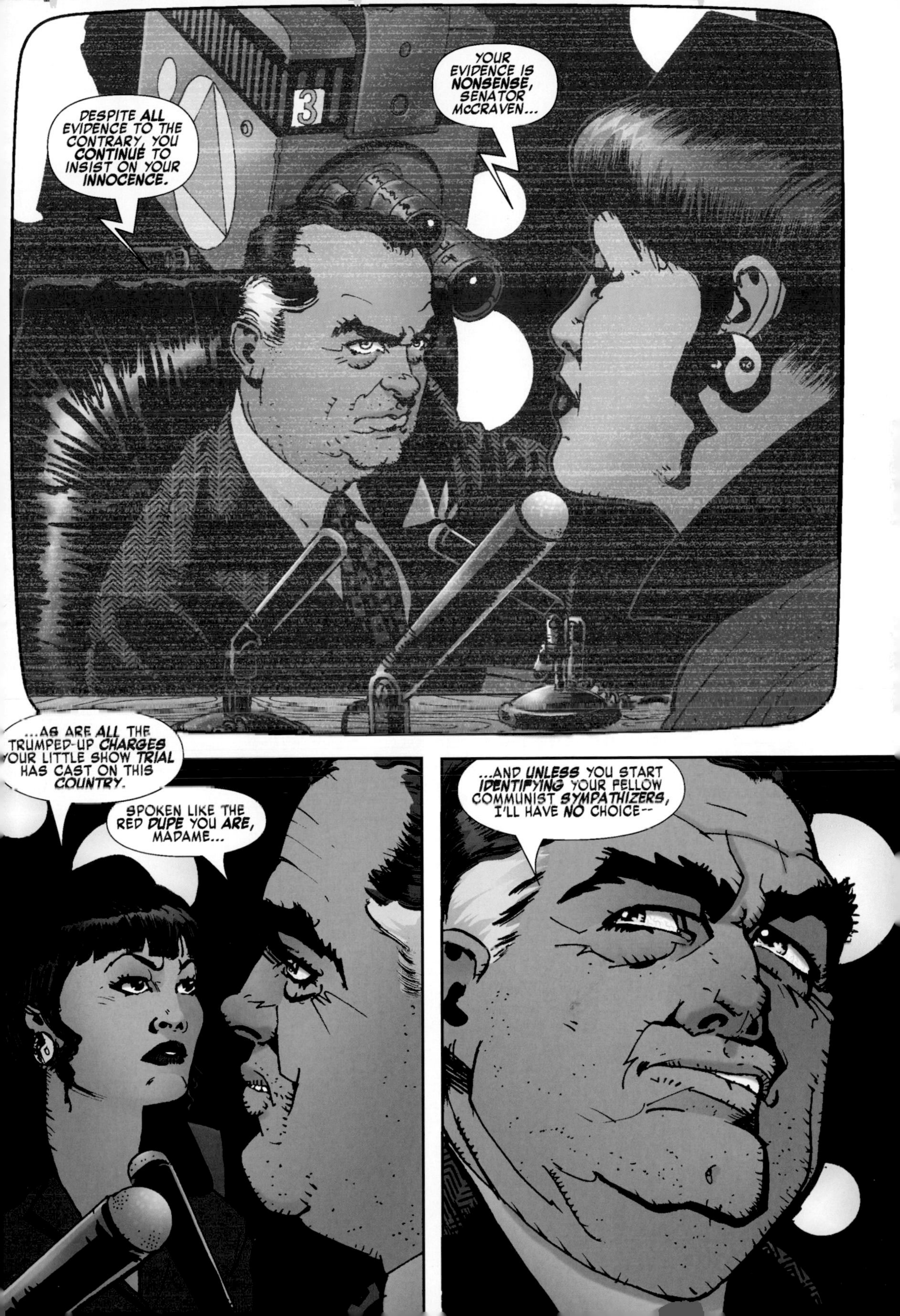
DESPITE ALL EVIDENCE TO THE CONTRARY, YOU CONTINUE TO INSIST ON YOUR INNOCENCE.
YOUR EVIDENCE IS NONSENSE, SENATOR McCRAVEN...
...AS ARE ALL THE TRUMPED-UP CHARGES YOUR LITTLE SHOW TRIAL HAS CAST ON THIS COUNTRY.
SPOKEN LIKE THE RED DUPE YOU ARE, MADAME...
...AND UNLESS YOU START IDENTIFYING YOUR FELLOW COMMUNIST SYMPATHIZERS, I'LL HAVE NO CHOICE--

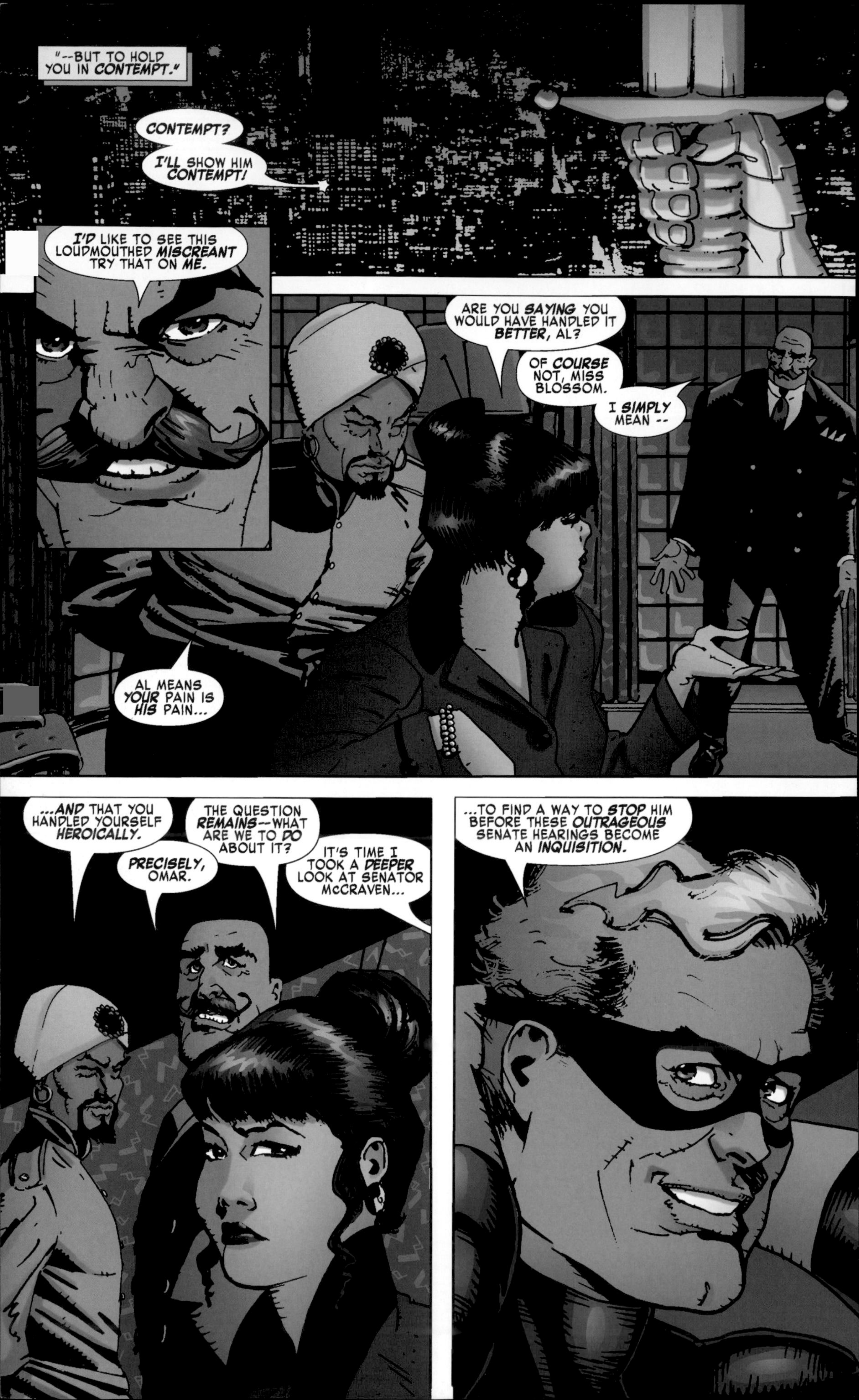
"--BUT TO HOLD YOU IN CONTEMPT."
CONTEMPT?
I'LL SHOW HIM CONTEMPT!
I'D LIKE TO SEE THIS LOUDMOUTHED MISCREANT TRY THAT ON ME.
ARE YOU SAYING YOU WOULD HAVE HANDLED IT BETTER, AL?
OF COURSE NOT, MISS BLOSSOM.
I SIMPLY MEAN --
AL MEANS YOUR PAIN IS HIS PAIN...
...AND THAT YOU HANDLED YOURSELF HEROICALLY.
PRECISELY, OMAR.
THE QUESTION REMAINS--WHAT ARE WE TO DO ABOUT IT?
IT'S TIME I TOOK A DEEPER LOOK AT SENATOR McCRAVEN...
...TO FIND A WAY TO STOP HIM BEFORE THESE OUTRAGEOUS SENATE HEARINGS BECOME AN INQUISITION.

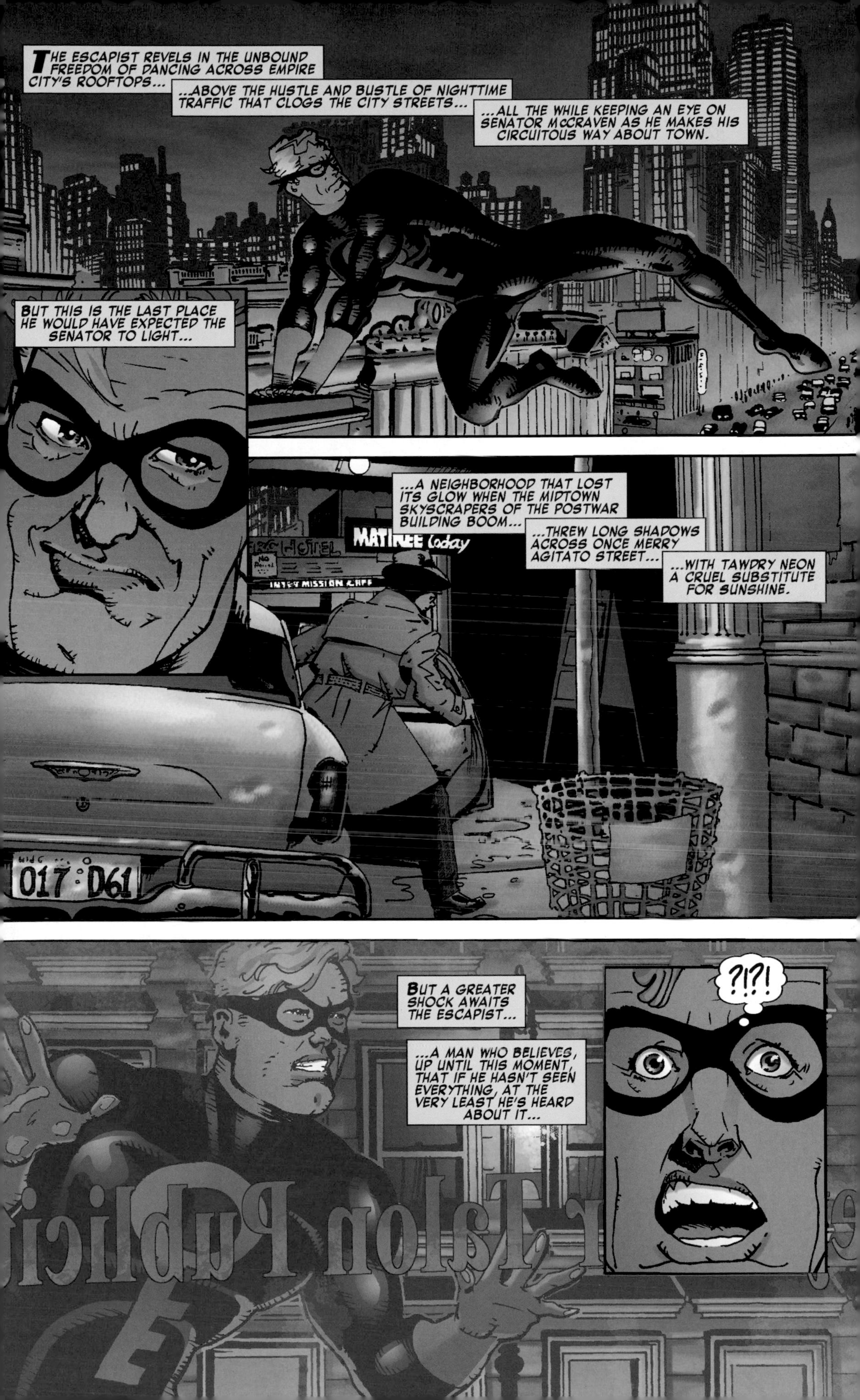
THE ESCAPIST REVELS IN THE UNBOUND FREEDOM OF DANCING ACROSS EMPIRE CITY'S ROOFTOPS...
...ABOVE THE HUSTLE AND BUSTLE OF NIGHTTIME TRAFFIC THAT CLOGS THE CITY STREETS...
...ALL THE WHILE KEEPING AN EYE ON SENATOR McCRAVEN AS HE MAKES HIS CIRCUITOUS WAY ABOUT TOWN.
BUT THIS IS THE LAST PLACE HE WOULD HAVE EXPECTED THE SENATOR TO LIGHT...
...A NEIGHBORHOOD THAT LOST ITS GLOW WHEN THE MIDTOWN SKYSCRAPERS OF THE POSTWAR BUILDING BOOM...
...THREW LONG SHADOWS ACROSS ONCE MERRY AGITATO STREET...
...WITH TAWDRY NEON A CRUEL SUBSTITUTE FOR SUNSHINE.
MATINEE today
HOTEL
INTERMISSION CAFE
017 D61
BUT A GREATER SHOCK AWAITS THE ESCAPIST...
...A MAN WHO BELIEVES, UP UNTIL THIS MOMENT, THAT IF HE HASN'T SEEN EVERYTHING, AT THE VERY LEAST HE'S HEARD ABOUT IT...
?!?!

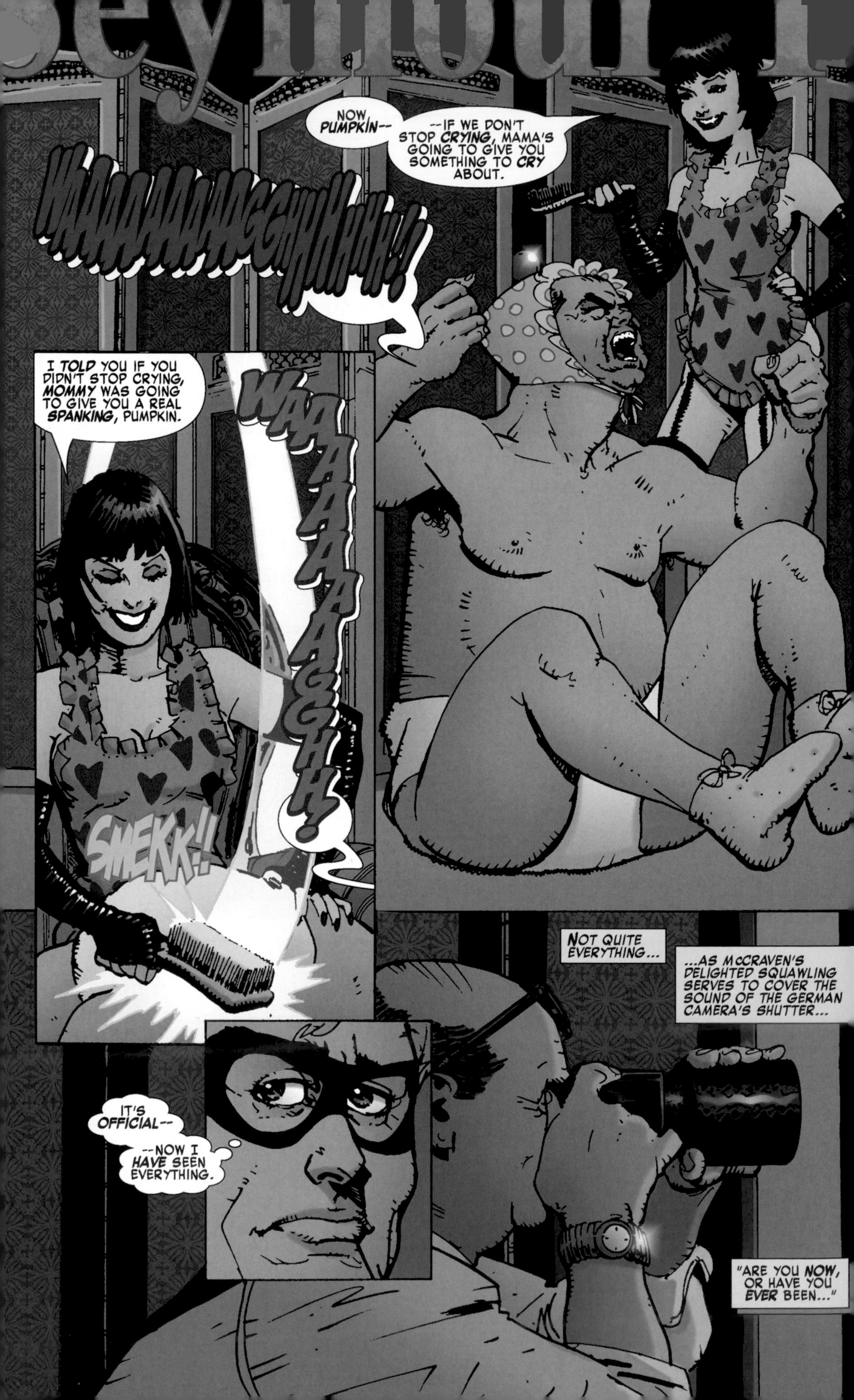

NOW PUMPKIN--
--IF WE DON'T STOP CRYING, MAMA'S GOING TO GIVE YOU SOMETHING TO CRY ABOUT.
WAAAAAAAAAGGHHHHHH!!
I TOLD YOU IF YOU DIDN'T STOP CRYING, MOMMY WAS GOING TO GIVE YOU A REAL SPANKING, PUMPKIN.
WAAAAAAAAAAGGHH!
SMEKK!!
NOT QUITE EVERYTHING...
...AS MCCRAVEN'S DELIGHTED SQUAWLING SERVES TO COVER THE SOUND OF THE GERMAN CAMERA'S SHUTTER...
IT'S OFFICIAL--
--NOW I HAVE SEEN EVERYTHING.
"ARE YOU NOW, OR HAVE YOU EVER BEEN..."

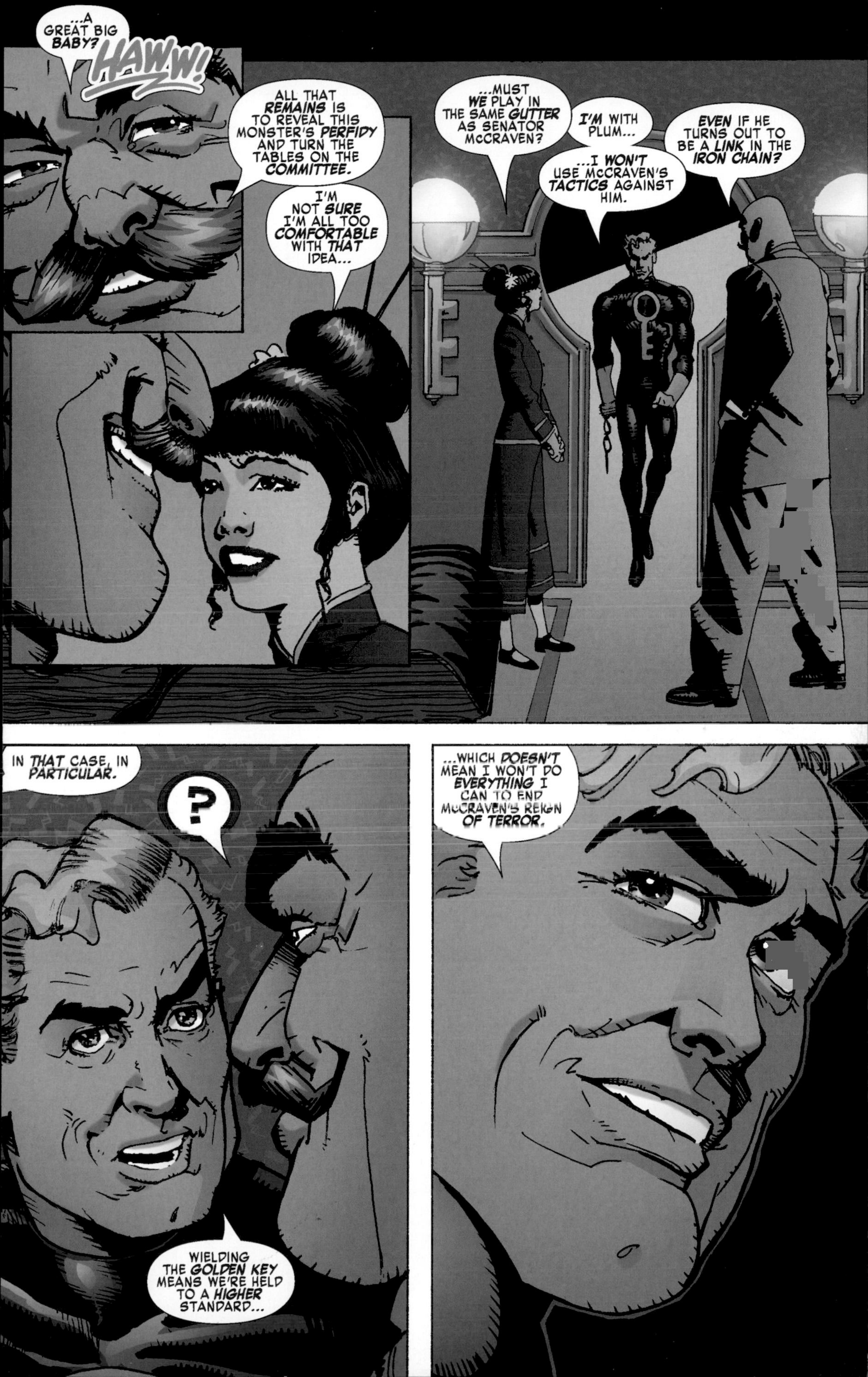
...A GREAT BIG BABY?
HAWW!
ALL THAT REMAINS IS TO REVEAL THIS MONSTER'S PERFIDY AND TURN THE TABLES ON THE COMMITTEE.
I'M NOT SURE I'M ALL TOO COMFORTABLE WITH THAT IDEA...
...MUST WE PLAY IN THE SAME GUTTER AS SENATOR McCRAVEN?
I'M WITH PLUM...
...I WON'T USE McCRAVEN'S TACTICS AGAINST HIM.
EVEN IF HE TURNS OUT TO BE A LINK IN THE IRON CHAIN?
IN THAT CASE, IN PARTICULAR.
?
WIELDING THE GOLDEN KEY MEANS WE'RE HELD TO A HIGHER STANDARD...
...WHICH DOESN'T MEAN I WON'T DO EVERYTHING I CAN TO END McCRAVEN'S REIGN OF TERROR.

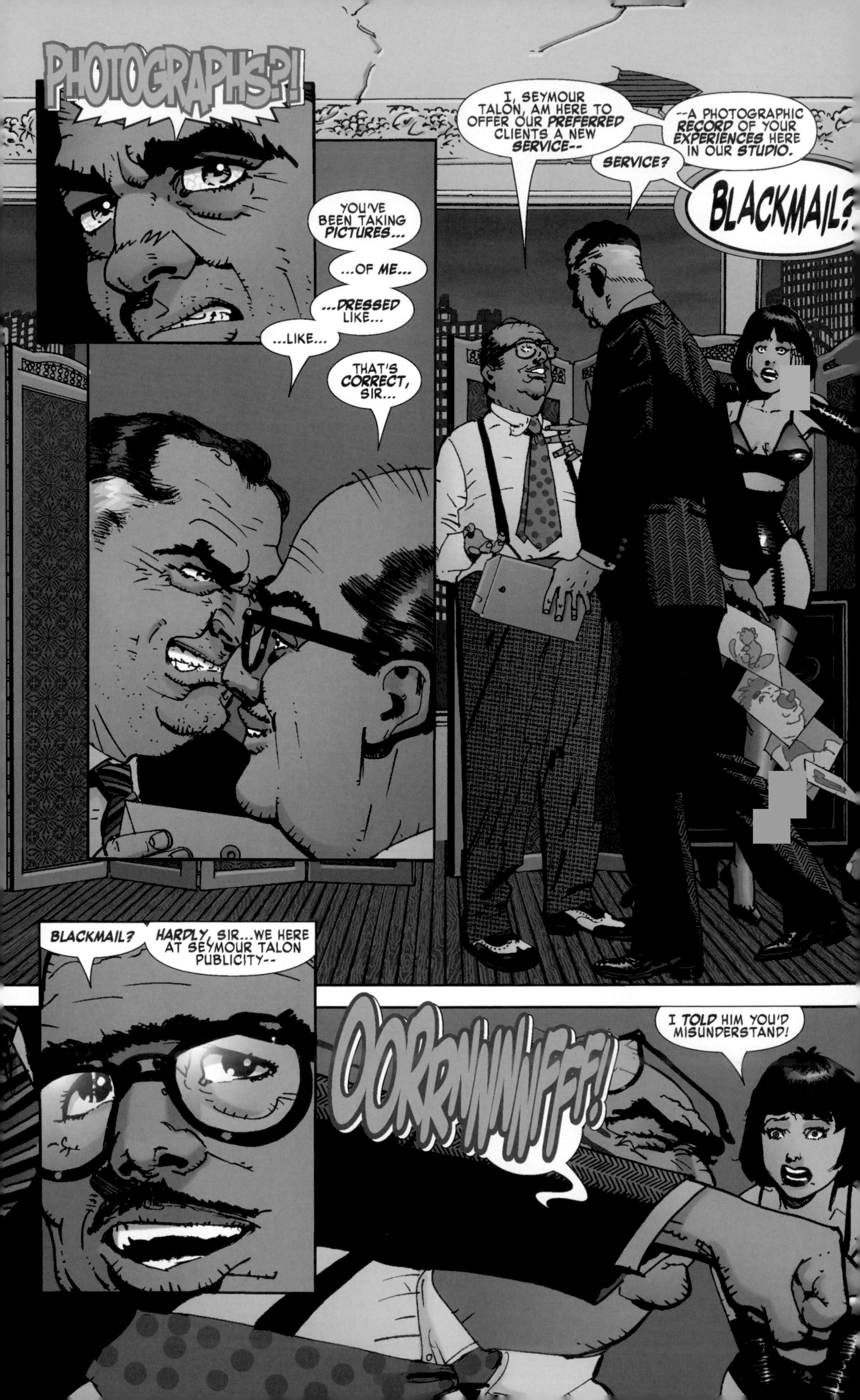
PHOTOGRAPHS?!
YOU'VE BEEN TAKING PICTURES...
...OF ME...
...DRESSED LIKE...
...LIKE...
THAT'S CORRECT, SIR...
I, SEYMOUR TALON, AM HERE TO OFFER OUR PREFERRED CLIENTS A NEW SERVICE--
SERVICE?
--A PHOTOGRAPHIC RECORD OF YOUR EXPERIENCES HERE IN OUR STUDIO.
BLACKMAIL?
BLACKMAIL?
HARDLY, SIR...WE HERE AT SEYMOUR TALON PUBLICITY--
OORRNNNNFFF!
I TOLD HIM YOU'D MISUNDERSTAND!

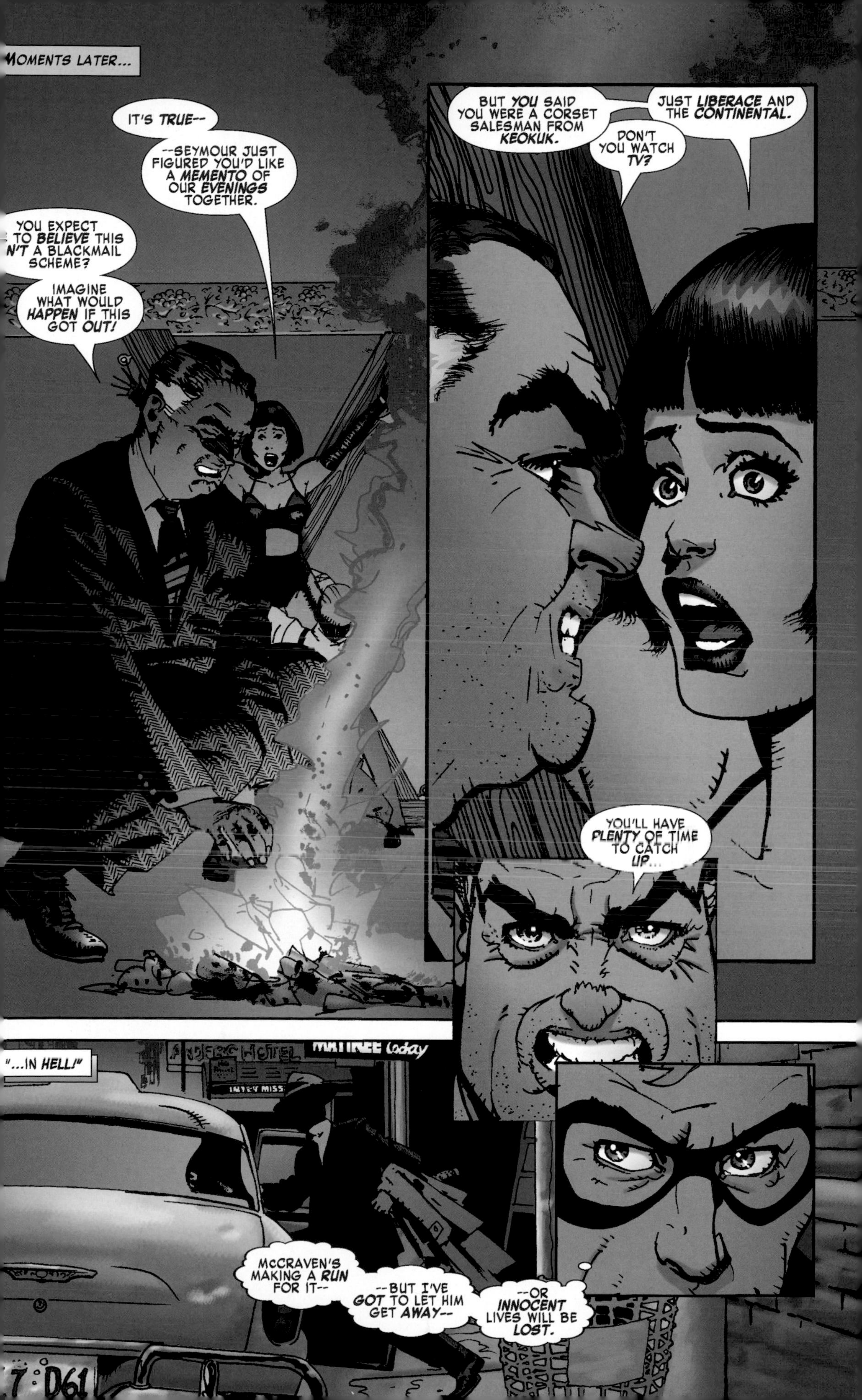
MOMENTS LATER...
IT'S TRUE--
--SEYMOUR JUST FIGURED YOU'D LIKE A MEMENTO OF OUR EVENINGS TOGETHER.
YOU EXPECT TO BELIEVE THIS N'T A BLACKMAIL SCHEME?
IMAGINE WHAT WOULD HAPPEN IF THIS GOT OUT!
BUT YOU SAID YOU WERE A CORSET SALESMAN FROM KEOKUK.
DON'T YOU WATCH TV?
JUST LIBERACE AND THE CONTINENTAL.
YOU'LL HAVE PLENTY OF TIME TO CATCH UP...
"...IN HELL!"
MATINEE today
HOTEL
McCRAVEN'S MAKING A RUN FOR IT--
--BUT I'VE GOT TO LET HIM GET AWAY--
--OR INNOCENT LIVES WILL BE LOST.
7 D61

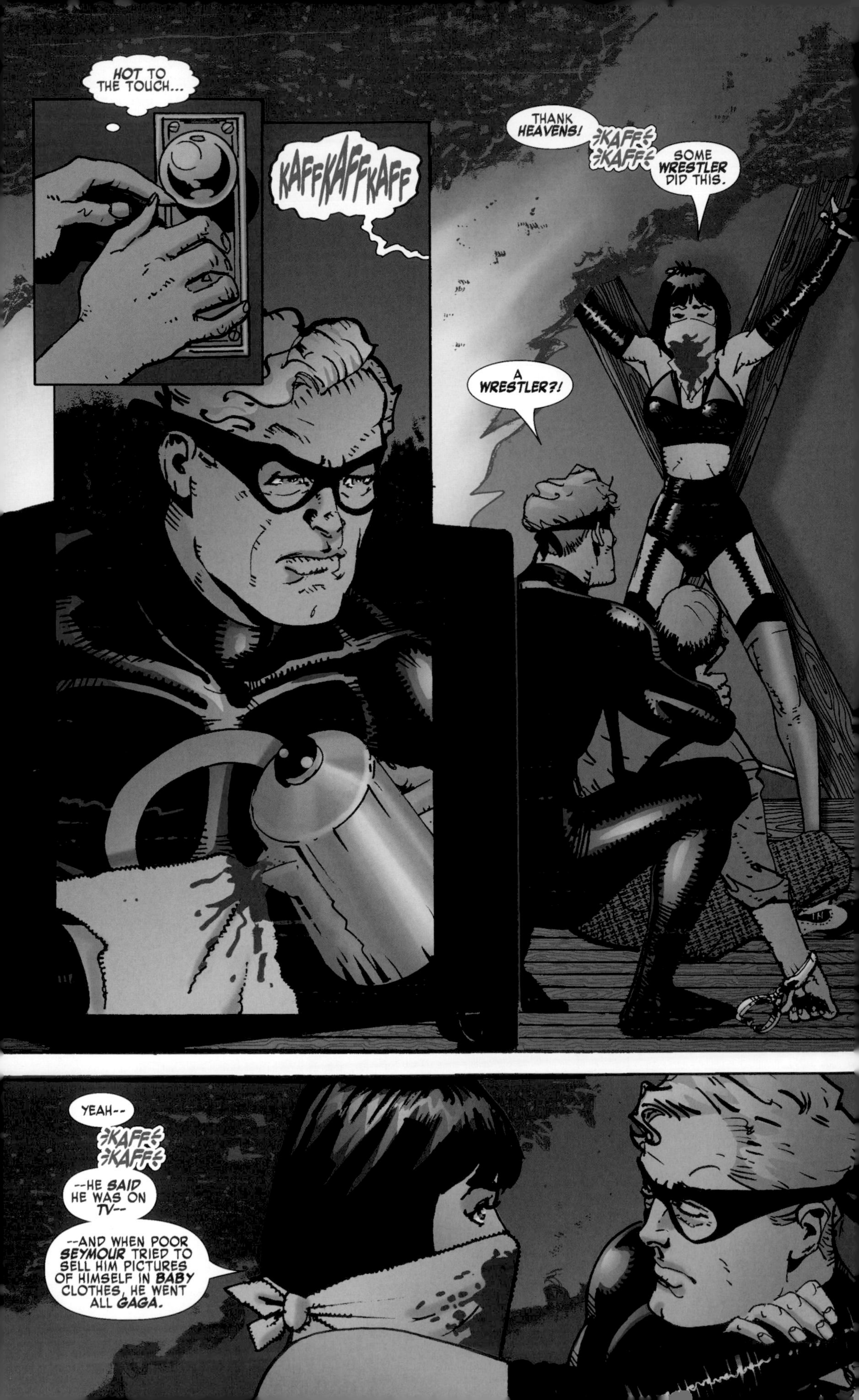

HOT TO THE TOUCH...
KAFFKAFFKAFF
THANK HEAVENS!
KAFF KAFF
SOME WRESTLER DID THIS.
A WRESTLER?!
YEAH--
KAFF KAFF
--HE SAID HE WAS ON TV--
--AND WHEN POOR SEYMOUR TRIED TO SELL HIM PICTURES OF HIMSELF IN BABY CLOTHES, HE WENT ALL GAGA.

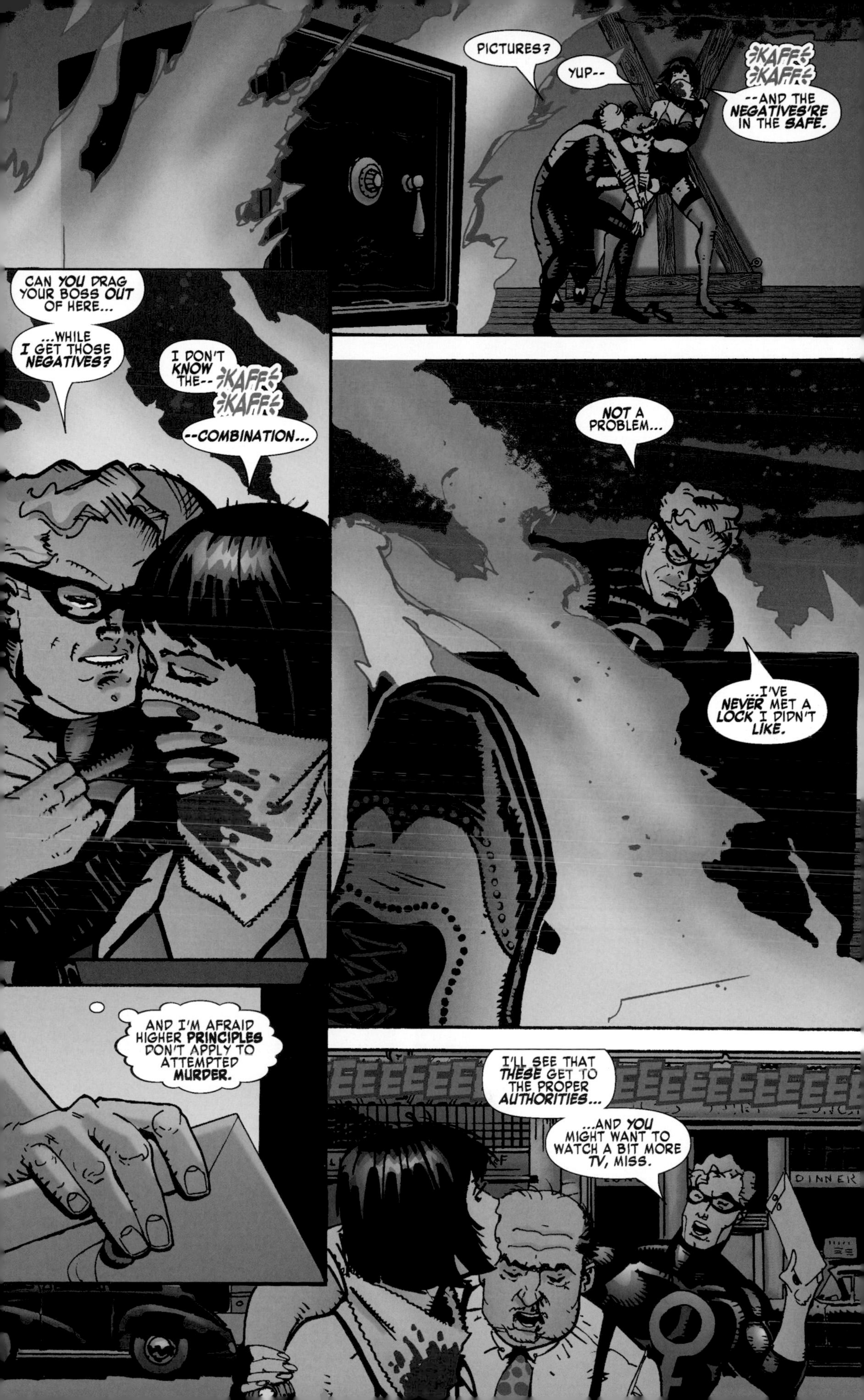
PICTURES?
YUP--
KAFF KAFF
--AND THE NEGATIVES'RE IN THE SAFE.
CAN YOU DRAG YOUR BOSS OUT OF HERE...
...WHILE I GET THOSE NEGATIVES?
I DON'T KNOW THE-- KAFF KAFF --COMBINATION...
NOT A PROBLEM...
...I'VE NEVER MET A LOCK I DIDN'T LIKE.
AND I'M AFRAID HIGHER PRINCIPLES DON'T APPLY TO ATTEMPTED MURDER.
I'LL SEE THAT THESE GET TO THE PROPER AUTHORITIES...
...AND YOU MIGHT WANT TO WATCH A BIT MORE TV, MISS.
DINNER

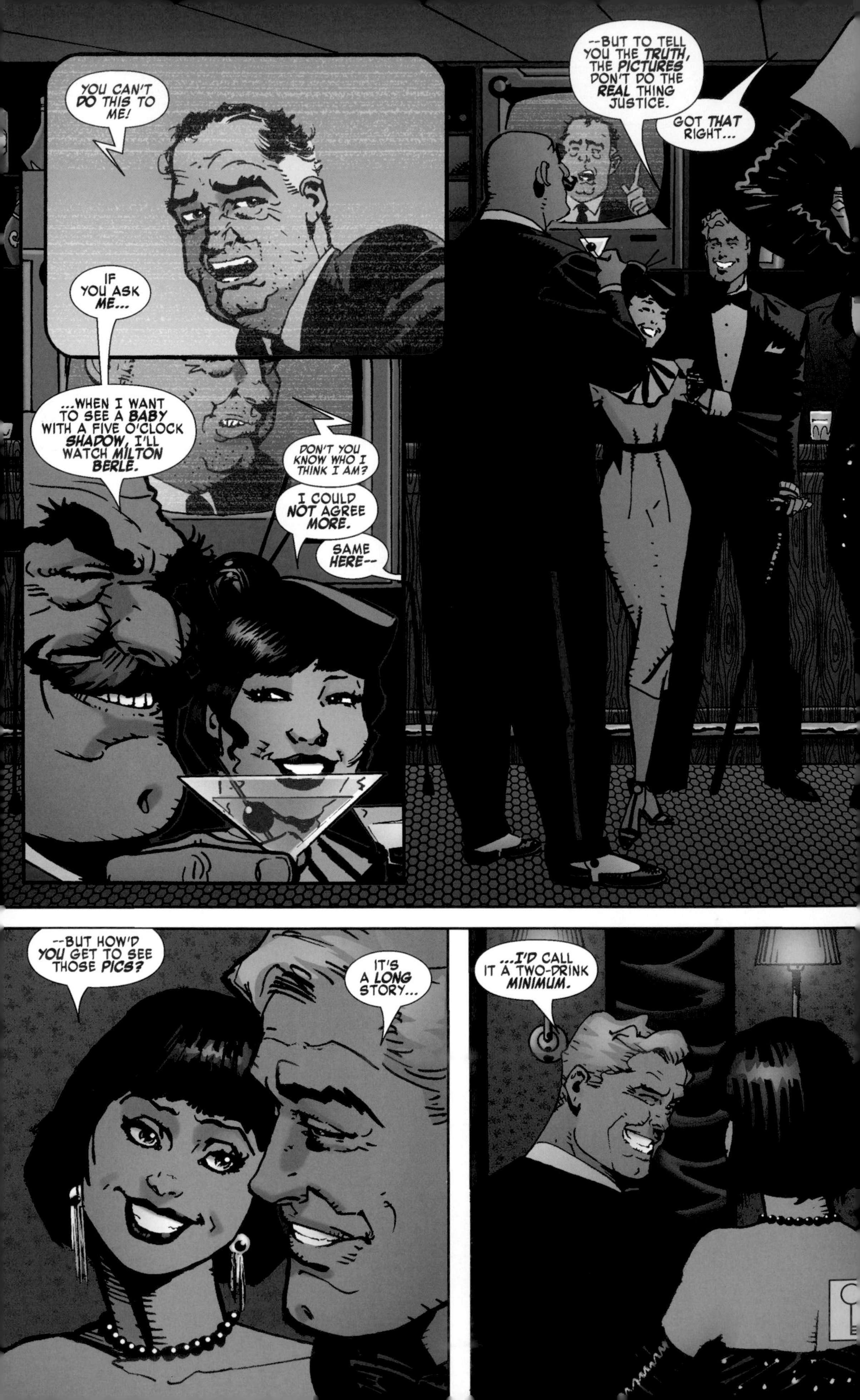
YOU CAN'T DO THIS TO ME!
IF YOU ASK ME...
...WHEN I WANT TO SEE A BABY WITH A FIVE O'CLOCK SHADOW, I'LL WATCH MILTON BERLE.
DON'T YOU KNOW WHO I THINK I AM?
I COULD NOT AGREE MORE.
SAME HERE--
--BUT TO TELL YOU THE TRUTH, THE PICTURES DON'T DO THE REAL THING JUSTICE.
GOT THAT RIGHT...
--BUT HOW'D YOU GET TO SEE THOSE PICS?
IT'S A LONG STORY...
...I'D CALL IT A TWO-DRINK MINIMUM.

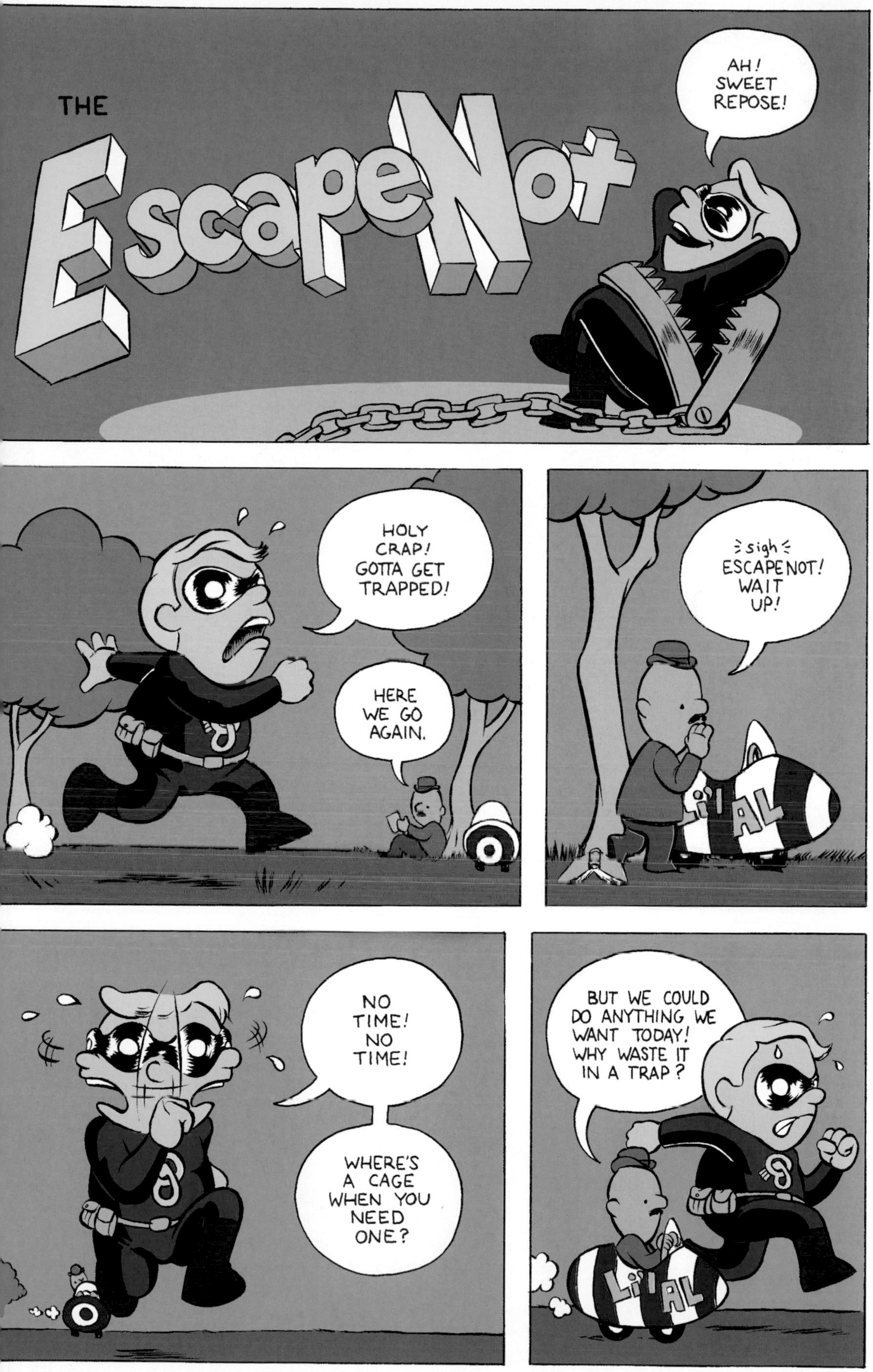
THE
EscapeNot
AH! SWEET REPOSE!
HOLY CRAP! GOTTA GET TRAPPED!
HERE WE GO AGAIN.
sigh
ESCAPENOT! WAIT UP!
LI'L AL
NO TIME! NO TIME!
WHERE'S A CAGE WHEN YOU NEED ONE?
BUT WE COULD DO ANYTHING WE WANT TODAY! WHY WASTE IT IN A TRAP?
LI'L AL

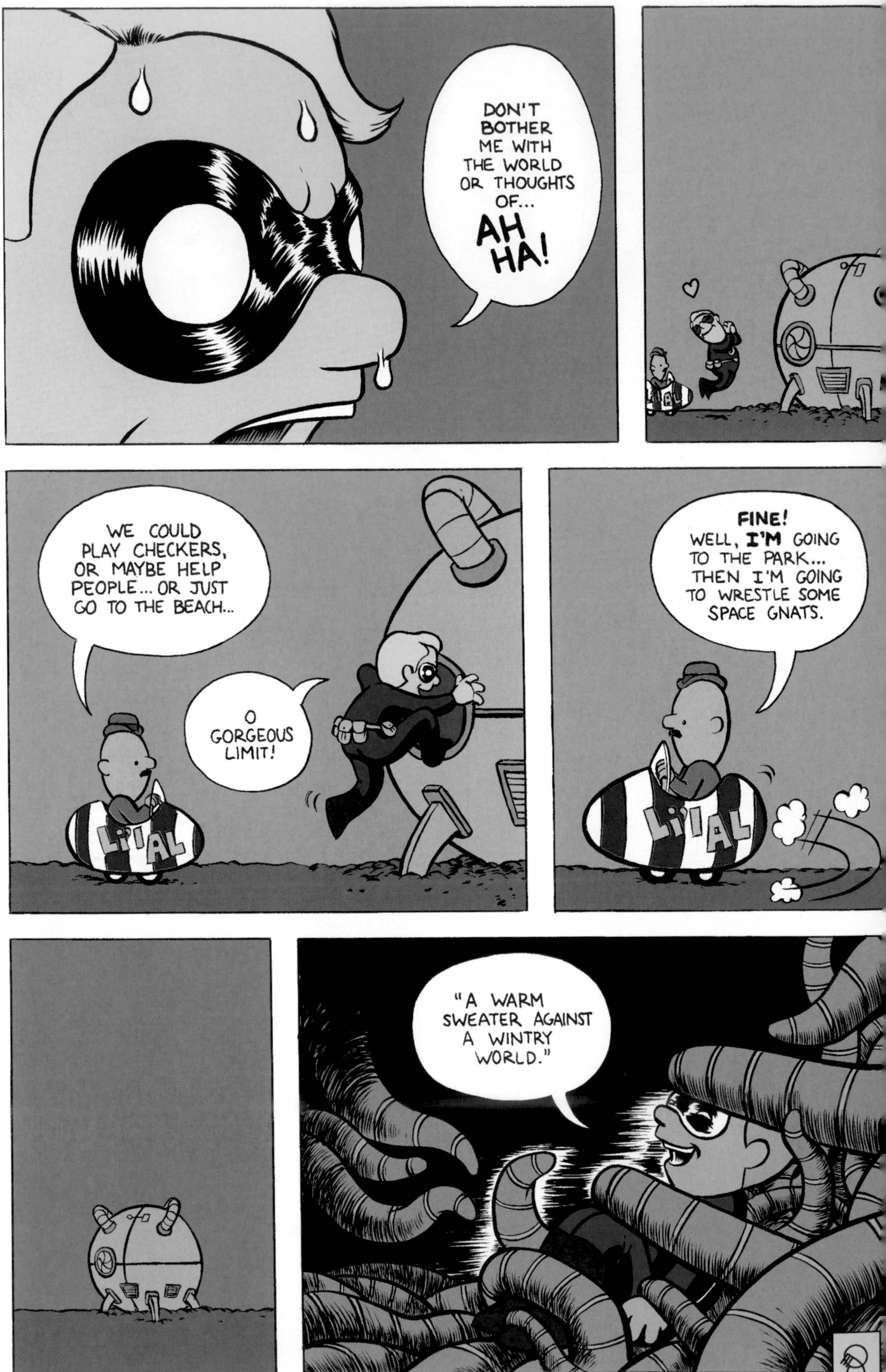
DON'T BOTHER ME WITH THE WORLD OR THOUGHTS OF... AH HA!
WE COULD PLAY CHECKERS, OR MAYBE HELP PEOPLE... OR JUST GO TO THE BEACH...
O GORGEOUS LIMIT!
LI'L AL
FINE! WELL, I'M GOING TO THE PARK... THEN I'M GOING TO WRESTLE SOME SPACE GNATS.
LI'L AL
"A WARM SWEATER AGAINST A WINTRY WORLD."

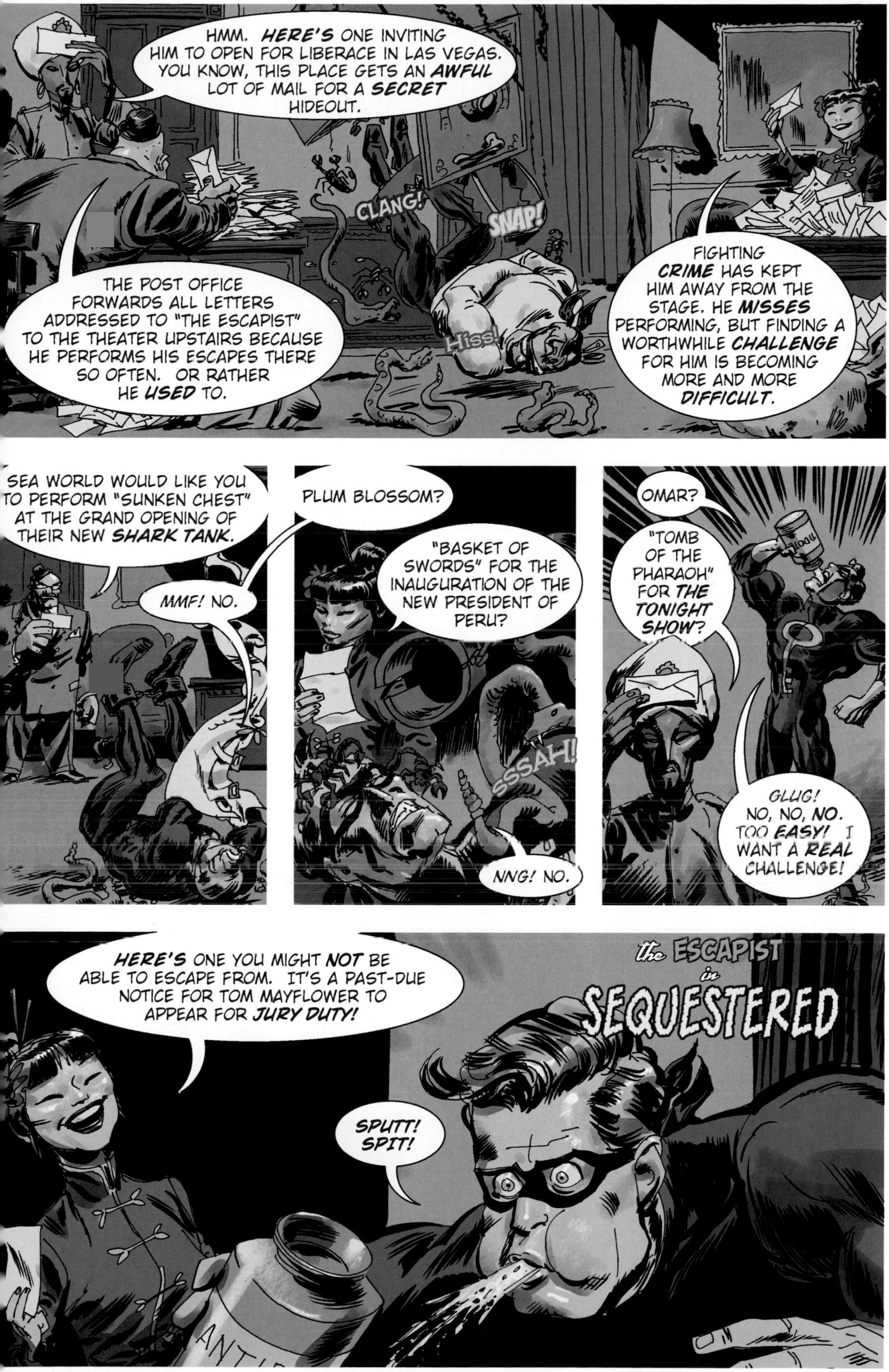
HMM. **HERE'S** ONE INVITING HIM TO OPEN FOR LIBERACE IN LAS VEGAS. YOU KNOW, THIS PLACE GETS AN **AWFUL** LOT OF MAIL FOR A **SECRET** HIDEOUT.
CLANG!
SNAP!
THE POST OFFICE FORWARDS ALL LETTERS ADDRESSED TO "THE ESCAPIST" TO THE THEATER UPSTAIRS BECAUSE HE PERFORMS HIS ESCAPES THERE SO OFTEN. OR RATHER HE **USED** TO.
Hiss!
FIGHTING **CRIME** HAS KEPT HIM AWAY FROM THE STAGE. HE **MISSES** PERFORMING, BUT FINDING A WORTHWHILE **CHALLENGE** FOR HIM IS BECOMING MORE AND MORE **DIFFICULT**.
SEA WORLD WOULD LIKE YOU TO PERFORM "SUNKEN CHEST" AT THE GRAND OPENING OF THEIR NEW **SHARK TANK**.
MMF! NO.
PLUM BLOSSOM?
"BASKET OF SWORDS" FOR THE INAUGURATION OF THE NEW PRESIDENT OF PERU?
SSSAH!
NNG! NO.
OMAR?
"TOMB OF THE PHARAOH" FOR **THE TONIGHT SHOW**?
GLUG! NO, NO, **NO**. TOO **EASY!** I WANT A **REAL** CHALLENGE!
**HERE'S** ONE YOU MIGHT **NOT** BE ABLE TO ESCAPE FROM. IT'S A PAST-DUE NOTICE FOR TOM MAYFLOWER TO APPEAR FOR **JURY DUTY!**
the ESCAPIST in SEQUESTERED
SPUTT! SPIT!

YOU DON'T **HAVE** TO GO THROUGH WITH THIS, YOU KNOW.

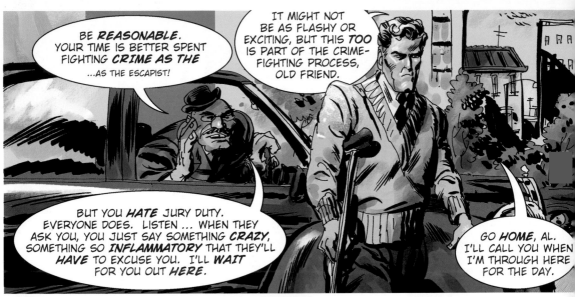

BE **REASONABLE**. YOUR TIME IS BETTER SPENT FIGHTING **CRIME AS THE**

...AS THE ESCAPIST!

IT MIGHT NOT BE AS FLASHY OR EXCITING, BUT THIS **TOO** IS PART OF THE CRIME-FIGHTING PROCESS, OLD FRIEND.

BUT YOU **HATE** JURY DUTY. EVERYONE DOES. LISTEN ... WHEN THEY ASK YOU, YOU JUST SAY SOMETHING **CRAZY**, SOMETHING SO **INFLAMMATORY** THAT THEY'LL **HAVE** TO EXCUSE YOU. I'LL **WAIT** FOR YOU OUT **HERE**.

GO **HOME**, AL. I'LL CALL YOU WHEN I'M THROUGH HERE FOR THE DAY.

HOURS LATER ...

I **HATE** JURY DUTY.

I JUST **LOVE** JURY DUTY, BOY. YESSIR, I DO!

I'M A VETERAN OF **TWO WARS**, BOY. I **LOVED** SERVING MY **COUNTRY**, BY GUM!

GUM?

THANK YOU.

SURE, SURE. JU DUTY LETS ME FE LIKE I'M **STILL** SERVING MY COUNTR SEE? GUYS LIKE YO AND **ME** -- BUM **LE** AND ALL -- WE CAN **ST** CONTRIBU AND **S** WHILE DOING IT!

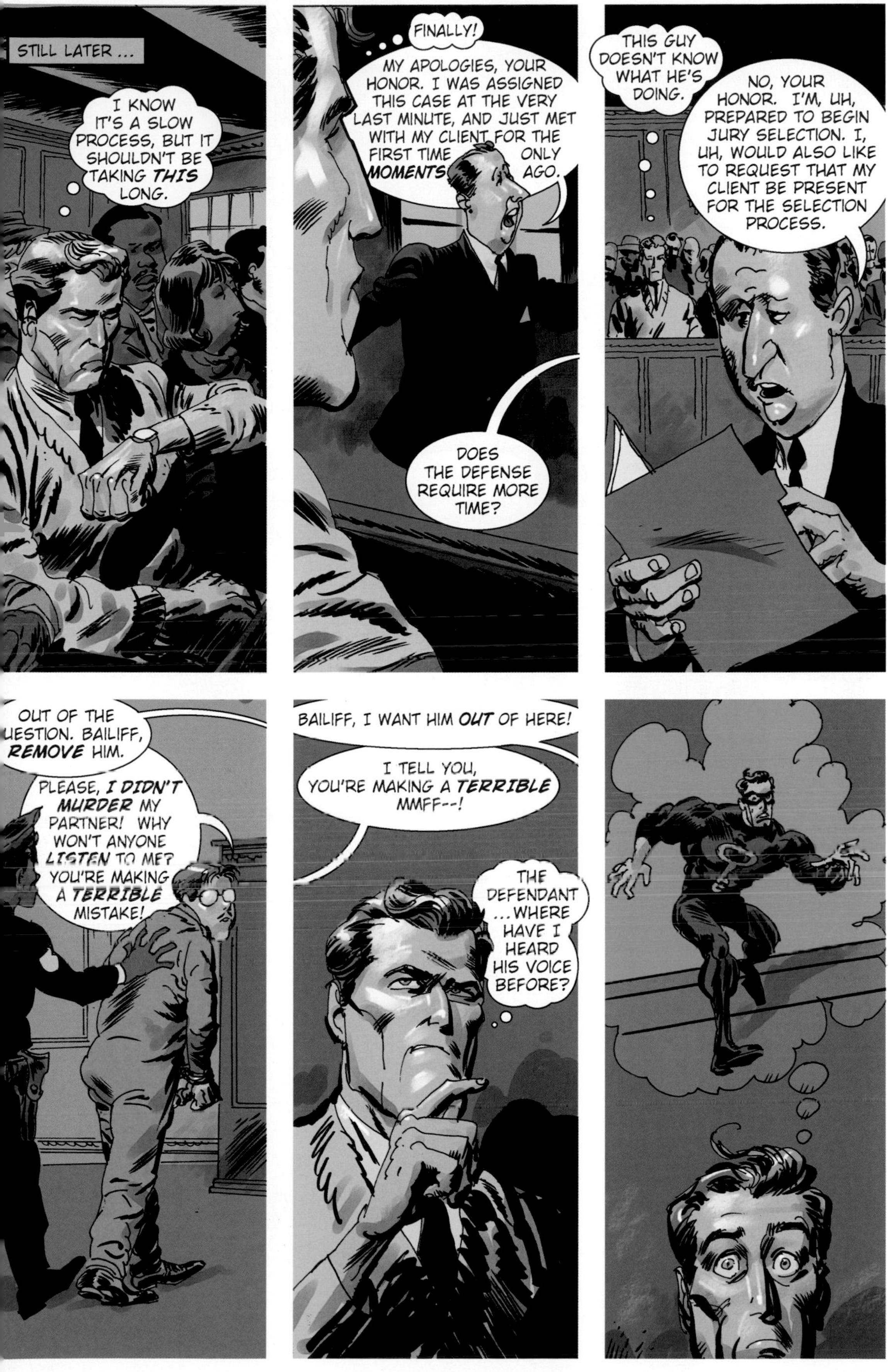
STILL LATER ...
I KNOW IT'S A SLOW PROCESS, BUT IT SHOULDN'T BE TAKING THIS LONG.
FINALLY!
MY APOLOGIES, YOUR HONOR. I WAS ASSIGNED THIS CASE AT THE VERY LAST MINUTE, AND JUST MET WITH MY CLIENT FOR THE FIRST TIME ONLY MOMENTS AGO.
DOES THE DEFENSE REQUIRE MORE TIME?
THIS GUY DOESN'T KNOW WHAT HE'S DOING.
NO, YOUR HONOR. I'M, UH, PREPARED TO BEGIN JURY SELECTION. I, UH, WOULD ALSO LIKE TO REQUEST THAT MY CLIENT BE PRESENT FOR THE SELECTION PROCESS.
OUT OF THE UESTION. BAILIFF, REMOVE HIM.
PLEASE, I DIDN'T MURDER MY PARTNER! WHY WON'T ANYONE LISTEN TO ME? YOU'RE MAKING A TERRIBLE MISTAKE!
BAILIFF, I WANT HIM OUT OF HERE!
I TELL YOU, YOU'RE MAKING A TERRIBLE MMFF--!
THE DEFENDANT ...WHERE HAVE I HEARD HIS VOICE BEFORE?

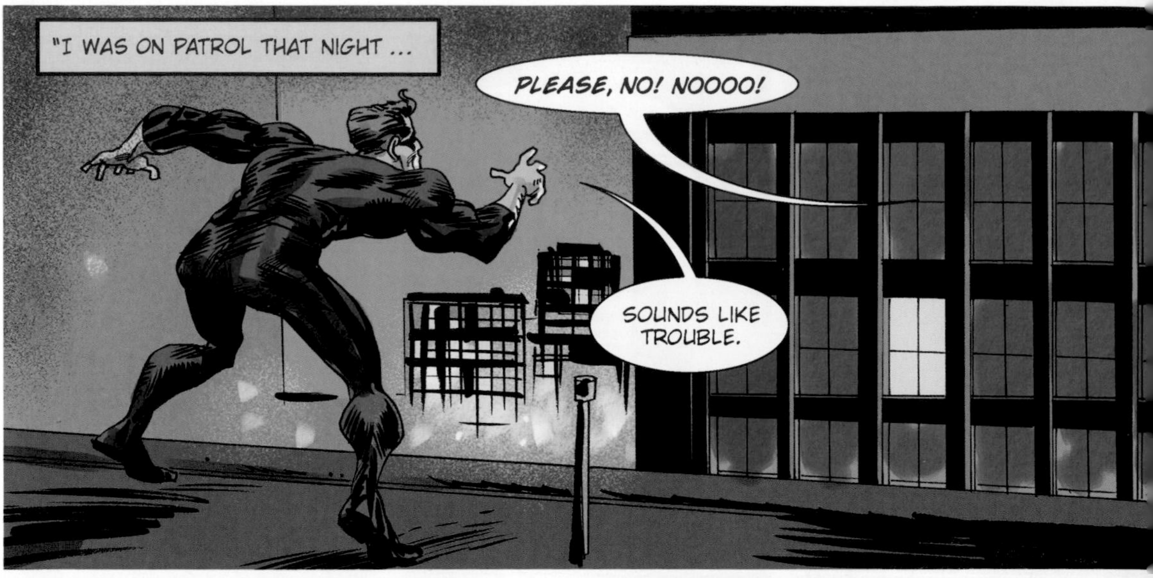
"I WAS ON PATROL THAT NIGHT ...
*PLEASE, NO! NOOOO!*
SOUNDS LIKE TROUBLE.

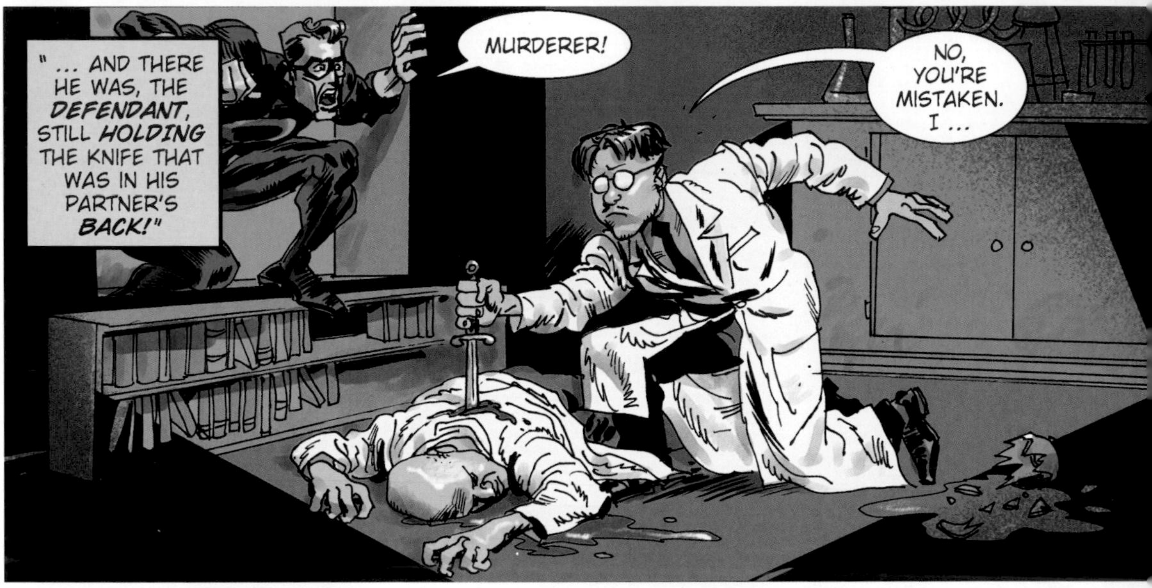
" ... AND THERE HE WAS, THE *DEFENDANT*, STILL *HOLDING* THE KNIFE THAT WAS IN HIS PARTNER'S *BACK!*"
MURDERER!
NO, YOU'RE MISTAKEN. I ...

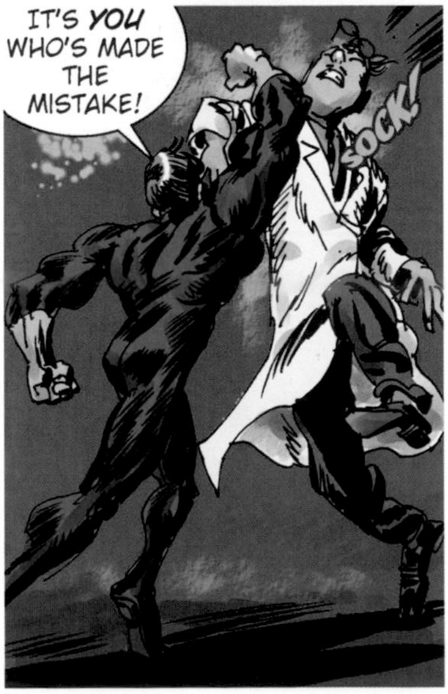
IT'S *YOU* WHO'S MADE THE MISTAKE!
SOCK!

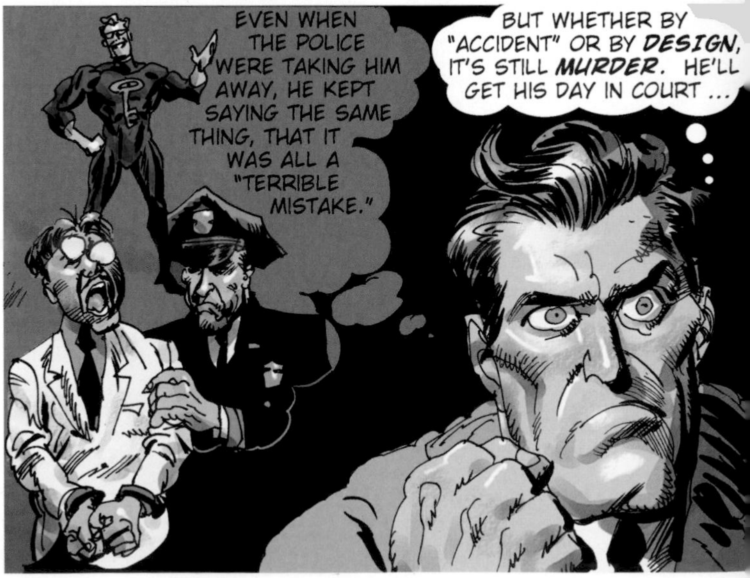
EVEN WHEN THE POLICE WERE TAKING HIM AWAY, HE KEPT SAYING THE SAME THING, THAT IT WAS ALL A "TERRIBLE MISTAKE."
BUT WHETHER BY "ACCIDENT" OR BY *DESIGN*, IT'S STILL *MURDER*. HE'LL GET HIS DAY IN COURT ...

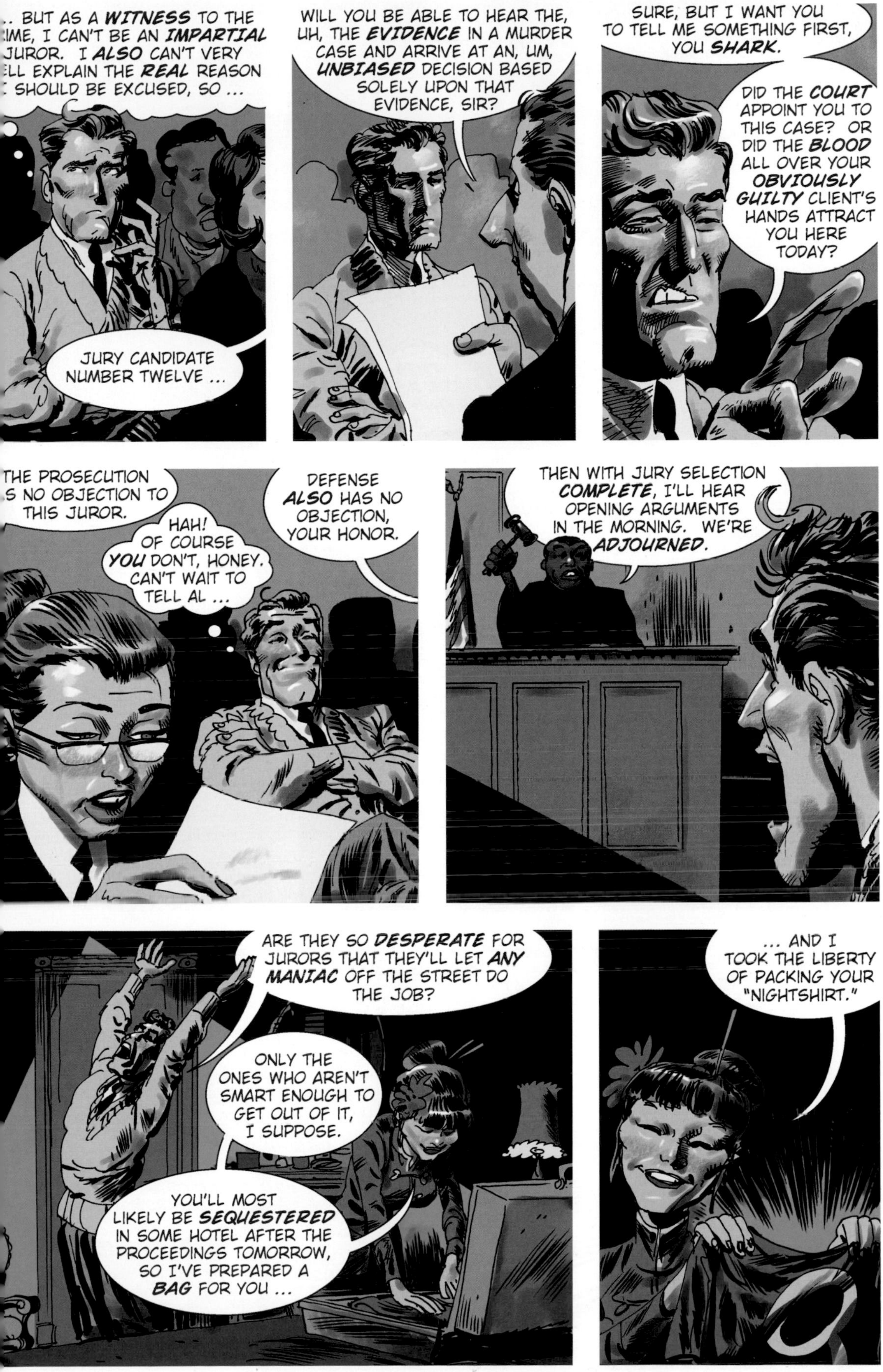
.. BUT AS A **WITNESS** TO THE IME, I CAN'T BE AN **IMPARTIAL** JUROR. I **ALSO** CAN'T VERY ELL EXPLAIN THE **REAL** REASON SHOULD BE EXCUSED, SO ...
JURY CANDIDATE NUMBER TWELVE ...
WILL YOU BE ABLE TO HEAR THE, UH, THE **EVIDENCE** IN A MURDER CASE AND ARRIVE AT AN, UM, **UNBIASED** DECISION BASED SOLELY UPON THAT EVIDENCE, SIR?
SURE, BUT I WANT YOU TO TELL ME SOMETHING FIRST, YOU **SHARK**.
DID THE **COURT** APPOINT YOU TO THIS CASE? OR DID THE **BLOOD** ALL OVER YOUR **OBVIOUSLY GUILTY** CLIENT'S HANDS ATTRACT YOU HERE TODAY?
THE PROSECUTION S NO OBJECTION TO THIS JUROR.
HAH! OF COURSE **YOU** DON'T, HONEY. CAN'T WAIT TO TELL AL ...
DEFENSE **ALSO** HAS NO OBJECTION, YOUR HONOR.
THEN WITH JURY SELECTION **COMPLETE**, I'LL HEAR OPENING ARGUMENTS IN THE MORNING. WE'RE **ADJOURNED**.
ARE THEY SO **DESPERATE** FOR JURORS THAT THEY'LL LET **ANY MANIAC** OFF THE STREET DO THE JOB?
ONLY THE ONES WHO AREN'T SMART ENOUGH TO GET OUT OF IT, I SUPPOSE.
YOU'LL MOST LIKELY BE **SEQUESTERED** IN SOME HOTEL AFTER THE PROCEEDINGS TOMORROW, SO I'VE PREPARED A **BAG** FOR YOU ...
... AND I TOOK THE LIBERTY OF PACKING YOUR "NIGHTSHIRT."

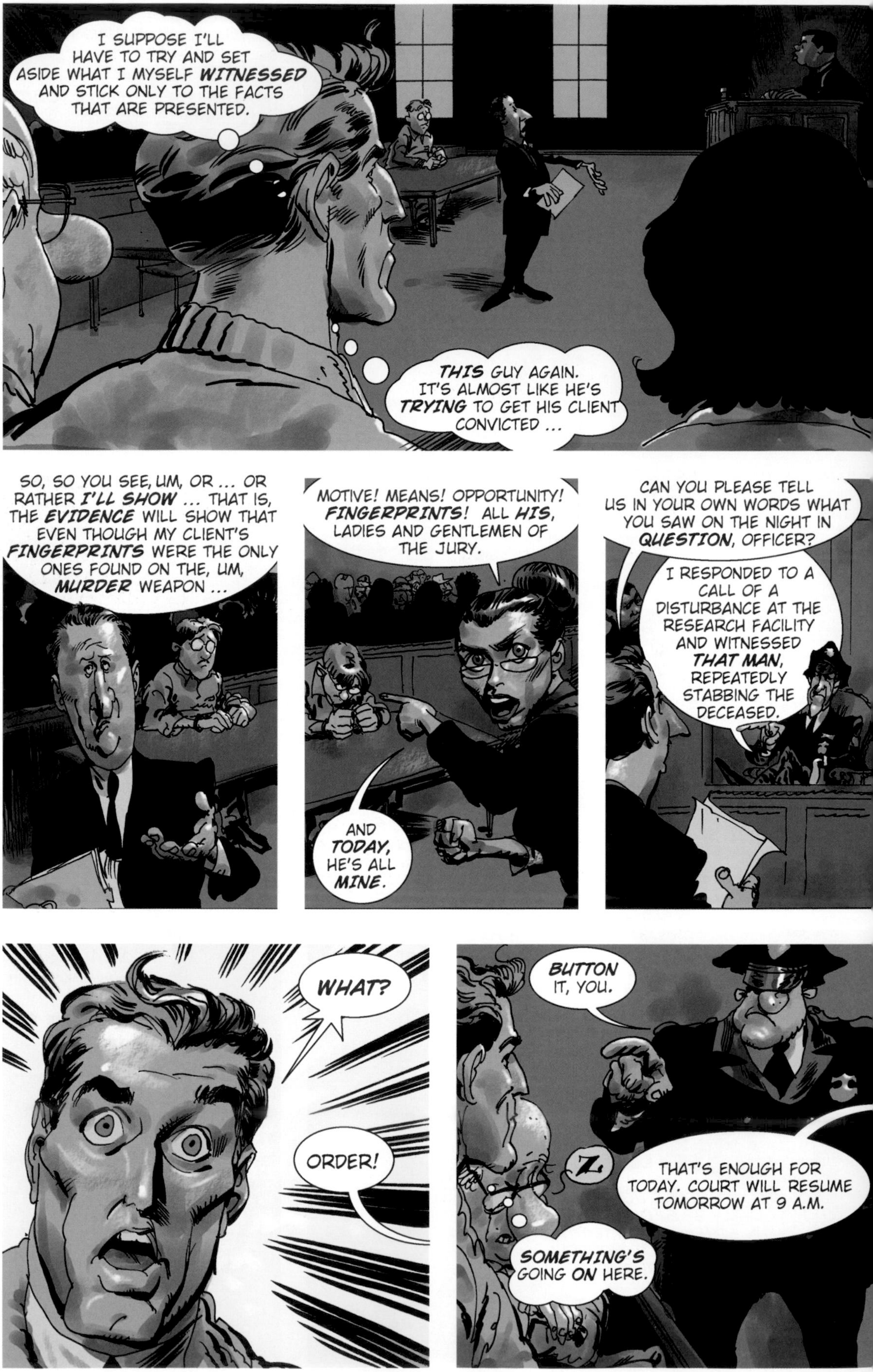
I SUPPOSE I'LL HAVE TO TRY AND SET ASIDE WHAT I MYSELF WITNESSED AND STICK ONLY TO THE FACTS THAT ARE PRESENTED.
THIS GUY AGAIN. IT'S ALMOST LIKE HE'S TRYING TO GET HIS CLIENT CONVICTED ...
SO, SO YOU SEE, UM, OR ... OR RATHER I'LL SHOW ... THAT IS, THE EVIDENCE WILL SHOW THAT EVEN THOUGH MY CLIENT'S FINGERPRINTS WERE THE ONLY ONES FOUND ON THE, UM, MURDER WEAPON ...
MOTIVE! MEANS! OPPORTUNITY! FINGERPRINTS! ALL HIS, LADIES AND GENTLEMEN OF THE JURY.
AND TODAY, HE'S ALL MINE.
CAN YOU PLEASE TELL US IN YOUR OWN WORDS WHAT YOU SAW ON THE NIGHT IN QUESTION, OFFICER?
I RESPONDED TO A CALL OF A DISTURBANCE AT THE RESEARCH FACILITY AND WITNESSED THAT MAN, REPEATEDLY STABBING THE DECEASED.
WHAT?
ORDER!
BUTTON IT, YOU.
Z
THAT'S ENOUGH FOR TODAY. COURT WILL RESUME TOMORROW AT 9 A.M.
SOMETHING'S GOING ON HERE.

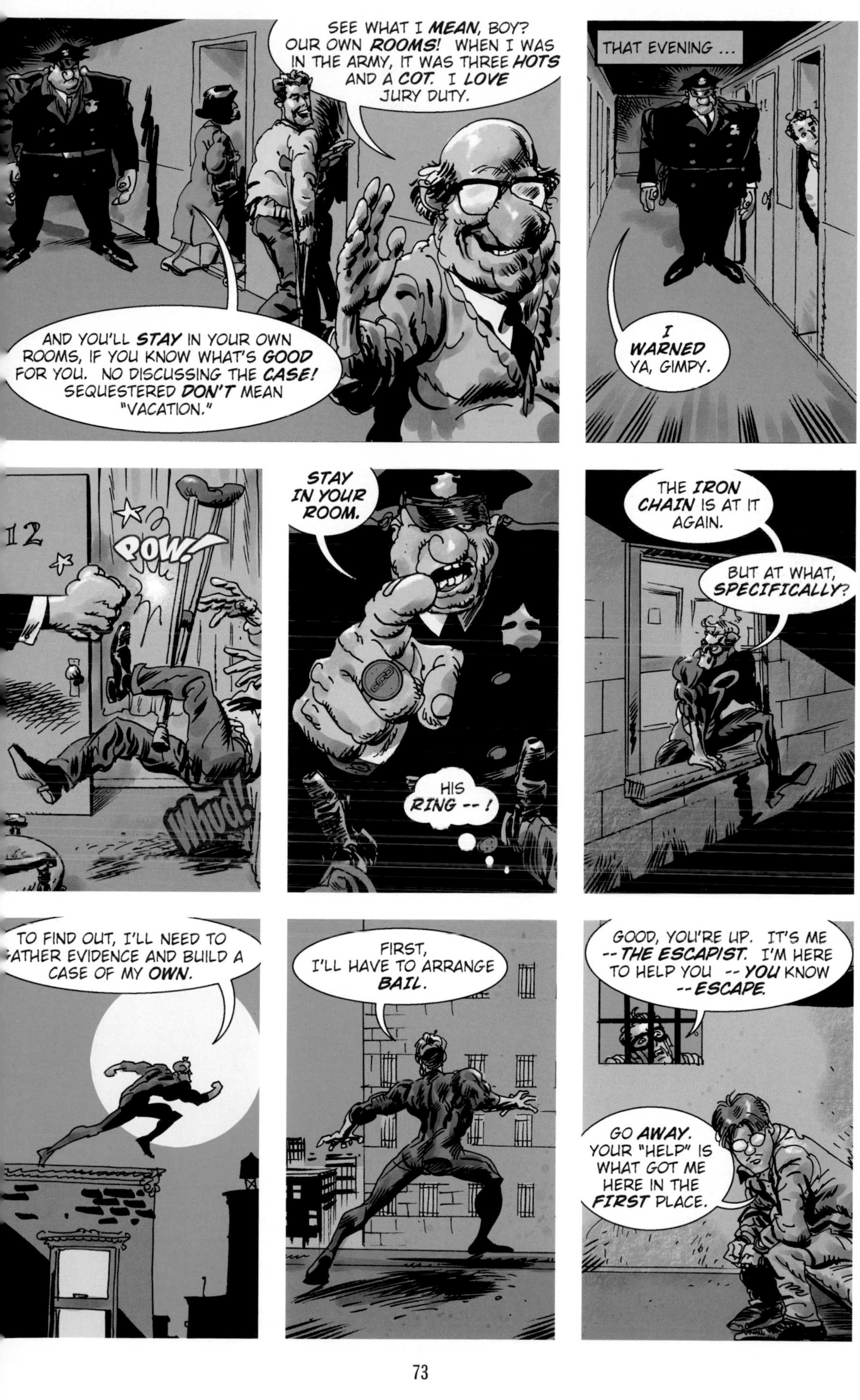
SEE WHAT I MEAN, BOY? OUR OWN ROOMS! WHEN I WAS IN THE ARMY, IT WAS THREE HOTS AND A COT. I LOVE JURY DUTY.
AND YOU'LL STAY IN YOUR OWN ROOMS, IF YOU KNOW WHAT'S GOOD FOR YOU. NO DISCUSSING THE CASE! SEQUESTERED DON'T MEAN "VACATION."
THAT EVENING ...
I WARNED YA, GIMPY.
12
POW!
WHUD!
STAY IN YOUR ROOM.
HIS RING -- !
THE IRON CHAIN IS AT IT AGAIN.
BUT AT WHAT, SPECIFICALLY?
TO FIND OUT, I'LL NEED TO GATHER EVIDENCE AND BUILD A CASE OF MY OWN.
FIRST, I'LL HAVE TO ARRANGE BAIL.
GOOD, YOU'RE UP. IT'S ME -- THE ESCAPIST. I'M HERE TO HELP YOU -- YOU KNOW -- ESCAPE.
GO AWAY. YOUR "HELP" IS WHAT GOT ME HERE IN THE FIRST PLACE.

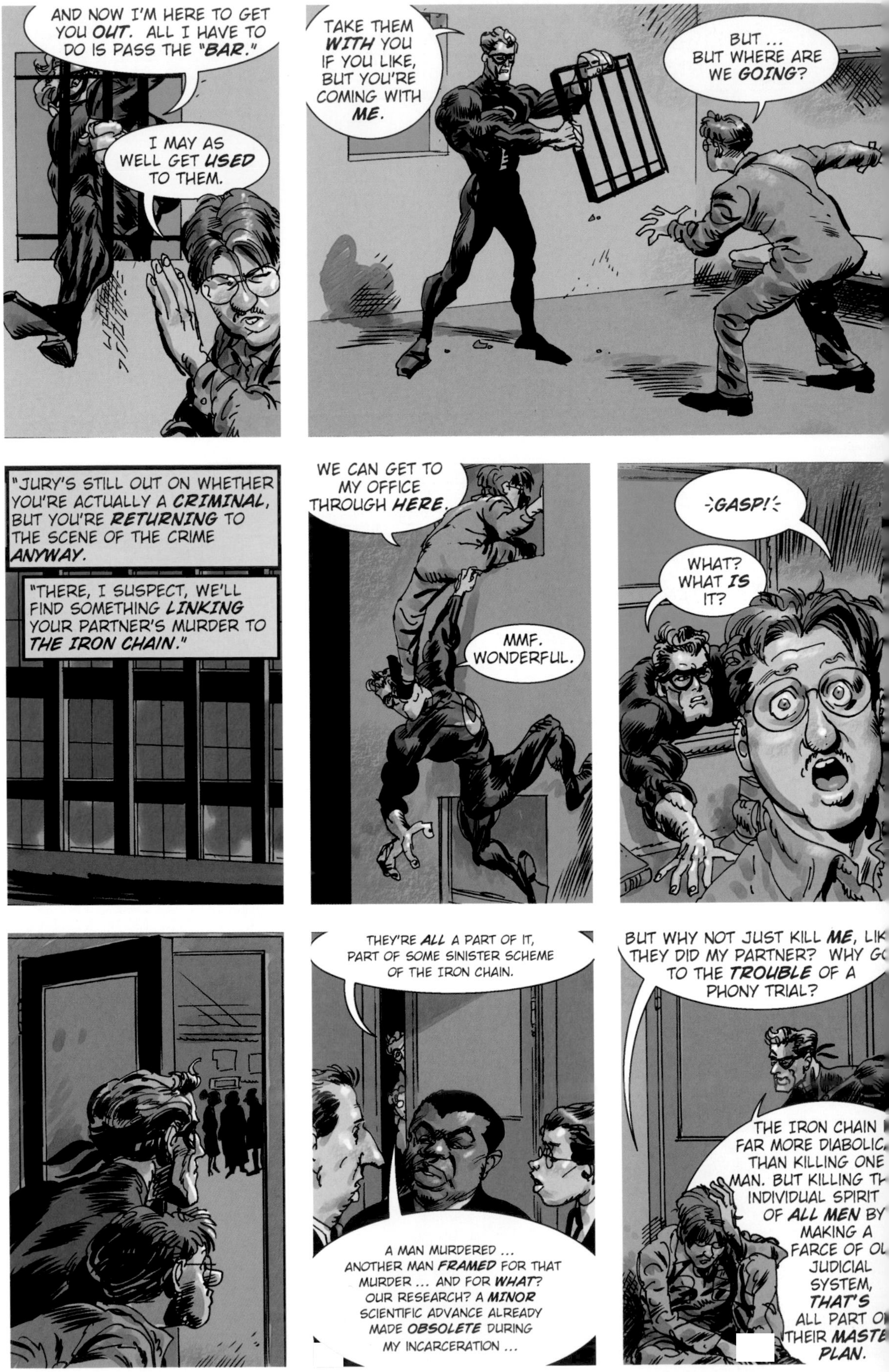
AND NOW I'M HERE TO GET YOU OUT. ALL I HAVE TO DO IS PASS THE "BAR."
I MAY AS WELL GET USED TO THEM.
TAKE THEM WITH YOU IF YOU LIKE, BUT YOU'RE COMING WITH ME.
BUT ... BUT WHERE ARE WE GOING?
"JURY'S STILL OUT ON WHETHER YOU'RE ACTUALLY A CRIMINAL, BUT YOU'RE RETURNING TO THE SCENE OF THE CRIME ANYWAY.
"THERE, I SUSPECT, WE'LL FIND SOMETHING LINKING YOUR PARTNER'S MURDER TO THE IRON CHAIN."
WE CAN GET TO MY OFFICE THROUGH HERE.
MMF. WONDERFUL.
GASP!
WHAT? WHAT IS IT?
THEY'RE ALL A PART OF IT, PART OF SOME SINISTER SCHEME OF THE IRON CHAIN.
A MAN MURDERED ... ANOTHER MAN FRAMED FOR THAT MURDER ... AND FOR WHAT? OUR RESEARCH? A MINOR SCIENTIFIC ADVANCE ALREADY MADE OBSOLETE DURING MY INCARCERATION ...
BUT WHY NOT JUST KILL ME, LIK THEY DID MY PARTNER? WHY G TO THE TROUBLE OF A PHONY TRIAL?
THE IRON CHAIN FAR MORE DIABOLIC THAN KILLING ONE MAN. BUT KILLING TH INDIVIDUAL SPIRIT OF ALL MEN BY MAKING A FARCE OF O JUDICIAL SYSTEM, THAT'S ALL PART O THEIR MASTE PLAN.

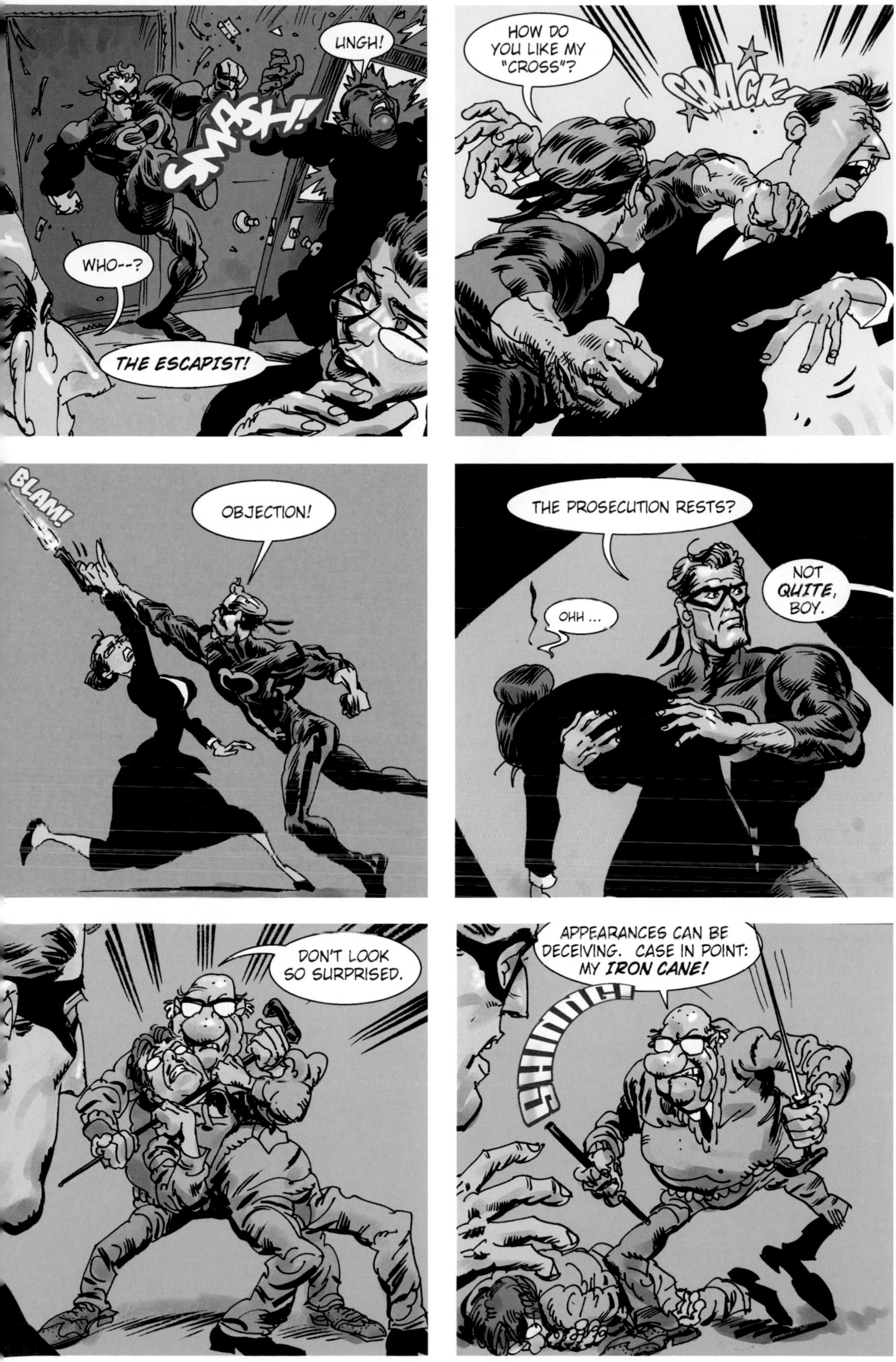
UNGH!
SMASH!
WHO--?
THE ESCAPIST!
HOW DO YOU LIKE MY "CROSS"?
CRACK
BLAM!
OBJECTION!
THE PROSECUTION RESTS?
OHH ...
NOT *QUITE*, BOY.
DON'T LOOK SO SURPRISED.
APPEARANCES CAN BE DECEIVING. CASE IN POINT: MY *IRON CANE!*

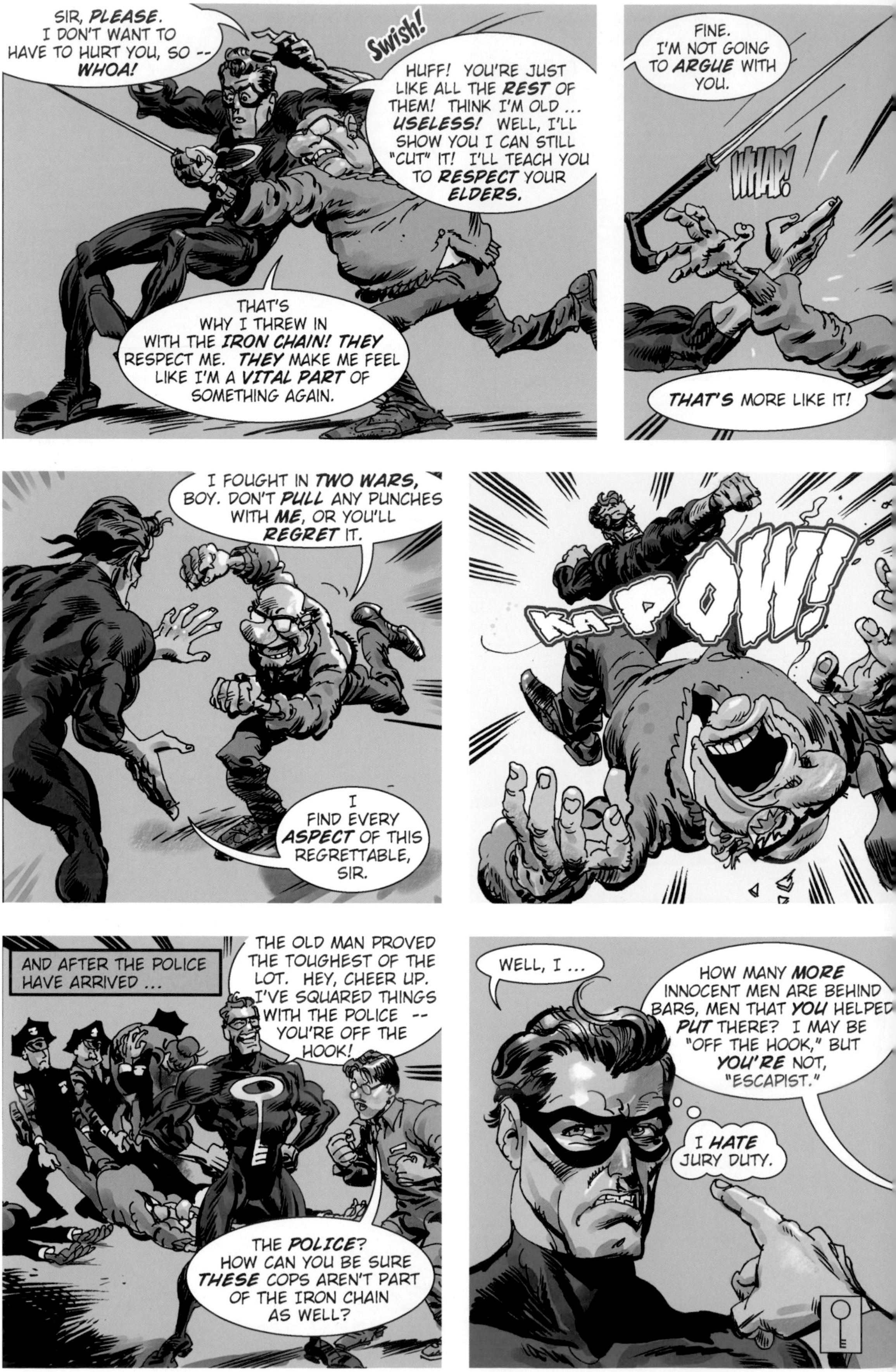
SIR, PLEASE. I DON'T WANT TO HAVE TO HURT YOU, SO -- WHOA!
Swish!
HUFF! YOU'RE JUST LIKE ALL THE REST OF THEM! THINK I'M OLD ... USELESS! WELL, I'LL SHOW YOU I CAN STILL "CUT" IT! I'LL TEACH YOU TO RESPECT YOUR ELDERS.
THAT'S WHY I THREW IN WITH THE IRON CHAIN! THEY RESPECT ME. THEY MAKE ME FEEL LIKE I'M A VITAL PART OF SOMETHING AGAIN.
FINE. I'M NOT GOING TO ARGUE WITH YOU.
WHAP!
THAT'S MORE LIKE IT!
I FOUGHT IN TWO WARS, BOY. DON'T PULL ANY PUNCHES WITH ME, OR YOU'LL REGRET IT.
I FIND EVERY ASPECT OF THIS REGRETTABLE, SIR.
KA-POW!
AND AFTER THE POLICE HAVE ARRIVED ...
THE OLD MAN PROVED THE TOUGHEST OF THE LOT. HEY, CHEER UP. I'VE SQUARED THINGS WITH THE POLICE -- YOU'RE OFF THE HOOK!
THE POLICE? HOW CAN YOU BE SURE THESE COPS AREN'T PART OF THE IRON CHAIN AS WELL?
WELL, I ...
HOW MANY MORE INNOCENT MEN ARE BEHIND BARS, MEN THAT YOU HELPED PUT THERE? I MAY BE "OFF THE HOOK," BUT YOU'RE NOT, "ESCAPIST."
I HATE JURY DUTY.

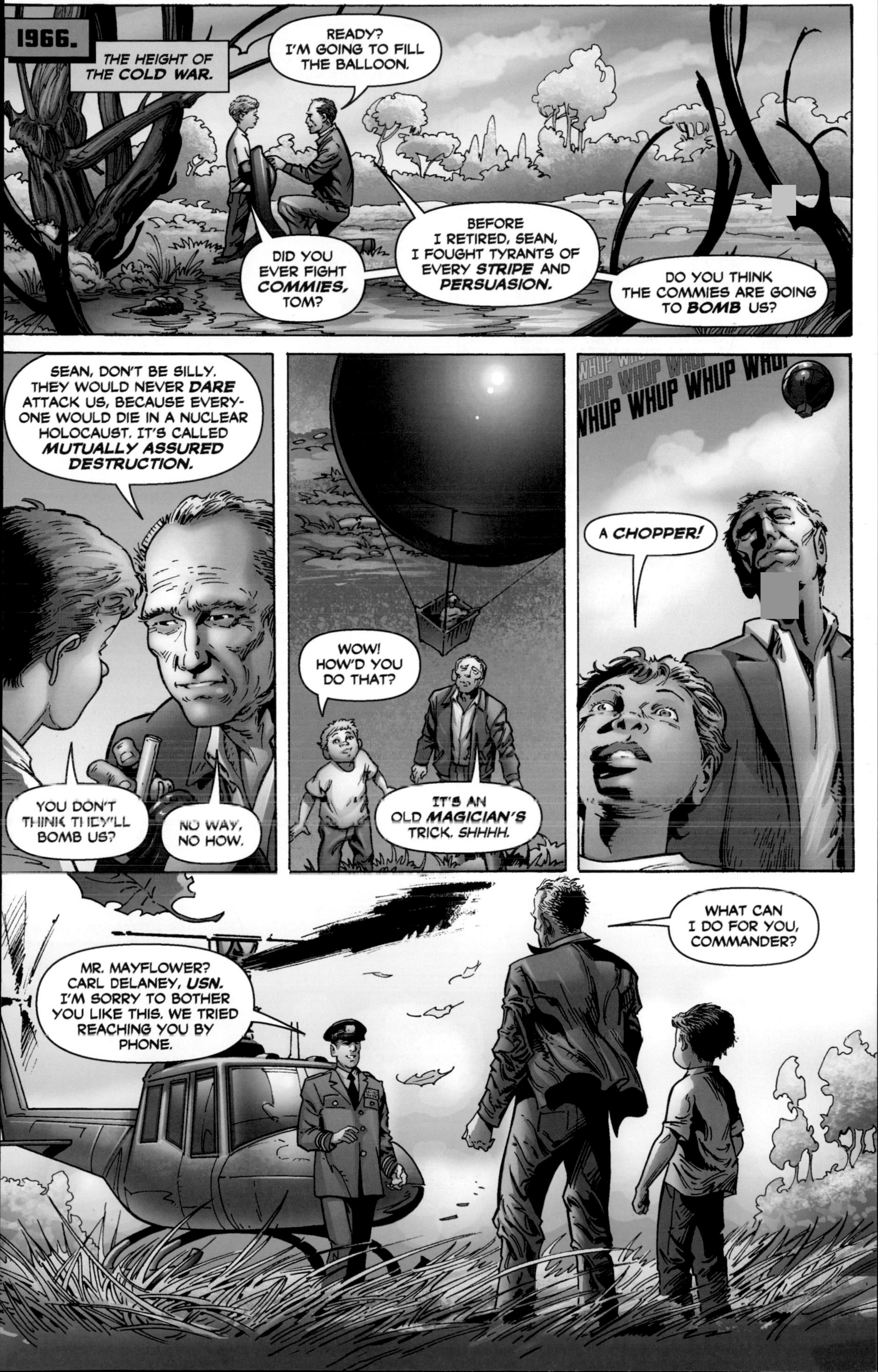
1966.
THE HEIGHT OF THE COLD WAR.
READY? I'M GOING TO FILL THE BALLOON.
DID YOU EVER FIGHT COMMIES, TOM?
BEFORE I RETIRED, SEAN, I FOUGHT TYRANTS OF EVERY STRIPE AND PERSUASION.
DO YOU THINK THE COMMIES ARE GOING TO BOMB US?
SEAN, DON'T BE SILLY. THEY WOULD NEVER DARE ATTACK US, BECAUSE EVERYONE WOULD DIE IN A NUCLEAR HOLOCAUST. IT'S CALLED MUTUALLY ASSURED DESTRUCTION.
YOU DON'T THINK THEY'LL BOMB US?
NO WAY, NO HOW.
WOW! HOW'D YOU DO THAT?
IT'S AN OLD MAGICIAN'S TRICK. SHHHH.
WHUP WHUP WHUP WHUP
A CHOPPER!
WHAT CAN I DO FOR YOU, COMMANDER?
MR. MAYFLOWER? CARL DELANEY, USN. I'M SORRY TO BOTHER YOU LIKE THIS. WE TRIED REACHING YOU BY PHONE.

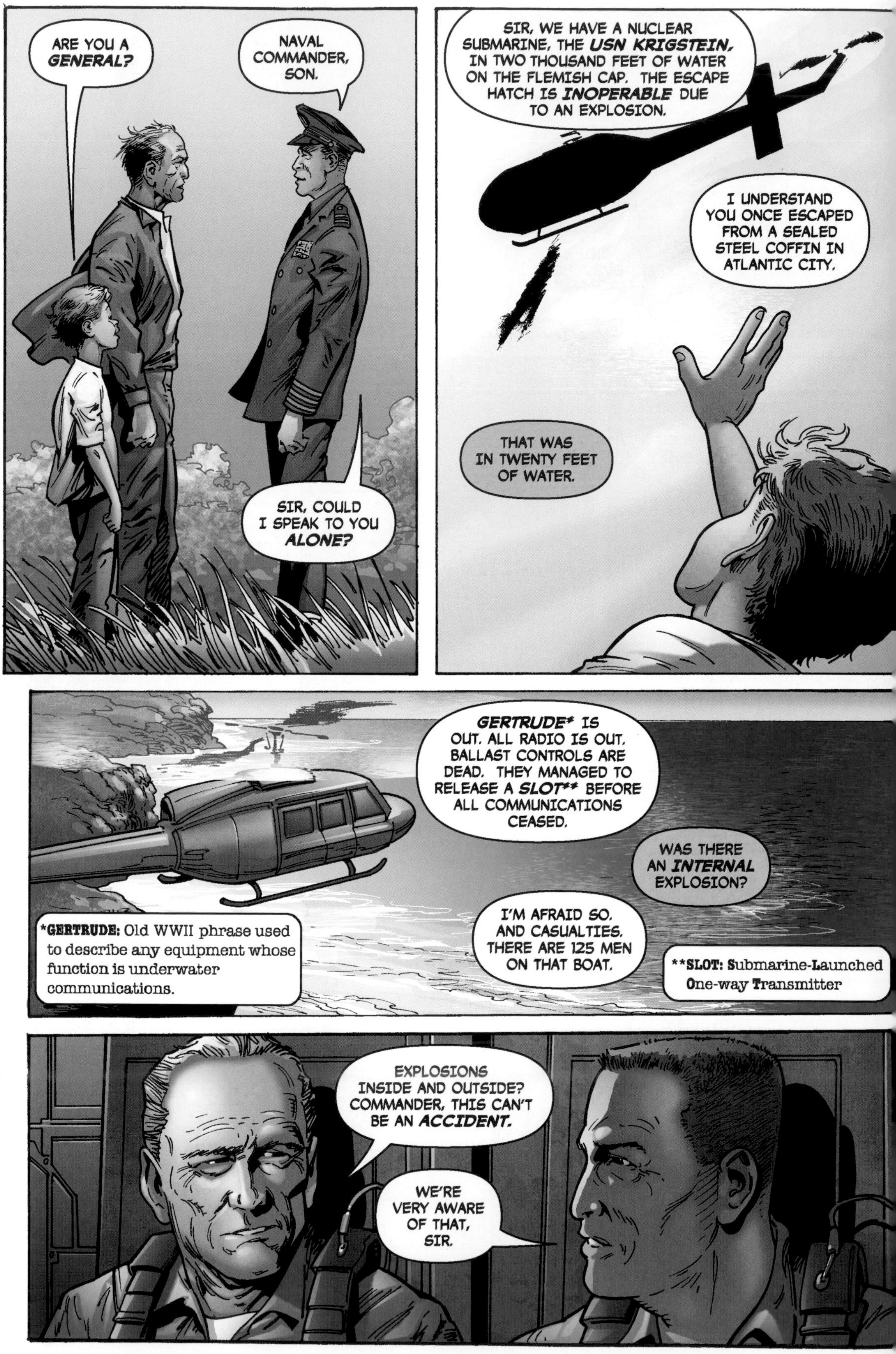
ARE YOU A GENERAL?
NAVAL COMMANDER, SON.
SIR, COULD I SPEAK TO YOU ALONE?
SIR, WE HAVE A NUCLEAR SUBMARINE, THE USN KRIGSTEIN, IN TWO THOUSAND FEET OF WATER ON THE FLEMISH CAP. THE ESCAPE HATCH IS INOPERABLE DUE TO AN EXPLOSION.
I UNDERSTAND YOU ONCE ESCAPED FROM A SEALED STEEL COFFIN IN ATLANTIC CITY.
THAT WAS IN TWENTY FEET OF WATER.
GERTRUDE* IS OUT. ALL RADIO IS OUT. BALLAST CONTROLS ARE DEAD. THEY MANAGED TO RELEASE A SLOT** BEFORE ALL COMMUNICATIONS CEASED.
WAS THERE AN INTERNAL EXPLOSION?
I'M AFRAID SO. AND CASUALTIES. THERE ARE 125 MEN ON THAT BOAT.
*GERTRUDE: Old WWII phrase used to describe any equipment whose function is underwater communications.
**SLOT: Submarine-Launched One-way Transmitter
EXPLOSIONS INSIDE AND OUTSIDE? COMMANDER, THIS CAN'T BE AN ACCIDENT.
WE'RE VERY AWARE OF THAT, SIR.

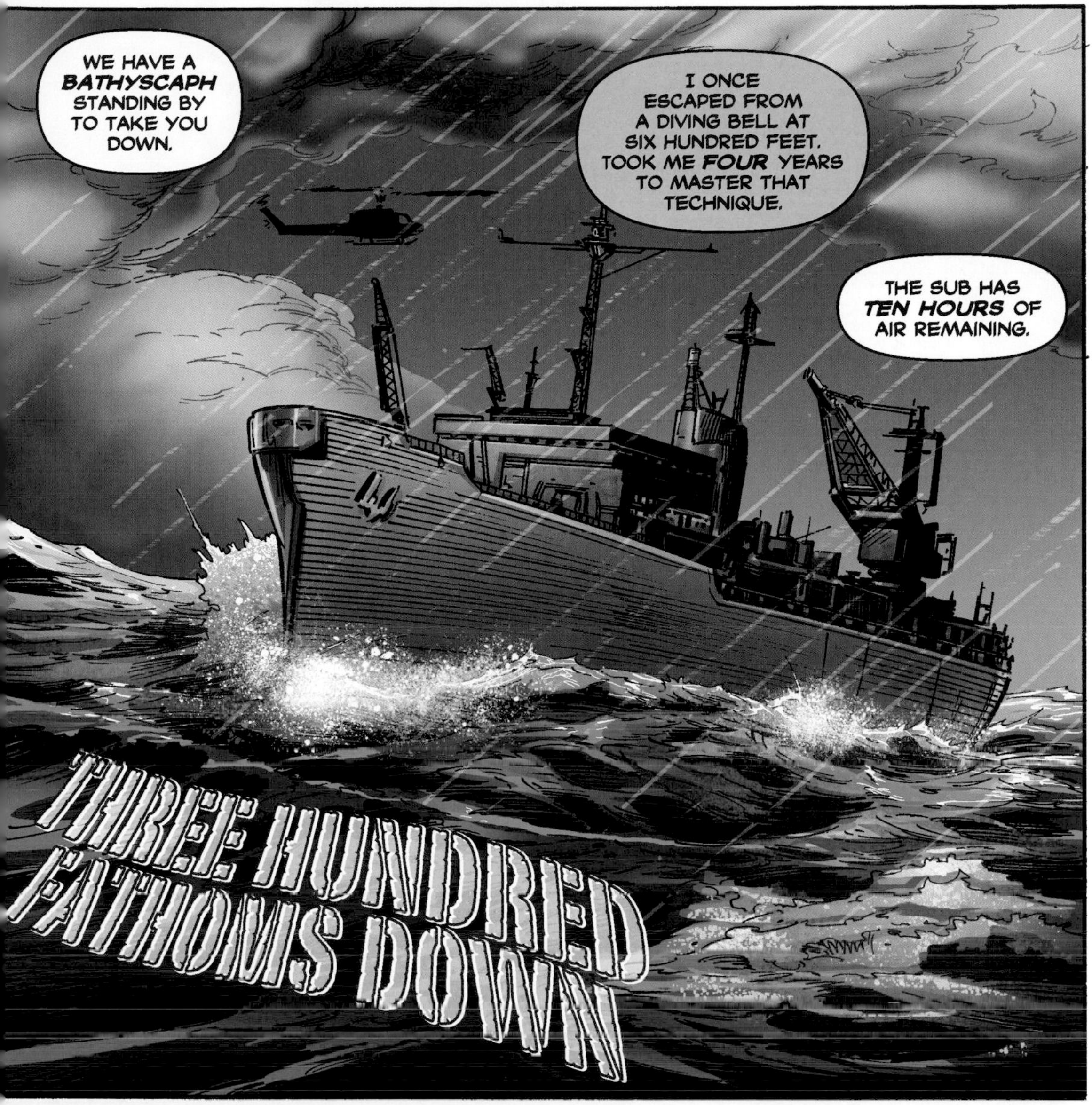
WE HAVE A BATHYSCAPH STANDING BY TO TAKE YOU DOWN.
I ONCE ESCAPED FROM A DIVING BELL AT SIX HUNDRED FEET. TOOK ME FOUR YEARS TO MASTER THAT TECHNIQUE.
THE SUB HAS TEN HOURS OF AIR REMAINING.
THREE HUNDRED FATHOMS DOWN

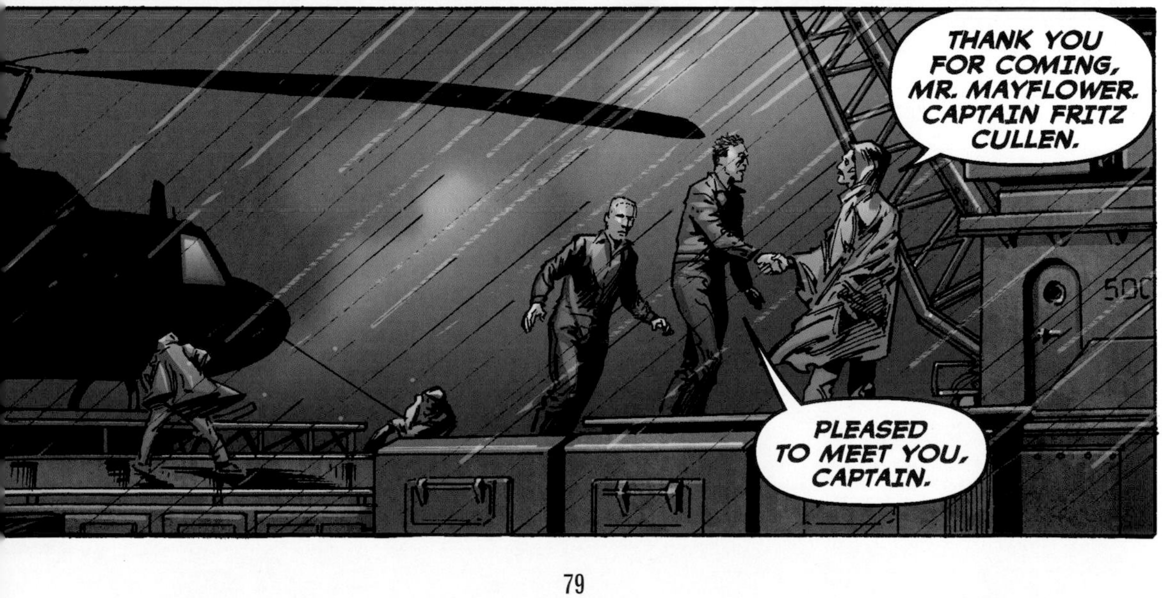
THANK YOU FOR COMING, MR. MAYFLOWER. CAPTAIN FRITZ CULLEN.
PLEASED TO MEET YOU, CAPTAIN.
500

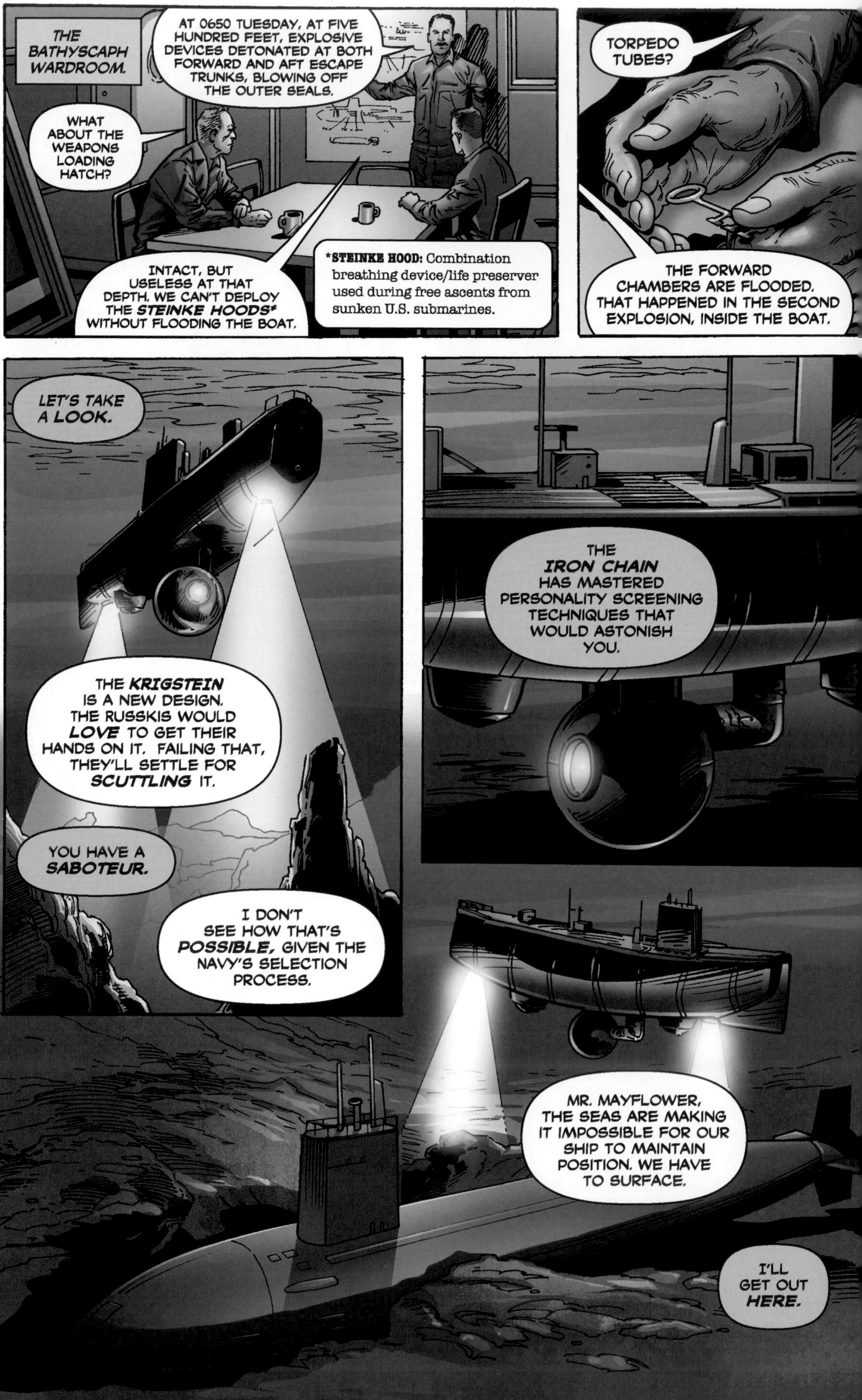
THE BATHYSCAPH WARDROOM.
AT 0650 TUESDAY, AT FIVE HUNDRED FEET, EXPLOSIVE DEVICES DETONATED AT BOTH FORWARD AND AFT ESCAPE TRUNKS, BLOWING OFF THE OUTER SEALS.
WHAT ABOUT THE WEAPONS LOADING HATCH?
INTACT, BUT USELESS AT THAT DEPTH. WE CAN'T DEPLOY THE STEINKE HOODS* WITHOUT FLOODING THE BOAT.
*STEINKE HOOD: Combination breathing device/life preserver used during free ascents from sunken U.S. submarines.
TORPEDO TUBES?
THE FORWARD CHAMBERS ARE FLOODED. THAT HAPPENED IN THE SECOND EXPLOSION, INSIDE THE BOAT.
LET'S TAKE A LOOK.
THE KRIGSTEIN IS A NEW DESIGN. THE RUSSKIS WOULD LOVE TO GET THEIR HANDS ON IT. FAILING THAT, THEY'LL SETTLE FOR SCUTTLING IT.
YOU HAVE A SABOTEUR.
I DON'T SEE HOW THAT'S POSSIBLE, GIVEN THE NAVY'S SELECTION PROCESS.
THE IRON CHAIN HAS MASTERED PERSONALITY SCREENING TECHNIQUES THAT WOULD ASTONISH YOU.
MR. MAYFLOWER, THE SEAS ARE MAKING IT IMPOSSIBLE FOR OUR SHIP TO MAINTAIN POSITION. WE HAVE TO SURFACE.
I'LL GET OUT HERE.

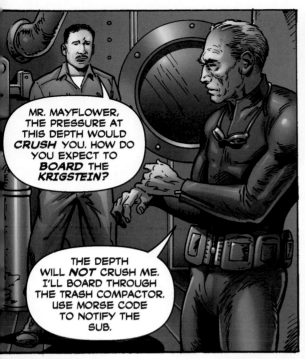

MR. MAYFLOWER, THE PRESSURE AT THIS DEPTH WOULD *CRUSH* YOU. HOW DO YOU EXPECT TO *BOARD* THE *KRIGSTEIN?*

THE DEPTH WILL *NOT* CRUSH ME. I'LL BOARD THROUGH THE TRASH COMPACTOR. USE MORSE CODE TO NOTIFY THE SUB.

IT WORKED AT SIX HUNDRED FEET. IT MUST WORK AT TWO THOUSAND.

MUST EXPEL ALL THE AIR IN MY LUNGS BEFORE I ENTER THE WATER.

SIXTY SECONDS BEFORE I BLACK OUT FROM OXYGEN DEPRIVATION.

PERMISSION TO COME ABOARD!

WELCOME, I'M CAPTAIN HENDERSON AND THIS IS MY *CBO*, ROLAND NEAME.

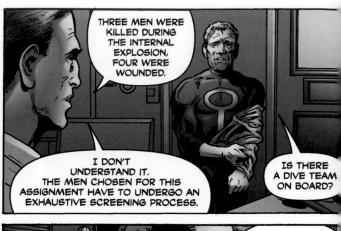

THREE MEN WERE KILLED DURING THE INTERNAL EXPLOSION, FOUR WERE WOUNDED.

I DON'T UNDERSTAND IT, THE MEN CHOSEN FOR THIS ASSIGNMENT HAVE TO UNDERGO AN EXHAUSTIVE SCREENING PROCESS.

IS THERE A DIVE TEAM ON BOARD?

WE CARRY A THREE-MAN DIVE TEAM, BUT THEY'RE ALL *SEALS*. IT'S UNTHINKABLE ONE OF *THEM* COULD BE A SABOTEUR.

I'D LIKE TO SEE THEIR FILES, THEN THE INJURED MEN.

FOR YOUR EYES ONLY.

We have obtained confirmation of "Project Deep Lung," a joint operation of the Soviet Union and the Iron Chain to genetically engineer soldiers who can survive at deep water pressures. Joint investigations between

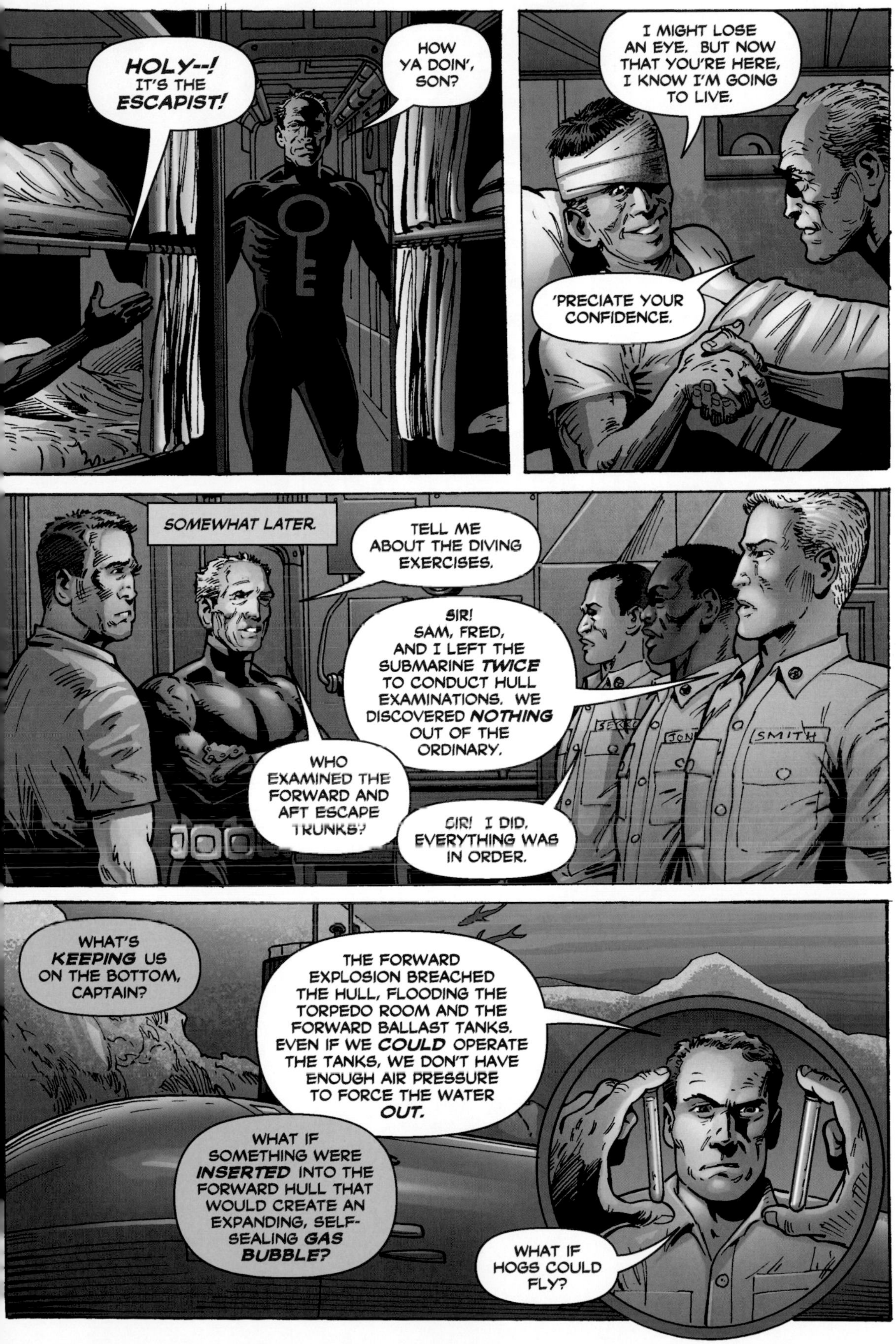
HOLY--! IT'S THE ESCAPIST!
HOW YA DOIN', SON?
I MIGHT LOSE AN EYE. BUT NOW THAT YOU'RE HERE, I KNOW I'M GOING TO LIVE.
'PRECIATE YOUR CONFIDENCE.
SOMEWHAT LATER.
TELL ME ABOUT THE DIVING EXERCISES.
SIR! SAM, FRED, AND I LEFT THE SUBMARINE TWICE TO CONDUCT HULL EXAMINATIONS. WE DISCOVERED NOTHING OUT OF THE ORDINARY.
SMITH
WHO EXAMINED THE FORWARD AND AFT ESCAPE TRUNKS?
SIR! I DID. EVERYTHING WAS IN ORDER.
WHAT'S KEEPING US ON THE BOTTOM, CAPTAIN?
THE FORWARD EXPLOSION BREACHED THE HULL, FLOODING THE TORPEDO ROOM AND THE FORWARD BALLAST TANKS. EVEN IF WE COULD OPERATE THE TANKS, WE DON'T HAVE ENOUGH AIR PRESSURE TO FORCE THE WATER OUT.
WHAT IF SOMETHING WERE INSERTED INTO THE FORWARD HULL THAT WOULD CREATE AN EXPANDING, SELF-SEALING GAS BUBBLE?
WHAT IF HOGS COULD FLY?

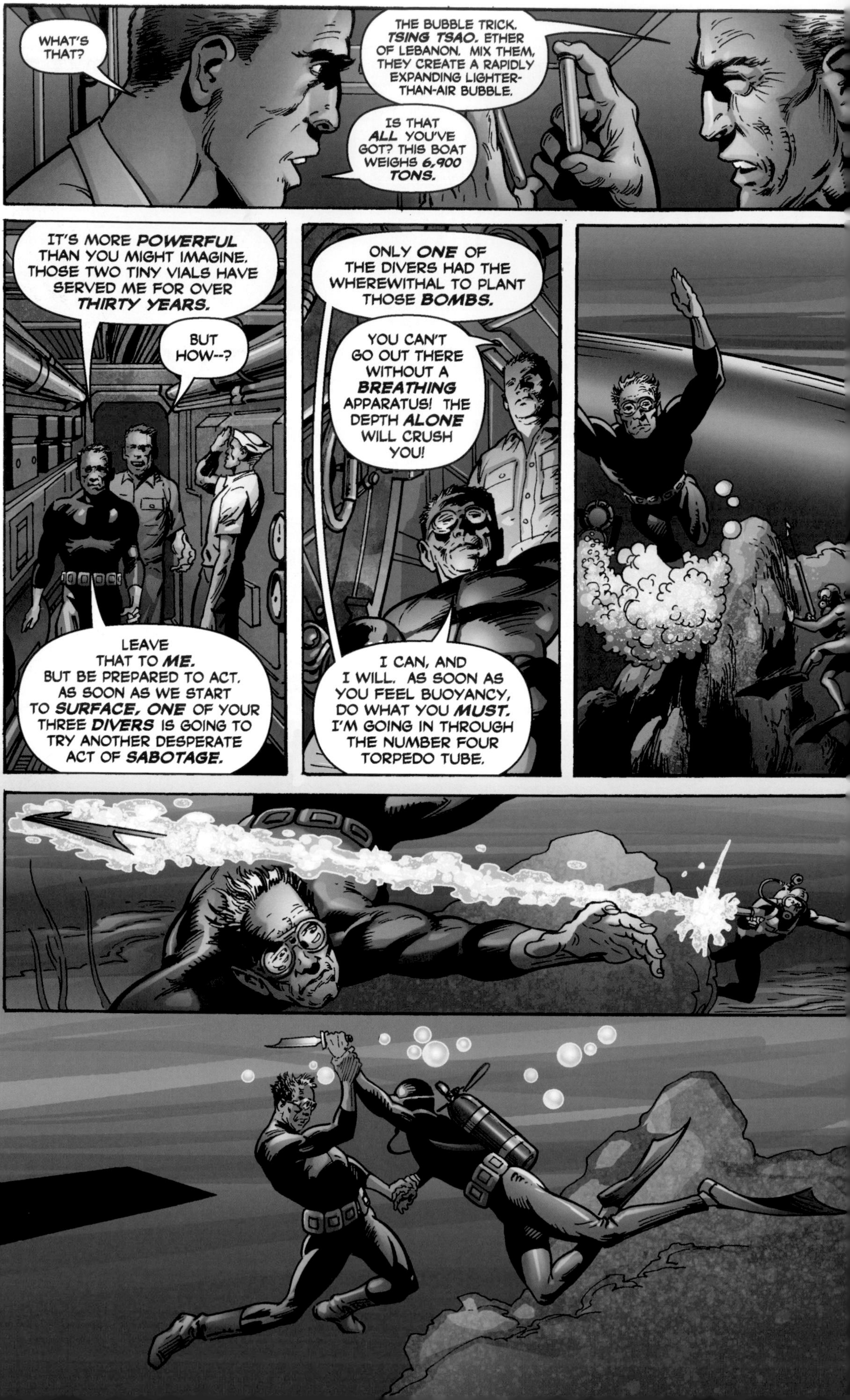
WHAT'S THAT?
THE BUBBLE TRICK. TSING TSAO. ETHER OF LEBANON. MIX THEM, THEY CREATE A RAPIDLY EXPANDING LIGHTER-THAN-AIR BUBBLE.
IS THAT ALL YOU'VE GOT? THIS BOAT WEIGHS 6,900 TONS.
IT'S MORE POWERFUL THAN YOU MIGHT IMAGINE. THOSE TWO TINY VIALS HAVE SERVED ME FOR OVER THIRTY YEARS.
BUT HOW--?
LEAVE THAT TO ME. BUT BE PREPARED TO ACT. AS SOON AS WE START TO SURFACE, ONE OF YOUR THREE DIVERS IS GOING TO TRY ANOTHER DESPERATE ACT OF SABOTAGE.
ONLY ONE OF THE DIVERS HAD THE WHEREWITHAL TO PLANT THOSE BOMBS.
YOU CAN'T GO OUT THERE WITHOUT A BREATHING APPARATUS! THE DEPTH ALONE WILL CRUSH YOU!
I CAN, AND I WILL. AS SOON AS YOU FEEL BUOYANCY, DO WHAT YOU MUST. I'M GOING IN THROUGH THE NUMBER FOUR TORPEDO TUBE.

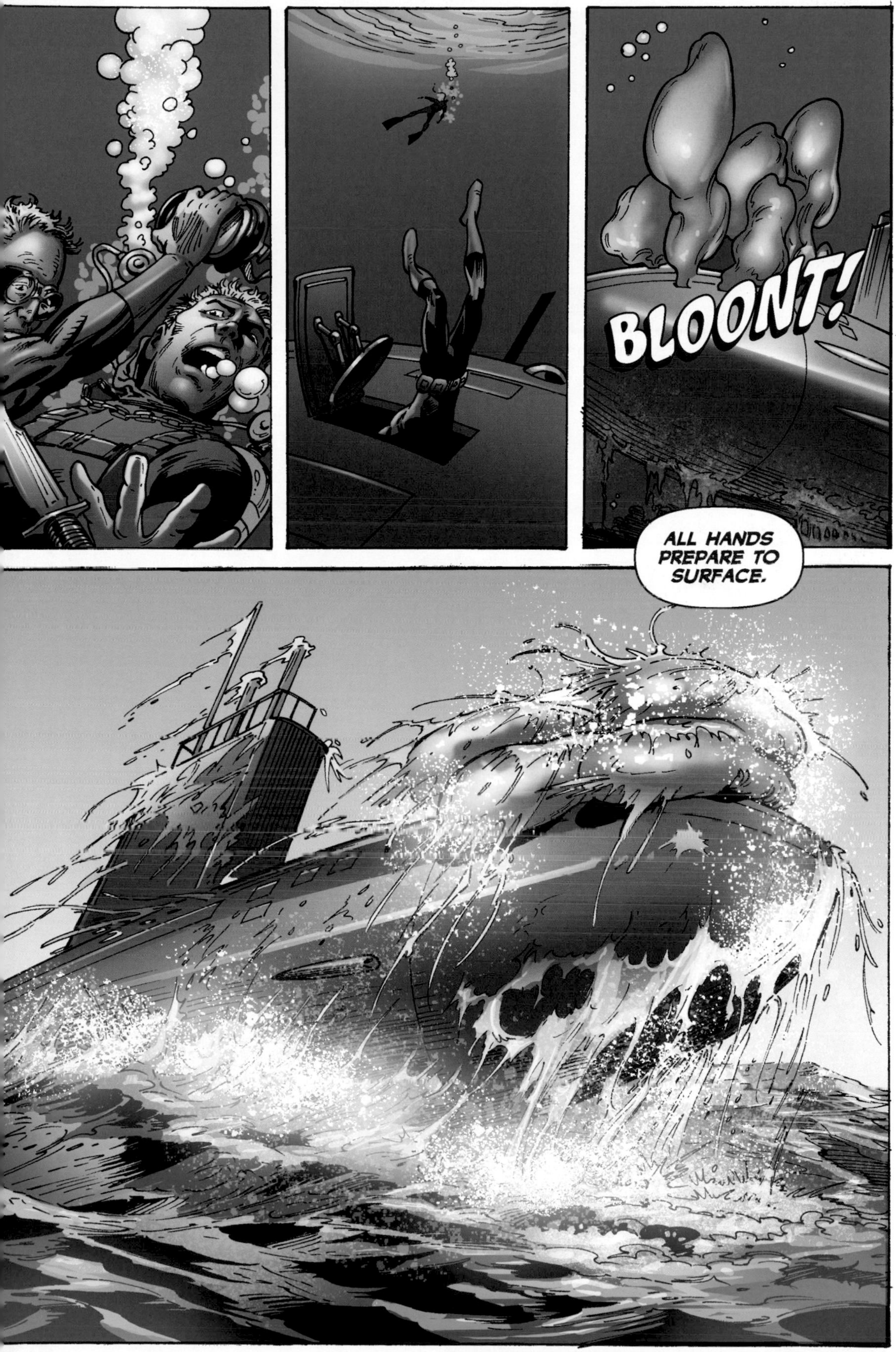
BLOONT!
ALL HANDS PREPARE TO SURFACE.

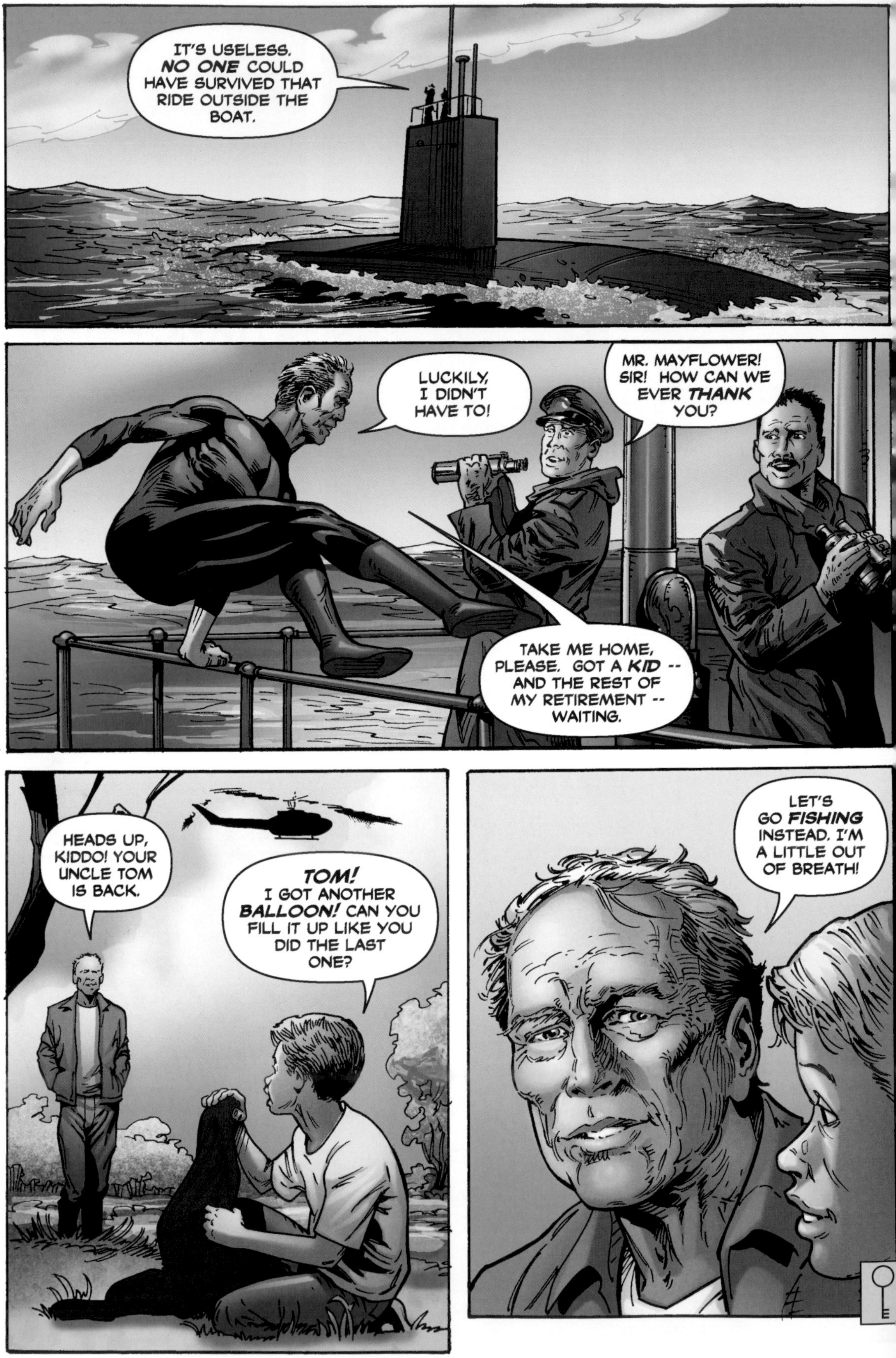
IT'S USELESS. NO ONE COULD HAVE SURVIVED THAT RIDE OUTSIDE THE BOAT.
LUCKILY, I DIDN'T HAVE TO!
MR. MAYFLOWER! SIR! HOW CAN WE EVER THANK YOU?
TAKE ME HOME, PLEASE. GOT A KID -- AND THE REST OF MY RETIREMENT -- WAITING.
HEADS UP, KIDDO! YOUR UNCLE TOM IS BACK.
TOM! I GOT ANOTHER BALLOON! CAN YOU FILL IT UP LIKE YOU DID THE LAST ONE?
LET'S GO FISHING INSTEAD. I'M A LITTLE OUT OF BREATH!

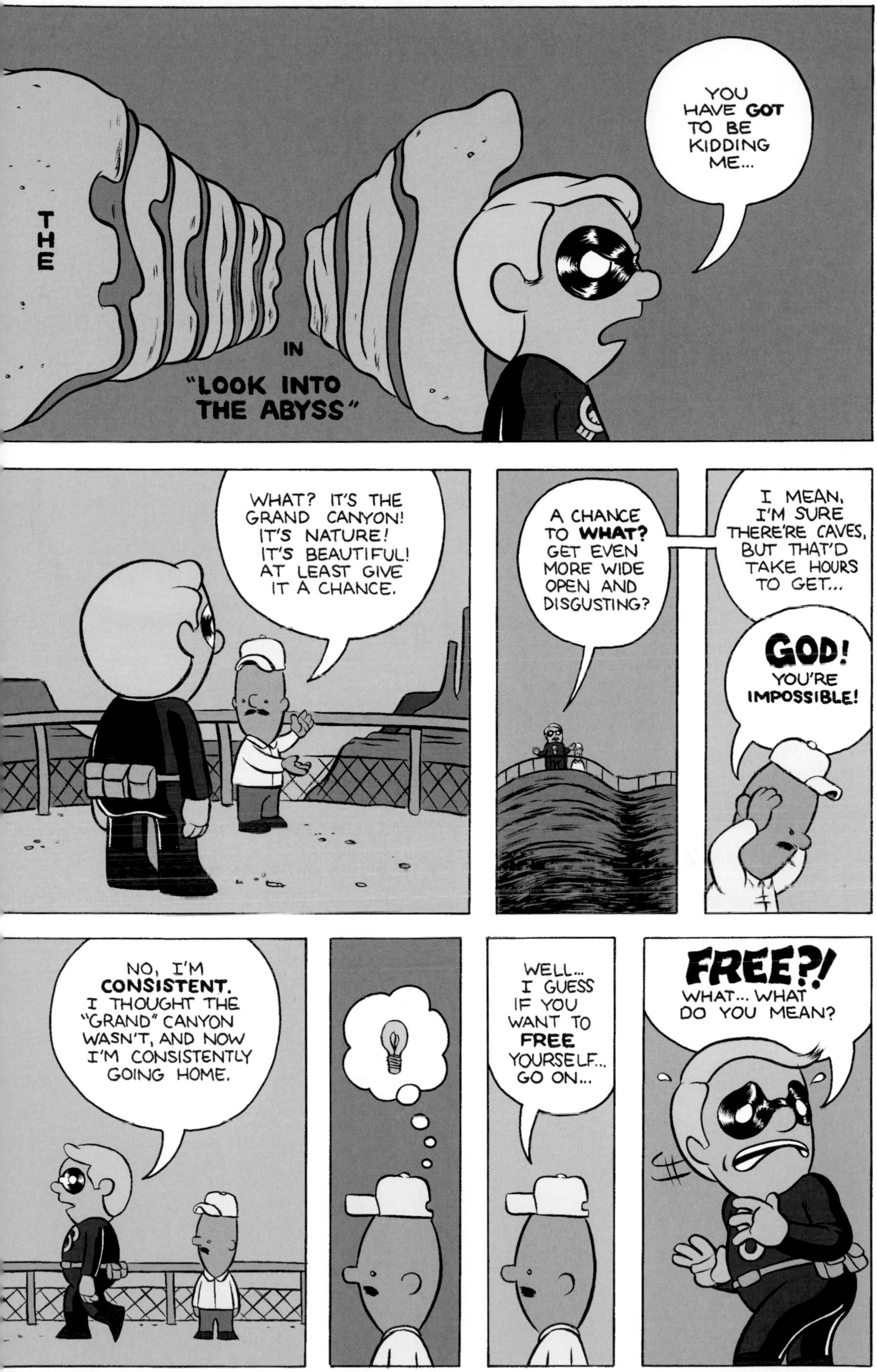
THE
IN
"LOOK INTO THE ABYSS"
YOU HAVE **GOT** TO BE KIDDING ME...
WHAT? IT'S THE GRAND CANYON! IT'S NATURE! IT'S BEAUTIFUL! AT LEAST GIVE IT A CHANCE.
A CHANCE TO **WHAT?** GET EVEN MORE WIDE OPEN AND DISGUSTING?
I MEAN, I'M SURE THERE'RE CAVES, BUT THAT'D TAKE HOURS TO GET...
**GOD!** YOU'RE **IMPOSSIBLE!**
NO, I'M **CONSISTENT.** I THOUGHT THE "GRAND" CANYON WASN'T, AND NOW I'M CONSISTENTLY GOING HOME.
WELL... I GUESS IF YOU WANT TO **FREE** YOURSELF... GO ON...
**FREE?!** WHAT... WHAT DO YOU MEAN?

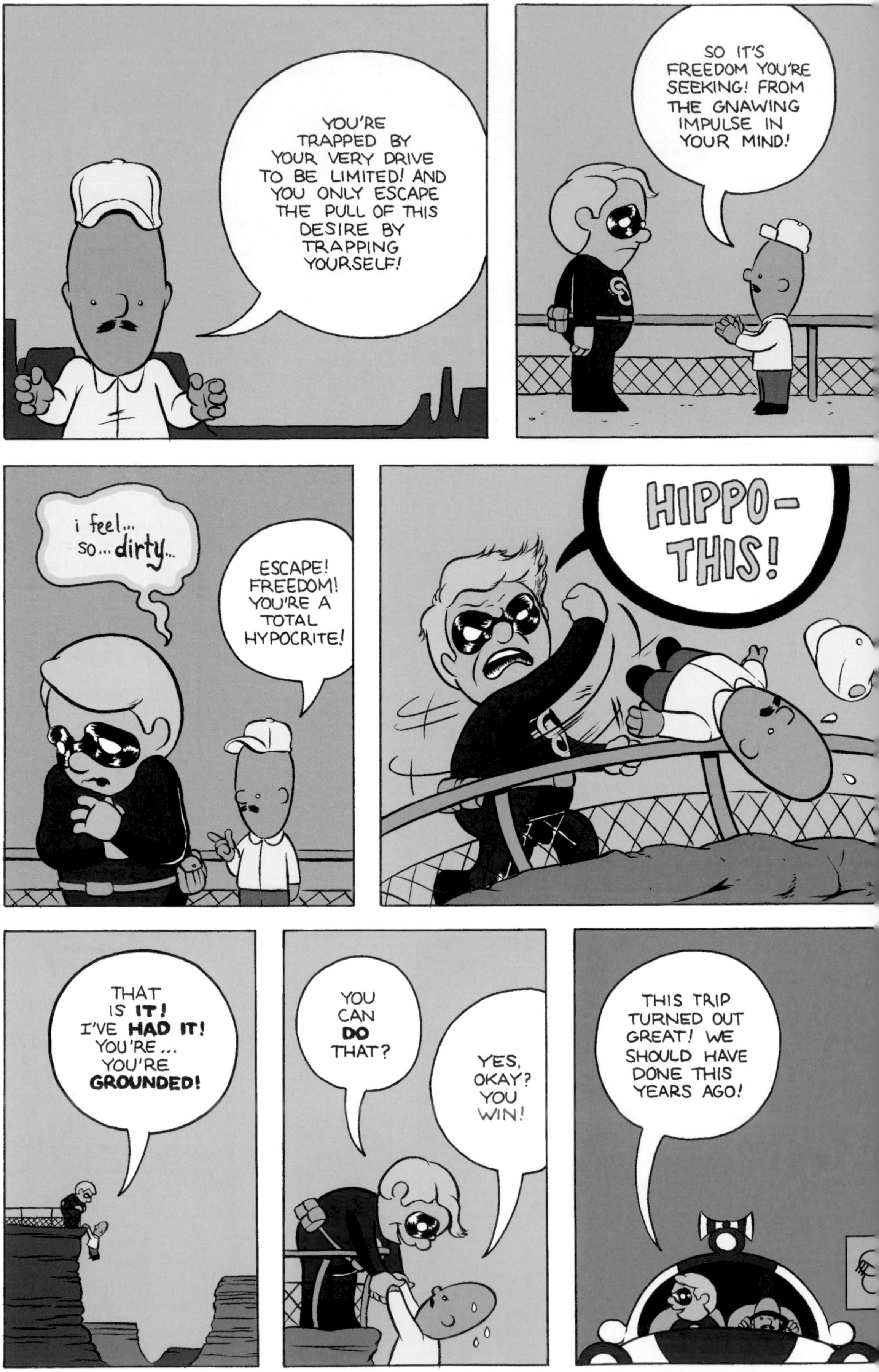
YOU'RE TRAPPED BY YOUR VERY DRIVE TO BE LIMITED! AND YOU ONLY ESCAPE THE PULL OF THIS DESIRE BY TRAPPING YOURSELF!
SO IT'S FREEDOM YOU'RE SEEKING! FROM THE GNAWING IMPULSE IN YOUR MIND!
i feel... so... dirty...
ESCAPE! FREEDOM! YOU'RE A TOTAL HYPOCRITE!
HIPPO-THIS!
THAT IS IT! I'VE HAD IT! YOU'RE... YOU'RE GROUNDED!
YOU CAN DO THAT?
YES, OKAY? YOU WIN!
THIS TRIP TURNED OUT GREAT! WE SHOULD HAVE DONE THIS YEARS AGO!

# "THE LADY OR THE TIGER"

*Preface*

## BY GLEN DAVID GOLD

COMICS ARE UNIQUE IN THE PRESENT DAY, IN THAT THE AUDIENCE HAS to wait for monthly installments, giving each episode weeks to steep in the memory before a new layer is added on. In this internet age, having to wait long enough to hit "refresh" on your browser toolbar strikes people as torture. To really find an antecedent for the lengthy comic book plot, one must look past even the intra-War era "Perils of Pauline"-type serials and back to serialized novels, such as those of Henry James.

*The Portrait of a Lady*, for instance, was the *Dark Knight Returns* of its day, taking up 13 months of *Macmillan's* in 1880–'81. In his prefaces to the New York edition (1907–'09), James refers to "the necessity, that is to say, of keeping the many narrative pots of slumgullion stew abubble" in explaining the art of how to end a chapter so that the reader won't just want to turn the page, but will want to buy another issue 30 days later.

Certain runs of 1970s to early '80s comic book epics carried a freight-train-like momentum. Consider the Kree-Skrull war, the Celestial Madonna, the Dark Phoenix story, the life and death (and life) of Elektra, and *The Escapist*'s own "Dark Lady" storyline. All of them were built on rising tensions and were resolved in spectacular climaxes. All except for *The Escapist*.

We needn't retell the difficult creative history *The Escapist* endured in the 1970s. Constant turnover of creative teams, shifting political winds, and the brief promise of Hollywood-style attention sent the storylines into turmoil. Not since the disastrous 1968 pinup in which the Escapist urged readers to "Escape reality! Turn on!" (forever alienating artist Steve Ditko, whose own pro-free-market caption had been statted over) had our hero so rapidly changed directions.

And yet there came 1976, the Escapist's miracle year. Having found a brilliant artist in the form of Gene Colan, whose tenure on *Daredevil and Tomb of Dracula* made him a perfect delineator,

Sunshine Comics editorial either relaxed—or rode roughshod (accounts differ)—on the writing team, who flourished. Quickly dropped were the child sidekicks (fandom had been loudly denouncing them in San Diego and in the *Reader* as coming from "Open Sesame Street") and the one-shot storylines. In their place was developed a fluid, multipart epic that showed a new seriousness and commitment to Tom Mayflower, the man and the hero.

By the sixth issue, a heady sort of rhythm had been established: each issue had a villain who was overcome with relative ease, but afterwards, each time, the Escapist paid some terrible price. First, wedges were placed between himself and the League, and then he grew grim and secretive around Omar, Plum Blossom, and Big Al himself. Alienated, lonely, he questioned how deeply the connection ran between himself and any of his allies.

Furthermore, he was tormented by dark dreams and waking visions of a woman whose face he couldn't quite see. During an otherwise easy tangle with Sagebrush, Tom Mayflower was so distracted by thoughts of this mysterious woman that he

The "Dark Lady" from *The Escapist* #53. © November 1976 Sunshine Media Group.

took a hard punch to the jaw that allowed the prickly supervillain to escape. Further, when Shiwan Khan, mystic of the Orient, attacked using the astral plane, Tom was led away by a vision of this woman—and directly into more danger. Was she good or evil? Everyone was dying to know.

The November 1976 issue set up a tense situation: The Gotham Sniper had kidnapped six children from a school under the Escapist's protection, and Tom Mayflower, who seemed almost criminally unprepared, vowed to retrieve them. But, more thrillingly, it was promised in the final blurb: "NEXT ISSUE: THE DARK WOMAN REVEALED."

Any fan can tell you what happened next. The December 1976 issue was, shockingly, a fill-in, pencilled by George Tuska and inked by the prime indicator of a rush job, Vince Colletta. There was an editor's note on the splash indicating that the "Dreaded Deadline Doom" had caught them unawares and that all would be resolved in the first issue of the new year.

When that issue finally did appear, after an *eight-year* hiatus, it was clear that nothing had been resolved. It was revealed that the "Dark Woman" had been a figment of the Escapist's imagination, brought on by too much stress. He agreed that he and his partners needed to go on a well-needed vacation, during which they reapplied themselves to effecting escapes. And that was that.

Officially, nothing *had* happened, but, clearly, something had happened. It was said that in the unpublished story, the Escapist had finally met his match in the form of a woman who would both rescue him and destroy him. Beyond that, details were hard to come by.

In his preface to *The American*, Henry James recalls the creation of art on a serial's timeline with a kind of head-shaking wonder: what if he'd fallen ill? "Would that a character who so nobly entered my consciousness as easily as if he wore his own passkey might somehow join society with a similar *frisson*, in the richest sense, of mass, so that the audience might think of the weight of his consciousness with the same 'drop' as did my own; the repetition of dwelling upon his mark would seem to make him upright and 'real' in the same sense of an uncle who once visited but whose carriage has been long delayed. Would that a 'ghost' had finished his tale, might it seem as if 'Uncle' had been carried away and an incubus put in his place?"

Which was exactly the complaint fandom had. After waiting eight years for resolution, they have had in fact to wait 20 more to find out what happened to "their" Escapist. Finally, the original artwork to this legendary story was recovered during Gene and Adrienne Colan's recent move from Vermont to Florida. It was still in its original pencil form, as the story had been suppressed before an inker had been assigned. So it is with great pleasure we bring you this missing puzzle piece, which isn't a "what if" so much as it is a "what was."

Original Colan pencil art for the woman of Tom Mayflower's dreams, before "remastered" coloring by Eisner Award nominee Paul Hornschemeier.

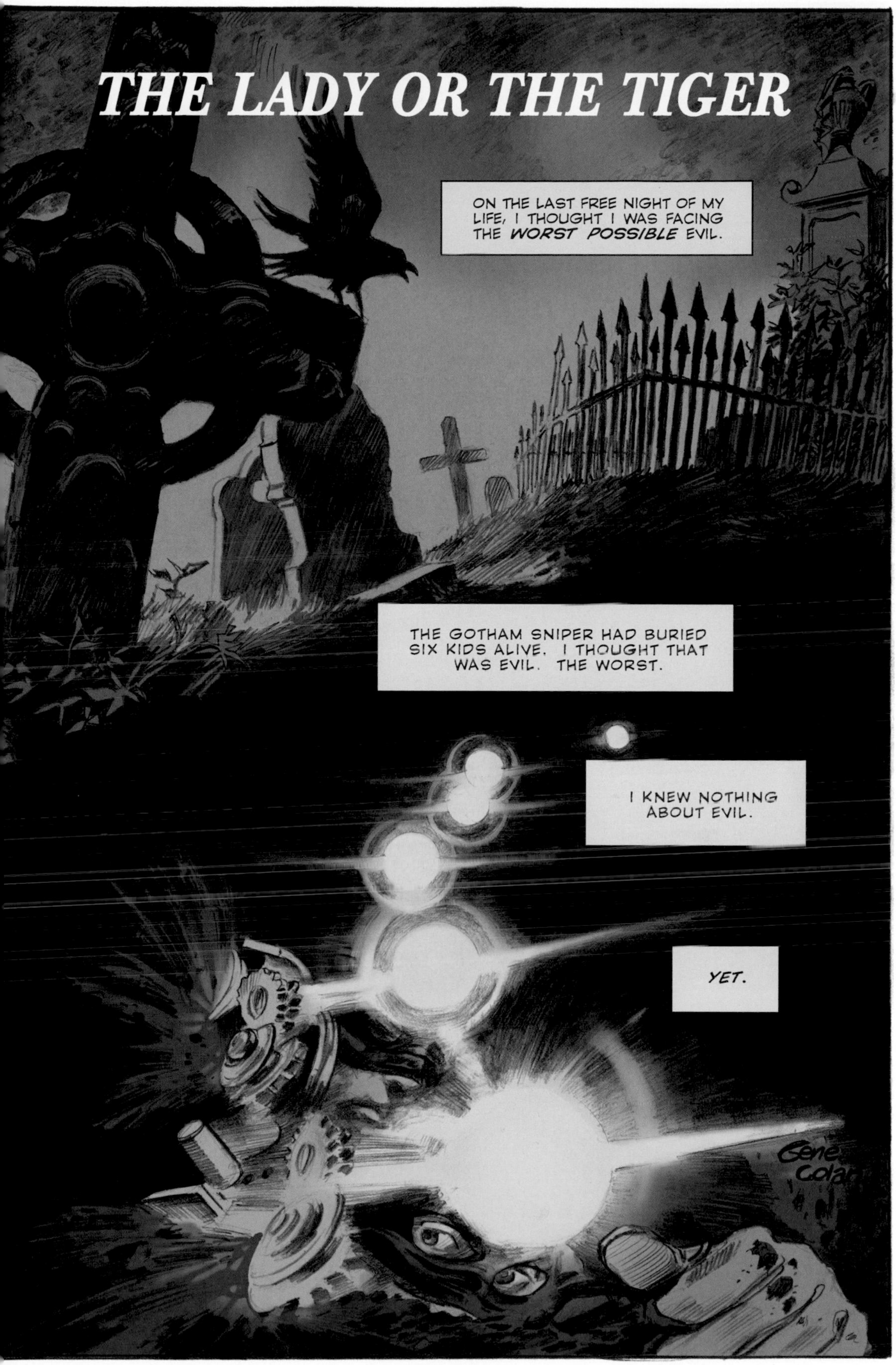
THE LADY OR THE TIGER
ON THE LAST FREE NIGHT OF MY LIFE, I THOUGHT I WAS FACING THE WORST POSSIBLE EVIL.
THE GOTHAM SNIPER HAD BURIED SIX KIDS ALIVE. I THOUGHT THAT WAS EVIL. THE WORST.
I KNEW NOTHING ABOUT EVIL.
YET.
Gene Colan

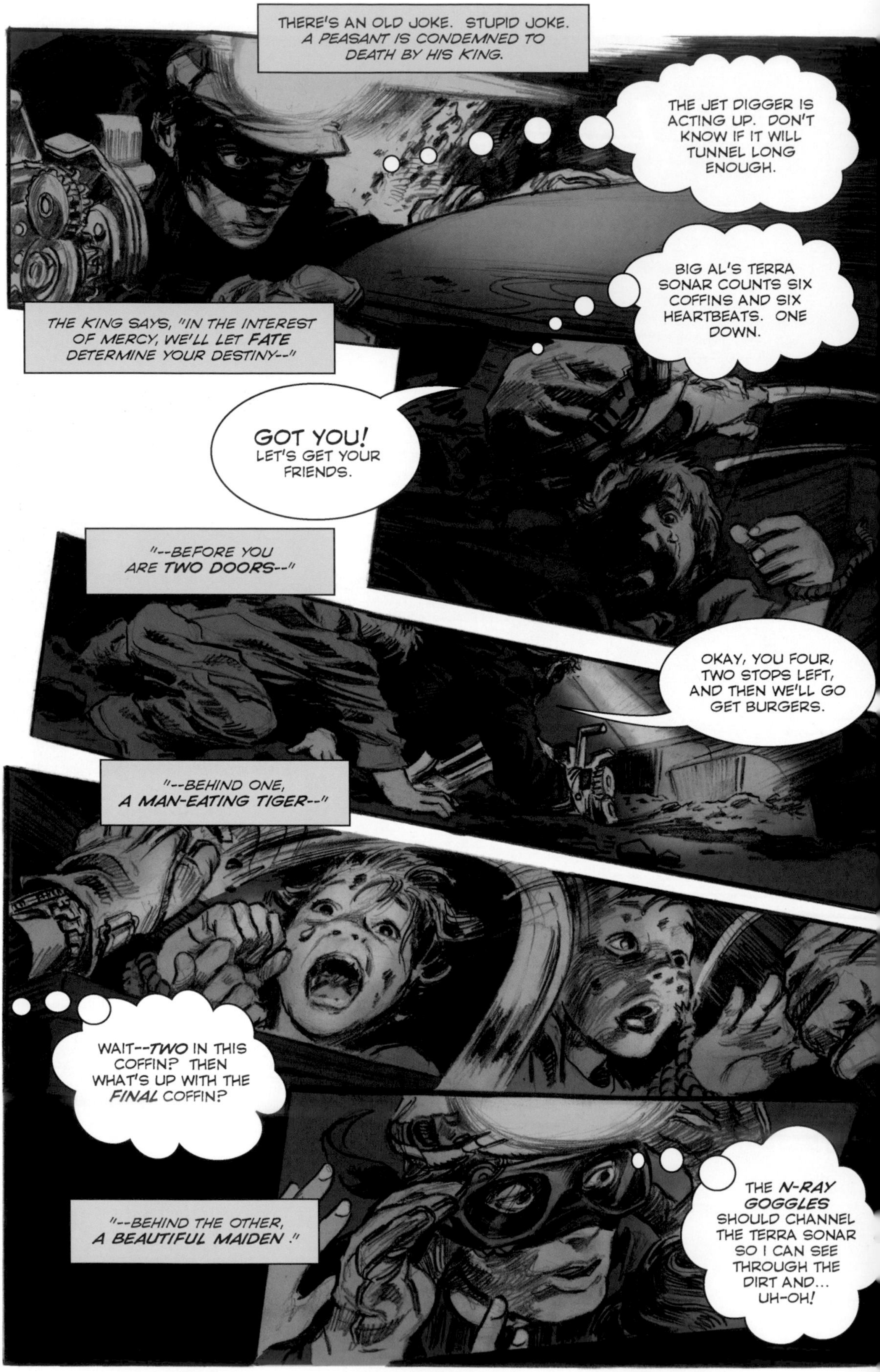
THERE'S AN OLD JOKE. STUPID JOKE. A PEASANT IS CONDEMNED TO DEATH BY HIS KING.
THE JET DIGGER IS ACTING UP. DON'T KNOW IF IT WILL TUNNEL LONG ENOUGH.
THE KING SAYS, "IN THE INTEREST OF MERCY, WE'LL LET FATE DETERMINE YOUR DESTINY--"
BIG AL'S TERRA SONAR COUNTS SIX COFFINS AND SIX HEARTBEATS. ONE DOWN.
GOT YOU! LET'S GET YOUR FRIENDS.
"--BEFORE YOU ARE TWO DOORS--"
OKAY, YOU FOUR, TWO STOPS LEFT, AND THEN WE'LL GO GET BURGERS.
"--BEHIND ONE, A MAN-EATING TIGER--"
WAIT--TWO IN THIS COFFIN? THEN WHAT'S UP WITH THE FINAL COFFIN?
"--BEHIND THE OTHER, A BEAUTIFUL MAIDEN."
THE N-RAY GOGGLES SHOULD CHANNEL THE TERRA SONAR SO I CAN SEE THROUGH THE DIRT AND... UH-OH!

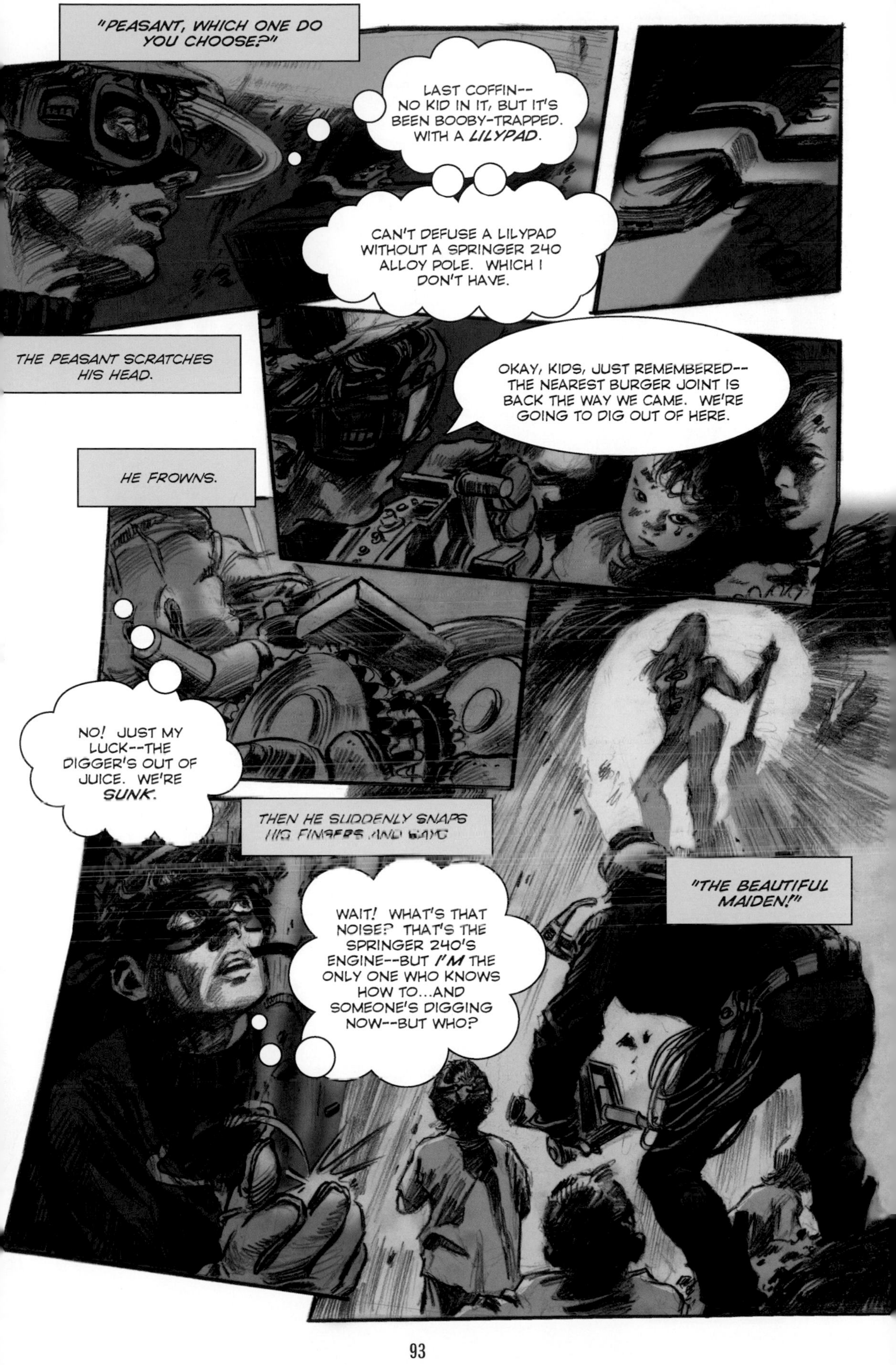
"PEASANT, WHICH ONE DO YOU CHOOSE?"
LAST COFFIN-- NO KID IN IT, BUT IT'S BEEN BOOBY-TRAPPED. WITH A LILYPAD.
CAN'T DEFUSE A LILYPAD WITHOUT A SPRINGER 240 ALLOY POLE. WHICH I DON'T HAVE.
THE PEASANT SCRATCHES HIS HEAD.
OKAY, KIDS, JUST REMEMBERED-- THE NEAREST BURGER JOINT IS BACK THE WAY WE CAME. WE'RE GOING TO DIG OUT OF HERE.
HE FROWNS.
NO! JUST MY LUCK--THE DIGGER'S OUT OF JUICE. WE'RE SUNK.
THEN HE SUDDENLY SNAPS HIS FINGERS AND SAYS
WAIT! WHAT'S THAT NOISE? THAT'S THE SPRINGER 240'S ENGINE--BUT I'M THE ONLY ONE WHO KNOWS HOW TO...AND SOMEONE'S DIGGING NOW--BUT WHO?
"THE BEAUTIFUL MAIDEN!"

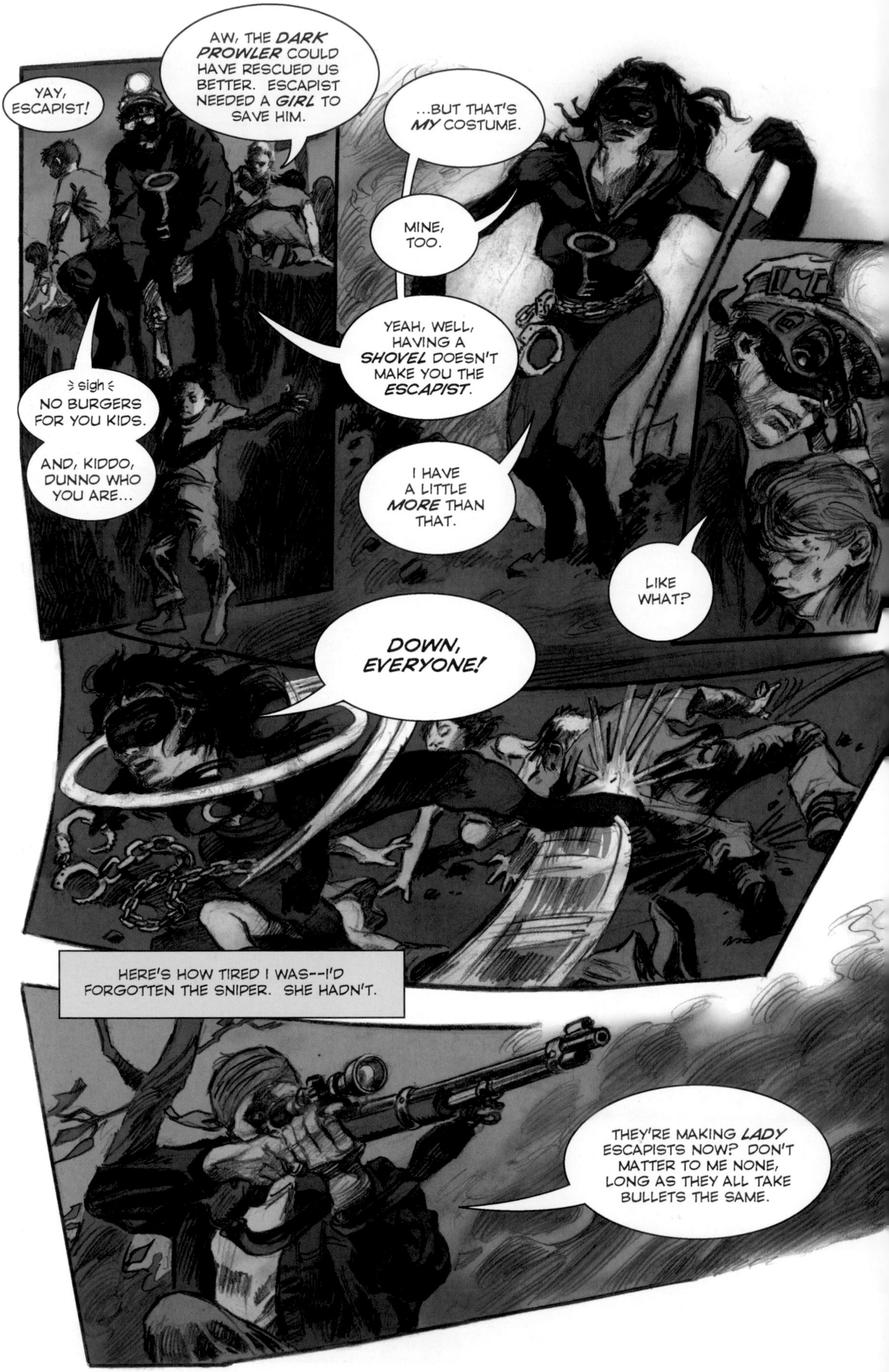

YAY, ESCAPIST!
AW, THE DARK PROWLER COULD HAVE RESCUED US BETTER. ESCAPIST NEEDED A GIRL TO SAVE HIM.
⪢ sigh ⪡ NO BURGERS FOR YOU KIDS.
AND, KIDDO, DUNNO WHO YOU ARE...
...BUT THAT'S MY COSTUME.
MINE, TOO.
YEAH, WELL, HAVING A SHOVEL DOESN'T MAKE YOU THE ESCAPIST.
I HAVE A LITTLE MORE THAN THAT.
LIKE WHAT?
DOWN, EVERYONE!
HERE'S HOW TIRED I WAS--I'D FORGOTTEN THE SNIPER. SHE HADN'T.
THEY'RE MAKING LADY ESCAPISTS NOW? DON'T MATTER TO ME NONE, LONG AS THEY ALL TAKE BULLETS THE SAME.

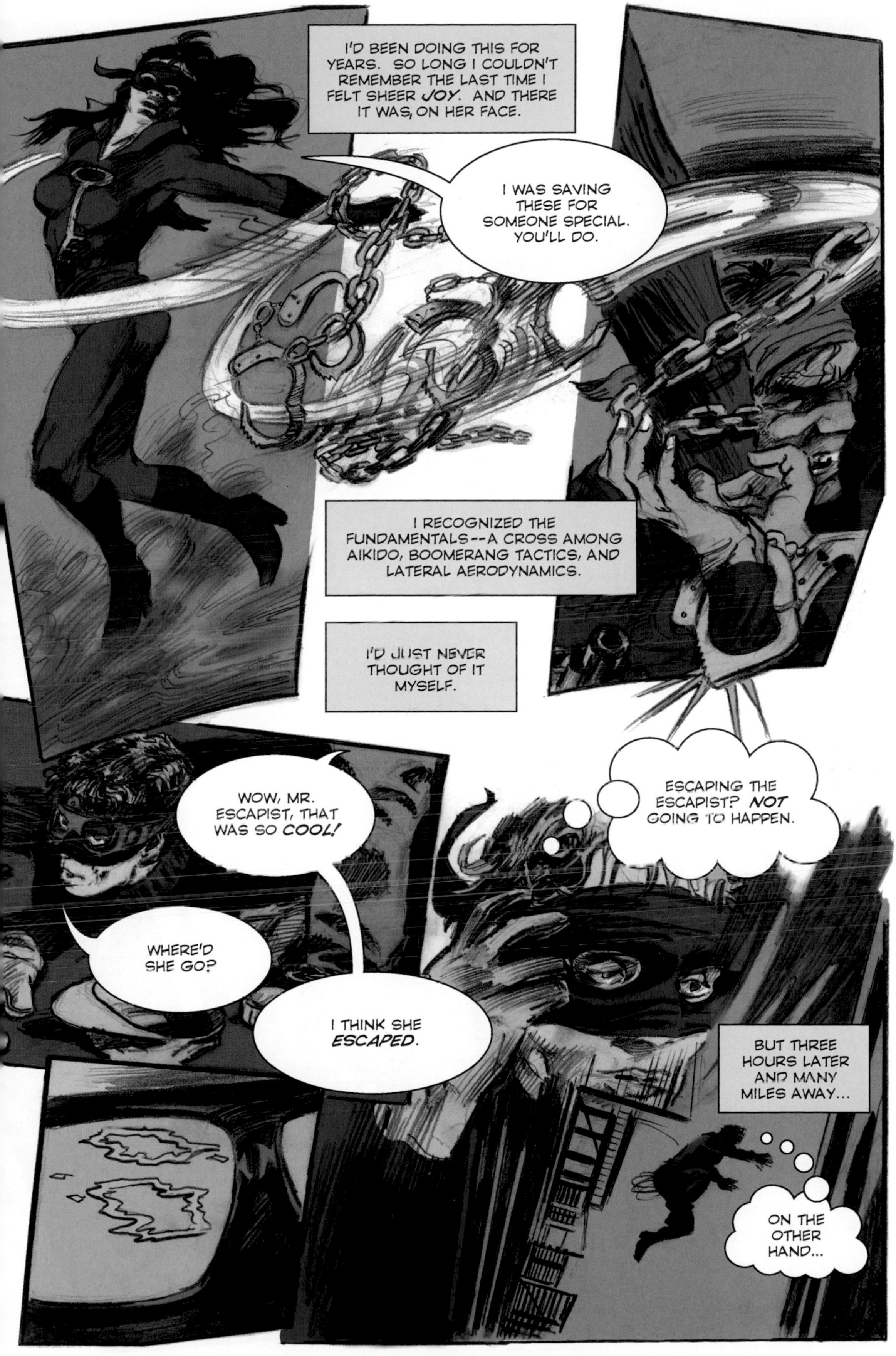
I'D BEEN DOING THIS FOR YEARS. SO LONG I COULDN'T REMEMBER THE LAST TIME I FELT SHEER *JOY*. AND THERE IT WAS, ON HER FACE.
I WAS SAVING THESE FOR SOMEONE SPECIAL. YOU'LL DO.
I RECOGNIZED THE FUNDAMENTALS--A CROSS AMONG AIKIDO, BOOMERANG TACTICS, AND LATERAL AERODYNAMICS.
I'D JUST NEVER THOUGHT OF IT MYSELF.
WOW, MR. ESCAPIST, THAT WAS SO *COOL!*
WHERE'D SHE GO?
I THINK SHE *ESCAPED*.
ESCAPING THE ESCAPIST? *NOT* GOING TO HAPPEN.
BUT THREE HOURS LATER AND MANY MILES AWAY...
ON THE OTHER HAND...

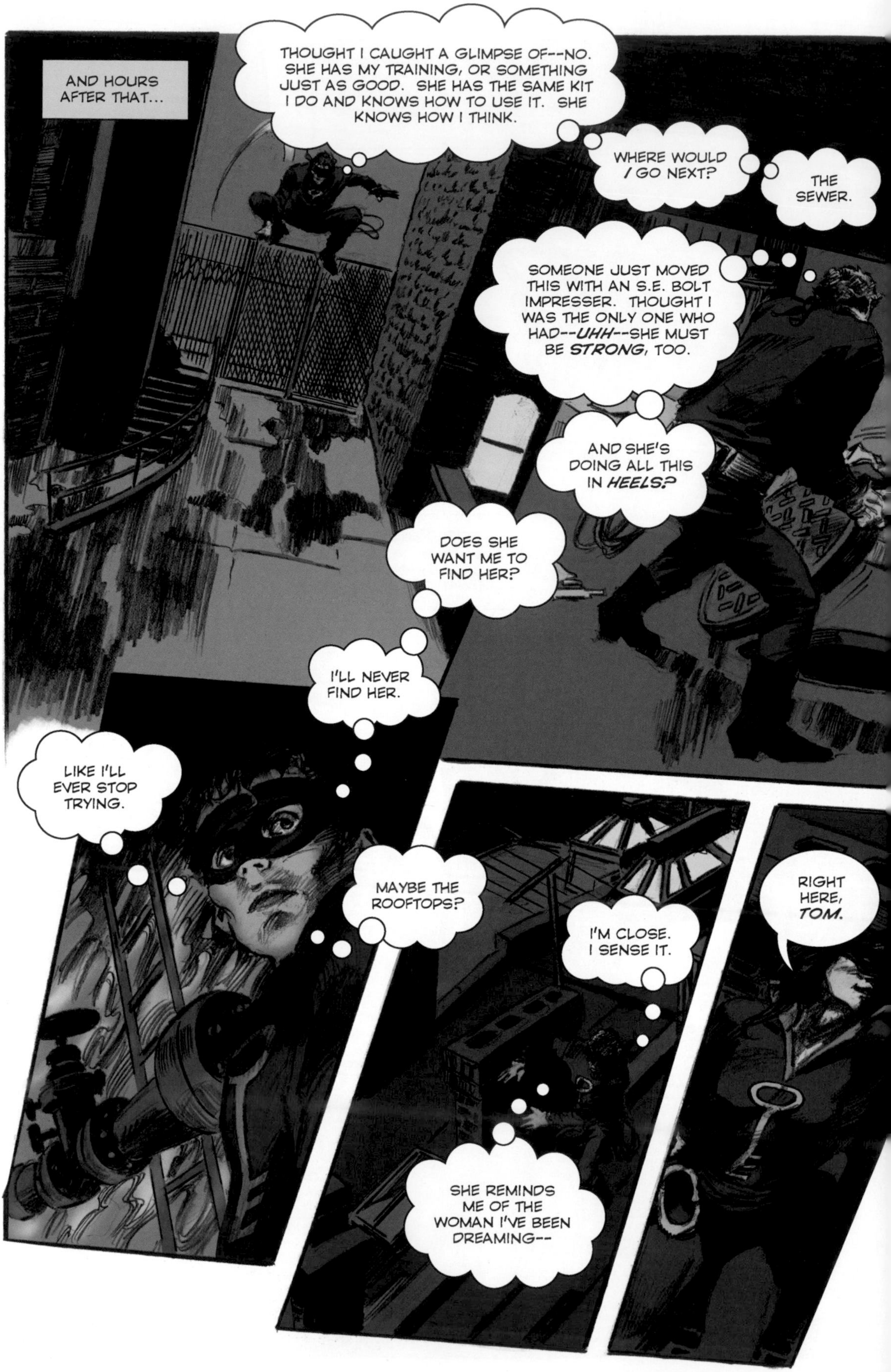
AND HOURS AFTER THAT...
THOUGHT I CAUGHT A GLIMPSE OF--NO. SHE HAS MY TRAINING, OR SOMETHING JUST AS GOOD. SHE HAS THE SAME KIT I DO AND KNOWS HOW TO USE IT. SHE KNOWS HOW I THINK.
WHERE WOULD *I* GO NEXT?
THE SEWER.
SOMEONE JUST MOVED THIS WITH AN S.E. BOLT IMPRESSER. THOUGHT I WAS THE ONLY ONE WHO HAD--*UHH*--SHE MUST BE *STRONG*, TOO.
AND SHE'S DOING ALL THIS IN *HEELS?*
DOES SHE WANT ME TO FIND HER?
I'LL NEVER FIND HER.
LIKE I'LL EVER STOP TRYING.
MAYBE THE ROOFTOPS?
I'M CLOSE. I SENSE IT.
SHE REMINDS ME OF THE WOMAN I'VE BEEN DREAMING--
RIGHT HERE, *TOM.*

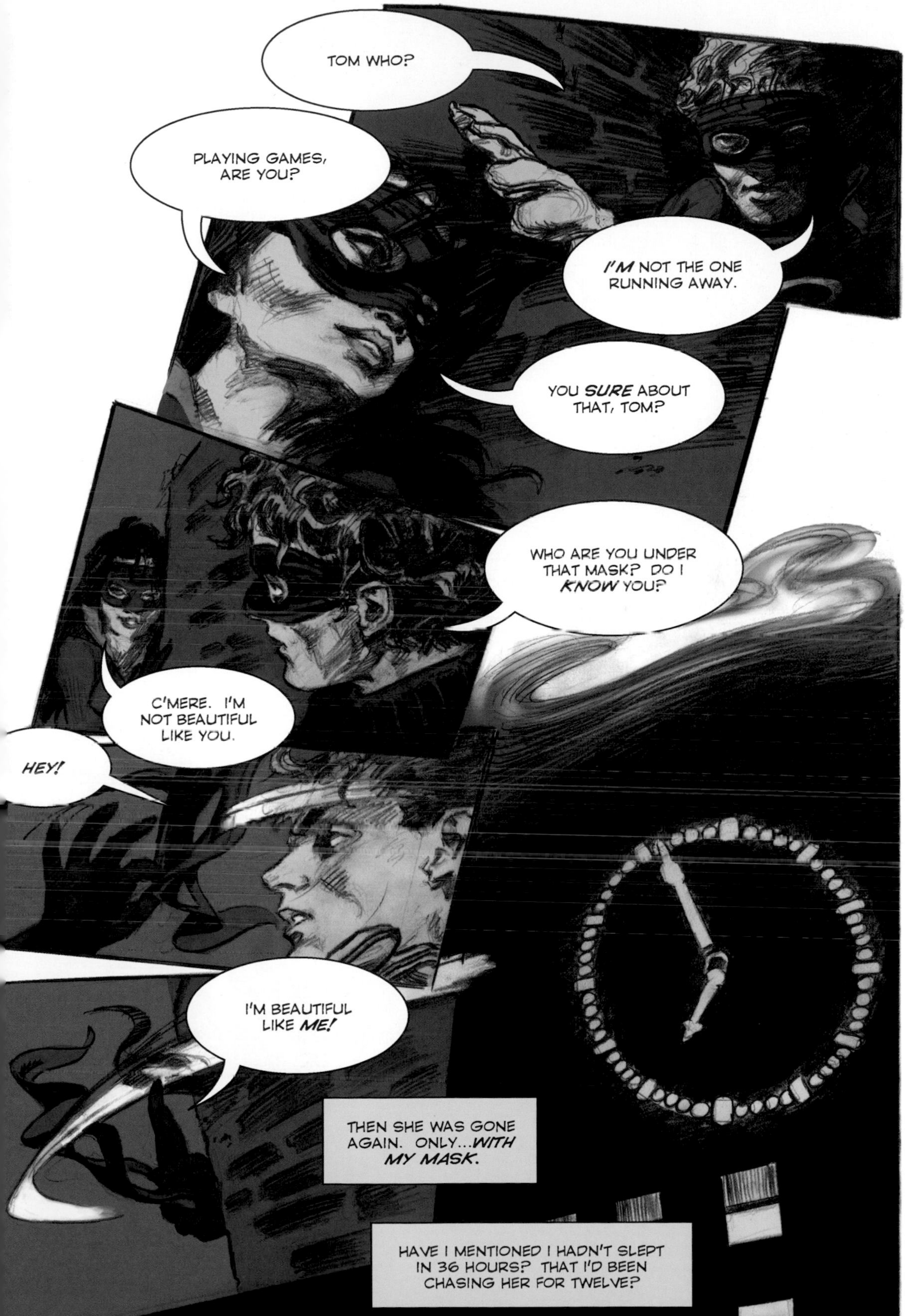
TOM WHO?
PLAYING GAMES, ARE YOU?
I'M NOT THE ONE RUNNING AWAY.
YOU SURE ABOUT THAT, TOM?
WHO ARE YOU UNDER THAT MASK? DO I KNOW YOU?
C'MERE. I'M NOT BEAUTIFUL LIKE YOU.
HEY!
I'M BEAUTIFUL LIKE ME!
THEN SHE WAS GONE AGAIN. ONLY...WITH MY MASK.
HAVE I MENTIONED I HADN'T SLEPT IN 36 HOURS? THAT I'D BEEN CHASING HER FOR TWELVE?

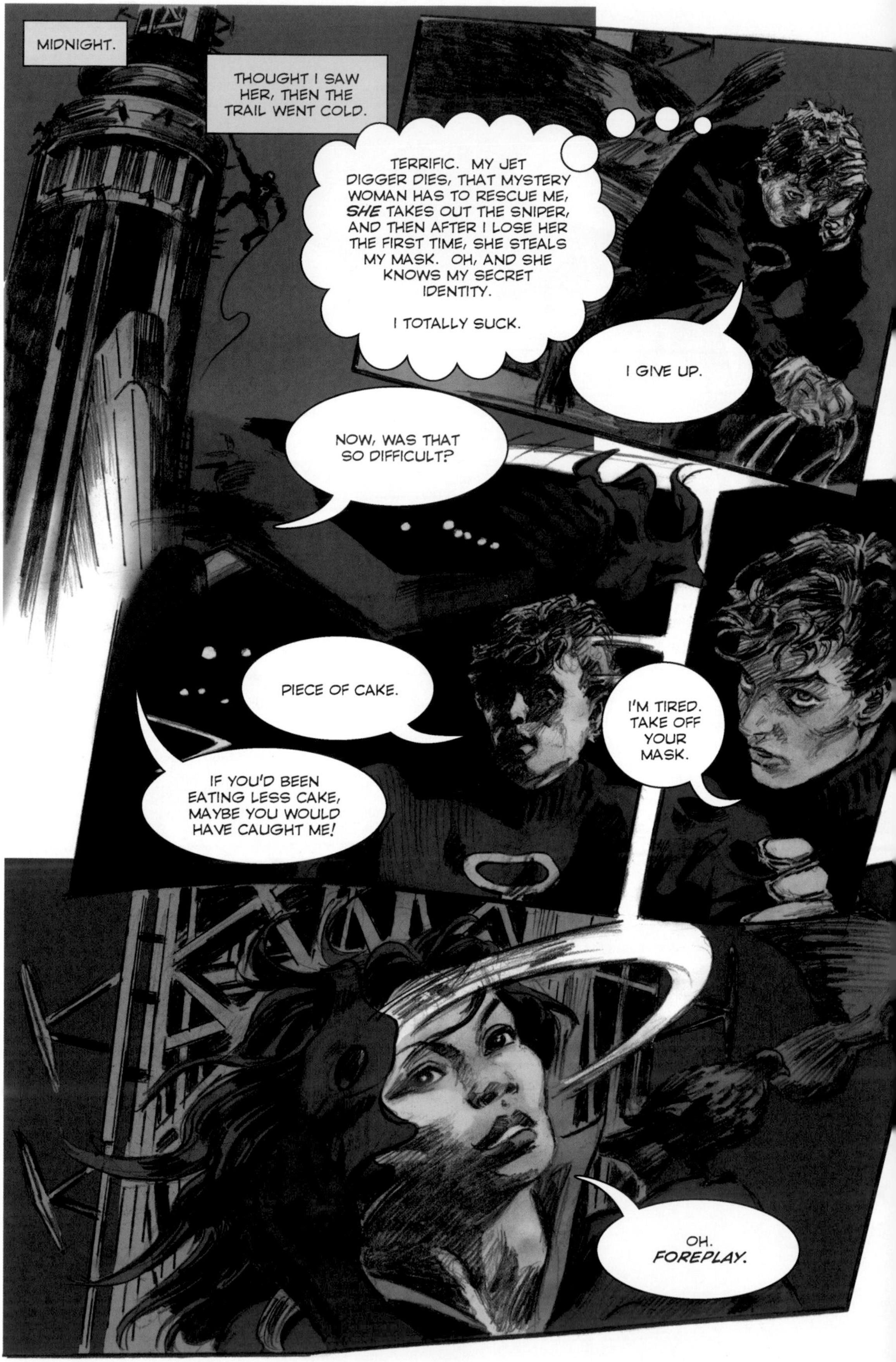

MIDNIGHT.
THOUGHT I SAW HER, THEN THE TRAIL WENT COLD.
TERRIFIC. MY JET DIGGER DIES, THAT MYSTERY WOMAN HAS TO RESCUE ME, *SHE* TAKES OUT THE SNIPER, AND THEN AFTER I LOSE HER THE FIRST TIME, SHE STEALS MY MASK. OH, AND SHE KNOWS MY SECRET IDENTITY.
I TOTALLY SUCK.
I GIVE UP.
NOW, WAS THAT SO DIFFICULT?
PIECE OF CAKE.
IF YOU'D BEEN EATING LESS CAKE, MAYBE YOU WOULD HAVE CAUGHT ME!
I'M TIRED. TAKE OFF YOUR MASK.
OH. *FOREPLAY.*

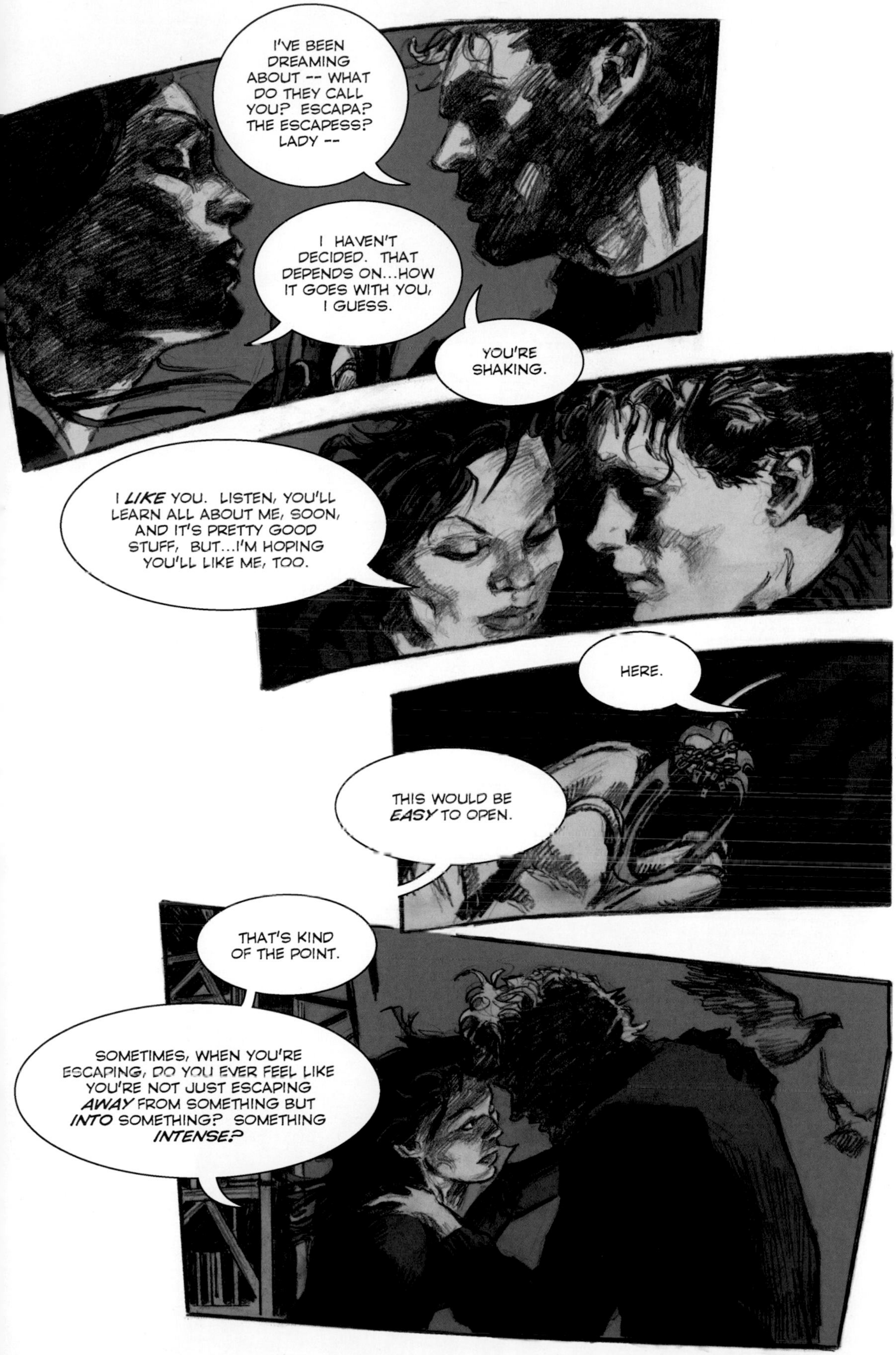
I'VE BEEN DREAMING ABOUT -- WHAT DO THEY CALL YOU? ESCAPA? THE ESCAPESS? LADY --
I HAVEN'T DECIDED. THAT DEPENDS ON...HOW IT GOES WITH YOU, I GUESS.
YOU'RE SHAKING.
I LIKE YOU. LISTEN, YOU'LL LEARN ALL ABOUT ME, SOON, AND IT'S PRETTY GOOD STUFF, BUT...I'M HOPING YOU'LL LIKE ME, TOO.
HERE.
THIS WOULD BE EASY TO OPEN.
THAT'S KIND OF THE POINT.
SOMETIMES, WHEN YOU'RE ESCAPING, DO YOU EVER FEEL LIKE YOU'RE NOT JUST ESCAPING AWAY FROM SOMETHING BUT INTO SOMETHING? SOMETHING INTENSE?

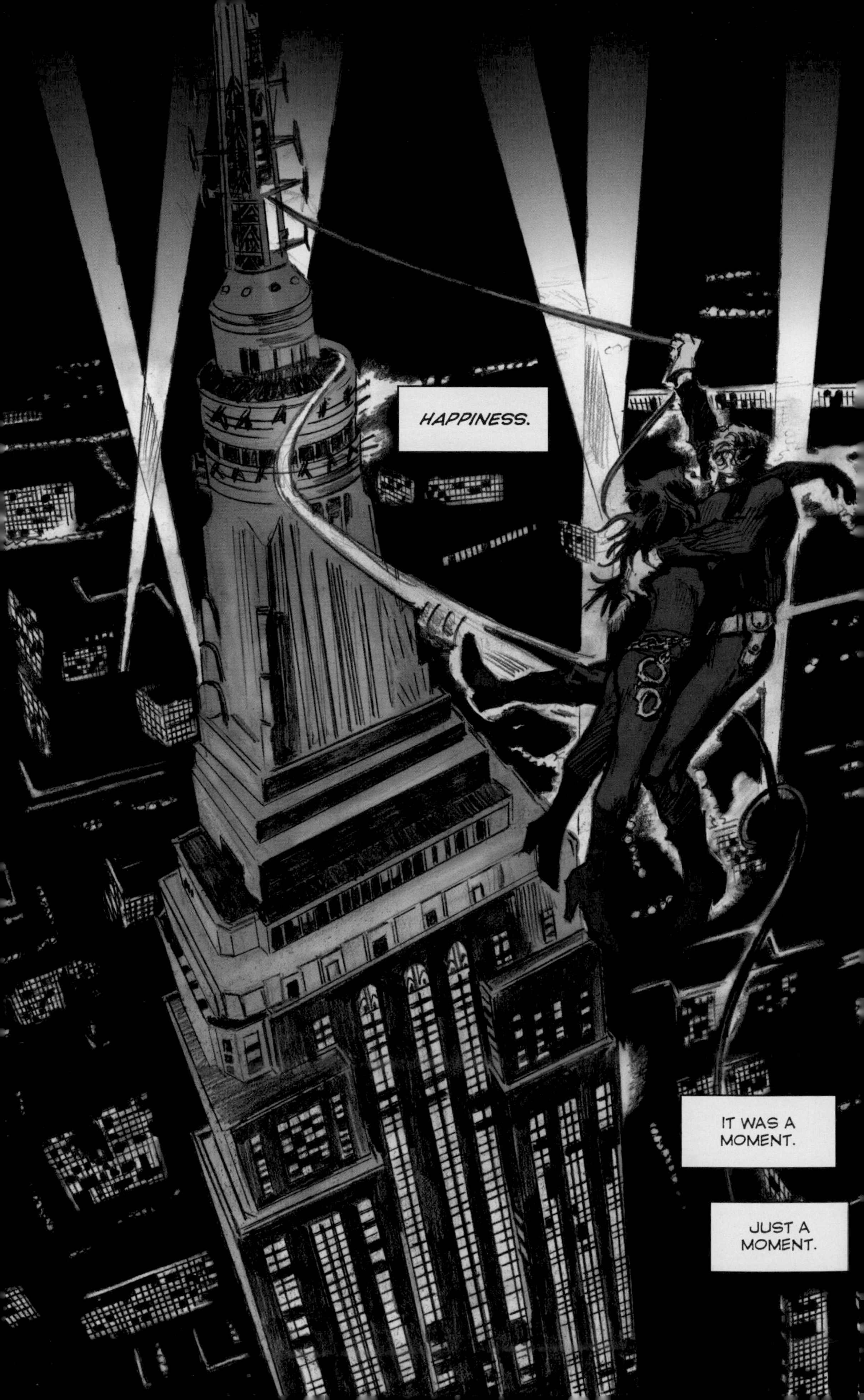
HAPPINESS.
IT WAS A MOMENT.
JUST A MOMENT.

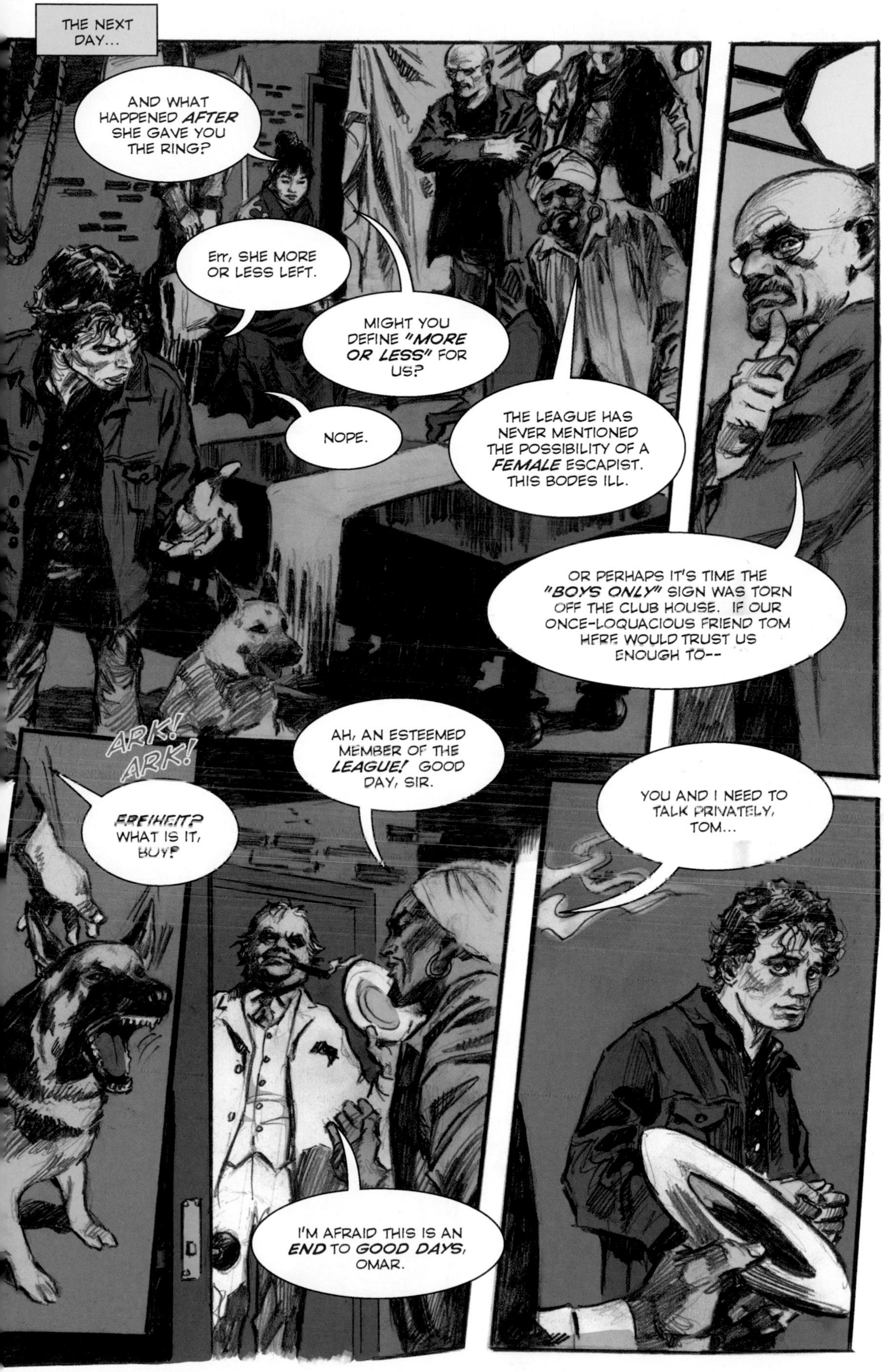
THE NEXT DAY...
AND WHAT HAPPENED *AFTER* SHE GAVE YOU THE RING?
Err, SHE MORE OR LESS LEFT.
MIGHT YOU DEFINE *"MORE OR LESS"* FOR US?
NOPE.
THE LEAGUE HAS NEVER MENTIONED THE POSSIBILITY OF A *FEMALE* ESCAPIST. THIS BODES ILL.
OR PERHAPS IT'S TIME THE *"BOYS ONLY"* SIGN WAS TORN OFF THE CLUB HOUSE. IF OUR ONCE-LOQUACIOUS FRIEND TOM HERE WOULD TRUST US ENOUGH TO--
ARK! ARK!
*FREIHEIT?* WHAT IS IT, BOY?
AH, AN ESTEEMED MEMBER OF THE *LEAGUE!* GOOD DAY, SIR.
I'M AFRAID THIS IS AN *END* TO *GOOD DAYS*, OMAR.
YOU AND I NEED TO TALK PRIVATELY, TOM...

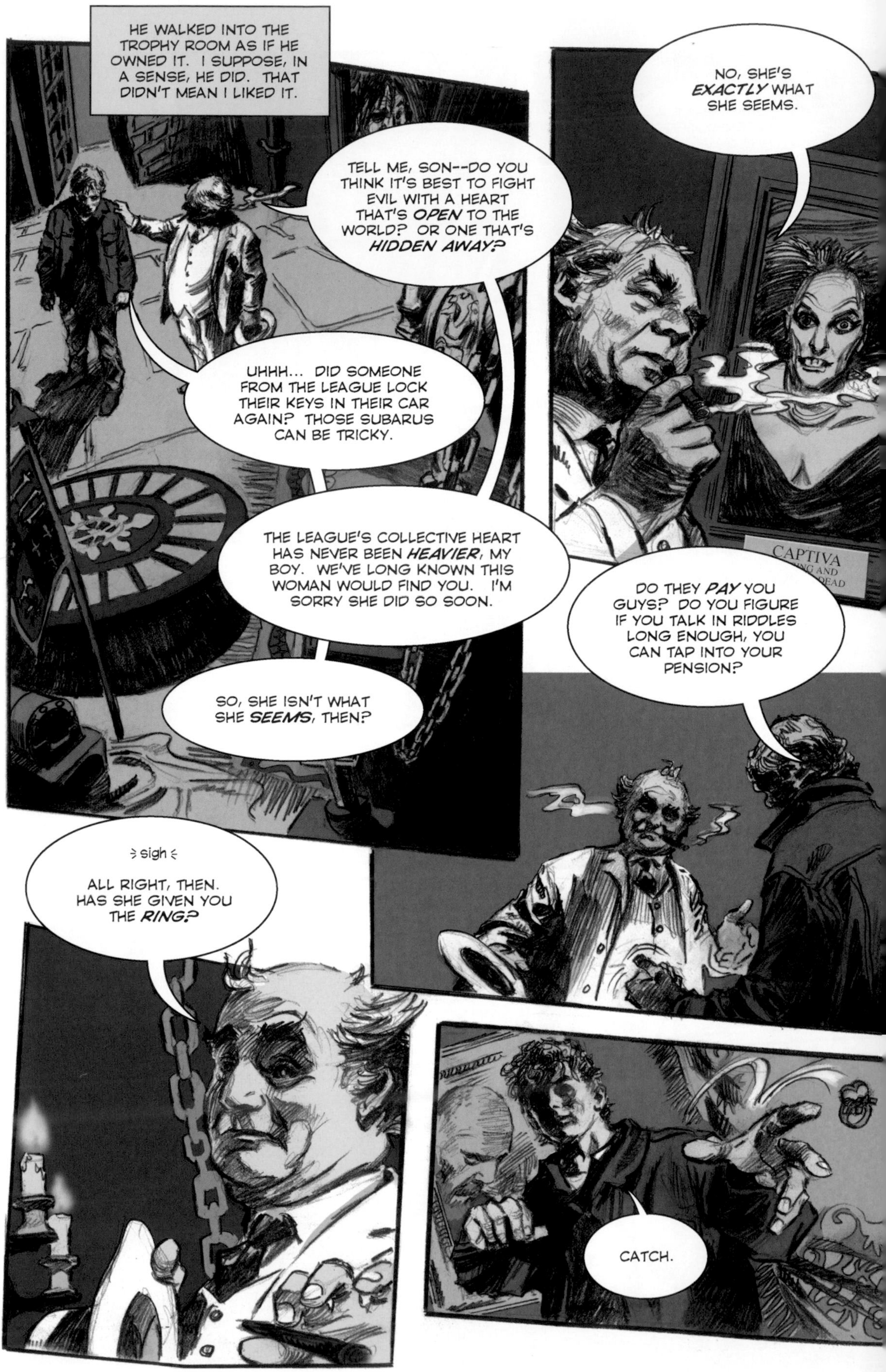

HE WALKED INTO THE TROPHY ROOM AS IF HE OWNED IT. I SUPPOSE, IN A SENSE, HE DID. THAT DIDN'T MEAN I LIKED IT.
TELL ME, SON--DO YOU THINK IT'S BEST TO FIGHT EVIL WITH A HEART THAT'S *OPEN* TO THE WORLD? OR ONE THAT'S ***HIDDEN AWAY?***
UHHH... DID SOMEONE FROM THE LEAGUE LOCK THEIR KEYS IN THEIR CAR AGAIN? THOSE SUBARUS CAN BE TRICKY.
THE LEAGUE'S COLLECTIVE HEART HAS NEVER BEEN ***HEAVIER***, MY BOY. WE'VE LONG KNOWN THIS WOMAN WOULD FIND YOU. I'M SORRY SHE DID SO SOON.
SO, SHE ISN'T WHAT SHE ***SEEMS***, THEN?
NO, SHE'S ***EXACTLY*** WHAT SHE SEEMS.
CAPTIVA
DO THEY ***PAY*** YOU GUYS? DO YOU FIGURE IF YOU TALK IN RIDDLES LONG ENOUGH, YOU CAN TAP INTO YOUR PENSION?
⊰ sigh ⊱
ALL RIGHT, THEN. HAS SHE GIVEN YOU THE ***RING?***
CATCH.

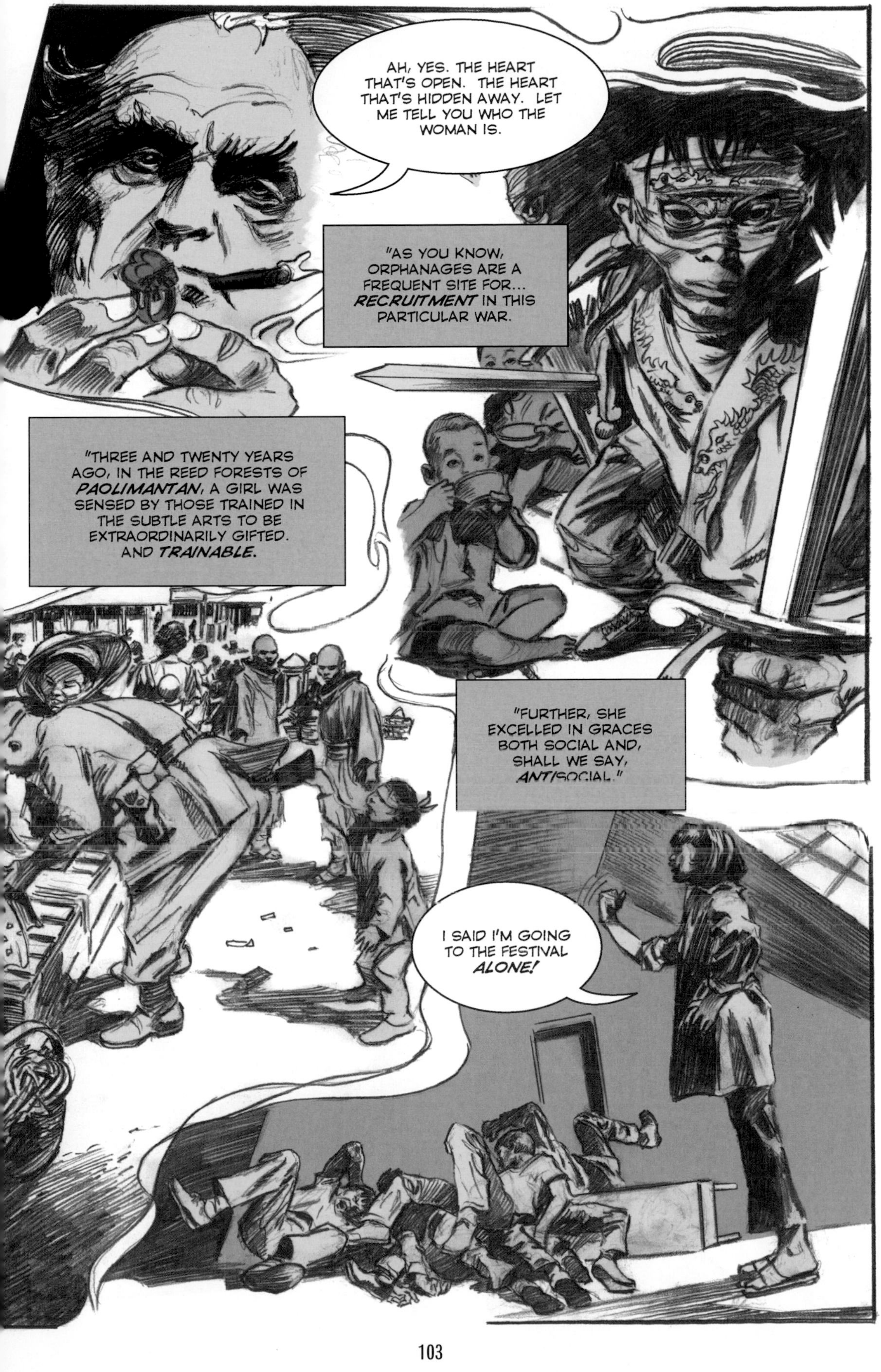
AH, YES. THE HEART THAT'S OPEN. THE HEART THAT'S HIDDEN AWAY. LET ME TELL YOU WHO THE WOMAN IS.
"AS YOU KNOW, ORPHANAGES ARE A FREQUENT SITE FOR... *RECRUITMENT* IN THIS PARTICULAR WAR.
"THREE AND TWENTY YEARS AGO, IN THE REED FORESTS OF *PAOLIMANTAN*, A GIRL WAS SENSED BY THOSE TRAINED IN THE SUBTLE ARTS TO BE EXTRAORDINARILY GIFTED. AND *TRAINABLE*.
"FURTHER, SHE EXCELLED IN GRACES BOTH SOCIAL AND, SHALL WE SAY, *ANTI*SOCIAL."
I SAID I'M GOING TO THE FESTIVAL *ALONE!*

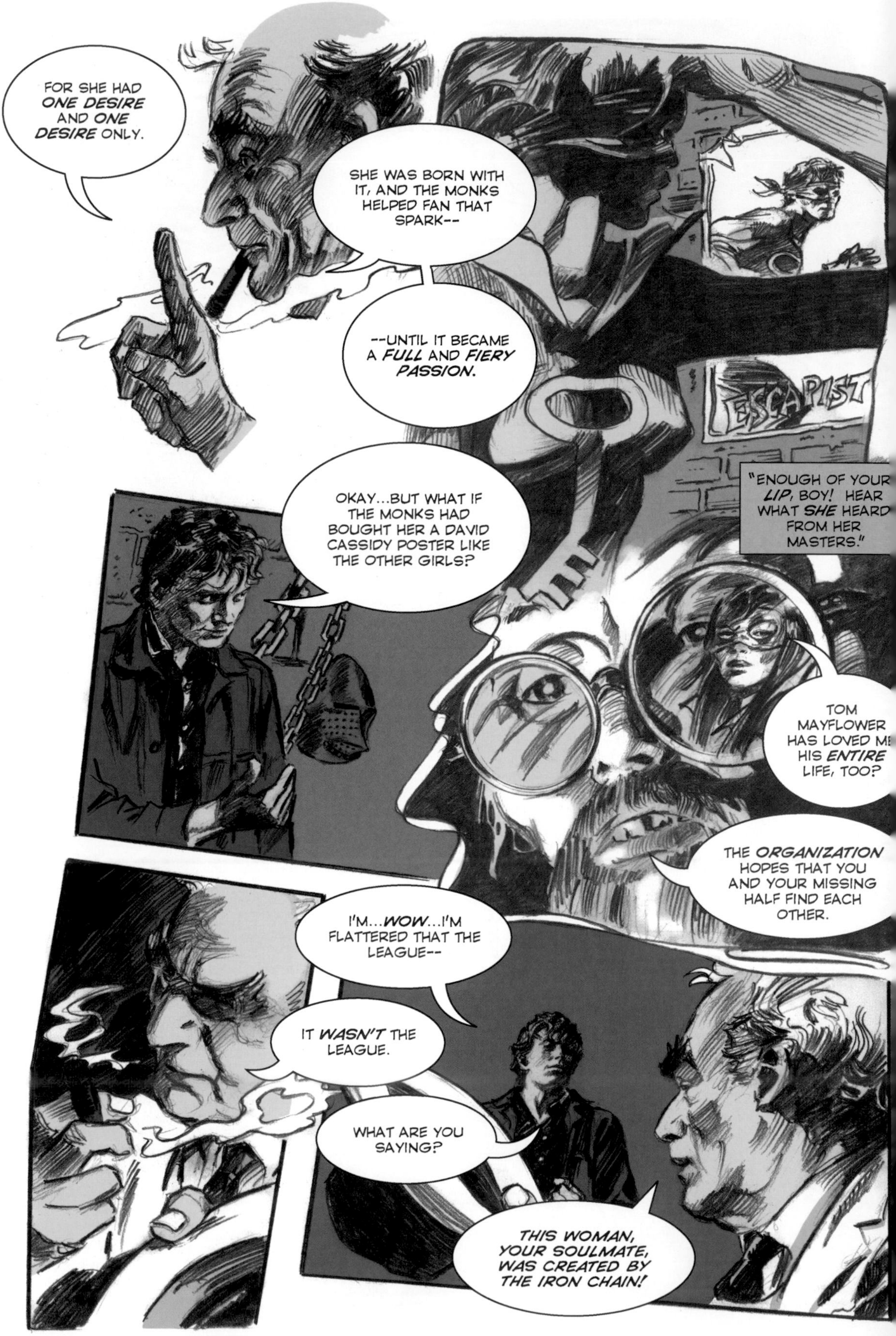

FOR SHE HAD ***ONE DESIRE*** AND ***ONE DESIRE*** ONLY.
SHE WAS BORN WITH IT, AND THE MONKS HELPED FAN THAT SPARK--
--UNTIL IT BECAME A ***FULL*** AND ***FIERY PASSION.***
ESCAPIST
OKAY...BUT WHAT IF THE MONKS HAD BOUGHT HER A DAVID CASSIDY POSTER LIKE THE OTHER GIRLS?
"ENOUGH OF YOUR ***LIP,*** BOY! HEAR WHAT ***SHE*** HEARD FROM HER MASTERS."
TOM MAYFLOWER HAS LOVED M HIS ***ENTIRE*** LIFE, TOO?
THE ***ORGANIZATION*** HOPES THAT YOU AND YOUR MISSING HALF FIND EACH OTHER.
I'M...***WOW***...I'M FLATTERED THAT THE LEAGUE--
IT ***WASN'T*** THE LEAGUE.
WHAT ARE YOU SAYING?
***THIS WOMAN, YOUR SOULMATE, WAS CREATED BY THE IRON CHAIN!***

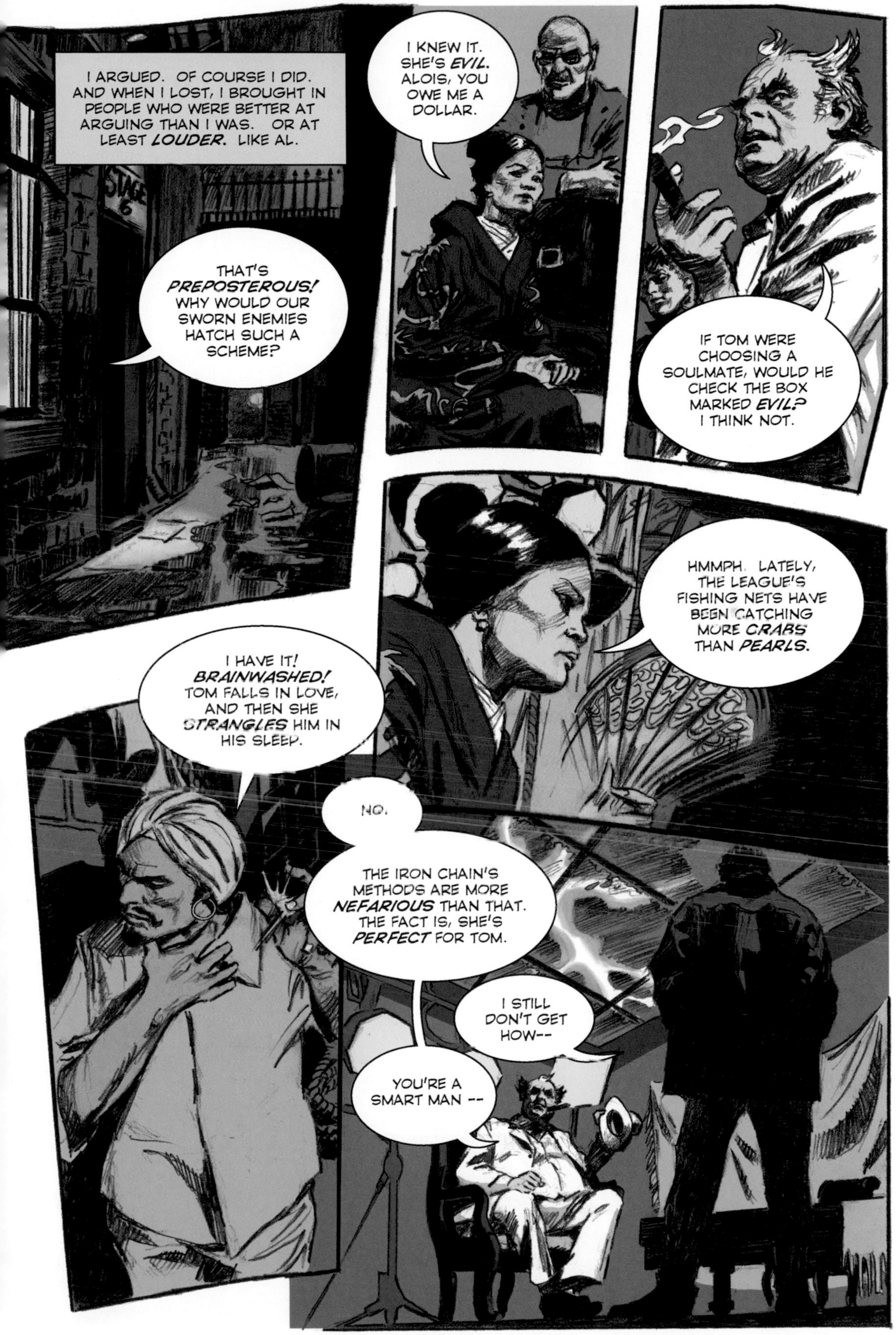
I ARGUED. OF COURSE I DID. AND WHEN I LOST, I BROUGHT IN PEOPLE WHO WERE BETTER AT ARGUING THAN I WAS. OR AT LEAST LOUDER. LIKE AL.
STAGE 6
THAT'S PREPOSTEROUS! WHY WOULD OUR SWORN ENEMIES HATCH SUCH A SCHEME?
I KNEW IT. SHE'S EVIL. ALOIS, YOU OWE ME A DOLLAR.
IF TOM WERE CHOOSING A SOULMATE, WOULD HE CHECK THE BOX MARKED EVIL? I THINK NOT.
HMMPH. LATELY, THE LEAGUE'S FISHING NETS HAVE BEEN CATCHING MORE CRABS THAN PEARLS.
I HAVE IT! BRAINWASHED! TOM FALLS IN LOVE, AND THEN SHE STRANGLES HIM IN HIS SLEEP.
NO.
THE IRON CHAIN'S METHODS ARE MORE NEFARIOUS THAN THAT. THE FACT IS, SHE'S PERFECT FOR TOM.
I STILL DON'T GET HOW--
YOU'RE A SMART MAN --

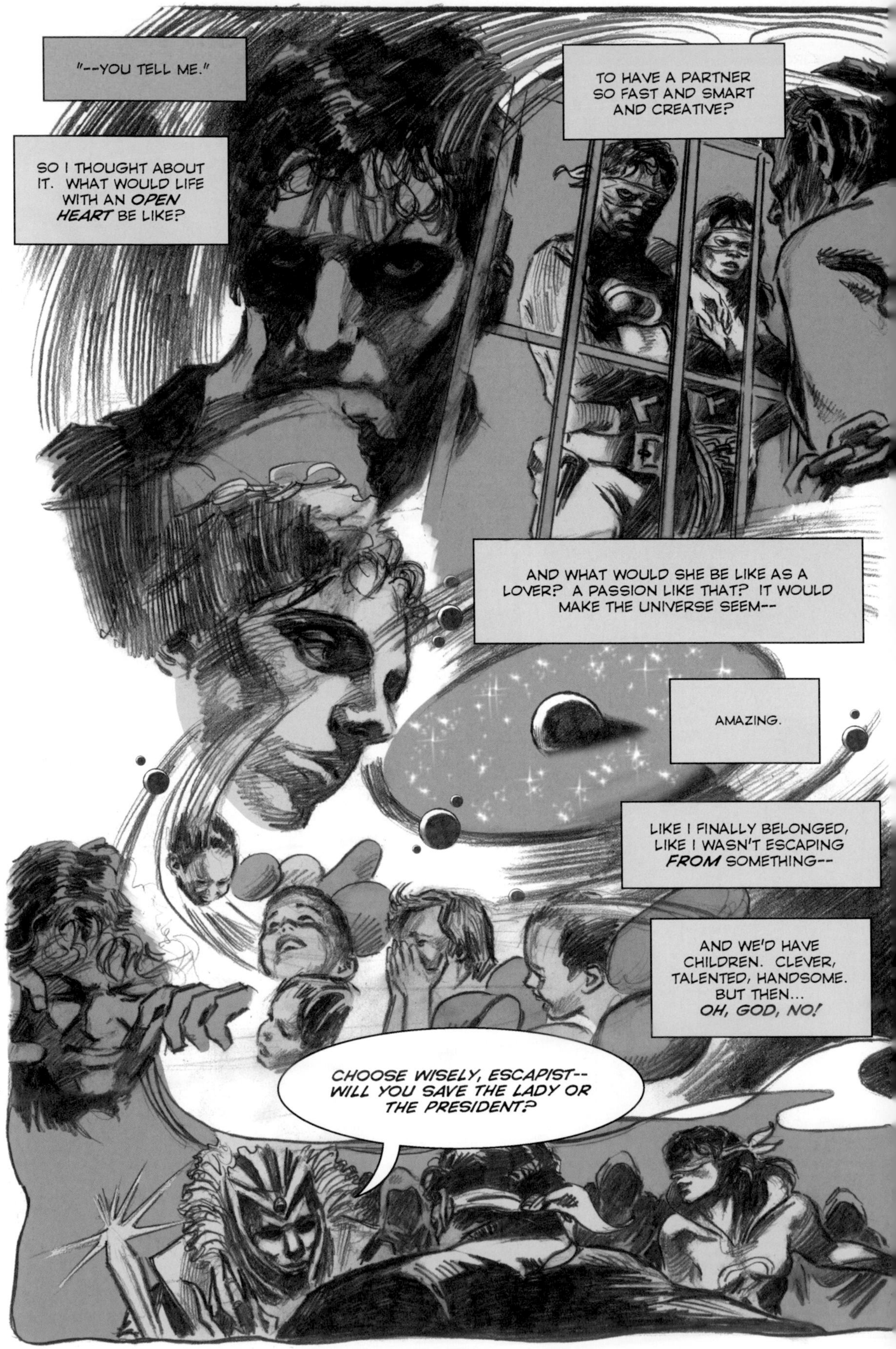
"--YOU TELL ME."
SO I THOUGHT ABOUT IT. WHAT WOULD LIFE WITH AN *OPEN HEART* BE LIKE?
TO HAVE A PARTNER SO FAST AND SMART AND CREATIVE?
AND WHAT WOULD SHE BE LIKE AS A LOVER? A PASSION LIKE THAT? IT WOULD MAKE THE UNIVERSE SEEM--
AMAZING.
LIKE I FINALLY BELONGED, LIKE I WASN'T ESCAPING *FROM* SOMETHING--
AND WE'D HAVE CHILDREN. CLEVER, TALENTED, HANDSOME. BUT THEN... *OH, GOD, NO!*
*CHOOSE WISELY, ESCAPIST-- WILL YOU SAVE THE LADY OR THE PRESIDENT?*

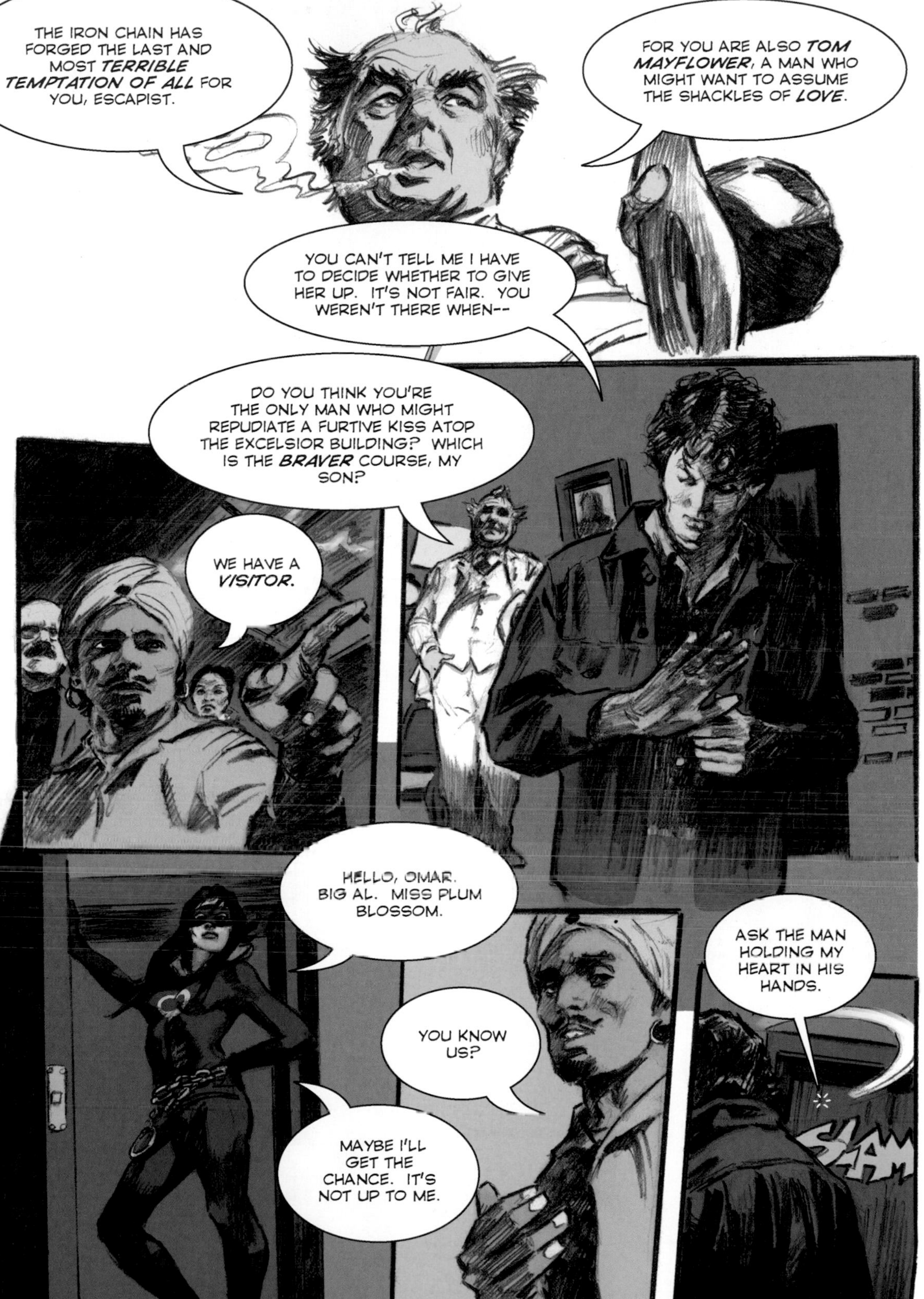
THE IRON CHAIN HAS FORGED THE LAST AND MOST TERRIBLE TEMPTATION OF ALL FOR YOU, ESCAPIST.
FOR YOU ARE ALSO TOM MAYFLOWER, A MAN WHO MIGHT WANT TO ASSUME THE SHACKLES OF LOVE.
YOU CAN'T TELL ME I HAVE TO DECIDE WHETHER TO GIVE HER UP. IT'S NOT FAIR. YOU WEREN'T THERE WHEN--
DO YOU THINK YOU'RE THE ONLY MAN WHO MIGHT REPUDIATE A FURTIVE KISS ATOP THE EXCELSIOR BUILDING? WHICH IS THE BRAVER COURSE, MY SON?
WE HAVE A VISITOR.
HELLO, OMAR. BIG AL. MISS PLUM BLOSSOM.
YOU KNOW US?
MAYBE I'LL GET THE CHANCE. IT'S NOT UP TO ME.
ASK THE MAN HOLDING MY HEART IN HIS HANDS.
SLAM

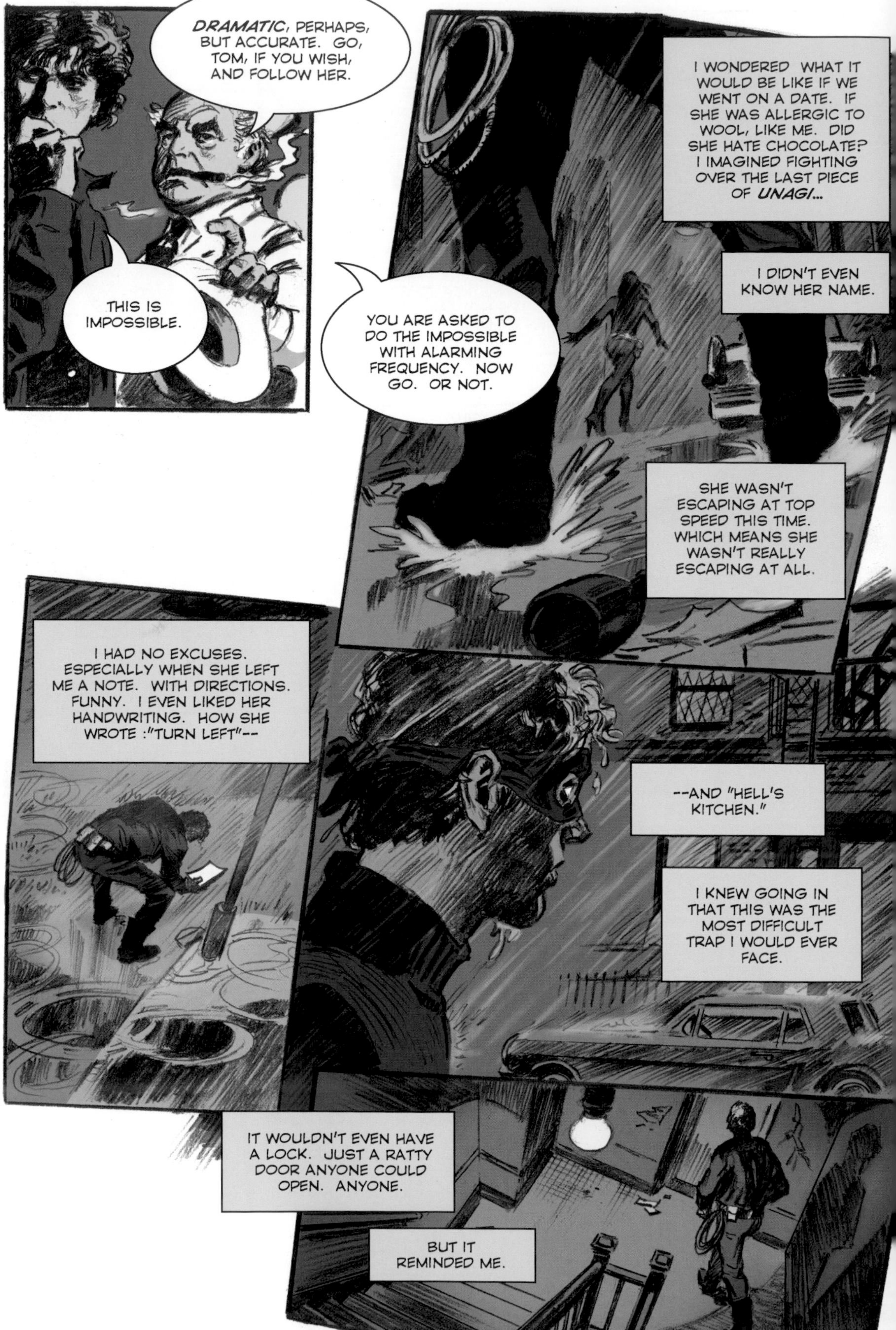
DRAMATIC, PERHAPS, BUT ACCURATE. GO, TOM, IF YOU WISH, AND FOLLOW HER.
THIS IS IMPOSSIBLE.
YOU ARE ASKED TO DO THE IMPOSSIBLE WITH ALARMING FREQUENCY. NOW GO. OR NOT.
I WONDERED WHAT IT WOULD BE LIKE IF WE WENT ON A DATE. IF SHE WAS ALLERGIC TO WOOL, LIKE ME. DID SHE HATE CHOCOLATE? I IMAGINED FIGHTING OVER THE LAST PIECE OF UNAGI...
I DIDN'T EVEN KNOW HER NAME.
SHE WASN'T ESCAPING AT TOP SPEED THIS TIME. WHICH MEANS SHE WASN'T REALLY ESCAPING AT ALL.
I HAD NO EXCUSES. ESPECIALLY WHEN SHE LEFT ME A NOTE. WITH DIRECTIONS. FUNNY. I EVEN LIKED HER HANDWRITING. HOW SHE WROTE :"TURN LEFT"--
--AND "HELL'S KITCHEN."
I KNEW GOING IN THAT THIS WAS THE MOST DIFFICULT TRAP I WOULD EVER FACE.
IT WOULDN'T EVEN HAVE A LOCK. JUST A RATTY DOOR ANYONE COULD OPEN. ANYONE.
BUT IT REMINDED ME.

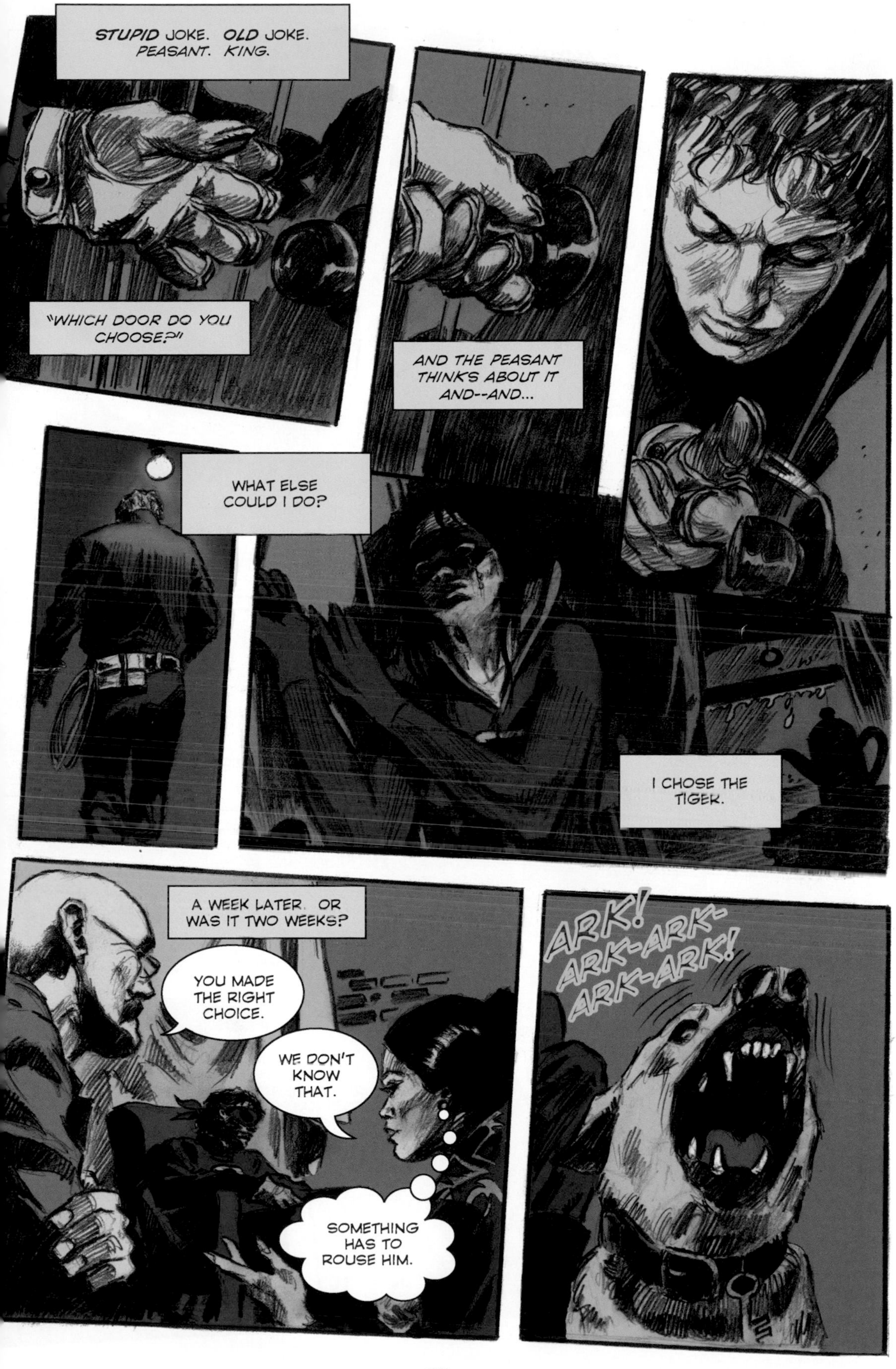
STUPID JOKE. OLD JOKE. PEASANT. KING.
"WHICH DOOR DO YOU CHOOSE?"
AND THE PEASANT THINKS ABOUT IT AND--AND...
WHAT ELSE COULD I DO?
I CHOSE THE TIGER.
A WEEK LATER. OR WAS IT TWO WEEKS?
YOU MADE THE RIGHT CHOICE.
WE DON'T KNOW THAT.
SOMETHING HAS TO ROUSE HIM.
ARK! ARK-ARK-ARK-ARK!

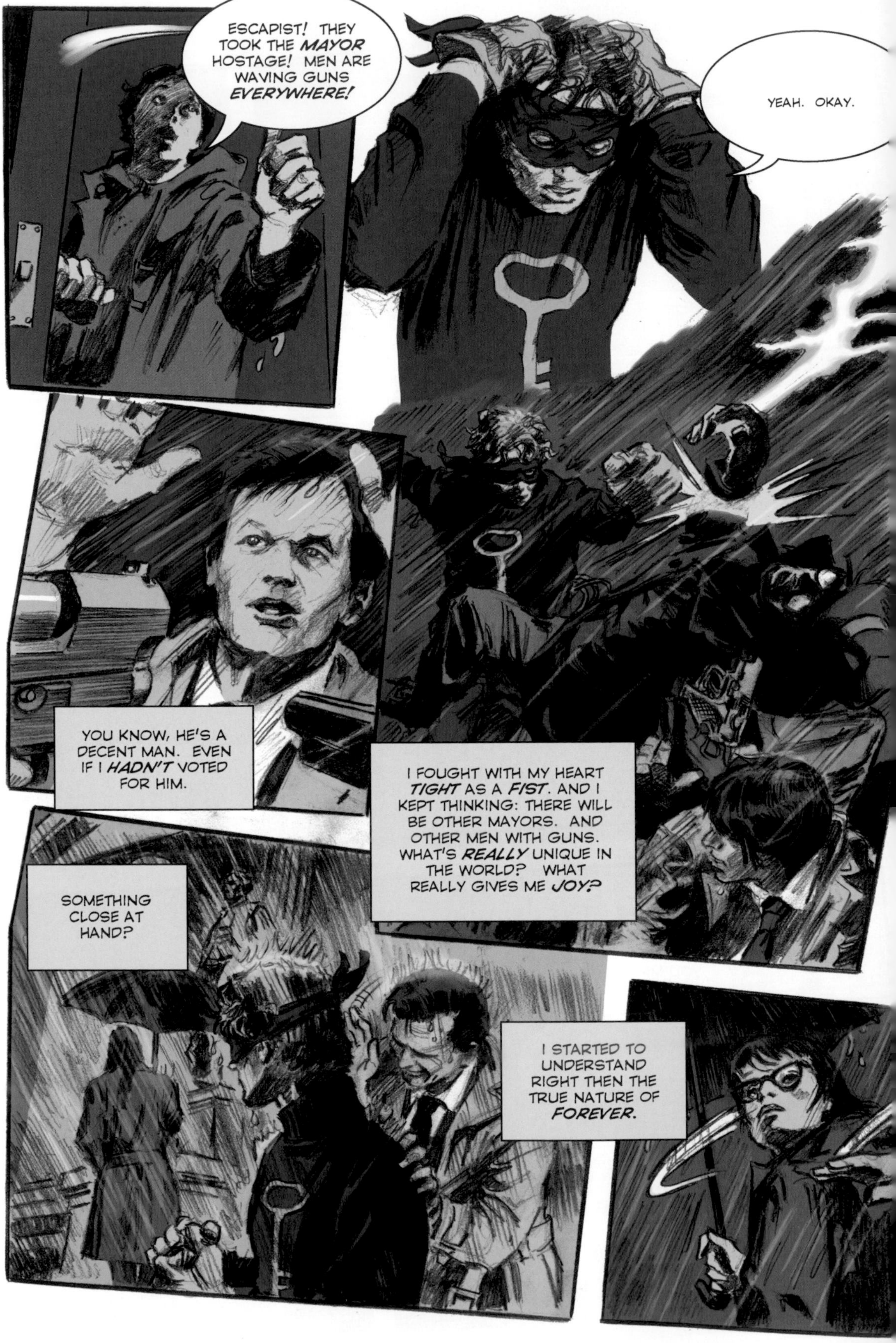
ESCAPIST! THEY TOOK THE *MAYOR* HOSTAGE! MEN ARE WAVING GUNS *EVERYWHERE!*
YEAH. OKAY.
YOU KNOW, HE'S A DECENT MAN. EVEN IF I *HADN'T* VOTED FOR HIM.
I FOUGHT WITH MY HEART *TIGHT* AS A *FIST*. AND I KEPT THINKING: THERE WILL BE OTHER MAYORS. AND OTHER MEN WITH GUNS. WHAT'S *REALLY* UNIQUE IN THE WORLD? WHAT REALLY GIVES ME *JOY?*
SOMETHING CLOSE AT HAND?
I STARTED TO UNDERSTAND RIGHT THEN THE TRUE NATURE OF *FOREVER*.

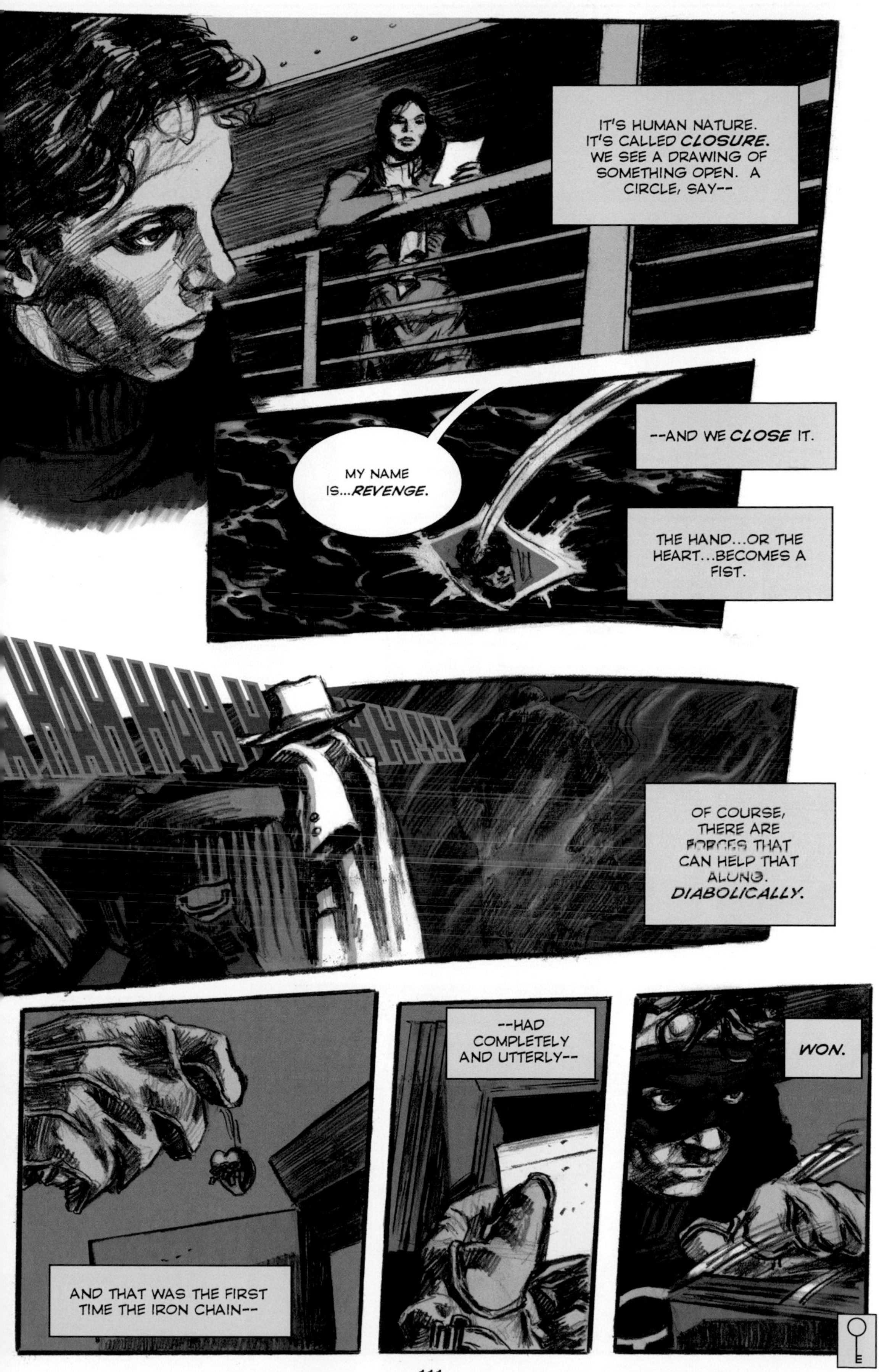
IT'S HUMAN NATURE. IT'S CALLED *CLOSURE.* WE SEE A DRAWING OF SOMETHING OPEN. A CIRCLE, SAY--
MY NAME IS...*REVENGE.*
--AND WE *CLOSE* IT.
THE HAND...OR THE HEART...BECOMES A FIST.
OF COURSE, THERE ARE FORCES THAT CAN HELP THAT ALONG. *DIABOLICALLY.*
AND THAT WAS THE FIRST TIME THE IRON CHAIN--
--HAD COMPLETELY AND UTTERLY--
*WON.*

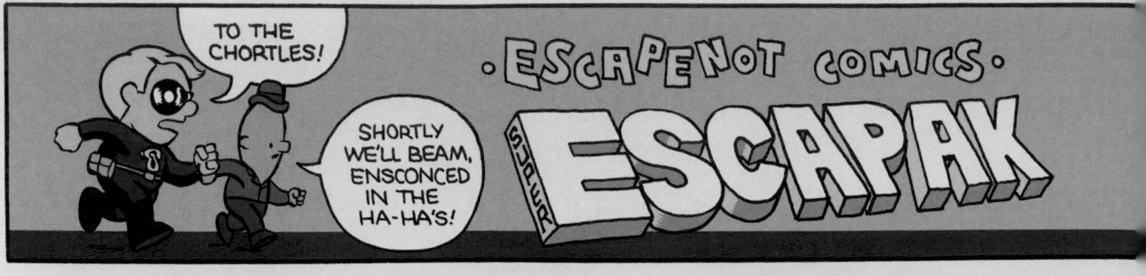
TO THE CHORTLES!
SHORTLY WE'LL BEAM, ENSCONCED IN THE HA-HA'S!
·ESCAPENOT COMICS·
SUPER
ESCAPAK

### LI'L AL'S KNEE-SLAPPERS

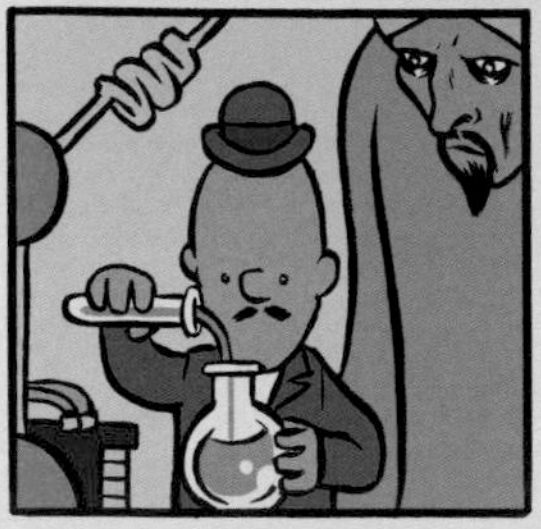

"Free will? Sorry, I thought you said unicorns."

### HILARITY HUNTERS

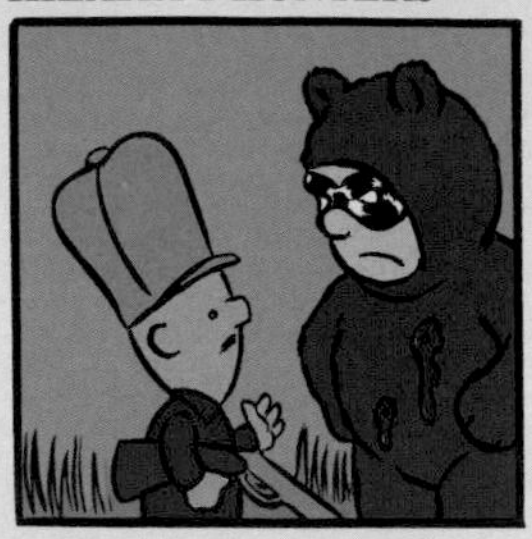

"Look, I can see your point, but I play the hand I'm dealt."

### NYUK-NYUKS AND SUCH

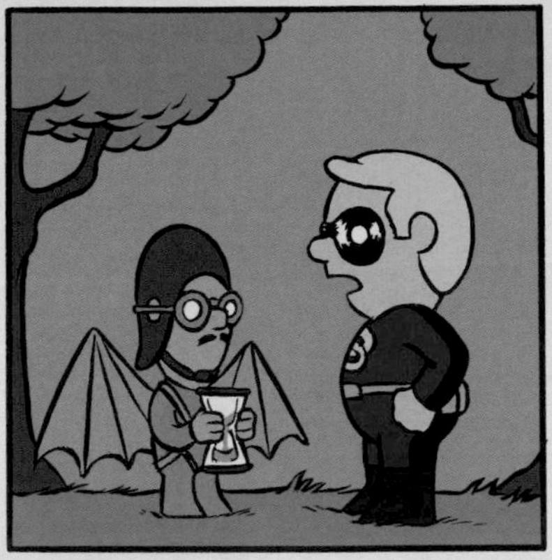

"I would question: is your statement a failed comedic attempt or, worse, a haphazard handling of general relativity? If one is to assume that, in your words, one is 'having fun,' why should the fourth dimension be appreciably affected? Further, stating that the fourth dimension should 'fly' while one is engaged in said amusement seems nonsensical entirely. To consider the aforementioned lazy employment of physical theory: if by 'fly,' you mean to 'move rapidly,' and one introduces the dubious premise that amusement is more easily procured at a great altitude (perhaps due to lack of oxygen's play on the brain and physiology), then, yes, I suppose time would here move more rapidly as compared to an amusement seeker on the Earth's surface, that amusement seeker being far closer to a massive body. But the difference between the two time passages, one at the greater altitude, and one closer to the massive body distorting space-time, would be negligible and hardly worthy of comment. So, then, I will presume your attire and statement to be, as mentioned, a crude stab at levity, an enterprise which serves only to dissuade the advancement of mankind and its civilization. For shame, sir. You look very much the fool."

### GOTTA PAY THE BILLS

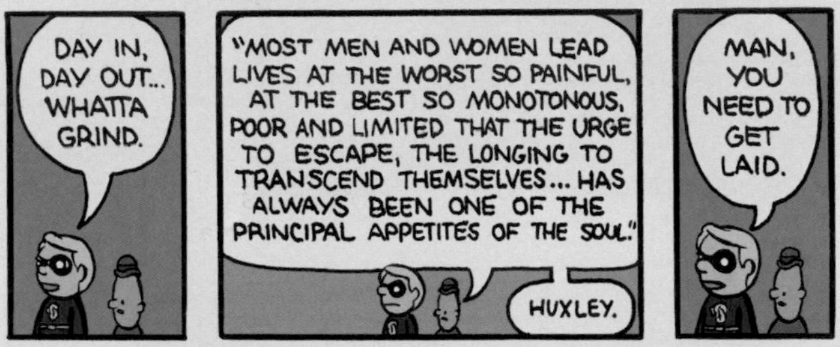
DAY IN, DAY OUT... WHATTA GRIND.
"MOST MEN AND WOMEN LEAD LIVES AT THE WORST SO PAINFUL, AT THE BEST SO MONOTONOUS, POOR AND LIMITED THAT THE URGE TO ESCAPE, THE LONGING TO TRANSCEND THEMSELVES... HAS ALWAYS BEEN ONE OF THE PRINCIPAL APPETITES OF THE SOUL."
HUXLEY.
MAN, YOU NEED TO GET LAID.

### THE GOLDEN KEY

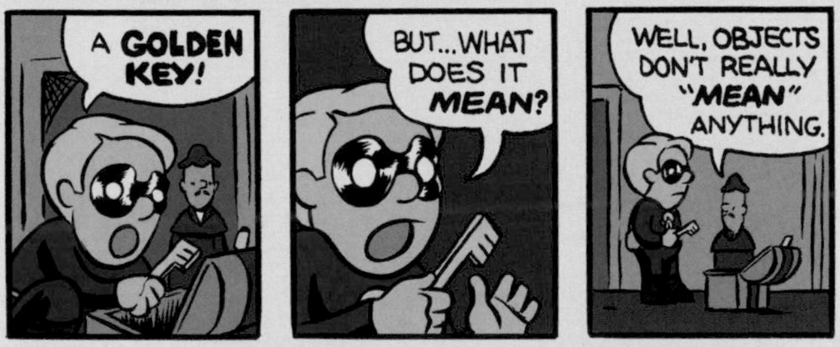
A **GOLDEN KEY!**
BUT...WHAT DOES IT ***MEAN?***
WELL, OBJECTS DON'T REALLY ***"MEAN"*** ANYTHING.

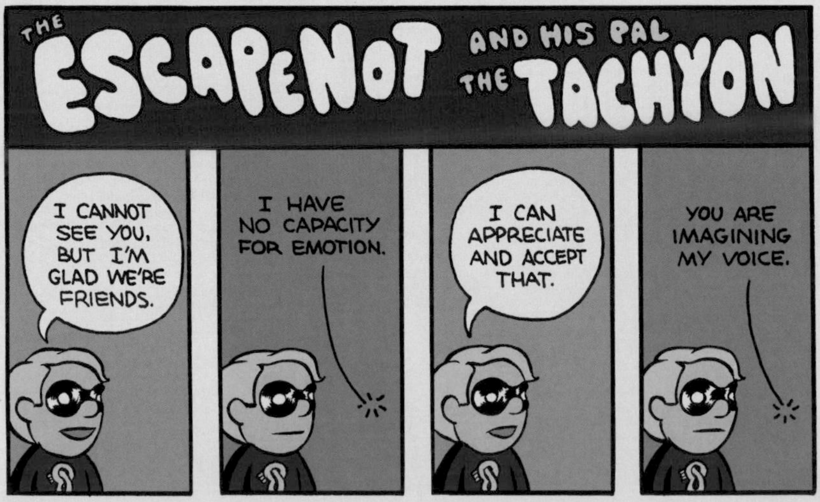
THE ESCAPENOT AND HIS PAL THE TACHYON
I CANNOT SEE YOU, BUT I'M GLAD WE'RE FRIENDS.
I HAVE NO CAPACITY FOR EMOTION.
I CAN APPRECIATE AND ACCEPT THAT.
YOU ARE IMAGINING MY VOICE.

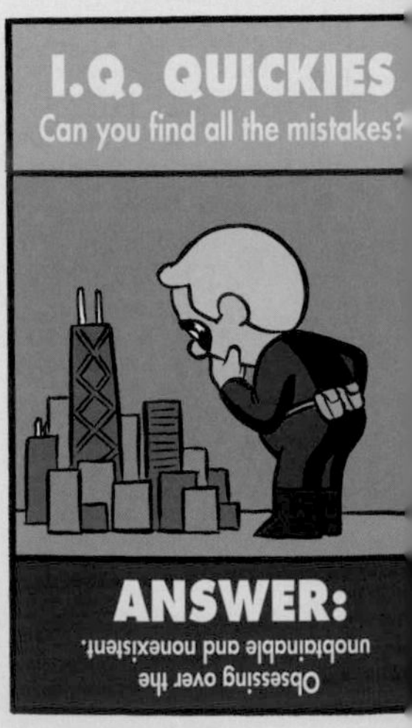
I.Q. QUICKIES
Can you find all the mistakes?
ANSWER:
Obsessing over the unobtainable and nonexistent.

# "DOUBLE OR NOTHING"

*Preface*

## BY KEN KRISTENSEN

*How Kavalier and Clay's Creation Escaped French Publication (Kinda Sorta)*

IN THE 1930S, STARTING WITH PAUL WINCKLER'S *JOURNAL DE MICKEY*, publishers in France and Belgium embraced the practice of translating American comic series for their market. Hundreds of comic magazines, including *Coeurs Vaillants*, *Hurrah*, and *Bravo*, struck deals with American copyright holders.

However, after the Nazi invasion all American imports were cut off. At first, creators like Jijé in *Spirou* and Edgar P. Jacobs in *Bravo* continued unfinished American stories of Superman and Flash Gordon, but soon the Nazis cracked down on even those homemade versions of American comics.

Without their US counterparts crowding the pages, French comic artists came into their own, filling the void with legions of new characters, sating the home market.

By war's end, French audiences had been successfully weaned away from American fare. Besides . . . a new law in 1949, engineered in part by the French communist party, prohibited most American comics, deemed "too adult," from being distributed to youth.

In 1959, comics writers Goscinny and Charlier, and artists Albert Uderzo and Jean Hébrard founded the now-legendary magazine *Pilote*. Three hundred thousand copies sold out in one day.

A year later the magazine was bought out by publisher Dargaud. With features like "Blueberry," "Lucky Luke," and "Achille Tallon," *Pilote* was a force of nature during the sixties and early seventies.

But as comics evolved and tastes began trending toward more mature subject matter, *Pilote* fell out of vogue. In 1974, sales ebbing, the publisher tried its best to update the magazine. But its star creators, Druillet and Giraud, decided to jump ship, founding the edgy fantasy and science fiction comic magazine *Metal Hurlant*.

Blindsided by their exit, *Pilote's* editor René Goscinny, was left with dozens of blank pages to fill. Frantically searching the "submissions" pile for new talent, Goscinny happened upon "Double or Nothing," an Escapist story in its entirety, by the then-unknown writer-artist team of Ken Kristensen and M.K. Perker.

Thanks to the Nazis, and later the communists, The Escapist had escaped ever being imported to France. So Goscinny assumed the character was an original work and immediately sent "Double or Nothing" to the printer. He mailed a check to the return address on the package.

A few days later he received a call from Perker and Kristensen who'd received the check. Barely in their teens, they were sons of American diplomats stationed in Nice. When Goscinny complemented them on their compelling creation, they told him the truth—this was an unauthorized "French spin" on an American hero. They'd sent it to him merely as a sample of their talent.

Perker, proudly explaining that he'd changed the costume's colors to those of the French flag, is said to have heard Goscinny drop the phone shouting, "Stop the presses!" But by then it was too late.

The printer had finished printing the issue. Fearing a lawsuit by the American copyright holder, hundreds of thousands of copies had to be scrapped.

Sadly, after that incident, Goscinny was replaced as editor-in-chief and Pilote was reduced from a weekly to a monthly.

Kristensen, bitter over his failure to become a published writer, turned his creative energies toward acts of vandalism and self mutilation. Embarrassed and ashamed, his parents sent him to "rest" in an asylum in Connecticut. He is now a member of the Writers Guild of America.

Perker was towed to Istanbul, his father's new embassy assignment. There he became one of the most sought-after artists in Turkey, a nation with a long history of supporting and celebrating copyright violators. He is now a member of the American Society of Illustrators.

A quick check of Snopes.com will dispel the persistent rumors that a few copies of the *Pilote* version of "Double or Nothing" survived the massive pulping in 1974. Only the original artwork survived.

This is the first time this story has been properly published.

IT'S DAY SIX OF THE HISTORIC MONTH-LONG FRANCO-SOVIET SPACE MISSION. OFFICIALS SAY ---

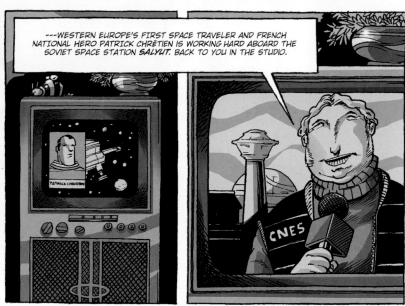

---WESTERN EUROPE'S FIRST SPACE TRAVELER AND FRENCH NATIONAL HERO PATRICK CHRÉTIEN IS WORKING HARD ABOARD THE SOVIET SPACE STATION *SALYUT*. BACK TO YOU IN THE STUDIO.

THANKS, PIERRE. I GUESS THE ONLY QUESTION NOW IS HOW WILL CHRÉTIEN SURVIVE FOR A MONTH ON RUSSIAN FOOD?

NOW, NILES RENAULT WITH THE WEATHER...

RUSSIAN *FOOD*--BLECH. WELL, SERGE, I PREDICT THE STARS WILL BE OUT TONIGHT FOR PATRICK CHRÉTIEN-- HEH HEH.

HOWEVER HERE IN PARIS CLOUDS ARE BEGINNING TO ROLL IN--

--PIECE OF JUNGLE NOBODY CARE ABOUT. IS *CRIMINAL*.

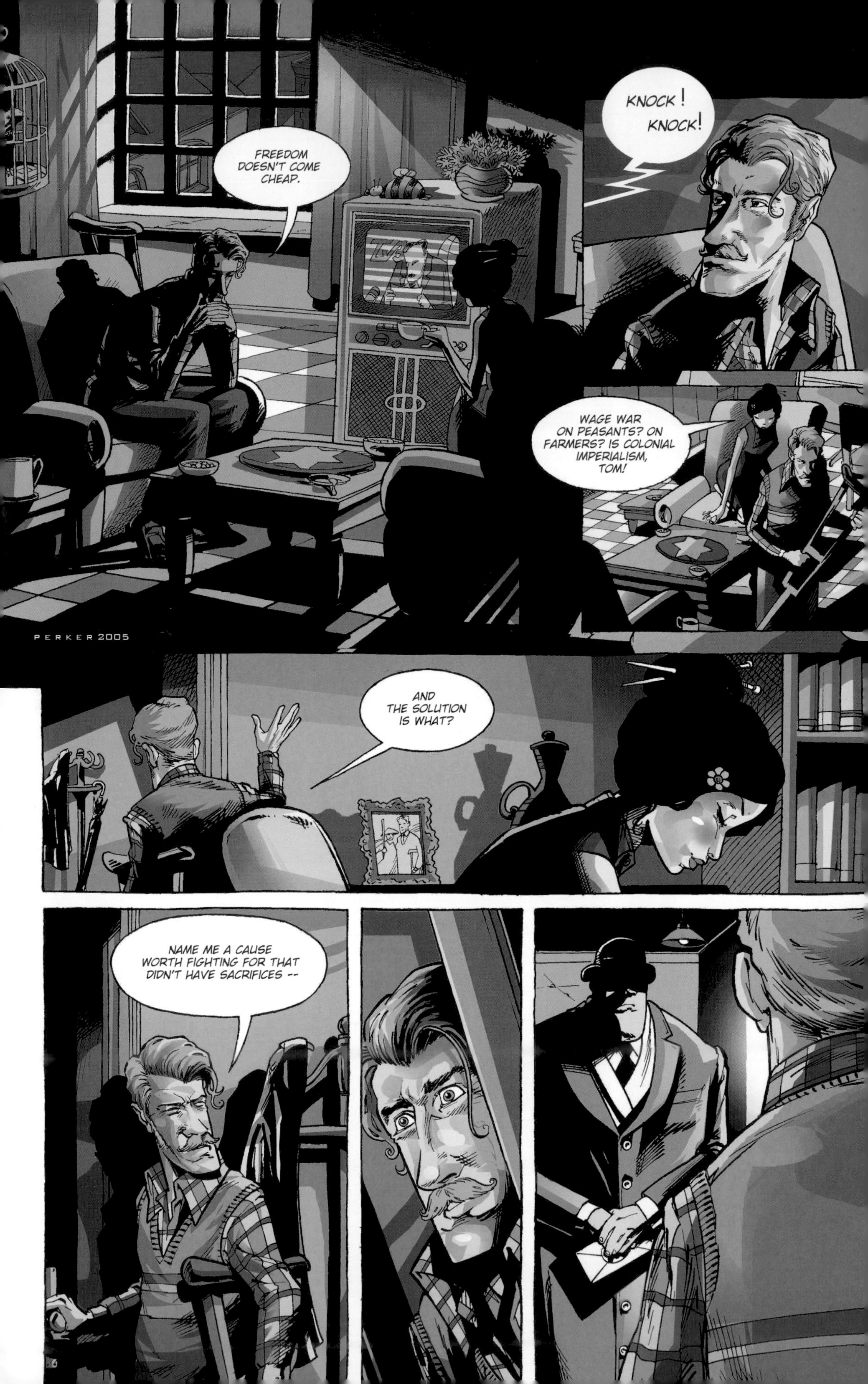
FREEDOM DOESN'T COME CHEAP.
PERKER 2005
KNOCK! KNOCK!
WAGE WAR ON PEASANTS? ON FARMERS? IS COLONIAL IMPERIALISM, TOM!
AND THE SOLUTION IS WHAT?
NAME ME A CAUSE WORTH FIGHTING FOR THAT DIDN'T HAVE SACRIFICES --

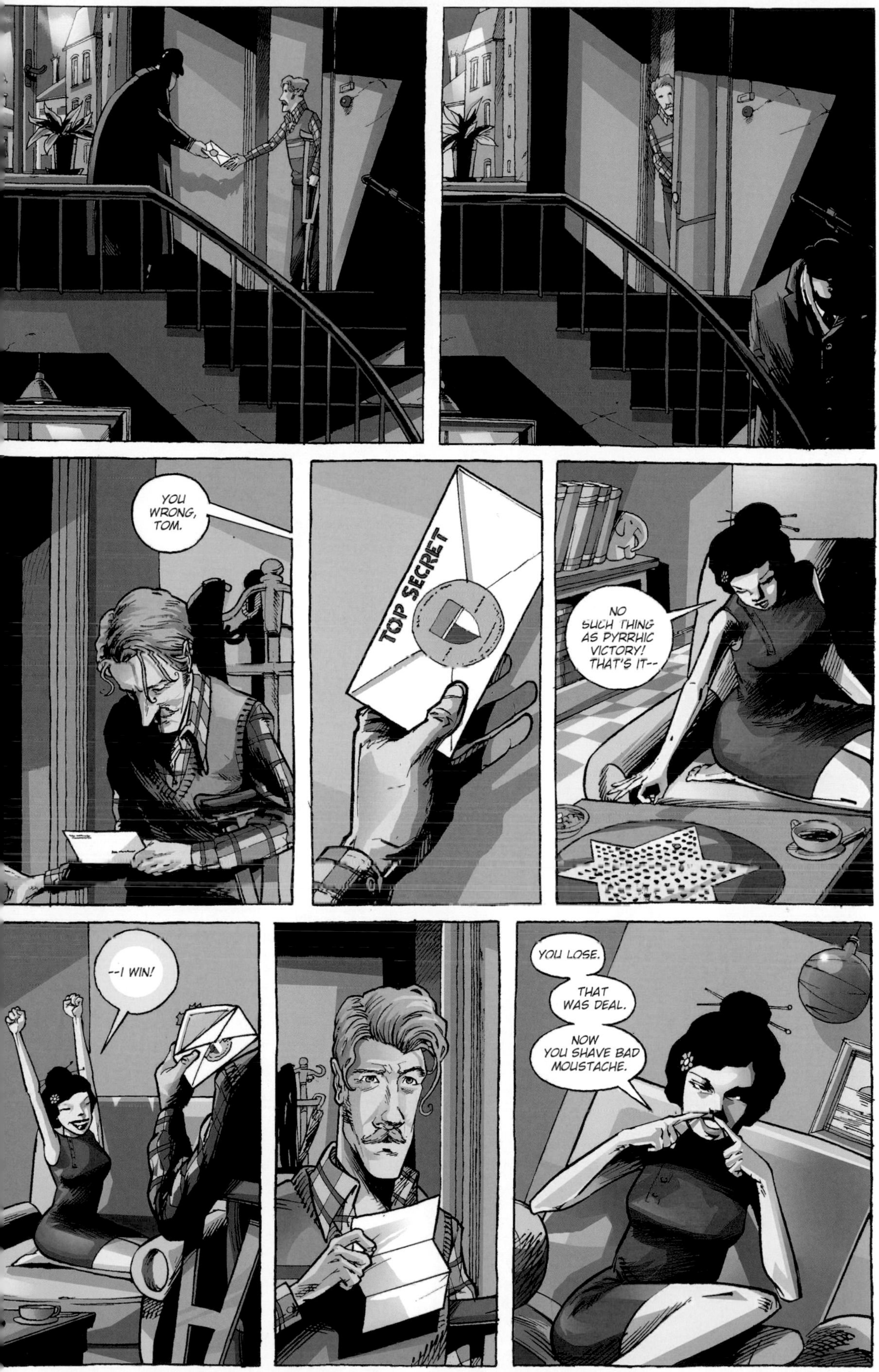
YOU WRONG, TOM.
TOP SECRET
NO SUCH THING AS PYRRHIC VICTORY! THAT'S IT--
--I WIN!
YOU LOSE.
THAT WAS DEAL.
NOW YOU SHAVE BAD MOUSTACHE.

Written by
**Monsieur KEN KRISTENSEN**

Art and Colors by
**Monsieur M.K. PERKER**

Edited by
**Mademoiselle DIANA SCHUTZ**

# DOUBLE or NOTHING

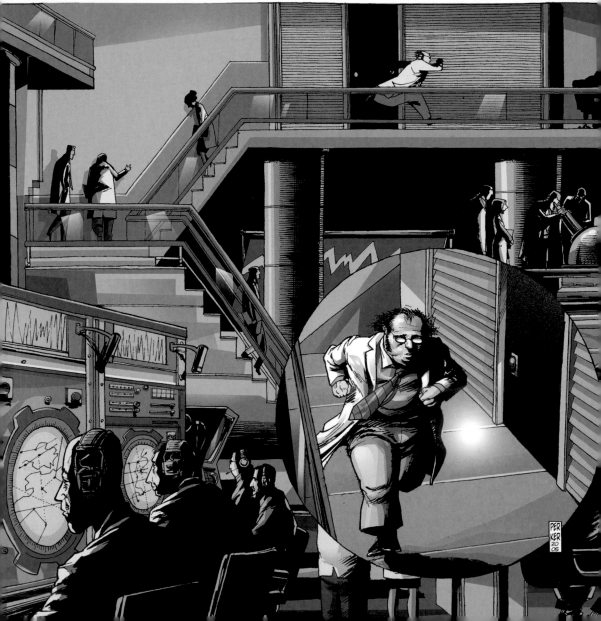

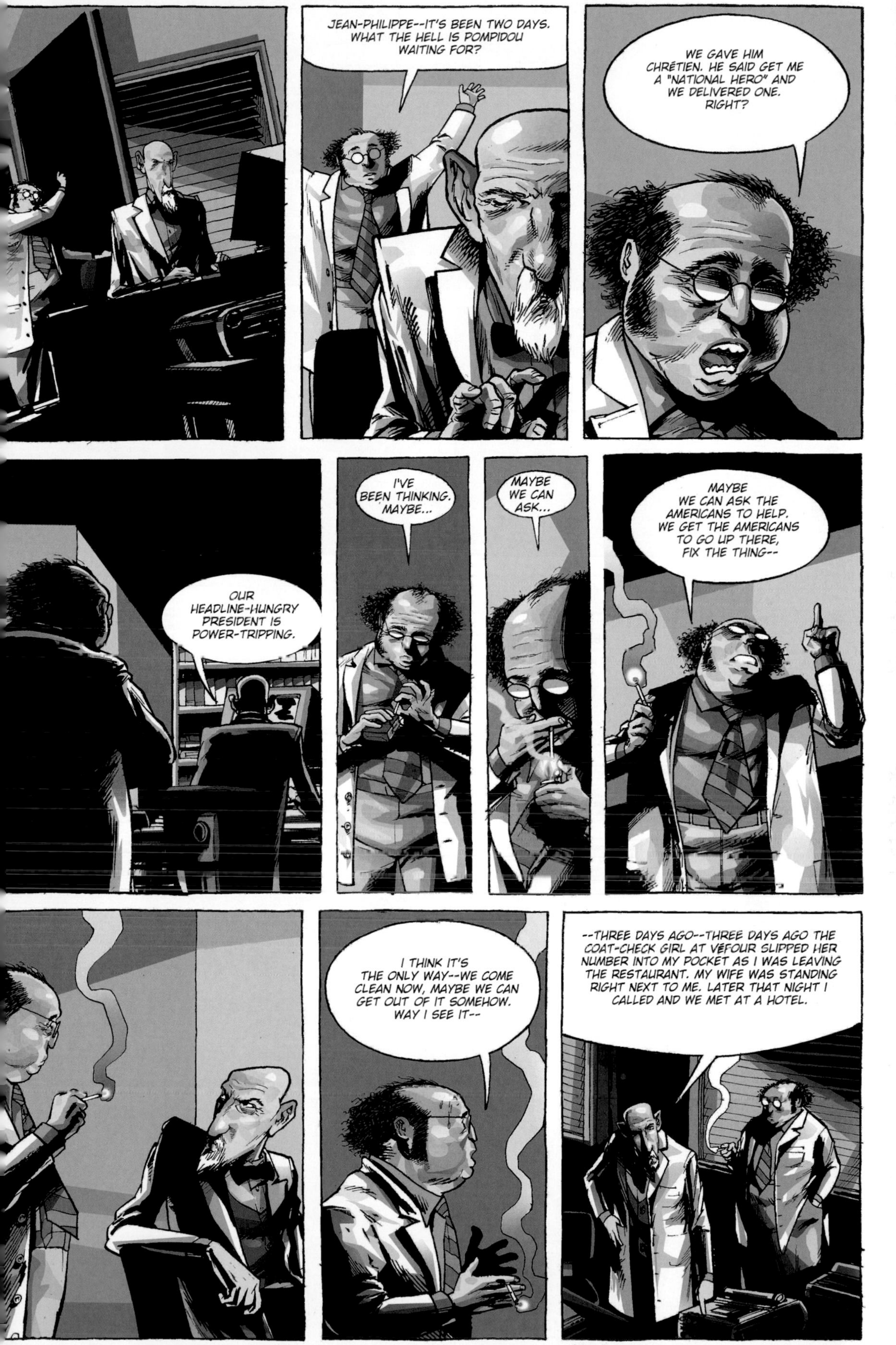
JEAN-PHILIPPE--IT'S BEEN TWO DAYS. WHAT THE HELL IS POMPIDOU WAITING FOR?
WE GAVE HIM CHRÉTIEN. HE SAID GET ME A "NATIONAL HERO" AND WE DELIVERED ONE. RIGHT?
OUR HEADLINE-HUNGRY PRESIDENT IS POWER-TRIPPING.
I'VE BEEN THINKING. MAYBE...
MAYBE WE CAN ASK...
MAYBE WE CAN ASK THE AMERICANS TO HELP. WE GET THE AMERICANS TO GO UP THERE, FIX THE THING--
I THINK IT'S THE ONLY WAY--WE COME CLEAN NOW, MAYBE WE CAN GET OUT OF IT SOMEHOW. WAY I SEE IT--
--THREE DAYS AGO--THREE DAYS AGO THE COAT-CHECK GIRL AT VÉFOUR SLIPPED HER NUMBER INTO MY POCKET AS I WAS LEAVING THE RESTAURANT. MY WIFE WAS STANDING RIGHT NEXT TO ME. LATER THAT NIGHT I CALLED AND WE MET AT A HOTEL.

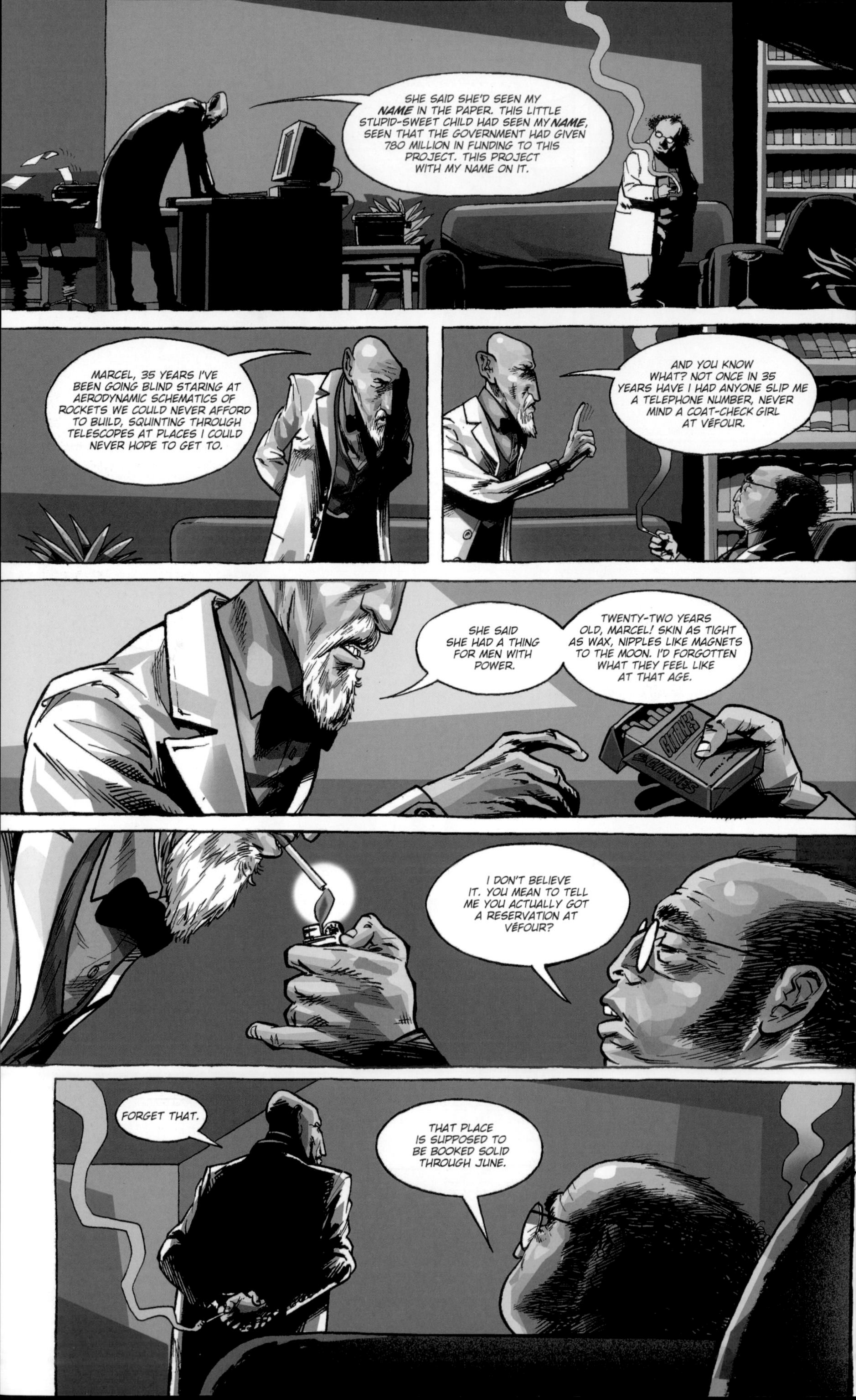
SHE SAID SHE'D SEEN MY **NAME** IN THE PAPER. THIS LITTLE STUPID-SWEET CHILD HAD SEEN MY **NAME**, SEEN THAT THE GOVERNMENT HAD GIVEN 780 MILLION IN FUNDING TO THIS PROJECT. THIS PROJECT WITH MY NAME ON IT.
MARCEL, 35 YEARS I'VE BEEN GOING BLIND STARING AT AERODYNAMIC SCHEMATICS OF ROCKETS WE COULD NEVER AFFORD TO BUILD, SQUINTING THROUGH TELESCOPES AT PLACES I COULD NEVER HOPE TO GET TO.
AND YOU KNOW WHAT? NOT ONCE IN 35 YEARS HAVE I HAD ANYONE SLIP ME A TELEPHONE NUMBER, NEVER MIND A COAT-CHECK GIRL AT VÉFOUR.
SHE SAID SHE HAD A THING FOR MEN WITH POWER.
TWENTY-TWO YEARS OLD, MARCEL! SKIN AS TIGHT AS WAX, NIPPLES LIKE MAGNETS TO THE MOON. I'D FORGOTTEN WHAT THEY FEEL LIKE AT THAT AGE.
GITANES
GITANES
I DON'T BELIEVE IT. YOU MEAN TO TELL ME YOU ACTUALLY GOT A RESERVATION AT VÉFOUR?
FORGET THAT.
THAT PLACE IS SUPPOSED TO BE BOOKED SOLID THROUGH JUNE.

FORGET VÉFOUR!

LISTEN, OUR ENTIRE OPERATION IS AFLOAT FOR ONE REASON AND ONE REASON ONLY--BECAUSE WE PROMISED TO DO THE IMPOSSIBLE--TO GET THE FIRST WESTERN EUROPEAN IN SPACE BEFORE THE GERMANS AND THE BRITISH.

YOU SAID IT YOURSELF, WE CREATED A "NATIONAL HERO", WE DID WHAT WE NEEDED TO DO.

WE WON, GODDAMMIT, AND I AM NOT GOING TO LET ANYONE SCREW IT UP FOR US.

WE'VE GOT TO DO *SOMETHING*--

--MAYBE WE CAN USE THE PRESS--LIGHT A FIRE UNDER POMPIDOU. TIME IS RUNNING OUT, JEAN!

NO! I DON'T WANT THE PRESS ANYWHERE NEAR THIS.

BUT YOU SAID WHAT POMPIDOU DOESN'T KNOW WON'T HURT US, THAT'S WHAT YOU SAID. WE'RE GONNA BURN IF ANYONE FINDS OUT THE TRUTH.

THE TRUTH?

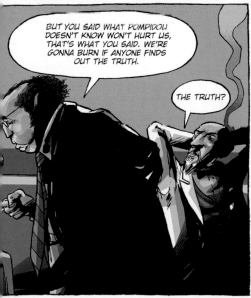

THE RUSSIANS AREN'T ABOUT TO TELL ANYONE--IT'S AS EMBARRASSING FOR THEM AS IT IS FOR THE TWO OF US.

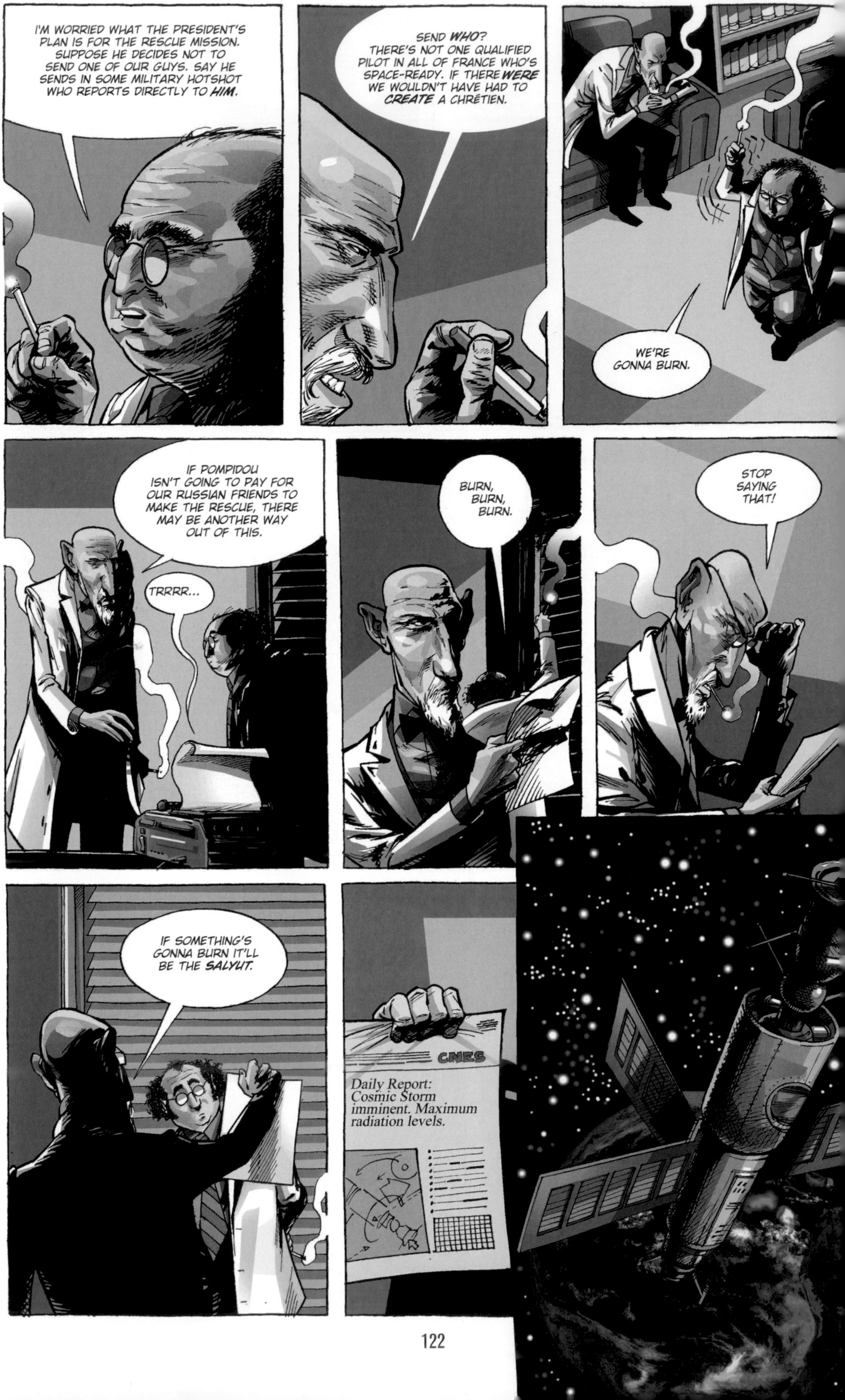
I'M WORRIED WHAT THE PRESIDENT'S PLAN IS FOR THE RESCUE MISSION. SUPPOSE HE DECIDES NOT TO SEND ONE OF OUR GUYS. SAY HE SENDS IN SOME MILITARY HOTSHOT WHO REPORTS DIRECTLY TO *HIM*.
SEND *WHO*? THERE'S NOT ONE QUALIFIED PILOT IN ALL OF FRANCE WHO'S SPACE-READY. IF THERE *WERE* WE WOULDN'T HAVE HAD TO *CREATE* A CHRÉTIEN.
WE'RE GONNA BURN.
IF POMPIDOU ISN'T GOING TO PAY FOR OUR RUSSIAN FRIENDS TO MAKE THE RESCUE, THERE MAY BE ANOTHER WAY OUT OF THIS.
TRRRR...
BURN, BURN, BURN.
STOP SAYING THAT!
IF SOMETHING'S GONNA BURN IT'LL BE THE *SALYUT*.
CNES
Daily Report: Cosmic Storm imminent. Maximum radiation levels.

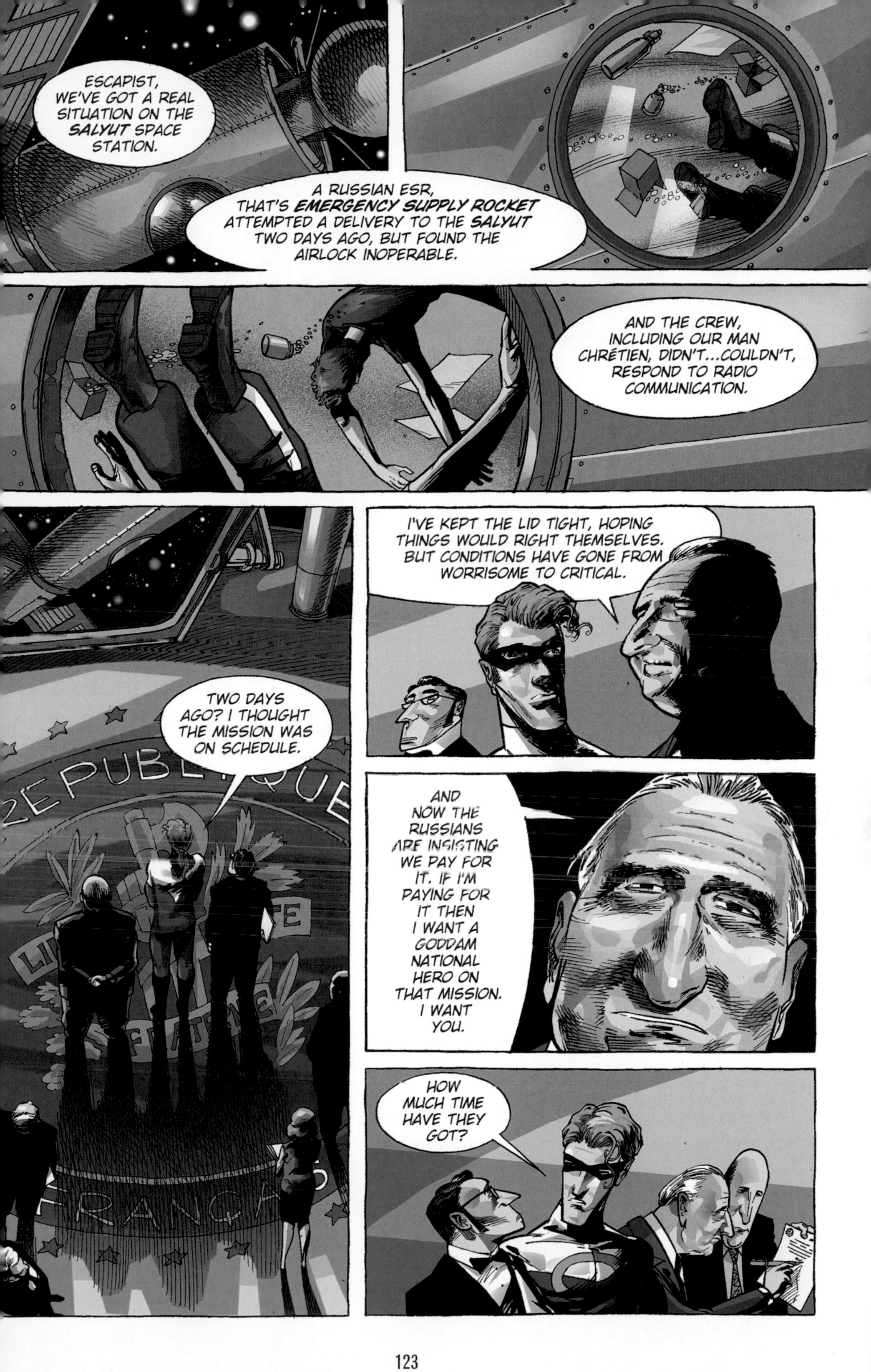
ESCAPIST, WE'VE GOT A REAL SITUATION ON THE SALYUT SPACE STATION.
A RUSSIAN ESR, THAT'S EMERGENCY SUPPLY ROCKET ATTEMPTED A DELIVERY TO THE SALYUT TWO DAYS AGO, BUT FOUND THE AIRLOCK INOPERABLE.
AND THE CREW, INCLUDING OUR MAN CHRÉTIEN, DIDN'T...COULDN'T, RESPOND TO RADIO COMMUNICATION.
TWO DAYS AGO? I THOUGHT THE MISSION WAS ON SCHEDULE.
I'VE KEPT THE LID TIGHT, HOPING THINGS WOULD RIGHT THEMSELVES. BUT CONDITIONS HAVE GONE FROM WORRISOME TO CRITICAL.
AND NOW THE RUSSIANS ARE INSISTING WE PAY FOR IT. IF I'M PAYING FOR IT THEN I WANT A GODDAM NATIONAL HERO ON THAT MISSION. I WANT YOU.
HOW MUCH TIME HAVE THEY GOT?

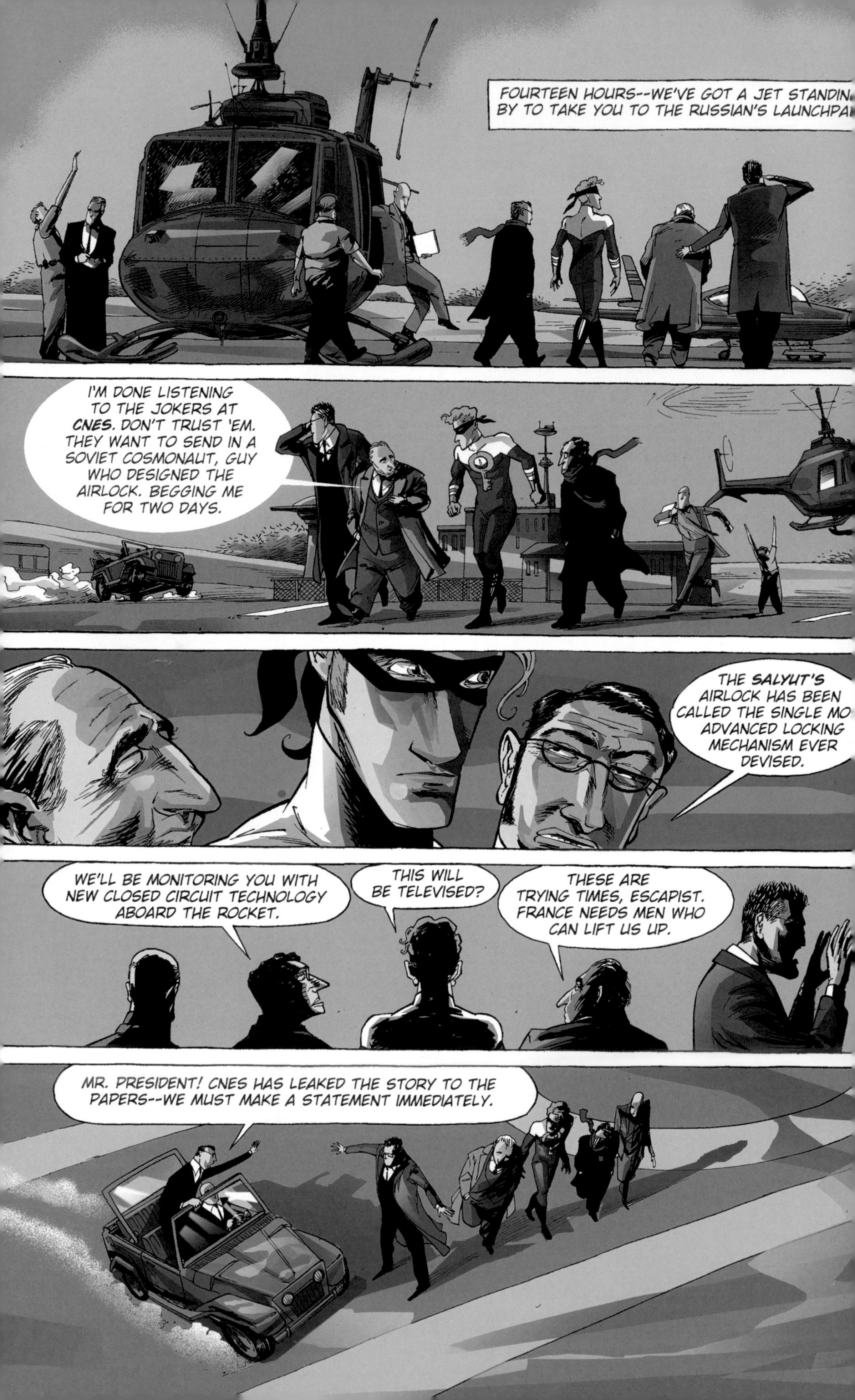

FOURTEEN HOURS--WE'VE GOT A JET STANDIN BY TO TAKE YOU TO THE RUSSIAN'S LAUNCHPA
I'M DONE LISTENING TO THE JOKERS AT CNES. DON'T TRUST 'EM. THEY WANT TO SEND IN A SOVIET COSMONAUT, GUY WHO DESIGNED THE AIRLOCK. BEGGING ME FOR TWO DAYS.
THE SALYUT'S AIRLOCK HAS BEEN CALLED THE SINGLE MO ADVANCED LOCKING MECHANISM EVER DEVISED.
WE'LL BE MONITORING YOU WITH NEW CLOSED CIRCUIT TECHNOLOGY ABOARD THE ROCKET.
THIS WILL BE TELEVISED?
THESE ARE TRYING TIMES, ESCAPIST. FRANCE NEEDS MEN WHO CAN LIFT US UP.
MR. PRESIDENT! CNES HAS LEAKED THE STORY TO THE PAPERS--WE MUST MAKE A STATEMENT IMMEDIATELY.

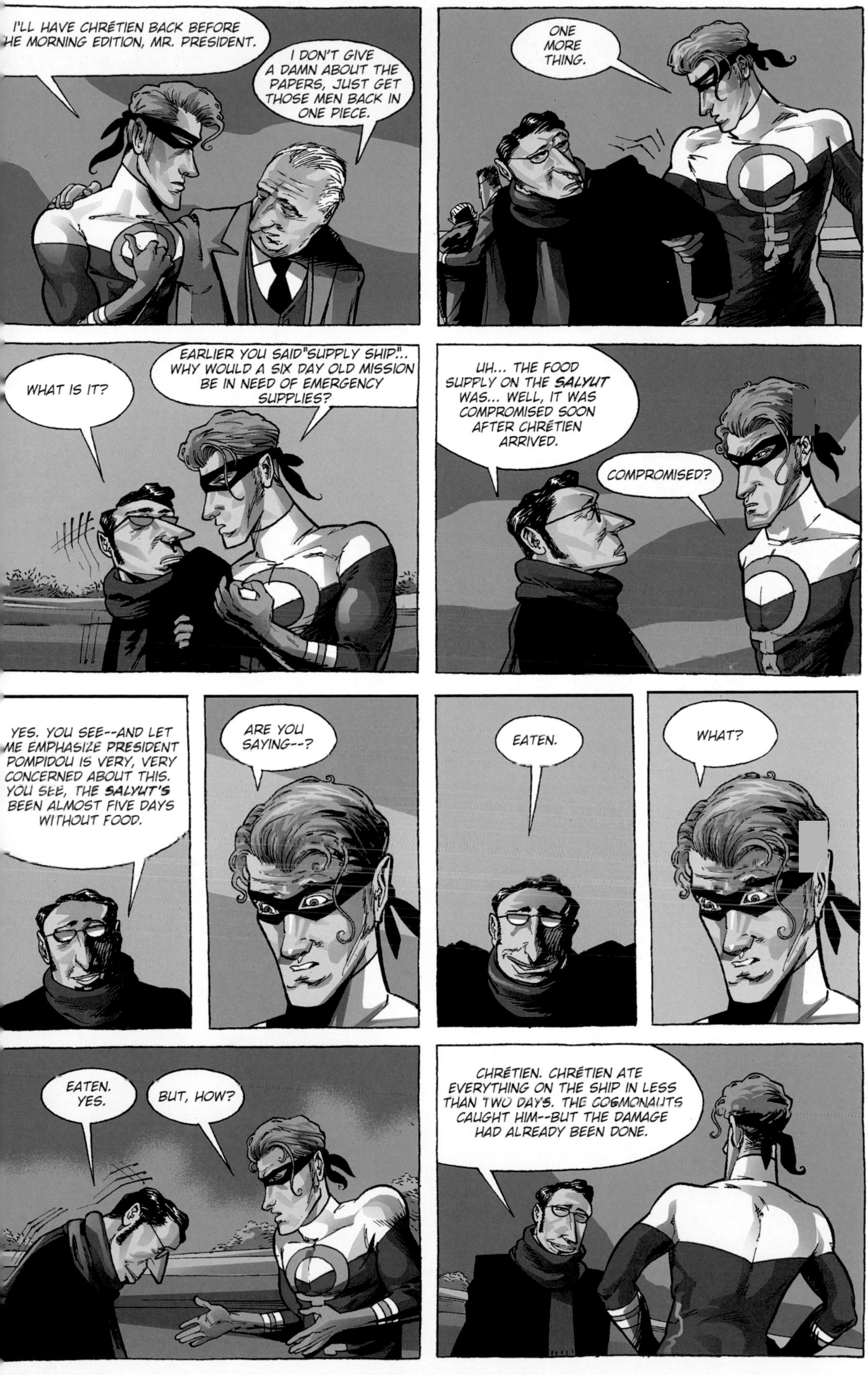
I'LL HAVE CHRÉTIEN BACK BEFORE THE MORNING EDITION, MR. PRESIDENT.
I DON'T GIVE A DAMN ABOUT THE PAPERS, JUST GET THOSE MEN BACK IN ONE PIECE.
ONE MORE THING.
WHAT IS IT?
EARLIER YOU SAID "SUPPLY SHIP"... WHY WOULD A SIX DAY OLD MISSION BE IN NEED OF EMERGENCY SUPPLIES?
UH... THE FOOD SUPPLY ON THE SALYUT WAS... WELL, IT WAS COMPROMISED SOON AFTER CHRÉTIEN ARRIVED.
COMPROMISED?
YES. YOU SEE--AND LET ME EMPHASIZE PRESIDENT POMPIDOU IS VERY, VERY CONCERNED ABOUT THIS. YOU SEE, THE SALYUT'S BEEN ALMOST FIVE DAYS WITHOUT FOOD.
ARE YOU SAYING--?
EATEN.
WHAT?
EATEN. YES.
BUT, HOW?
CHRÉTIEN. CHRÉTIEN ATE EVERYTHING ON THE SHIP IN LESS THAN TWO DAYS. THE COSMONAUTS CAUGHT HIM--BUT THE DAMAGE HAD ALREADY BEEN DONE.

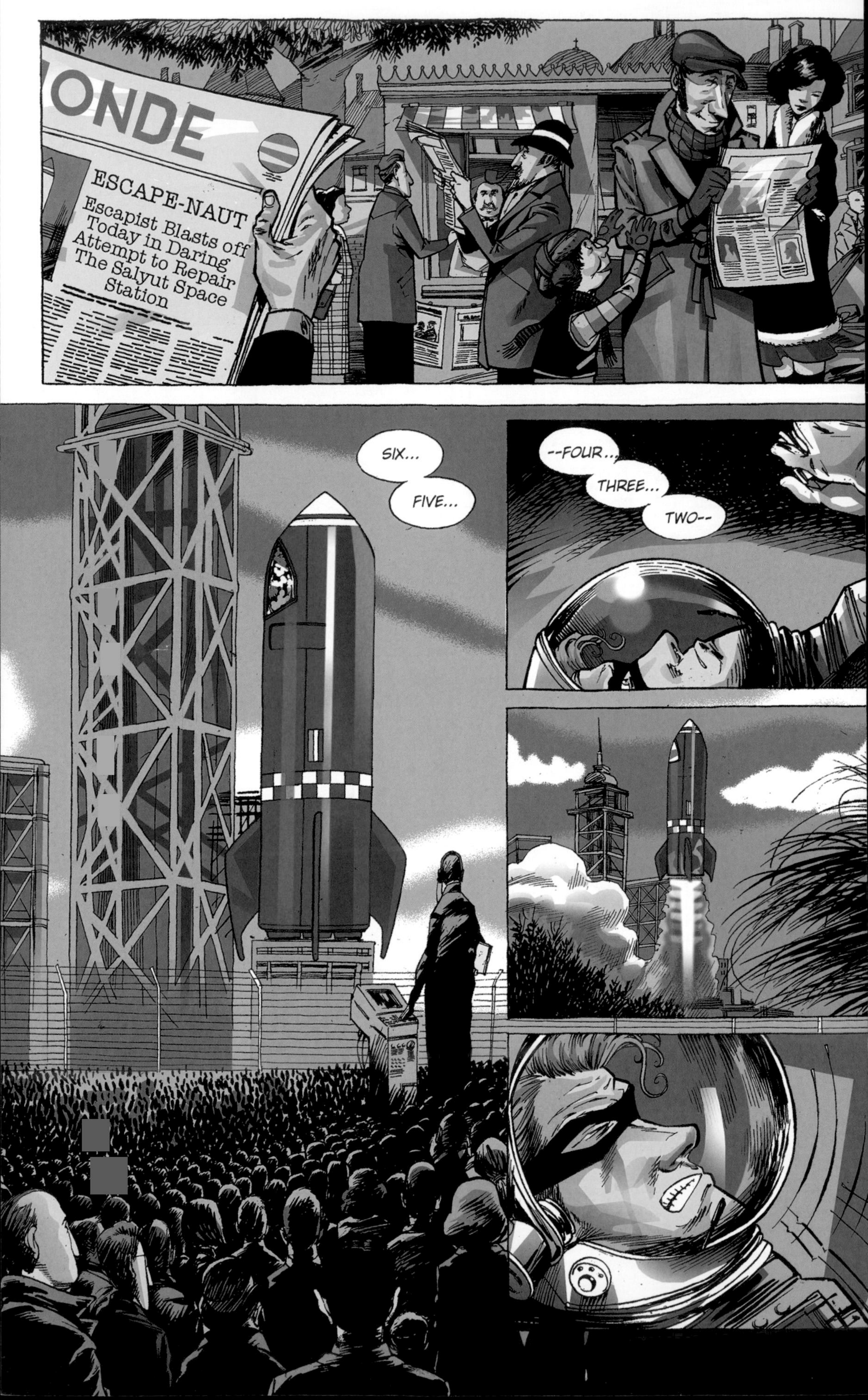
ONDE
ESCAPE-NAUT
Escapist Blasts off Today in Daring Attempt to Repair The Salyut Space Station
SIX...
FIVE...
--FOUR...
THREE...
TWO--

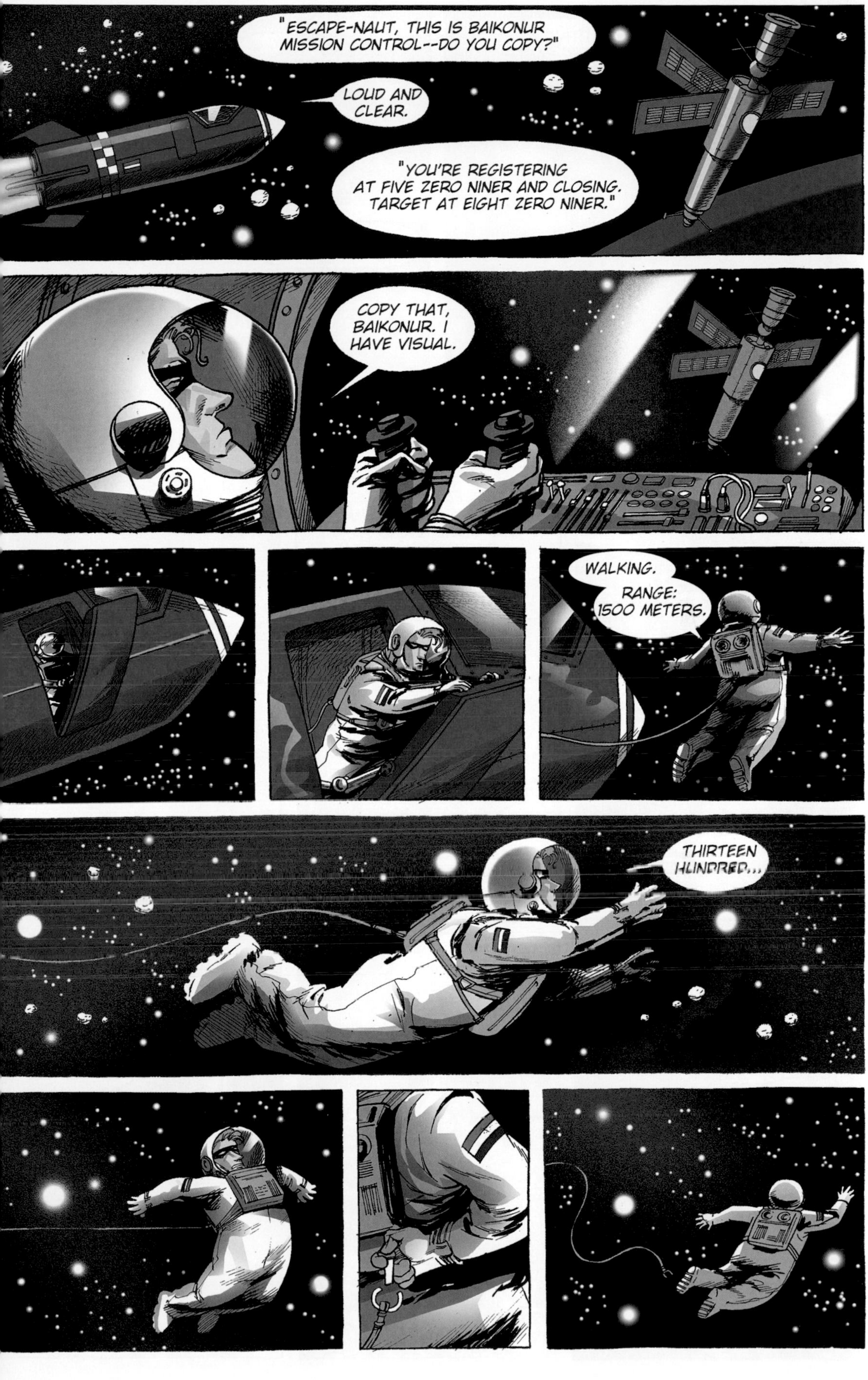
"ESCAPE-NAUT, THIS IS BAIKONUR MISSION CONTROL--DO YOU COPY?"
LOUD AND CLEAR.
"YOU'RE REGISTERING AT FIVE ZERO NINER AND CLOSING. TARGET AT EIGHT ZERO NINER."
COPY THAT, BAIKONUR. I HAVE VISUAL.
WALKING.
RANGE: 1500 METERS.
THIRTEEN HUNDRED...

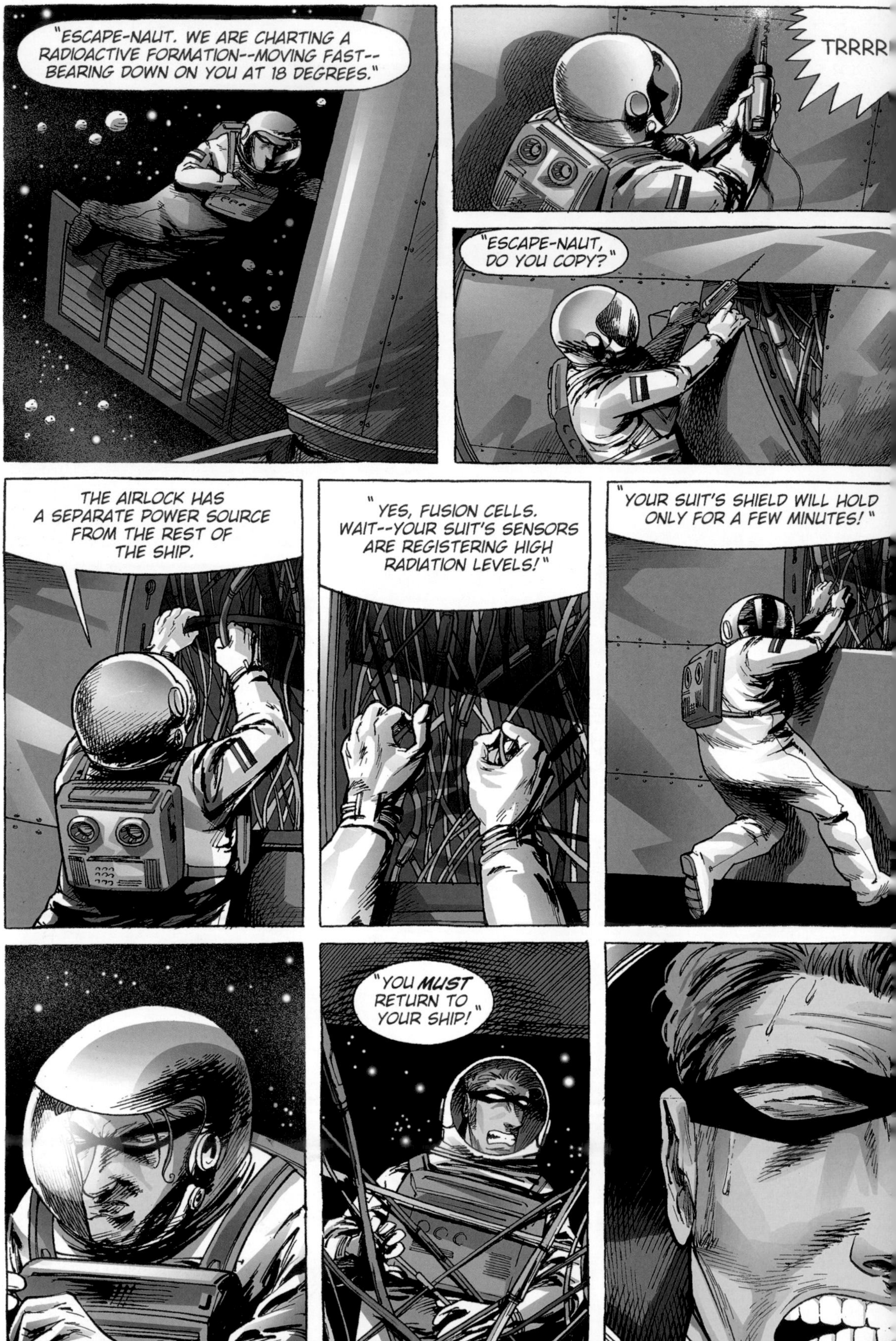
"ESCAPE-NAUT. WE ARE CHARTING A RADIOACTIVE FORMATION--MOVING FAST--BEARING DOWN ON YOU AT 18 DEGREES."
TRRRR
"ESCAPE-NAUT, DO YOU COPY?"
THE AIRLOCK HAS A SEPARATE POWER SOURCE FROM THE REST OF THE SHIP.
"YES, FUSION CELLS. WAIT--YOUR SUIT'S SENSORS ARE REGISTERING HIGH RADIATION LEVELS!"
"YOUR SUIT'S SHIELD WILL HOLD ONLY FOR A FEW MINUTES!"
"YOU MUST RETURN TO YOUR SHIP!"

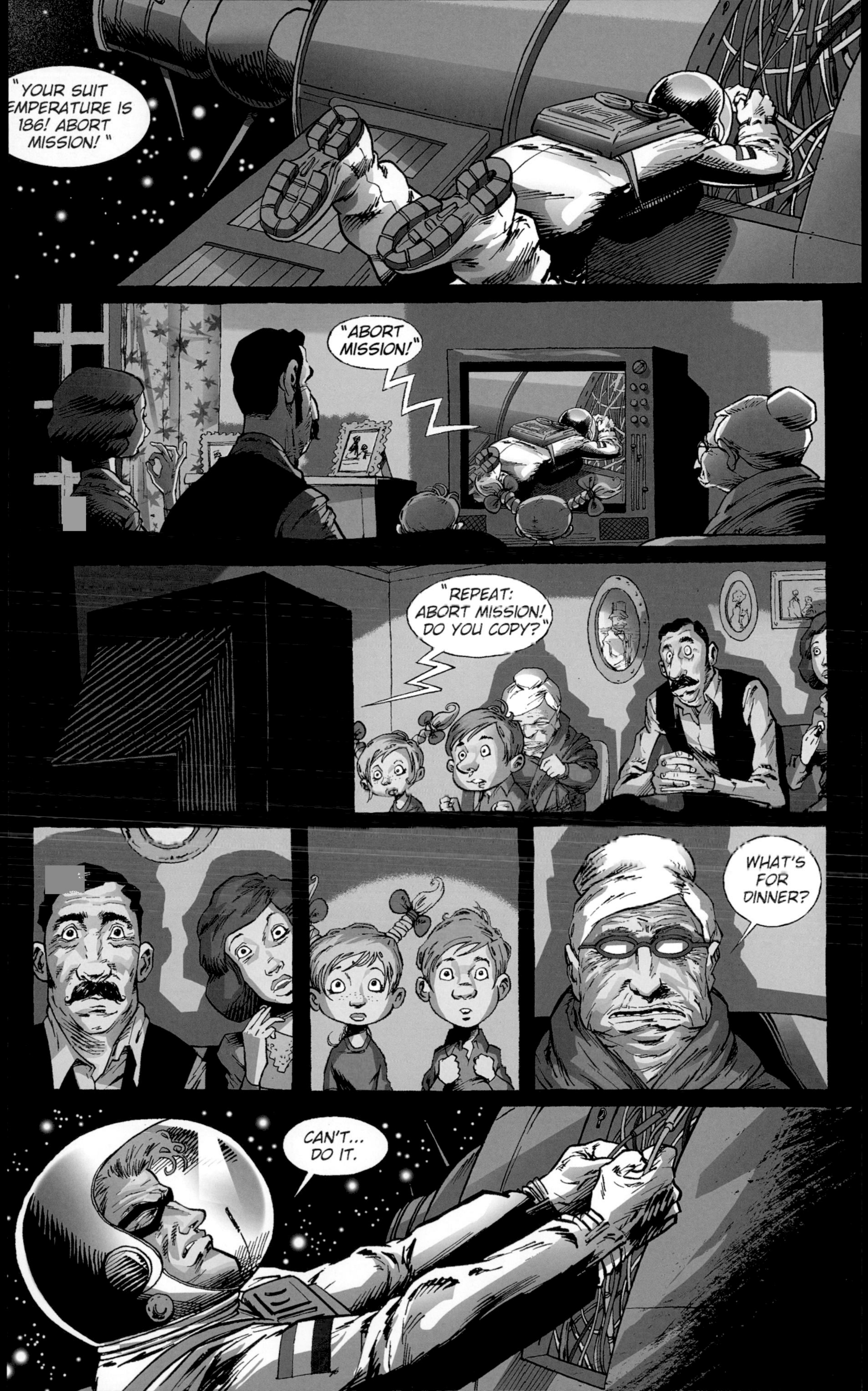
"YOUR SUIT
EMPERATURE IS 186! ABORT MISSION!"
"ABORT MISSION!"
"REPEAT: ABORT MISSION! DO YOU COPY?"
WHAT'S FOR DINNER?
CAN'T... DO IT.

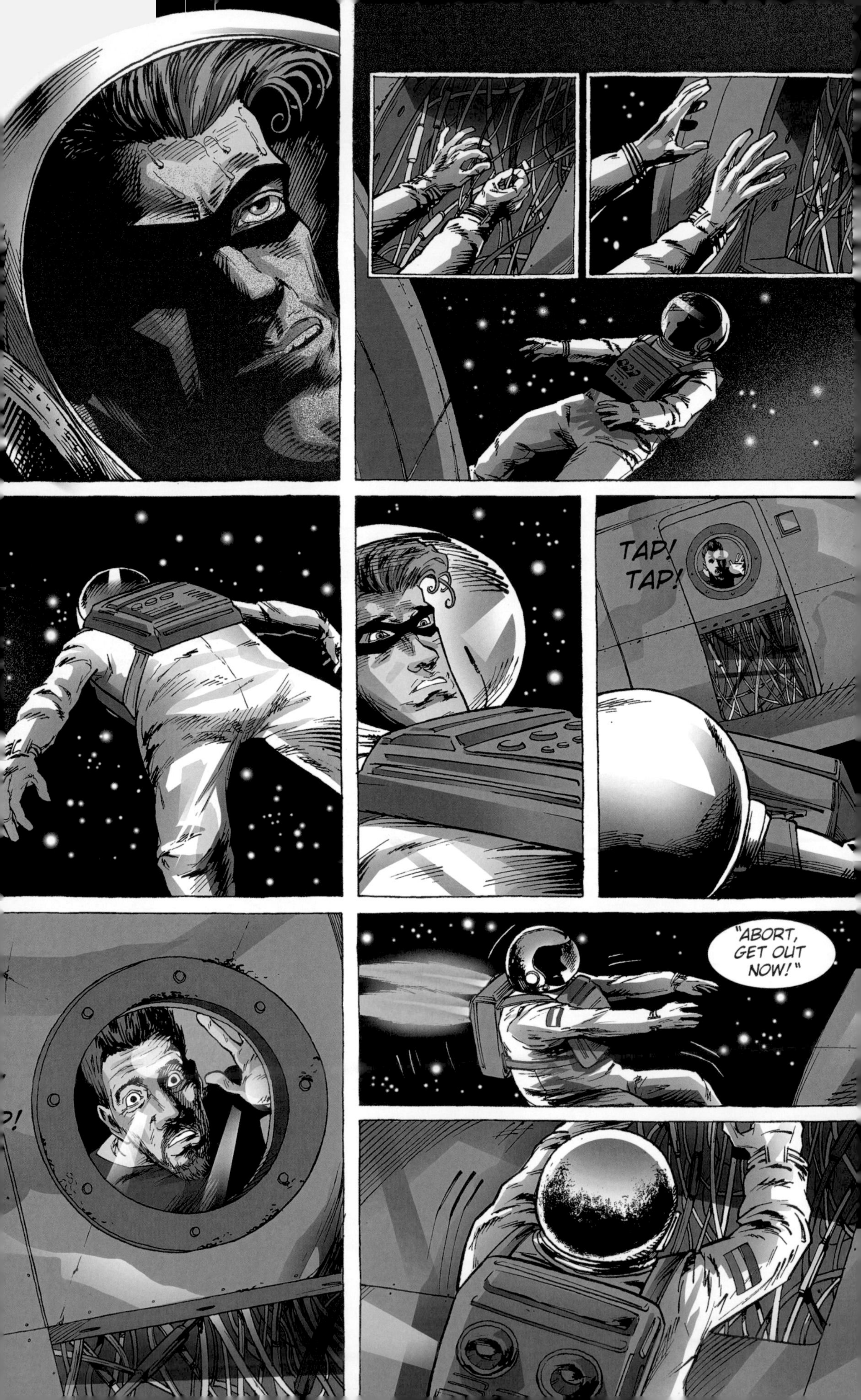
TAP!
TAP!
"ABORT, GET OUT NOW!"

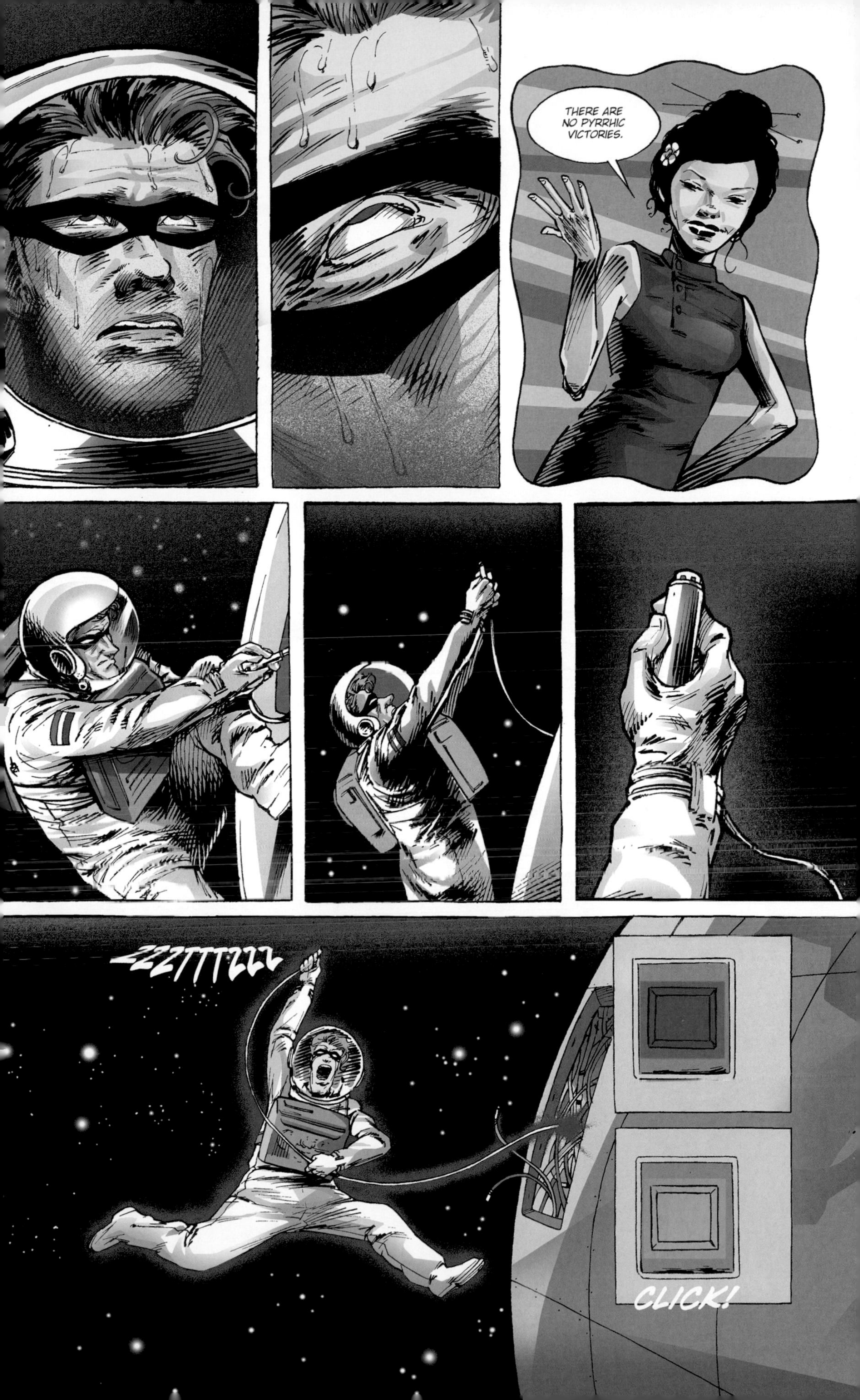
THERE ARE NO PYRRHIC VICTORIES.
ZZZTTTZZZ
CLICK!

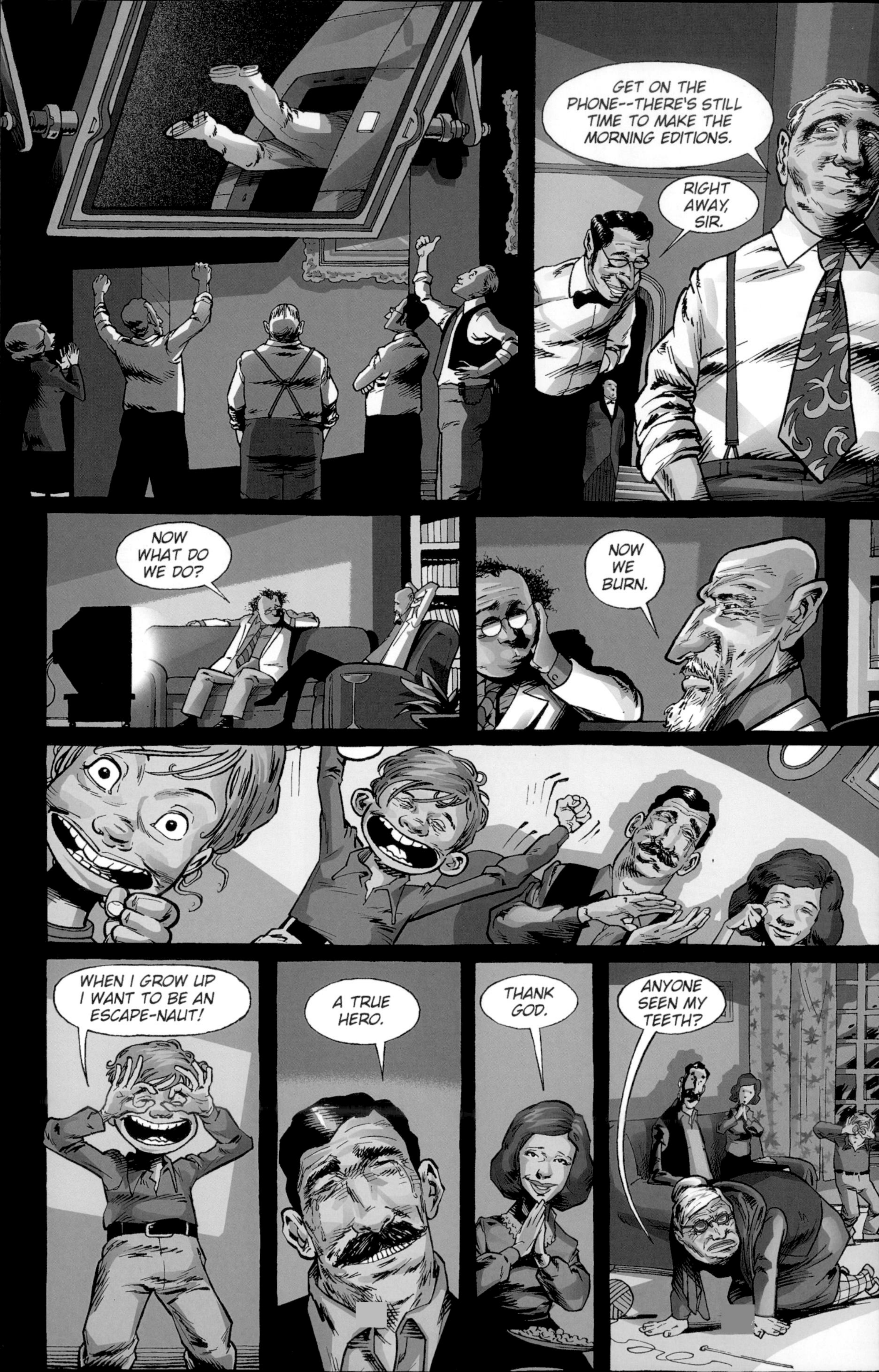
GET ON THE PHONE--THERE'S STILL TIME TO MAKE THE MORNING EDITIONS.
RIGHT AWAY, SIR.
NOW WHAT DO WE DO?
NOW WE BURN.
WHEN I GROW UP I WANT TO BE AN ESCAPE-NAUT!
A TRUE HERO.
THANK GOD.
ANYONE SEEN MY TEETH?

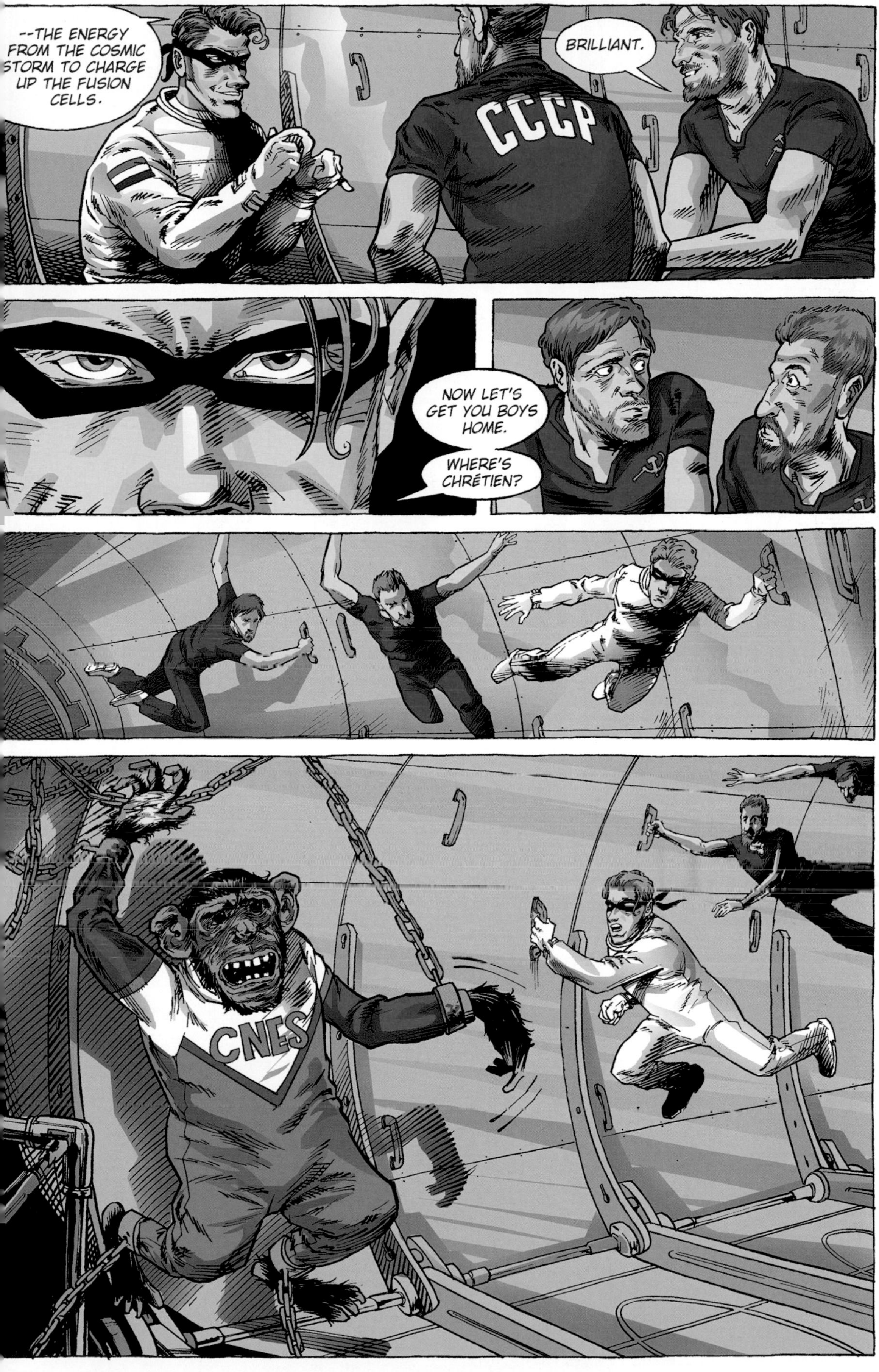
--THE ENERGY FROM THE COSMIC STORM TO CHARGE UP THE FUSION CELLS.
BRILLIANT.
CCCP
NOW LET'S GET YOU BOYS HOME.
WHERE'S CHRÉTIEN?
CNES

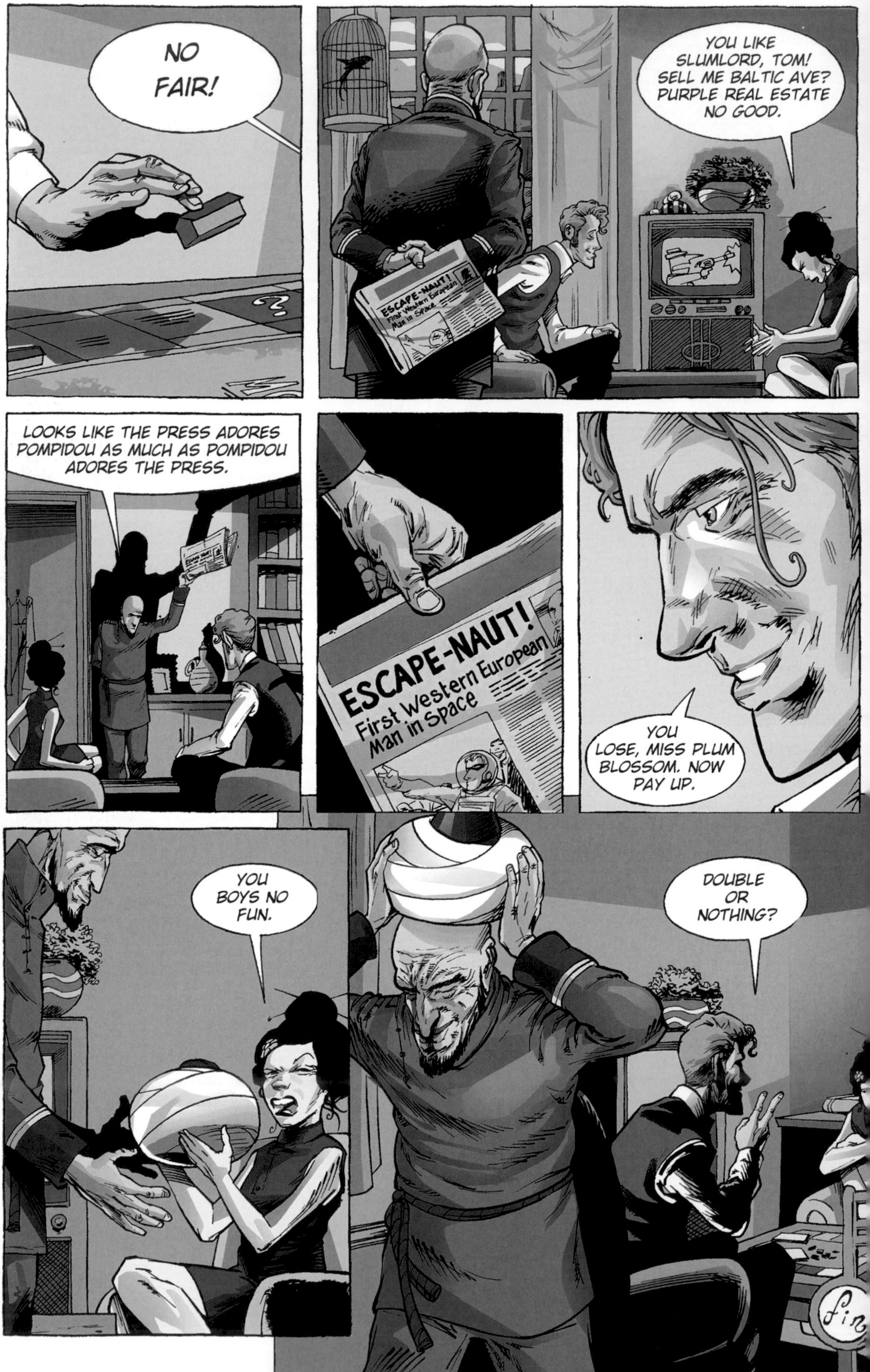
NO FAIR!
YOU LIKE SLUMLORD, TOM! SELL ME BALTIC AVE? PURPLE REAL ESTATE NO GOOD.
ESCAPE-NAUT! First Western European Man in Space
LOOKS LIKE THE PRESS ADORES POMPIDOU AS MUCH AS POMPIDOU ADORES THE PRESS.
ESCAPE-NAUT!
ESCAPE-NAUT! First Western European Man in Space
YOU LOSE, MISS PLUM BLOSSOM. NOW PAY UP.
YOU BOYS NO FUN.
DOUBLE OR NOTHING?
fin

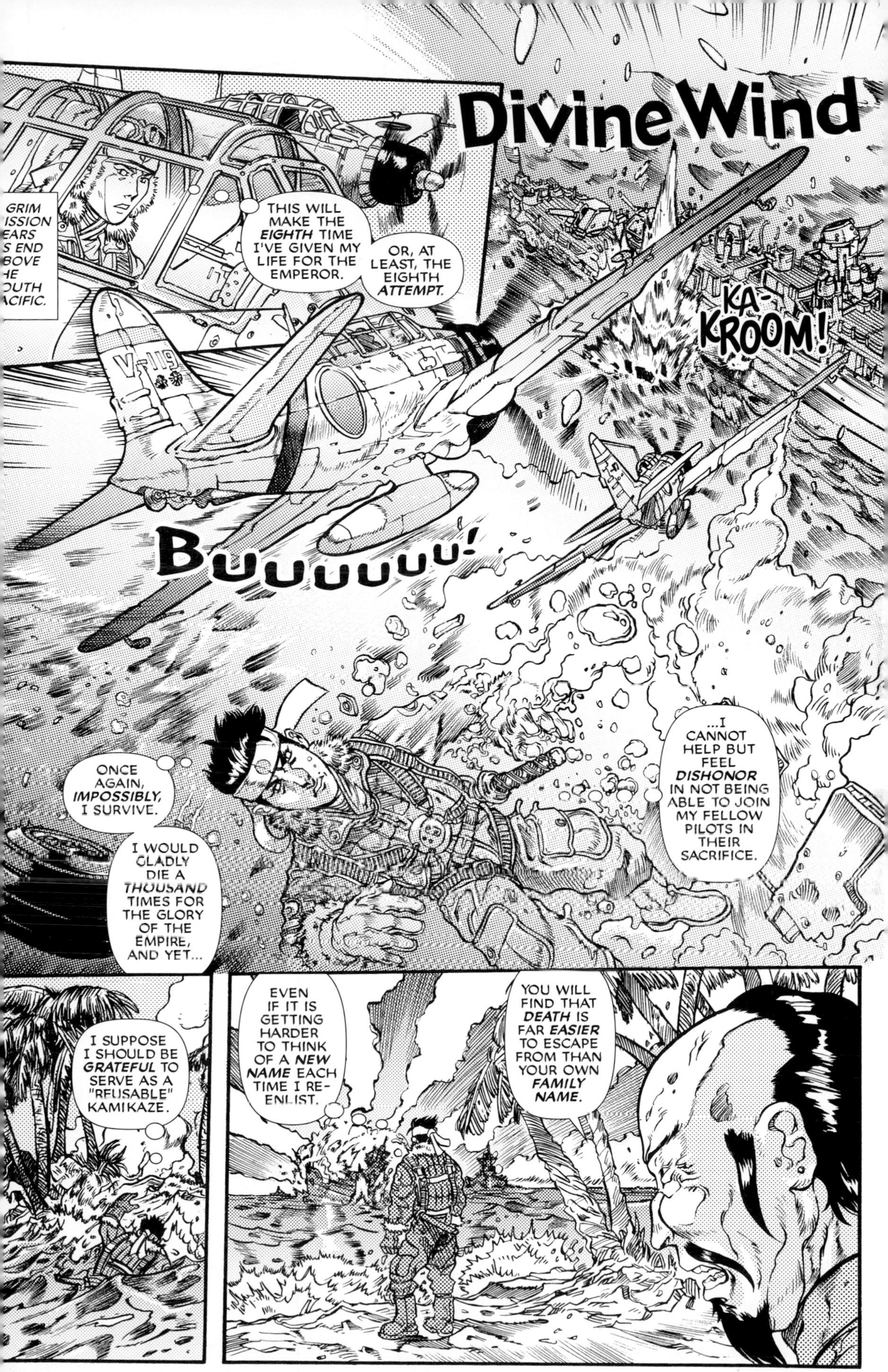
GRIM ISSION EARS S END BOVE HE OUTH ACIFIC.
Divine Wind
THIS WILL MAKE THE *EIGHTH* TIME I'VE GIVEN MY LIFE FOR THE EMPEROR.
OR, AT LEAST, THE EIGHTH *ATTEMPT.*
KA-KROOM!
BUUUUUUU!
ONCE AGAIN, *IMPOSSIBLY,* I SURVIVE.
I WOULD GLADLY DIE A *THOUSAND* TIMES FOR THE GLORY OF THE EMPIRE, AND YET...
...I CANNOT HELP BUT FEEL *DISHONOR* IN NOT BEING ABLE TO JOIN MY FELLOW PILOTS IN THEIR SACRIFICE.
I SUPPOSE I SHOULD BE *GRATEFUL* TO SERVE AS A "REFUSABLE" KAMIKAZE.
EVEN IF IT IS GETTING HARDER TO THINK OF A *NEW NAME* EACH TIME I RE-ENLIST.
YOU WILL FIND THAT *DEATH* IS FAR *EASIER* TO ESCAPE FROM THAN YOUR OWN *FAMILY NAME.*

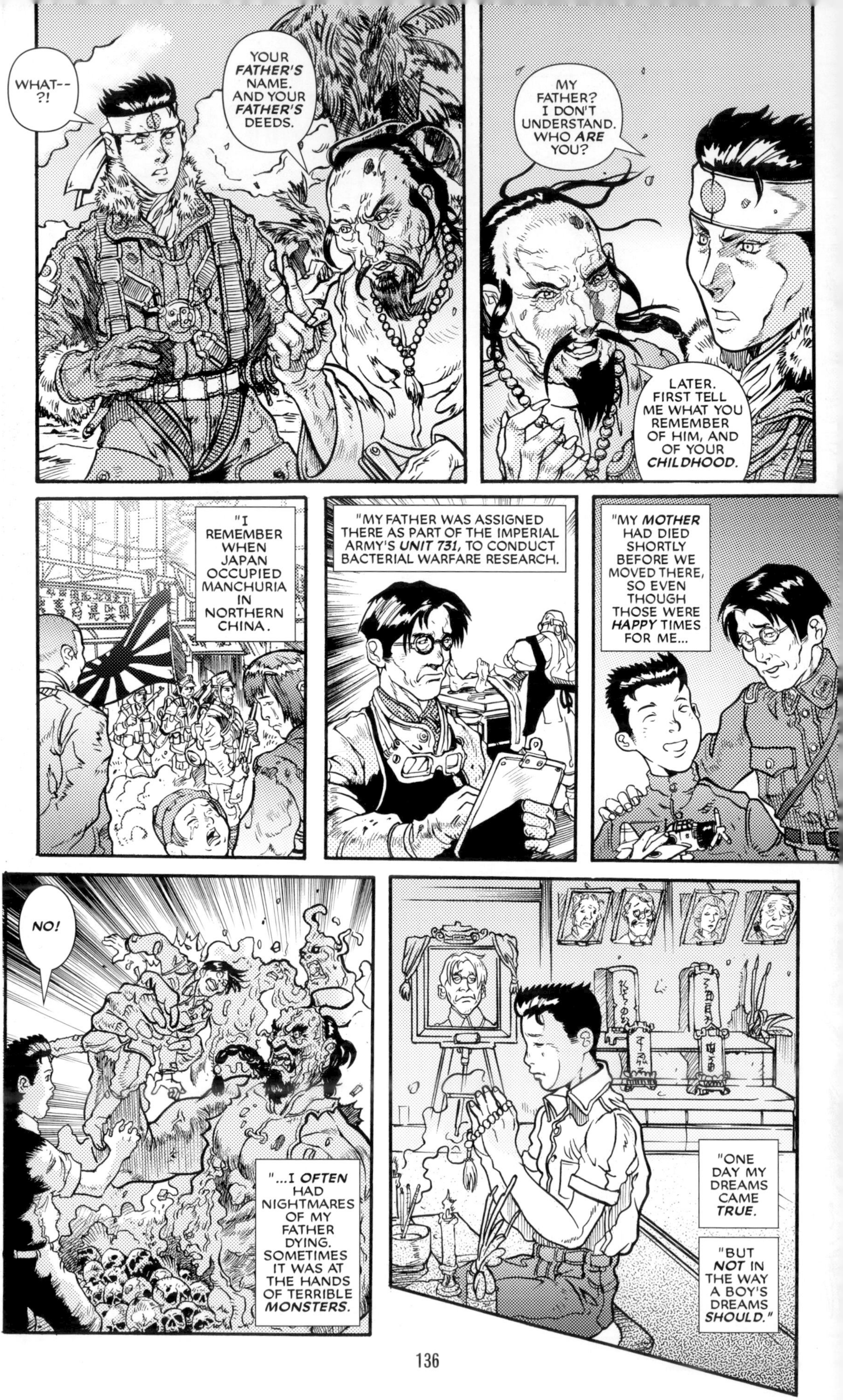
WHAT-- ?!
YOUR FATHER'S NAME. AND YOUR FATHER'S DEEDS.
MY FATHER? I DON'T UNDERSTAND. WHO ARE YOU?
LATER. FIRST TELL ME WHAT YOU REMEMBER OF HIM, AND OF YOUR CHILDHOOD.
"I REMEMBER WHEN JAPAN OCCUPIED MANCHURIA IN NORTHERN CHINA.
"MY FATHER WAS ASSIGNED THERE AS PART OF THE IMPERIAL ARMY'S UNIT 731, TO CONDUCT BACTERIAL WARFARE RESEARCH.
"MY MOTHER HAD DIED SHORTLY BEFORE WE MOVED THERE, SO EVEN THOUGH THOSE WERE HAPPY TIMES FOR ME...
NO!
"...I OFTEN HAD NIGHTMARES OF MY FATHER DYING. SOMETIMES IT WAS AT THE HANDS OF TERRIBLE MONSTERS.
"ONE DAY MY DREAMS CAME TRUE.
"BUT NOT IN THE WAY A BOY'S DREAMS SHOULD."

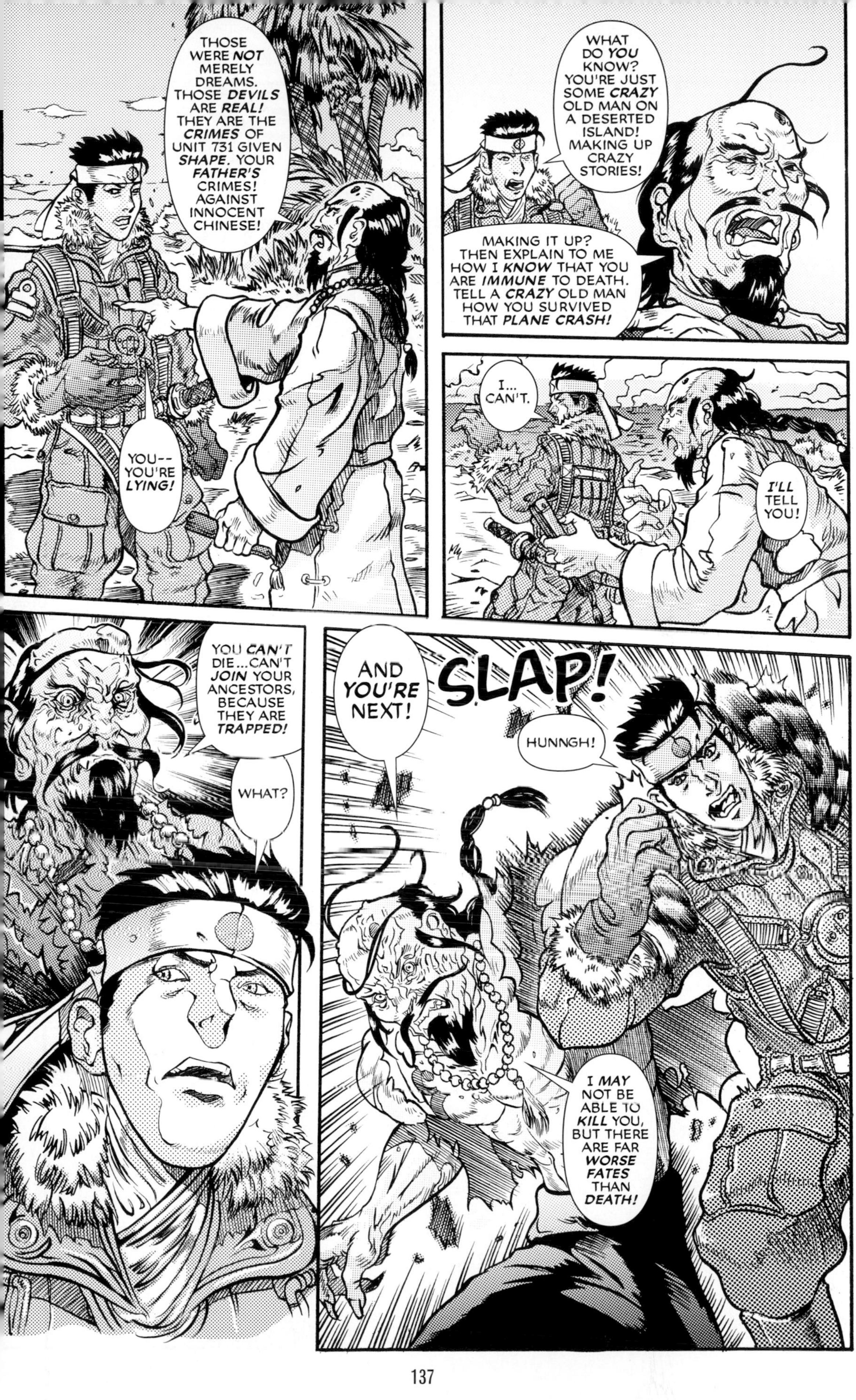
THOSE WERE NOT MERELY DREAMS. THOSE DEVILS ARE REAL! THEY ARE THE CRIMES OF UNIT 731 GIVEN SHAPE. YOUR FATHER'S CRIMES! AGAINST INNOCENT CHINESE!
YOU-- YOU'RE LYING!
WHAT DO YOU KNOW? YOU'RE JUST SOME CRAZY OLD MAN ON A DESERTED ISLAND! MAKING UP CRAZY STORIES!
MAKING IT UP? THEN EXPLAIN TO ME HOW I KNOW THAT YOU ARE IMMUNE TO DEATH. TELL A CRAZY OLD MAN HOW YOU SURVIVED THAT PLANE CRASH!
I... CAN'T.
I'LL TELL YOU!
YOU CAN'T DIE...CAN'T JOIN YOUR ANCESTORS, BECAUSE THEY ARE TRAPPED!
WHAT?
AND YOU'RE NEXT!
SLAP!
HUNNGH!
I MAY NOT BE ABLE TO KILL YOU, BUT THERE ARE FAR WORSE FATES THAN DEATH!

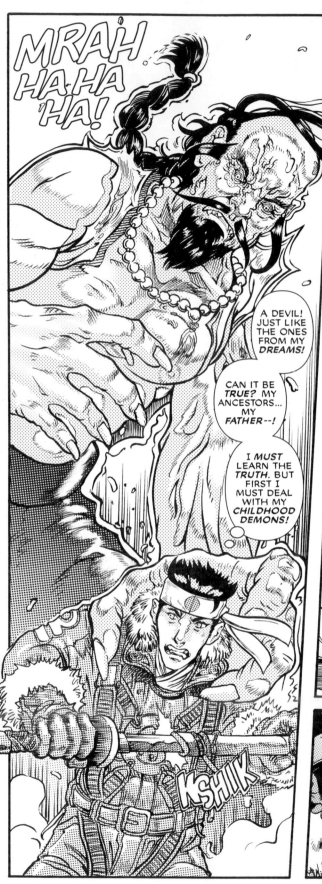

MRAH HA HA HA!

A DEVIL! JUST LIKE THE ONES FROM MY *DREAMS!*

CAN IT BE *TRUE?* MY ANCESTORS... MY *FATHER*--!

I *MUST* LEARN THE *TRUTH.* BUT FIRST I MUST DEAL WITH MY *CHILDHOOD DEMONS!*

KSHIIK

YOU'LL LIVE *FOREVER*... IN MY *BELLY!*

NNNG!

?

WH-CHOK

MUH-- MOTHER?

YES, MY SON. YOU'VE RELEASED MY SPIRIT FROM THIS CREATURE.

BAH!

IT IS UP TO YOU TO DO THE SAME FOR *ALL* OF US.

I WILL. I *SWEAR* IT!

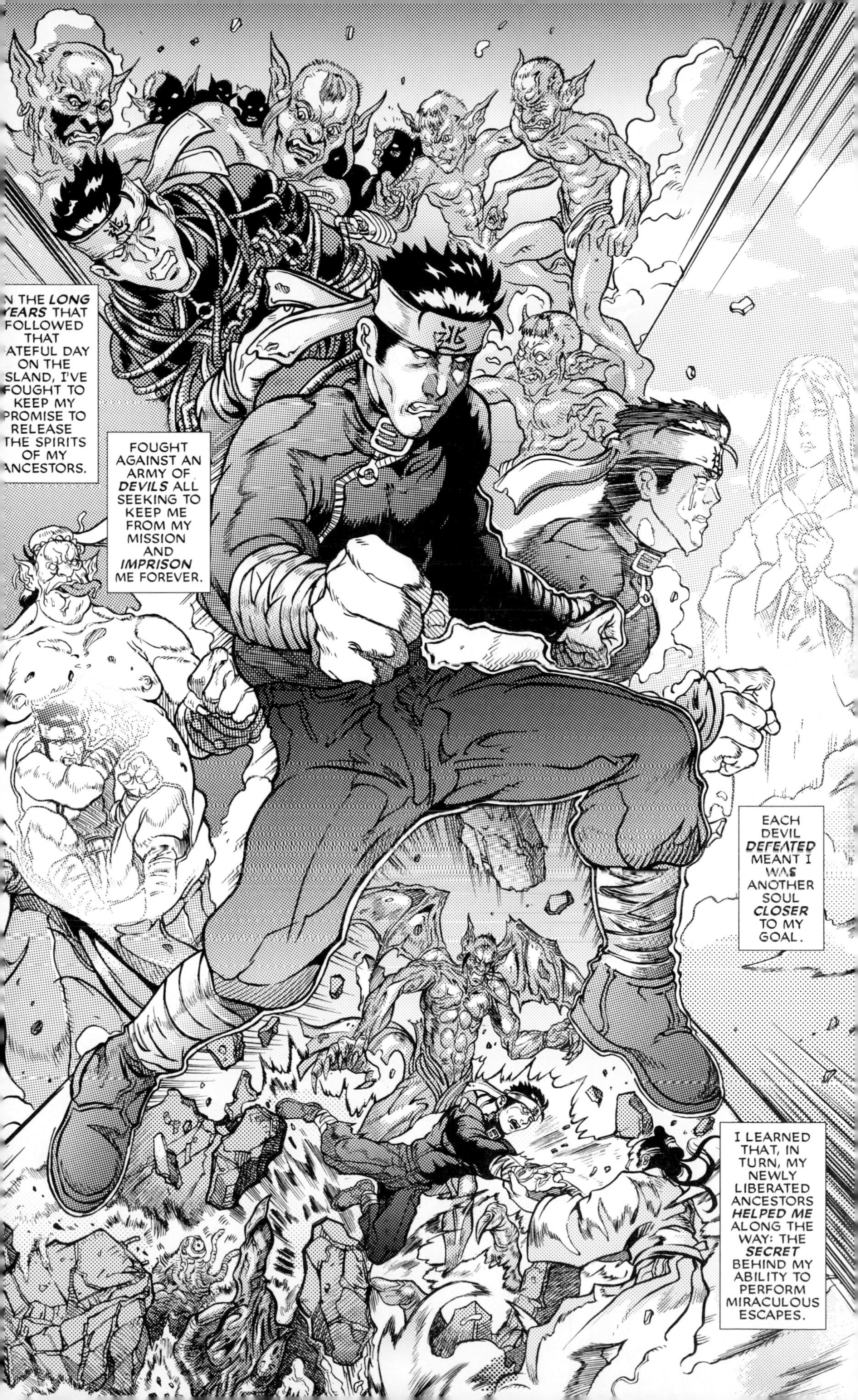
N THE LONG YEARS THAT FOLLOWED THAT FATEFUL DAY ON THE ISLAND, I'VE FOUGHT TO KEEP MY PROMISE TO RELEASE THE SPIRITS OF MY ANCESTORS.
FOUGHT AGAINST AN ARMY OF DEVILS ALL SEEKING TO KEEP ME FROM MY MISSION AND IMPRISON ME FOREVER.
EACH DEVIL DEFEATED MEANT I WAS ANOTHER SOUL CLOSER TO MY GOAL.
I LEARNED THAT, IN TURN, MY NEWLY LIBERATED ANCESTORS HELPED ME ALONG THE WAY: THE SECRET BEHIND MY ABILITY TO PERFORM MIRACULOUS ESCAPES.

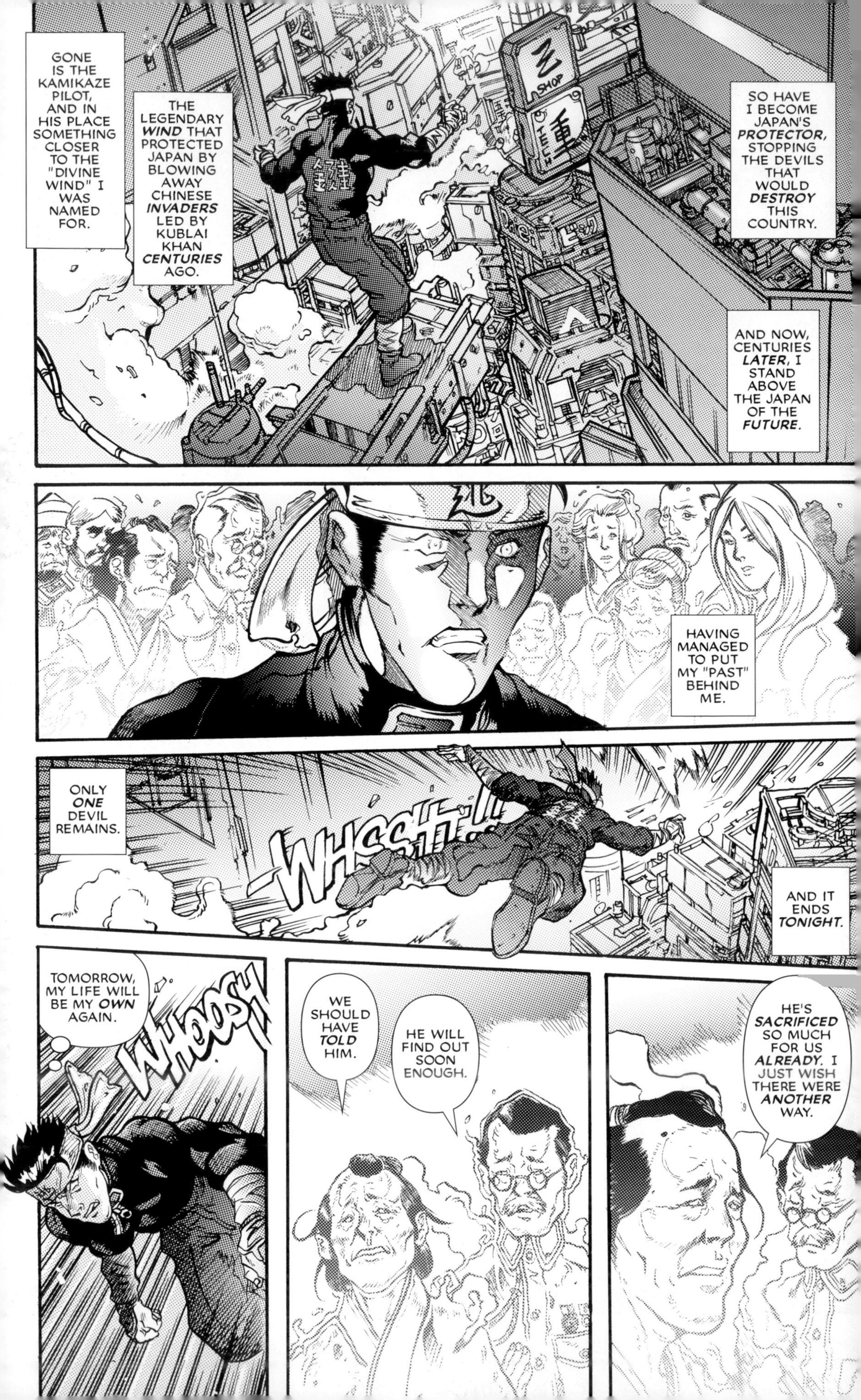

GONE IS THE KAMIKAZE PILOT, AND IN HIS PLACE SOMETHING CLOSER TO THE "DIVINE WIND" I WAS NAMED FOR.
THE LEGENDARY *WIND* THAT PROTECTED JAPAN BY BLOWING AWAY CHINESE *INVADERS* LED BY KUBLAI KHAN *CENTURIES* AGO.
SO HAVE I BECOME JAPAN'S *PROTECTOR*, STOPPING THE DEVILS THAT WOULD *DESTROY* THIS COUNTRY.
AND NOW, CENTURIES *LATER*, I STAND ABOVE THE JAPAN OF THE *FUTURE*.
HAVING MANAGED TO PUT MY "PAST" BEHIND ME.
ONLY *ONE* DEVIL REMAINS.
WHSSH!!
AND IT ENDS *TONIGHT*.
TOMORROW, MY LIFE WILL BE MY *OWN* AGAIN.
WHOOSH
WE SHOULD HAVE *TOLD* HIM.
HE WILL FIND OUT SOON ENOUGH.
HE'S *SACRIFICED* SO MUCH FOR US *ALREADY*. I JUST WISH THERE WERE *ANOTHER* WAY.

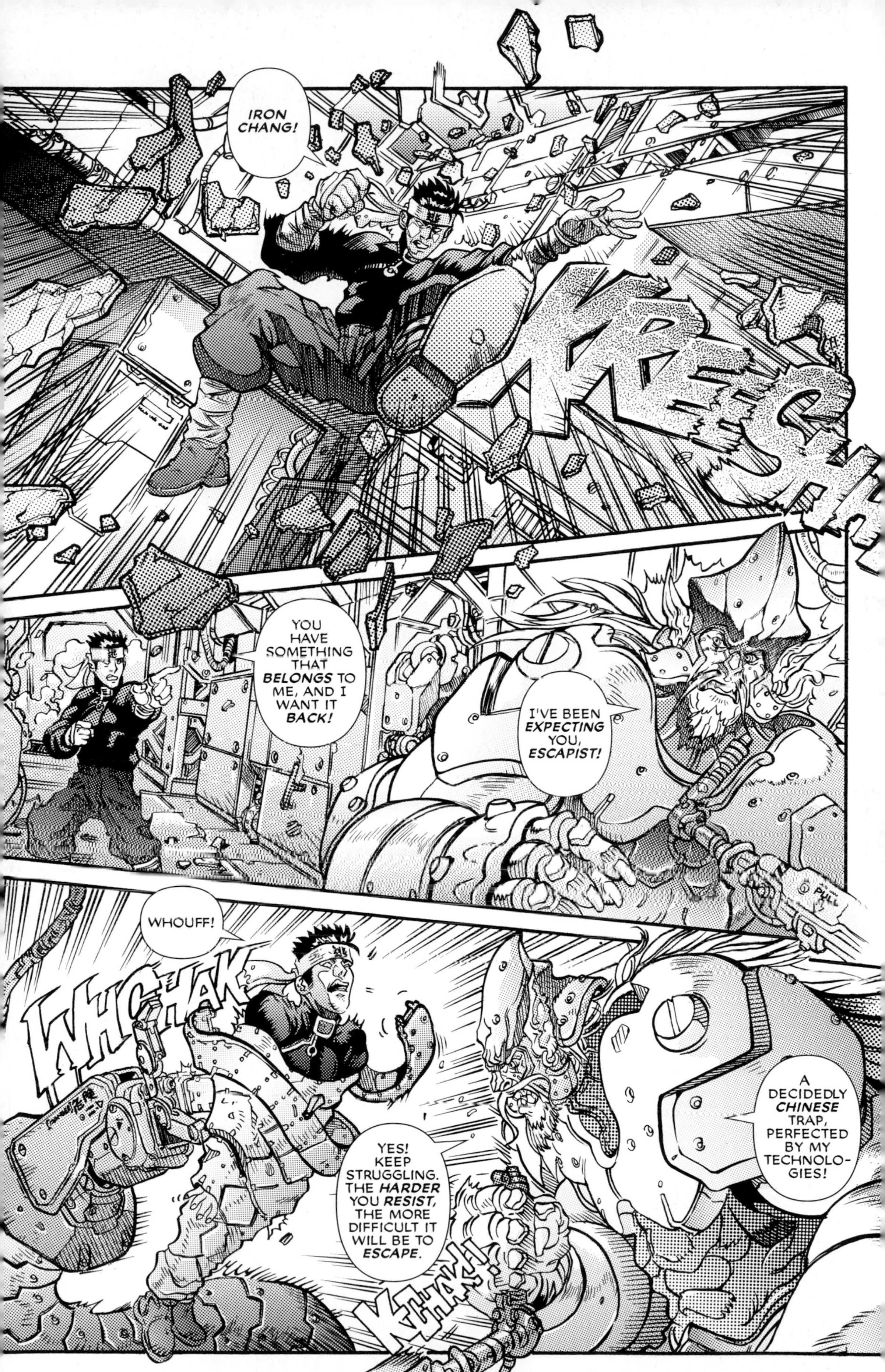
IRON CHANG!
KRESSH
YOU HAVE SOMETHING THAT BELONGS TO ME, AND I WANT IT BACK!
I'VE BEEN EXPECTING YOU, ESCAPIST!
PULL
WHOUFF!
WHCHAK
A DECIDEDLY CHINESE TRAP, PERFECTED BY MY TECHNOLOGIES!
YES! KEEP STRUGGLING. THE HARDER YOU RESIST, THE MORE DIFFICULT IT WILL BE TO ESCAPE.
KCHAK!

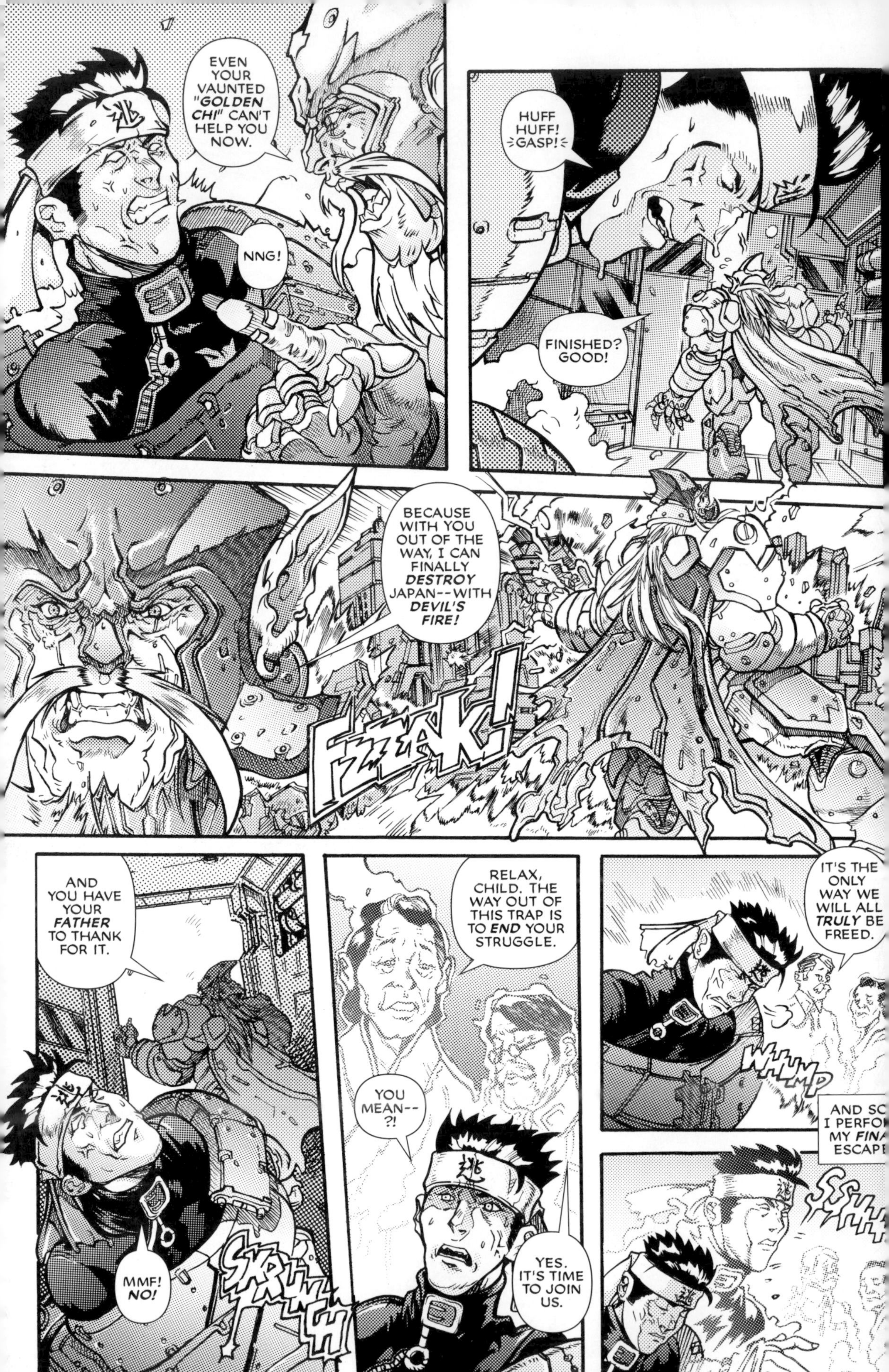
EVEN YOUR VAUNTED "GOLDEN CHI" CAN'T HELP YOU NOW.
NNG!
HUFF HUFF! GASP!
FINISHED? GOOD!
BECAUSE WITH YOU OUT OF THE WAY, I CAN FINALLY DESTROY JAPAN--WITH DEVIL'S FIRE!
FZZAK!
AND YOU HAVE YOUR FATHER TO THANK FOR IT.
MMF! NO!
RELAX, CHILD. THE WAY OUT OF THIS TRAP IS TO END YOUR STRUGGLE.
YOU MEAN-- ?!
YES. IT'S TIME TO JOIN US.
IT'S THE ONLY WAY WE WILL ALL TRULY BE FREED.
WHUMP
AND SO I PERFO MY FINA ESCAPE

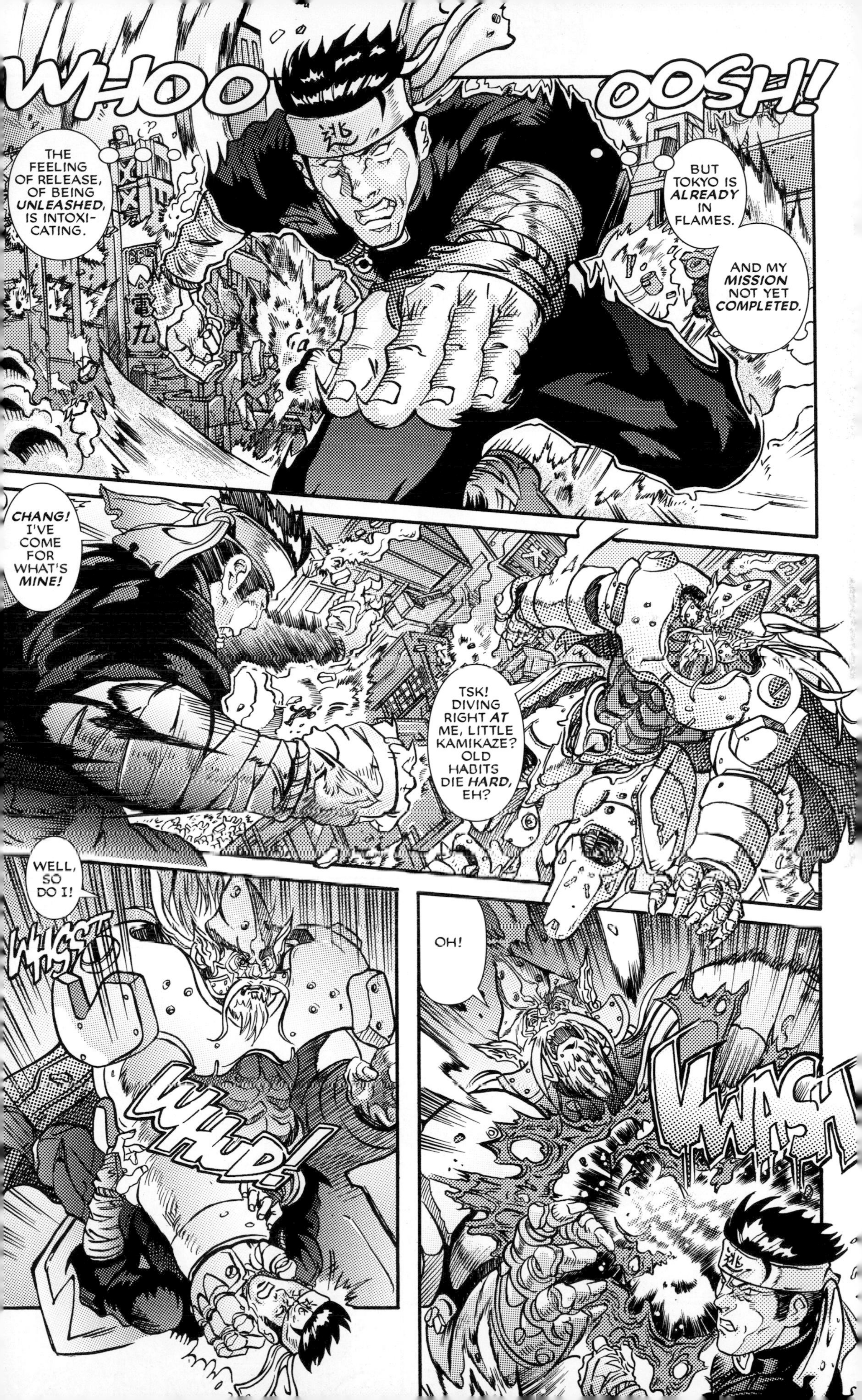

WHOO
OOSH!
THE FEELING OF RELEASE, OF BEING *UNLEASHED,* IS INTOXICATING.
BUT TOKYO IS *ALREADY* IN FLAMES.
AND MY *MISSION* NOT YET *COMPLETED.*
*CHANG!* I'VE COME FOR WHAT'S *MINE!*
TSK! DIVING RIGHT *AT* ME, LITTLE KAMIKAZE? OLD HABITS DIE *HARD,* EH?
WELL, SO DO I!
WHUD!
OH!

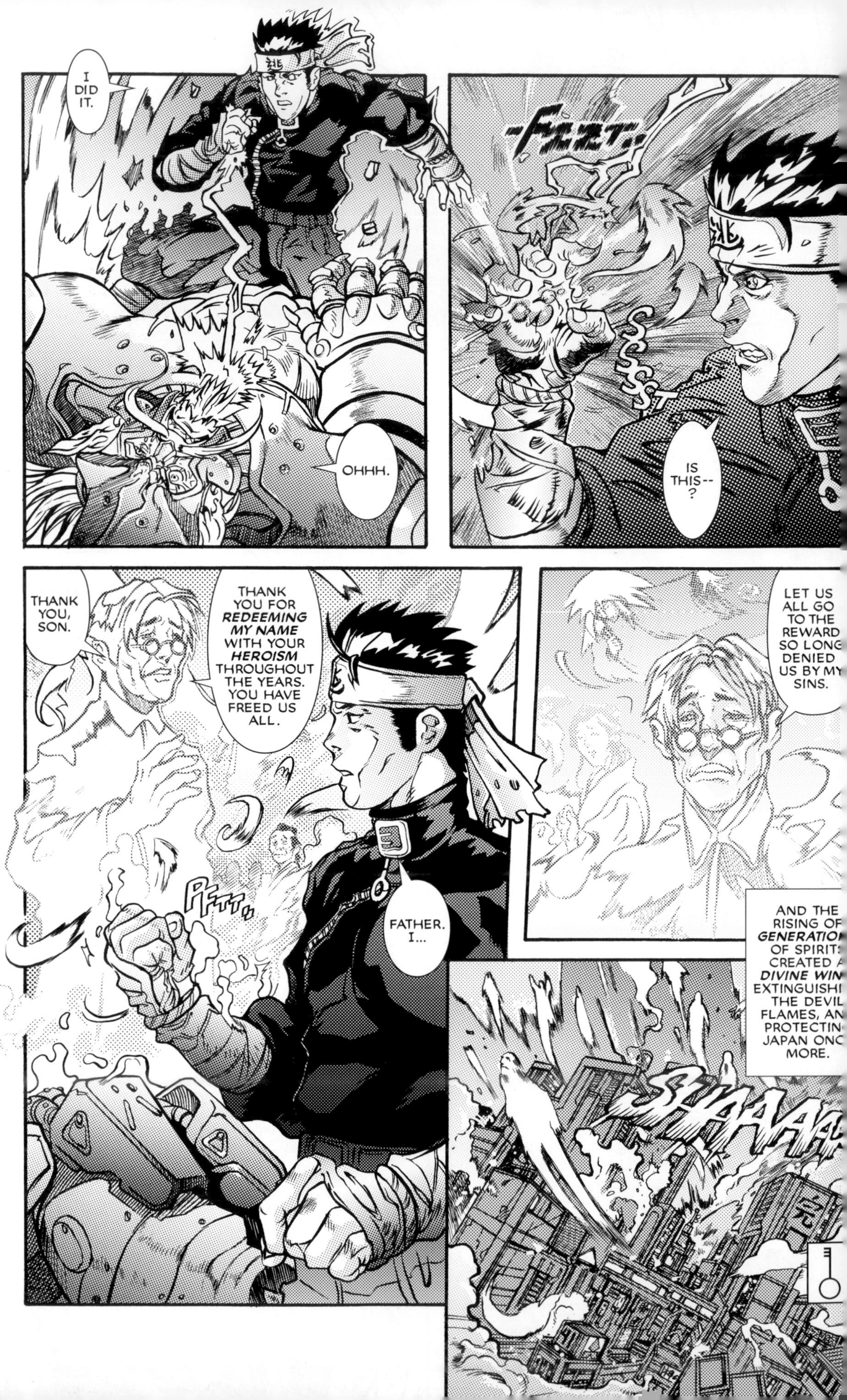
I DID IT.
OHHH.
-FZZT-
IS THIS--?
THANK YOU, SON.
THANK YOU FOR ***REDEEMING MY NAME*** WITH YOUR ***HEROISM*** THROUGHOUT THE YEARS. YOU HAVE FREED US ALL.
FATHER. I...
LET US ALL GO TO THE REWARD SO LONG DENIED US BY MY SINS.
AND THE RISING OF ***GENERATIO*** OF SPIRITS CREATED A ***DIVINE WIN*** EXTINGUISHI THE DEVIL FLAMES, AN PROTECTIN JAPAN ONC MORE.

# "DIVINE WIND"

*Post Script*

## BY KEVIN McCARTHY

THE DESIRE TO EXPLOIT THE INCREASING POPULARITY OF JAPANESE COMIC BOOKS —or manga—in the U.S. led to the rediscovery, some twenty years later, of one of the better-kept secrets in the long and checkered history of Kavalier & Clay's Escapist.

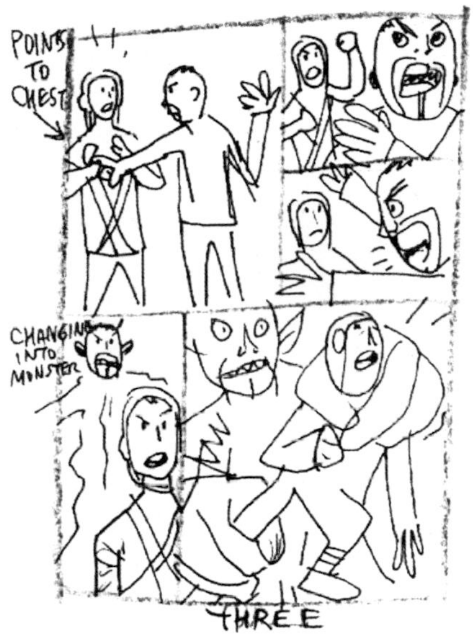
POINTS TO CHEST
CHANGING INTO MONSTER
THREE

An original manga Escapist layout page, with English-language notes, lends some credence to the supposition that Sam Clay wrote these stories for the Japanese market. *From the McCarthy collection.*

In 1983, the Omnigrip Corporation had licensed to Kodansha, on a one-year trial basis, the rights to publish original *Escapist* material in Japan, where the renowned master manga artist known only as "Tonikoro" produced an astounding twenty pages of artwork per week, depicting all-new and decidedly different adventures of a Japanese Escapist for Kodansha's *Shukan Shonen Magazine* (Weekly Boys' Magazine).

The writer—or writers—for the 1000-plus pages was never credited, but one persistent rumor has it that it was none other than Sammy Clay himself who penned (with the aid of a translator) the adventures of a young kamikaze pilot who became "The God of Escapes," thereby giving Japan one of its most controversial *manga* of all time.

Supporting the Clay-as-author rumor is the inclusion of "politically sensitive" material such as an anti-imperialist subtext and at least one direct reference to a shameful event in Japan's history—the biological warfare research conducted by the Japanese Army in Manchuria in the 1930s and 1940s—as evidenced in the preceding story. Some experts submit than only a "barbarian" like Clay would even have *considered* the use of such touchy subject matter.

It is felt that this controversy is what kept the Escapist manga from selling as well as it could have . . . but the limited scope of the Omnigrip license (which prohibited the production of toys or animation) is what really prevented the Escapist serial from becoming the "break-out" success it should have been. Kodansha's *Escapist* license expired in 1984 and was not renewed. Two years later, when Katsuhiro Otomo's *Akira* exploded on the scene, Otomo would cite Tonikoro's version of the Escapist as an influence.

Truly, it is the draftsmanship of Tonikoro that makes the *manga* Escapist—and the encapsulation of that epic story reprinted herein—such a treasure. Among other things, the artist was especially notorious for his attention to detail (witness the inverted Escapist key logo created by the zipper and collar of the hero's costume).

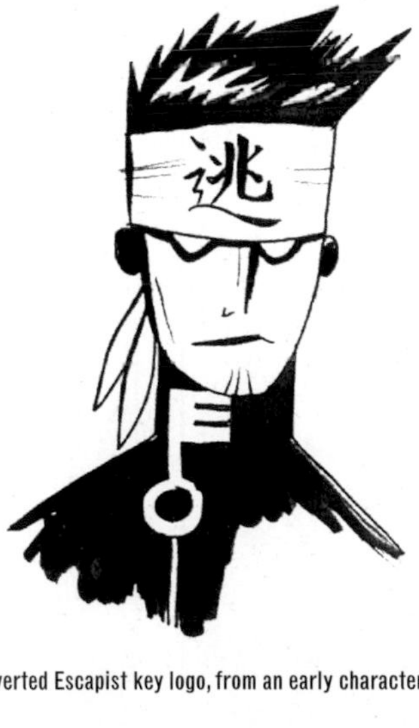
逃

Tonikoro's inverted Escapist key logo, from an early character design sheet.

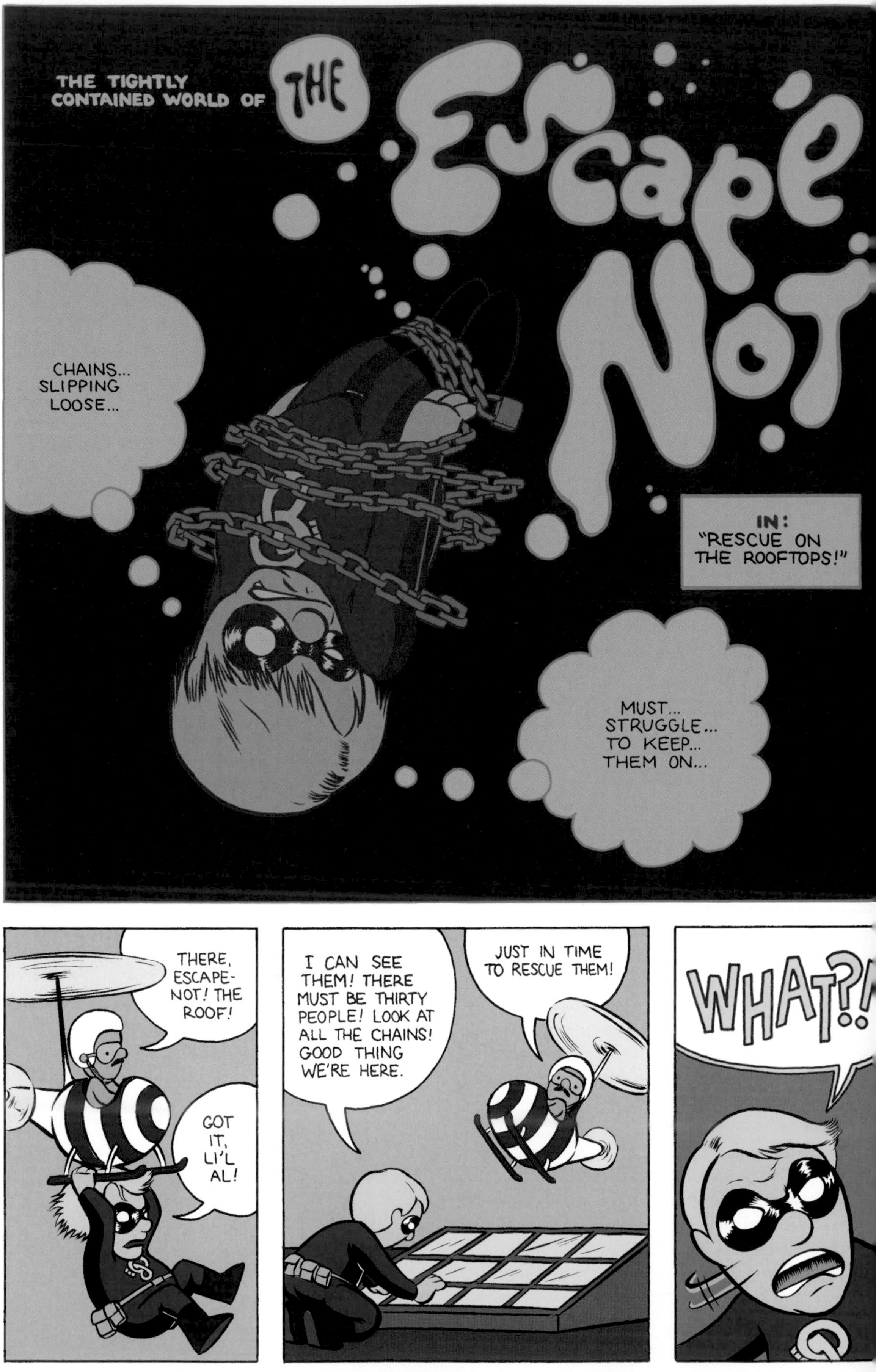
THE TIGHTLY CONTAINED WORLD OF THE Escape Not
CHAINS... SLIPPING LOOSE...
IN: "RESCUE ON THE ROOFTOPS!"
MUST... STRUGGLE... TO KEEP... THEM ON...
THERE, ESCAPE-NOT! THE ROOF!
GOT IT, LI'L AL!
I CAN SEE THEM! THERE MUST BE THIRTY PEOPLE! LOOK AT ALL THE CHAINS! GOOD THING WE'RE HERE.
JUST IN TIME TO RESCUE THEM!
WHAT?!

"I WAS HAVING RAMO COVER ME IN ONE OF MY FAMOUS LEAD-AND-POTATO SALADS...

"... WHEN YOU RUSHED IN, SCREAMING ABOUT SOME PEOPLE WANTING TO TRAP ME.

MY LEGS HAVE LOST ALL FEELING! COOL! LET'S CONCENTRATE ON THE HEAD NOW.

"I'LL ADMIT, I WAS INTRIGUED."

I'LL ADMIT, I AM INTRIGUED.

SO WE JUMPED ON THE... UHH... THE FLITTY THING.

THE ESCOPTER.

RIGHT. WHATEVER.

POINT IS: I CAME OUT HERE BECAUSE "MORE THAN A DOZEN PEOPLE NEED TO TRAP THE ESCAPENOT."

" ARE TRAPPED AND NEED THE ESCAPENOT'S **HELP!**" YOU HAD LEAD AND POTATO IN YOUR EARS!

THAT DOESN'T CHANGE THE FACT THAT **I** NEED TO BE TRAPPED, AND **THEY'RE** HOGGING ALL THE CHAINS!

COME TO YOUR **SENSES**, MAN! EVEN THE HUMAN CAVEFISH WOULD HELP THESE PEOPLE, AND **HE'S** LEGALLY BLIND!

**SO?** HE AND I DISAGREE ABOUT... WELL, ABOUT A LOT OF THINGS!

"I MEAN, HAVE YOU **SEEN** HIS COSTUME?"

Yeesh!

**ESCAPENOT!** THIS **ISN'T** A DEBATE! WE **HAVE** TO HELP THESE PEOPLE!

WAIT A MINUTE...

DID YOU EVEN ASK THESE PEOPLE IF THEY **WANT** TO BE FREE?

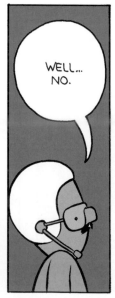

WELL... NO.

AND WHO'S TO SAY, EVEN IF YOU DID ASK, THAT THEY'D BE HONEST WITH YOU, OR THEMSELVES?

I'M OUTTA HER

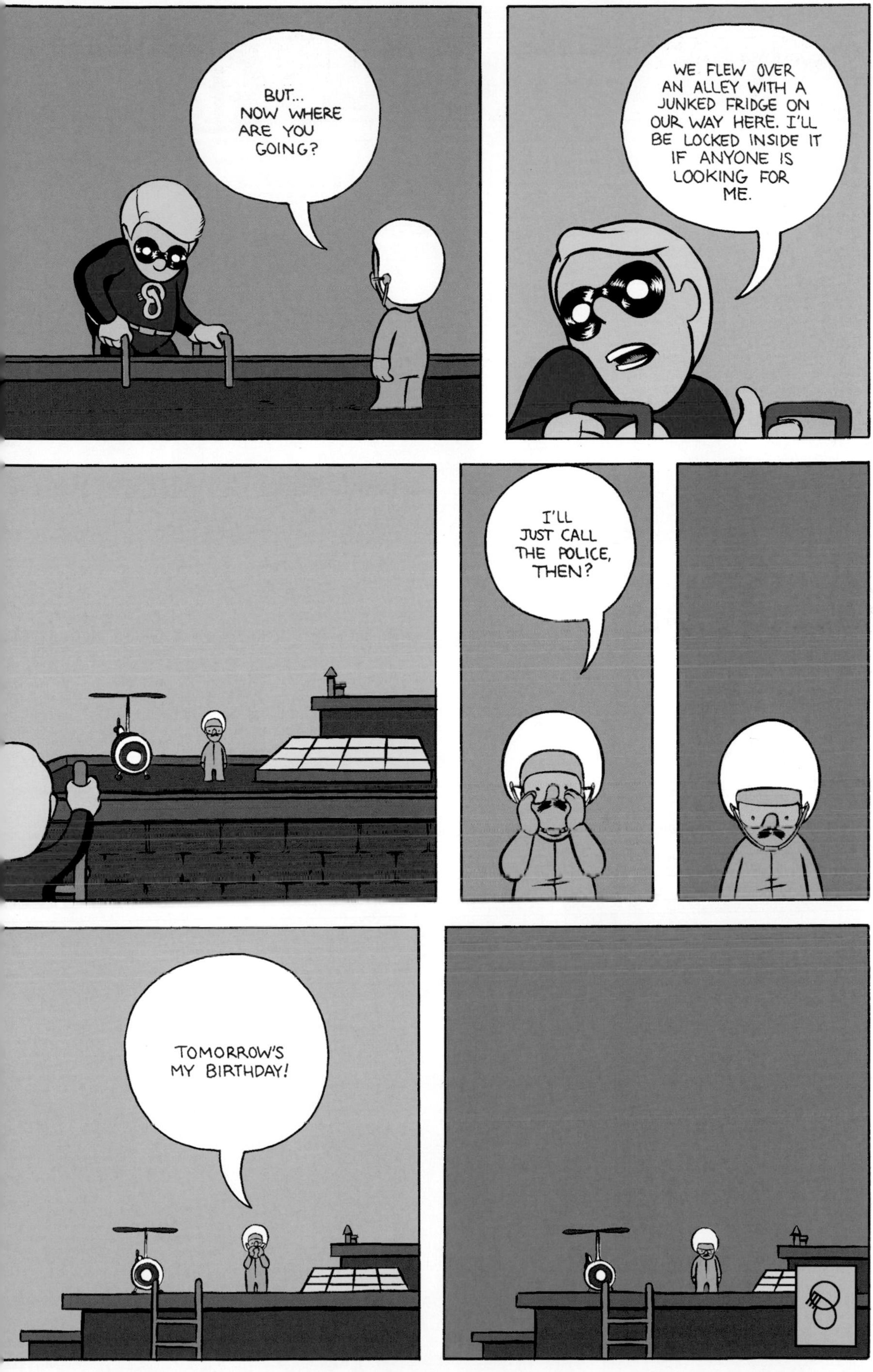
BUT... NOW WHERE ARE YOU GOING?
WE FLEW OVER AN ALLEY WITH A JUNKED FRIDGE ON OUR WAY HERE. I'LL BE LOCKED INSIDE IT IF ANYONE IS LOOKING FOR ME.
I'LL JUST CALL THE POLICE, THEN?
TOMORROW'S MY BIRTHDAY!

# The ESCAPIST in THE TRAP

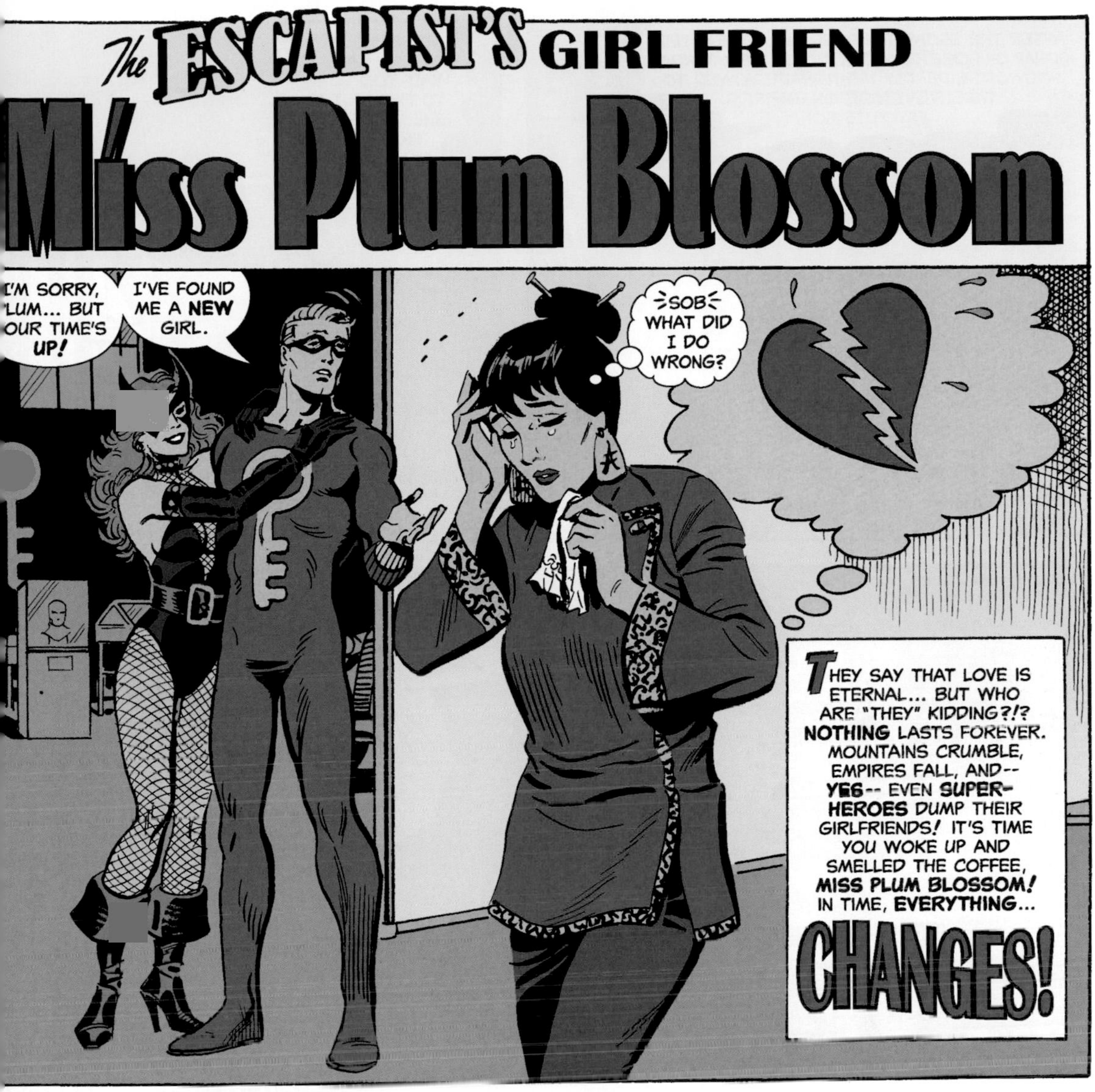
The ESCAPIST'S GIRL FRIEND
Miss Plum Blossom
I'M SORRY, LUM... BUT OUR TIME'S UP!
I'VE FOUND ME A NEW GIRL.
SOB WHAT DID I DO WRONG?
THEY SAY THAT LOVE IS ETERNAL... BUT WHO ARE "THEY" KIDDING?!? NOTHING LASTS FOREVER. MOUNTAINS CRUMBLE, EMPIRES FALL, AND-- YES-- EVEN SUPER-HEROES DUMP THEIR GIRLFRIENDS! IT'S TIME YOU WOKE UP AND SMELLED THE COFFEE, MISS PLUM BLOSSOM! IN TIME, EVERYTHING...
CHANGES!

CRIPT: JUMPIN' AMES PEATY — ART: ELEGANT EDUARDO BARRETO — LETTERING: TITANIC TOM ORZECHOWSKI — COLORING: LUCKY LOVERN KINDZIERSKI — EDITS: DIZZY DIANA SCHUTZ

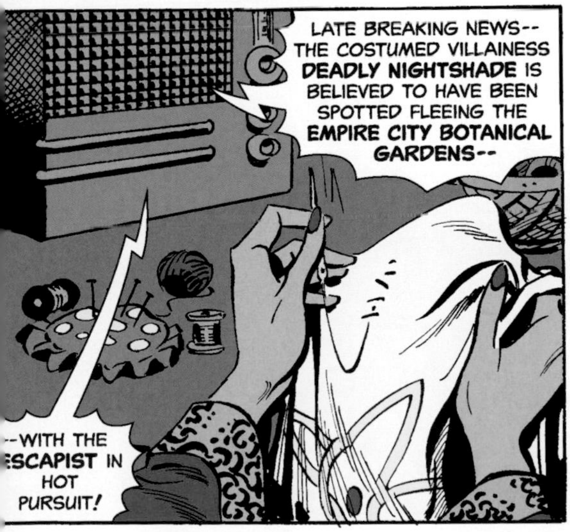
LATE BREAKING NEWS-- THE COSTUMED VILLAINESS DEADLY NIGHTSHADE IS BELIEVED TO HAVE BEEN SPOTTED FLEEING THE EMPIRE CITY BOTANICAL GARDENS--
--WITH THE ESCAPIST IN HOT PURSUIT!

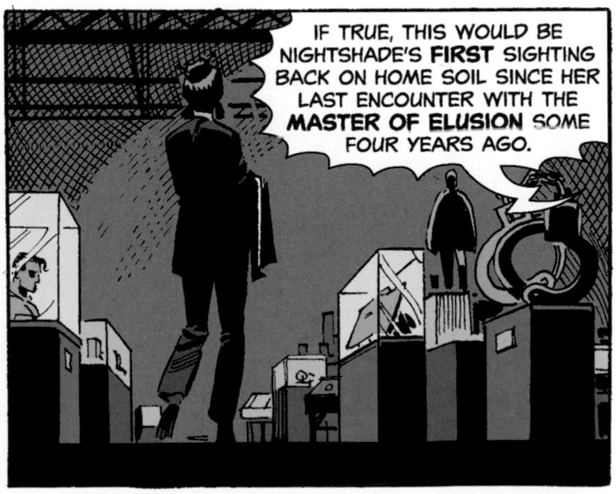
IF TRUE, THIS WOULD BE NIGHTSHADE'S FIRST SIGHTING BACK ON HOME SOIL SINCE HER LAST ENCOUNTER WITH THE MASTER OF ELUSION SOME FOUR YEARS AGO.

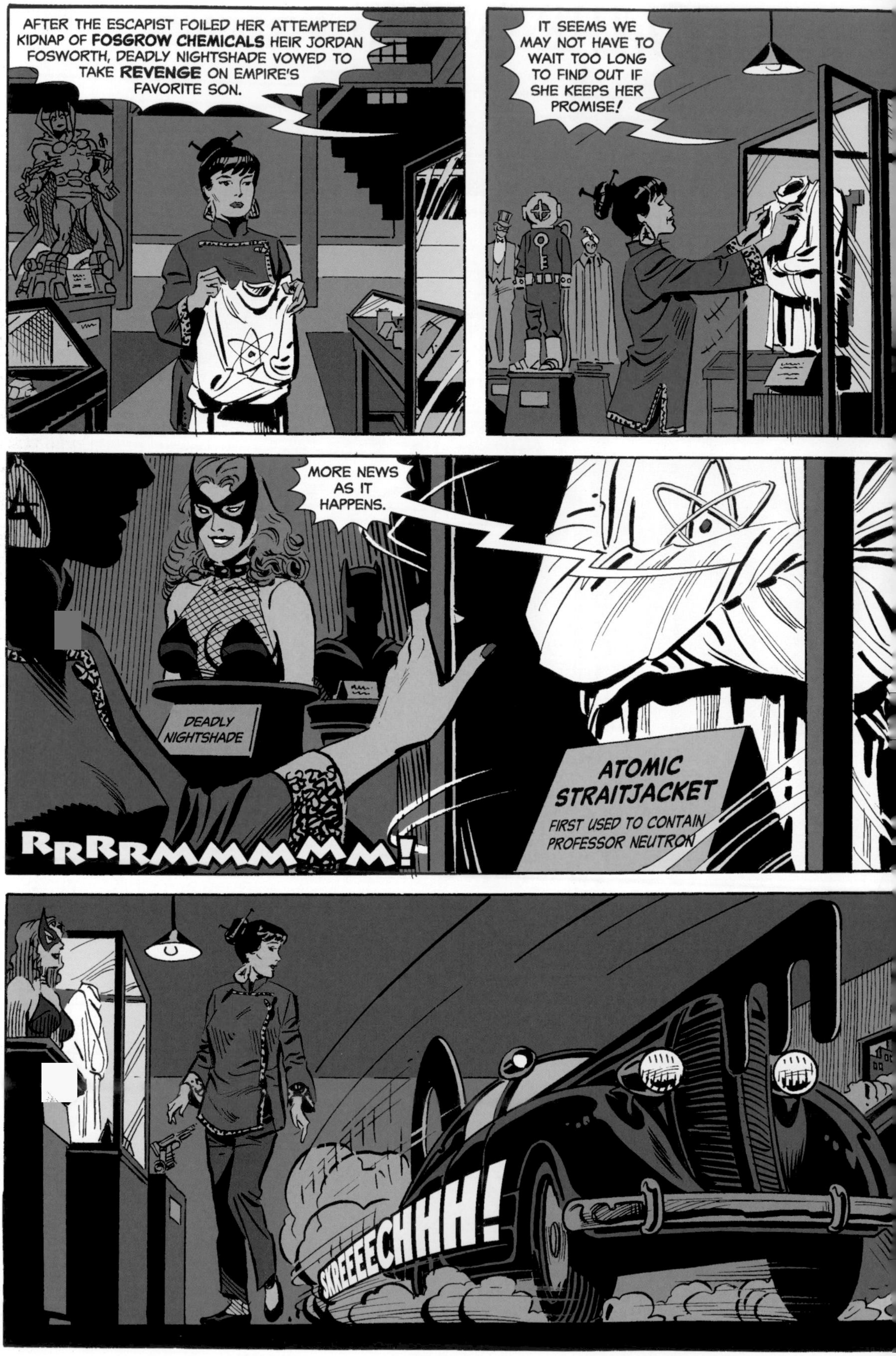
AFTER THE ESCAPIST FOILED HER ATTEMPTED KIDNAP OF **FOSGROW CHEMICALS** HEIR JORDAN FOSWORTH, DEADLY NIGHTSHADE VOWED TO TAKE **REVENGE** ON EMPIRE'S FAVORITE SON.
IT SEEMS WE MAY NOT HAVE TO WAIT TOO LONG TO FIND OUT IF SHE KEEPS HER PROMISE!
MORE NEWS AS IT HAPPENS.
DEADLY NIGHTSHADE
ATOMIC STRAITJACKET
FIRST USED TO CONTAIN PROFESSOR NEUTRON
RRRRMMMMMM!
SKREEEECHHH!

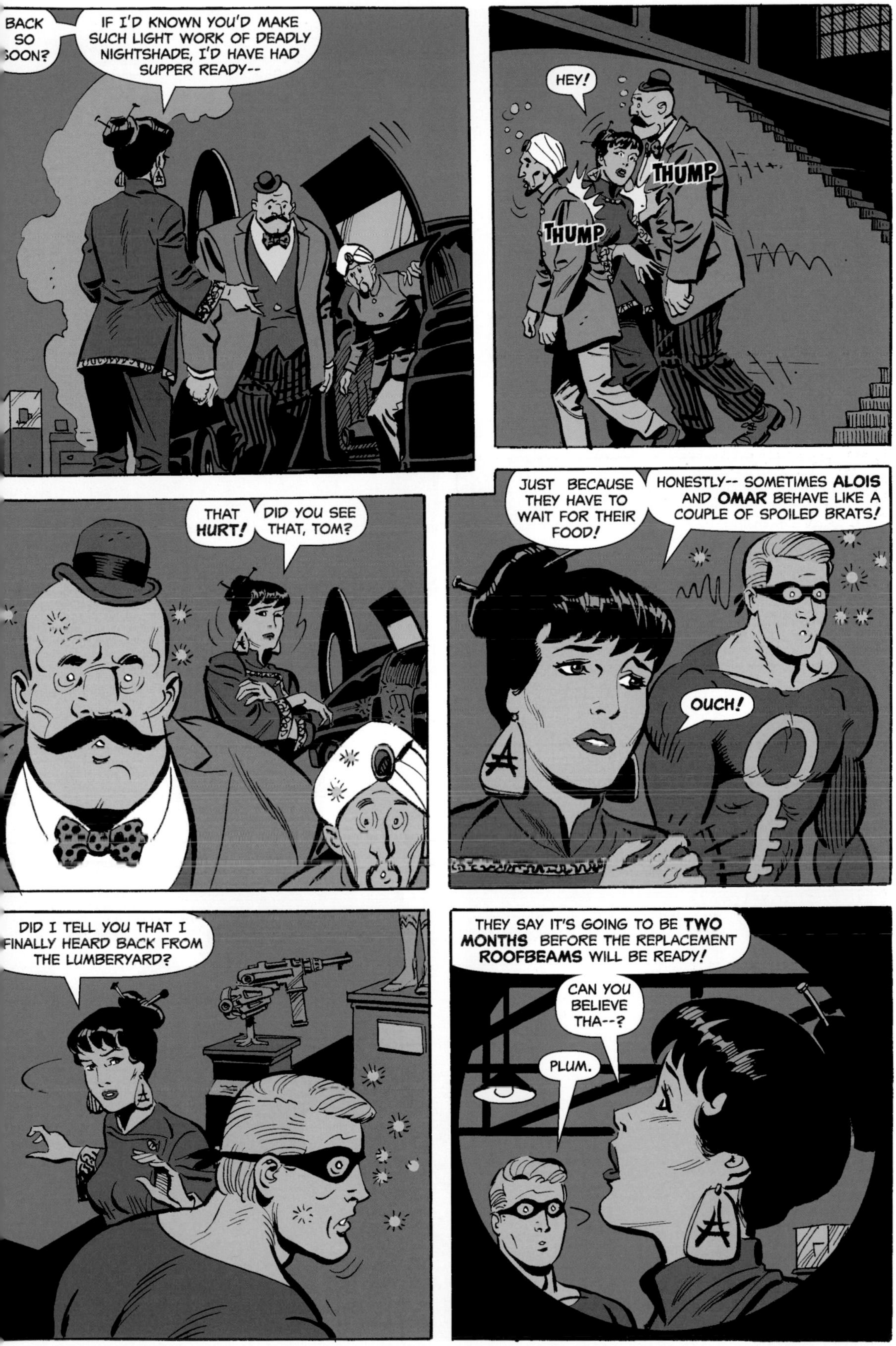

BACK SO SOON?
IF I'D KNOWN YOU'D MAKE SUCH LIGHT WORK OF DEADLY NIGHTSHADE, I'D HAVE HAD SUPPER READY--
HEY!
THUMP
THUMP
THAT HURT!
DID YOU SEE THAT, TOM?
JUST BECAUSE THEY HAVE TO WAIT FOR THEIR FOOD!
HONESTLY-- SOMETIMES ALOIS AND OMAR BEHAVE LIKE A COUPLE OF SPOILED BRATS!
OUCH!
DID I TELL YOU THAT I FINALLY HEARD BACK FROM THE LUMBERYARD?
THEY SAY IT'S GOING TO BE TWO MONTHS BEFORE THE REPLACEMENT ROOFBEAMS WILL BE READY!
CAN YOU BELIEVE THA--?
PLUM.

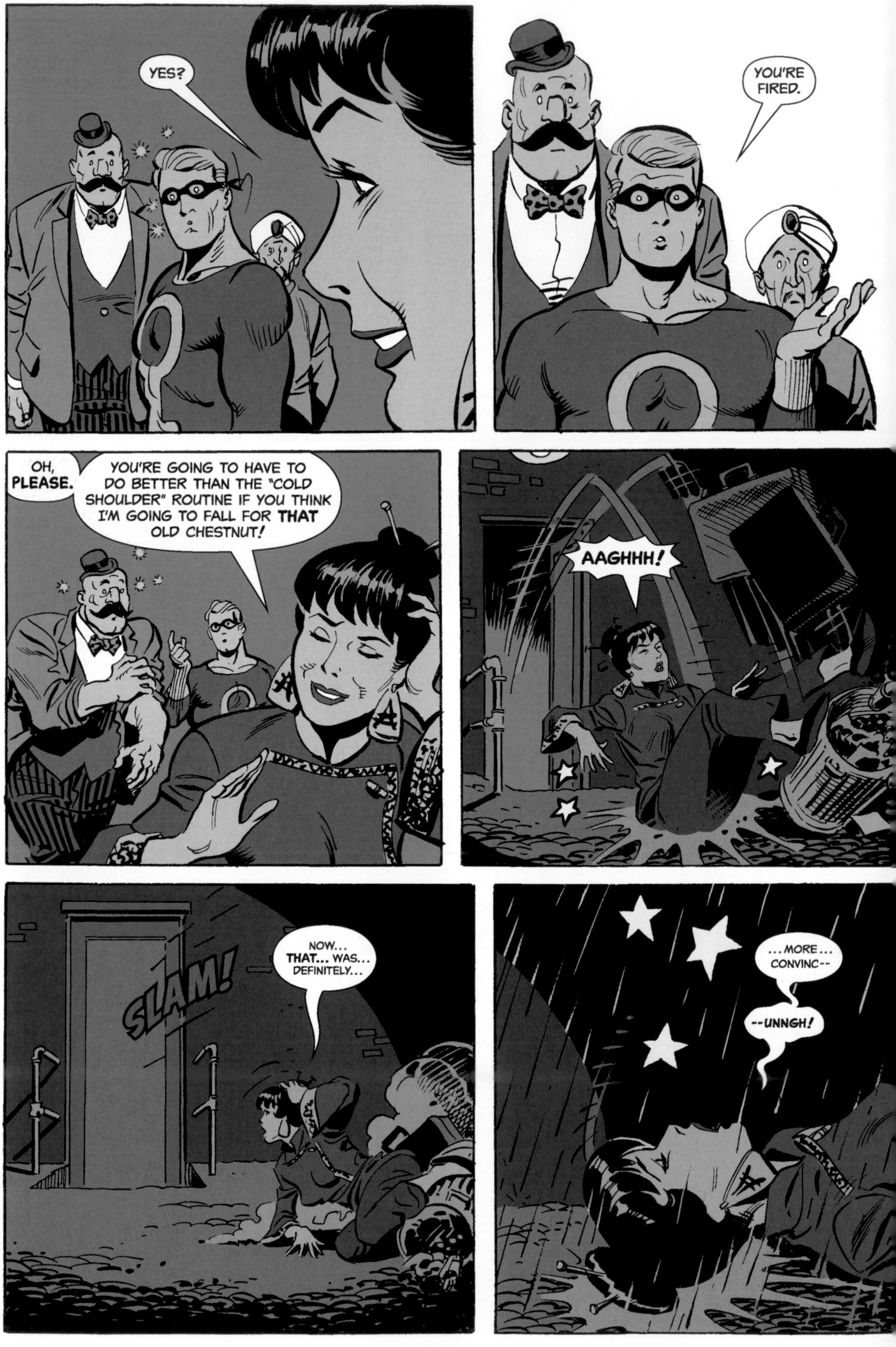
YES?
YOU'RE FIRED.
OH, PLEASE.
YOU'RE GOING TO HAVE TO DO BETTER THAN THE "COLD SHOULDER" ROUTINE IF YOU THINK I'M GOING TO FALL FOR THAT OLD CHESTNUT!
AAGHHH!
SLAM!
NOW... THAT... WAS... DEFINITELY...
...MORE... CONVINC--
--UNNGH!

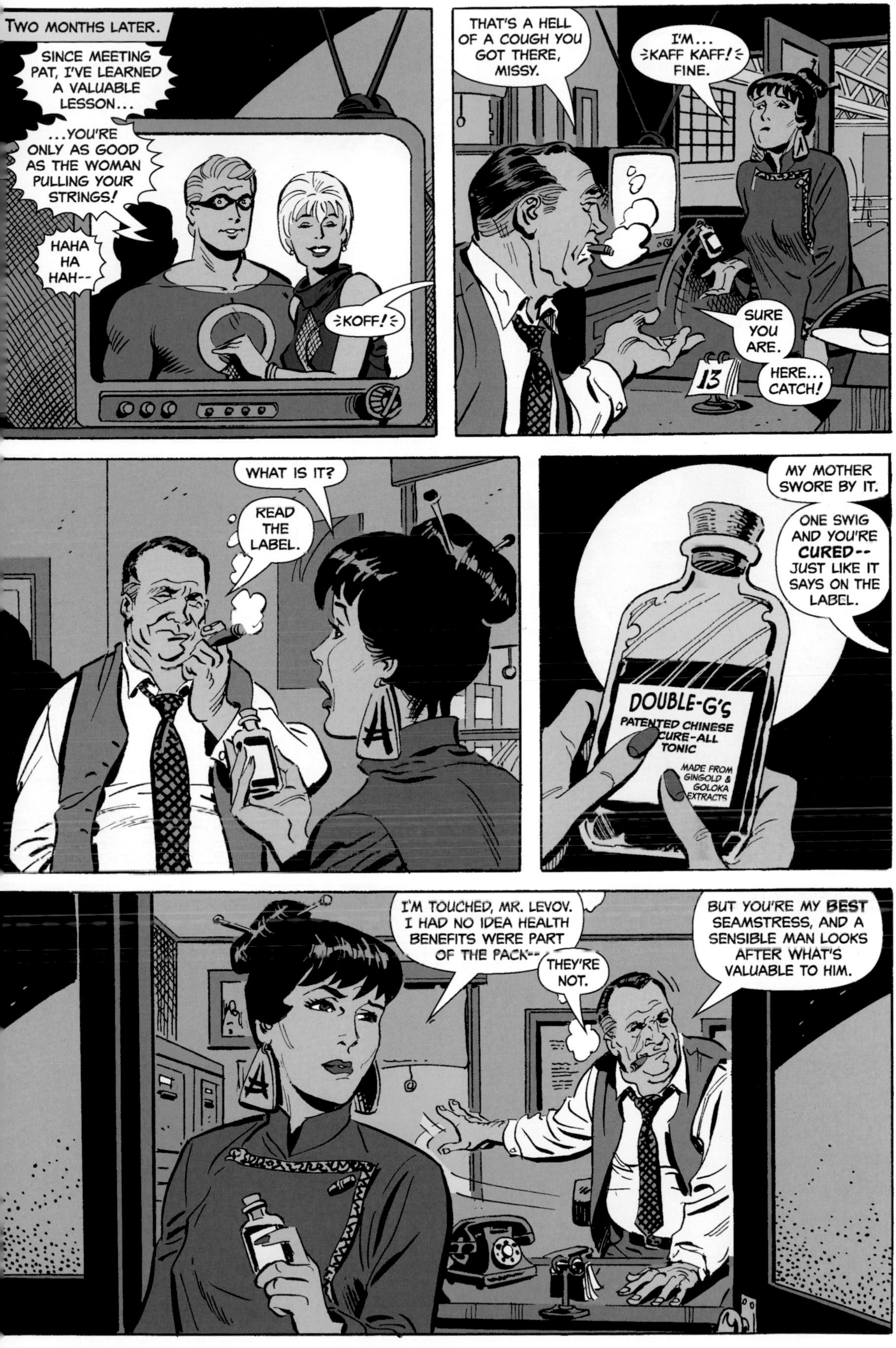

TWO MONTHS LATER.
SINCE MEETING PAT, I'VE LEARNED A VALUABLE LESSON...
...YOU'RE ONLY AS GOOD AS THE WOMAN PULLING YOUR STRINGS!
HAHA HA HAH--
KOFF!
THAT'S A HELL OF A COUGH YOU GOT THERE, MISSY.
I'M... KAFF KAFF! FINE.
SURE YOU ARE.
13
HERE... CATCH!
WHAT IS IT?
READ THE LABEL.
MY MOTHER SWORE BY IT.
ONE SWIG AND YOU'RE CURED-- JUST LIKE IT SAYS ON THE LABEL.
DOUBLE-G's
PATENTED CHINESE CURE-ALL TONIC
MADE FROM GINGOLD & GOLOKA EXTRACTS
I'M TOUCHED, MR. LEVOV. I HAD NO IDEA HEALTH BENEFITS WERE PART OF THE PACK--
THEY'RE NOT.
BUT YOU'RE MY BEST SEAMSTRESS, AND A SENSIBLE MAN LOOKS AFTER WHAT'S VALUABLE TO HIM.

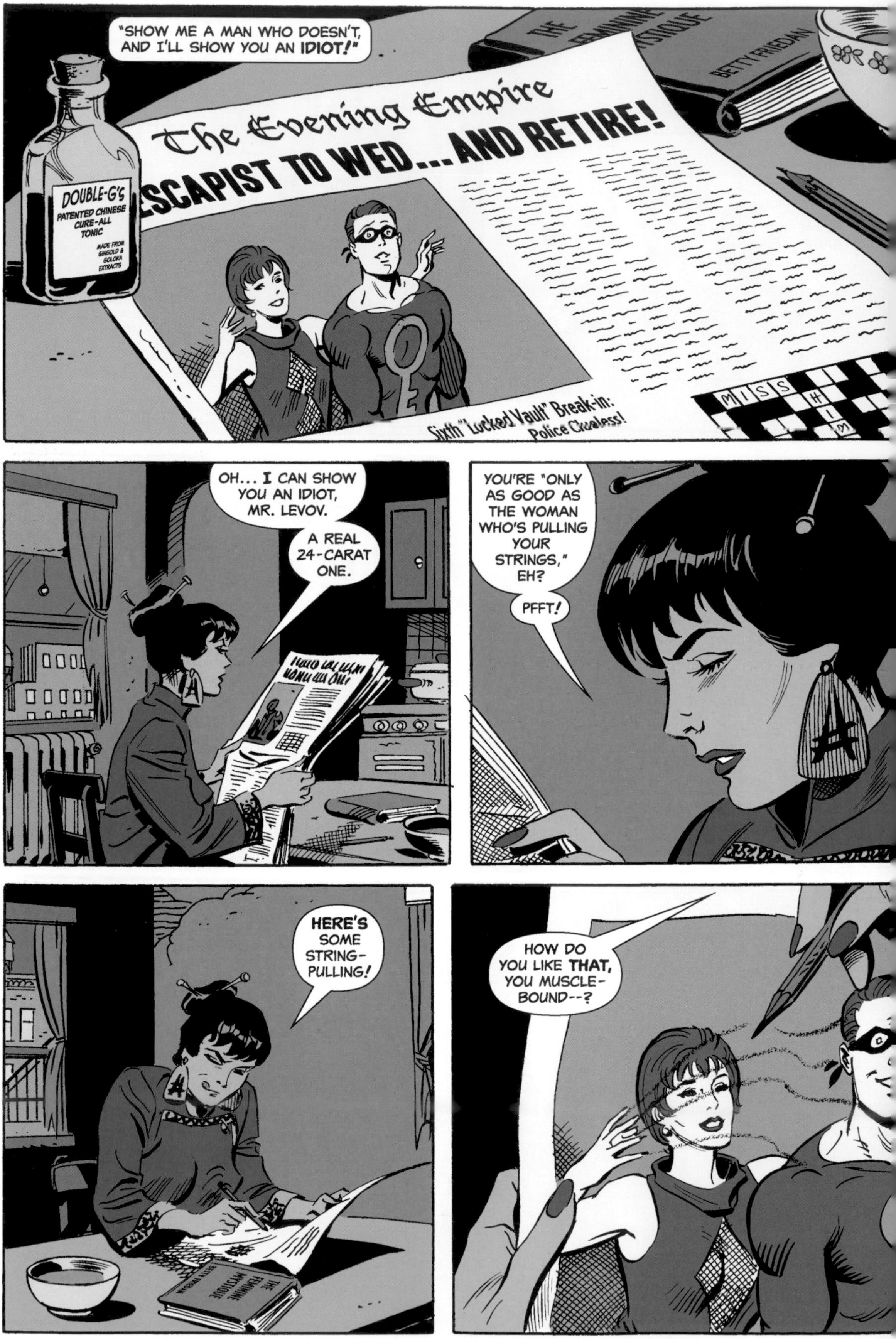
"SHOW ME A MAN WHO DOESN'T, AND I'LL SHOW YOU AN **IDIOT!**"
DOUBLE-G's PATENTED CHINESE CURE-ALL TONIC MADE FROM GINGOLD & GOLOKA EXTRACTS
The Evening Empire
ESCAPIST TO WED... AND RETIRE!
Sixth "Locked Vault" Break-in: Police Clueless!
THE FEMININE MYSTIQUE BETTY FRIEDAN
MISS
HIM
OH... **I** CAN SHOW YOU AN IDIOT, MR. LEVOV.
A REAL 24-CARAT ONE.
YOU'RE "ONLY AS GOOD AS THE WOMAN WHO'S PULLING YOUR STRINGS," EH?
PFFT!
**HERE'S** SOME STRING-PULLING!
THE FEMININE MYSTIQUE BETTY FRIEDAN
HOW DO YOU LIKE **THAT**, YOU MUSCLE-BOUND--?

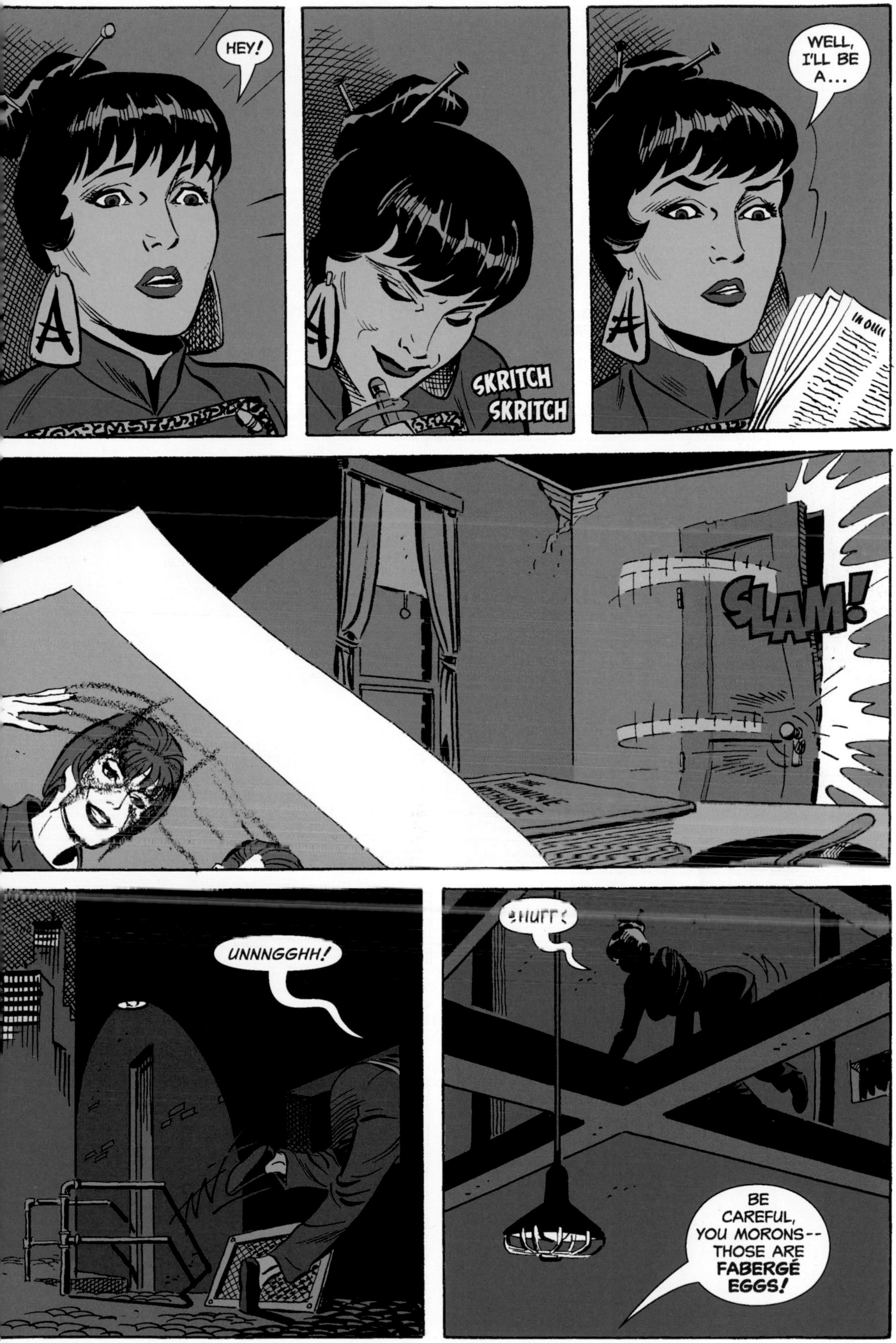
HEY!
SKRITCH
SKRITCH
WELL, I'LL BE A...
SLAM!
UNNNGGHH!
BE CAREFUL, YOU MORONS-- THOSE ARE FABERGÉ EGGS!

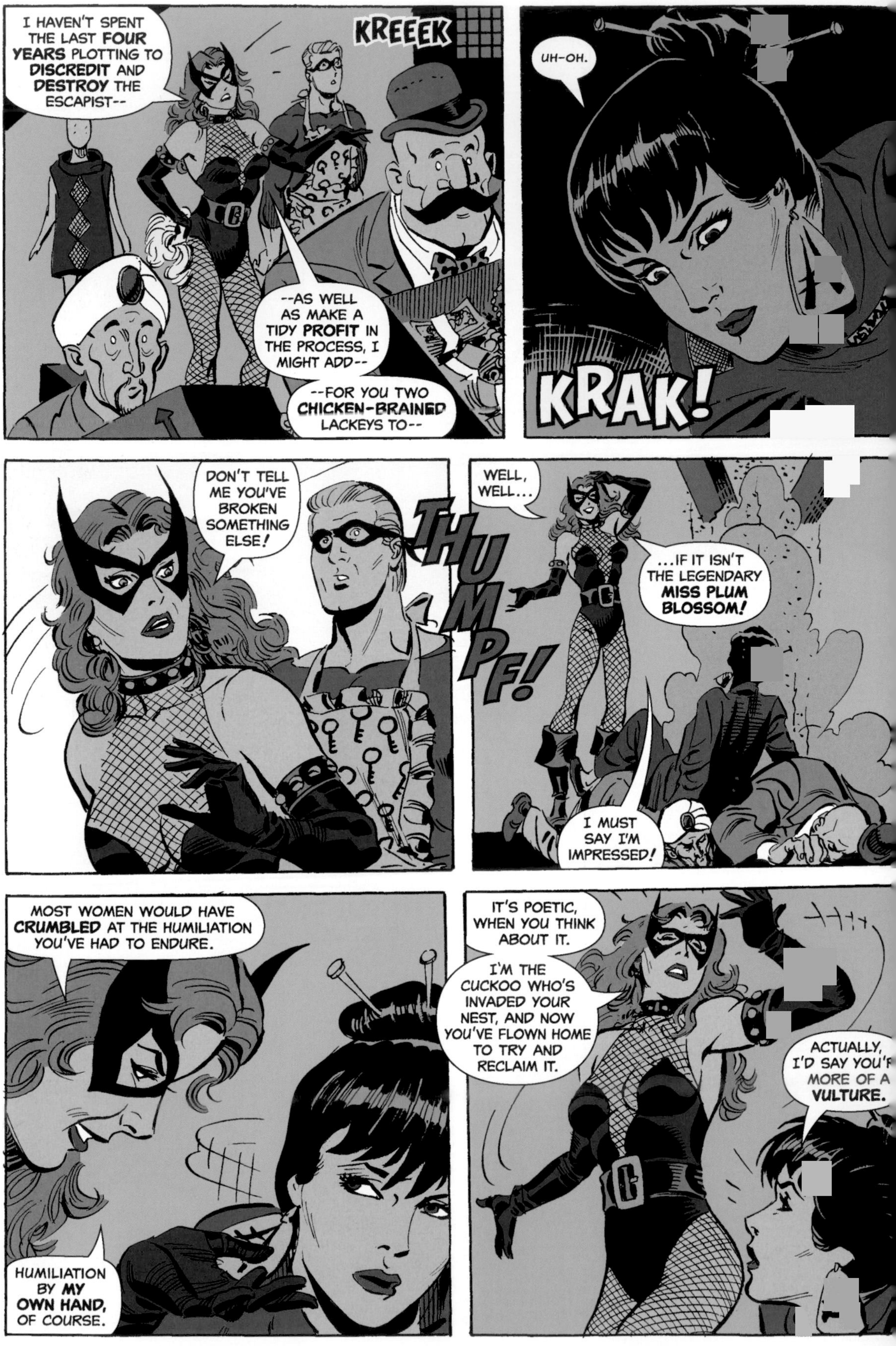

I HAVEN'T SPENT THE LAST FOUR YEARS PLOTTING TO DISCREDIT AND DESTROY THE ESCAPIST--
KREEEK
--AS WELL AS MAKE A TIDY PROFIT IN THE PROCESS, I MIGHT ADD--
--FOR YOU TWO CHICKEN-BRAINED LACKEYS TO--
UH-OH.
KRAK!
DON'T TELL ME YOU'VE BROKEN SOMETHING ELSE!
THUMPF!
WELL, WELL...
...IF IT ISN'T THE LEGENDARY MISS PLUM BLOSSOM!
I MUST SAY I'M IMPRESSED!
MOST WOMEN WOULD HAVE CRUMBLED AT THE HUMILIATION YOU'VE HAD TO ENDURE.
HUMILIATION BY MY OWN HAND, OF COURSE.
IT'S POETIC, WHEN YOU THINK ABOUT IT.
I'M THE CUCKOO WHO'S INVADED YOUR NEST, AND NOW YOU'VE FLOWN HOME TO TRY AND RECLAIM IT.
ACTUALLY, I'D SAY YOU'R MORE OF A VULTURE.

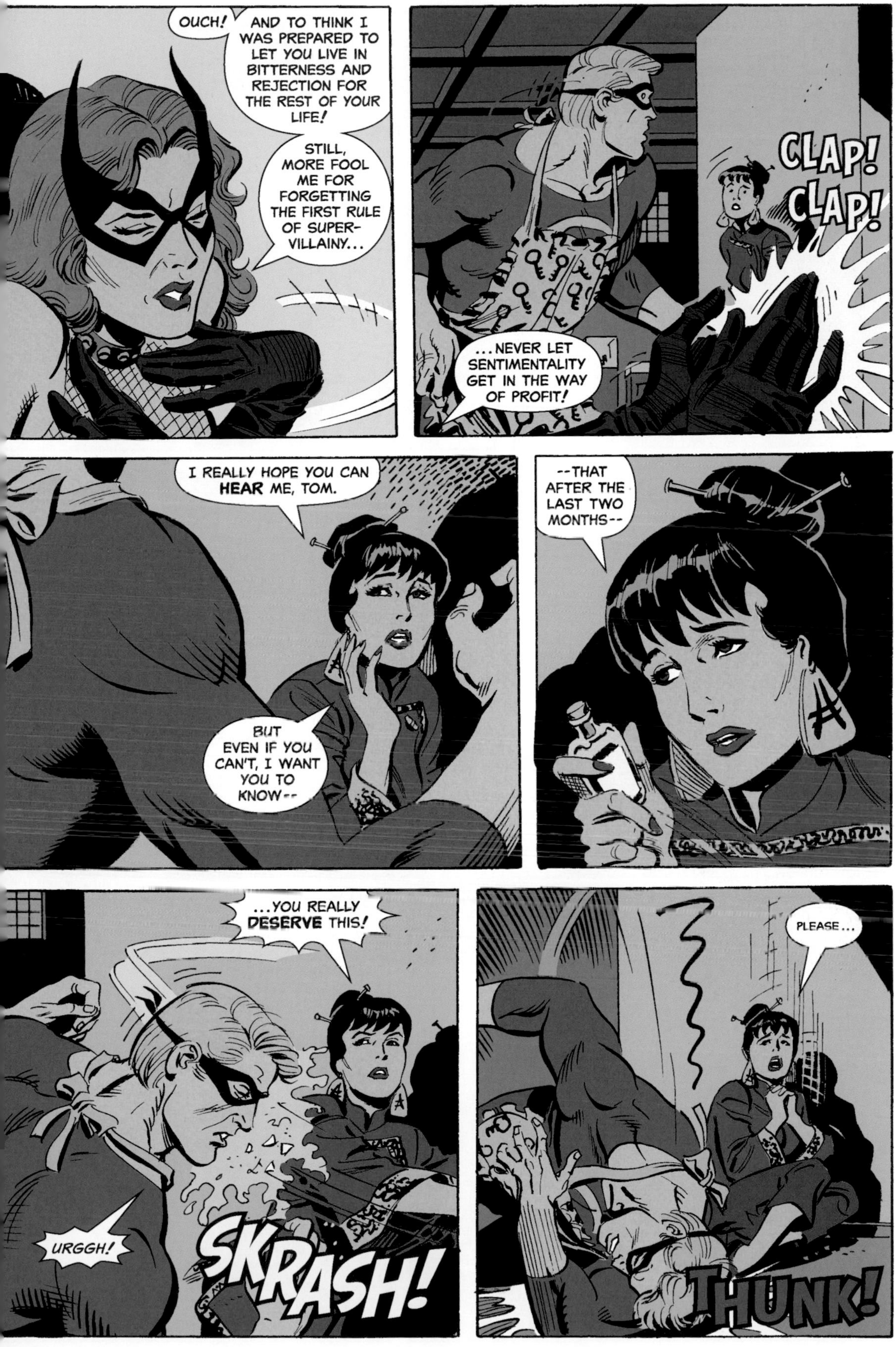
OUCH!
AND TO THINK I WAS PREPARED TO LET YOU LIVE IN BITTERNESS AND REJECTION FOR THE REST OF YOUR LIFE!
STILL, MORE FOOL ME FOR FORGETTING THE FIRST RULE OF SUPER-VILLAINY...
CLAP! CLAP!
...NEVER LET SENTIMENTALITY GET IN THE WAY OF PROFIT!
I REALLY HOPE YOU CAN HEAR ME, TOM.
BUT EVEN IF YOU CAN'T, I WANT YOU TO KNOW--
--THAT AFTER THE LAST TWO MONTHS--
...YOU REALLY DESERVE THIS!
URGGH!
SKRASH!
PLEASE...
THUNK!

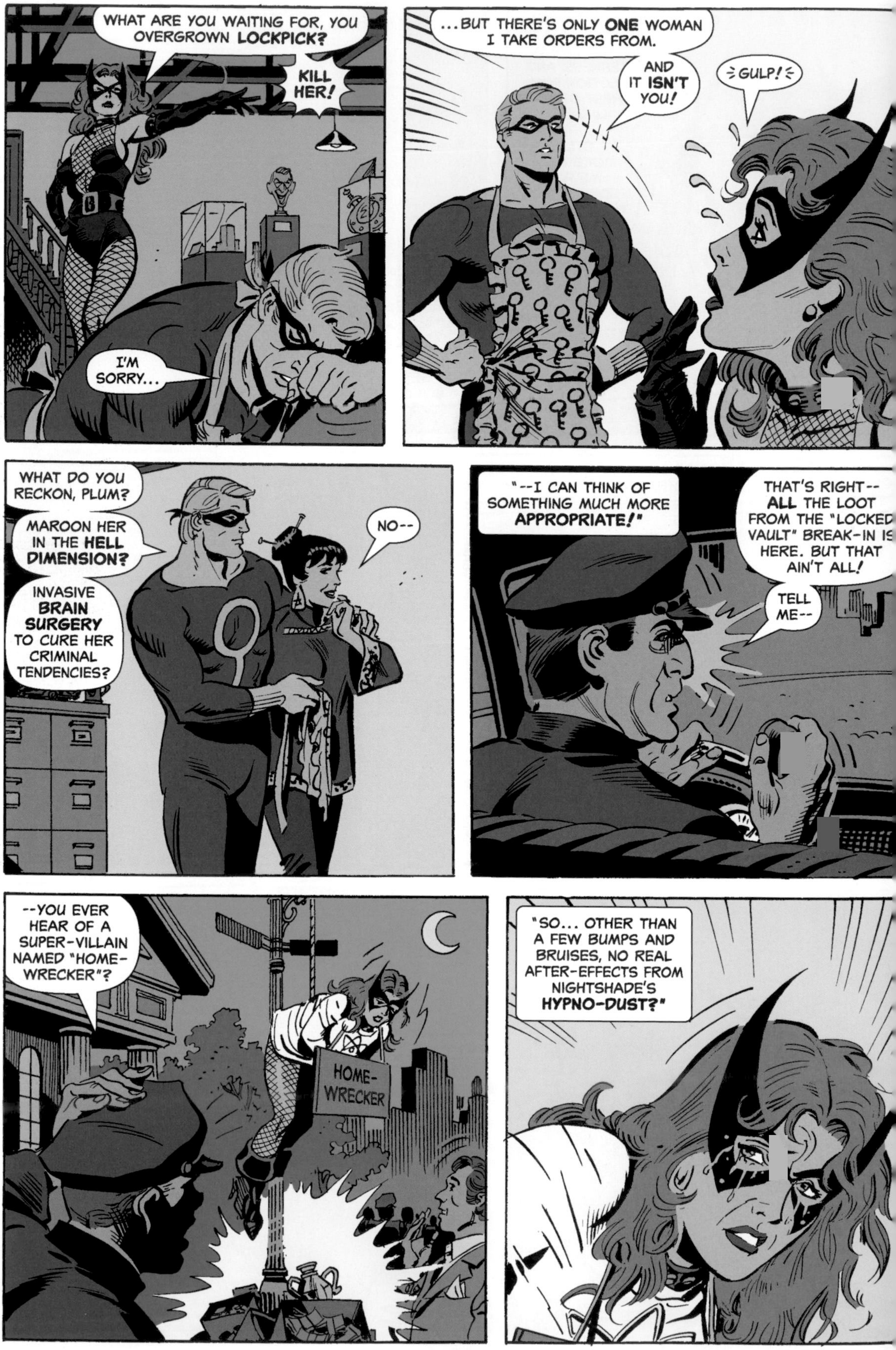
WHAT ARE YOU WAITING FOR, YOU OVERGROWN LOCKPICK?
KILL HER!
I'M SORRY...
...BUT THERE'S ONLY ONE WOMAN I TAKE ORDERS FROM.
AND IT ISN'T YOU!
GULP!
WHAT DO YOU RECKON, PLUM?
MAROON HER IN THE HELL DIMENSION?
INVASIVE BRAIN SURGERY TO CURE HER CRIMINAL TENDENCIES?
NO--
"--I CAN THINK OF SOMETHING MUCH MORE APPROPRIATE!"
THAT'S RIGHT-- ALL THE LOOT FROM THE "LOCKED VAULT" BREAK-IN IS HERE. BUT THAT AIN'T ALL!
TELL ME--
--YOU EVER HEAR OF A SUPER-VILLAIN NAMED "HOME-WRECKER"?
HOME-WRECKER
"SO... OTHER THAN A FEW BUMPS AND BRUISES, NO REAL AFTER-EFFECTS FROM NIGHTSHADE'S HYPNO-DUST?"

THREE DAYS LATER...

YOU MEAN **APART** FROM DEEP-SEATED EMOTIONAL TRAUMA **AND** A BROKEN HEART?

PLUM-- I WAS TALKING TO AL AND OMAR!

OF **COURSE** YOU WERE.

BUT THEN, THAT'S **YOU.**

NEVER ANY THOUGHT FOR THE "LITTLE WOMAN" WHO DARNS YOUR SOCKS AND MENDS YOUR COSTUMES.

**HEY!** WHAT'S THE MATTER?

THE MATTER, TOM MAYFLOWER, IS THAT **YOU** THINK NOTHING'S **CHANGED.**

NOW, COME ON...

PLUM... WHAT ARE YOU **DOING?!**

GETTING READY.

**KRASH!**

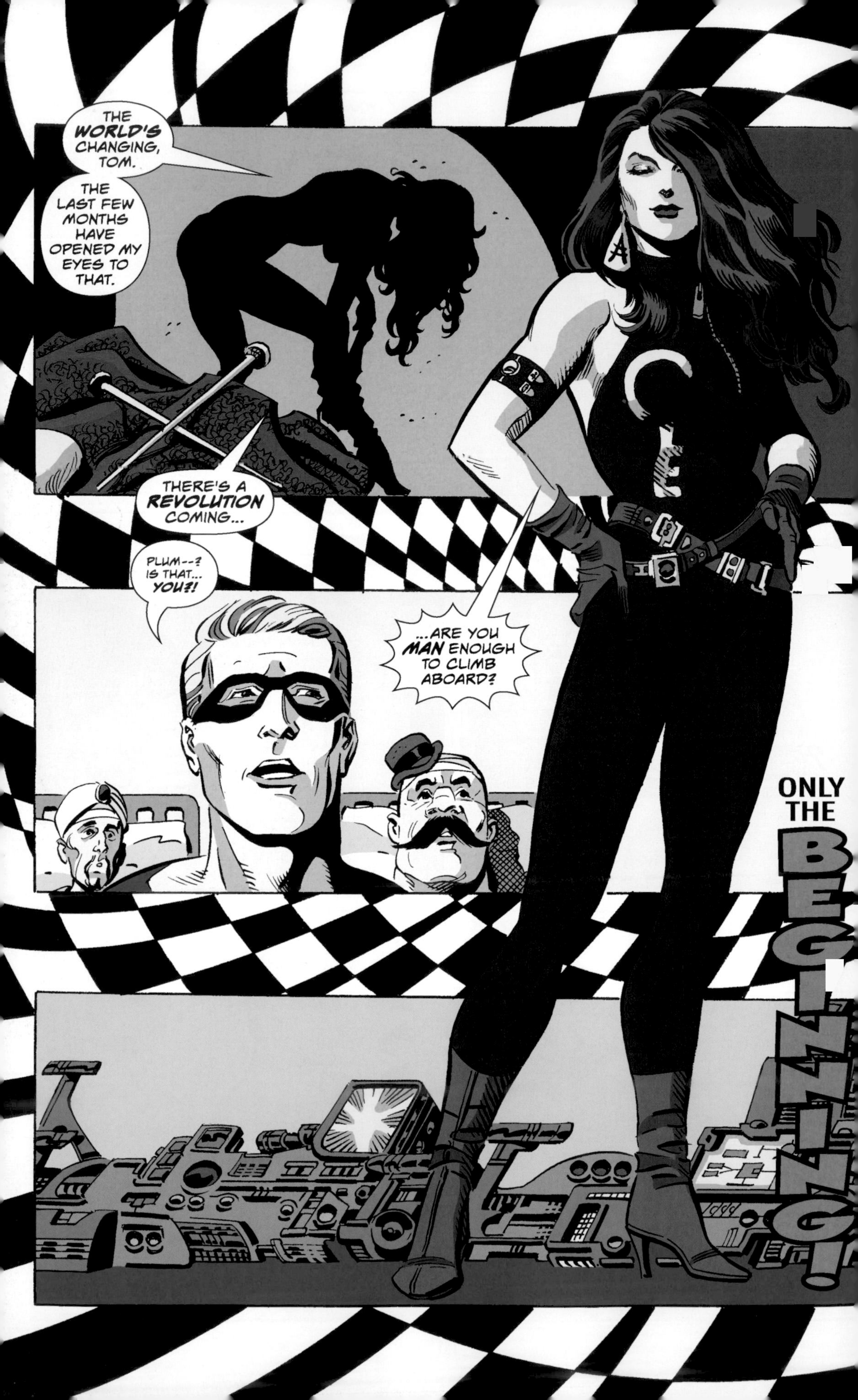
THE WORLD'S CHANGING, TOM.
THE LAST FEW MONTHS HAVE OPENED MY EYES TO THAT.
THERE'S A REVOLUTION COMING...
PLUM--? IS THAT... YOU?!
...ARE YOU MAN ENOUGH TO CLIMB ABOARD?
ONLY THE BEGINNING!

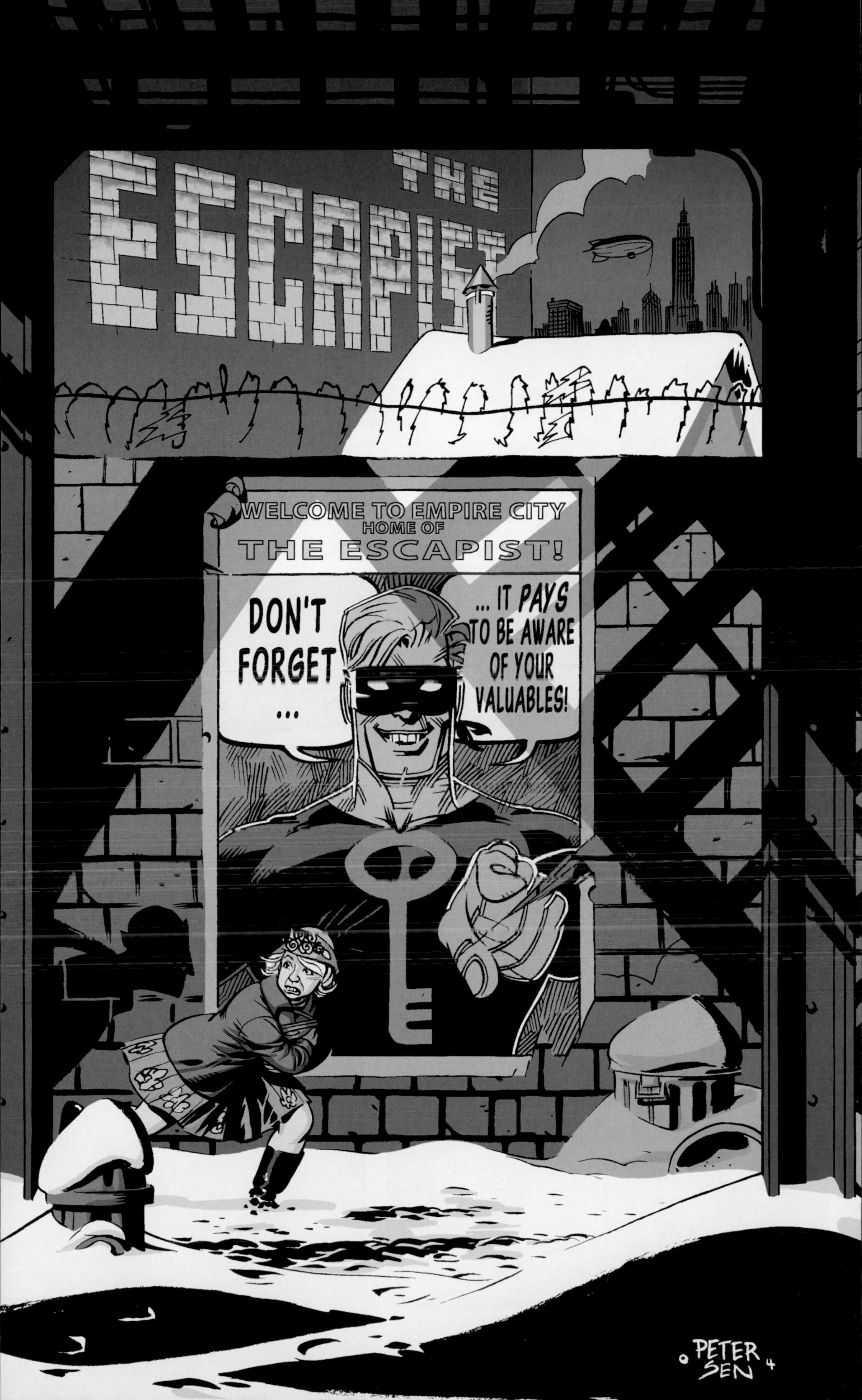
THE ESCAPIST
WELCOME TO EMPIRE CITY
HOME OF
THE ESCAPIST!
DON'T FORGET ...
... IT PAYS TO BE AWARE OF YOUR VALUABLES!
PETERSEN

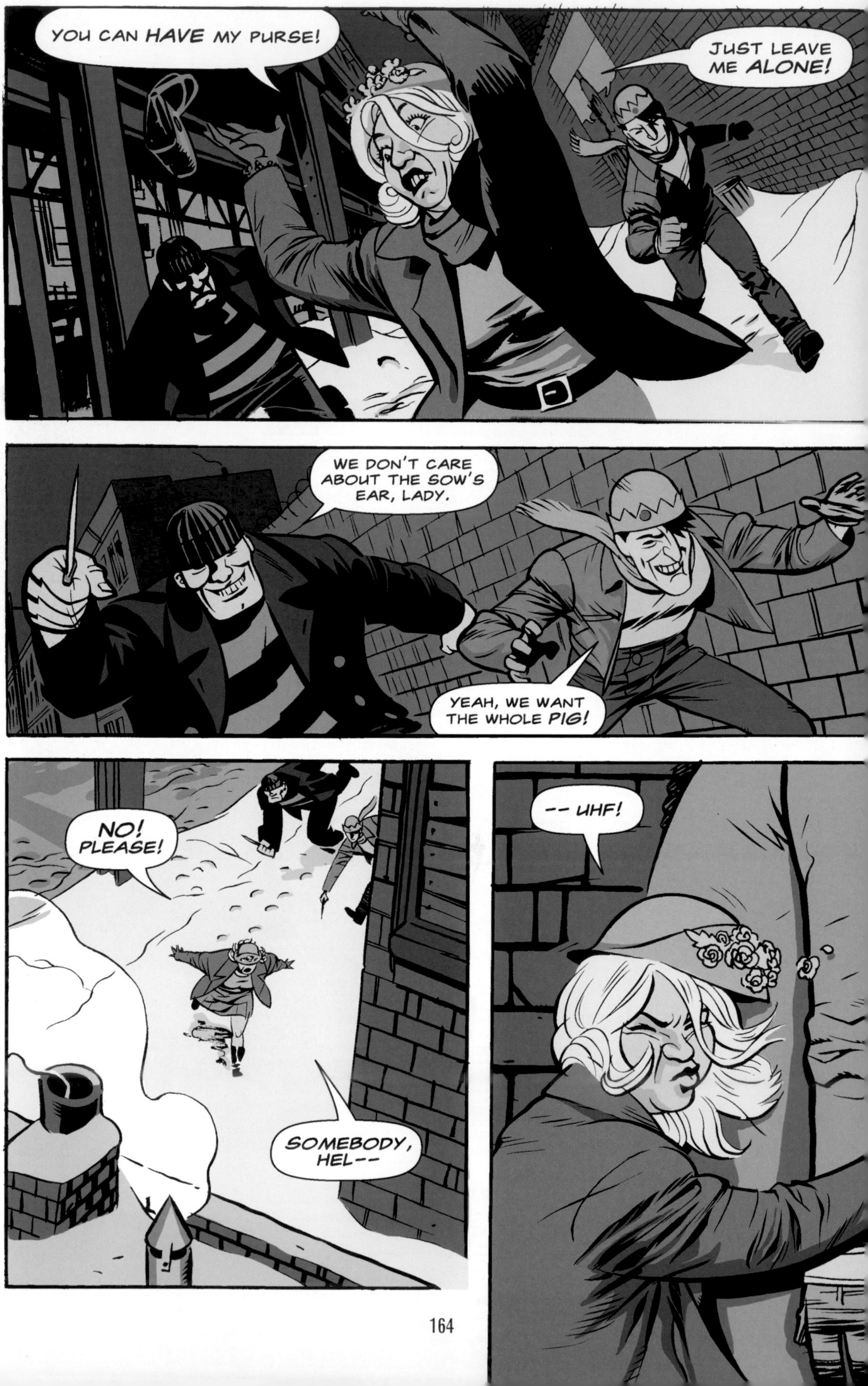
YOU CAN HAVE MY PURSE!
JUST LEAVE ME ALONE!
WE DON'T CARE ABOUT THE SOW'S EAR, LADY.
YEAH, WE WANT THE WHOLE PIG!
NO! PLEASE!
SOMEBODY, HEL--
-- UHF!

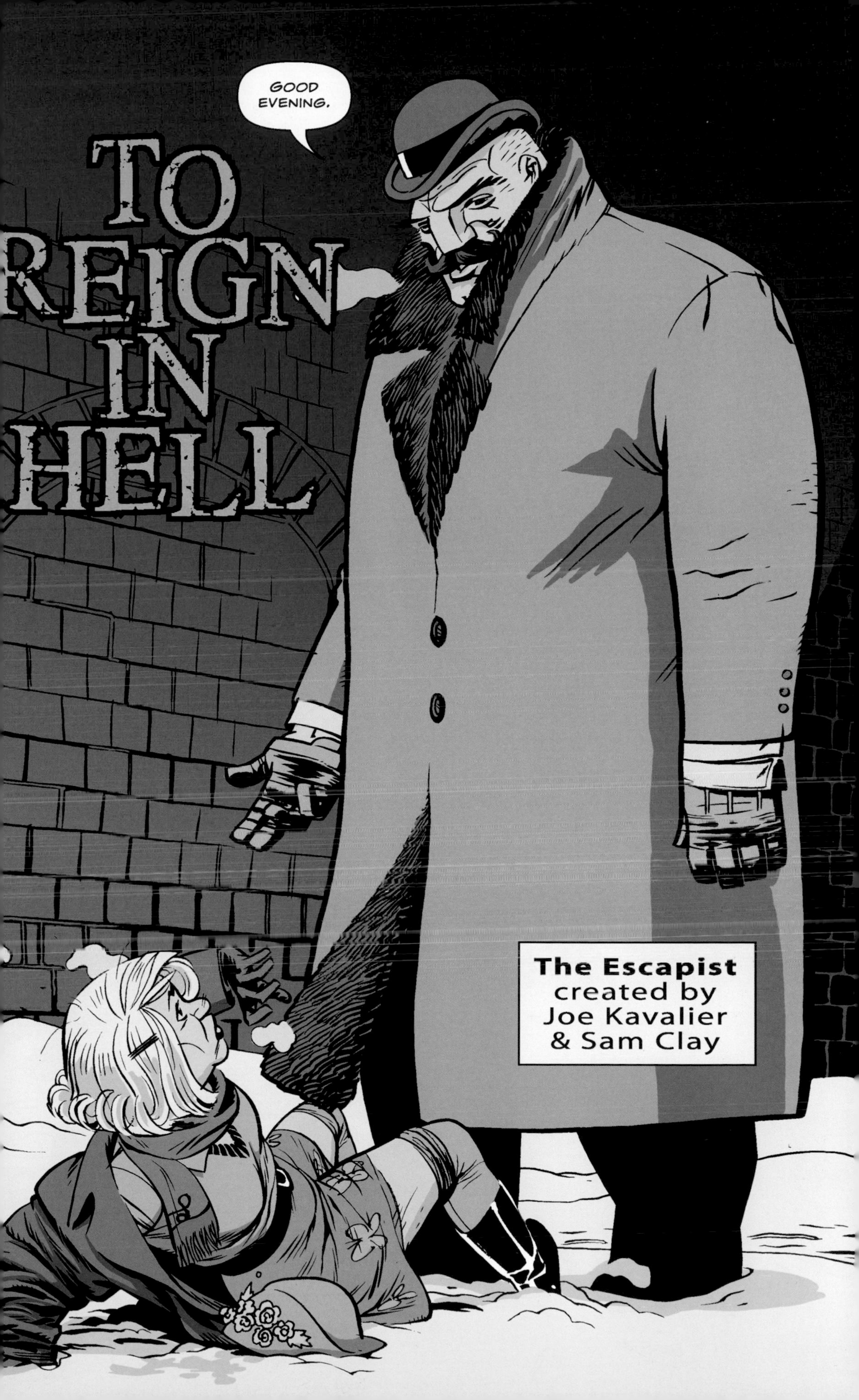
GOOD EVENING.
TO REIGN IN HELL
The Escapist created by Joe Kavalier & Sam Clay

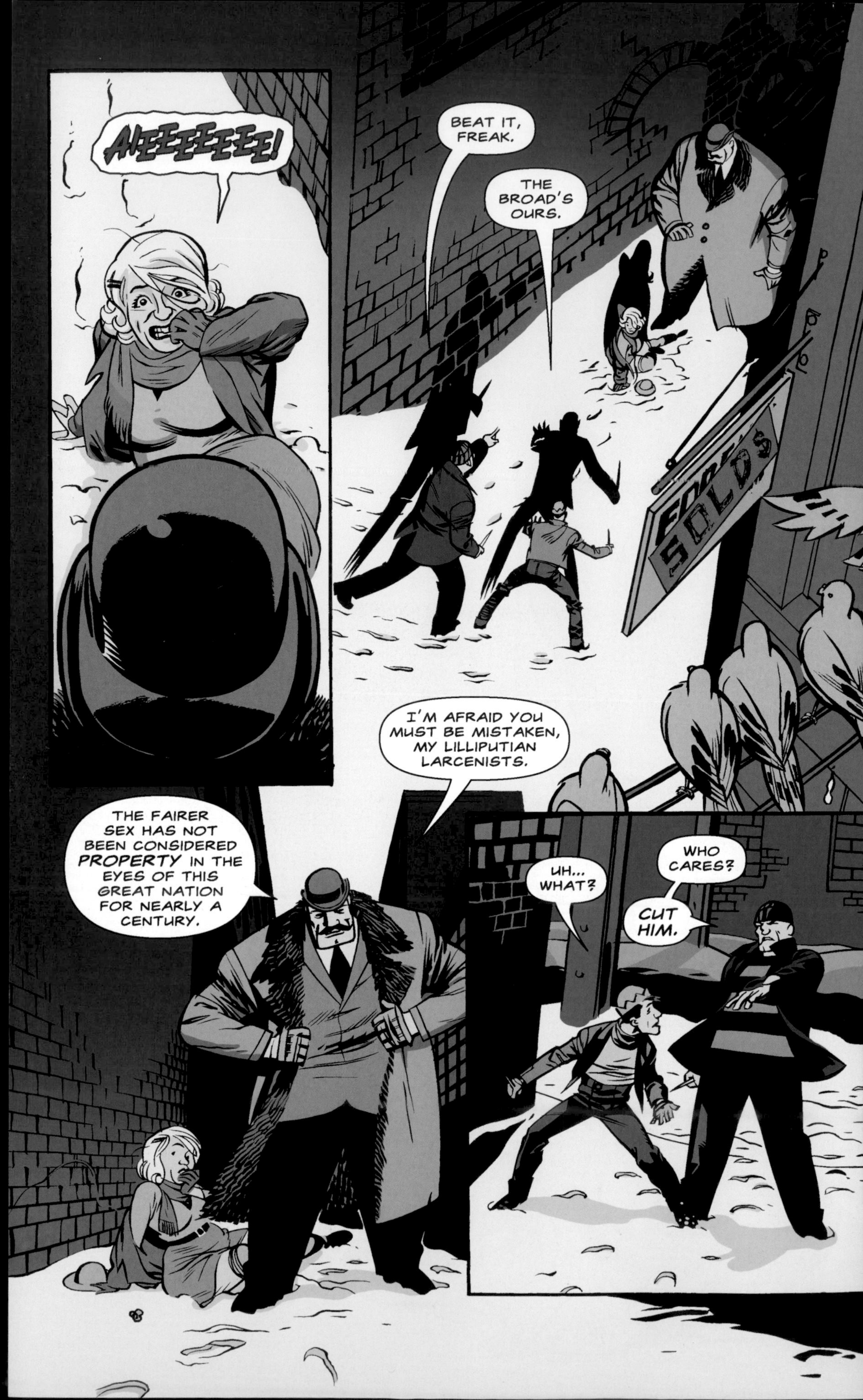
AIEEEEEEEE!
BEAT IT, FREAK.
THE BROAD'S OURS.
I'M AFRAID YOU MUST BE MISTAKEN, MY LILLIPUTIAN LARCENISTS.
THE FAIRER SEX HAS NOT BEEN CONSIDERED PROPERTY IN THE EYES OF THIS GREAT NATION FOR NEARLY A CENTURY.
UH... WHAT?
WHO CARES?
CUT HIM.

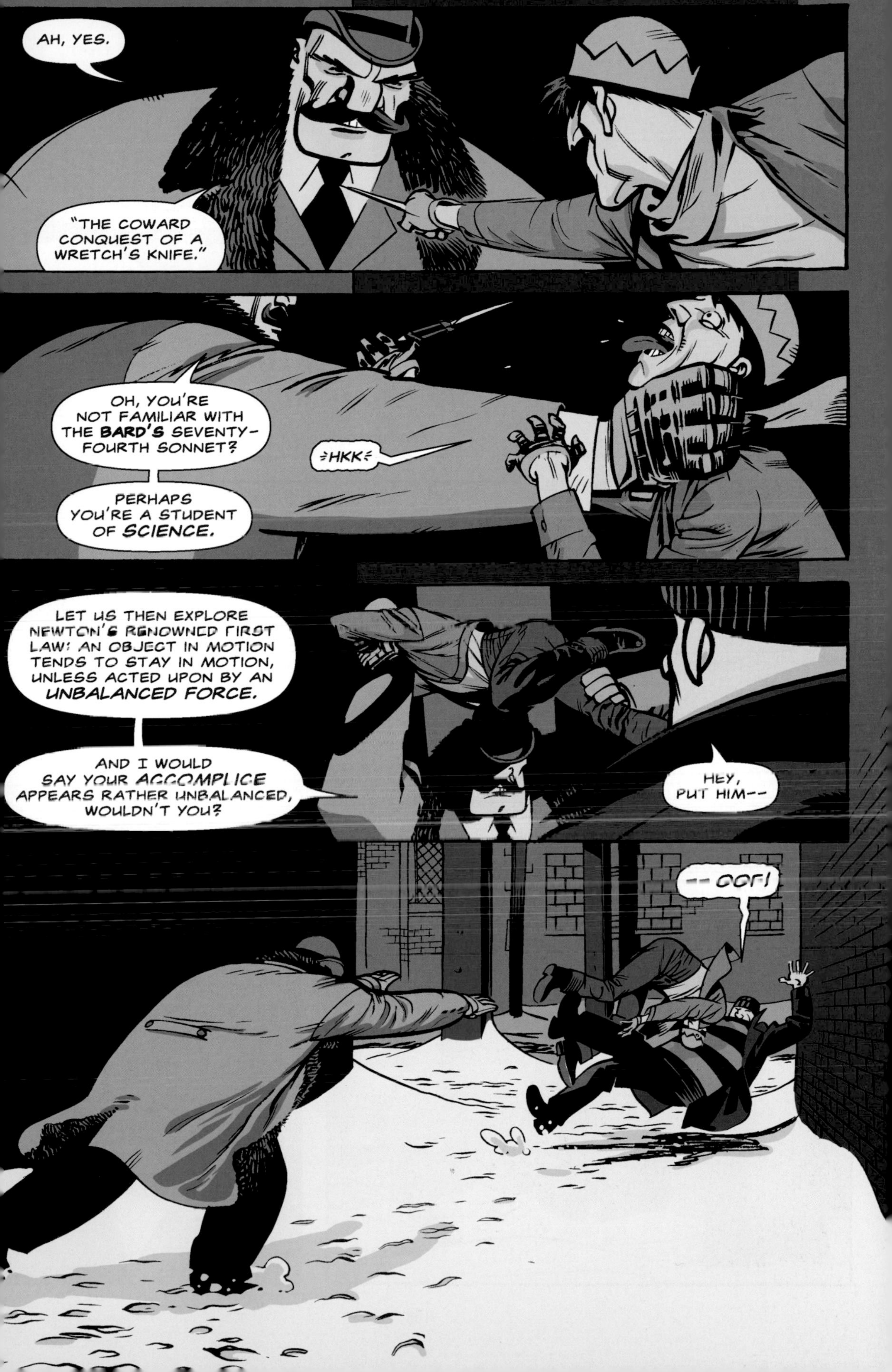
AH, YES.
"THE COWARD CONQUEST OF A WRETCH'S KNIFE."
OH, YOU'RE NOT FAMILIAR WITH THE BARD'S SEVENTY-FOURTH SONNET?
PERHAPS YOU'RE A STUDENT OF SCIENCE.
HKK
LET US THEN EXPLORE NEWTON'S RENOWNED FIRST LAW: AN OBJECT IN MOTION TENDS TO STAY IN MOTION, UNLESS ACTED UPON BY AN UNBALANCED FORCE.
AND I WOULD SAY YOUR ACCOMPLICE APPEARS RATHER UNBALANCED, WOULDN'T YOU?
HEY, PUT HIM--
--OOF!

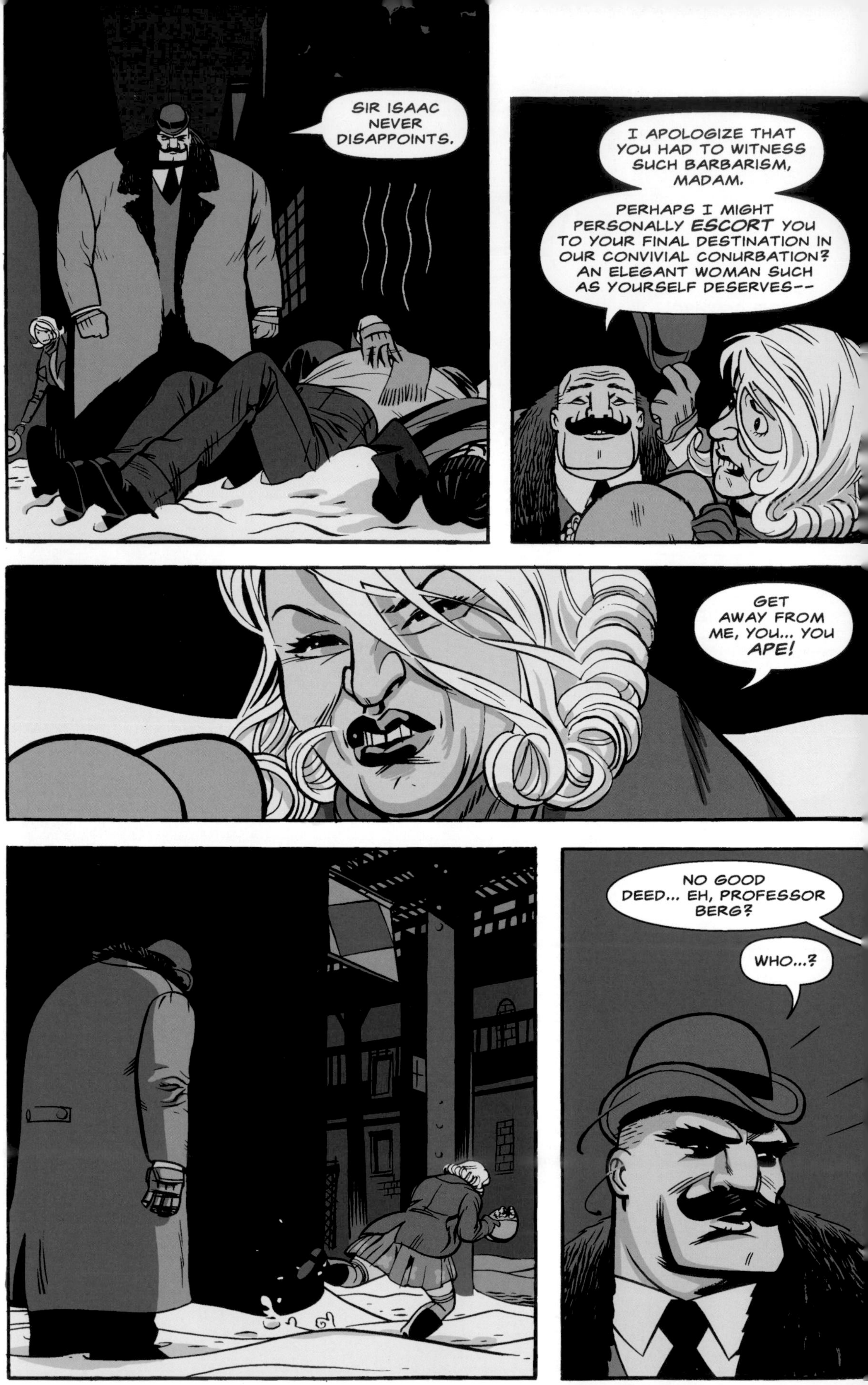
SIR ISAAC NEVER DISAPPOINTS.
I APOLOGIZE THAT YOU HAD TO WITNESS SUCH BARBARISM, MADAM.
PERHAPS I MIGHT PERSONALLY ESCORT YOU TO YOUR FINAL DESTINATION IN OUR CONVIVIAL CONURBATION? AN ELEGANT WOMAN SUCH AS YOURSELF DESERVES--
GET AWAY FROM ME, YOU... YOU APE!
NO GOOD DEED... EH, PROFESSOR BERG?
WHO...?

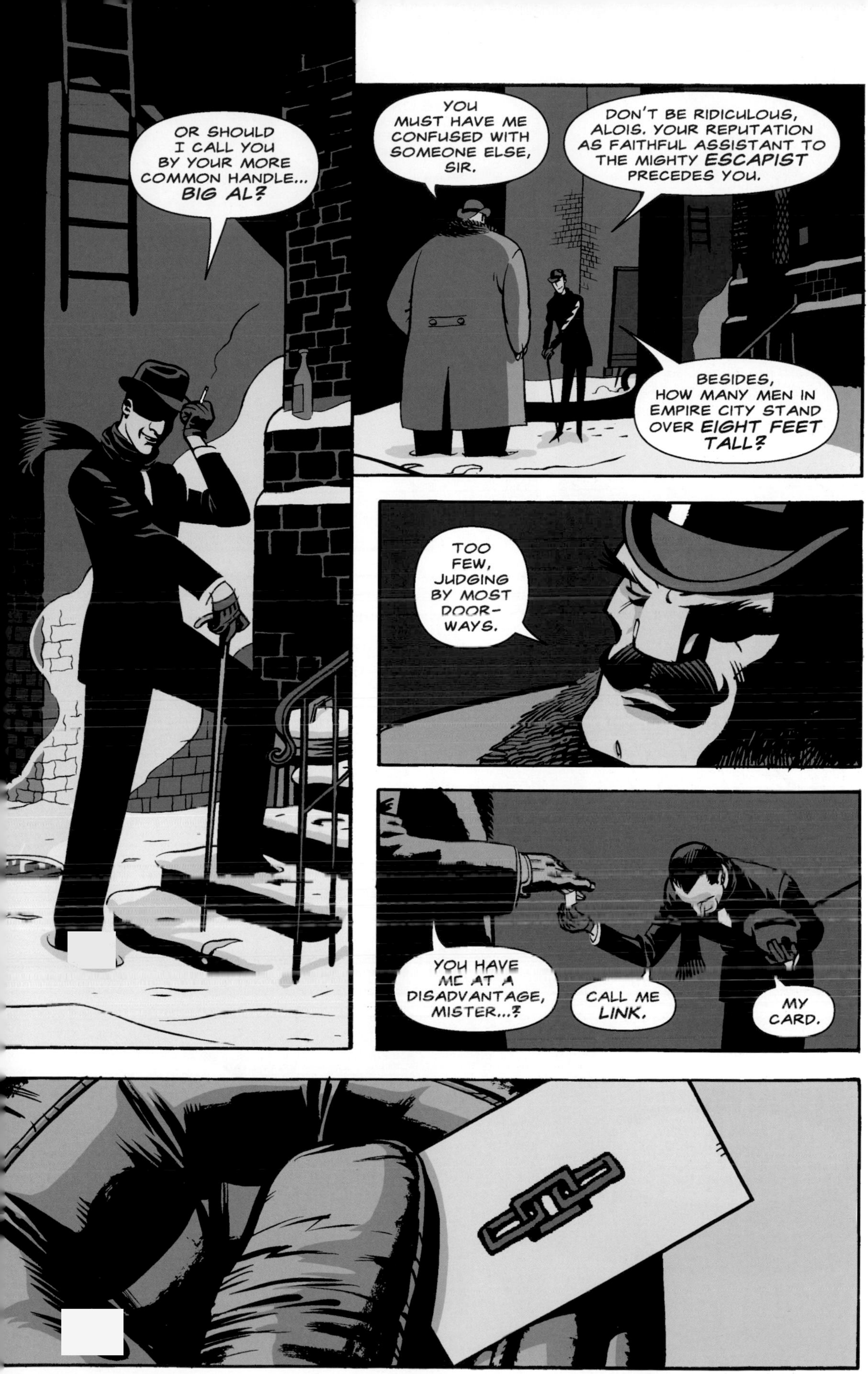
OR SHOULD I CALL YOU BY YOUR MORE COMMON HANDLE... BIG AL?
YOU MUST HAVE ME CONFUSED WITH SOMEONE ELSE, SIR.
DON'T BE RIDICULOUS, ALOIS. YOUR REPUTATION AS FAITHFUL ASSISTANT TO THE MIGHTY ESCAPIST PRECEDES YOU.
BESIDES, HOW MANY MEN IN EMPIRE CITY STAND OVER EIGHT FEET TALL?
TOO FEW, JUDGING BY MOST DOORWAYS.
YOU HAVE ME AT A DISADVANTAGE, MISTER...?
CALL ME LINK.
MY CARD.

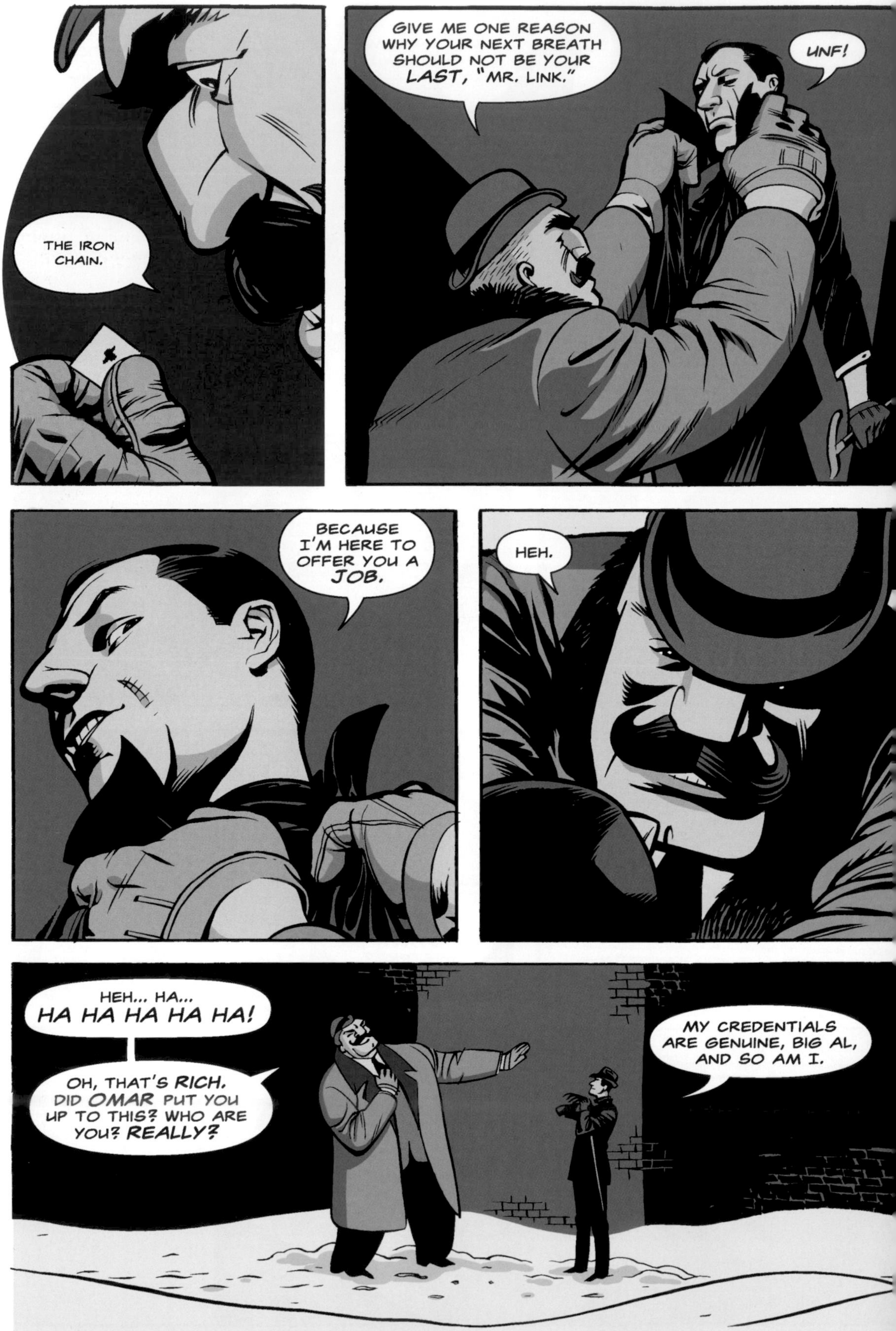
THE IRON CHAIN.
GIVE ME ONE REASON WHY YOUR NEXT BREATH SHOULD NOT BE YOUR LAST, "MR. LINK."
UNF!
BECAUSE I'M HERE TO OFFER YOU A JOB.
HEH.
HEH... HA... HA HA HA HA HA!
OH, THAT'S RICH. DID OMAR PUT YOU UP TO THIS? WHO ARE YOU? REALLY?
MY CREDENTIALS ARE GENUINE, BIG AL, AND SO AM I.

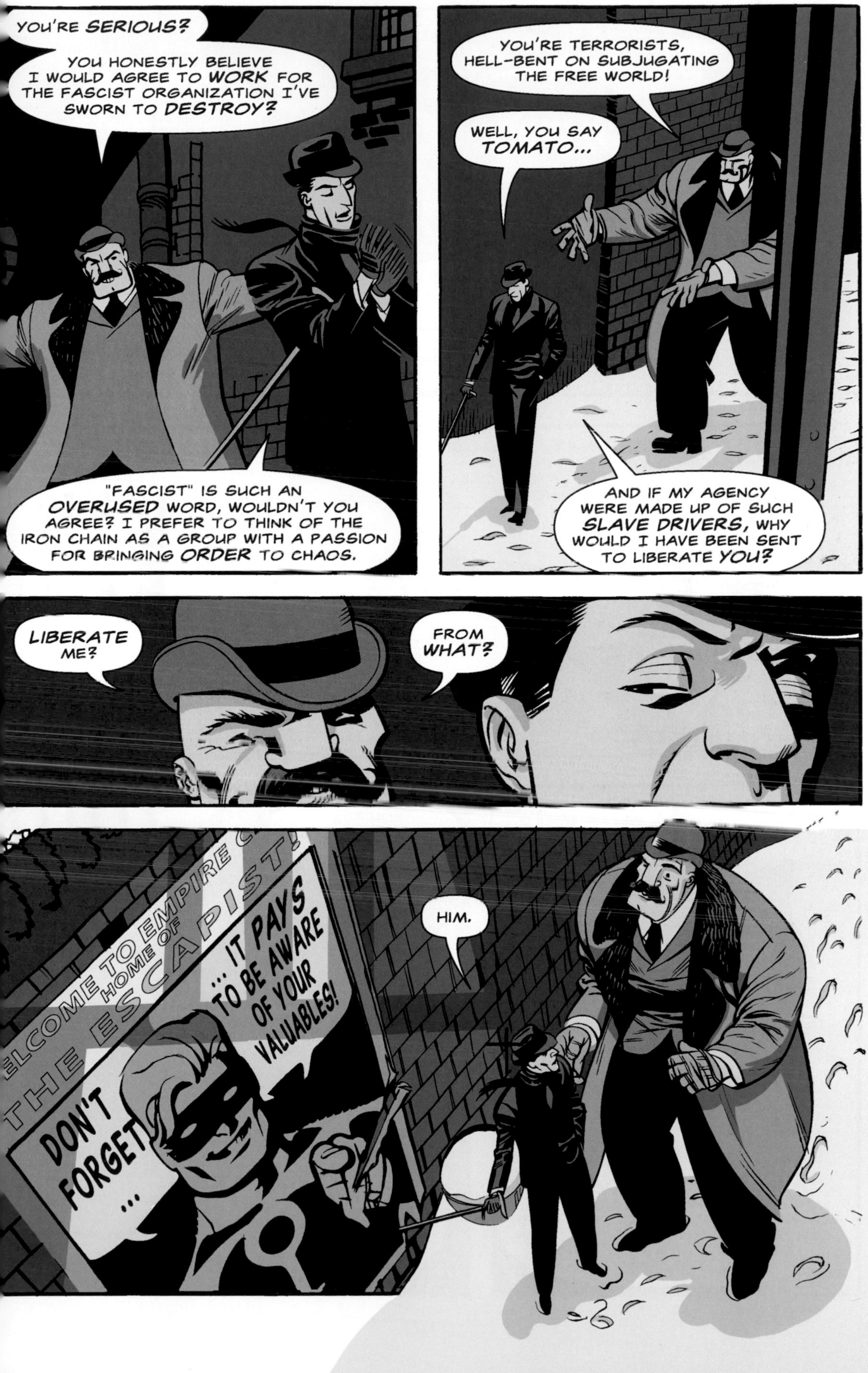
YOU'RE SERIOUS?
YOU HONESTLY BELIEVE I WOULD AGREE TO WORK FOR THE FASCIST ORGANIZATION I'VE SWORN TO DESTROY?
"FASCIST" IS SUCH AN OVERUSED WORD, WOULDN'T YOU AGREE? I PREFER TO THINK OF THE IRON CHAIN AS A GROUP WITH A PASSION FOR BRINGING ORDER TO CHAOS.
YOU'RE TERRORISTS, HELL-BENT ON SUBJUGATING THE FREE WORLD!
WELL, YOU SAY TOMATO...
AND IF MY AGENCY WERE MADE UP OF SUCH SLAVE DRIVERS, WHY WOULD I HAVE BEEN SENT TO LIBERATE YOU?
LIBERATE ME?
FROM WHAT?
ELCOME TO EMPIRE C
HOME OF
THE ESCAPIST!
... IT PAYS TO BE AWARE OF YOUR VALUABLES!
DON'T FORGET ...
HIM.

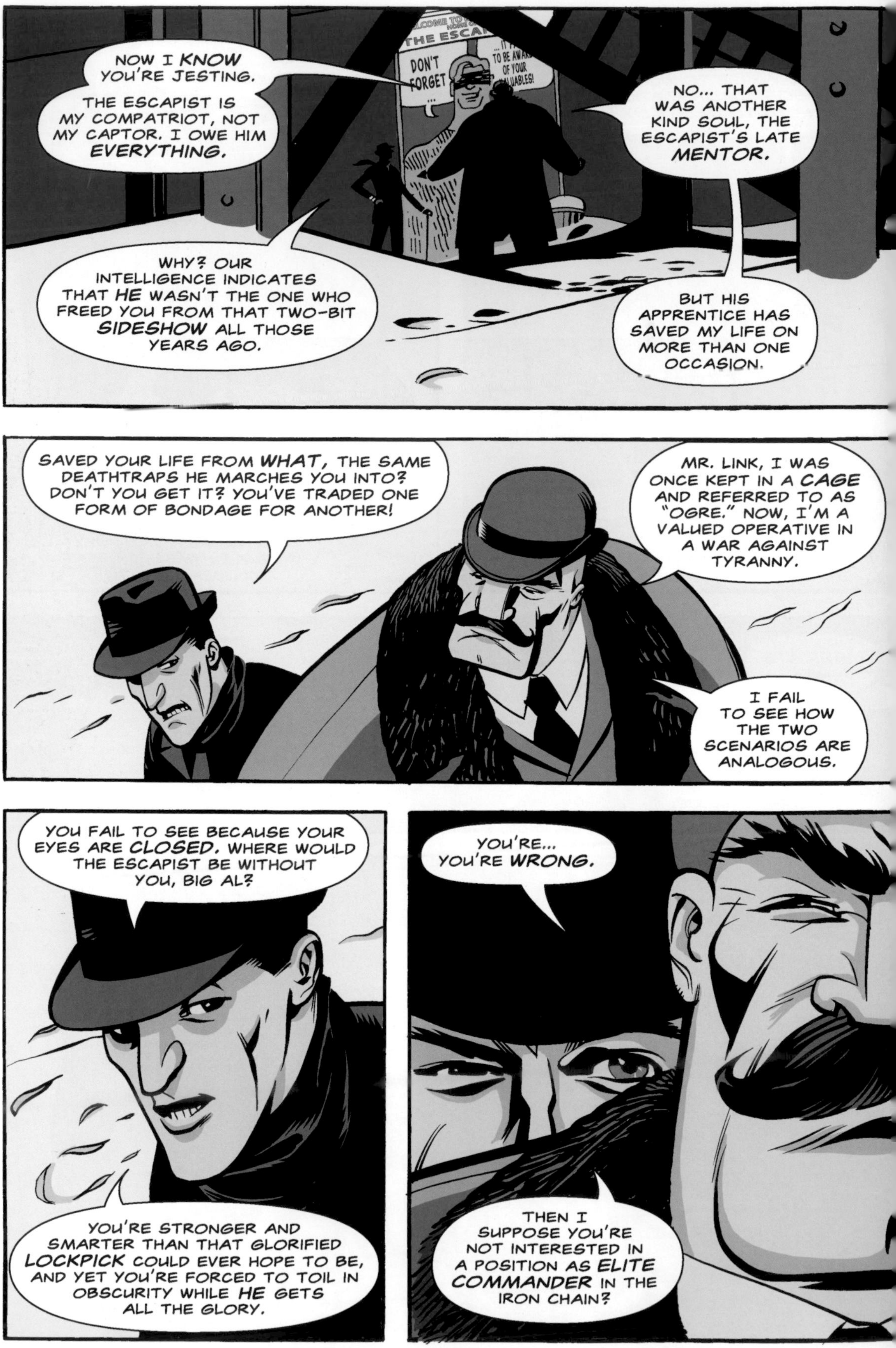
DON'T FORGET
NOW I KNOW YOU'RE JESTING.
THE ESCAPIST IS MY COMPATRIOT, NOT MY CAPTOR. I OWE HIM EVERYTHING.
NO... THAT WAS ANOTHER KIND SOUL, THE ESCAPIST'S LATE MENTOR.
WHY? OUR INTELLIGENCE INDICATES THAT HE WASN'T THE ONE WHO FREED YOU FROM THAT TWO-BIT SIDESHOW ALL THOSE YEARS AGO.
BUT HIS APPRENTICE HAS SAVED MY LIFE ON MORE THAN ONE OCCASION.
SAVED YOUR LIFE FROM WHAT, THE SAME DEATHTRAPS HE MARCHES YOU INTO? DON'T YOU GET IT? YOU'VE TRADED ONE FORM OF BONDAGE FOR ANOTHER!
MR. LINK, I WAS ONCE KEPT IN A CAGE AND REFERRED TO AS "OGRE." NOW, I'M A VALUED OPERATIVE IN A WAR AGAINST TYRANNY.
I FAIL TO SEE HOW THE TWO SCENARIOS ARE ANALOGOUS.
YOU FAIL TO SEE BECAUSE YOUR EYES ARE CLOSED. WHERE WOULD THE ESCAPIST BE WITHOUT YOU, BIG AL?
YOU'RE STRONGER AND SMARTER THAN THAT GLORIFIED LOCKPICK COULD EVER HOPE TO BE, AND YET YOU'RE FORCED TO TOIL IN OBSCURITY WHILE HE GETS ALL THE GLORY.
YOU'RE... YOU'RE WRONG.
THEN I SUPPOSE YOU'RE NOT INTERESTED IN A POSITION AS ELITE COMMANDER IN THE IRON CHAIN?

"ELITE COMMANDER"?

YOU'LL HAVE ABSOLUTE CONTROL OVER ONE OF OUR LARGEST DIVISIONS, WITH FULL ACCESS TO THE CONSIDERABLE RESOURCES OF OUR EMPIRE.

ANY EXPERIMENT YOU'VE EVER HOPED TO PERFORM WILL RECEIVE THE COMPLETE SUPPORT OF A VAST NETWORK THAT ACTUALLY *APPRECIATES* YOUR GENIUS.

BUT... WHAT GOOD ARE RESPECT AND ACCLAIM WHEN ONE IS PART OF AN *UNDERGROUND CABAL*?

OH, WE MAY EMPLOY THE *SECRECY* OF THE INFAMOUS, BUT WE ENJOY THE *LIFESTYLES* OF THE FAMOUS.

UNLIMITED WEALTH, WINE...

... AND *WOMEN*.

BE RATIONAL, PROFESSOR.

DON'T FORGET

...IT PAYS TO BE AWARE OF YOUR VALUABLES!

WHY CONTINUE ANONYMOUSLY SERVICING SOME COSTUMED ICON, WHEN YOU COULD PURSUE YOUR *OWN* DREAMS?

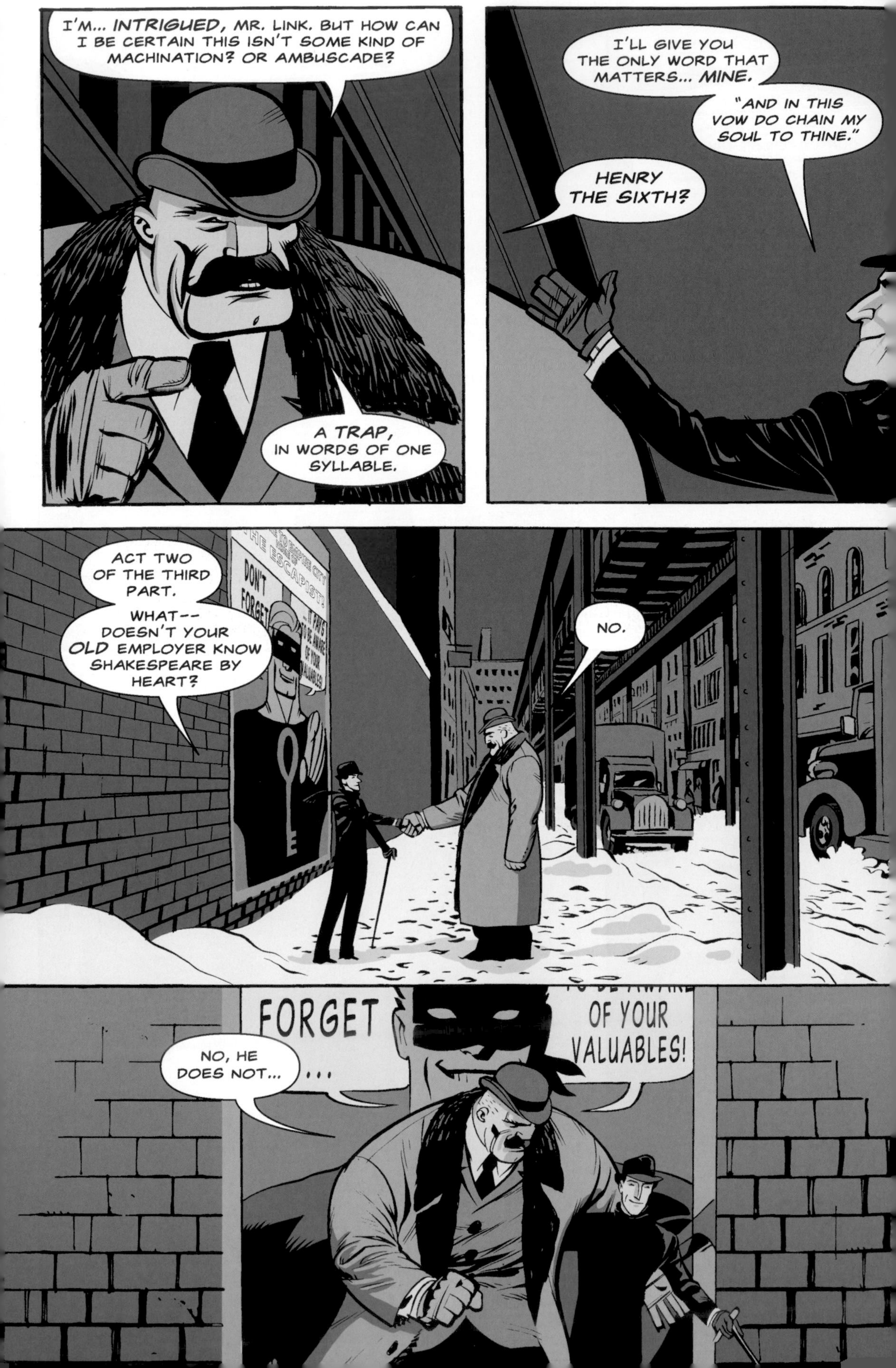
I'M... INTRIGUED, MR. LINK. BUT HOW CAN I BE CERTAIN THIS ISN'T SOME KIND OF MACHINATION? OR AMBUSCADE?
A TRAP, IN WORDS OF ONE SYLLABLE.
I'LL GIVE YOU THE ONLY WORD THAT MATTERS... MINE.
"AND IN THIS VOW DO CHAIN MY SOUL TO THINE."
HENRY THE SIXTH?
ACT TWO OF THE THIRD PART.
WHAT-- DOESN'T YOUR OLD EMPLOYER KNOW SHAKESPEARE BY HEART?
DON'T FORGET
THE ESCAPIST!
...IT PAYS TO BE AWARE OF YOUR VALUABLES!
NO.
FORGET
OF YOUR VALUABLES!
NO, HE DOES NOT...
...

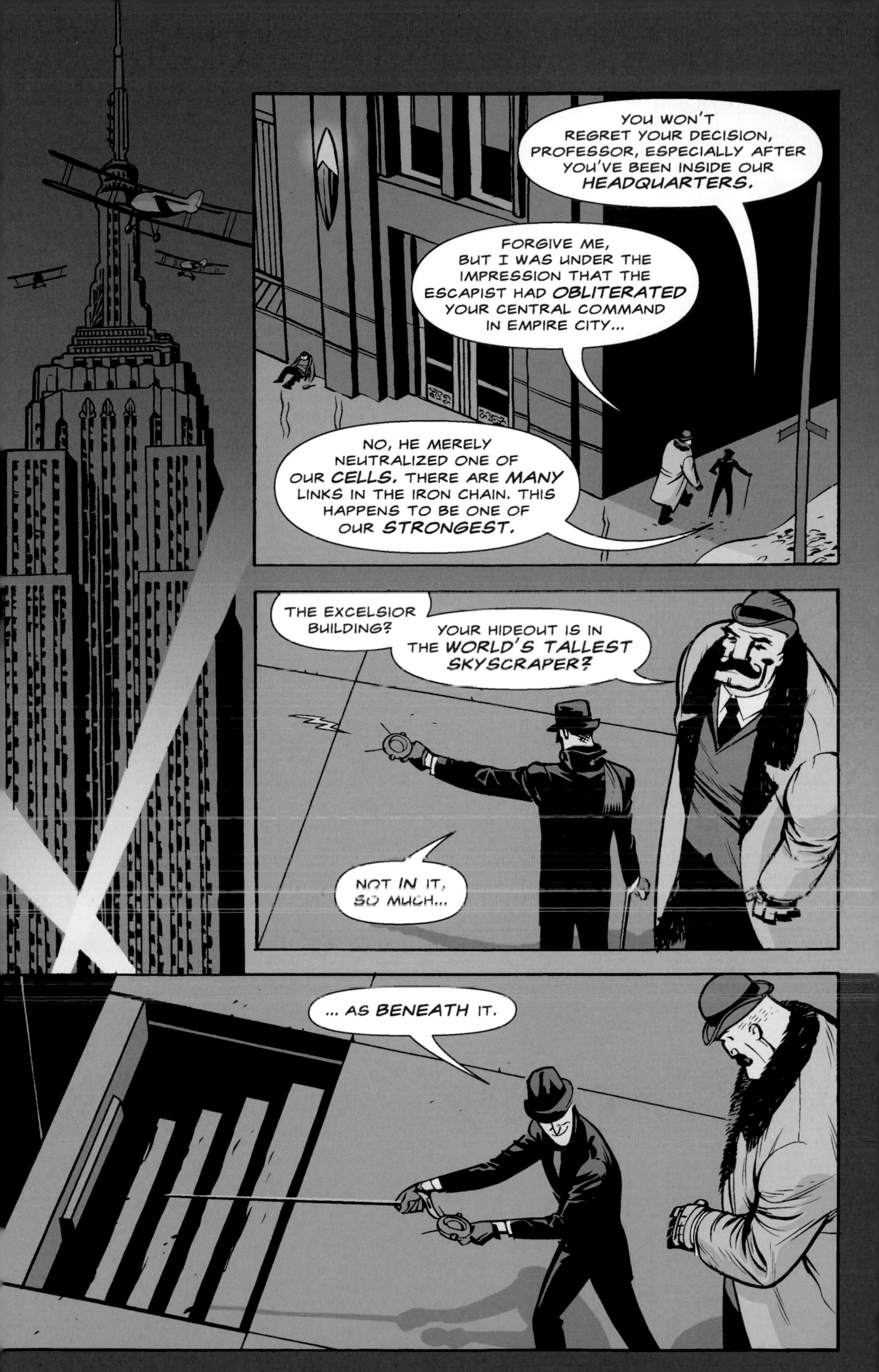
YOU WON'T REGRET YOUR DECISION, PROFESSOR, ESPECIALLY AFTER YOU'VE BEEN INSIDE OUR HEADQUARTERS.
FORGIVE ME, BUT I WAS UNDER THE IMPRESSION THAT THE ESCAPIST HAD OBLITERATED YOUR CENTRAL COMMAND IN EMPIRE CITY...
NO, HE MERELY NEUTRALIZED ONE OF OUR CELLS. THERE ARE MANY LINKS IN THE IRON CHAIN. THIS HAPPENS TO BE ONE OF OUR STRONGEST.
THE EXCELSIOR BUILDING?
YOUR HIDEOUT IS IN THE WORLD'S TALLEST SKYSCRAPER?
NOT IN IT, SO MUCH...
... AS BENEATH IT.

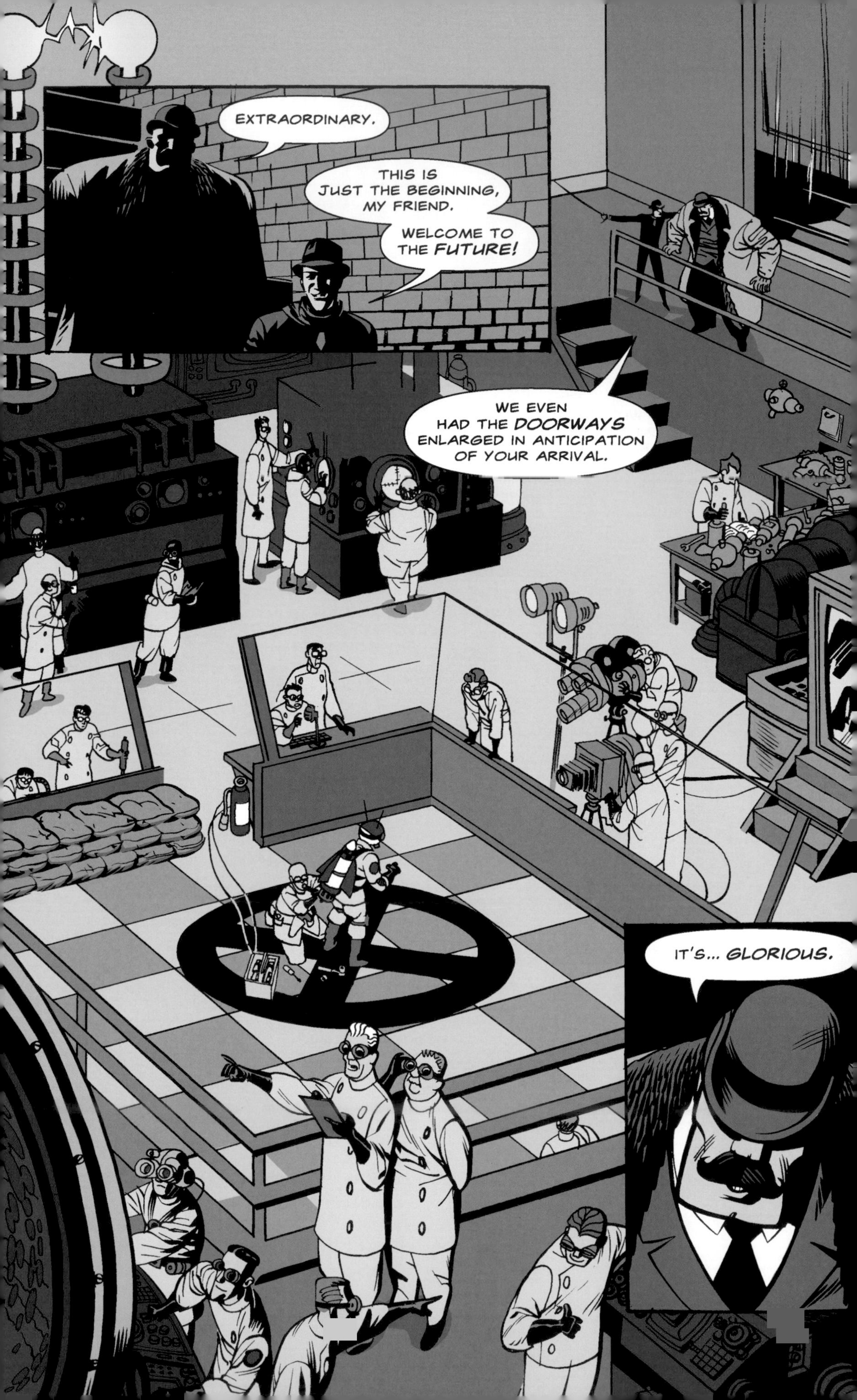
EXTRAORDINARY.
THIS IS JUST THE BEGINNING, MY FRIEND.
WELCOME TO THE *FUTURE!*
WE EVEN HAD THE *DOORWAYS* ENLARGED IN ANTICIPATION OF YOUR ARRIVAL.
IT'S... *GLORIOUS.*

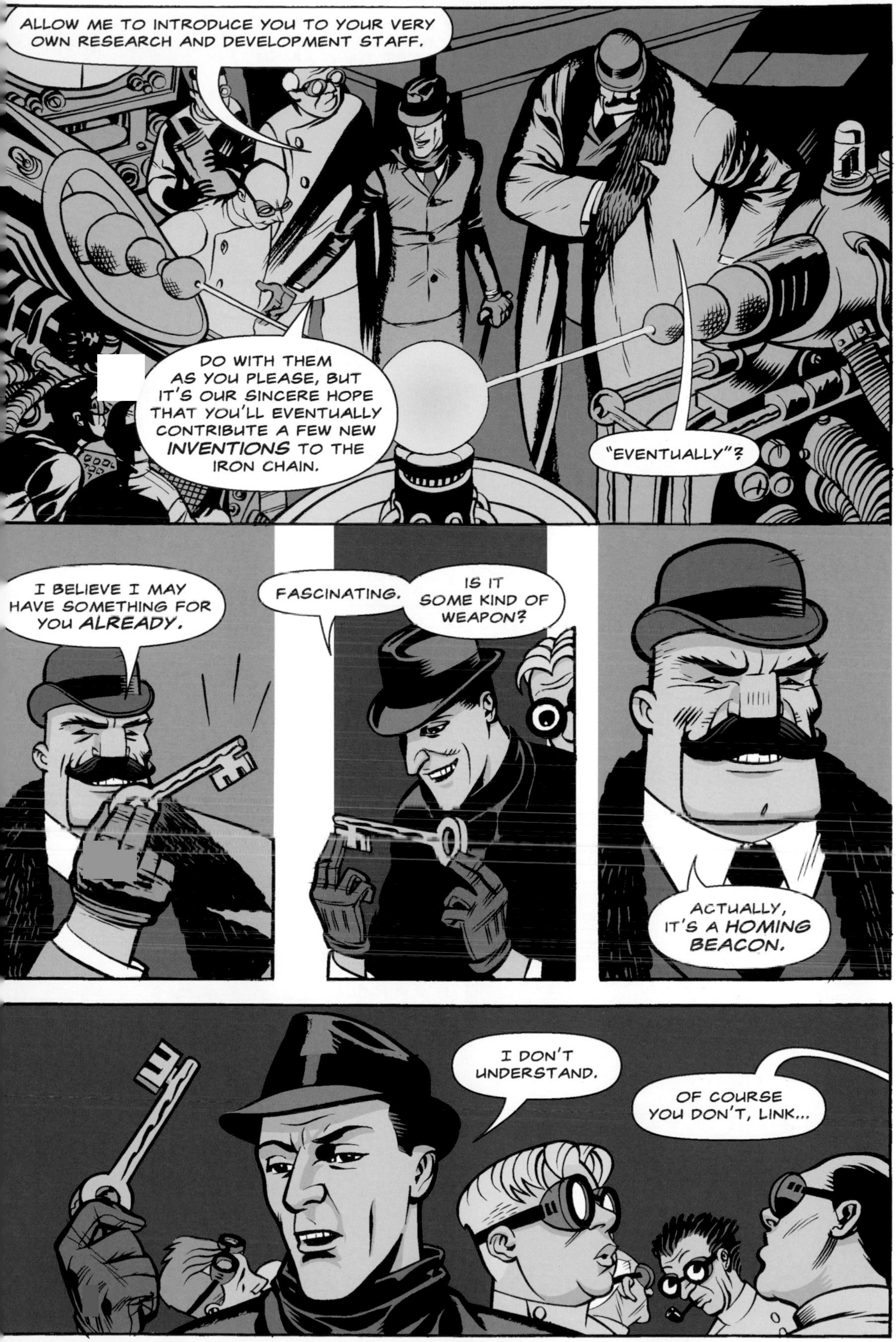
ALLOW ME TO INTRODUCE YOU TO YOUR VERY OWN RESEARCH AND DEVELOPMENT STAFF.
DO WITH THEM AS YOU PLEASE, BUT IT'S OUR SINCERE HOPE THAT YOU'LL EVENTUALLY CONTRIBUTE A FEW NEW *INVENTIONS* TO THE IRON CHAIN.
"EVENTUALLY"?
I BELIEVE I MAY HAVE SOMETHING FOR YOU *ALREADY*.
FASCINATING.
IS IT SOME KIND OF WEAPON?
ACTUALLY, IT'S A *HOMING BEACON*.
I DON'T UNDERSTAND.
OF COURSE YOU DON'T, LINK...

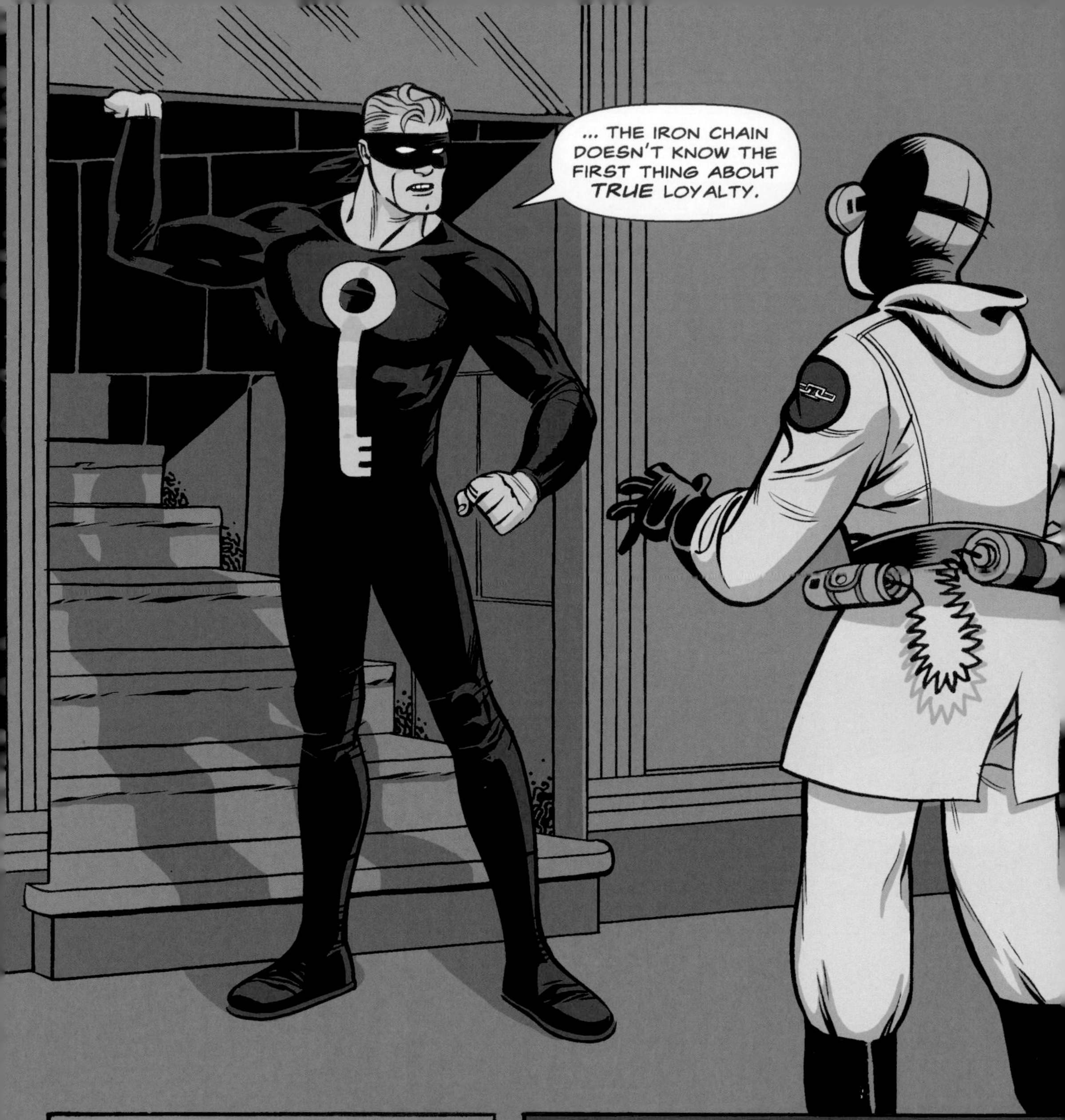
... THE IRON CHAIN DOESN'T KNOW THE FIRST THING ABOUT TRUE LOYALTY.
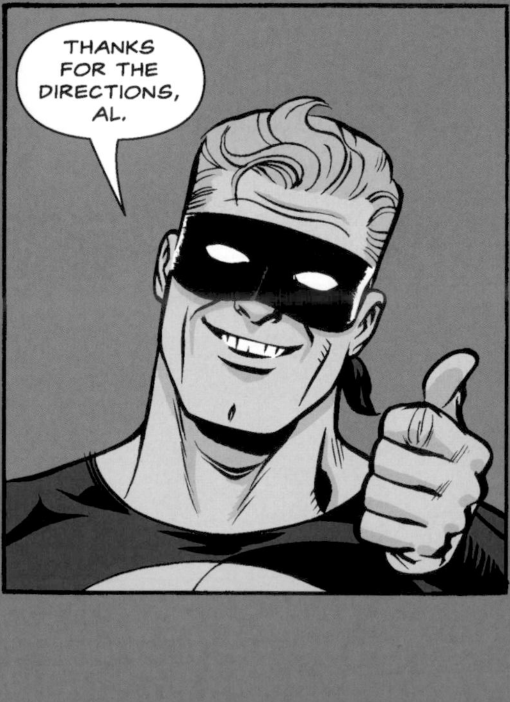
THANKS FOR THE DIRECTIONS, AL.
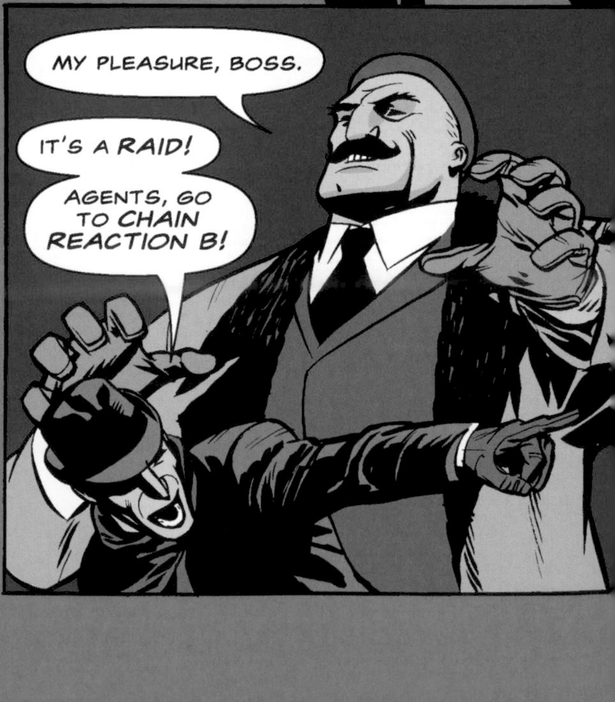
MY PLEASURE, BOSS.
IT'S A RAID!
AGENTS, GO TO CHAIN REACTION B!

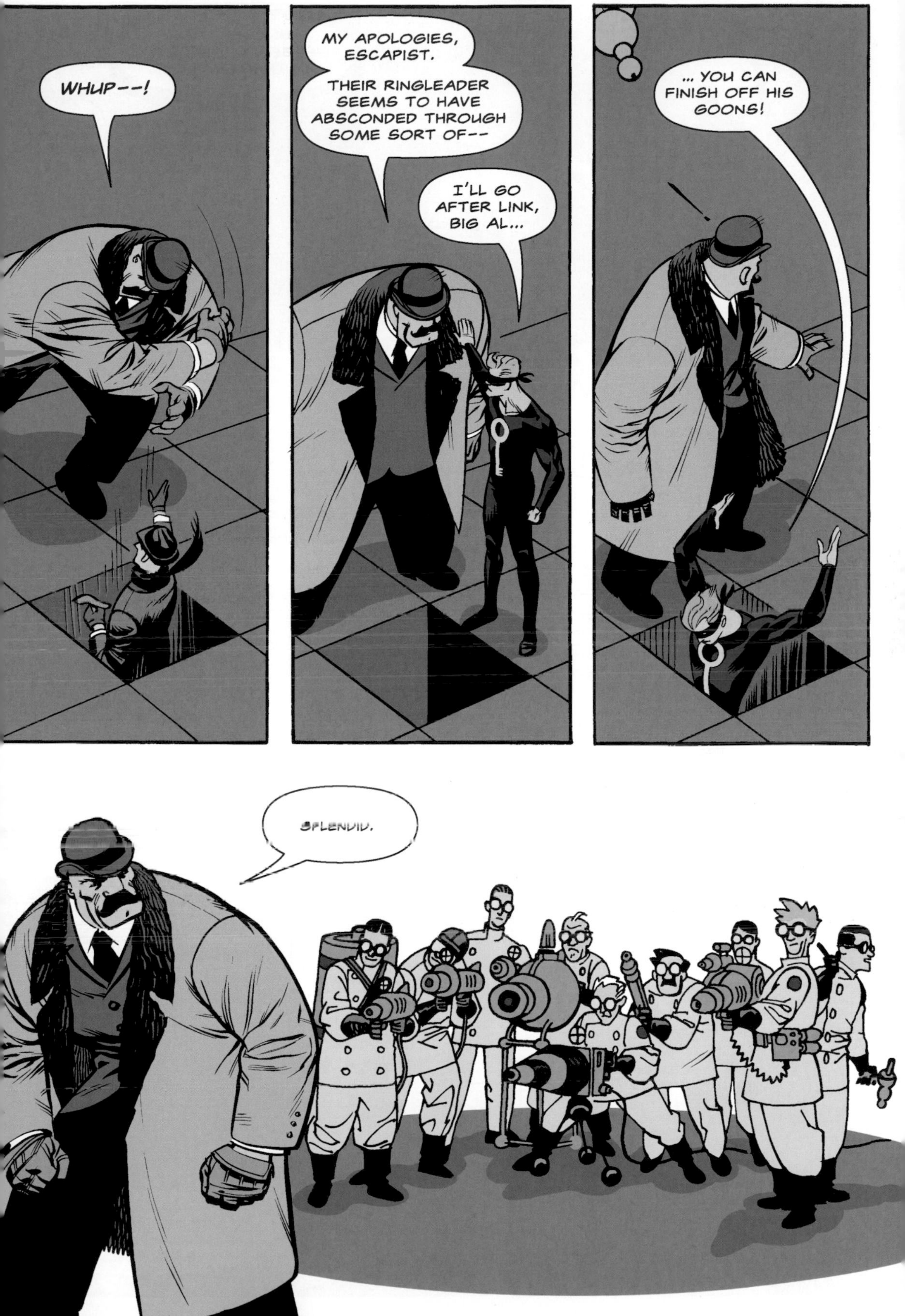
WHUP--!
MY APOLOGIES, ESCAPIST.
THEIR RINGLEADER SEEMS TO HAVE ABSCONDED THROUGH SOME SORT OF--
I'LL GO AFTER LINK, BIG AL...
... YOU CAN FINISH OFF HIS GOONS!
SPLENDID.

... BUT YOU ALSO POSSESS *MISERABLE MARKSMANSHIP.*

GENTLEMEN, YOU MAY HAVE FORMIDABLE FIREPOWER...

NOW THEN, WHAT SAY WE AGREE TO AN AMICABLE ARMISTICE...

... BEFORE I RUN OUT OF ANNOYING ALLITERATION!

RELAX, WE... WE *SURRENDER!*

WE'RE *SCIENTISTS,* NOT SOLDIERS!

YEAH, IT'S TOUGH TO FIND BRAINS AND BRAWN IN THE SAME PACKAGE...

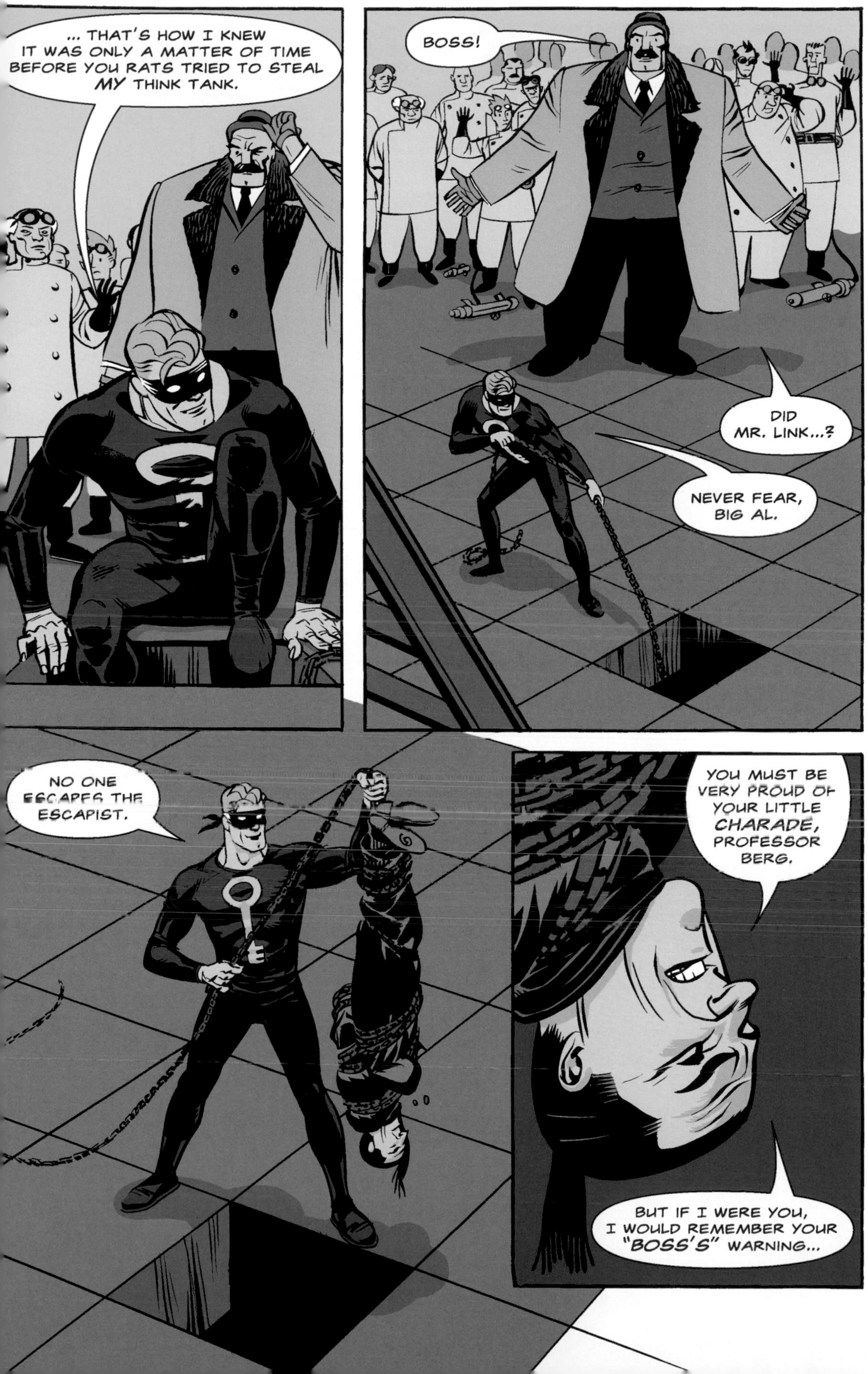
... THAT'S HOW I KNEW IT WAS ONLY A MATTER OF TIME BEFORE YOU RATS TRIED TO STEAL MY THINK TANK.
BOSS!
DID MR. LINK...?
NEVER FEAR, BIG AL.
NO ONE ESCAPES THE ESCAPIST.
YOU MUST BE VERY PROUD OF YOUR LITTLE CHARADE, PROFESSOR BERG.
BUT IF I WERE YOU, I WOULD REMEMBER YOUR "BOSS'S" WARNING...

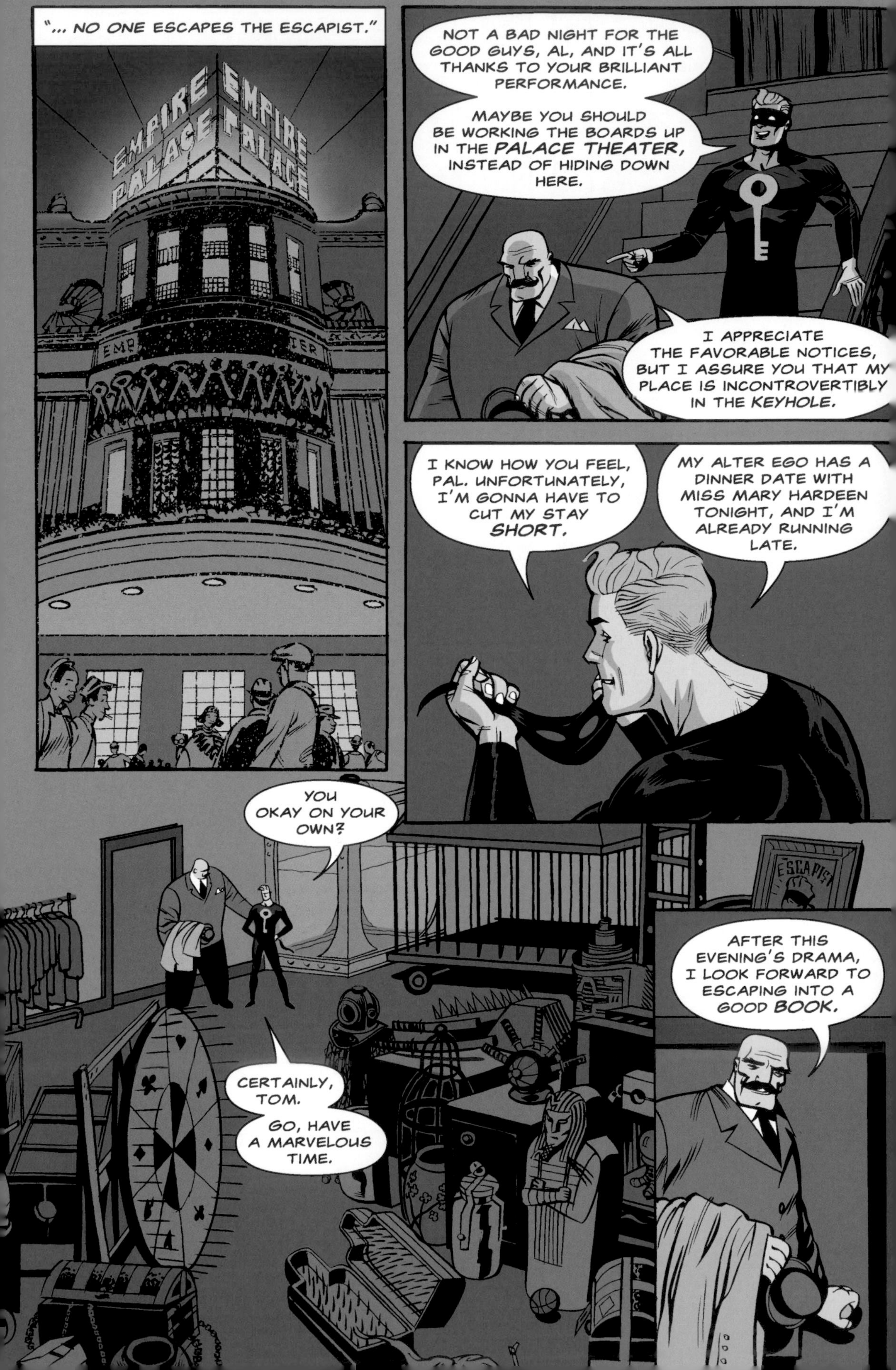
"... NO ONE ESCAPES THE ESCAPIST."
EMPIRE PALACE
EMPIRE PALACE
NOT A BAD NIGHT FOR THE GOOD GUYS, AL, AND IT'S ALL THANKS TO YOUR BRILLIANT PERFORMANCE.
MAYBE YOU SHOULD BE WORKING THE BOARDS UP IN THE PALACE THEATER, INSTEAD OF HIDING DOWN HERE.
I APPRECIATE THE FAVORABLE NOTICES, BUT I ASSURE YOU THAT MY PLACE IS INCONTROVERTIBLY IN THE KEYHOLE.
I KNOW HOW YOU FEEL, PAL. UNFORTUNATELY, I'M GONNA HAVE TO CUT MY STAY SHORT.
MY ALTER EGO HAS A DINNER DATE WITH MISS MARY HARDEEN TONIGHT, AND I'M ALREADY RUNNING LATE.
YOU OKAY ON YOUR OWN?
CERTAINLY, TOM.
GO, HAVE A MARVELOUS TIME.
ESCAPIST
AFTER THIS EVENING'S DRAMA, I LOOK FORWARD TO ESCAPING INTO A GOOD BOOK.

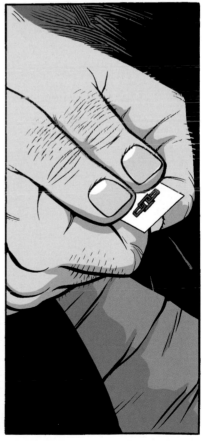

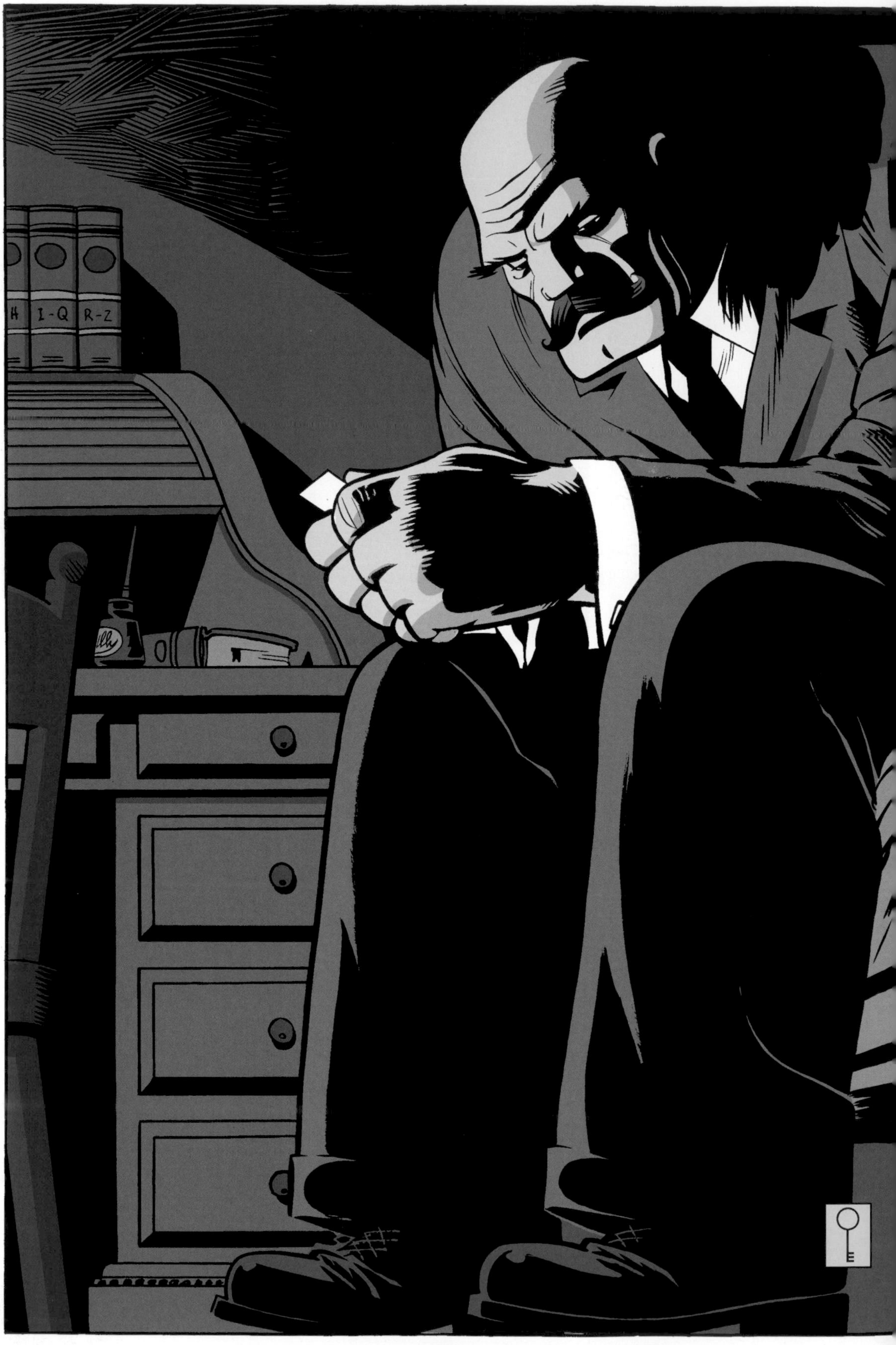
I-Q
R-Z

THOUGH THE ESCAPIST IS THE ***GREATEST HERO*** THE ***FORCES OF LIBERATION*** HAVE EVER KNOWN, EVEN ***HE*** CANNOT ELUDE ***DEATH*** FOREVER! SOMEDAY, IN THE FUTURE, ***OTHERS*** WILL CARRY ON THE MANTLE OF THE ***ESCAPIST...*** AS SEEN IN THIS CLASSIC STORY BY AWARD-WINNING SCI-FI SCRIBE ***CYRIL M. CUTTER.*** CUTTER PENNED DOZENS OF TELEPLAYS, EDITED A VARIETY OF GENERAL INTEREST MAGAZINES, AND WROTE HUNDREDS OF LEGENDARY SHORT STORIES. SADLY, HE IS NO LONGER WITH US...BUT IN THIS VERY SPECIAL ***EDITOR'S CHOICE REPRINT***, YOU, READER, CAN ONCE AGAIN ***THRILL*** TO THE ***ROCKET-BLASTING ADVENTURES OF...***

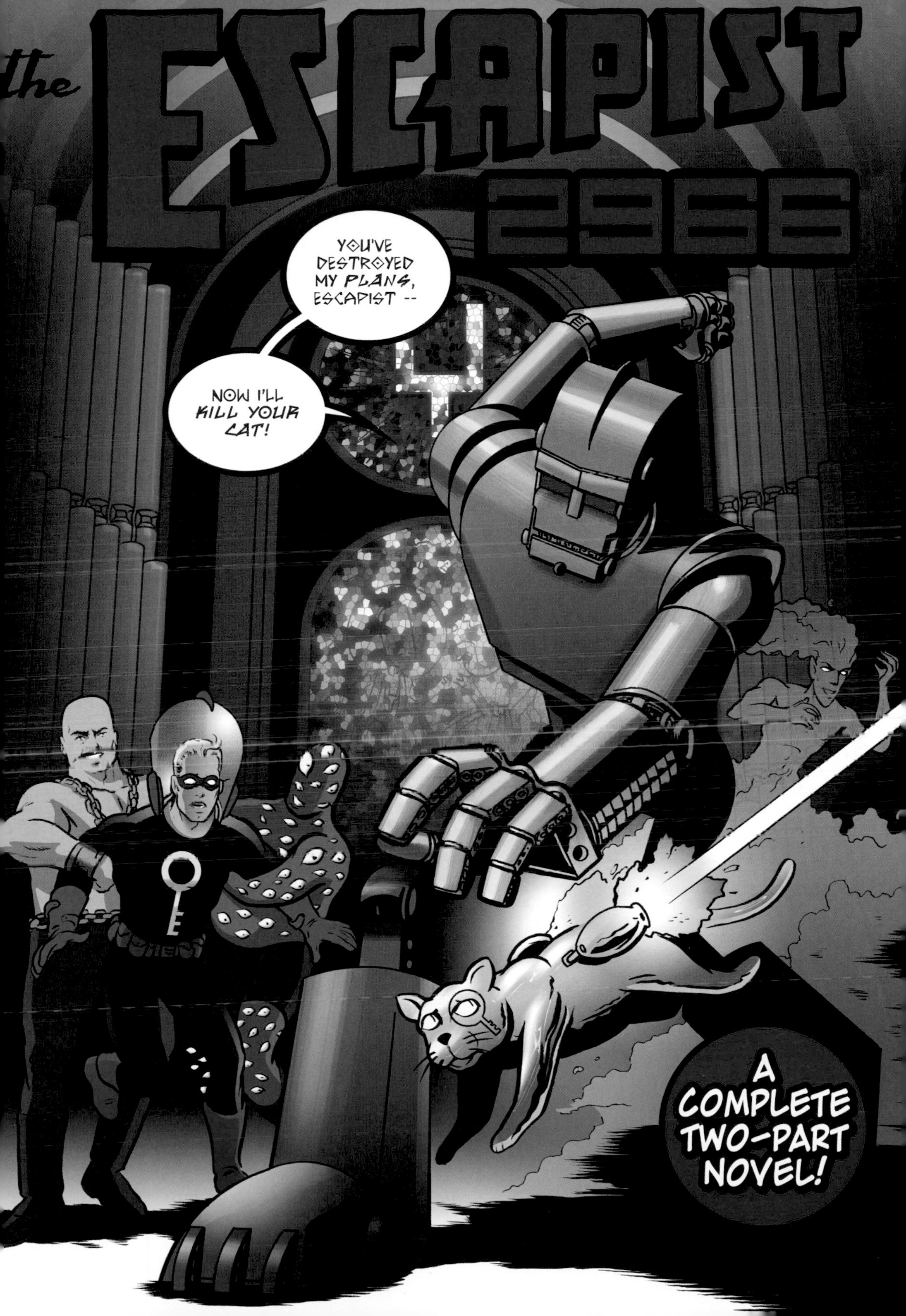
the ESCAPIST 2966
YOU'VE DESTROYED MY *PLANS*, ESCAPIST --
NOW I'LL *KILL YOUR CAT!*
A COMPLETE TWO-PART NOVEL!

...AND WHAT OF THE ESCAPIST?

THIS IS A **TOUGH** ONE!

MY ARCH-ENEMIES, THE **IRON CHAIN**, HAVE TRAPPED ME IN THIS **GIANT CLAM** -- AT THE BOTTOM OF THE **MARIANAS TRENCH**\*...

*EDITOR'S NOTE: AT 32,842 FEET BELOW SEA LEVEL, THE MARIANAS TRENCH IS THE DEEPEST POINT ON THE OCEAN FLOOR!*

...AND IF I **DO** BREAK LOOSE, THE EXPLOSION FROM THIS **TORPEX DEPTH CHARGE**\* WILL **KILL** ME!

BUT I'VE **GOT** TO GET **FREE!** THOSE MONSTERS ARE GOING TO **KILL** PRESIDENT **JOHNSON!**

*EDITOR'S NOTE: TORPEX, WHICH IS 50% MORE POWERFUL THAN TNT, WAS USED IN DEPTH CHARGES BEGINNING LATE IN WORLD WAR II!*

LET'S SEE -- THAT DEPTH CHARGE IS DETONATED BY **IMPACT**, NOT **HEAT** --

SO IF I CAN JUST **WARM UP** THE SURROUNDING **WATER** WITH THIS **OXY-ACETYLENE TORCH** --

VOILÀ!

JUST LIKE **COOKING CLAMS** FOR DINNER -- THEY OPEN BY **THEMSELVES!**

GOOD THING I'VE GOT ON MY **SCUBA**\* GEAR!

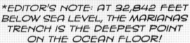

*EDITOR'S NOTE: SCUBA: SELF-CONTAINED UNDERWATER BREATHING APPARATUS!*

TIME TO LIVE UP TO MY REPUTATION AS THE **CHAMPION OF DEMOCRACY**\* --

*EDITOR'S NOTE: DEMOCRACY -- THE ONLY FORM OF GOVERNMENT IN THE DAMN WORLD WORTH FIGHTING FOR -- DATES BACK*

DAYDREAMING AGAIN?

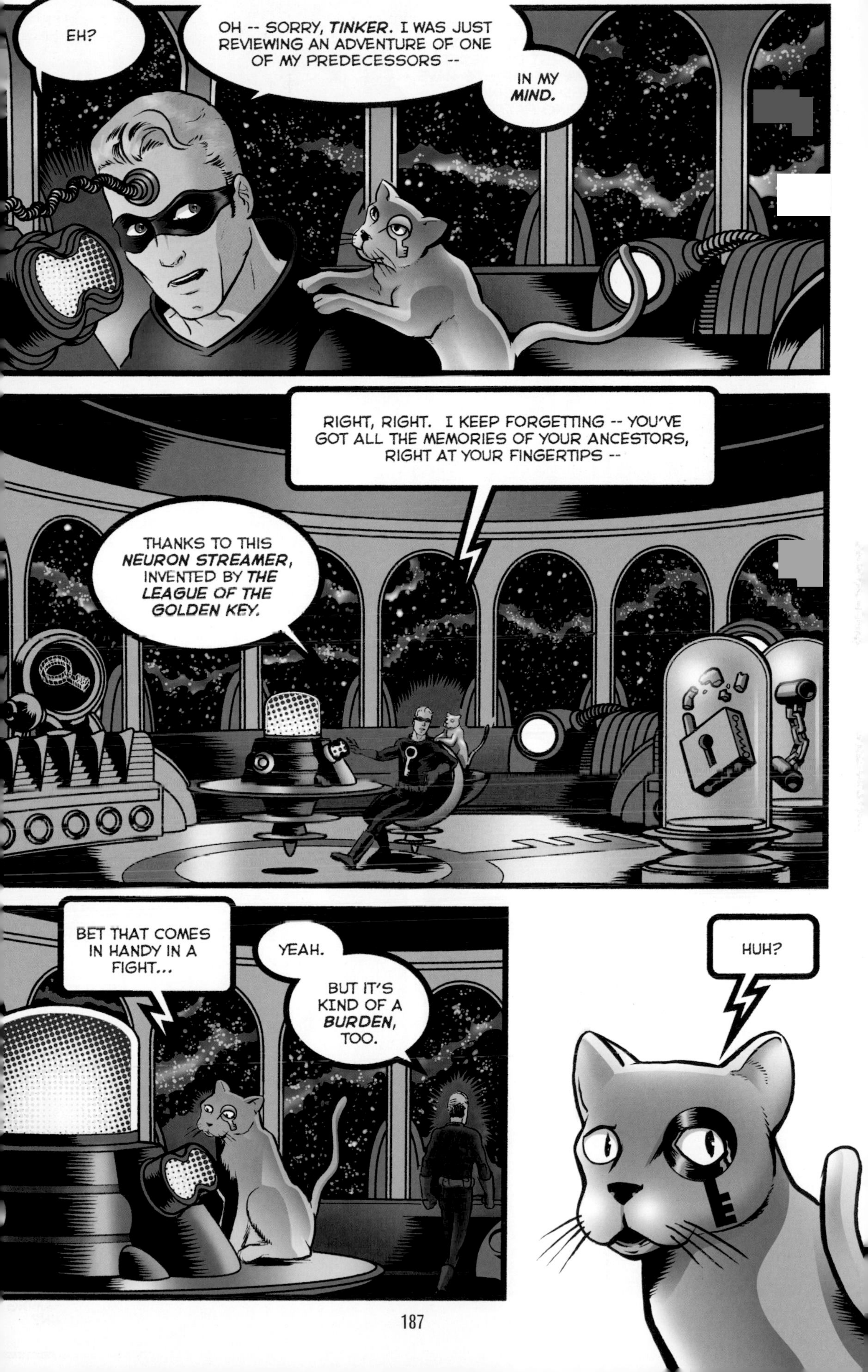
EH?
OH -- SORRY, *TINKER.* I WAS JUST REVIEWING AN ADVENTURE OF ONE OF MY PREDECESSORS --
IN MY *MIND.*
RIGHT, RIGHT. I KEEP FORGETTING -- YOU'VE GOT ALL THE MEMORIES OF YOUR ANCESTORS, RIGHT AT YOUR FINGERTIPS --
THANKS TO THIS *NEURON STREAMER,* INVENTED BY *THE LEAGUE OF THE GOLDEN KEY.*
BET THAT COMES IN HANDY IN A FIGHT...
YEAH.
BUT IT'S KIND OF A *BURDEN,* TOO.
HUH?

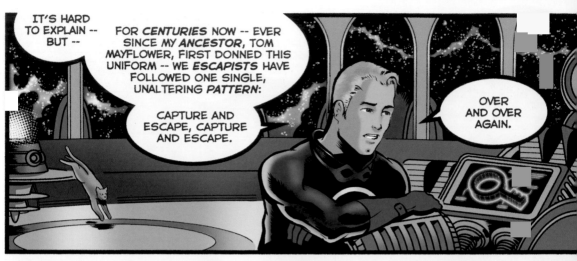

IT'S HARD TO EXPLAIN -- BUT --

FOR *CENTURIES* NOW -- EVER SINCE *MY ANCESTOR,* TOM MAYFLOWER, FIRST DONNED THIS UNIFORM -- WE *ESCAPISTS* HAVE FOLLOWED ONE SINGLE, UNALTERING *PATTERN:*

CAPTURE AND ESCAPE, CAPTURE AND ESCAPE.

OVER AND OVER AGAIN.

AND IT'S...IT'S STARTING TO FEEL LIKE A *TRAP,* YOU KNOW?

LIKE A COSMIC CIRCLE THAT ALWAYS LEADS RIGHT BACK WHERE IT STARTED. *FOREVER.*

TAKE THE *LEAGUE*...THEY'VE BEEN FIGHTING THE IRON CHAIN FOR *ALL OF HUMAN HISTORY.*

WHERE HAS IT *GOTTEN* THEM?

SHOULDN'T THEY HAVE *WON* BY NOW?

EVEN AFTER ALL THESE CENTURIES, THE LEAGUE IS STILL A *MYSTERY.* THEY'VE GIVEN ME THE NEURON STREAMER, THIS KEY-SATELLITE, AND *YOU* --

BUT SOMETIMES... IT FEELS LIKE *THEY'RE* THE ONES WHO'VE GOT ME CORNERED.

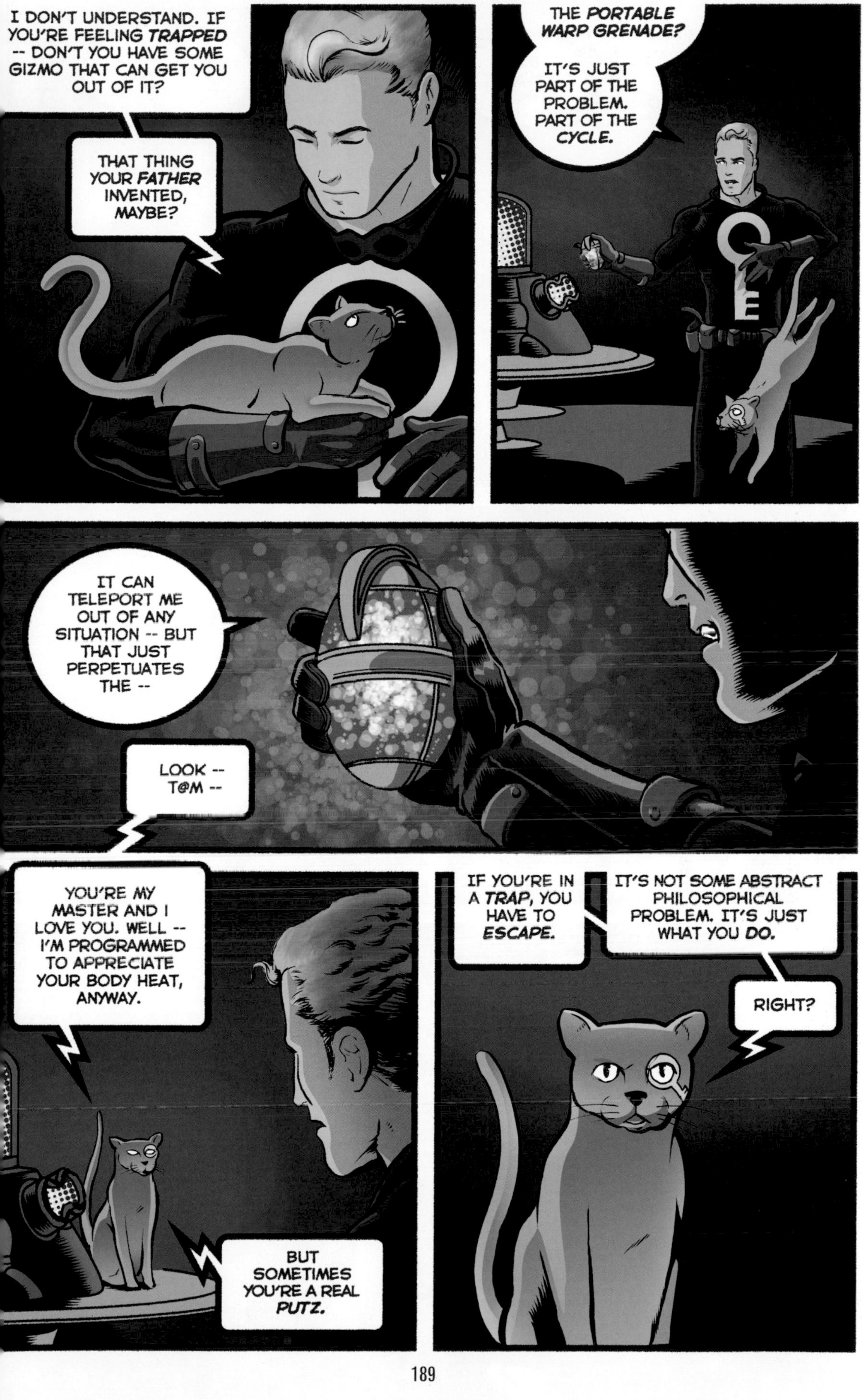
I DON'T UNDERSTAND. IF YOU'RE FEELING *TRAPPED* -- DON'T YOU HAVE SOME GIZMO THAT CAN GET YOU OUT OF IT?
THAT THING YOUR *FATHER* INVENTED, MAYBE?
THE *PORTABLE WARP GRENADE?*
IT'S JUST PART OF THE PROBLEM. PART OF THE *CYCLE.*
IT CAN TELEPORT ME OUT OF ANY SITUATION -- BUT THAT JUST PERPETUATES THE --
LOOK -- T@M --
YOU'RE MY MASTER AND I LOVE YOU. WELL -- I'M PROGRAMMED TO APPRECIATE YOUR BODY HEAT, ANYWAY.
BUT SOMETIMES YOU'RE A REAL *PUTZ.*
IF YOU'RE IN A *TRAP,* YOU HAVE TO *ESCAPE.*
IT'S NOT SOME ABSTRACT PHILOSOPHICAL PROBLEM. IT'S JUST WHAT YOU *DO.*
RIGHT?

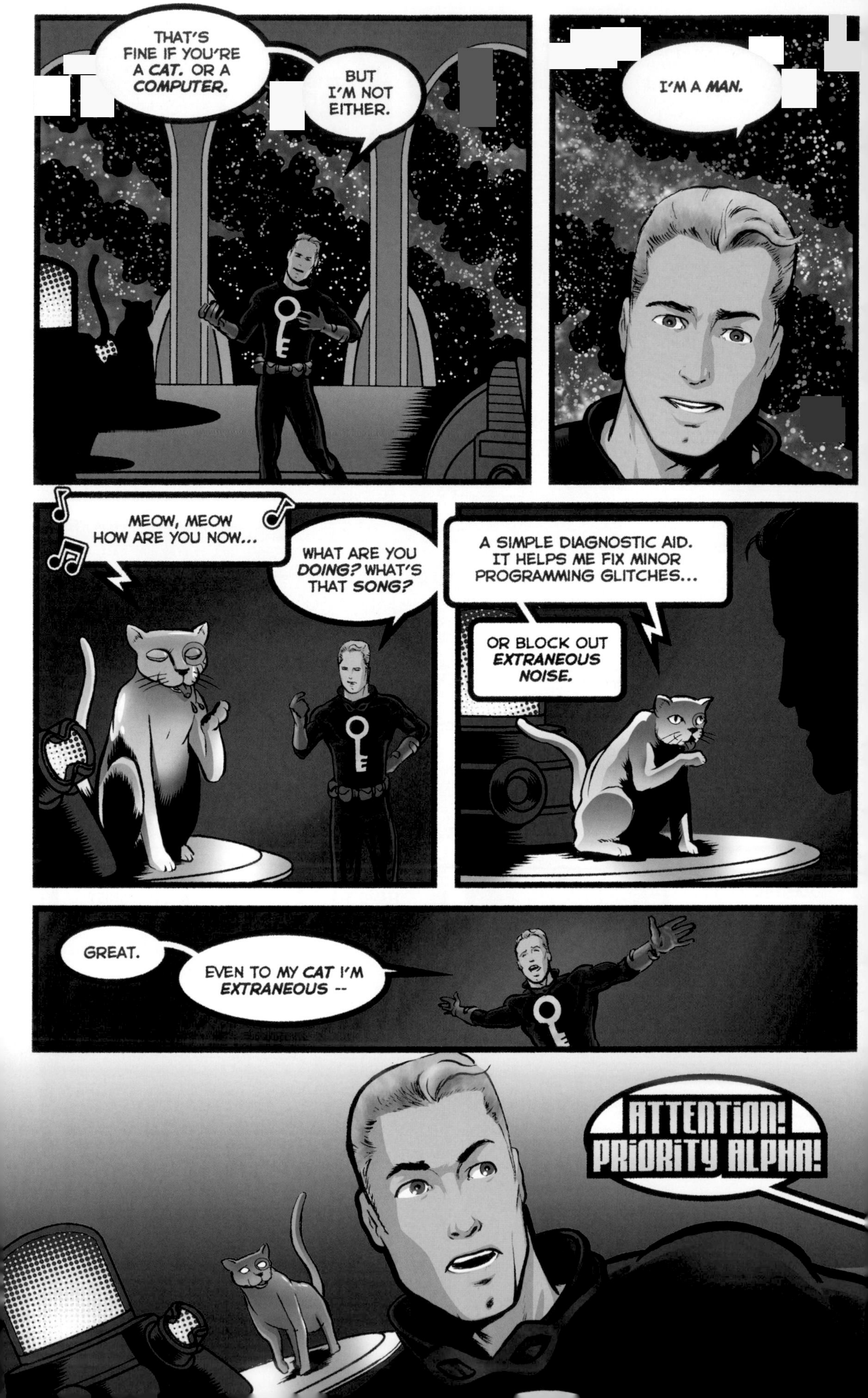
THAT'S FINE IF YOU'RE A *CAT.* OR A *COMPUTER.*
BUT I'M NOT EITHER.
I'M A *MAN.*
MEOW, MEOW HOW ARE YOU NOW...
WHAT ARE YOU *DOING?* WHAT'S THAT *SONG?*
A SIMPLE DIAGNOSTIC AID. IT HELPS ME FIX MINOR PROGRAMMING GLITCHES...
OR BLOCK OUT *EXTRANEOUS NOISE.*
GREAT.
EVEN TO *MY CAT* I'M *EXTRANEOUS* --
ATTENTION! PRIORITY ALPHA!

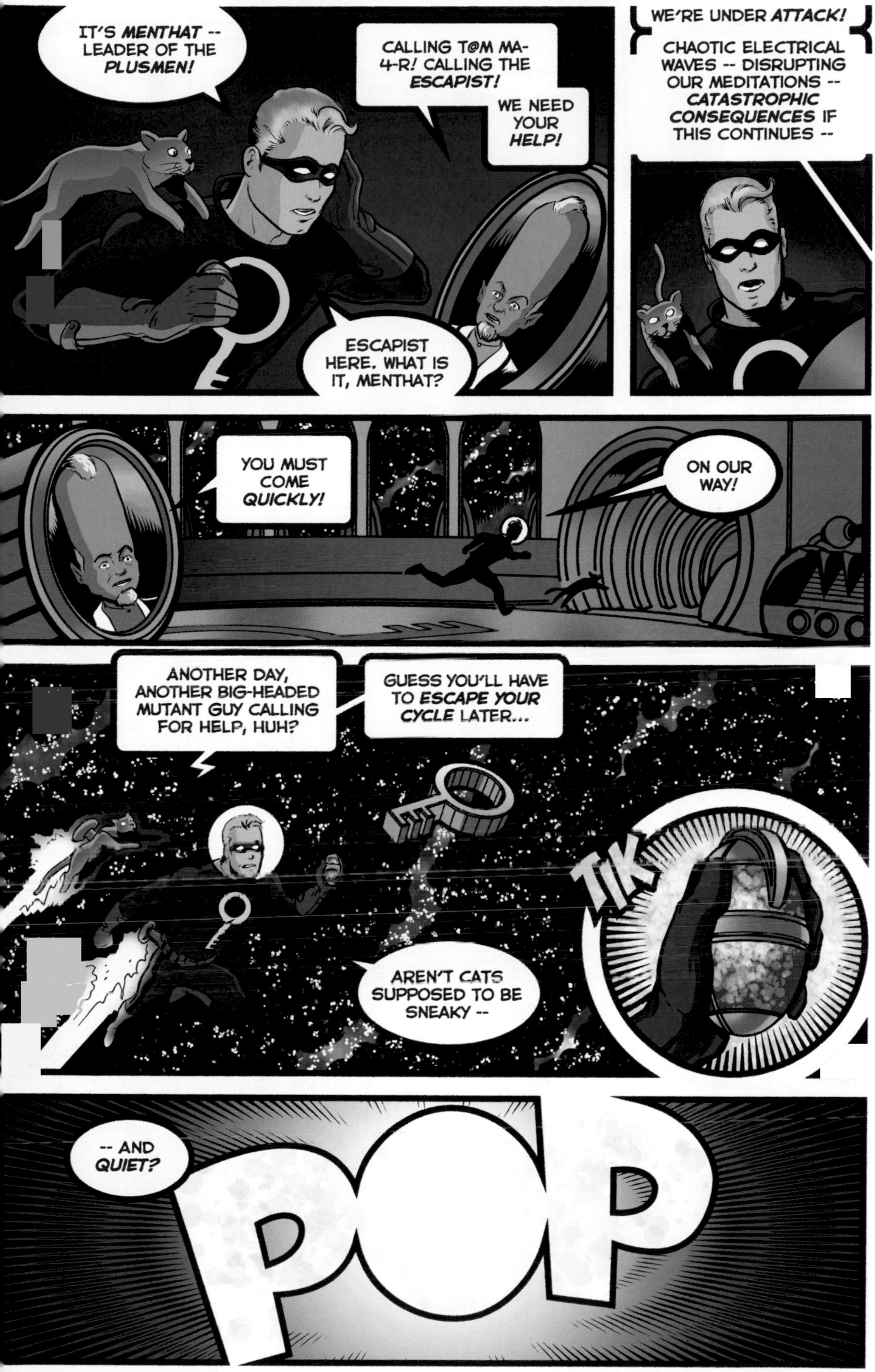
IT'S MENTHAT -- LEADER OF THE PLUSMEN!
CALLING T@M MA-4-R! CALLING THE ESCAPIST!
WE NEED YOUR HELP!
ESCAPIST HERE. WHAT IS IT, MENTHAT?
WE'RE UNDER ATTACK!
CHAOTIC ELECTRICAL WAVES -- DISRUPTING OUR MEDITATIONS -- CATASTROPHIC CONSEQUENCES IF THIS CONTINUES --
YOU MUST COME QUICKLY!
ON OUR WAY!
ANOTHER DAY, ANOTHER BIG-HEADED MUTANT GUY CALLING FOR HELP, HUH?
GUESS YOU'LL HAVE TO ESCAPE YOUR CYCLE LATER...
TIK
AREN'T CATS SUPPOSED TO BE SNEAKY --
-- AND QUIET?
POP

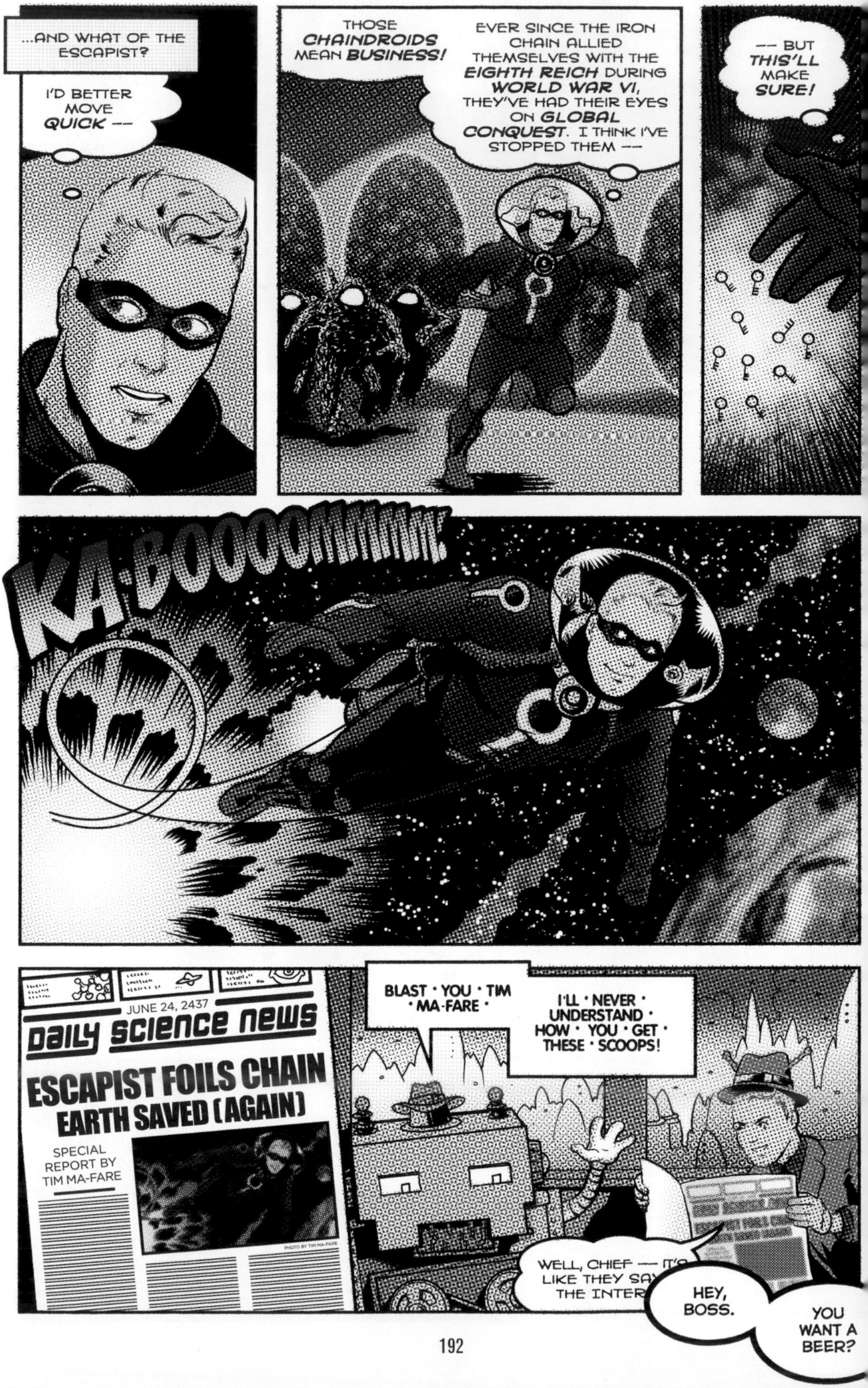

...AND WHAT OF THE ESCAPIST?
I'D BETTER MOVE *QUICK* ––
THOSE *CHAINDROIDS* MEAN *BUSINESS!*
EVER SINCE THE IRON CHAIN ALLIED THEMSELVES WITH THE *EIGHTH REICH* DURING *WORLD WAR VI*, THEY'VE HAD THEIR EYES ON *GLOBAL CONQUEST*. I THINK I'VE STOPPED THEM ––
–– BUT *THIS'LL* MAKE *SURE!*
KA-BOOOOOMMMMM!
JUNE 24, 2437
DAILY SCIENCE NEWS
ESCAPIST FOILS CHAIN
EARTH SAVED (AGAIN)
SPECIAL REPORT BY TIM MA-FARE
PHOTO BY TIM MA-FARE
BLAST · YOU · TIM · MA-FARE ·
I'LL · NEVER · UNDERSTAND · HOW · YOU · GET · THESE · SCOOPS!
WELL, CHIEF –– IT'S LIKE THEY SA THE INTER
HEY, BOSS.
YOU WANT A BEER?

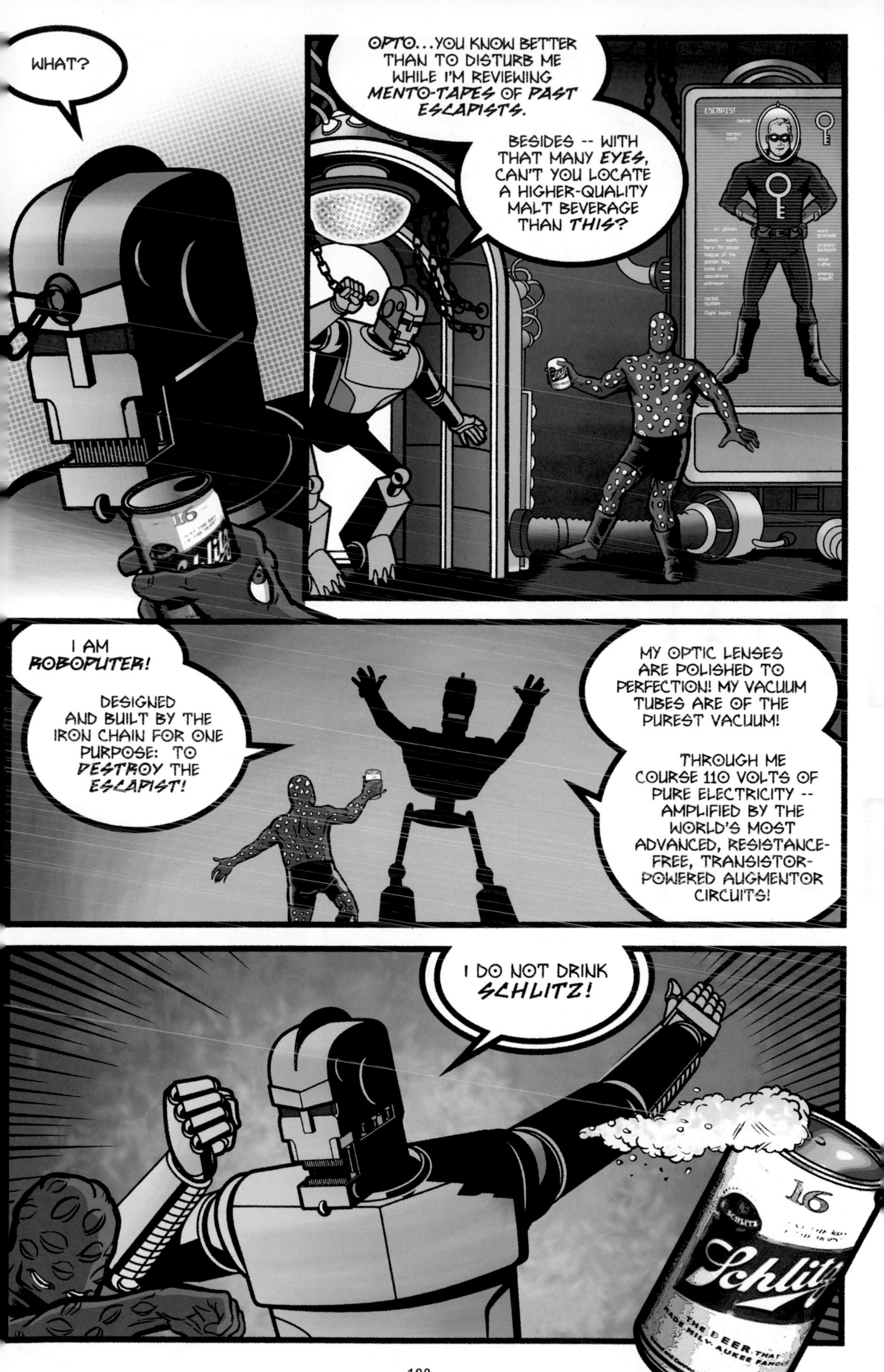
WHAT?
OPTO...YOU KNOW BETTER THAN TO DISTURB ME WHILE I'M REVIEWING MENTO-TAPES OF PAST ESCAPISTS.
BESIDES -- WITH THAT MANY EYES, CAN'T YOU LOCATE A HIGHER-QUALITY MALT BEVERAGE THAN THIS?
ESCAPIST
I AM ROBOPUTER!
DESIGNED AND BUILT BY THE IRON CHAIN FOR ONE PURPOSE: TO DESTROY THE ESCAPIST!
MY OPTIC LENSES ARE POLISHED TO PERFECTION! MY VACUUM TUBES ARE OF THE PUREST VACUUM!
THROUGH ME COURSE 110 VOLTS OF PURE ELECTRICITY -- AMPLIFIED BY THE WORLD'S MOST ADVANCED, RESISTANCE-FREE, TRANSISTOR-POWERED AUGMENTOR CIRCUITS!
I DO NOT DRINK SCHLITZ!
16
Schlitz

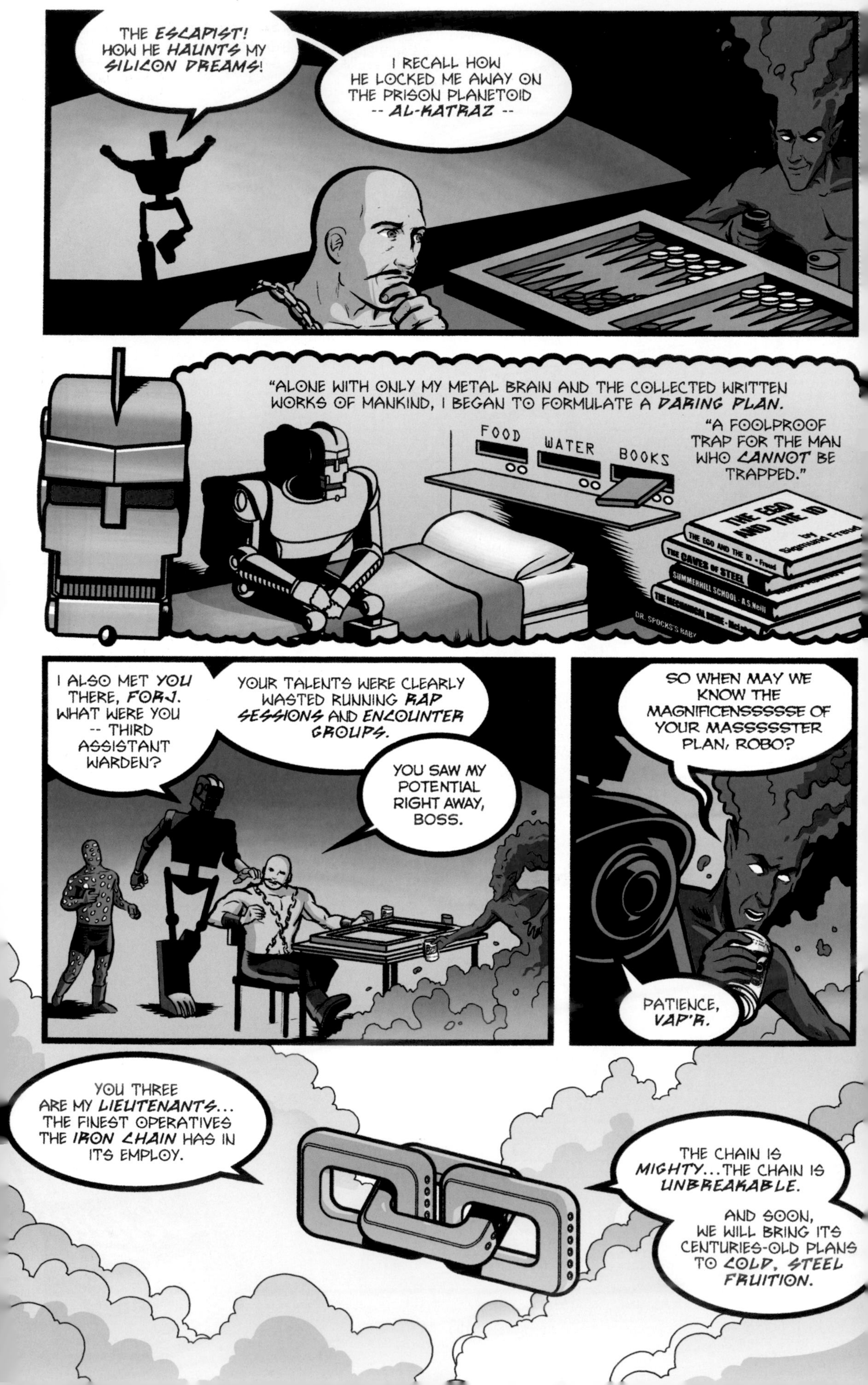
THE ESCAPIST! HOW HE HAUNTS MY SILICON DREAMS!
I RECALL HOW HE LOCKED ME AWAY ON THE PRISON PLANETOID -- AL-KATRAZ --
"ALONE WITH ONLY MY METAL BRAIN AND THE COLLECTED WRITTEN WORKS OF MANKIND, I BEGAN TO FORMULATE A DARING PLAN.
FOOD
WATER
BOOKS
"A FOOLPROOF TRAP FOR THE MAN WHO CANNOT BE TRAPPED."
THE EGO AND THE ID by Sigmund Freud
THE EGO AND THE ID • Freud
THE CAVES OF STEEL
SUMMERHILL SCHOOL • A.S.Neill
DR. SPOCKS'S BABY
I ALSO MET YOU THERE, FORJ. WHAT WERE YOU -- THIRD ASSISTANT WARDEN?
YOUR TALENTS WERE CLEARLY WASTED RUNNING RAP SESSIONS AND ENCOUNTER GROUPS.
YOU SAW MY POTENTIAL RIGHT AWAY, BOSS.
SO WHEN MAY WE KNOW THE MAGNIFICENSSSSSE OF YOUR MASSSSSTER PLAN, ROBO?
PATIENCE, VAP'R.
YOU THREE ARE MY LIEUTENANTS... THE FINEST OPERATIVES THE IRON CHAIN HAS IN ITS EMPLOY.
THE CHAIN IS MIGHTY...THE CHAIN IS UNBREAKABLE.
AND SOON, WE WILL BRING ITS CENTURIES-OLD PLANS TO COLD, STEEL FRUITION.

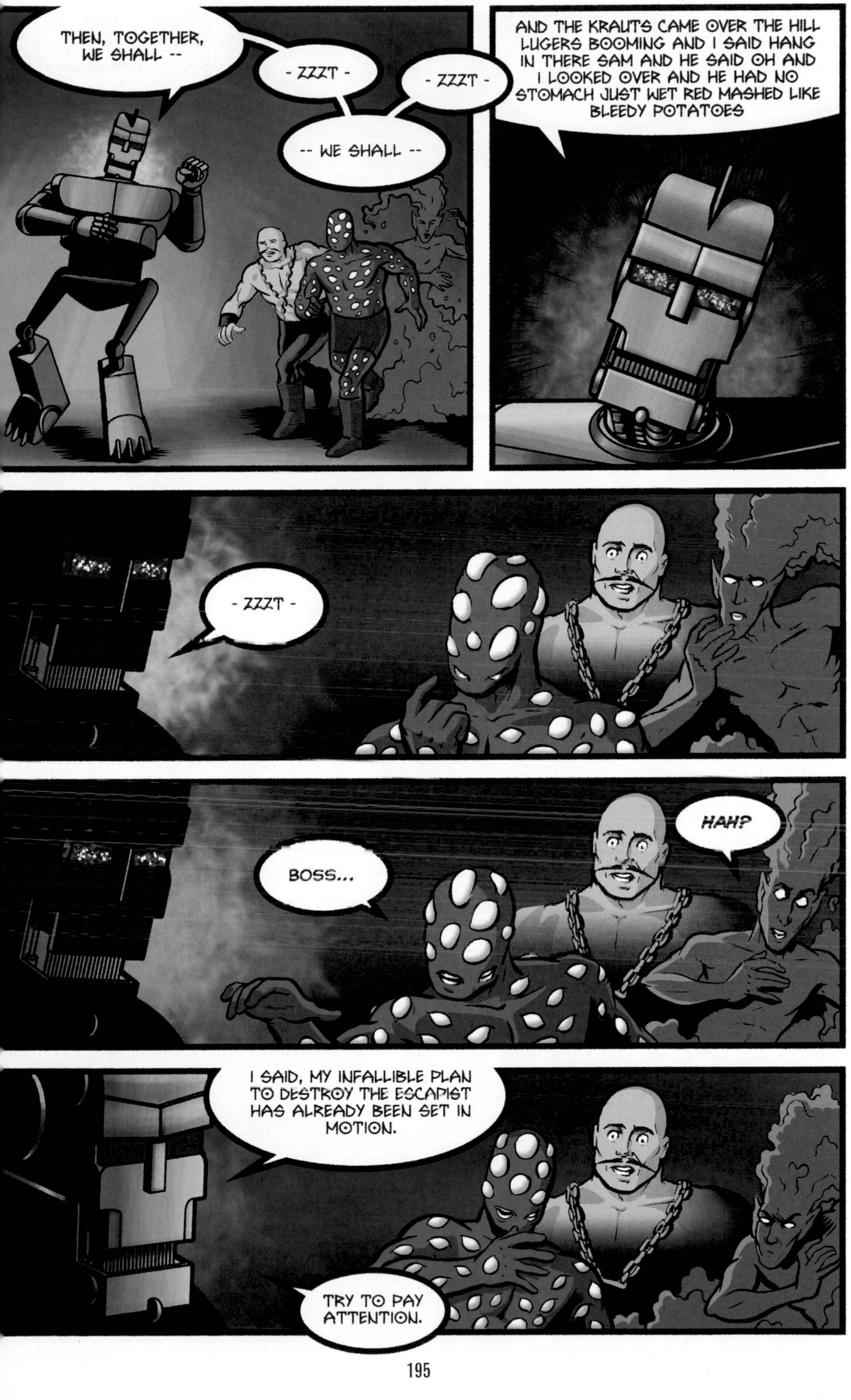
THEN, TOGETHER, WE SHALL --
- ZZZT -
- ZZZT -
-- WE SHALL --
AND THE KRAUTS CAME OVER THE HILL LUGERS BOOMING AND I SAID HANG IN THERE SAM AND HE SAID OH AND I LOOKED OVER AND HE HAD NO STOMACH JUST WET RED MASHED LIKE BLEEDY POTATOES
- ZZZT -
BOSS...
HAH?
I SAID, MY INFALLIBLE PLAN TO DESTROY THE ESCAPIST HAS ALREADY BEEN SET IN MOTION.
TRY TO PAY ATTENTION.

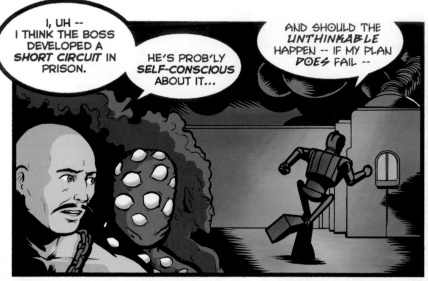

I, UH -- I THINK THE BOSS DEVELOPED A *SHORT CIRCUIT* IN PRISON.

HE'S PROB'LY *SELF-CONSCIOUS* ABOUT IT...

AND SHOULD THE *UNTHINKABLE* HAPPEN -- IF MY PLAN *DOES* FAIL --

THERE IS *THIS.*

IN THIS BOX RESTS THE *ULTIMATE WEAPON.*

IT CAN DESTROY *ANYONE* -- INCLUDING THE *ESCAPIST.*

BOSS -- NO DISRESPECT, BUT --

WE'RE *TIRED* OF SITTIN' AROUND, WAITIN'.

FORJ HERE HAS BUILT AN UNBREAKABLE INER -- INER --

INERTRONIUM

INTERMONIUM COFFIN. WE WANNA GO FIND THE ESCAPIST --

YESSS! AND *SSSSNARE* HIM!

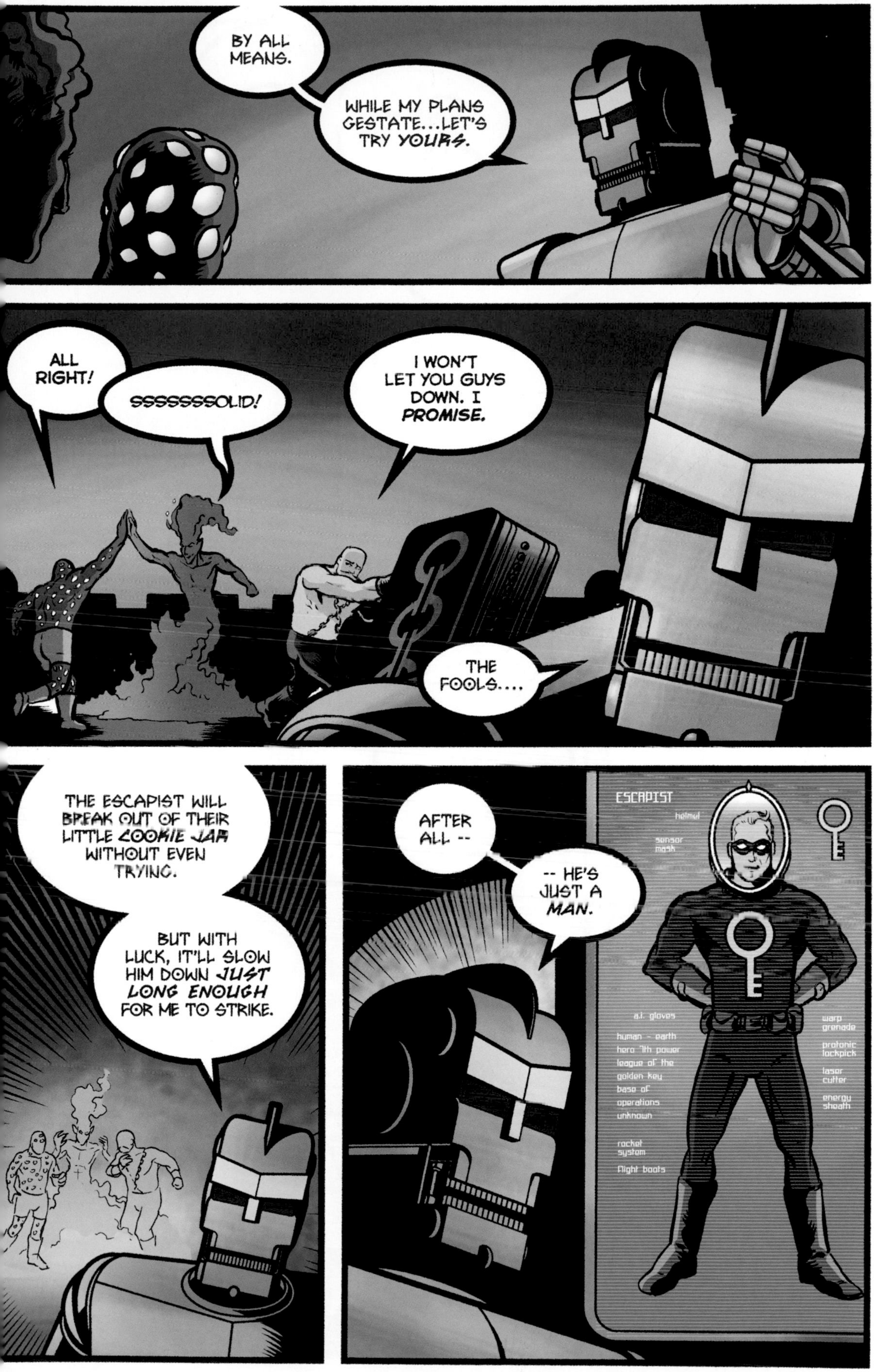
BY ALL MEANS.
WHILE MY PLANS GESTATE...LET'S TRY *YOURS.*
ALL RIGHT!
SSSSSSSOLID!
I WON'T LET YOU GUYS DOWN. I *PROMISE.*
THE FOOLS....
THE ESCAPIST WILL BREAK OUT OF THEIR LITTLE *COOKIE JAR* WITHOUT EVEN TRYING.
BUT WITH LUCK, IT'LL SLOW HIM DOWN *JUST LONG ENOUGH* FOR ME TO STRIKE.
AFTER ALL --
-- HE'S JUST A *MAN.*
ESCAPIST
helmet
sensor mask
a.i. gloves
human - earth
hero 7th power
league of the golden key
base of operations unknown
rocket system
flight boots
warp grenade
protonic lockpick
laser cutter
energy sheath

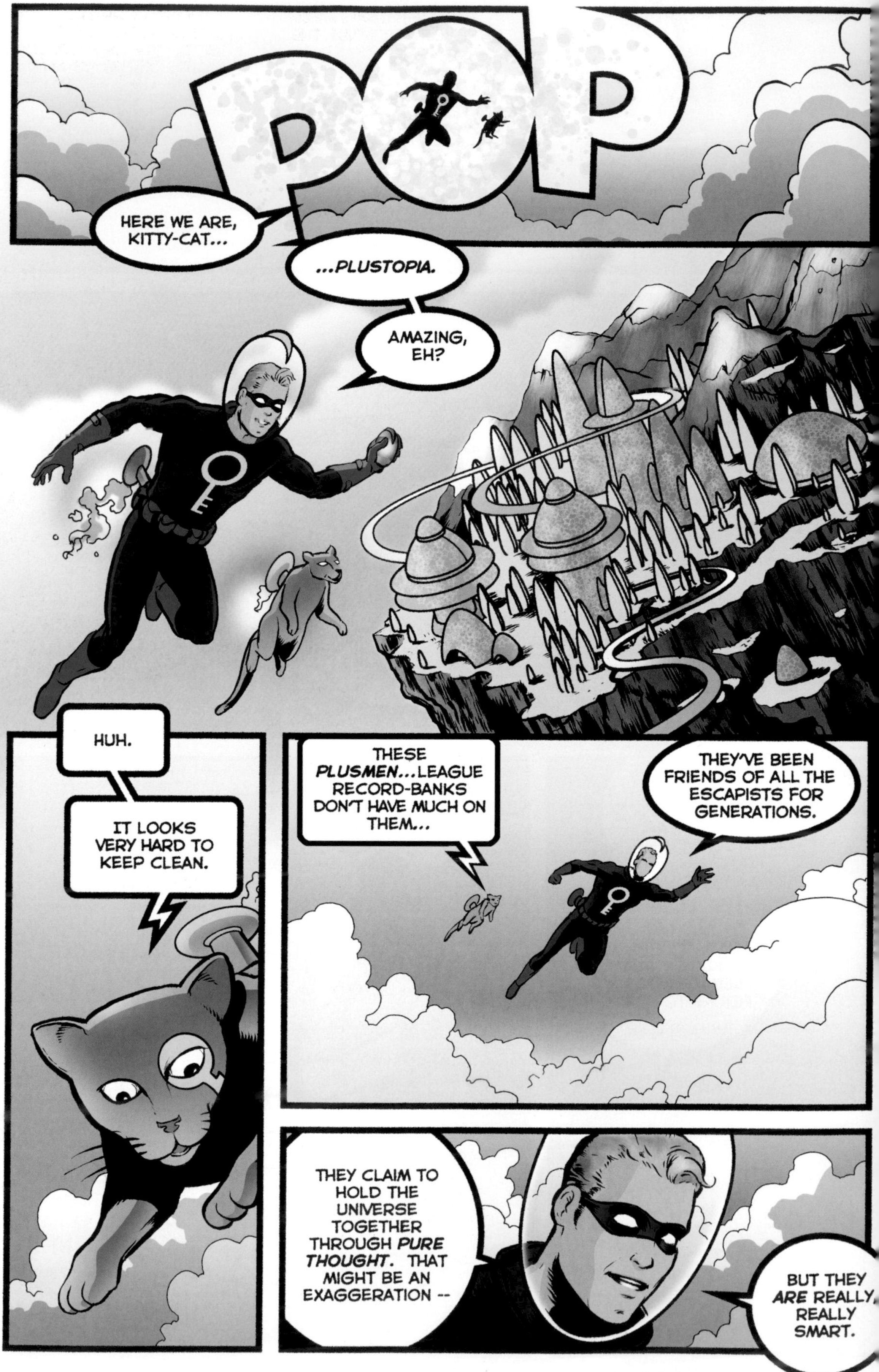
POP
HERE WE ARE, KITTY-CAT...
...PLUSTOPIA.
AMAZING, EH?
HUH.
IT LOOKS VERY HARD TO KEEP CLEAN.
THESE PLUSMEN...LEAGUE RECORD-BANKS DON'T HAVE MUCH ON THEM...
THEY'VE BEEN FRIENDS OF ALL THE ESCAPISTS FOR GENERATIONS.
THEY CLAIM TO HOLD THE UNIVERSE TOGETHER THROUGH PURE THOUGHT. THAT MIGHT BE AN EXAGGERATION --
BUT THEY ARE REALLY, REALLY SMART.

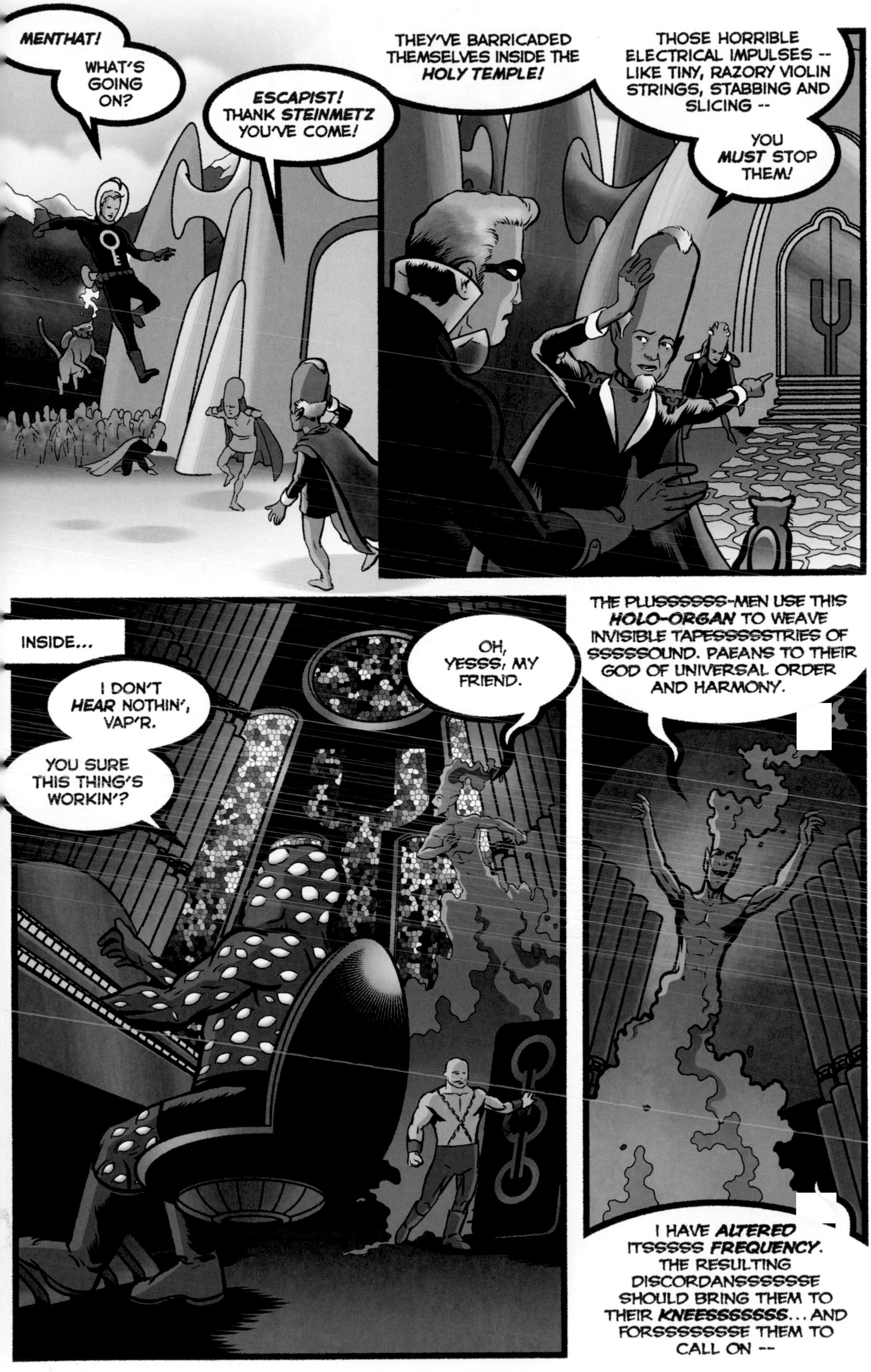
MENTHAT!
WHAT'S GOING ON?
ESCAPIST! THANK STEINMETZ YOU'VE COME!
THEY'VE BARRICADED THEMSELVES INSIDE THE HOLY TEMPLE!
THOSE HORRIBLE ELECTRICAL IMPULSES -- LIKE TINY, RAZORY VIOLIN STRINGS, STABBING AND SLICING --
YOU MUST STOP THEM!
INSIDE...
I DON'T HEAR NOTHIN', VAP'R.
YOU SURE THIS THING'S WORKIN'?
OH, YESSS, MY FRIEND.
THE PLUSSSSSS-MEN USE THIS HOLO-ORGAN TO WEAVE INVISIBLE TAPESSSSSTRIES OF SSSSSOUND. PAEANS TO THEIR GOD OF UNIVERSAL ORDER AND HARMONY.
I HAVE ALTERED ITSSSSS FREQUENCY. THE RESULTING DISCORDANSSSSSSE SHOULD BRING THEM TO THEIR KNEESSSSSSS... AND FORSSSSSSSE THEM TO CALL ON --

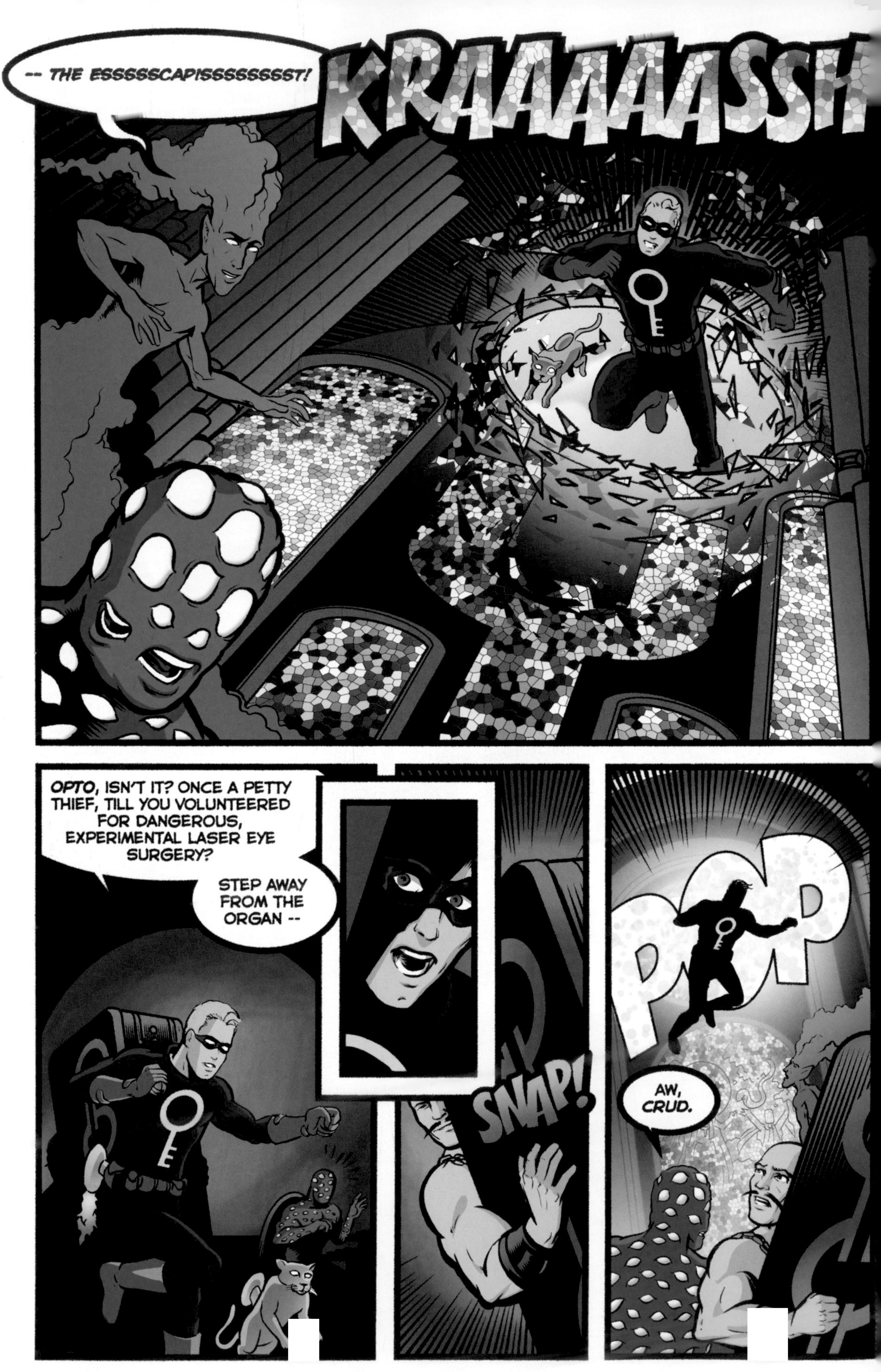
-- THE ESSSSSCAPISSSSSSSST!
KRAAAAAASSH
OPTO, ISN'T IT? ONCE A PETTY THIEF, TILL YOU VOLUNTEERED FOR DANGEROUS, EXPERIMENTAL LASER EYE SURGERY?
STEP AWAY FROM THE ORGAN --
SNAP!
POP
AW, CRUD.

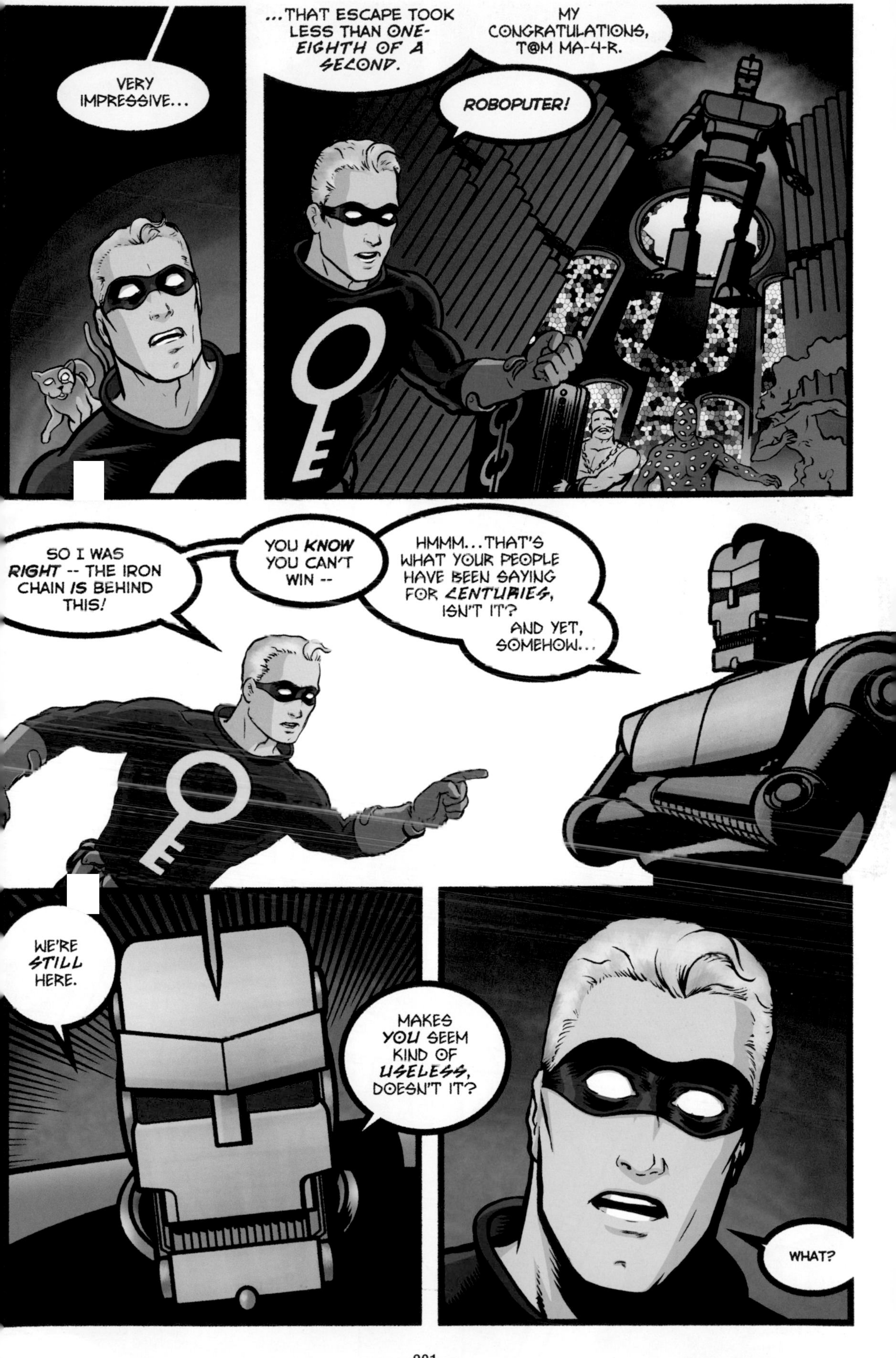
VERY IMPRESSIVE...
...THAT ESCAPE TOOK LESS THAN ONE-EIGHTH OF A SECOND.
MY CONGRATULATIONS, T@M MA-4-R.
ROBOPUTER!
SO I WAS RIGHT -- THE IRON CHAIN IS BEHIND THIS!
YOU KNOW YOU CAN'T WIN --
HMMM...THAT'S WHAT YOUR PEOPLE HAVE BEEN SAYING FOR CENTURIES, ISN'T IT?
AND YET, SOMEHOW...
WE'RE STILL HERE.
MAKES YOU SEEM KIND OF USELESS, DOESN'T IT?
WHAT?

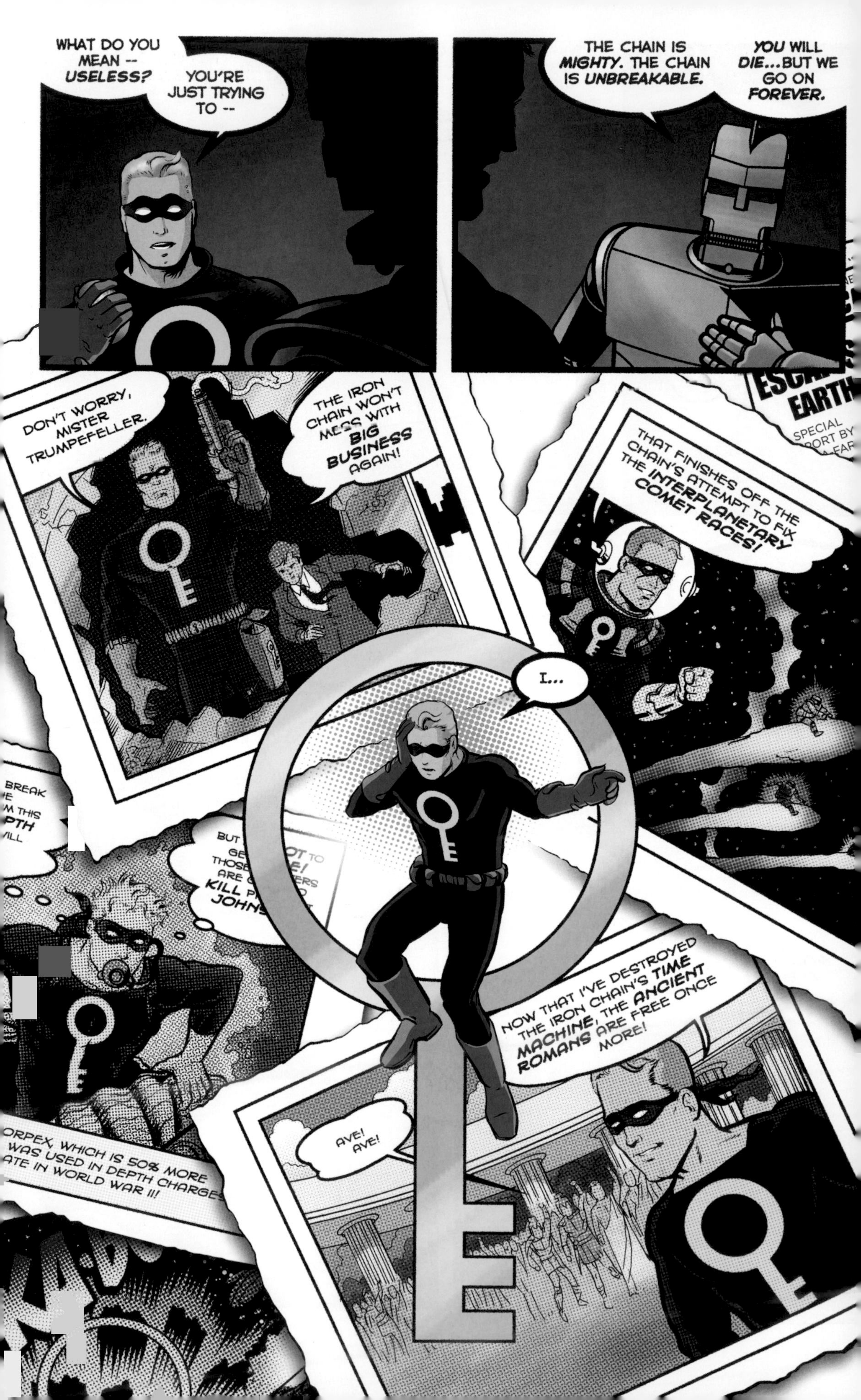
WHAT DO YOU MEAN -- USELESS?
YOU'RE JUST TRYING TO --
THE CHAIN IS MIGHTY. THE CHAIN IS UNBREAKABLE.
YOU WILL DIE...BUT WE GO ON FOREVER.
DON'T WORRY, MISTER TRUMPEFELLER.
THE IRON CHAIN WON'T MESS WITH BIG BUSINESS AGAIN!
EARTH
SPECIAL
THAT FINISHES OFF THE CHAIN'S ATTEMPT TO FIX THE INTERPLANETARY COMET RACES!
I...
NOW THAT I'VE DESTROYED THE IRON CHAIN'S TIME MACHINE, THE ANCIENT ROMANS ARE FREE ONCE MORE!
AVE! AVE!

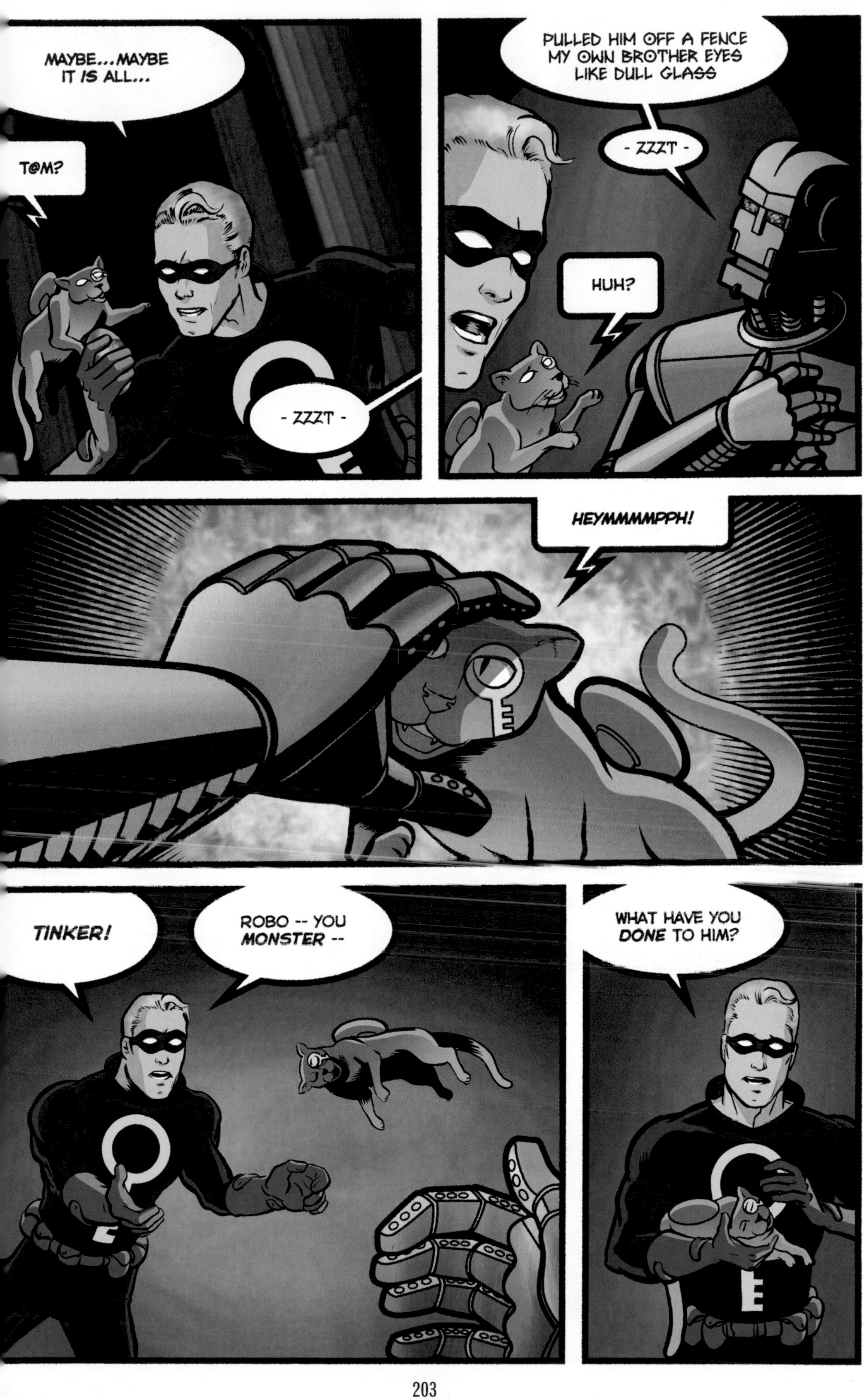
MAYBE...MAYBE IT IS ALL...
T@M?
- ZZZT -
PULLED HIM OFF A FENCE MY OWN BROTHER EYES LIKE DULL GLASS
- ZZZT -
HUH?
HEYMMMMPPH!
TINKER!
ROBO -- YOU MONSTER --
WHAT HAVE YOU DONE TO HIM?

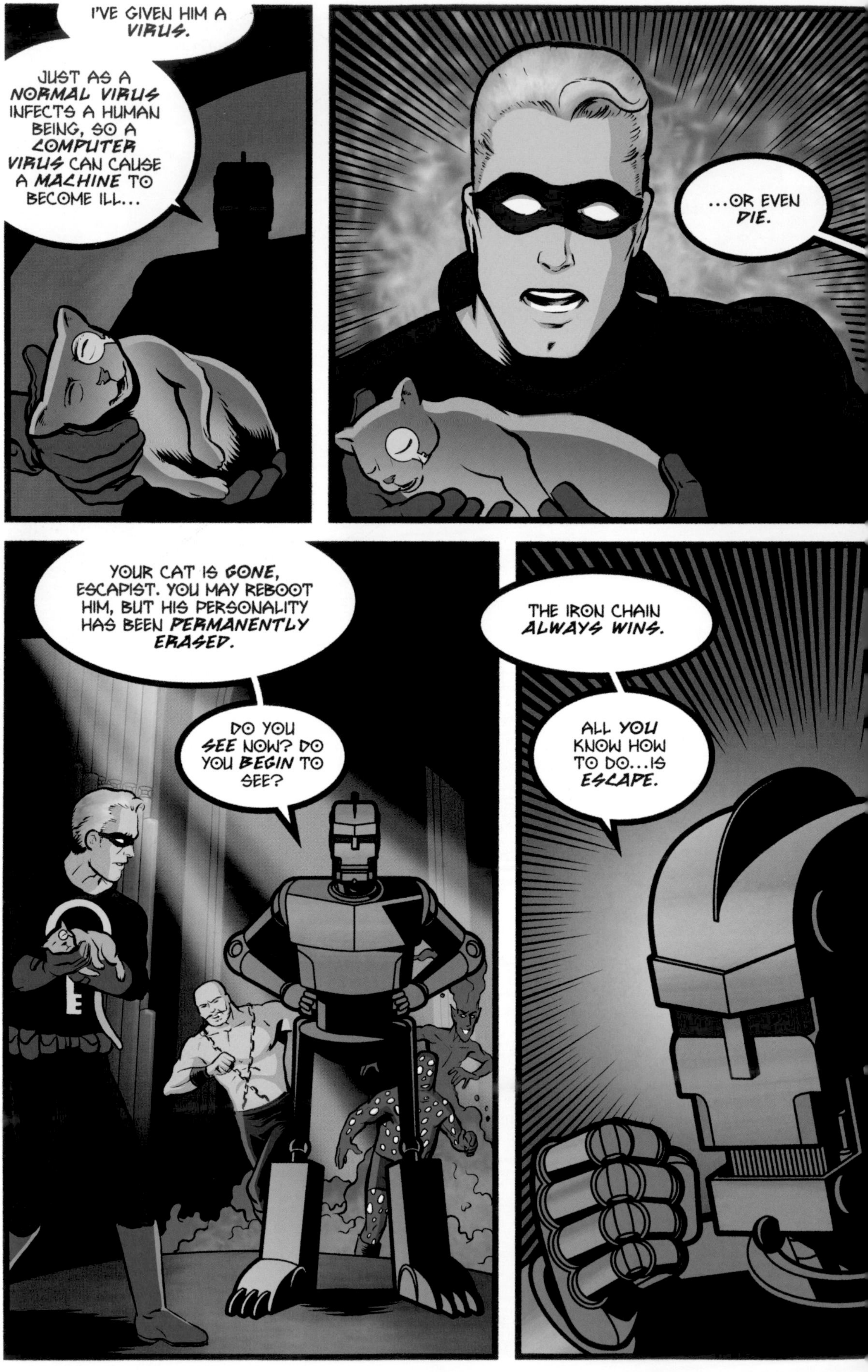
I'VE GIVEN HIM A VIRUS.
JUST AS A NORMAL VIRUS INFECTS A HUMAN BEING, SO A COMPUTER VIRUS CAN CAUSE A MACHINE TO BECOME ILL...
...OR EVEN DIE.
YOUR CAT IS GONE, ESCAPIST. YOU MAY REBOOT HIM, BUT HIS PERSONALITY HAS BEEN PERMANENTLY ERASED.
DO YOU SEE NOW? DO YOU BEGIN TO SEE?
THE IRON CHAIN ALWAYS WINS.
ALL YOU KNOW HOW TO DO...IS ESCAPE.

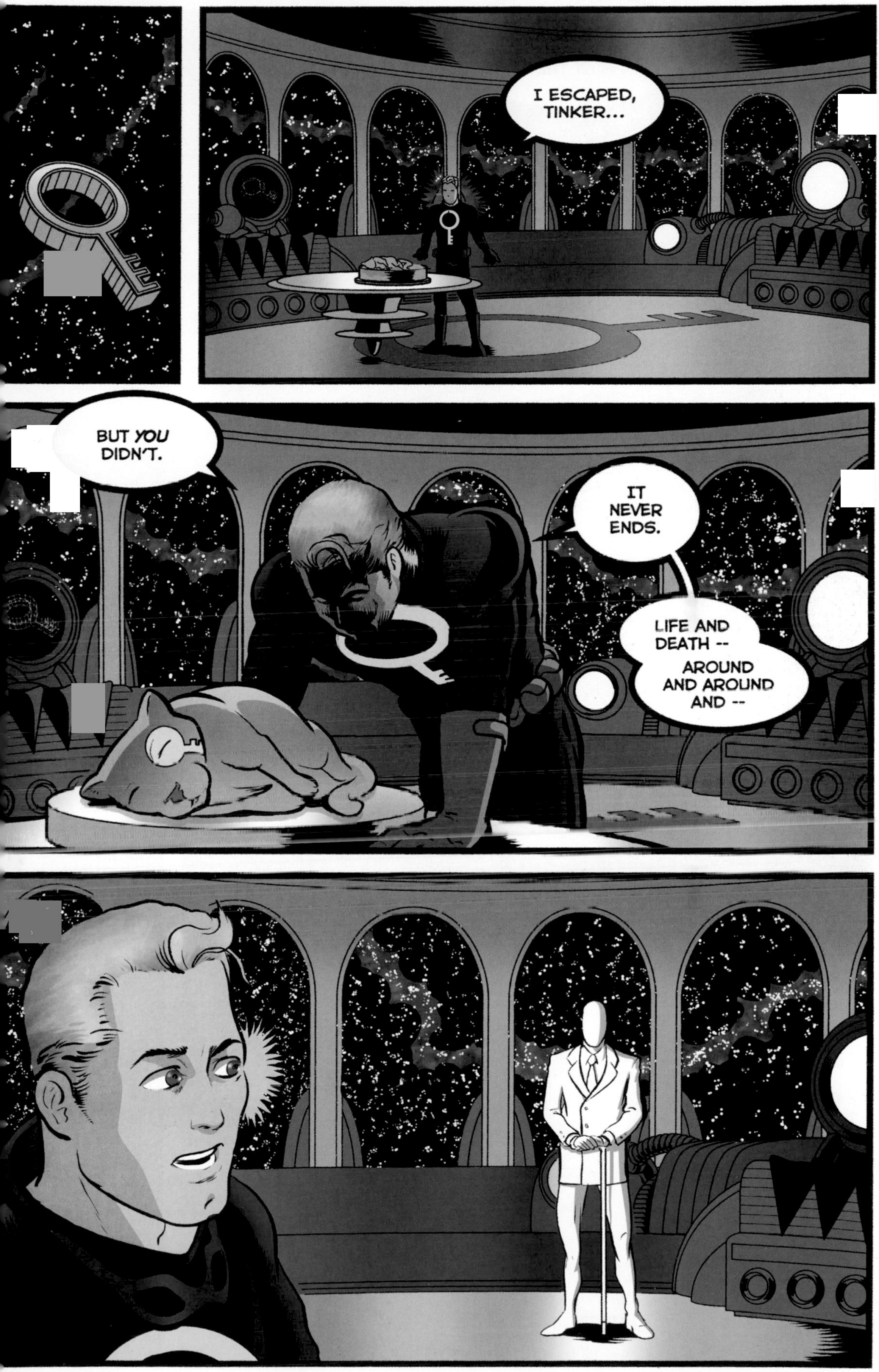
I ESCAPED, TINKER...
BUT *YOU* DIDN'T.
IT NEVER ENDS.
LIFE AND DEATH -- AROUND AND AROUND AND --

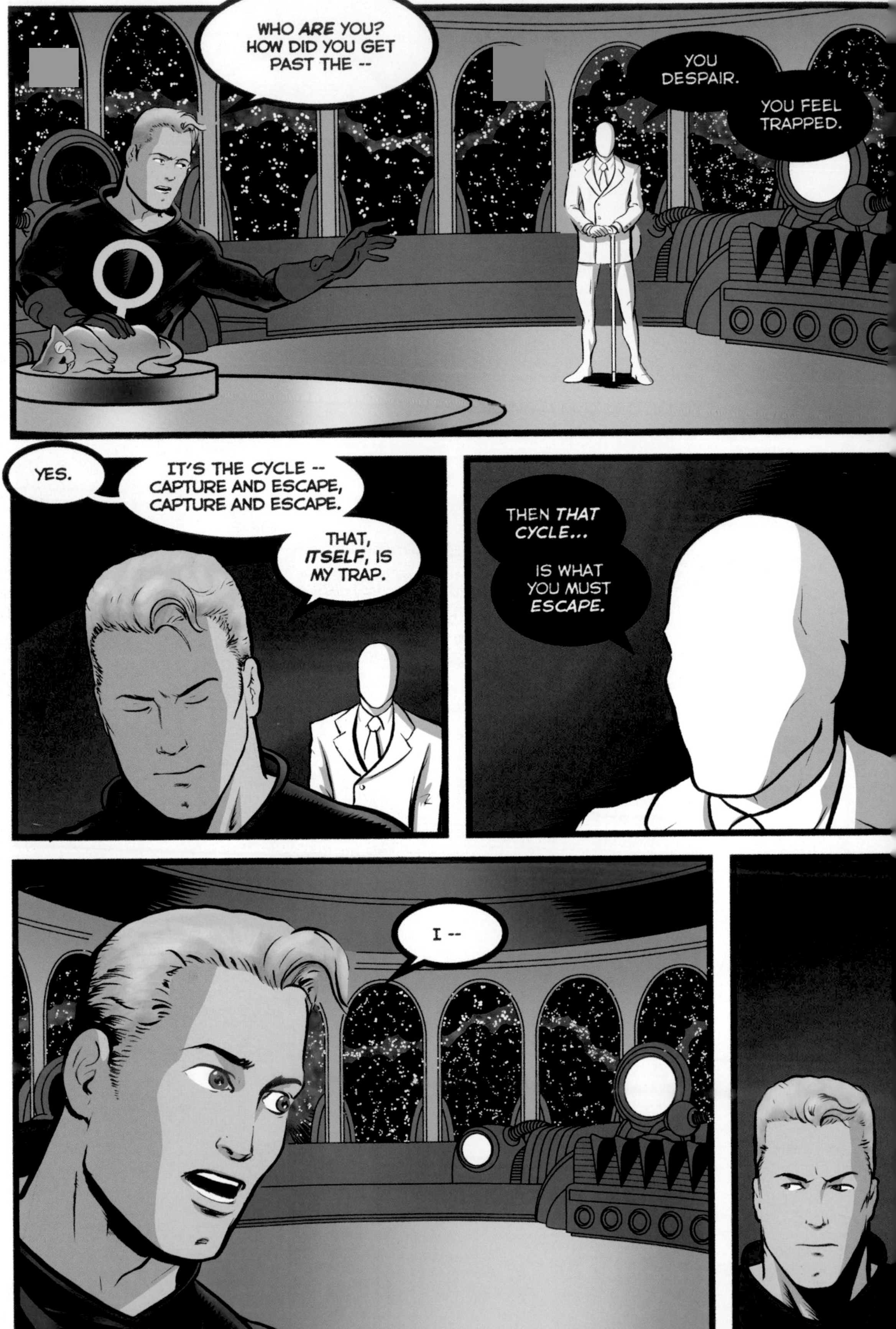
WHO *ARE* YOU? HOW DID YOU GET PAST THE --
YOU DESPAIR.
YOU FEEL TRAPPED.
YES.
IT'S THE CYCLE -- CAPTURE AND ESCAPE, CAPTURE AND ESCAPE.
THAT, *ITSELF*, IS MY TRAP.
THEN *THAT CYCLE...*
IS WHAT YOU MUST *ESCAPE.*
I --

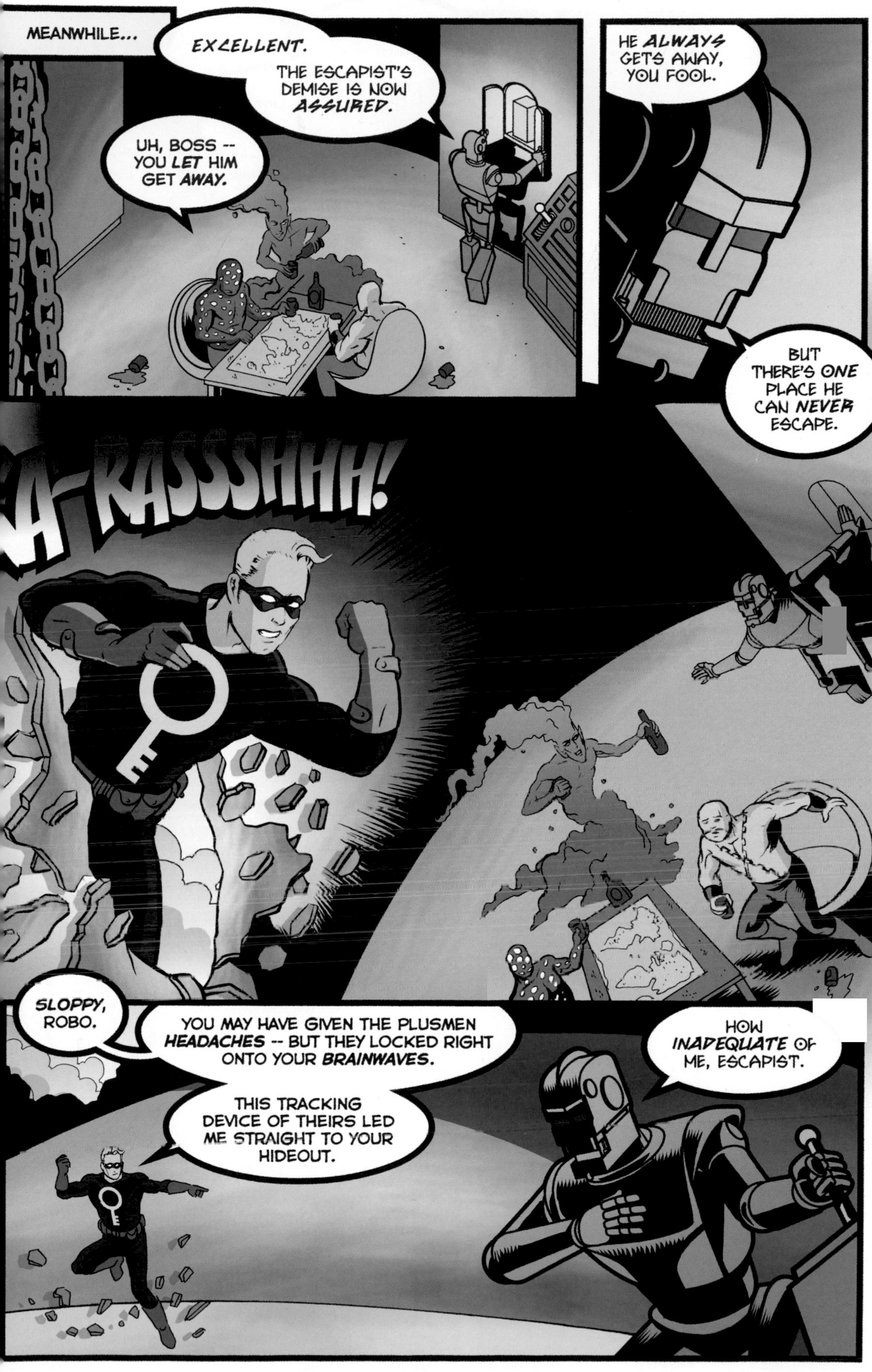
MEANWHILE...
EXCELLENT.
THE ESCAPIST'S DEMISE IS NOW ASSURED.
UH, BOSS -- YOU LET HIM GET AWAY.
HE ALWAYS GETS AWAY, YOU FOOL.
BUT THERE'S ONE PLACE HE CAN NEVER ESCAPE.
A-RASSSHHH!
SLOPPY, ROBO.
YOU MAY HAVE GIVEN THE PLUSMEN HEADACHES -- BUT THEY LOCKED RIGHT ONTO YOUR BRAINWAVES.
THIS TRACKING DEVICE OF THEIRS LED ME STRAIGHT TO YOUR HIDEOUT.
HOW INADEQUATE OF ME, ESCAPIST.

UNLESS, OF COURSE --

I *WANTED* YOU HERE.

UUHH!

HAH!

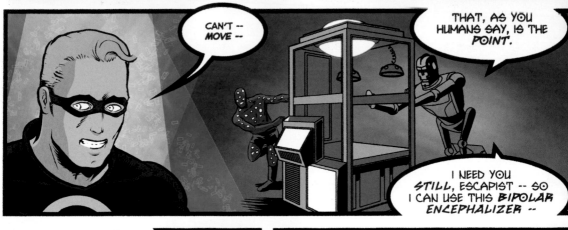

CAN'T -- MOVE --

THAT, AS YOU HUMANS SAY, IS THE *POINT.*

I NEED YOU *STILL,* ESCAPIST -- SO I CAN USE THIS *BIPOLAR ENCEPHALIZER* --

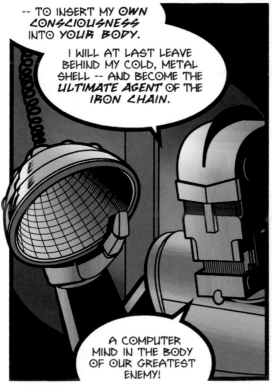

-- TO INSERT MY *OWN CONSCIOUSNESS* INTO *YOUR BODY.*

I WILL AT LAST LEAVE BEHIND MY COLD, METAL SHELL -- AND BECOME THE *ULTIMATE AGENT* OF THE *IRON CHAIN.*

A COMPUTER MIND IN THE BODY OF OUR GREATEST ENEMY!

OF COURSE --

*YOUR* CONSCIOUSNESS WILL THEN HAVE NOWHERE TO GO.

I'M AFRAID IT'LL JUST... *DISSIPATE.*

YESS! YESSSSSSS! *DISSSSSSSSSSIPATE!*

210

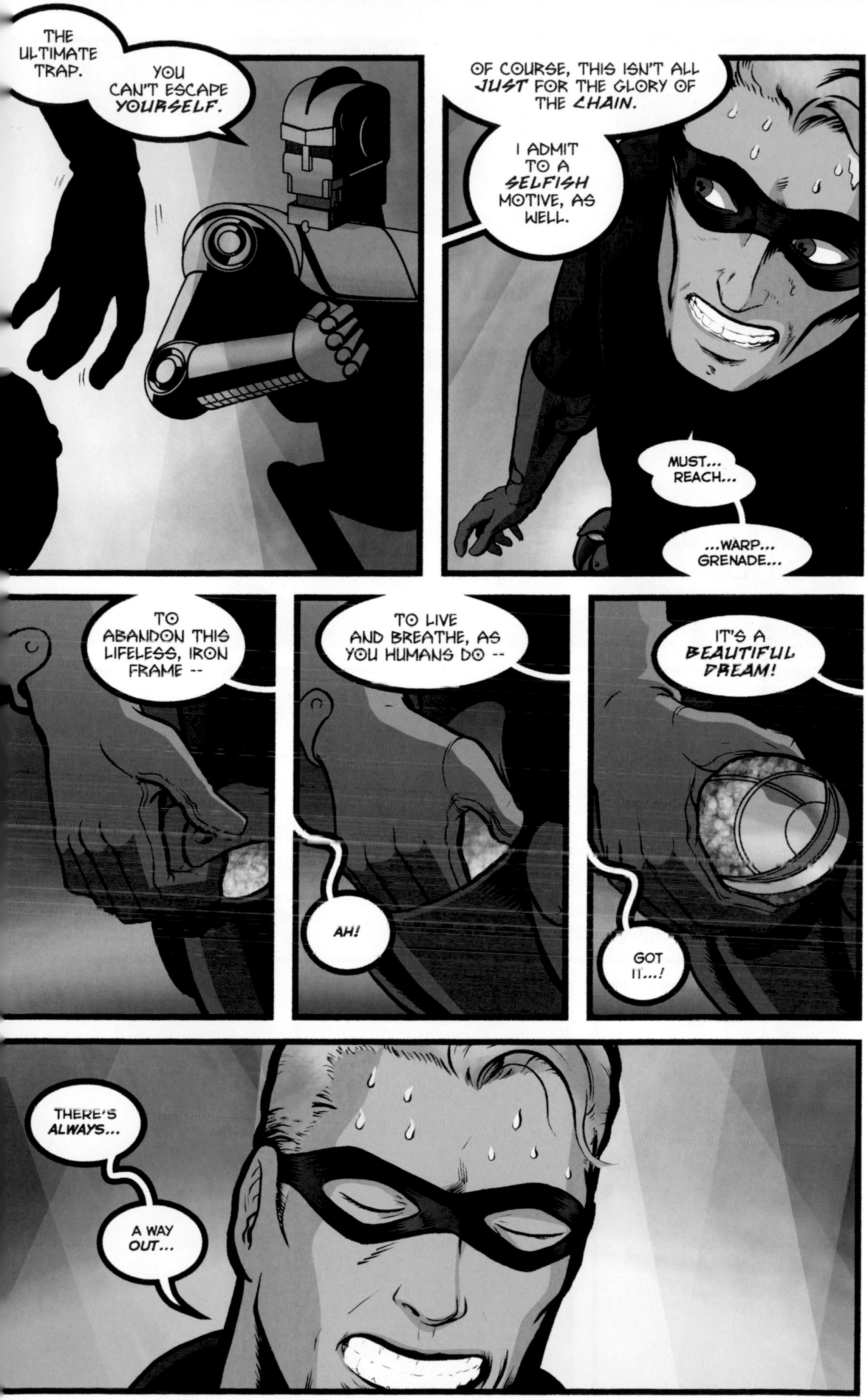
THE ULTIMATE TRAP.
YOU CAN'T ESCAPE YOURSELF.
OF COURSE, THIS ISN'T ALL JUST FOR THE GLORY OF THE CHAIN.
I ADMIT TO A SELFISH MOTIVE, AS WELL.
MUST... REACH...
...WARP... GRENADE...
TO ABANDON THIS LIFELESS, IRON FRAME --
TO LIVE AND BREATHE, AS YOU HUMANS DO --
AH!
IT'S A BEAUTIFUL DREAM!
GOT IT...!
THERE'S ALWAYS...
A WAY OUT...

BUT...

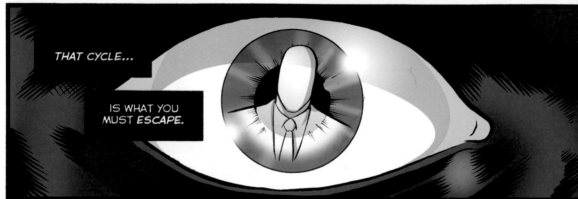

THAT CYCLE...

IS WHAT YOU MUST *ESCAPE*.

BOP

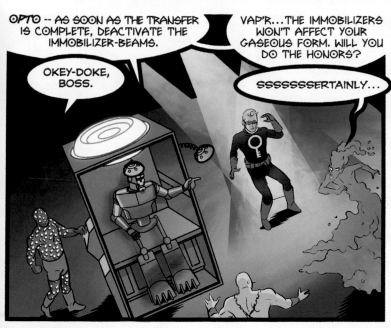

OPTO -- AS SOON AS THE TRANSFER IS COMPLETE, DEACTIVATE THE IMMOBILIZER-BEAMS.

OKEY-DOKE, BOSS.

VAP'R...THE IMMOBILIZERS WON'T AFFECT YOUR GASEOUS FORM. WILL YOU DO THE HONORS?

SSSSSSSSERTAINLY...

SSSSAY "SSSSSSSSAYONARA," ESSSSSSCAPIST!

AHH...

WONDROUS...!

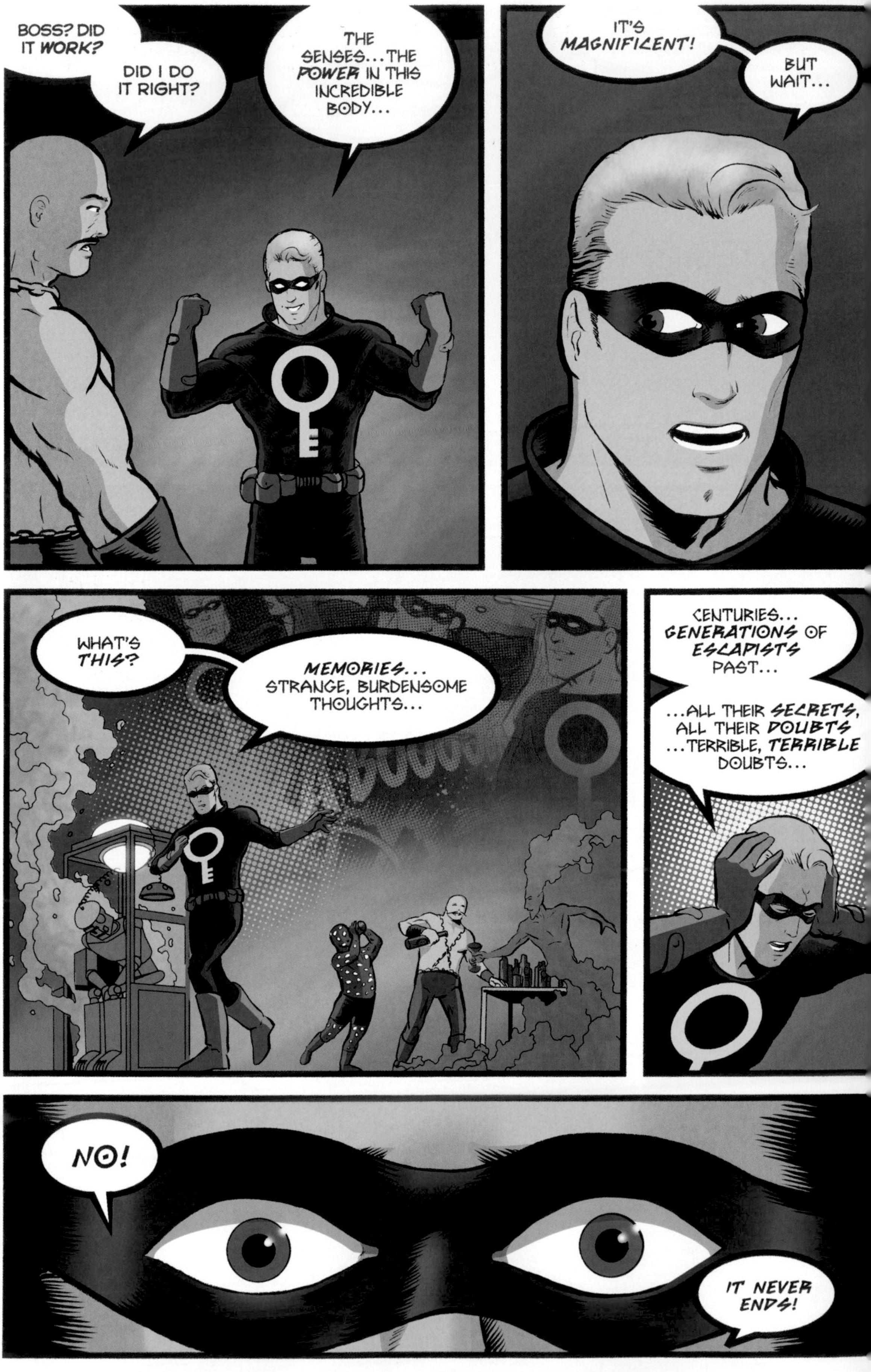
BOSS? DID IT WORK?
DID I DO IT RIGHT?
THE SENSES...THE POWER IN THIS INCREDIBLE BODY...
IT'S MAGNIFICENT!
BUT WAIT...
WHAT'S THIS?
MEMORIES... STRANGE, BURDENSOME THOUGHTS...
CENTURIES... GENERATIONS OF ESCAPISTS PAST...
...ALL THEIR SECRETS, ALL THEIR DOUBTS ...TERRIBLE, TERRIBLE DOUBTS...
NO!
IT NEVER ENDS!

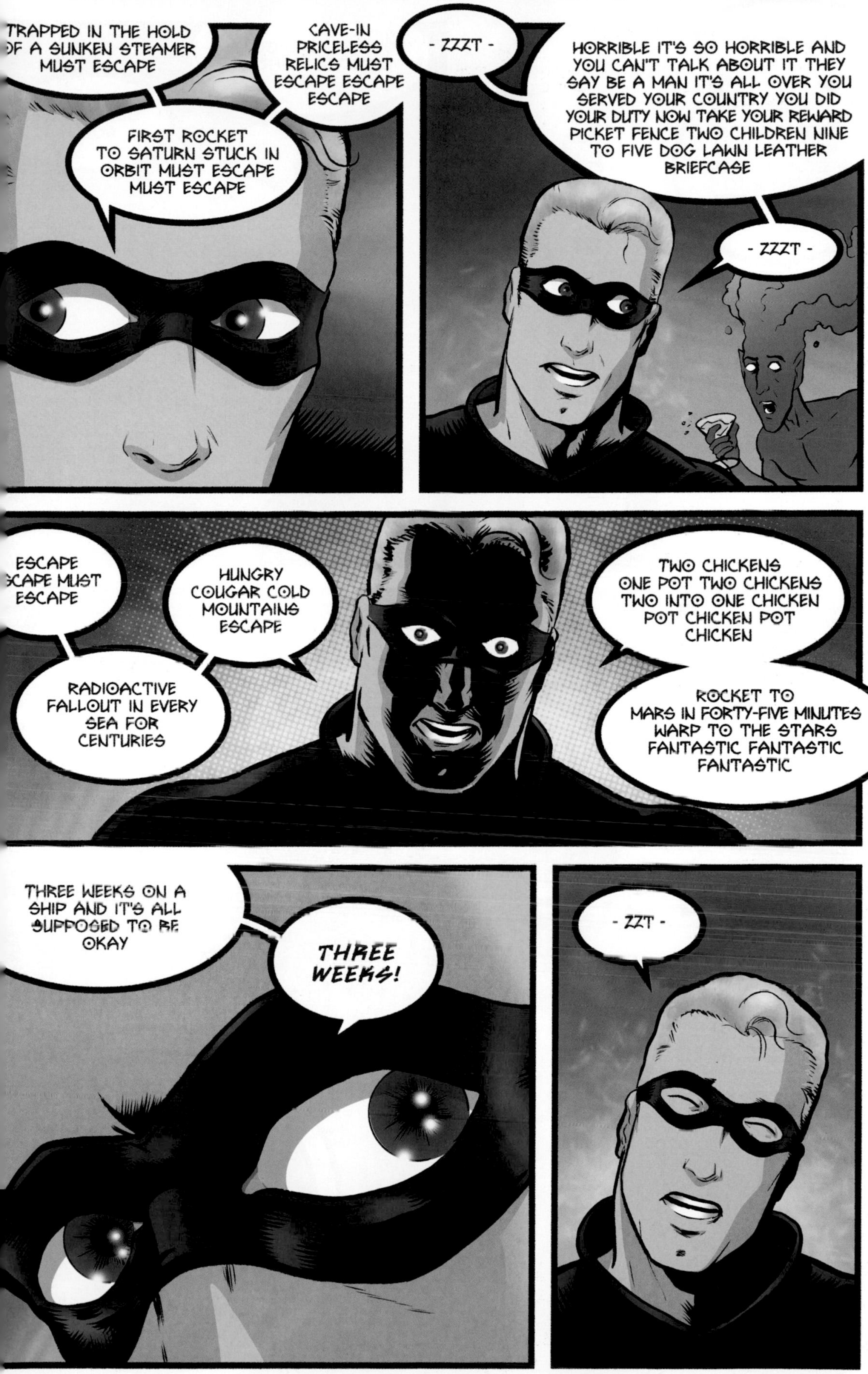
TRAPPED IN THE HOLD OF A SUNKEN STEAMER MUST ESCAPE
CAVE-IN PRICELESS RELICS MUST ESCAPE ESCAPE ESCAPE
FIRST ROCKET TO SATURN STUCK IN ORBIT MUST ESCAPE MUST ESCAPE
- ZZZT -
HORRIBLE IT'S SO HORRIBLE AND YOU CAN'T TALK ABOUT IT THEY SAY BE A MAN IT'S ALL OVER YOU SERVED YOUR COUNTRY YOU DID YOUR DUTY NOW TAKE YOUR REWARD PICKET FENCE TWO CHILDREN NINE TO FIVE DOG LAWN LEATHER BRIEFCASE
- ZZZT -
ESCAPE SCAPE MUST ESCAPE
HUNGRY COUGAR COLD MOUNTAINS ESCAPE
RADIOACTIVE FALLOUT IN EVERY SEA FOR CENTURIES
TWO CHICKENS ONE POT TWO CHICKENS TWO INTO ONE CHICKEN POT CHICKEN POT CHICKEN
ROCKET TO MARS IN FORTY-FIVE MINUTES WARP TO THE STARS FANTASTIC FANTASTIC FANTASTIC
THREE WEEKS ON A SHIP AND IT'S ALL SUPPOSED TO BE OKAY
THREE WEEKS!
- ZZT -

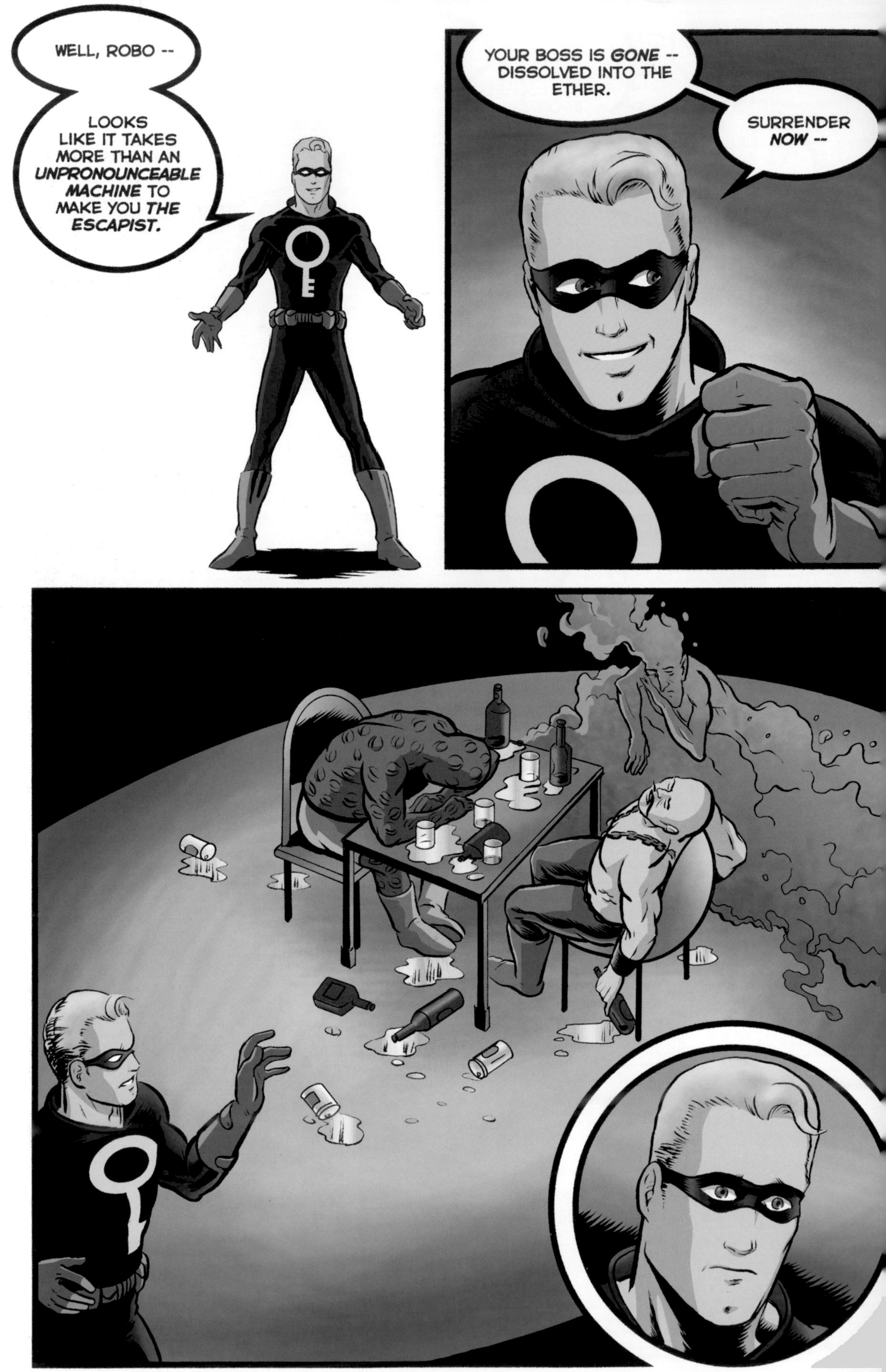
WELL, ROBO --
LOOKS LIKE IT TAKES MORE THAN AN UNPRONOUNCEABLE MACHINE TO MAKE YOU THE ESCAPIST.
YOUR BOSS IS GONE -- DISSOLVED INTO THE ETHER.
SURRENDER NOW --

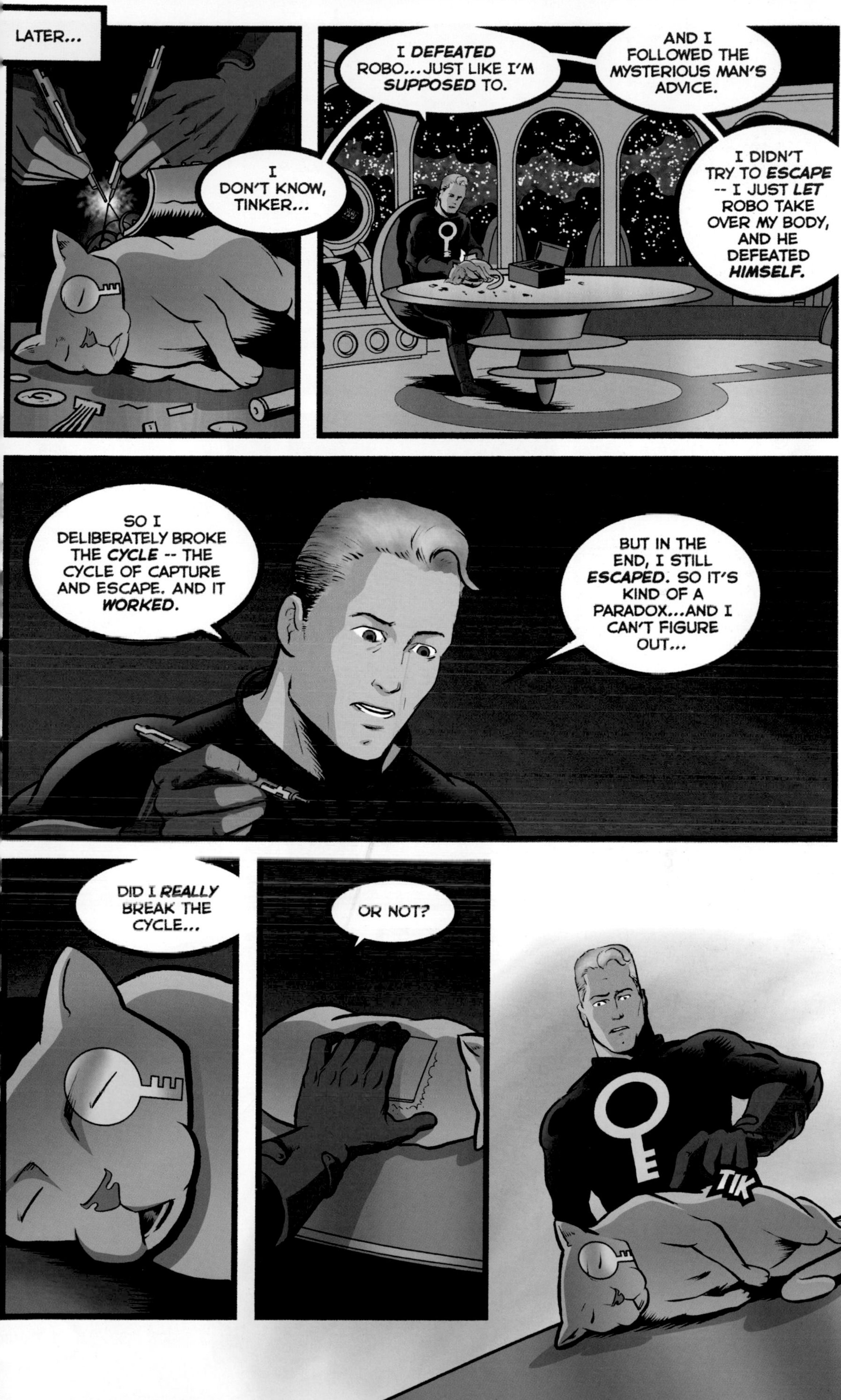
LATER...
I DON'T KNOW, TINKER...
I DEFEATED ROBO...JUST LIKE I'M SUPPOSED TO.
AND I FOLLOWED THE MYSTERIOUS MAN'S ADVICE.
I DIDN'T TRY TO ESCAPE -- I JUST LET ROBO TAKE OVER MY BODY, AND HE DEFEATED HIMSELF.
SO I DELIBERATELY BROKE THE CYCLE -- THE CYCLE OF CAPTURE AND ESCAPE. AND IT WORKED.
BUT IN THE END, I STILL ESCAPED. SO IT'S KIND OF A PARADOX...AND I CAN'T FIGURE OUT...
DID I REALLY BREAK THE CYCLE...
OR NOT?
TIK

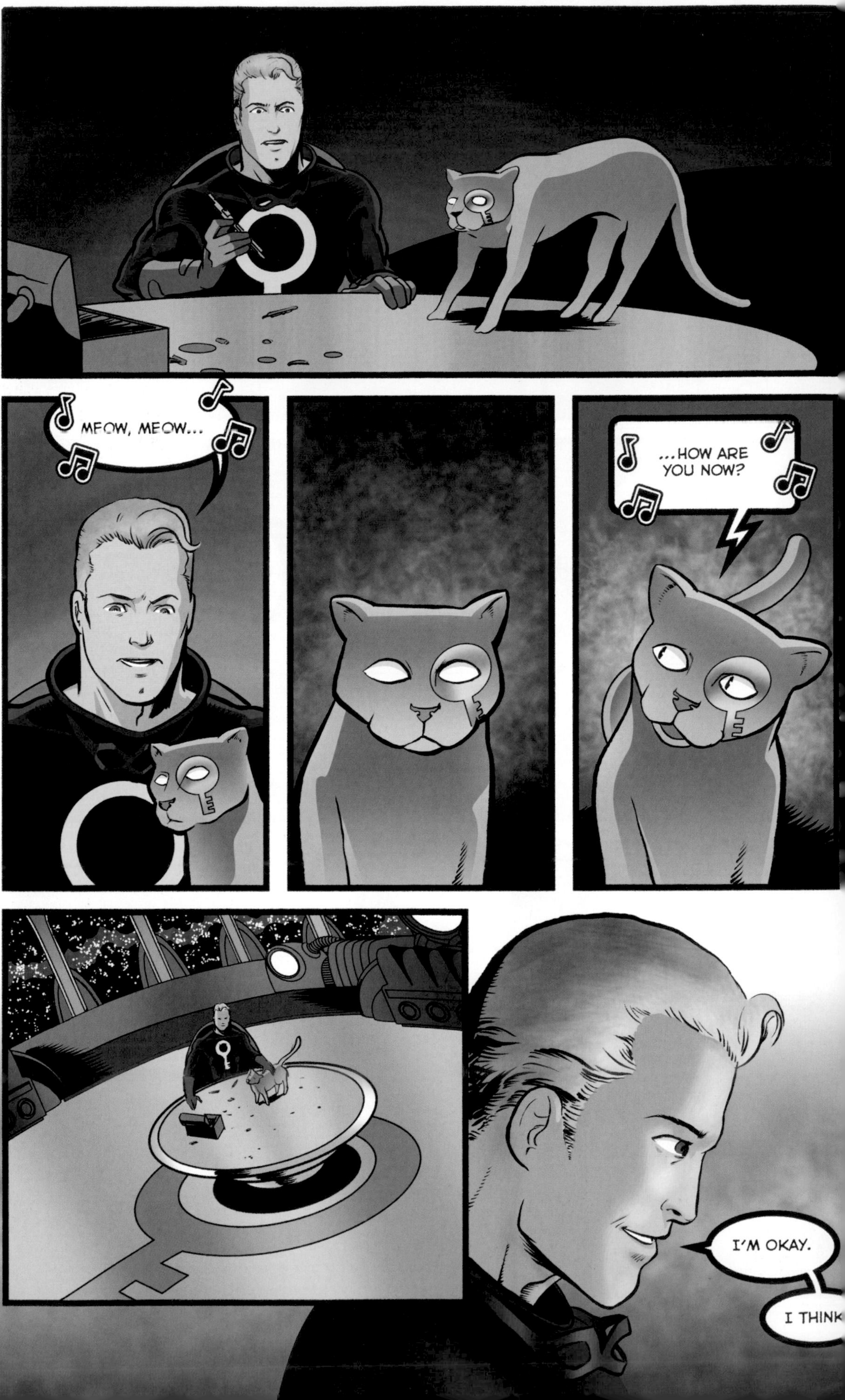
MEOW, MEOW...
...HOW ARE YOU NOW?
I'M OKAY.
I THINK

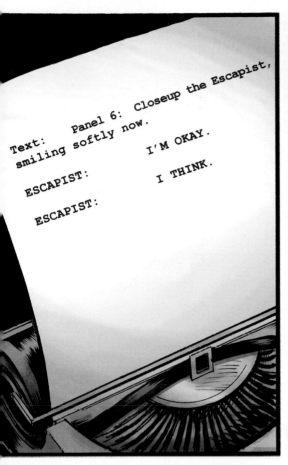

Text: Panel 6: Closeup the Escapist, smiling softly now.
ESCAPIST: I'M OKAY.
ESCAPIST: I THINK.
Text: Panel 6: smiling softly now.
ESCAPIST: I'M OKAY.
ESCAPIST: I THINK.
RRRIIP
THE ESCAPIST 2966
SCRIPT
Cyril M. Cutter
FAB COMICS
LOOK DEEP INTO THESE EYES!
IS IT LOVE, HATE OR MURDER?
THEY'RE THE EYES OF
HUMPHREY
BOGART
In A
Lonely Place
Gloria GRAHAME

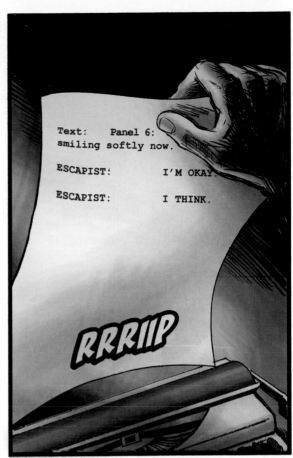

Writers Guild Award
CYRIL M. CUTTER
Best Teleplay - 1961
"The Fire on Main Street"
Series: The Inner Mind

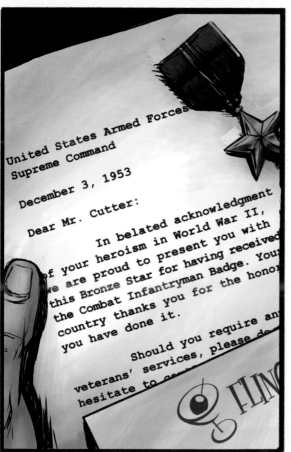

United States Armed Forces
Supreme Command

December 3, 1953

Dear Mr. Cutter:

In belated acknowledgment
of your heroism in World War II,
we are proud to present you with
this Bronze Star for having received
the Combat Infantryman Badge. Your
country thanks you for the honor
you have done it.

Should you require any
veterans' services, please do
hesitate to

FLING

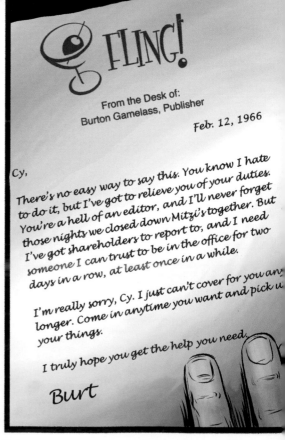

**FLING!**

From the Desk of:
Burton Gamelass, Publisher

Feb. 12, 1966

Cy,

There's no easy way to say this. You know I hate
to do it, but I've got to relieve you of your duties.
You're a hell of an editor, and I'll never forget
those nights we closed down Mitzi's together. But
I've got shareholders to report to, and I need
someone I can trust to be in the office for two
days in a row, at least once in a while.

I'm really sorry, Cy. I just can't cover for you any
longer. Come in anytime you want and pick up
your things.

I truly hope you get the help you need.

Burt

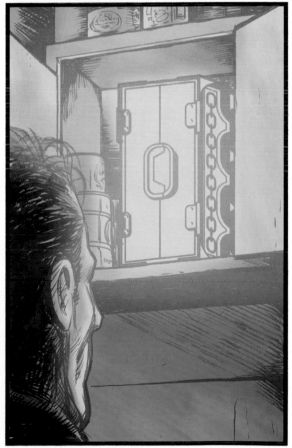

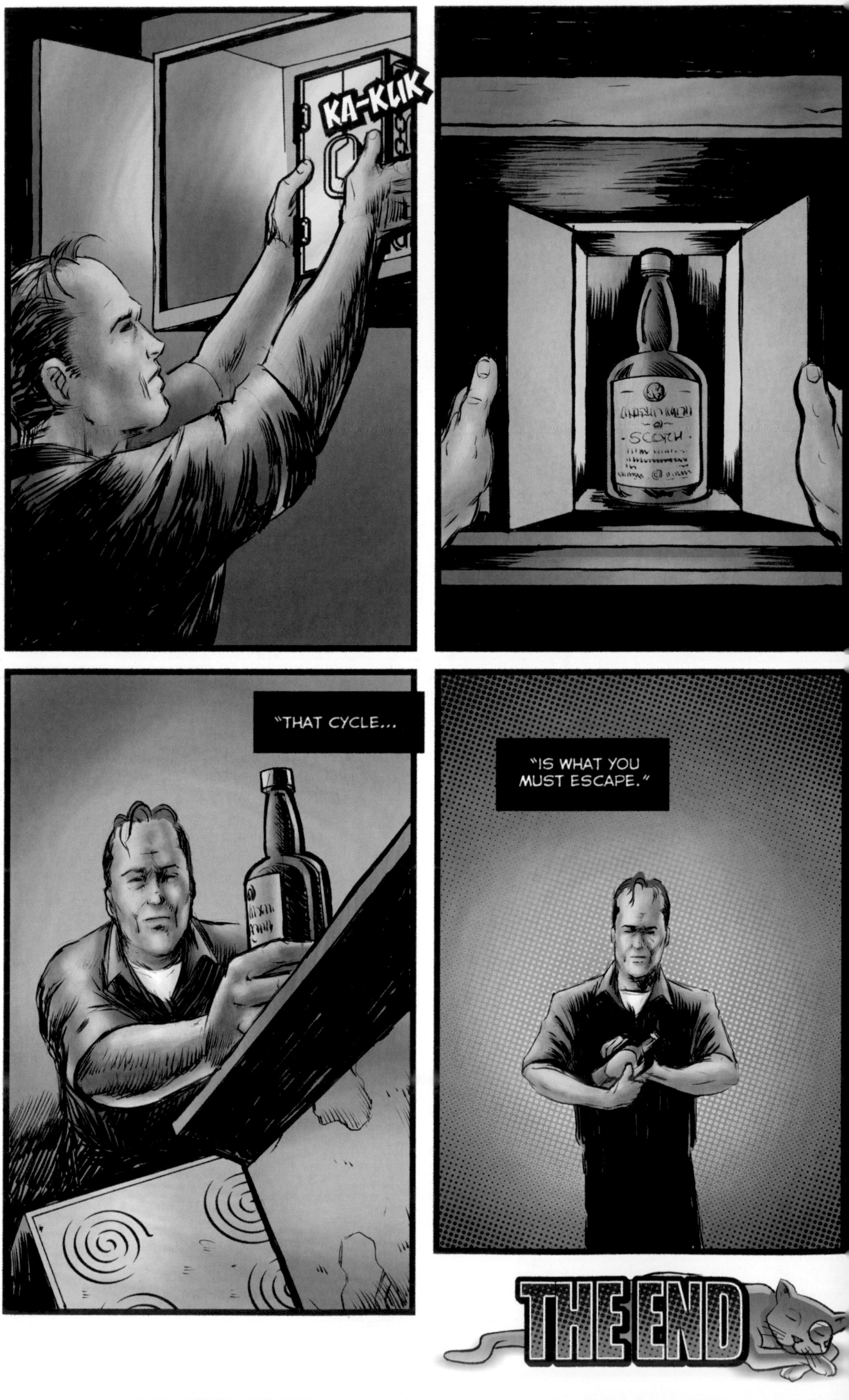
KA-KLIK
SCOTCH
"THAT CYCLE...
"IS WHAT YOU MUST ESCAPE."
THE END

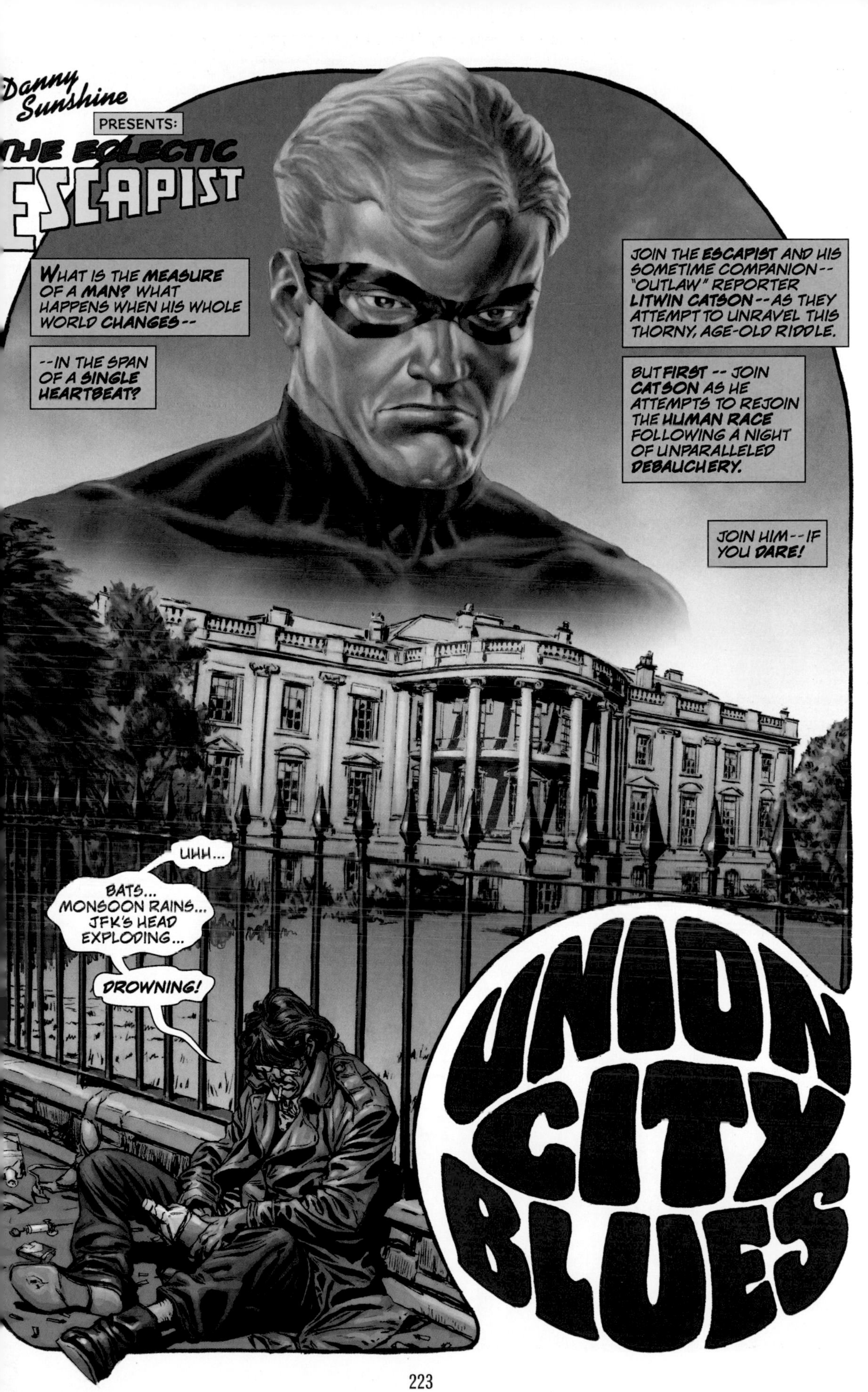

Danny Sunshine
PRESENTS:
THE ECLECTIC ESCAPIST
WHAT IS THE MEASURE OF A MAN? WHAT HAPPENS WHEN HIS WHOLE WORLD CHANGES--
--IN THE SPAN OF A SINGLE HEARTBEAT?
JOIN THE ESCAPIST AND HIS SOMETIME COMPANION-- "OUTLAW" REPORTER LITWIN CATSON--AS THEY ATTEMPT TO UNRAVEL THIS THORNY, AGE-OLD RIDDLE.
BUT FIRST -- JOIN CATSON AS HE ATTEMPTS TO REJOIN THE HUMAN RACE FOLLOWING A NIGHT OF UNPARALLELED DEBAUCHERY.
JOIN HIM--IF YOU DARE!
UHH...
BATS... MONSOON RAINS... JFK'S HEAD EXPLODING...
DROWNING!
UNION CITY BLUES

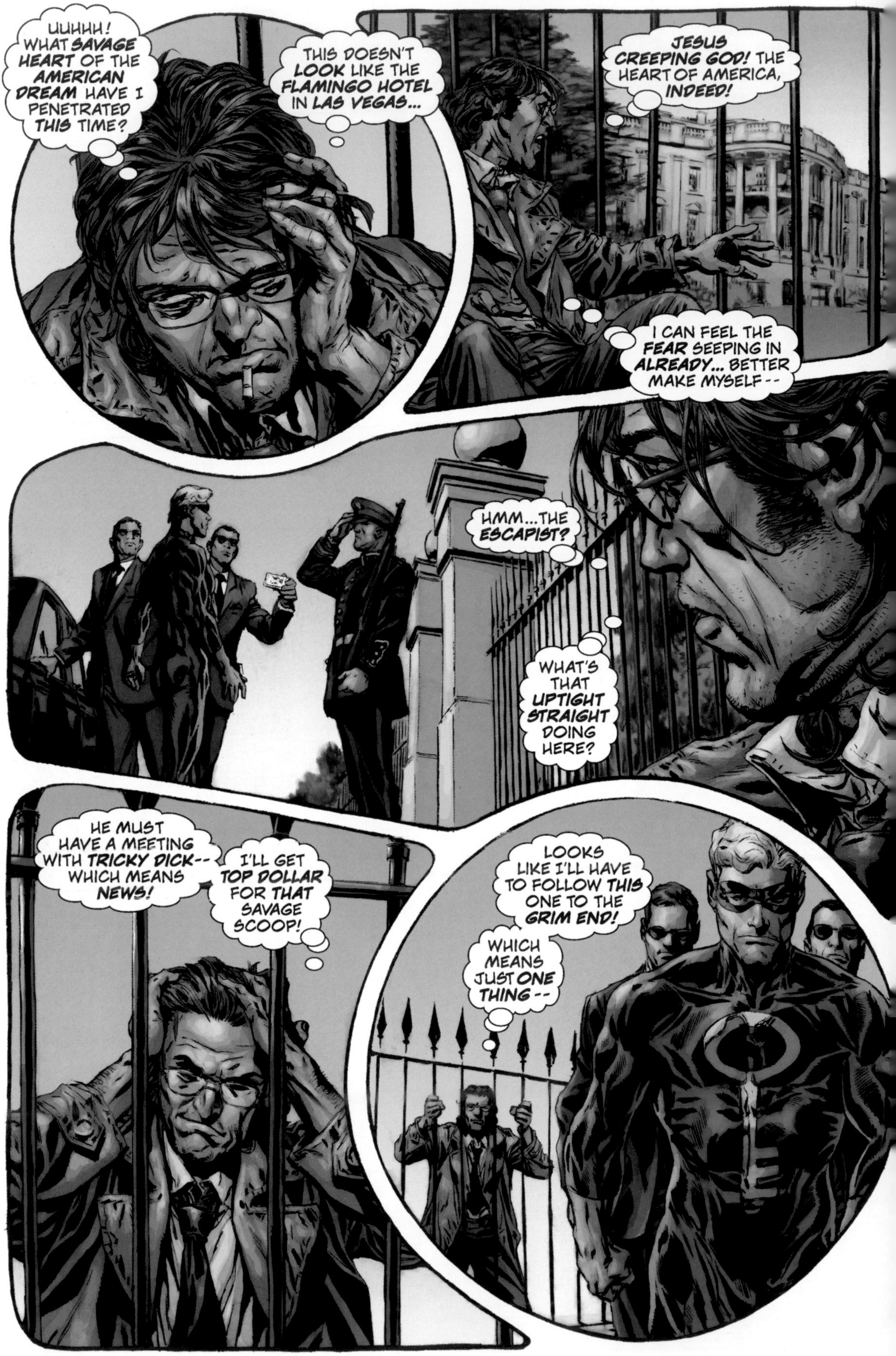
UUHHH! WHAT SAVAGE HEART OF THE AMERICAN DREAM HAVE I PENETRATED THIS TIME?
THIS DOESN'T LOOK LIKE THE FLAMINGO HOTEL IN LAS VEGAS...
JESUS CREEPING GOD! THE HEART OF AMERICA, INDEED!
I CAN FEEL THE FEAR SEEPING IN ALREADY... BETTER MAKE MYSELF--
HMM...THE ESCAPIST?
WHAT'S THAT UPTIGHT STRAIGHT DOING HERE?
HE MUST HAVE A MEETING WITH TRICKY DICK-- WHICH MEANS NEWS!
I'LL GET TOP DOLLAR FOR THAT SAVAGE SCOOP!
LOOKS LIKE I'LL HAVE TO FOLLOW THIS ONE TO THE GRIM END!
WHICH MEANS JUST ONE THING--

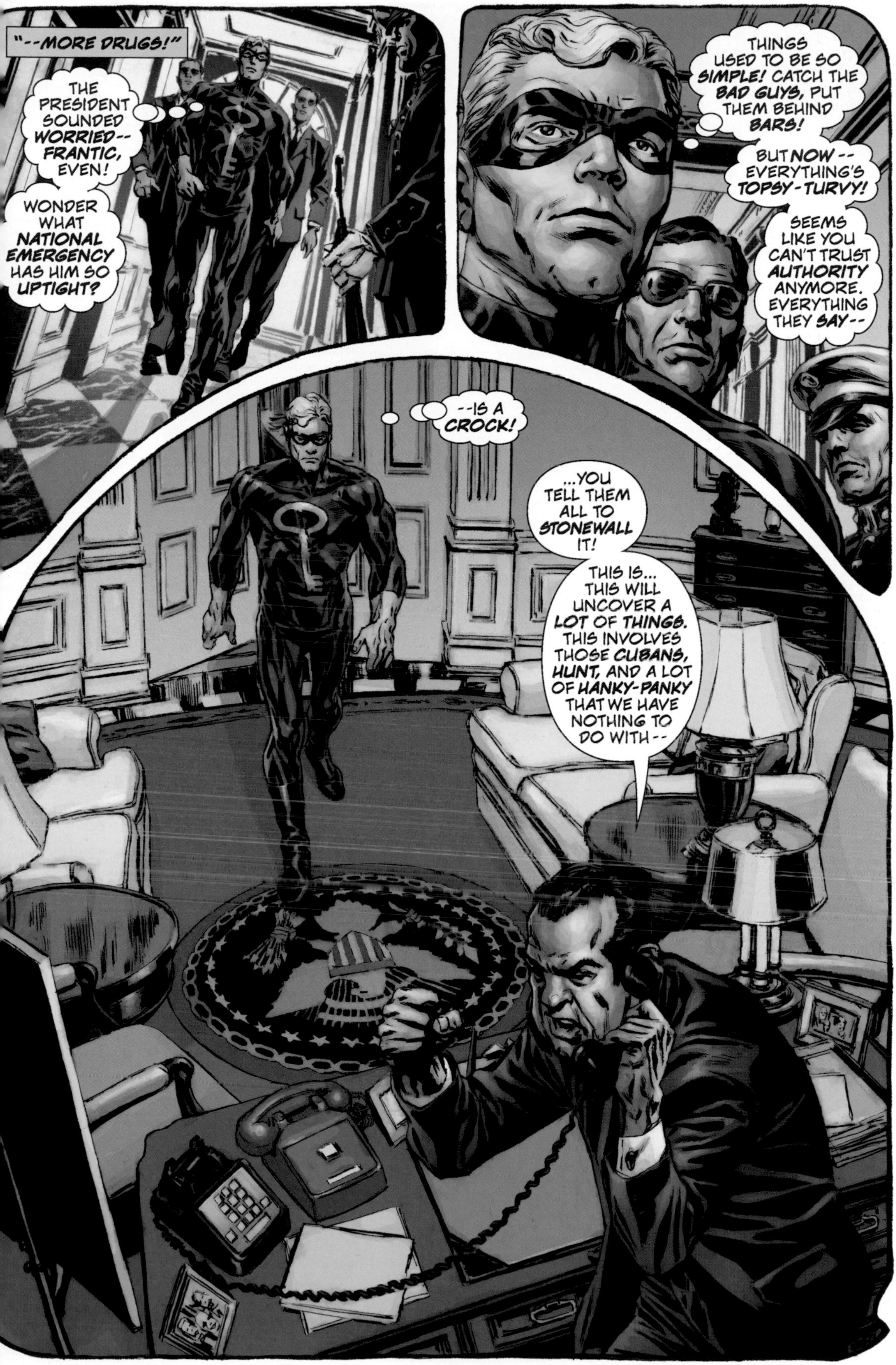
"--MORE DRUGS!"
THE PRESIDENT SOUNDED WORRIED-- FRANTIC, EVEN!
WONDER WHAT NATIONAL EMERGENCY HAS HIM SO UPTIGHT?
THINGS USED TO BE SO SIMPLE! CATCH THE BAD GUYS, PUT THEM BEHIND BARS!
BUT NOW -- EVERYTHING'S TOPSY-TURVY!
SEEMS LIKE YOU CAN'T TRUST AUTHORITY ANYMORE. EVERYTHING THEY SAY--
--IS A CROCK!
...YOU TELL THEM ALL TO STONEWALL IT!
THIS IS... THIS WILL UNCOVER A LOT OF THINGS. THIS INVOLVES THOSE CUBANS, HUNT, AND A LOT OF HANKY-PANKY THAT WE HAVE NOTHING TO DO WITH--

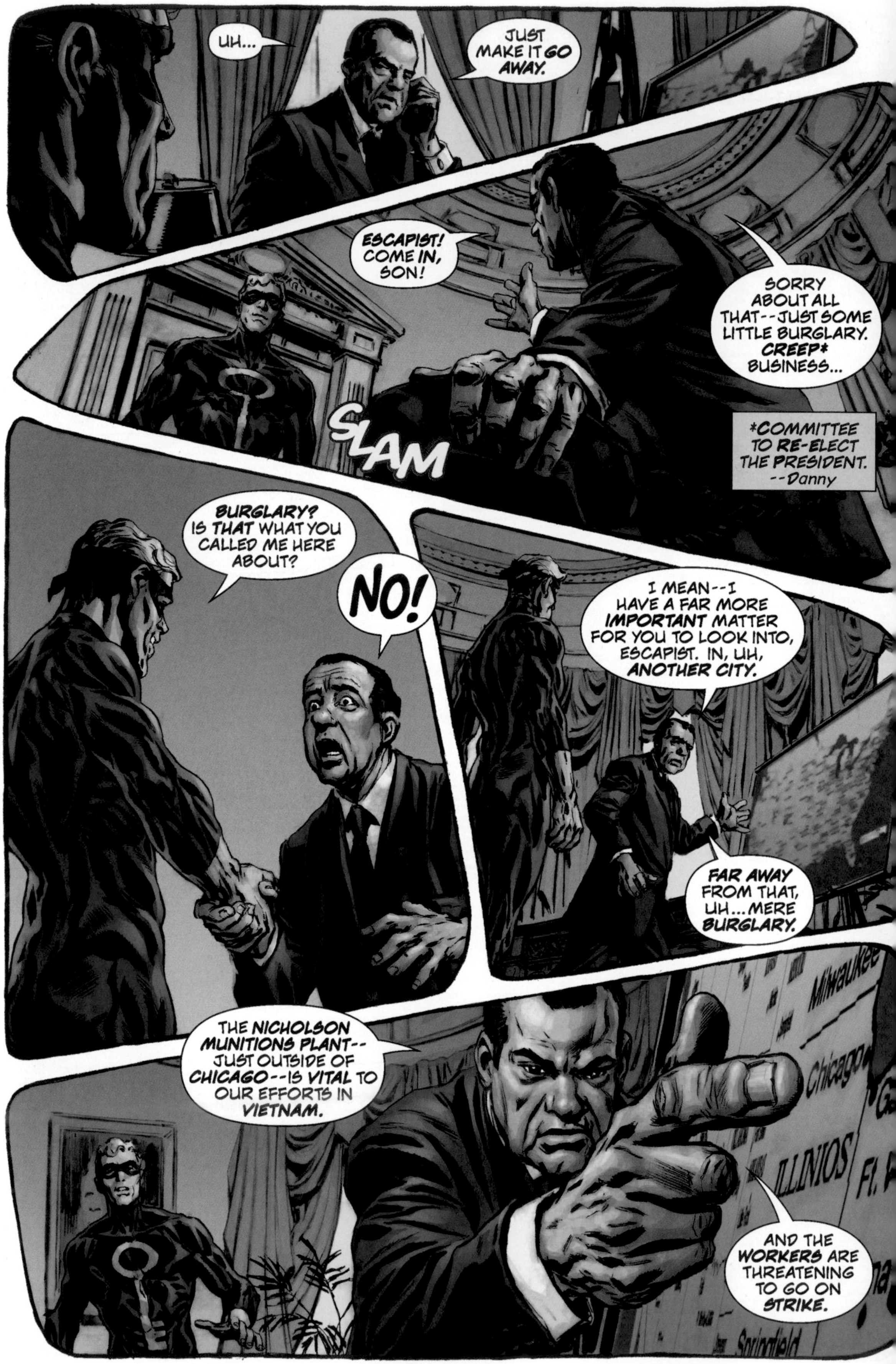
UH...
JUST MAKE IT GO AWAY.
ESCAPIST! COME IN, SON!
SORRY ABOUT ALL THAT--JUST SOME LITTLE BURGLARY. CREEP* BUSINESS...
SLAM
*COMMITTEE TO RE-ELECT THE PRESIDENT. --Danny
BURGLARY? IS THAT WHAT YOU CALLED ME HERE ABOUT?
NO!
I MEAN--I HAVE A FAR MORE IMPORTANT MATTER FOR YOU TO LOOK INTO, ESCAPIST. IN, UH, ANOTHER CITY.
FAR AWAY FROM THAT, UH... MERE BURGLARY.
THE NICHOLSON MUNITIONS PLANT--JUST OUTSIDE OF CHICAGO--IS VITAL TO OUR EFFORTS IN VIETNAM.
Milwaukee
Chicago
ILLINIOS
AND THE WORKERS ARE THREATENING TO GO ON STRIKE.

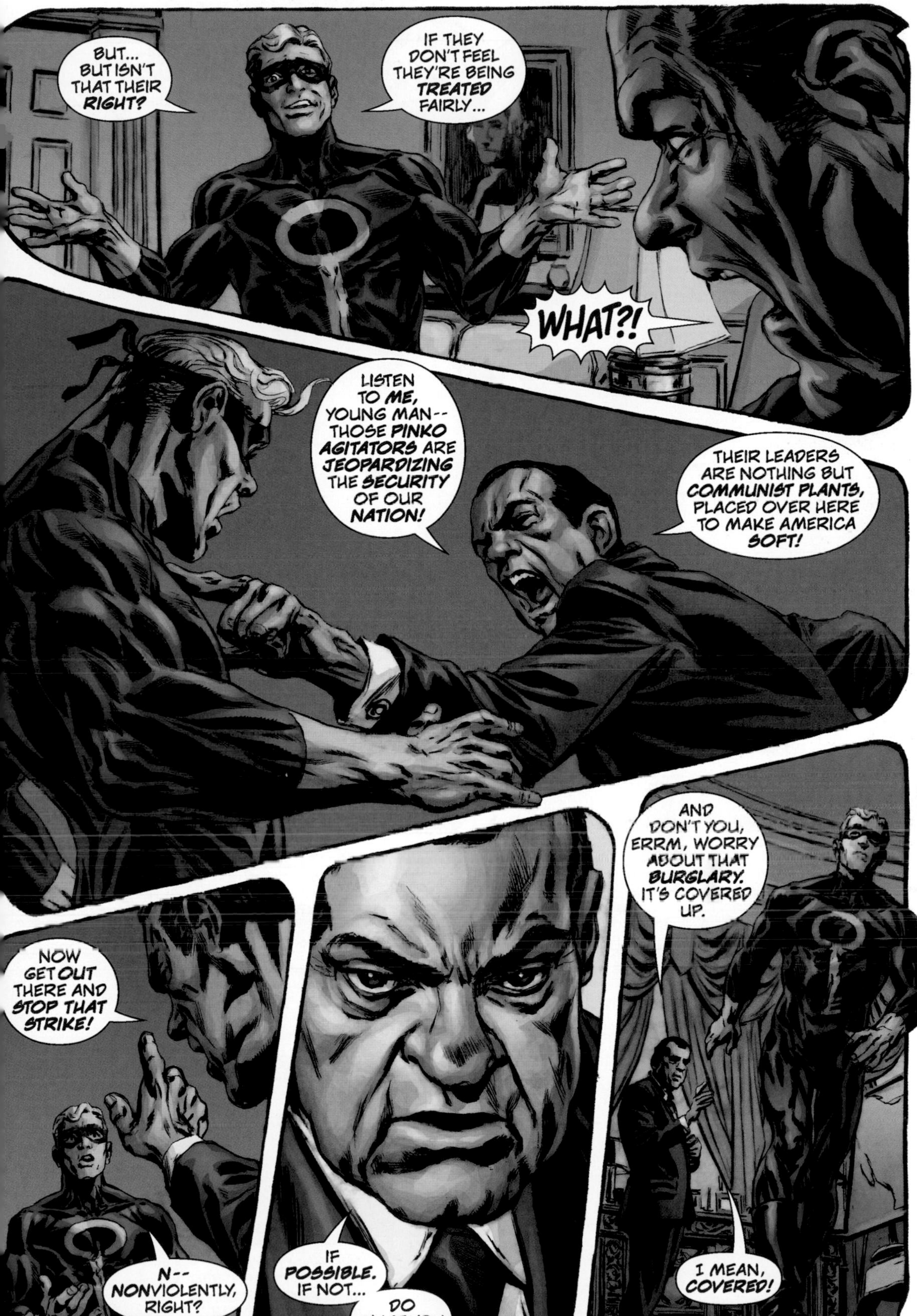
BUT... BUT ISN'T THAT THEIR RIGHT?
IF THEY DON'T FEEL THEY'RE BEING TREATED FAIRLY...
WHAT?!
LISTEN TO ME, YOUNG MAN-- THOSE PINKO AGITATORS ARE JEOPARDIZING THE SECURITY OF OUR NATION!
THEIR LEADERS ARE NOTHING BUT COMMUNIST PLANTS, PLACED OVER HERE TO MAKE AMERICA SOFT!
NOW GET OUT THERE AND STOP THAT STRIKE!
N-- NONVIOLENTLY, RIGHT?
IF POSSIBLE. IF NOT...
DO WHAT YOU HAVE TO.
AND DON'T YOU, ERRM, WORRY ABOUT THAT BURGLARY. IT'S COVERED UP.
I MEAN, COVERED!

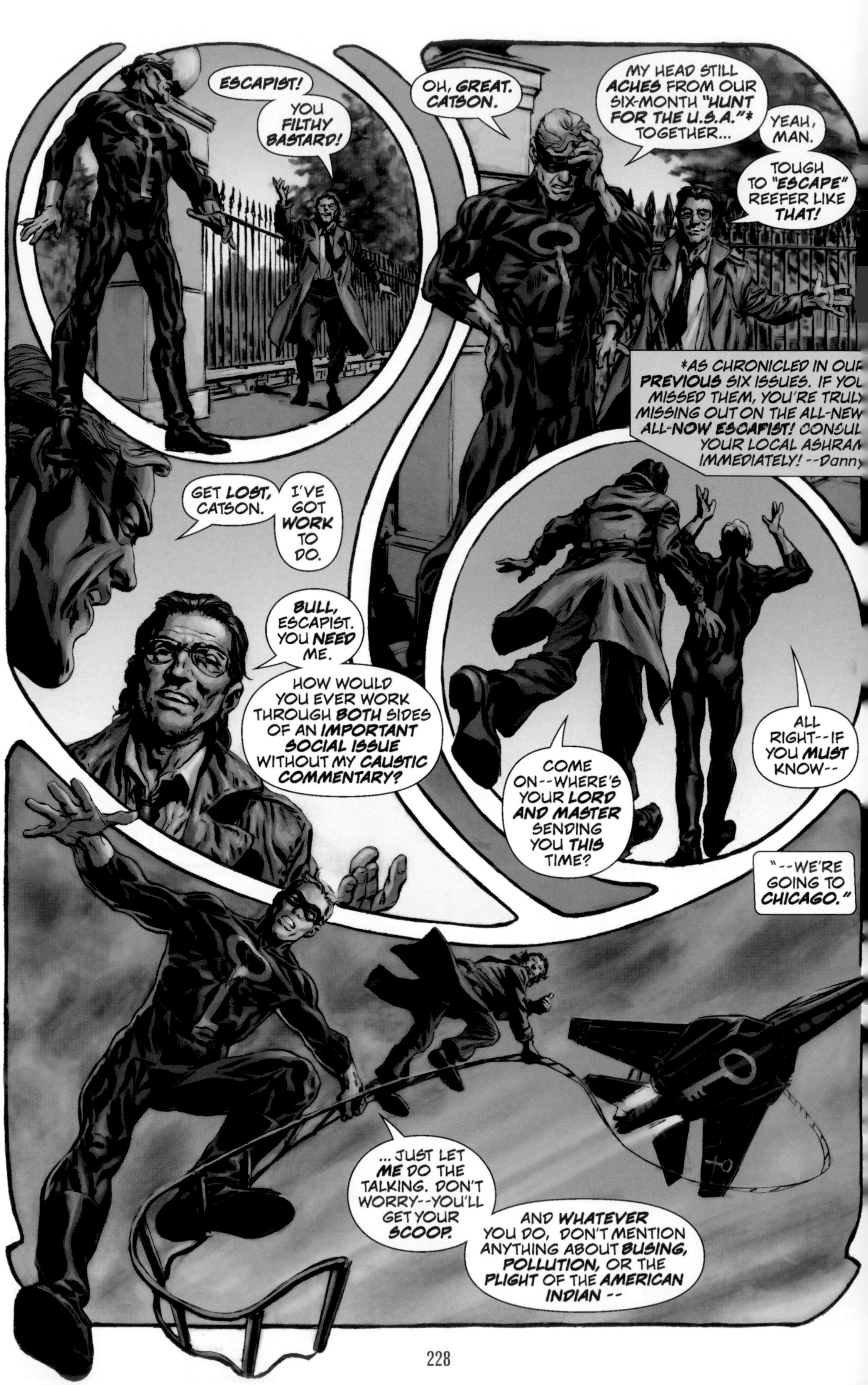

ESCAPIST!
YOU FILTHY BASTARD!
OH, GREAT. CATSON.
MY HEAD STILL ACHES FROM OUR SIX-MONTH "HUNT FOR THE U.S.A."* TOGETHER...
YEAH, MAN.
TOUGH TO "ESCAPE" REEFER LIKE THAT!
*AS CHRONICLED IN OUR PREVIOUS SIX ISSUES. IF YOU MISSED THEM, YOU'RE TRULY MISSING OUT ON THE ALL-NEW ALL-NOW ESCAFIST! CONSULT YOUR LOCAL ASHRAM IMMEDIATELY! --Danny
GET LOST, CATSON.
I'VE GOT WORK TO DO.
BULL, ESCAPIST. YOU NEED ME.
HOW WOULD YOU EVER WORK THROUGH BOTH SIDES OF AN IMPORTANT SOCIAL ISSUE WITHOUT MY CAUSTIC COMMENTARY?
COME ON--WHERE'S YOUR LORD AND MASTER SENDING YOU THIS TIME?
ALL RIGHT--IF YOU MUST KNOW--
"--WE'RE GOING TO CHICAGO."
... JUST LET ME DO THE TALKING. DON'T WORRY--YOU'LL GET YOUR SCOOP.
AND WHATEVER YOU DO, DON'T MENTION ANYTHING ABOUT BUSING, POLLUTION, OR THE PLIGHT OF THE AMERICAN INDIAN --

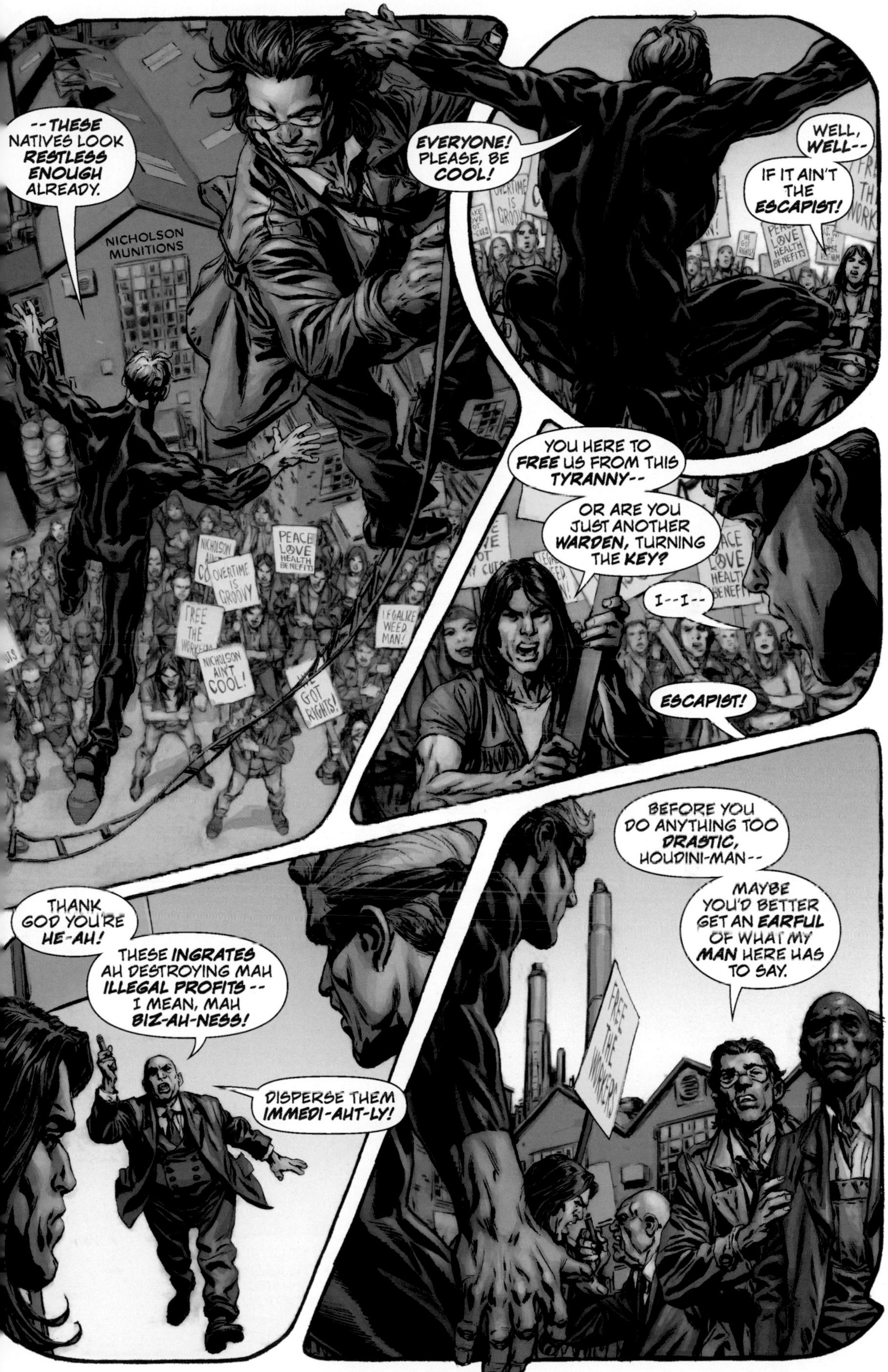
--THESE NATIVES LOOK RESTLESS ENOUGH ALREADY.
NICHOLSON MUNITIONS
EVERYONE! PLEASE, BE COOL!
PEACE LOVE HEALTH BENEFITS
OVERTIME IS GROOVY
FREE THE WORKERS
LEGALIZE WEED MAN!
NICHOLSON AIN'T COOL!
WE GOT RIGHTS!
WELL, WELL--
IF IT AIN'T THE ESCAPIST!
YOU HERE TO FREE US FROM THIS TYRANNY--
OR ARE YOU JUST ANOTHER WARDEN, TURNING THE KEY?
I--I--
ESCAPIST!
THANK GOD YOU'RE HE-AH!
THESE INGRATES AH DESTROYING MAH ILLEGAL PROFITS -- I MEAN, MAH BIZ-AH-NESS!
DISPERSE THEM IMMEDI-AHT-LY!
BEFORE YOU DO ANYTHING TOO DRASTIC, HOUDINI-MAN--
MAYBE YOU'D BETTER GET AN EARFUL OF WHAT MY MAN HERE HAS TO SAY.
FREE THE WORKERS

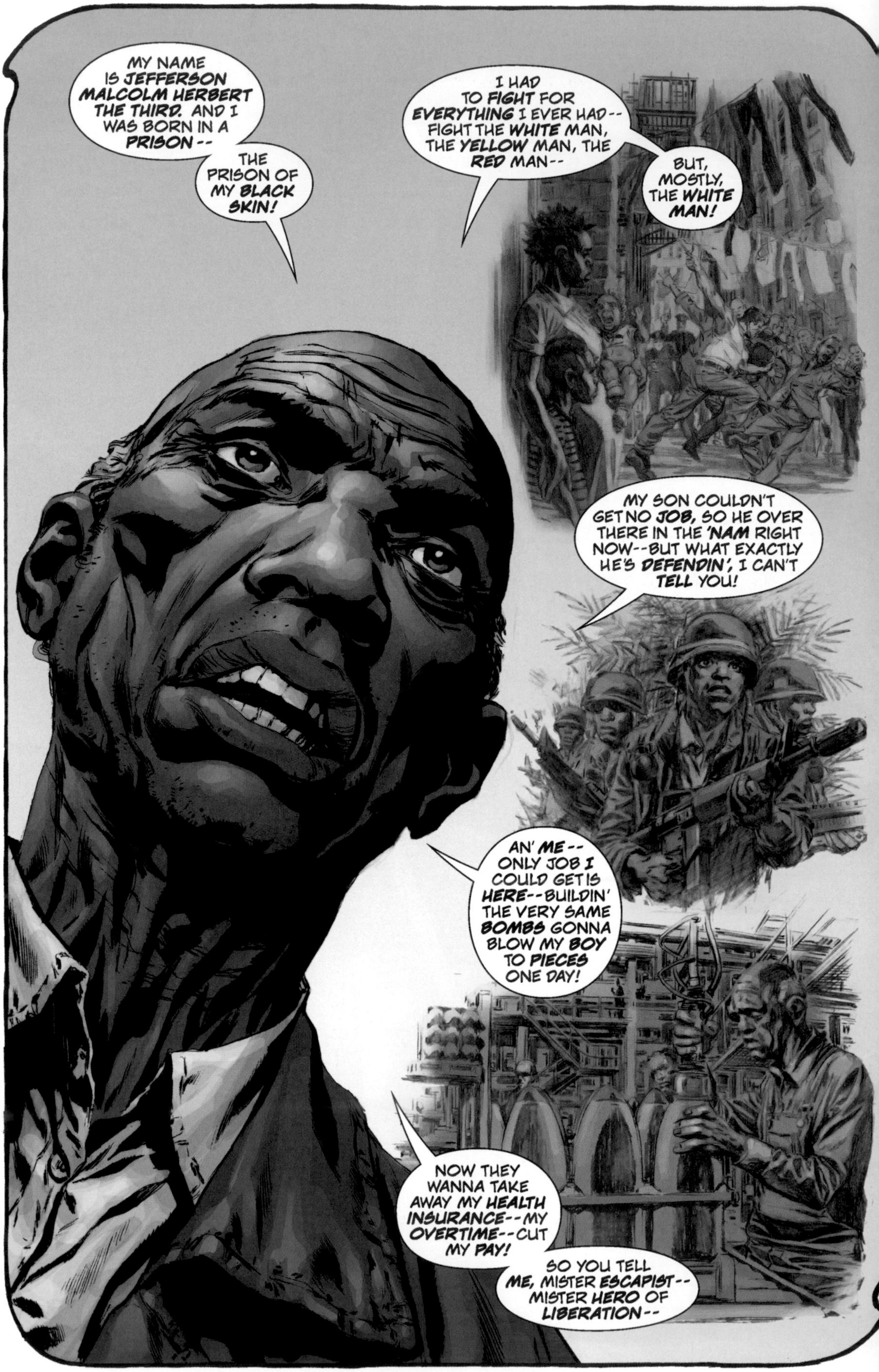
MY NAME IS JEFFERSON MALCOLM HERBERT THE THIRD. AND I WAS BORN IN A PRISON--
THE PRISON OF MY BLACK SKIN!
I HAD TO FIGHT FOR EVERYTHING I EVER HAD--FIGHT THE WHITE MAN, THE YELLOW MAN, THE RED MAN--
BUT, MOSTLY, THE WHITE MAN!
MY SON COULDN'T GET NO JOB, SO HE OVER THERE IN THE 'NAM RIGHT NOW--BUT WHAT EXACTLY HE'S DEFENDIN', I CAN'T TELL YOU!
AN' ME--ONLY JOB I COULD GET IS HERE--BUILDIN' THE VERY SAME BOMBS GONNA BLOW MY BOY TO PIECES ONE DAY!
NOW THEY WANNA TAKE AWAY MY HEALTH INSURANCE--MY OVERTIME--CUT MY PAY!
SO YOU TELL ME, MISTER ESCAPIST--MISTER HERO OF LIBERATION--

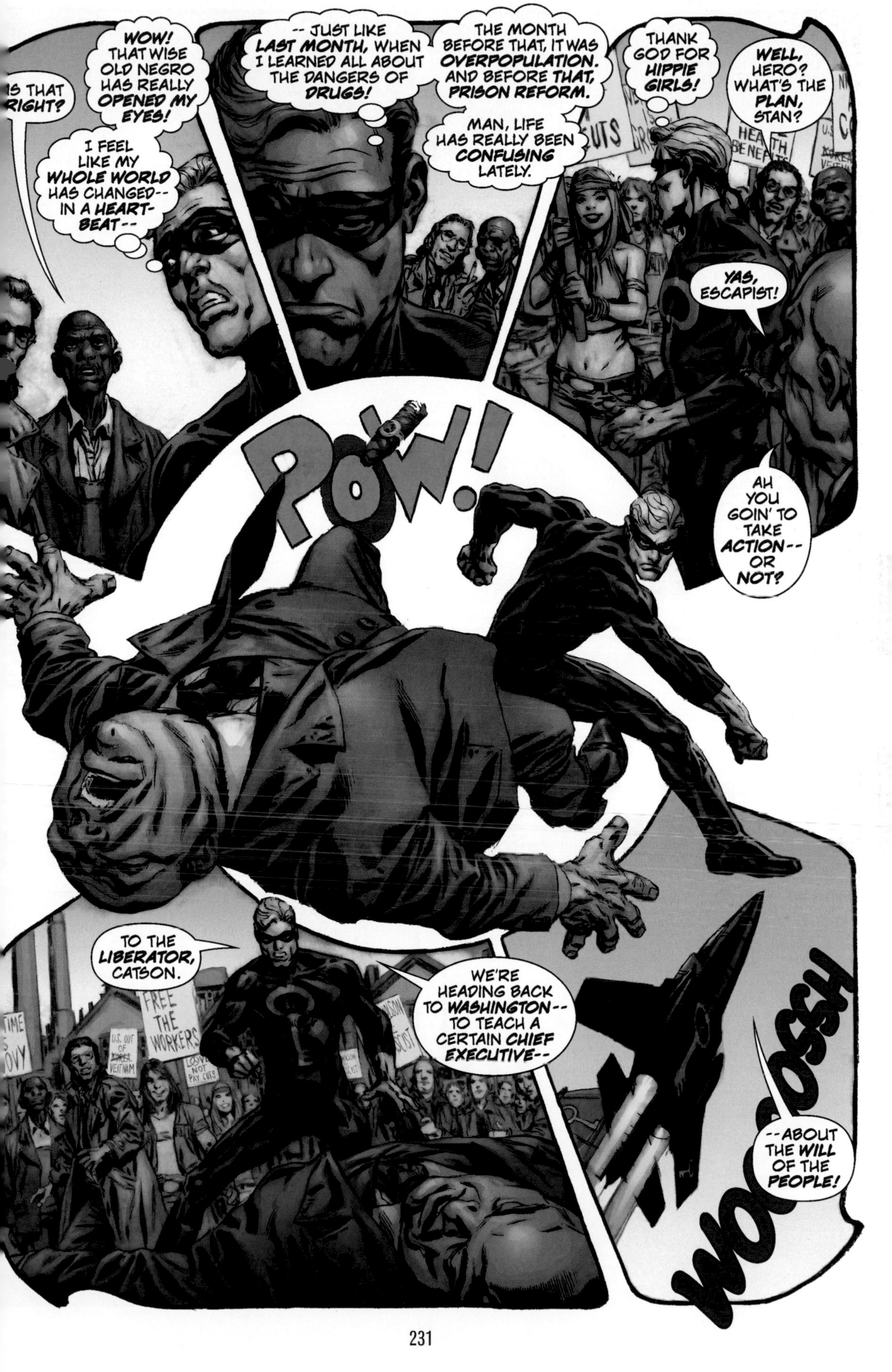
IS THAT RIGHT?
WOW! THAT WISE OLD NEGRO HAS REALLY OPENED MY EYES!
I FEEL LIKE MY WHOLE WORLD HAS CHANGED-- IN A HEART-BEAT--
-- JUST LIKE LAST MONTH, WHEN I LEARNED ALL ABOUT THE DANGERS OF DRUGS!
THE MONTH BEFORE THAT, IT WAS OVERPOPULATION. AND BEFORE THAT, PRISON REFORM.
MAN, LIFE HAS REALLY BEEN CONFUSING LATELY.
THANK GOD FOR HIPPIE GIRLS!
WELL, HERO? WHAT'S THE PLAN, STAN?
YAS, ESCAPIST!
AH YOU GOIN' TO TAKE ACTION-- OR NOT?
POW!
TO THE LIBERATOR, CATSON.
FREE THE WORKERS
LOVE NOT PAY CUTS
WE'RE HEADING BACK TO WASHINGTON-- TO TEACH A CERTAIN CHIEF EXECUTIVE--
WOOOSSH
--ABOUT THE WILL OF THE PEOPLE!

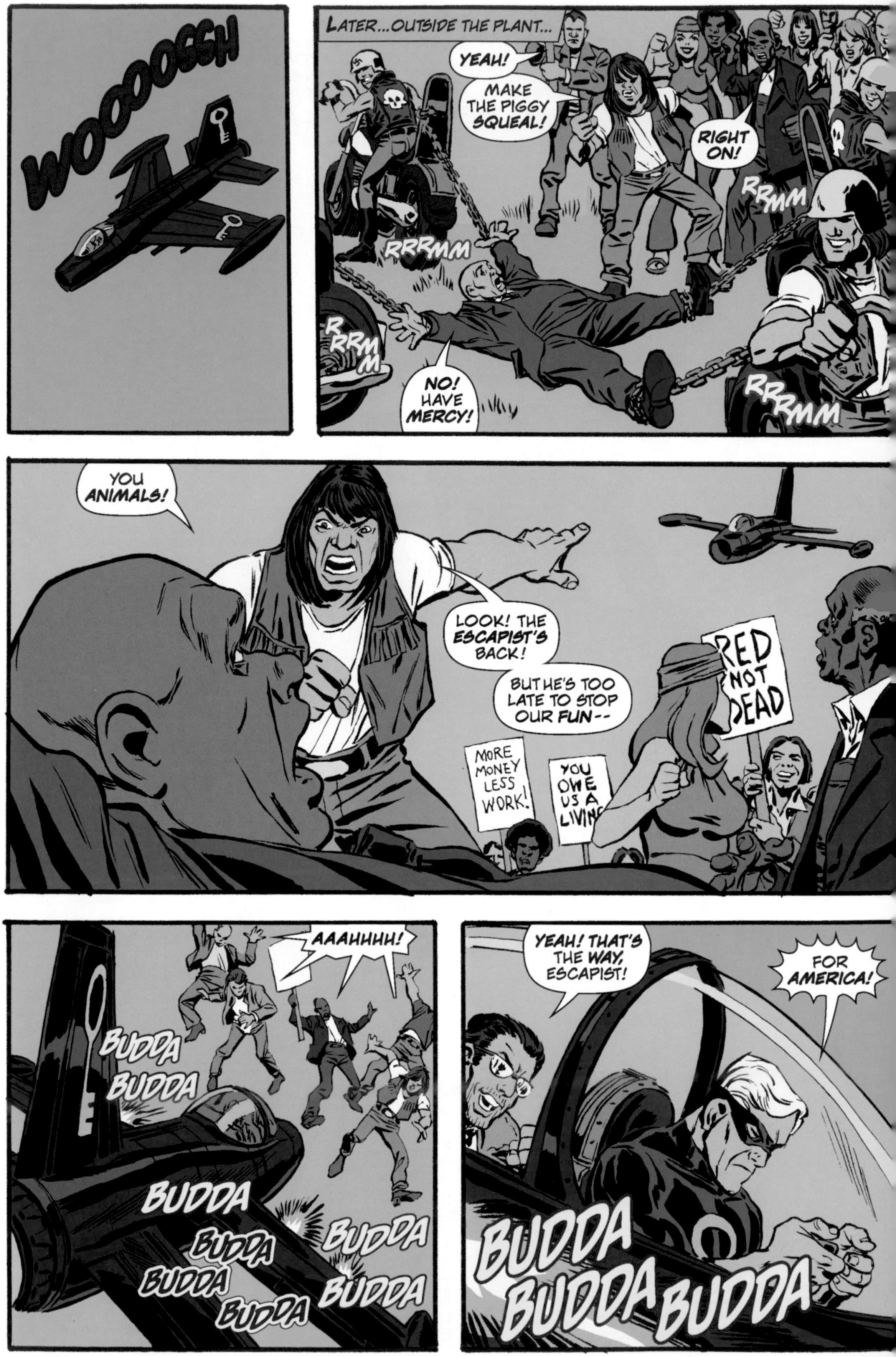
WOOOOSSH
LATER...OUTSIDE THE PLANT...
YEAH!
MAKE THE PIGGY SQUEAL!
RIGHT ON!
RRMM
RRRMM
RRRMM
NO! HAVE MERCY!
RRRMM
YOU ANIMALS!
LOOK! THE ESCAPIST'S BACK!
BUT HE'S TOO LATE TO STOP OUR FUN--
RED NOT DEAD
MORE MONEY LESS WORK!
YOU OWE US A LIVIN
AAAHHHH!
BUDDA BUDDA
BUDDA BUDDA BUDDA BUDDA
BUDDA BUDDA
YEAH! THAT'S THE WAY, ESCAPIST!
FOR AMERICA!
BUDDA BUDDA BUDDA

ATTENTION! YOU--THE SURVIVORS!

RETURN TO WORK IMMEDIATELY!

AND IF ANY OF YOU *EVER* THINK AGAIN ABOUT *BETRAYING* YOUR *COUNTRY*--

JUST *REMEMBER*-- YOU CAN'T *ESCAPE* THE *ESCAPIST!*

YOU *FASCIST BASTARD!* THAT WAS *INSPIRING!*

MAKES ME WANT TO BREAK OUT THE OLD *TYPER* AND WRITE A *SAVAGE* STORY!

IT HAD TO BE *DONE*, CATSON.

FREEDOM ISN'T *FREE.* IF YOU DON'T SUPPORT THE *ADMINISTRATION*--

YOU DON'T SUPPORT THE *TROOPS.*

AND, FRIEND, THAT'S NOT *MY* AMERICA!

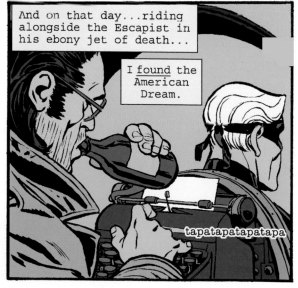

And on that day...riding alongside the Escapist in his ebony jet of death...

I found the American Dream.

*tapatapatapatapa*

233

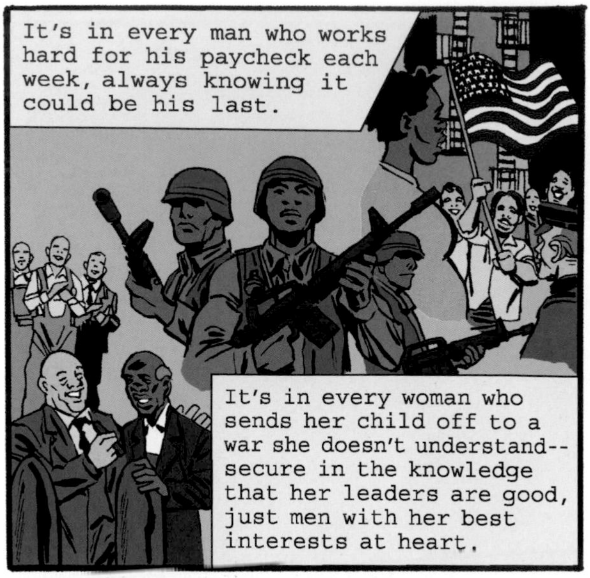
It's in every man who works hard for his paycheck each week, always knowing it could be his last.
It's in every woman who sends her child off to a war she doesn't understand--secure in the knowledge that her leaders are good, just men with her best interests at heart.

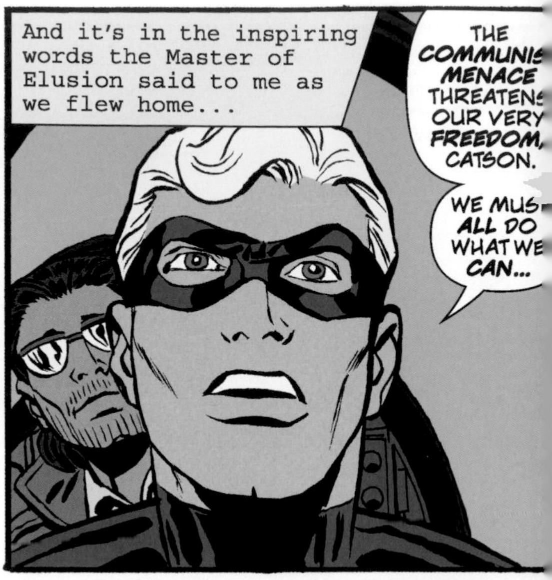
And it's in the inspiring words the Master of Elusion said to me as we flew home...
THE COMMUNIS MENACE THREATENS OUR VERY FREEDOM, CATSON.
WE MUS ALL DO WHAT WE CAN...

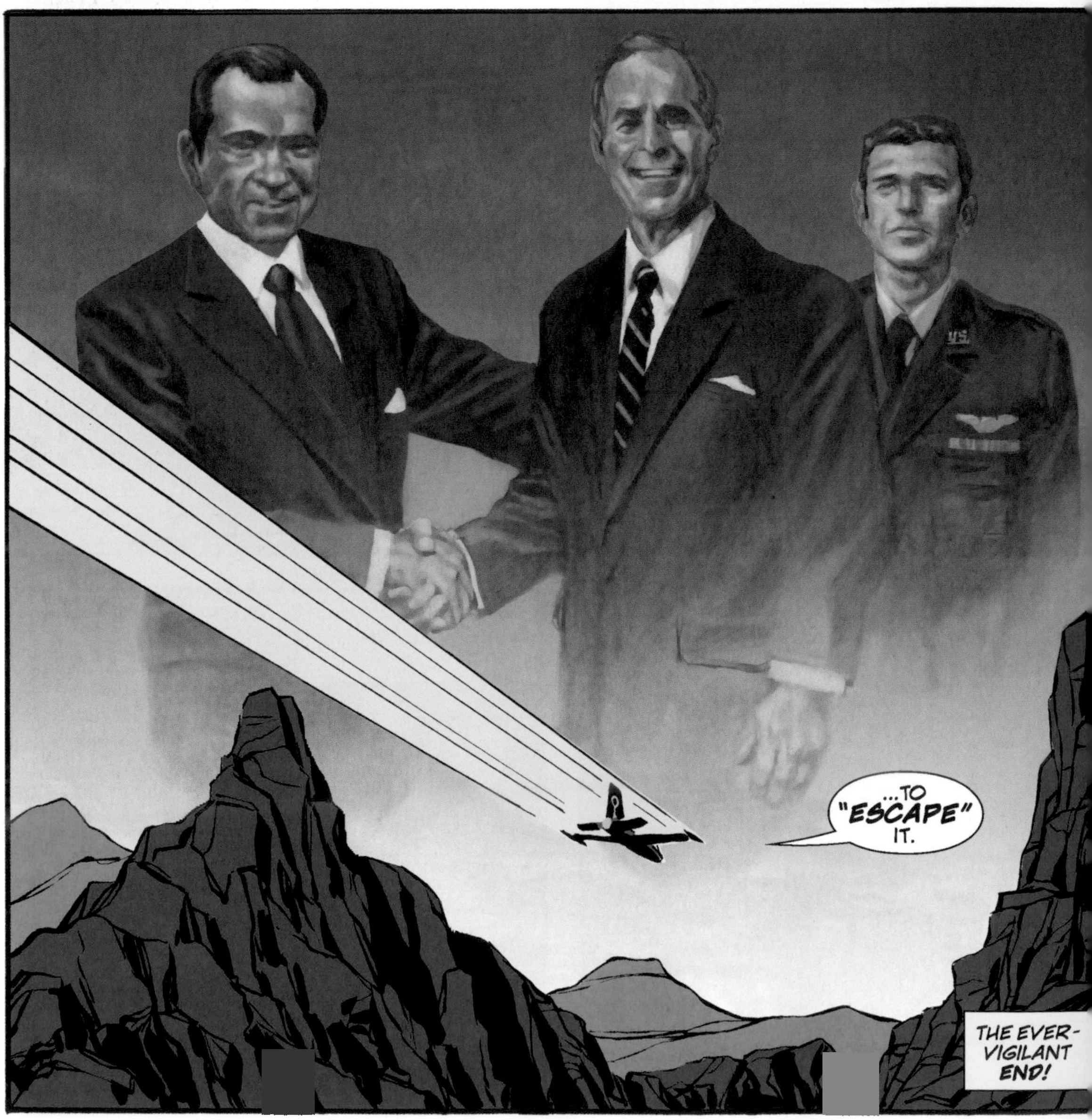
...TO "ESCAPE" IT.
THE EVER-VIGILANT END!

# DANNY'S DIALOG

WRITE TO: 909 THIRD AVENUE, NEW YORK, N.Y. 10022

Hola, **Sunbeams.** Pull up a beanbag and let's rap!

In keeping with Sunshine Media Group's new policy of honesty with our readers, I'm here to give you the story behind the story you just read.

First off: Since assuming control of Sunshine Media from my fascist, money-grubbing father, I've worked hard to create a place where inspired creative people can come together in a communal atmosphere of peace, harmony, and mutual support.

Unfortunately, every Eden has its serpents. In this case it was **Bob Eider** and **Curt Schnaffler,** the original writer and artist of "Union City Blues."

Bob and Curt -- unable to see the beauty and love that, praise Buddha, I have worked so hard to instill into the Escapist line -- insisted that the Sunshine Group needed a freelancers' union. Something about reprint rates and insurance -- a petty, mortal-coil matter.

I was stunned. Just like the Escapist, my whole world had changed -- in the span of a single heartbeat!

Anyway -- once Bob and Curt were escorted from the premises, poor Danny was left with half a story -- and a looming deadline. Did Lenin have days like this?

Thankfully, thirteen-year-old prodigy **Slim Farger** stepped in and dialogued the rest of the story, putting his own "edgy" '70s spin on the Escapist. Meanwhile, old pro **Lou Pintz** stepped out of retirement -- and the V.A. hospital -- to finish the mind-blowing art.

It's great to be working with people who truly understand the beautiful **Sunshine** philosophy. And no talk of unions anymore, either. Slim's too young to sign anything, and Lou's just grateful for the work. Very, very grateful.

Anyway -- I've gone on longer than I intended, **Sunbeams.** May peace be with you as you go about your daily ablutions. And be grateful you don't have to put up with the crap old Danny deals with every day.

Mahalo,
-- Danny

P.S. We're raising the price to 25 cents next month. Nembutsu, nembutsu, nembutsu!

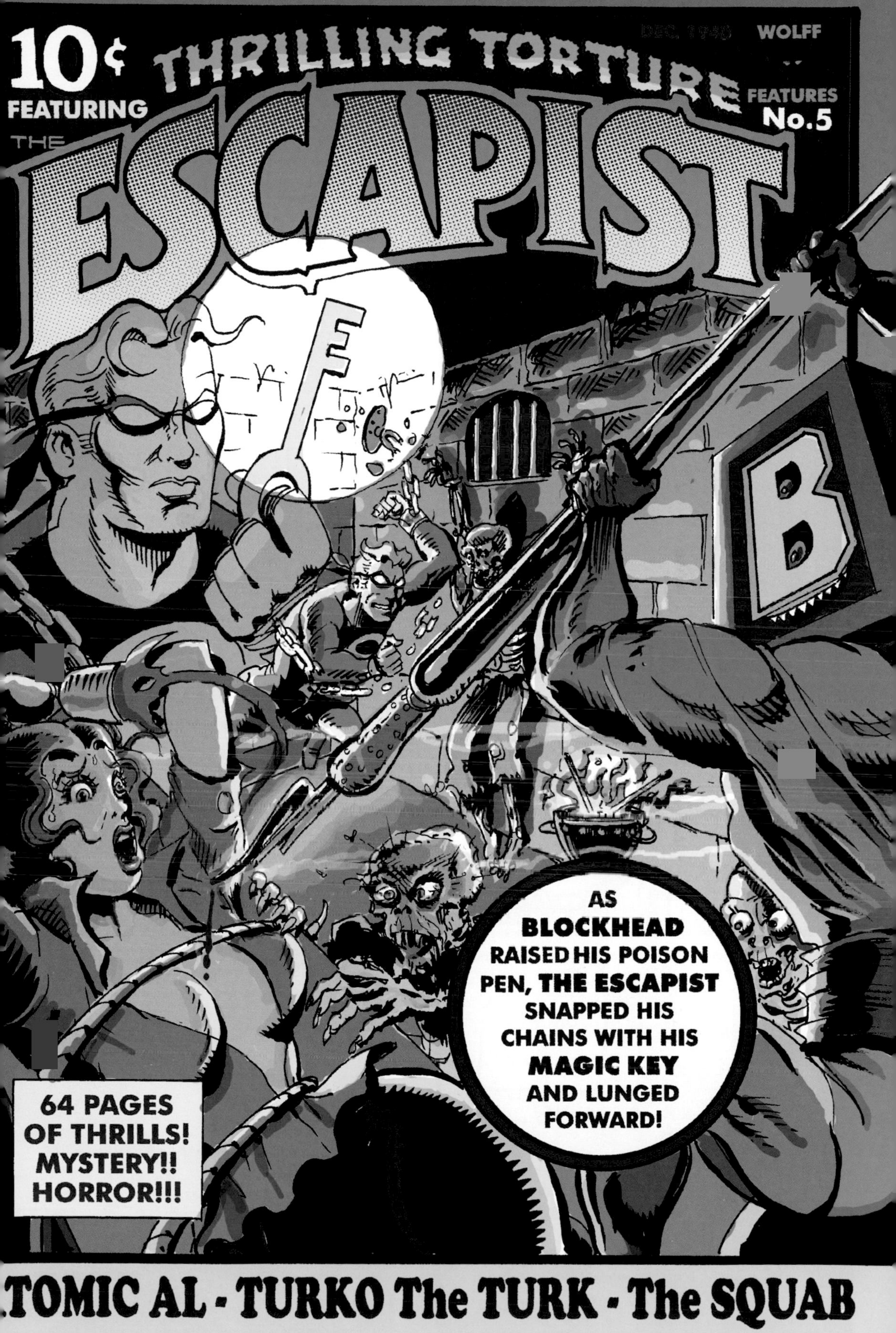
10¢
FEATURING
THE
THRILLING TORTURE
DEC. 1940
WOLFF
FEATURES
No.5
ESCAPIST
AS BLOCKHEAD RAISED HIS POISON PEN, THE ESCAPIST SNAPPED HIS CHAINS WITH HIS MAGIC KEY AND LUNGED FORWARD!
64 PAGES OF THRILLS! MYSTERY!! HORROR!!!
TOMIC AL - TURKO The TURK - The SQUAB

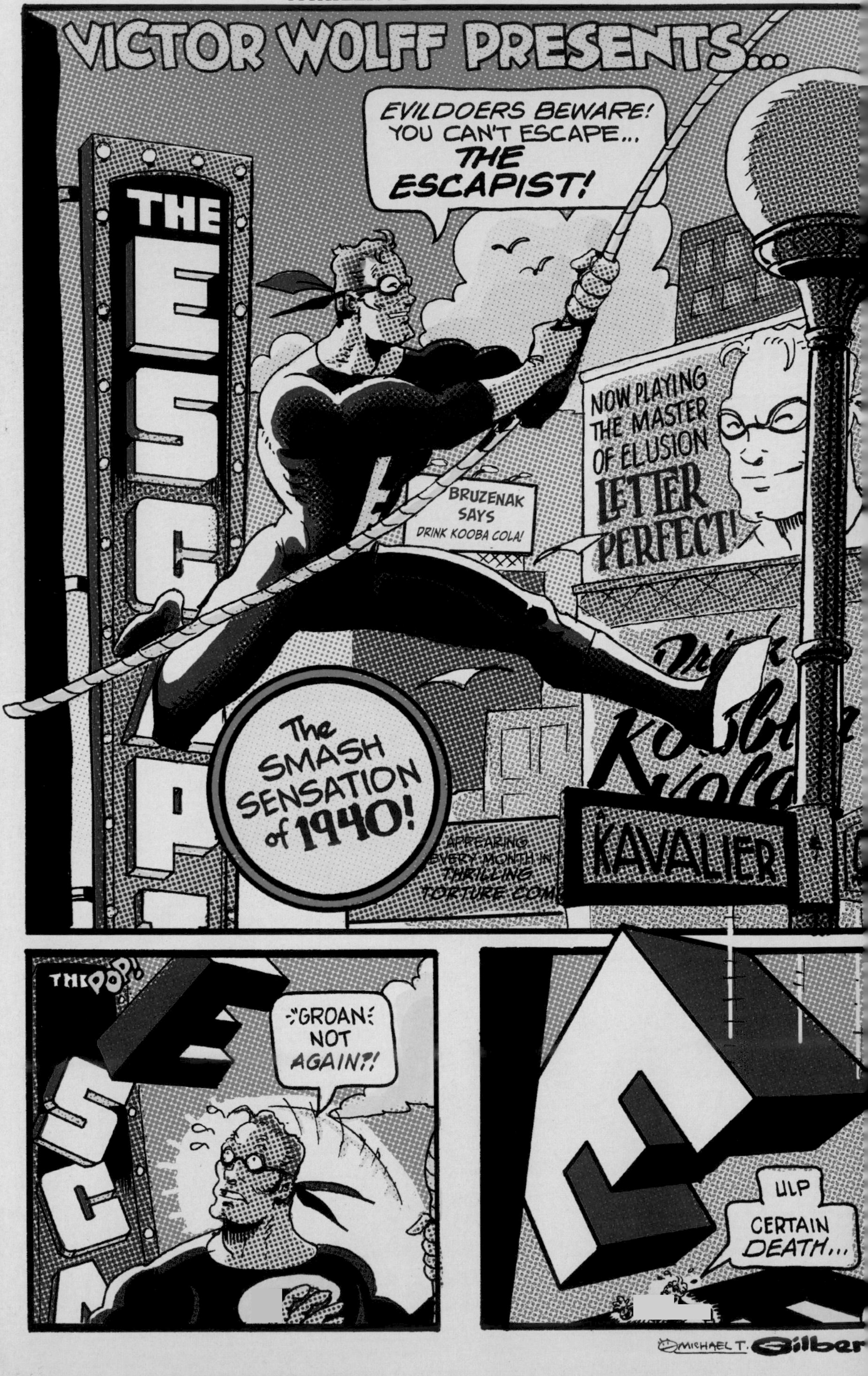
VICTOR WOLFF PRESENTS...
EVILDOERS BEWARE! YOU CAN'T ESCAPE... THE ESCAPIST!
BRUZENAK SAYS DRINK KOOBA COLA!
NOW PLAYING THE MASTER OF ELUSION LETTER PERFECT!
The SMASH SENSATION of 1940!
APPEARING EVERY MONTH IN THRILLING
KAVALIER
THOOP!
GROAN NOT AGAIN?!
ULP
CERTAIN DEATH...
MICHAEL T. Gilbert

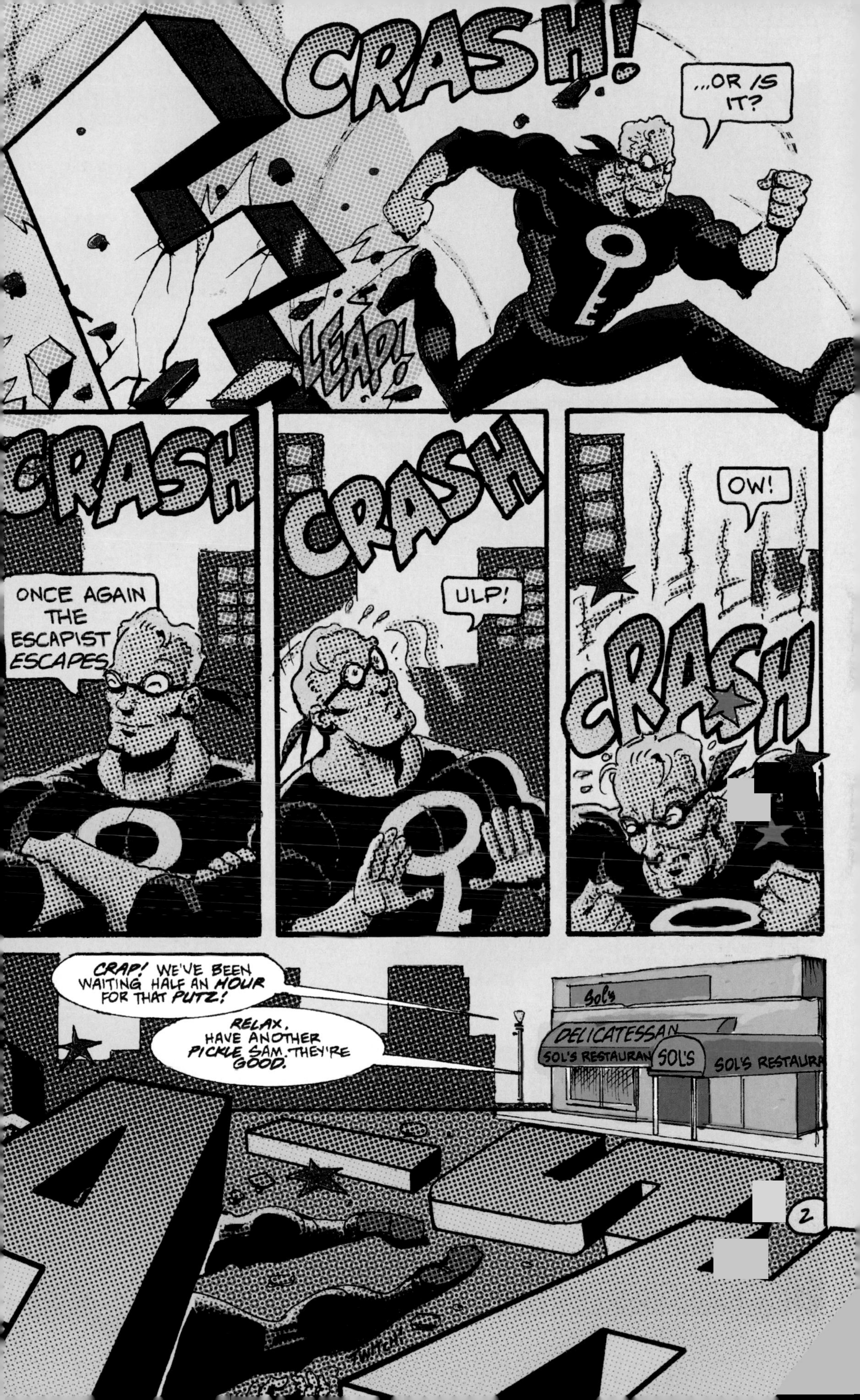
CRASH!
...OR IS IT?
LEAP!
CRASH
ONCE AGAIN THE ESCAPIST *ESCAPES*
CRASH
ULP!
OW!
CRASH
*CRAP!* WE'VE BEEN WAITING HALF AN *HOUR* FOR THAT *PUTZ!*
*RELAX.* HAVE ANOTHER *PICKLE* SAM. THEY'RE *GOOD.*
SOL'S
DELICATESSAN
SOL'S RESTAURAN
SOL'S
SOL'S RESTAURA
TWITCH!

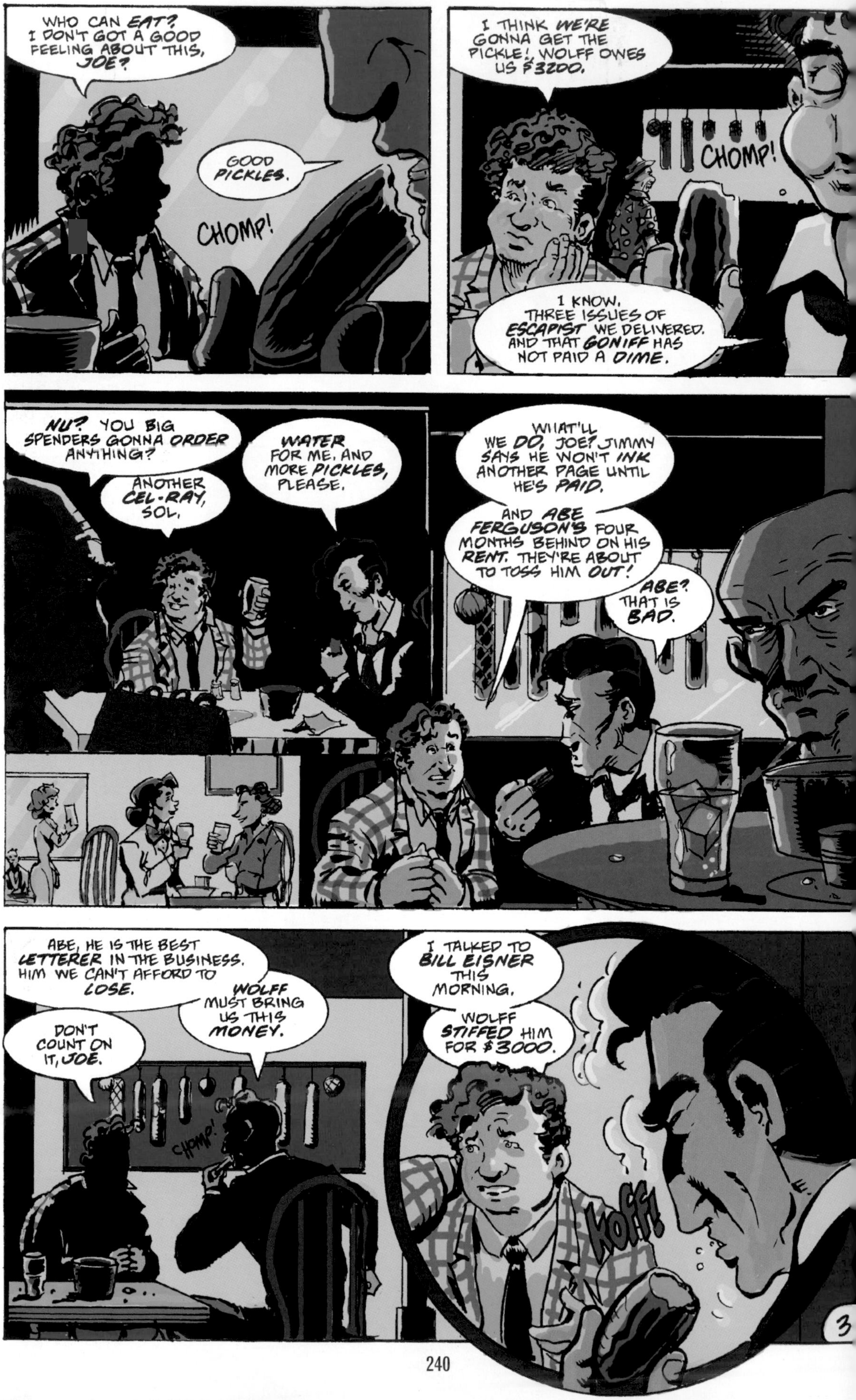

WHO CAN EAT? I DON'T GOT A GOOD FEELING ABOUT THIS, JOE?
GOOD PICKLES.
CHOMP!
I THINK WE'RE GONNA GET THE PICKLE! WOLFF OWES US $3200.
CHOMP!
I KNOW. THREE ISSUES OF ESCAPIST WE DELIVERED. AND THAT GONIFF HAS NOT PAID A DIME.
NU? YOU BIG SPENDERS GONNA ORDER ANYTHING?
ANOTHER CEL-RAY, SOL.
WATER FOR ME. AND MORE PICKLES, PLEASE.
WHAT'LL WE DO, JOE? JIMMY SAYS HE WON'T INK ANOTHER PAGE UNTIL HE'S PAID.
AND ABE FERGUSON'S FOUR MONTHS BEHIND ON HIS RENT. THEY'RE ABOUT TO TOSS HIM OUT!
ABE? THAT IS BAD.
ABE, HE IS THE BEST LETTERER IN THE BUSINESS. HIM WE CAN'T AFFORD TO LOSE.
WOLFF MUST BRING US THIS MONEY.
DON'T COUNT ON IT, JOE.
CHOMP!
I TALKED TO BILL EISNER THIS MORNING.
WOLFF STIFFED HIM FOR $3000.
KOFF!
3

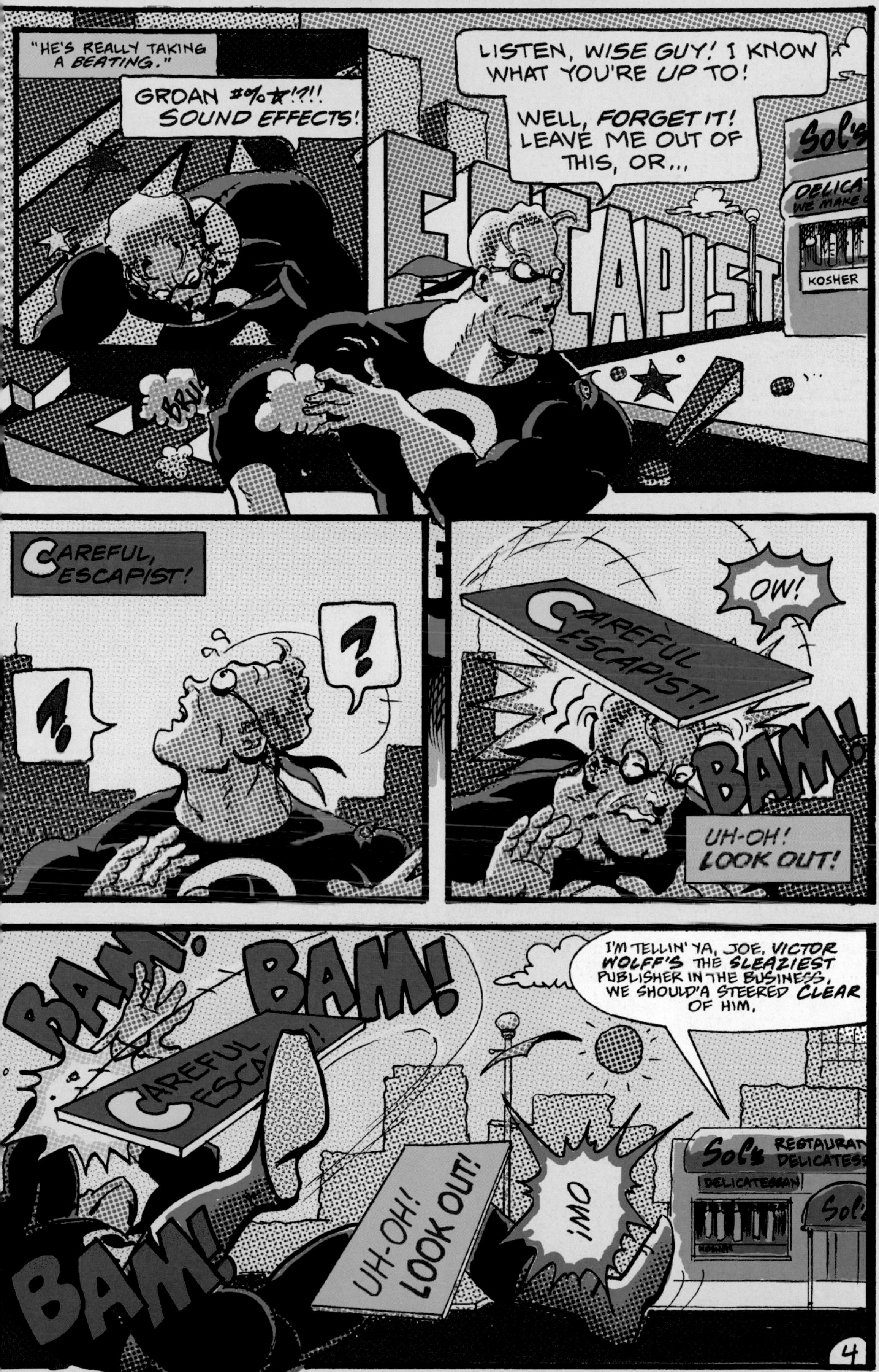
"HE'S REALLY TAKING A BEATING."
GROAN #%★!?!! SOUND EFFECTS!
LISTEN, WISE GUY! I KNOW WHAT YOU'RE UP TO!
WELL, FORGET IT! LEAVE ME OUT OF THIS, OR...
Sol's
KOSHER
CAREFUL, ESCAPIST!
?
?
OW!
CAREFUL ESCAPIST!
BAM!
UH-OH! LOOK OUT!
BAM!
BAM!
I'M TELLIN' YA, JOE. VICTOR WOLFF'S THE SLEAZIEST PUBLISHER IN THE BUSINESS. WE SHOULD'A STEERED CLEAR OF HIM.
UH-OH! LOOK OUT!
OW!
Sol's
DELICATESSAN
BAM!
4

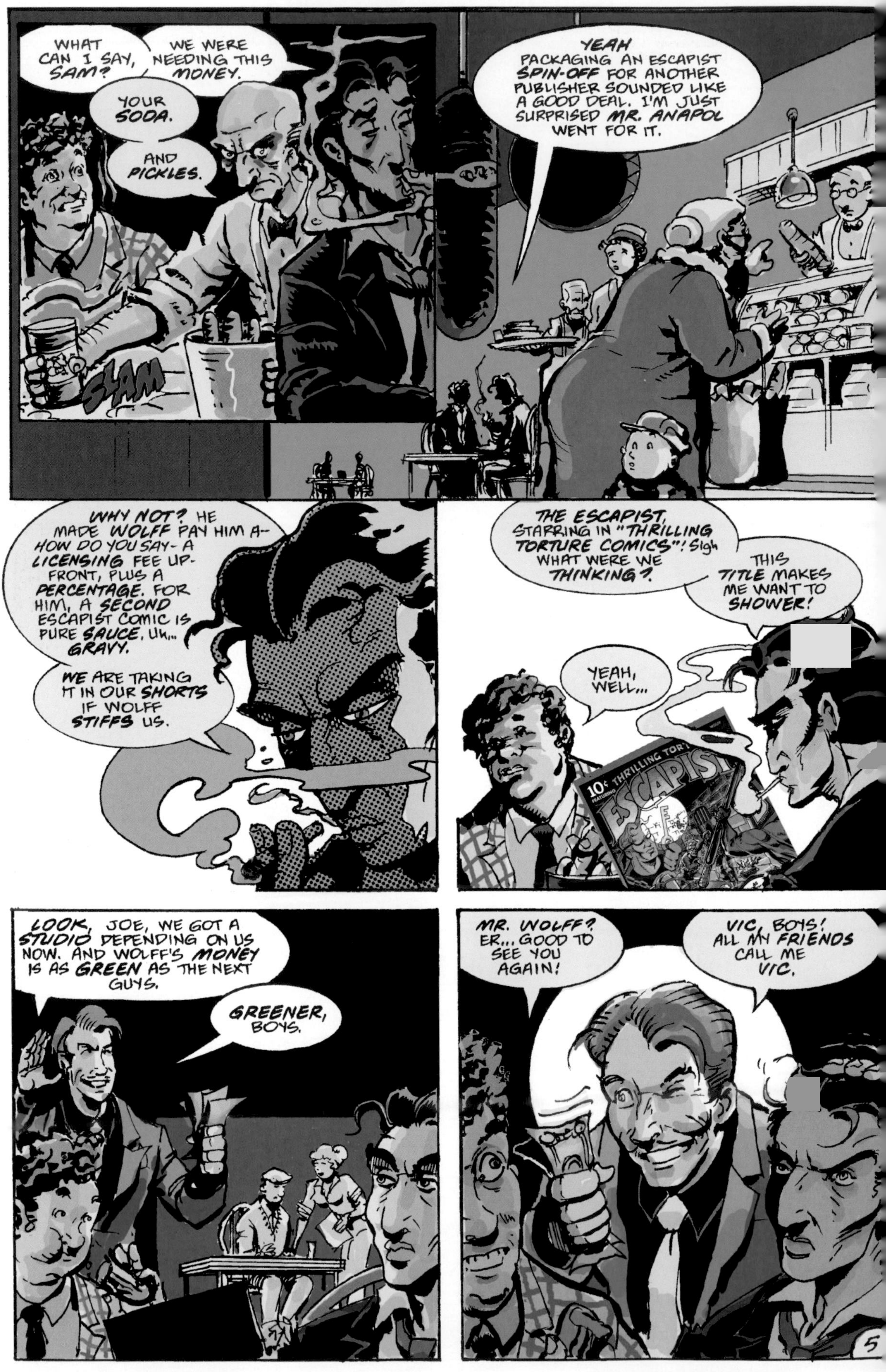
WHAT CAN I SAY, SAM?
WE WERE NEEDING THIS MONEY.
YOUR SODA.
AND PICKLES.
SLAM
YEAH
PACKAGING AN ESCAPIST SPIN-OFF FOR ANOTHER PUBLISHER SOUNDED LIKE A GOOD DEAL. I'M JUST SURPRISED MR. ANAPOL WENT FOR IT.
WHY NOT? HE MADE WOLFF PAY HIM A-- HOW DO YOU SAY- A LICENSING FEE UP-FRONT, PLUS A PERCENTAGE. FOR HIM, A SECOND ESCAPIST COMIC IS PURE SAUCE, UH... GRAVY.
WE ARE TAKING IT IN OUR SHORTS IF WOLFF STIFFS US.
THE ESCAPIST, STARRING IN "THRILLING TORTURE COMICS"! Sigh WHAT WERE WE THINKING?
THIS TITLE MAKES ME WANT TO SHOWER!
YEAH, WELL...
10¢
ESCAPIST
LOOK, JOE, WE GOT A STUDIO DEPENDING ON US NOW. AND WOLFF'S MONEY IS AS GREEN AS THE NEXT GUYS.
GREENER, BOYS.
MR. WOLFF? ER... GOOD TO SEE YOU AGAIN!
VIC, BOYS! ALL MY FRIENDS CALL ME VIC.
5

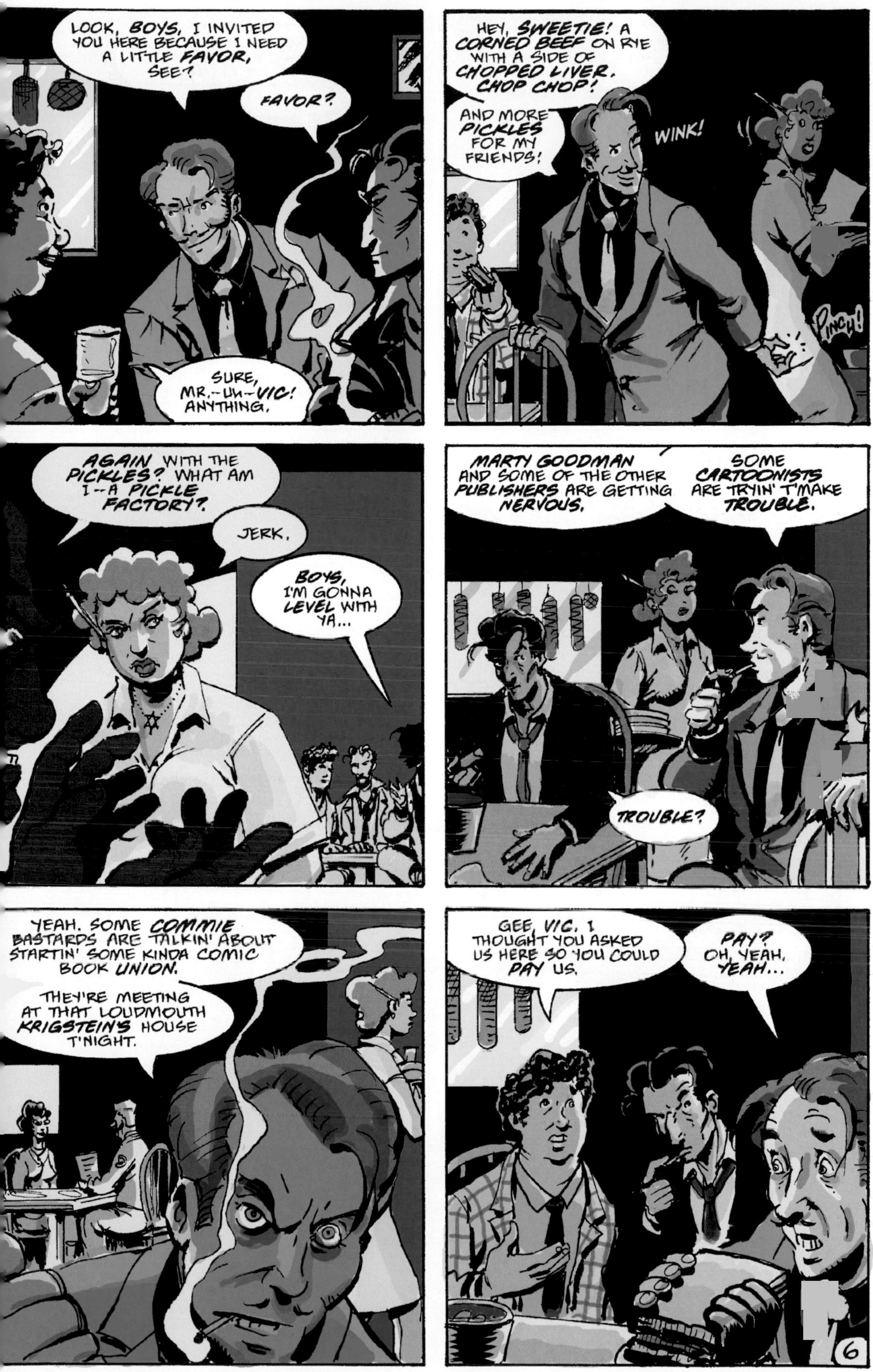
LOOK, BOYS, I INVITED YOU HERE BECAUSE I NEED A LITTLE FAVOR, SEE?
FAVOR?
SURE, MR.--UH--VIC! ANYTHING.
HEY, SWEETIE! A CORNED BEEF ON RYE WITH A SIDE OF CHOPPED LIVER. CHOP CHOP!
AND MORE PICKLES FOR MY FRIENDS!
WINK!
PINCH!
AGAIN WITH THE PICKLES? WHAT AM I--A PICKLE FACTORY?
JERK.
BOYS, I'M GONNA LEVEL WITH YA...
MARTY GOODMAN AND SOME OF THE OTHER PUBLISHERS ARE GETTING NERVOUS.
SOME CARTOONISTS ARE TRYIN' T'MAKE TROUBLE.
TROUBLE?
YEAH. SOME COMMIE BASTARDS ARE TALKIN' ABOUT STARTIN' SOME KINDA COMIC BOOK UNION.
THEY'RE MEETING AT THAT LOUDMOUTH KRIGSTEIN'S HOUSE T'NIGHT.
GEE, VIC, I THOUGHT YOU ASKED US HERE SO YOU COULD PAY US.
PAY? OH, YEAH, YEAH...
6

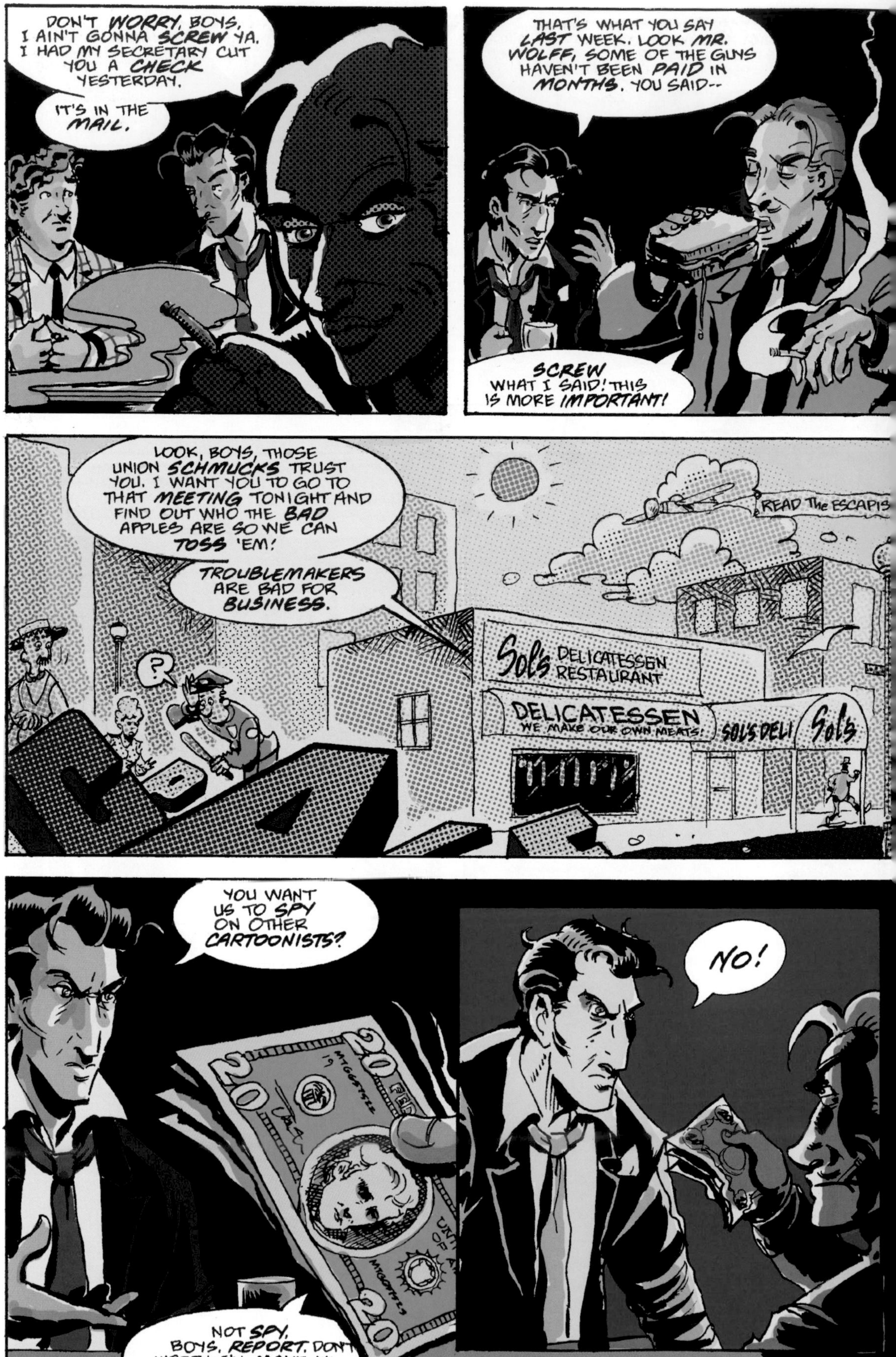
DON'T WORRY, BOYS, I AIN'T GONNA SCREW YA. I HAD MY SECRETARY CUT YOU A CHECK YESTERDAY.
IT'S IN THE MAIL.
THAT'S WHAT YOU SAY LAST WEEK. LOOK MR. WOLFF, SOME OF THE GUYS HAVEN'T BEEN PAID IN MONTHS. YOU SAID--
SCREW WHAT I SAID! THIS IS MORE IMPORTANT!
LOOK, BOYS, THOSE UNION SCHMUCKS TRUST YOU. I WANT YOU TO GO TO THAT MEETING TONIGHT AND FIND OUT WHO THE BAD APPLES ARE SO WE CAN TOSS 'EM!
TROUBLEMAKERS ARE BAD FOR BUSINESS.
READ The ESCAPIS
Sol's DELICATESSEN RESTAURANT
DELICATESSEN
WE MAKE OUR OWN MEATS!
SOL'S DELI
Sol's
?
YOU WANT US TO SPY ON OTHER CARTOONISTS?
NOT SPY, BOYS, REPORT. DON'T WORRY--I'LL MAKE IT WORTH YOUR WHILE!
NO!
7

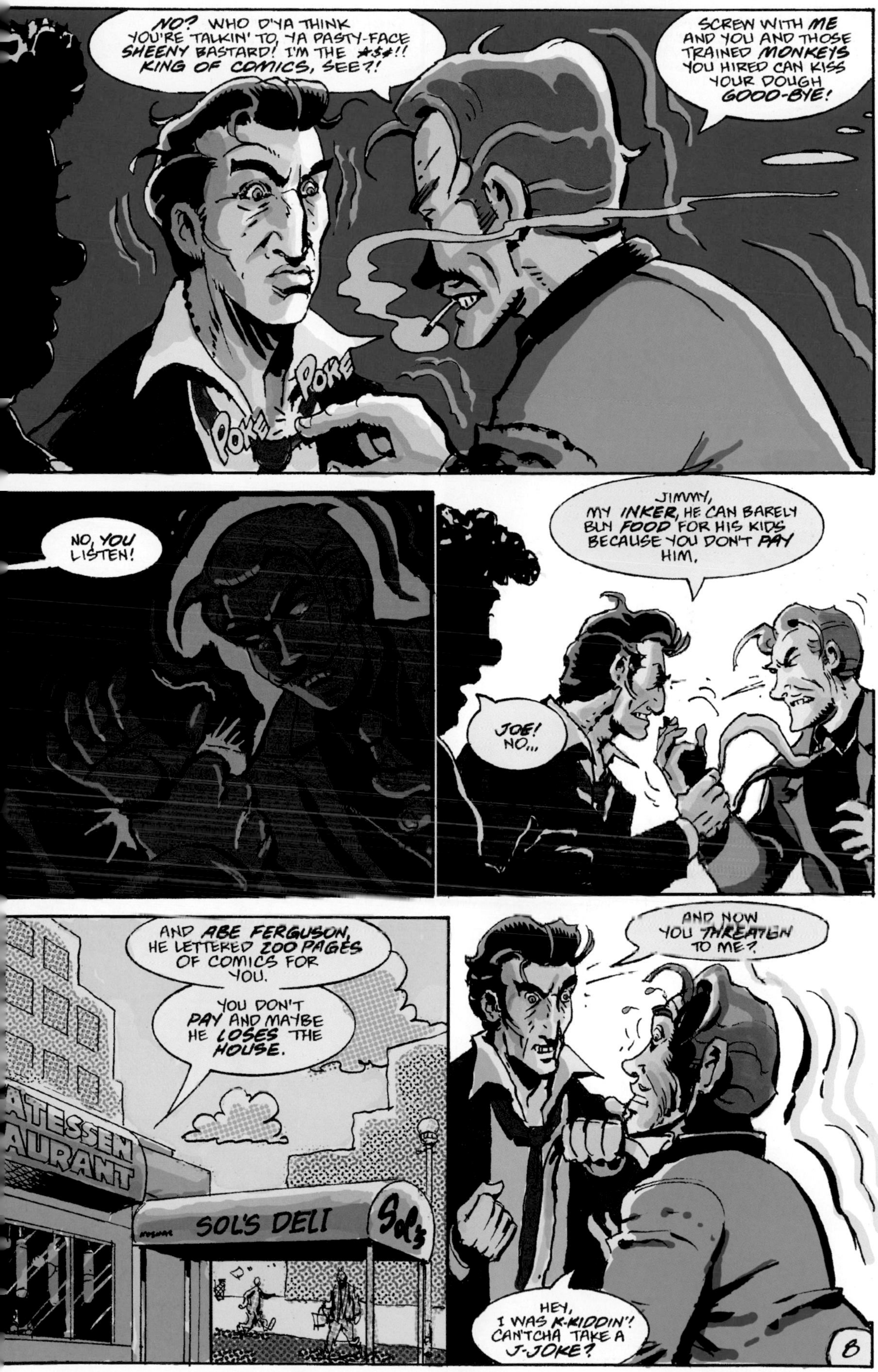
NO? WHO D'YA THINK YOU'RE TALKIN' TO, YA PASTY-FACE SHEENY BASTARD! I'M THE *$#!! KING OF COMICS, SEE?!
SCREW WITH ME AND YOU AND THOSE TRAINED MONKEYS YOU HIRED CAN KISS YOUR DOUGH GOOO-BYE!
POKE
POKE
NO, YOU LISTEN!
JIMMY, MY INKER, HE CAN BARELY BUY FOOD FOR HIS KIDS BECAUSE YOU DON'T PAY HIM.
JOE! NO...
AND ABE FERGUSON, HE LETTERED 200 PAGES OF COMICS FOR YOU.
YOU DON'T PAY AND MAYBE HE LOSES THE HOUSE.
ATESSEN
AURANT
SOL'S DELI
Sol's
AND NOW YOU THREATEN TO ME?
HEY, I WAS K-KIDDIN'! CAN'TCHA TAKE A J-JOKE?
8

F'GET THE *MEETING*, OKAY? LOOK, I GOT YOUR *DOUGH*, SEE? I'LL *PAY* YA RIGHT NOW T'SHOW YOU I'M ON TH' *LEVEL*.

GEE, *VIC*, WE—

HEY, *HOLD* THAT *THOUGHT*, WILLYA. I GOTTA HIT THE *CAN* FIRST.

LOOK, YOU BOYS GET A PIECE OF *KUGEL* OR SOMETHIN'-- *MY TREAT!* I'LL BE BACK IN A *MINUTE*.

ME

*JEEZ, JOE*. WHAT'D Y'DO *THAT* FOR?

THAT GUY I DON'T *LIKE*, HE HAS NO *HEART*.

**M**EANWHILE...

OH, NO YOU *DON'T!*

HA! I'M NOT FALLING FOR *THAT* GAG AGAIN!

MEANWHILE...

SNOOOSH!

MPHH?

FWAP!

NEWS STAN

BEWAR ESCAPI

EXTRA! ESCAPIST BATTLES MYSTERIO FOE

9

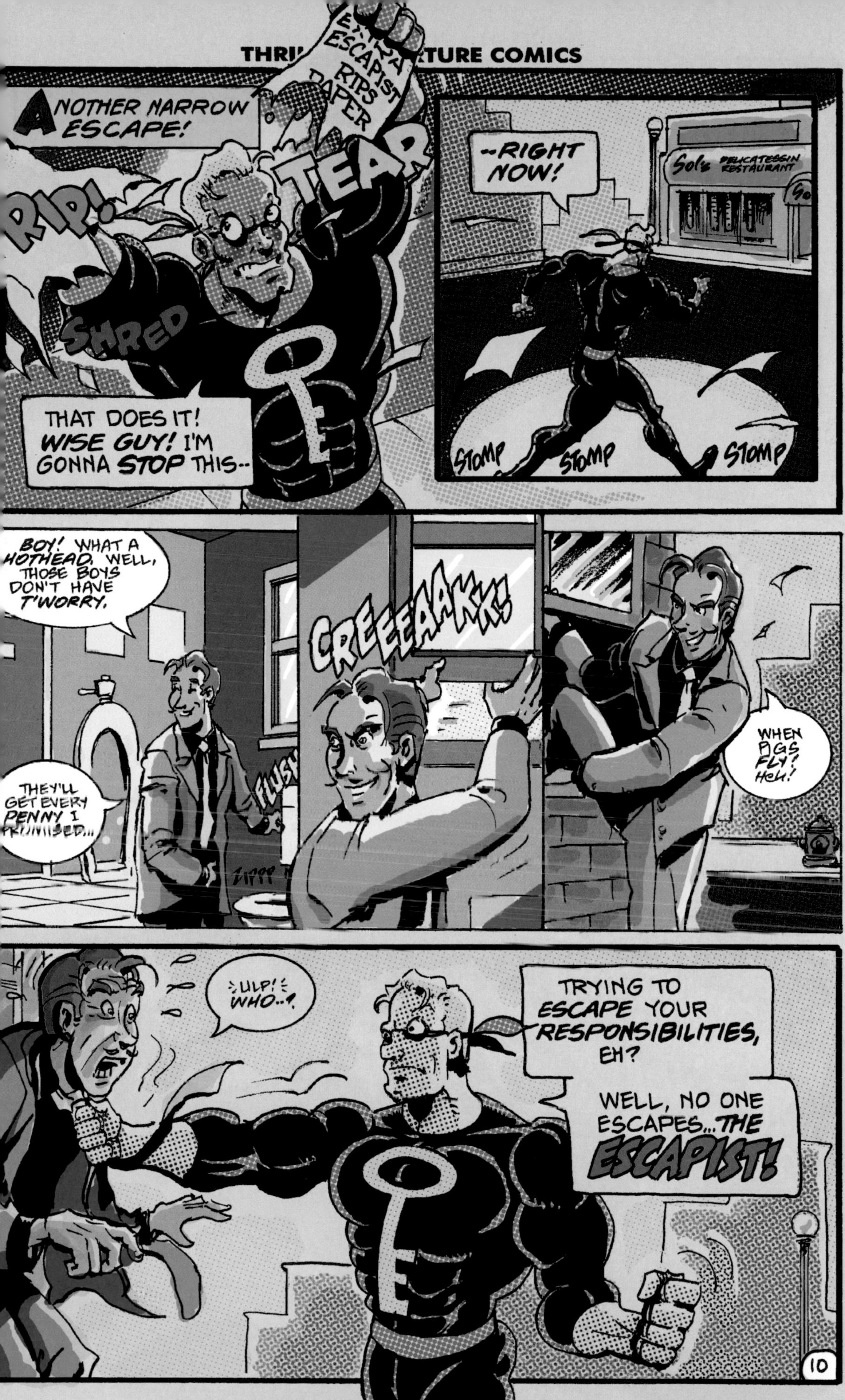
ANOTHER NARROW ESCAPE!
EXTRA ESCAPIST RIPS PAPER
RIP!
TEAR
SHRED
THAT DOES IT! WISE GUY! I'M GONNA STOP THIS--
--RIGHT NOW!
Sol's DELICATESSEN RESTAURANT
STOMP
STOMP
STOMP
BOY! WHAT A HOTHEAD. WELL, THOSE BOYS DON'T HAVE T'WORRY.
THEY'LL GET EVERY PENNY I PROMISED...
FLUS
ZIPPP
CREEEAAKK!
WHEN PIGS FLY! Heh!
ULP! WHO--?
TRYING TO ESCAPE YOUR RESPONSIBILITIES, EH?
WELL, NO ONE ESCAPES... THE ESCAPIST!

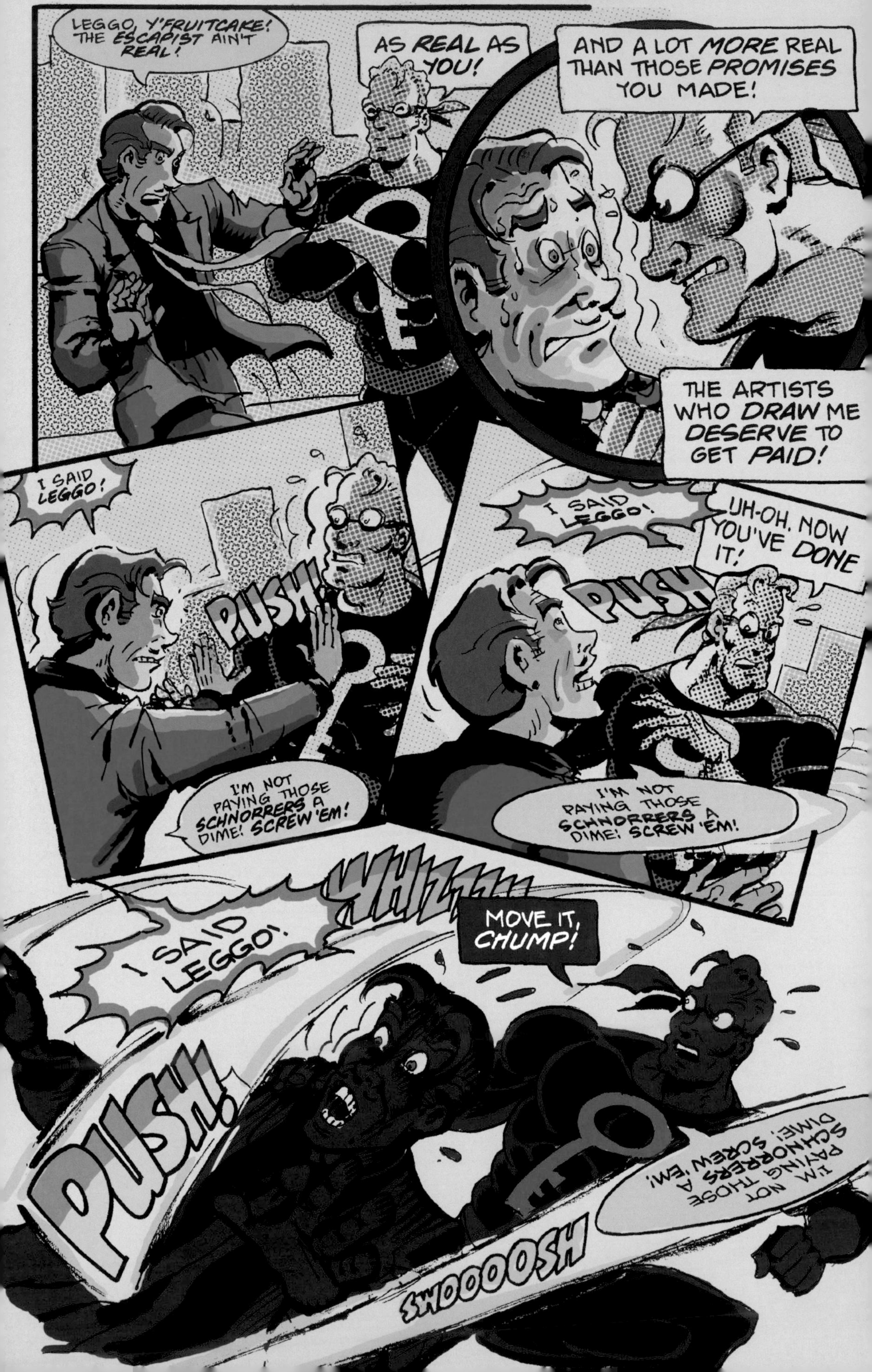
LEGGO, Y'FRUITCAKE! THE ESCAPIST AIN'T REAL!
AS REAL AS YOU!
AND A LOT MORE REAL THAN THOSE PROMISES YOU MADE!
THE ARTISTS WHO DRAW ME DESERVE TO GET PAID!
I SAID LEGGO!
PUSH!
I'M NOT PAYING THOSE SCHNORRERS A DIME! SCREW 'EM!
I SAID LEGGO!
UH-OH. NOW YOU'VE DONE IT!
PUSH
I'M NOT PAYING THOSE SCHNORRERS A DIME! SCREW 'EM!
I SAID LEGGO!
WHIZZ
MOVE IT, CHUMP!
PUSH!!
I'M NOT PAYING THOSE SCHNORRERS A DIME! SCREW 'EM!
SWOOOOSH

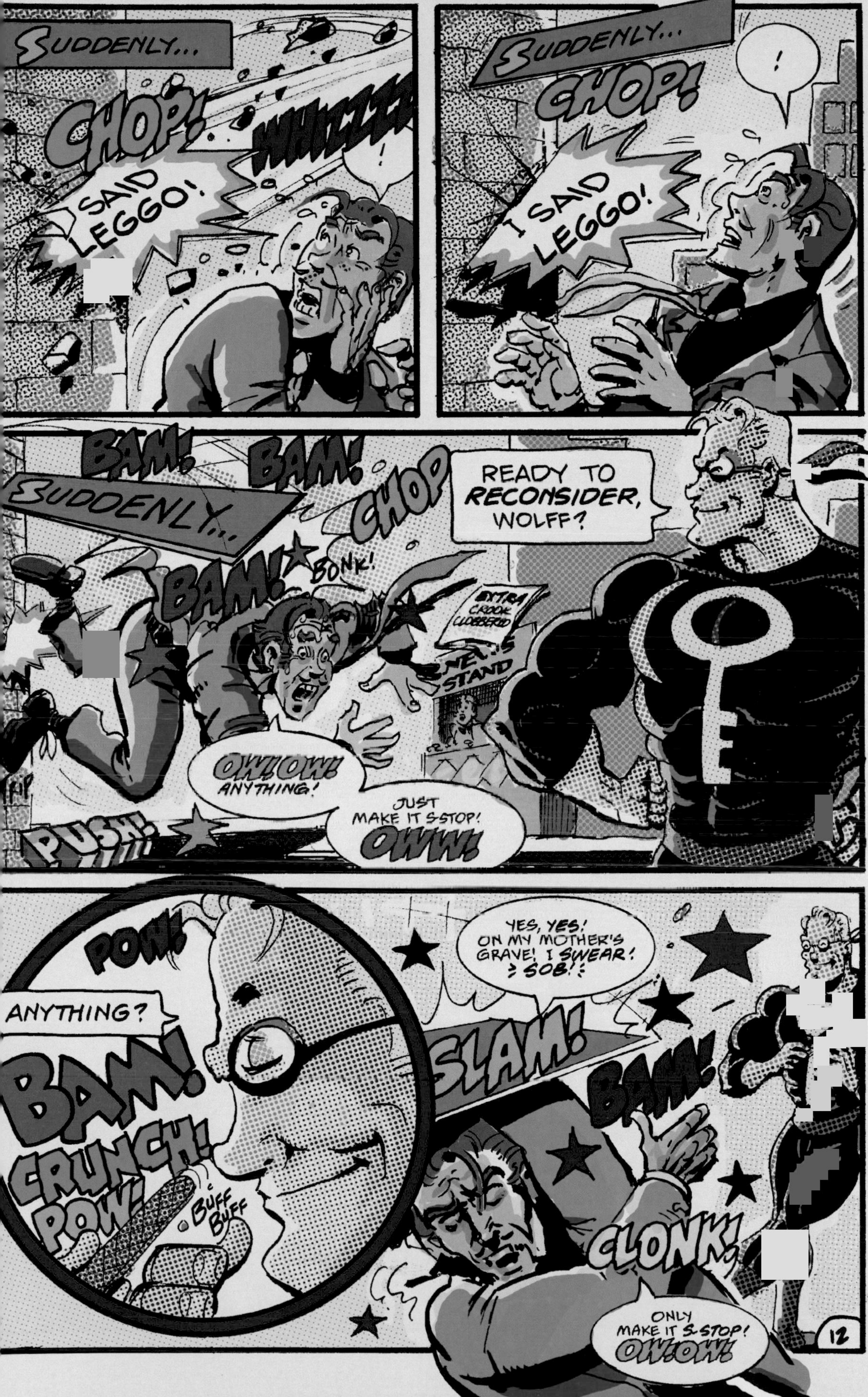
SUDDENLY...
CHOP!
WHIZZZ
SAID LEGGO!
!
SUDDENLY...
CHOP!
!
I SAID LEGGO!
BAM!
BAM!
SUDDENLY...
CHOP
BAM!
BONK!
READY TO RECONSIDER, WOLFF?
EXTRA CROOK CLOBBERED
OW! OW! ANYTHING!
JUST MAKE IT S-STOP! OWW!
PUSH!
POW!
ANYTHING?
BAM!
CRUNCH!
POW!
BUFF BUFF
YES, YES! ON MY MOTHER'S GRAVE! I SWEAR! SOB!
SLAM!
BAM!
CLONK!
ONLY MAKE IT S-STOP! OW! OW!
12

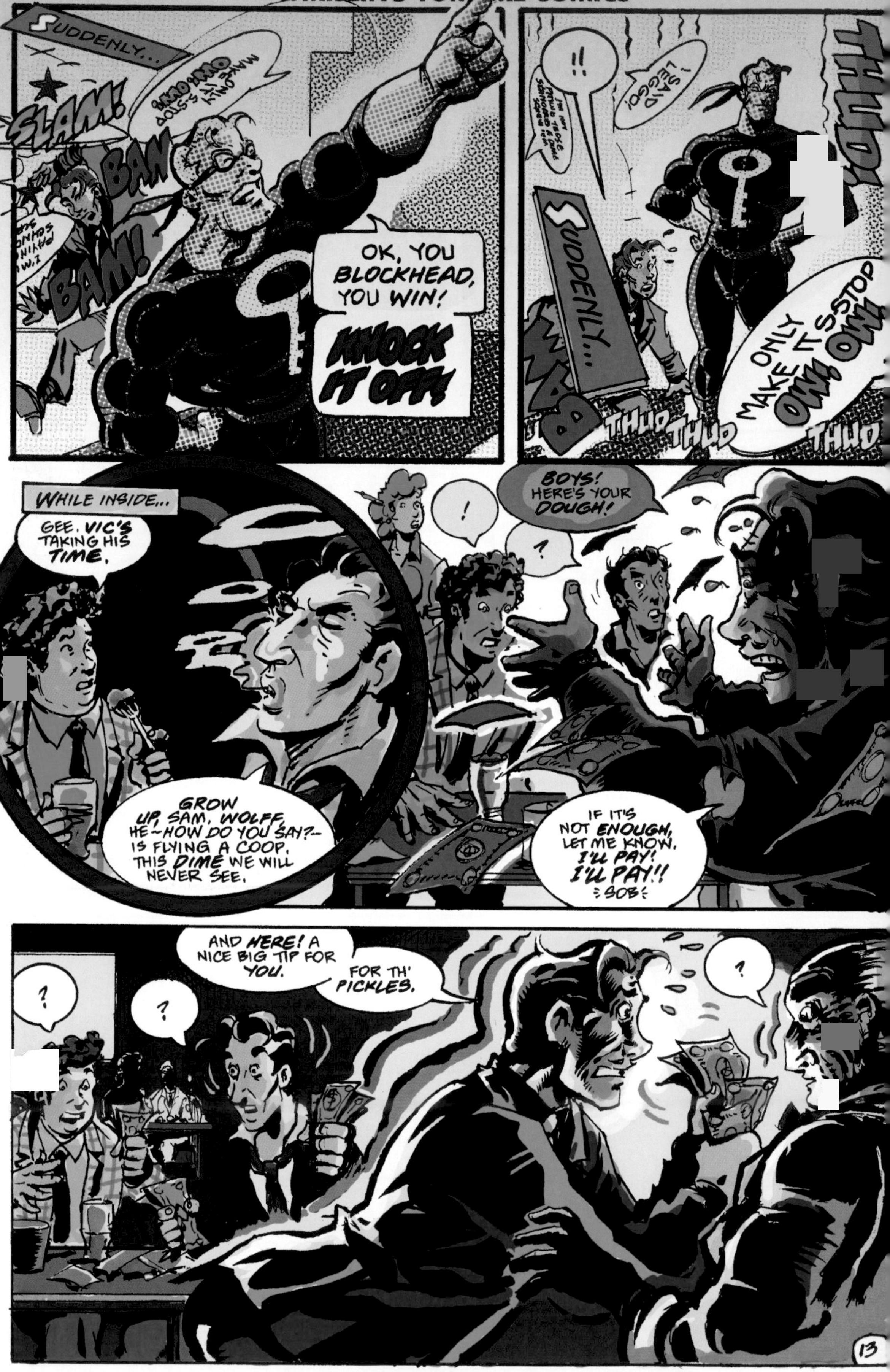
SUDDENLY...
SLAM!
BAN
BAM!
OK, YOU BLOCKHEAD, YOU WIN!
KNOCK IT OFF!
!!
I SAID LEGGO!
SUDDENLY...
THUD!
BAM
THUD THUD
MAKE IT S-STOP ONLY OW! OW!
THUD
WHILE INSIDE...
GEE. VIC'S TAKING HIS TIME.
GROW UP, SAM. WOLFF, HE--HOW DO YOU SAY?--IS FLYING A COOP. THIS DIME WE WILL NEVER SEE.
!
BOYS! HERE'S YOUR DOUGH!
?
IF IT'S NOT ENOUGH, LET ME KNOW. I'LL PAY! I'LL PAY!! SOB
?
?
AND HERE! A NICE BIG TIP FOR YOU.
FOR TH' PICKLES.
?
13

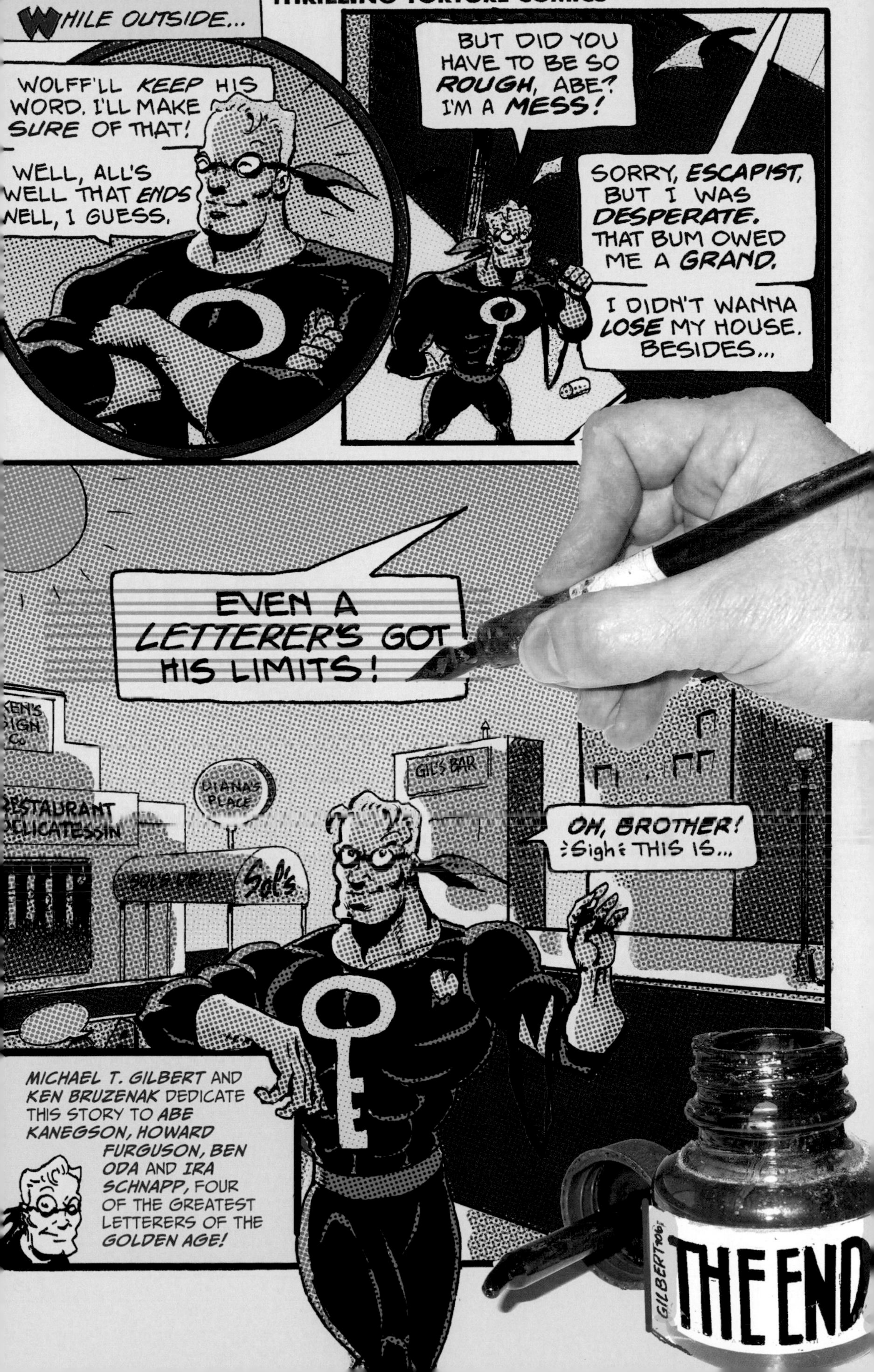
WHILE OUTSIDE...
WOLFF'LL KEEP HIS WORD. I'LL MAKE SURE OF THAT!
WELL, ALL'S WELL THAT ENDS WELL, I GUESS.
BUT DID YOU HAVE TO BE SO ROUGH, ABE? I'M A MESS!
SORRY, ESCAPIST, BUT I WAS DESPERATE. THAT BUM OWED ME A GRAND.
I DIDN'T WANNA LOSE MY HOUSE. BESIDES...
EVEN A LETTERER'S GOT HIS LIMITS!
KEN'S SIGN Co
GIL'S BAR
DIANA'S PLACE
RESTAURANT DELICATESSIN
SOL'S DELI
Sol's
OH, BROTHER! :Sigh: THIS IS...
MICHAEL T. GILBERT AND KEN BRUZENAK DEDICATE THIS STORY TO ABE KANEGSON, HOWARD FURGUSON, BEN ODA AND IRA SCHNAPP, FOUR OF THE GREATEST LETTERERS OF THE GOLDEN AGE!
GILBERT'06
THE END

# COLLECTING THE GOLDEN AGE ESCAPIST

## BY STEVE DUIN

THERE ARE SO MANY REASONS TO BE JADED, to regard the collecting of Golden Age comics with weary cynicism. There are eBay scams; clumsy, surreptitious restoration; and, of course, the travesty of a professional grading service that insists the color, action, and continuity inside a comic book no longer matter.

But all is not lost—except, perhaps, for the legendary (and mythical?) *All Doll* #47. There is still the joy of chasing the Escapist and, on the best days, trapping him inside a Mylar sleeve.

Compared to the pursuit of Timelys and DCs, that chase is quirky and unpredictable. While the classic adventures spun by the young Kavalier & Clay are predictably rare, there constantly appears, on the convention circuit or in *Comics Buyer's Guide*, the curious tale of the *Escapist* mysteriously popping up at an antique show, a garage sale, or a small-town pharmacy that still sports a spinner rack. Often the seller is as stunned to see the book as the giddy buyer.

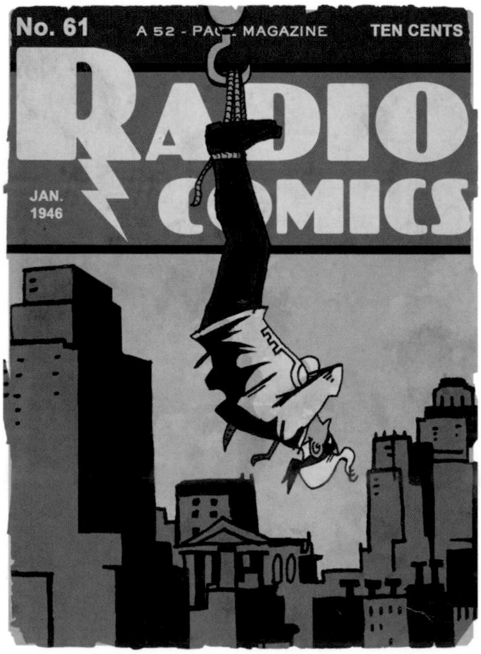
No. 61
A 52 - PAGE MAGAZINE
TEN CENTS
RADIO
COMICS
JAN.
1946

Golden Age comics featuring the Escapist are as elusive as the title character.

They can't believe they set the comic out. They don't remember fixing a price to its backer board.

This much, I think, is clear: there are few, if any, complete runs of the Empire books locked away in safe-deposit boxes or in Steve Geppi's glass cases at Diamond International Galleries. Perhaps the Escapist hasn't lost his touch for eluding permanent confinement, but I suspect there is a simpler explanation: because no funny books were better read than Empire Comics in the '40s, no comics are in worse shape sixty years later. Those battered Radio and *Triumph Comics* are disdained by the condition freaks. Reader copies of *Pharaoh* and *All Doll* tend to mock the 9.4 fanatics.

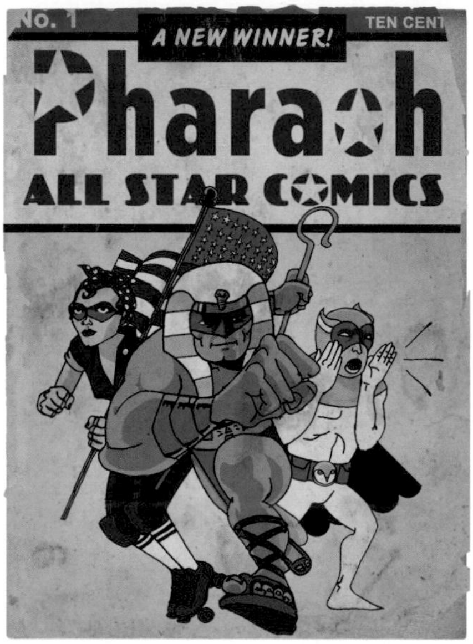
No. 1
A NEW WINNER!
TEN CENT
Pharaoh
ALL STAR COMICS

All comics accompanying this article are courtesy of the Jashar Awan Collection, including this battered copy of *Pharoah* #1.

The ardors of pursuing the Escapist, curiously enough, were not significantly altered by what most Golden Age collectors consider the seminal event of the last twenty years, the 1989 publication of Ernie Gerber's *Photo-Journal Guide to Comic Books*.

Gerber's two-volume set—a gallery of 22,000 Golden Age covers—drastically increased the popularity of the Quality, Fiction House, and Standard-Nedor books because it introduced

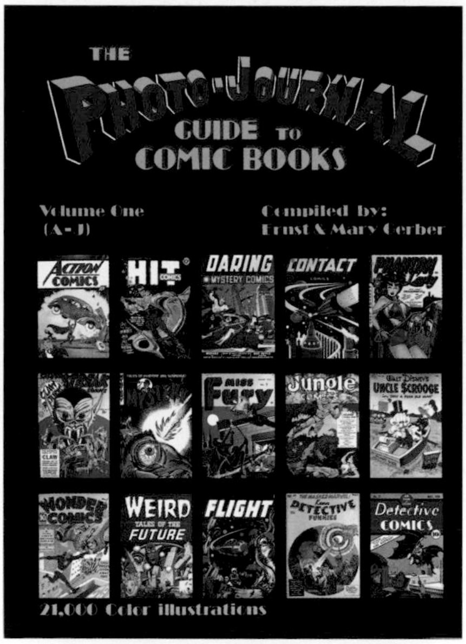
THE
PHOTO-JOURNAL
GUIDE TO
COMIC BOOKS
Volume One
(A-J)
Compiled by:
Ernst & Mary Gerber
21,000 Color illustrations

Ernst & Mary Gerber's two-volume *Photo-Journal Guide to Comic Books* has provided a valuable resource for all collectors.

another generation of fans to the cover art of such legends as Alex Schomburg, Lou Fine, and Bob Lubbers.

Empire kingpin Sheldon Anapol, of course, was far too cheap to fork over $50 per cover for illustrations from the best artists in the field. Joe Kavalier did the icon covers for the early issues of *Amazing Midget Radio Comics*, and I still believe that several of the best *All Doll* cat fights reveal the breezy signature of Schomburg's airbrush. But once Kavalier joined the Navy, Anapol generally showed his disdain for cover art by hiring anonymous industry hacks to pencil the images and color in the numbers. Gerber was so unimpressed with several of the later books in the Empire line that he failed to include them in the *Photo-Journal*.

Lest we forget, what's impressive about those comics is between the covers, especially while Joe Kavalier and Sam Clay were joined at the hip. Two of the most creative minds of that era, Bill Finger and Jack Kirby, long ago confessed that they were inspired and intimidated by the complex, inventive Escapist story lines, particularly the "magical run" (to quote amateur historian Michael Chabon) that began in *Radio Comics* #19 (July 1941) and illuminated *All Doll, Triumph, Pharoah, Radio, The Monitor,* and *Escapist Adventures* for the next nine months. That run is the heart of any Empire collection, and those comics remain some of the more difficult to track down. That's been the case for years. Some of those keys are even missing from the storied Edgar Church collection, which suggests that either Anapol's distribution was lousy in the Denver area, where Church carefully stored his comics in a cold, dry basement, or that the Colorado collector, an aspiring artist, shared Ernie Gerber's disdain for the covers.

*Amazing Midget Radio Comics* #1 had a print run of 300,000. The seminal 1941 issues from Empire probably sold half a million each, yet in some cases, less than fifty copies of an issue survive. There are, of course, the usual problems with comics published before 1943: The paper was notoriously bad, the distribution uneven, and fandom was not yet in place to play the pack rat. Small wonder a garage-sale sighting occasions such delight. And if you are puzzled as to why, given that rarity, *Radio Comics* #19–27 or *All Doll* #7–15 don't command higher prices in the *Overstreet Price Guide*, perhaps the enterprising Mr. Overstreet, like so many of us, is still trying to complete his set.

Most of the 1941 Empire comics are, like the Matt Baker romance books or the Dan Zolnerovich covers at Fiction House, severely undervalued in the *Price Guide*, regardless of grade. *Radio Comics* #4, the first appearance of the League of the Golden

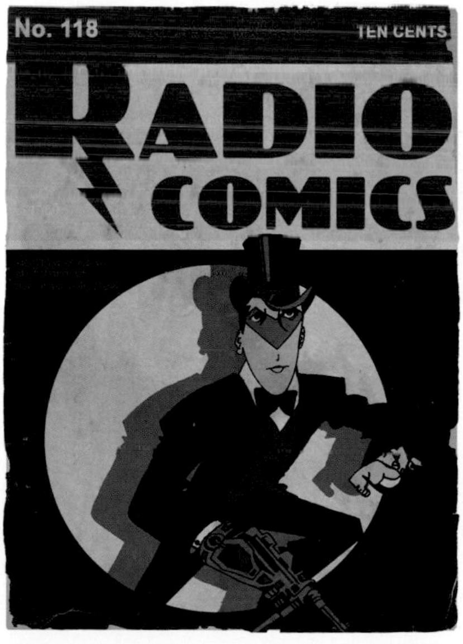
No. 118
TEN CENTS
RADIO
COMICS

*Radio Comics* was home to other Kavalier & Clay creations, most notably Mr. Machine Gun.

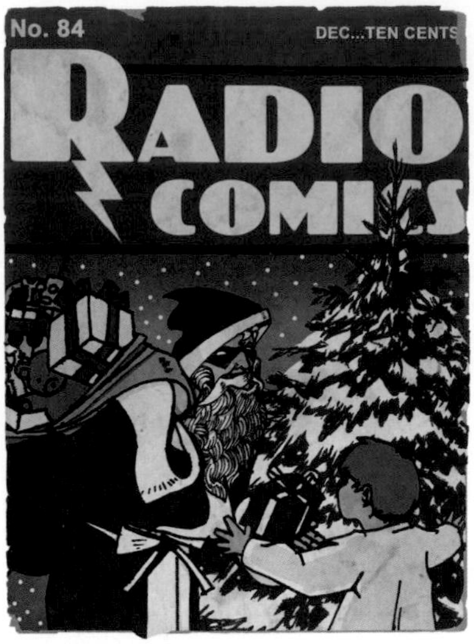
No. 84
DEC...TEN CENTS
RADIO
COMICS

It's unlikely this Christmas cover was actually drawn by Joe Kavalier.

Key's "secret mountain sanctum," is a far more important book than *Batman* #5, the first appearance of the Batmobile, yet is "valued" at less than half the latter's price. In Overstreet's world, you might think you would need to trade three copies of *Radio* #19, the herald of Kavalier & Clay's best work, to acquire a single copy of *Master* #21, the first appearance of Captain Nazi. Luna Moth's first

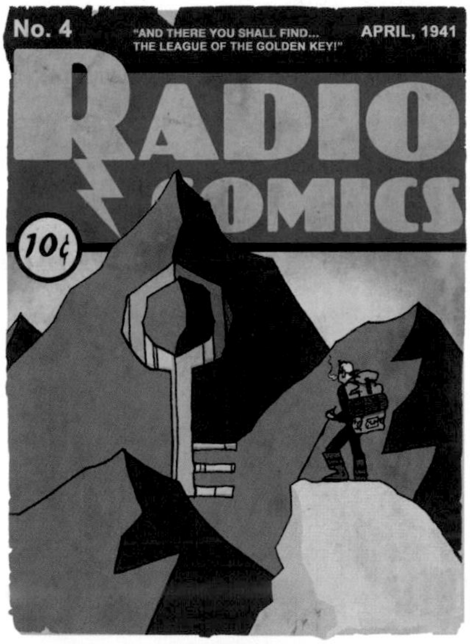
No. 4
"AND THERE YOU SHALL FIND...
THE LEAGUE OF THE GOLDEN KEY!"
APRIL, 1941
RADIO
COMICS
10¢

The "severely undervalued" ***Radio Comics*** **#4.**

appearance in *All Doll* #1 predates Wonder Woman's debut in *All-Star* #8 by almost a year, yet has a "near-mint" value of $12,000 compared to the $45,000 sticker plastered on the Amazon's chest.

Money, then, is not the primary obstacle to stalking the Escapist, sixty-five years after he knocked Hitler for a loop. Collectors will need time, patience, and a gift for matching keys with keyholes when they set out after the Four Freedoms, Mr. Machine Gun, or the final sighting of Fan, the Korean houseboy. They will need a discerning eye to find the curious covers—*Pharoah* #18 and *Triumph* #13—where Kavalier pays tribute (a reflection in a store window, an anagram on a billboard) to the indelible Rosa Saks.

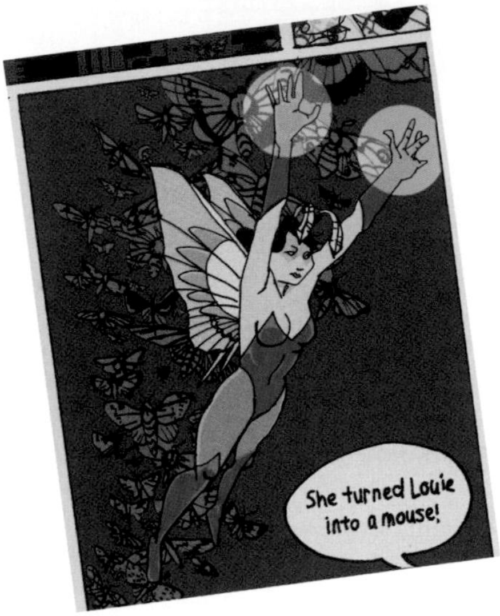
She turned Louie into a mouse!

A classic panel from the first issue of *All Doll*, which introduced the legendary Luna Moth.

And they may need all the conceits of the Escapist himself—save, perhaps, that trick with the artillery shells—to find the long-lost grail that is *All Doll* #47, reportedly published but never found. Just between you and me, I'd look to find our hero and his harem peeking out from inside a translucent green cellophane school folder that is carefully tucked inside an old wine crate, a crate you'd swear wasn't under that canvas tarp at the back of the garage the last time you looked.

---

Steve Duin is the Metro columnist for *The Oregonian*, Portland's daily paper, as well as the author of *Father Time* and *Oil and Water*, and co-author of both *Comics Between the Panels* and *Blast Off!*

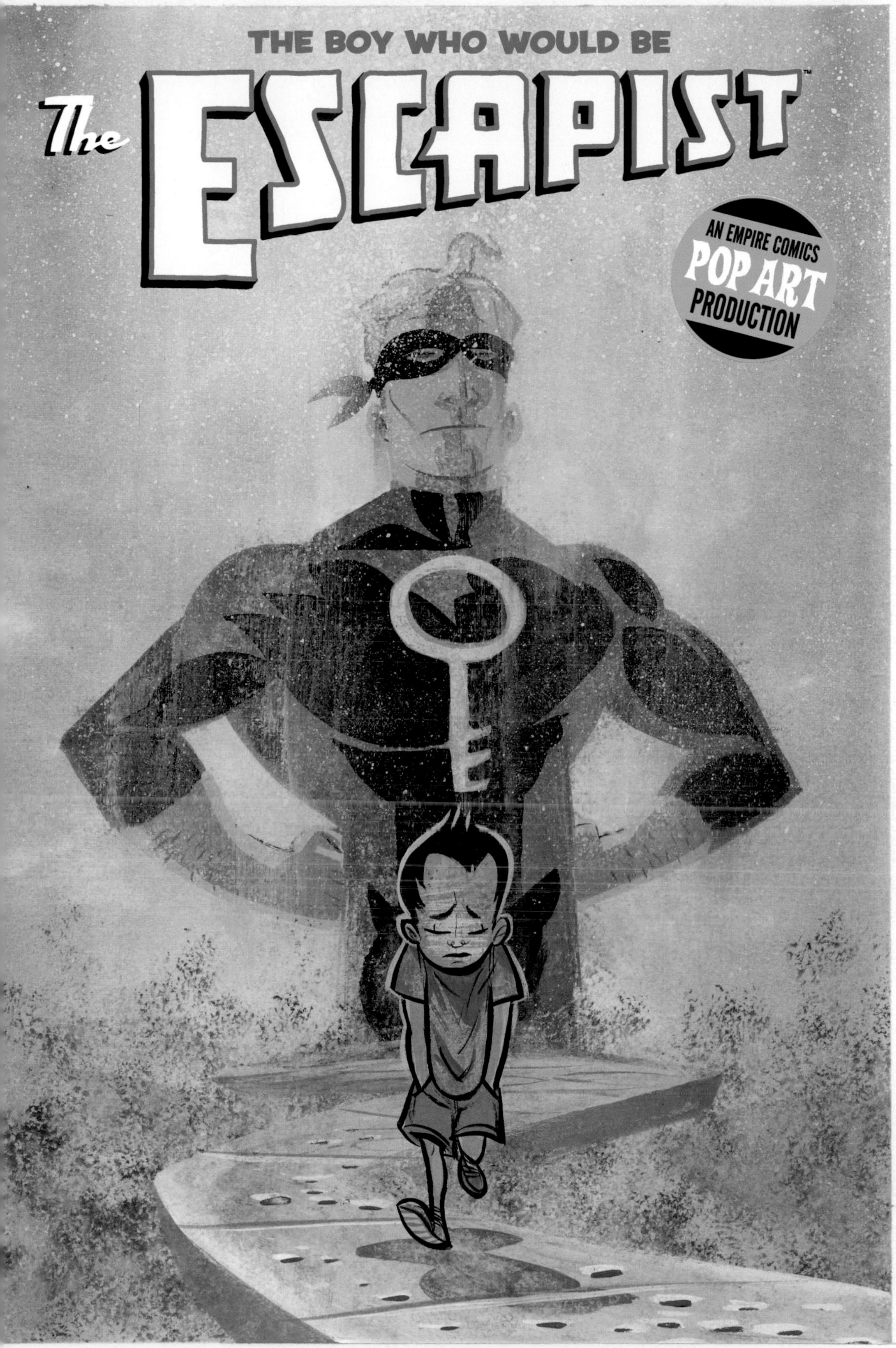
THE BOY WHO WOULD BE
The ESCAPIST™
AN EMPIRE COMICS
POP ART
PRODUCTION

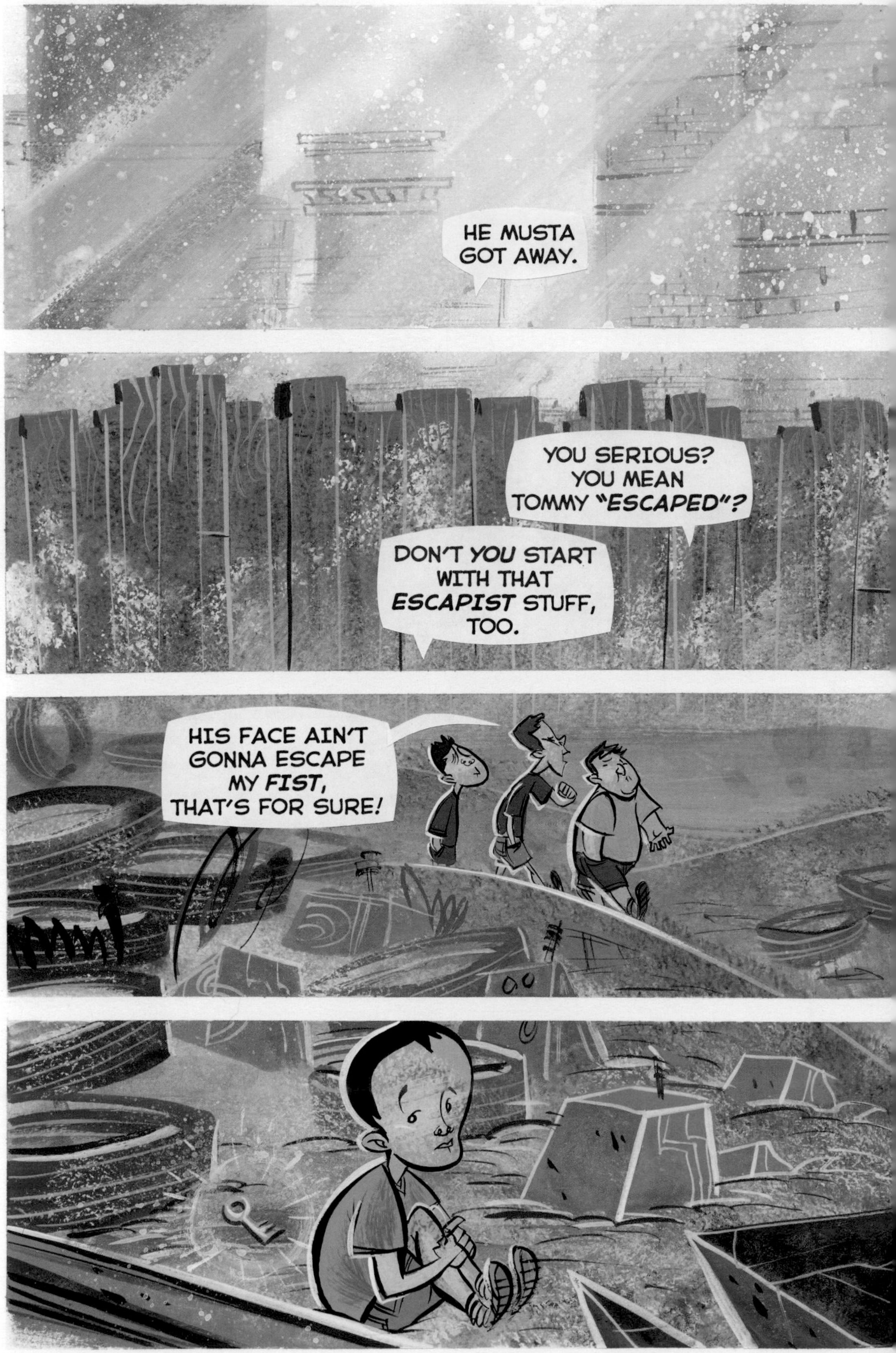
HE MUSTA GOT AWAY.
YOU SERIOUS? YOU MEAN TOMMY "*ESCAPED*"?
DON'T *YOU* START WITH THAT *ESCAPIST* STUFF, TOO.
HIS FACE AIN'T GONNA ESCAPE MY *FIST*, THAT'S FOR SURE!

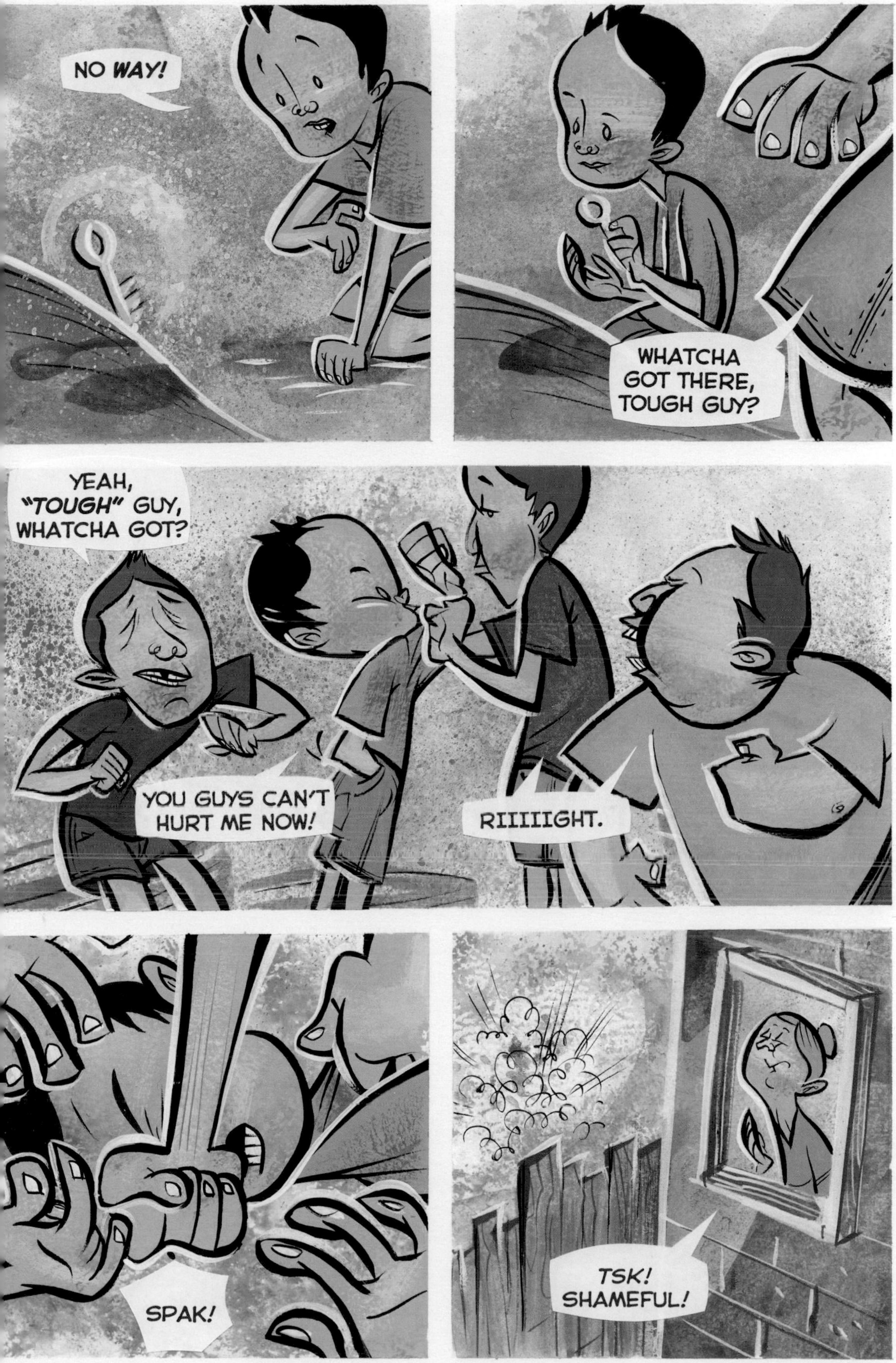
NO *WAY!*
WHATCHA GOT THERE, TOUGH GUY?
YEAH, *"TOUGH"* GUY, WHATCHA GOT?
YOU GUYS CAN'T HURT ME NOW!
RIIIIIGHT.
SPAK!
*TSK! SHAMEFUL!*

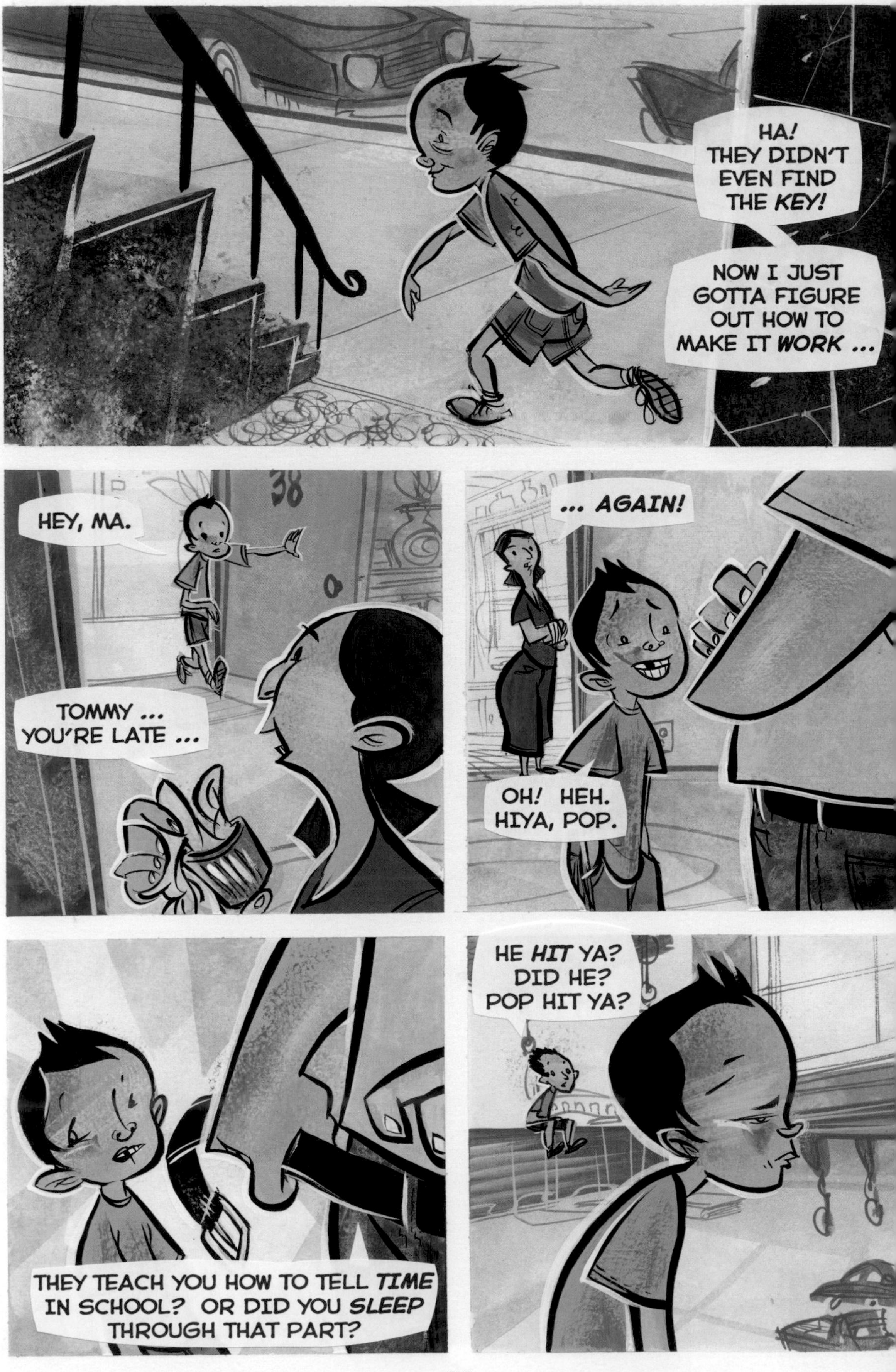
HA! THEY DIDN'T EVEN FIND THE *KEY!*
NOW I JUST GOTTA FIGURE OUT HOW TO MAKE IT *WORK* ...
HEY, MA.
TOMMY ... YOU'RE LATE ...
... *AGAIN!*
OH! HEH. HIYA, POP.
THEY TEACH YOU HOW TO TELL *TIME* IN SCHOOL? OR DID YOU *SLEEP* THROUGH THAT PART?
HE *HIT* YA? DID HE? POP HIT YA?

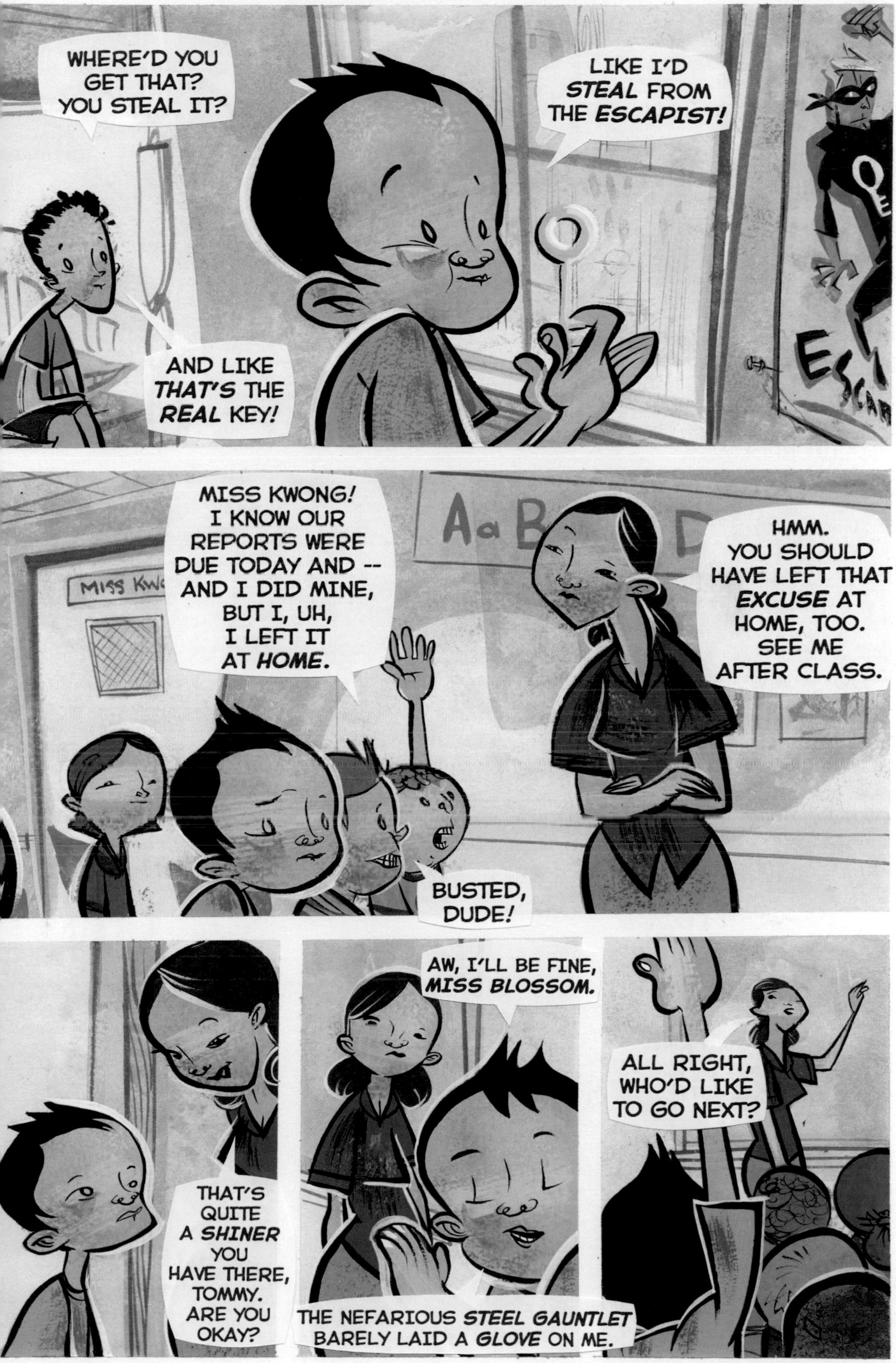
WHERE'D YOU GET THAT? YOU STEAL IT?
LIKE I'D *STEAL* FROM THE *ESCAPIST!*
AND LIKE *THAT'S* THE *REAL* KEY!
MISS KWONG! I KNOW OUR REPORTS WERE DUE TODAY AND -- AND I DID MINE, BUT I, UH, I LEFT IT AT *HOME*.
HMM. YOU SHOULD HAVE LEFT THAT *EXCUSE* AT HOME, TOO. SEE ME AFTER CLASS.
BUSTED, DUDE!
THAT'S QUITE A *SHINER* YOU HAVE THERE, TOMMY. ARE YOU OKAY?
AW, I'LL BE FINE, *MISS BLOSSOM.*
THE NEFARIOUS *STEEL GAUNTLET* BARELY LAID A *GLOVE* ON ME.
ALL RIGHT, WHO'D LIKE TO GO NEXT?

TOMMY'S REPORT IS ABOUT HIS *HERO*, THE ESCAPIST.

MY ... "HERO"?

AH, YES. *SECRET IDENTITY* AND ALL THAT. GOOD *SAVE*, PLUM BLOSSOM.

KNOWN THROUGHOUT THE WORLD AS THE *MASTER OF ELUSION*, THE ESCAPIST FIGHTS...

HAW! MORE LIKE "MASTER OF *DELUSION*!"

AND I'VE GOT AN IDEA FOR HIS NEW *ADVENTURE*!

?

BANG! BANG! BA-BANGA! BANG! BANG!

TOMMY? MOST ESCAPE ARTISTS WORK *AGAINST* THE CLOCK. HAVE YOU BEEN IN THERE ALL *AFTERNOON*?

I WAS JUST ABOUT TO ESCAPE ON MY *OWN*!

STILL, I APPRECIATE THE *ASSIST*, MISS BLOSSOM.

"ASSIST"? THIS LITTLE BOY NEEDS *HELP*, ALL RIGHT.

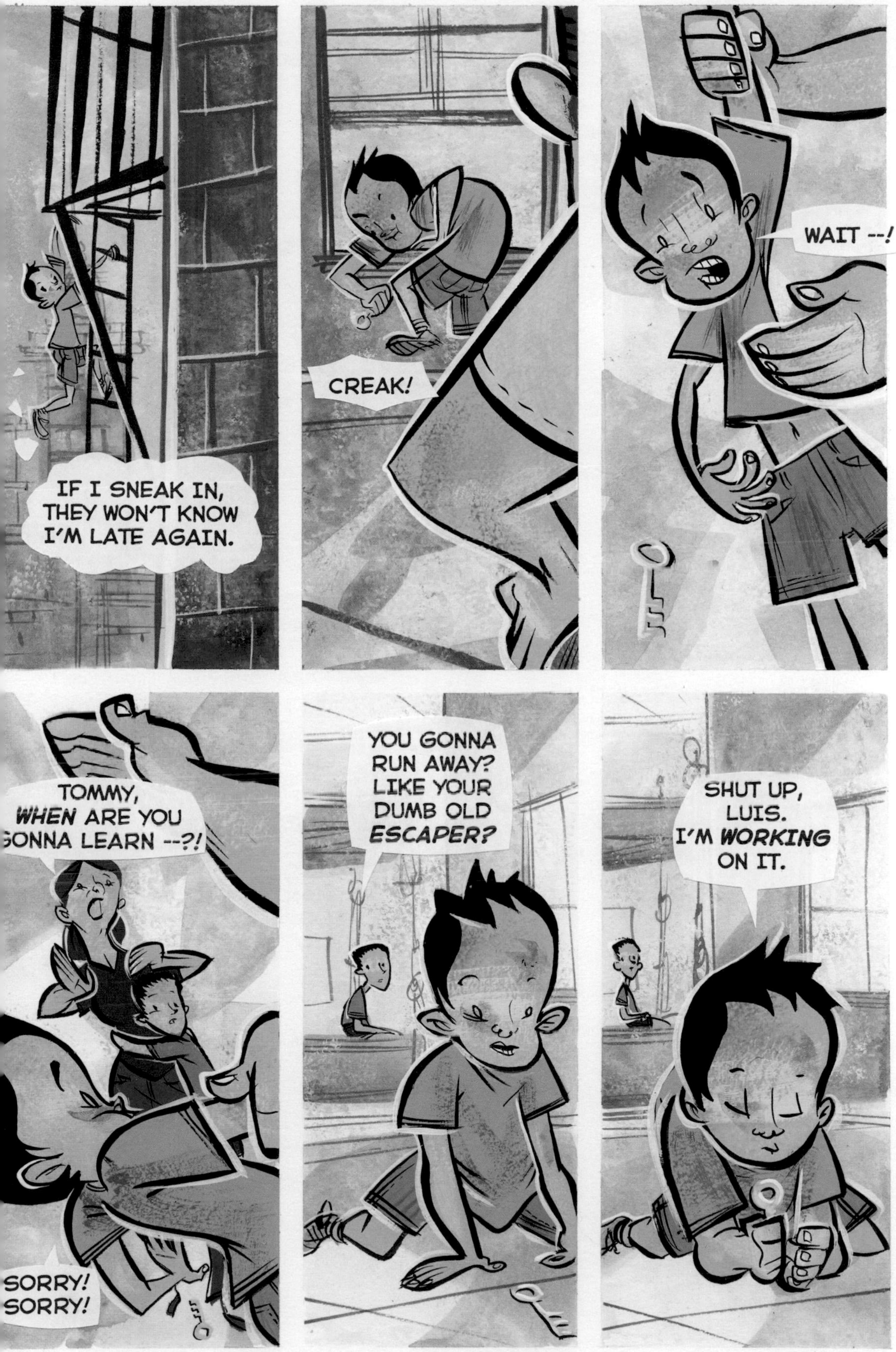
IF I SNEAK IN, THEY WON'T KNOW I'M LATE AGAIN.
CREAK!
WAIT --!
TOMMY, WHEN ARE YOU GONNA LEARN --?!
SORRY! SORRY!
YOU GONNA RUN AWAY? LIKE YOUR DUMB OLD ESCAPER?
SHUT UP, LUIS. I'M WORKING ON IT.

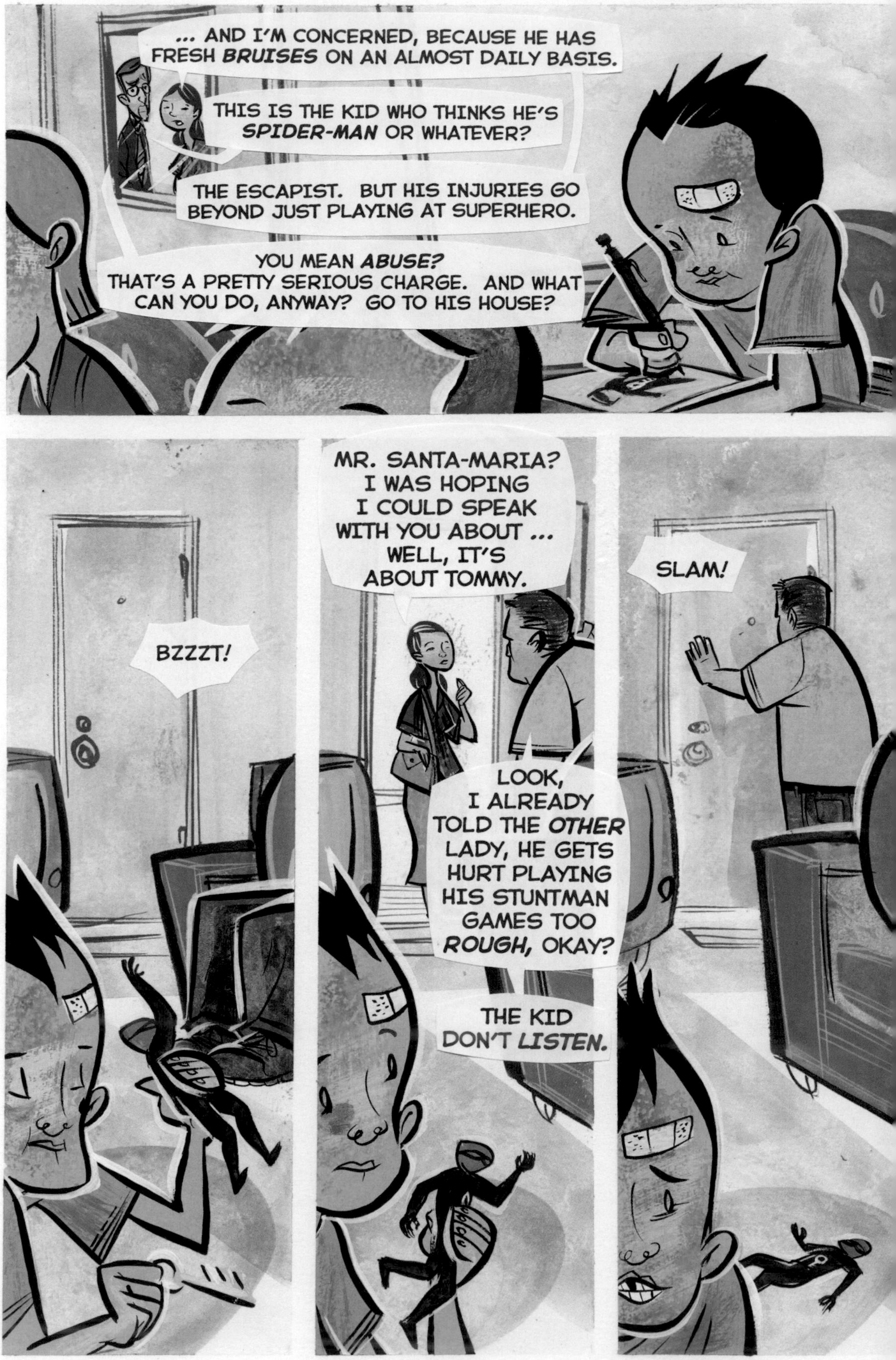
... AND I'M CONCERNED, BECAUSE HE HAS FRESH *BRUISES* ON AN ALMOST DAILY BASIS.
THIS IS THE KID WHO THINKS HE'S *SPIDER-MAN* OR WHATEVER?
THE ESCAPIST. BUT HIS INJURIES GO BEYOND JUST PLAYING AT SUPERHERO.
YOU MEAN *ABUSE?* THAT'S A PRETTY SERIOUS CHARGE. AND WHAT CAN YOU DO, ANYWAY? GO TO HIS HOUSE?
BZZZT!
MR. SANTA-MARIA? I WAS HOPING I COULD SPEAK WITH YOU ABOUT ... WELL, IT'S ABOUT TOMMY.
LOOK, I ALREADY TOLD THE *OTHER* LADY, HE GETS HURT PLAYING HIS STUNTMAN GAMES TOO *ROUGH,* OKAY?
THE KID DON'T *LISTEN.*
SLAM!

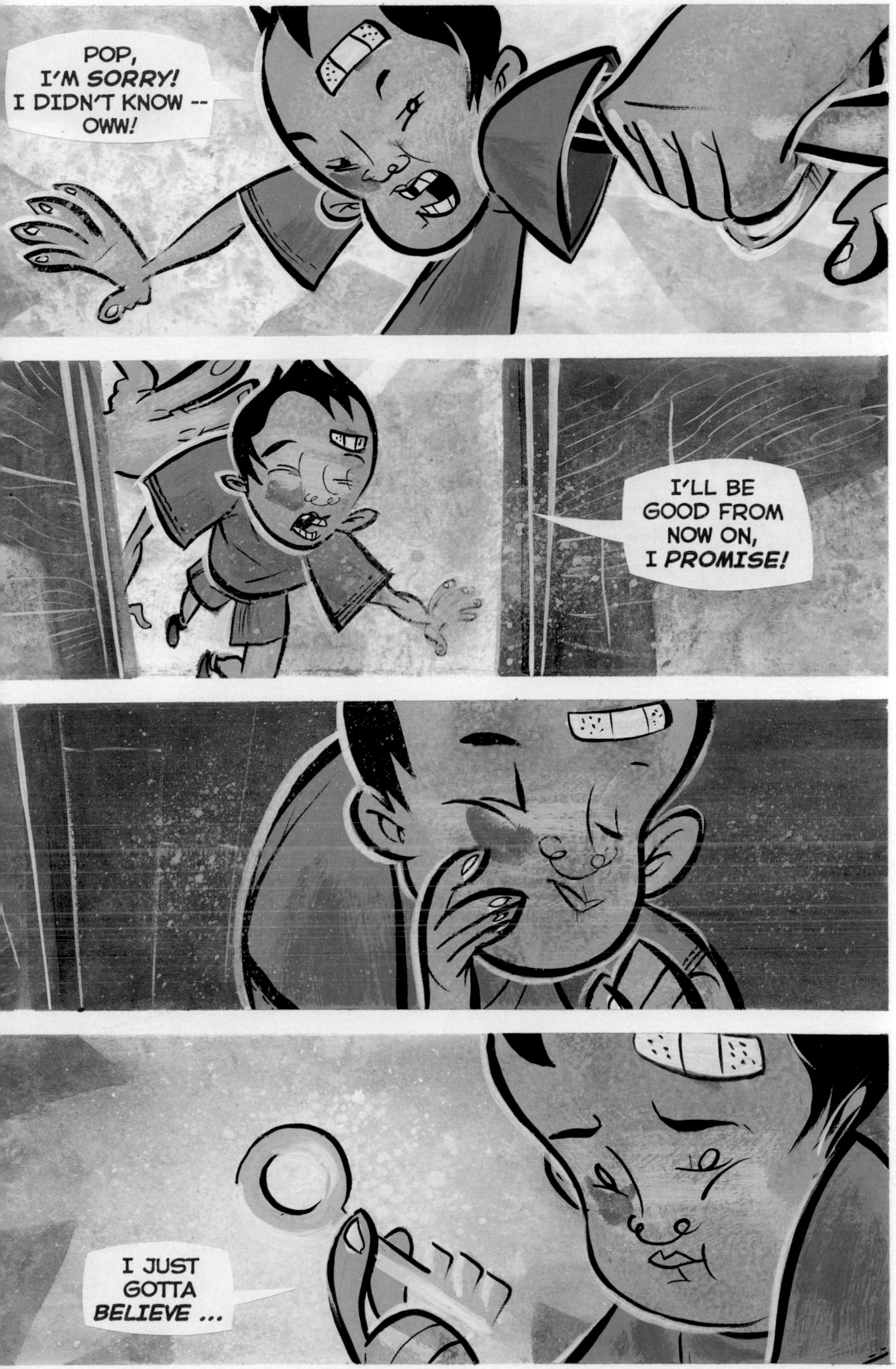
POP, I'M SORRY! I DIDN'T KNOW -- OWW!
I'LL BE GOOD FROM NOW ON, I PROMISE!
I JUST GOTTA BELIEVE ...

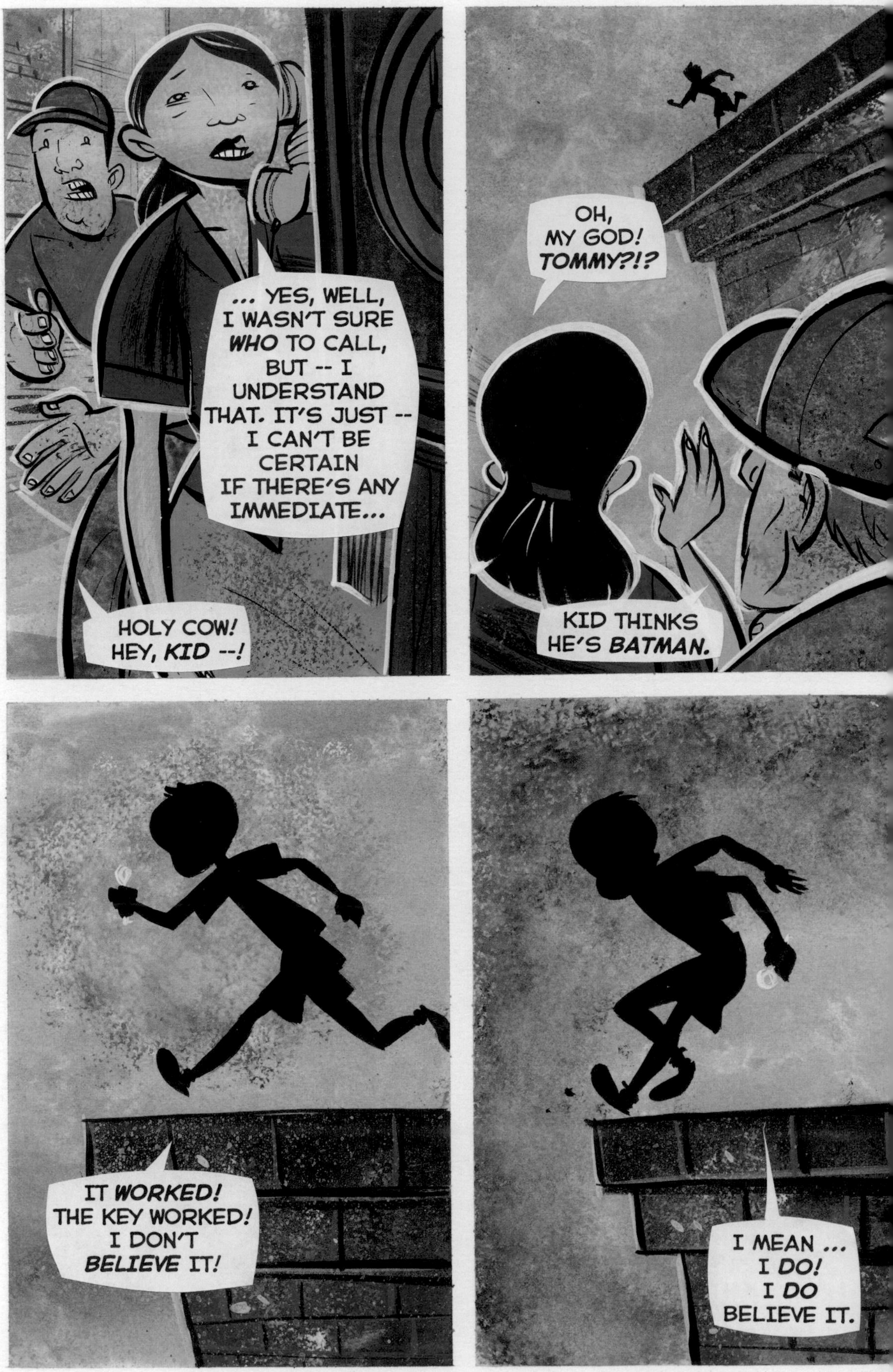
... YES, WELL, I WASN'T SURE *WHO* TO CALL, BUT -- I UNDERSTAND THAT. IT'S JUST -- I CAN'T BE CERTAIN IF THERE'S ANY IMMEDIATE...
HOLY COW! HEY, *KID* --!
OH, MY GOD! *TOMMY?!?*
KID THINKS HE'S *BATMAN.*
IT *WORKED!* THE KEY WORKED! I DON'T *BELIEVE* IT!
I MEAN ... I *DO!* I *DO* BELIEVE IT.

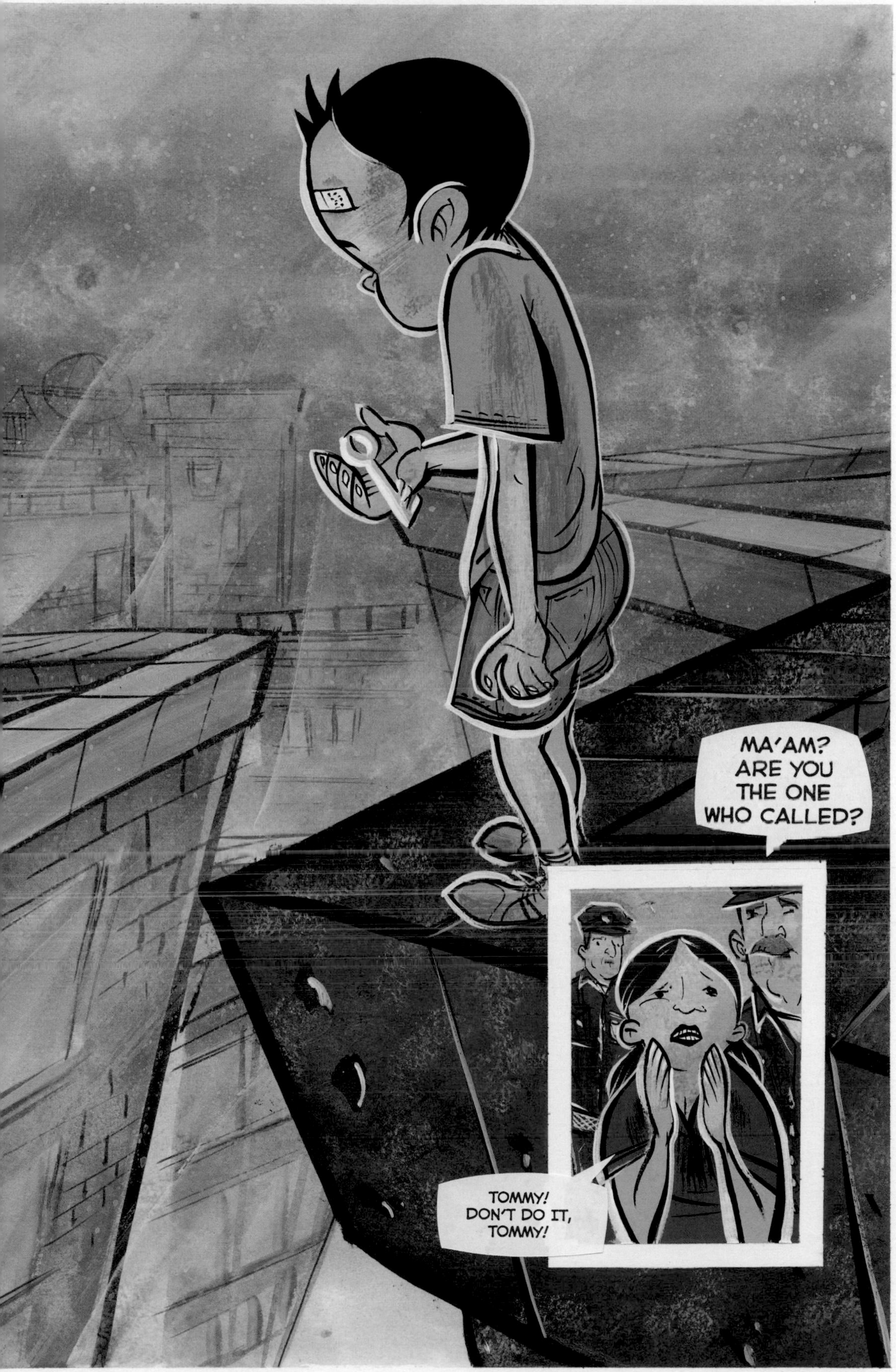
MA'AM? ARE YOU THE ONE WHO CALLED?
TOMMY! DON'T DO IT, TOMMY!

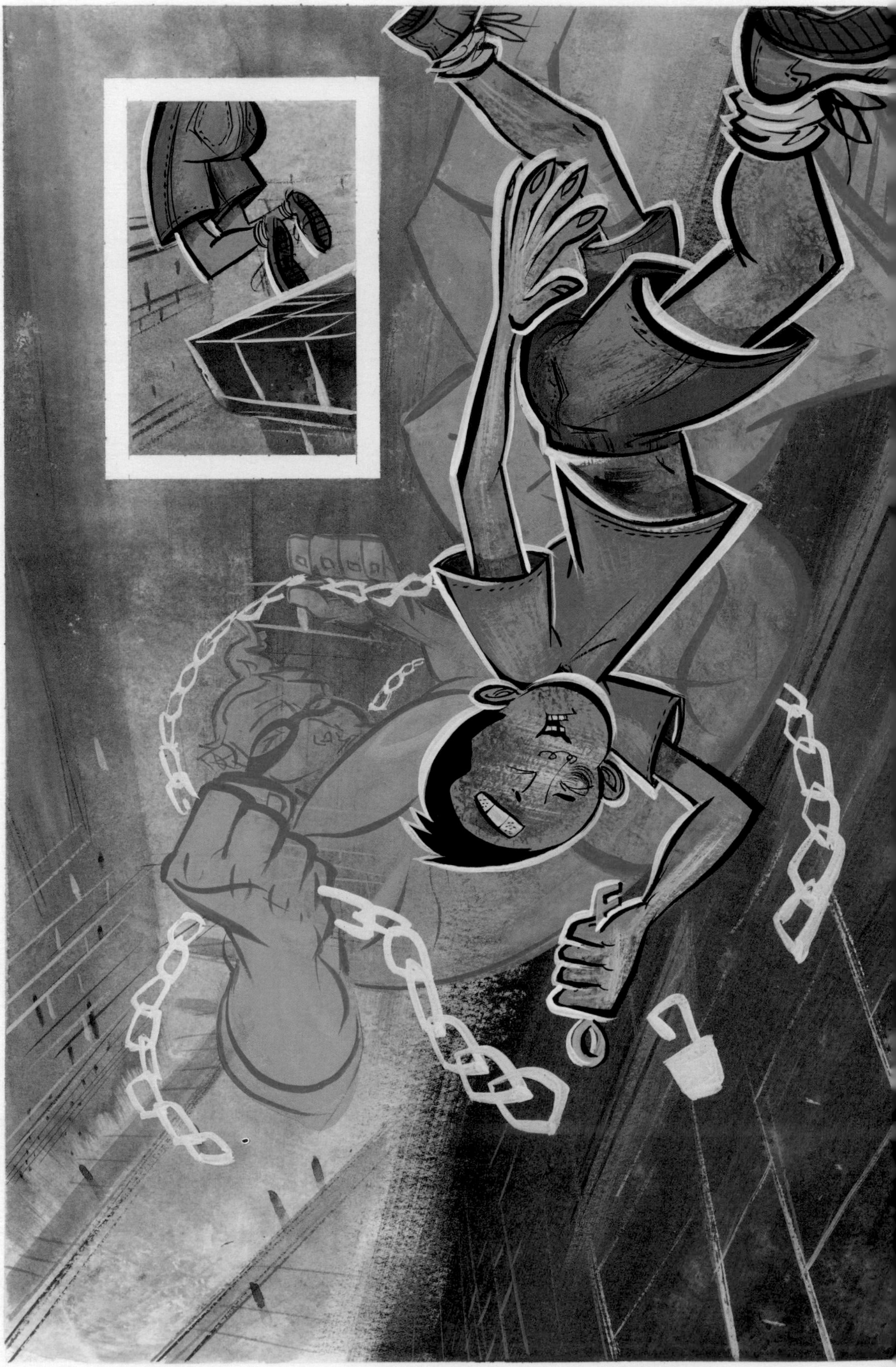

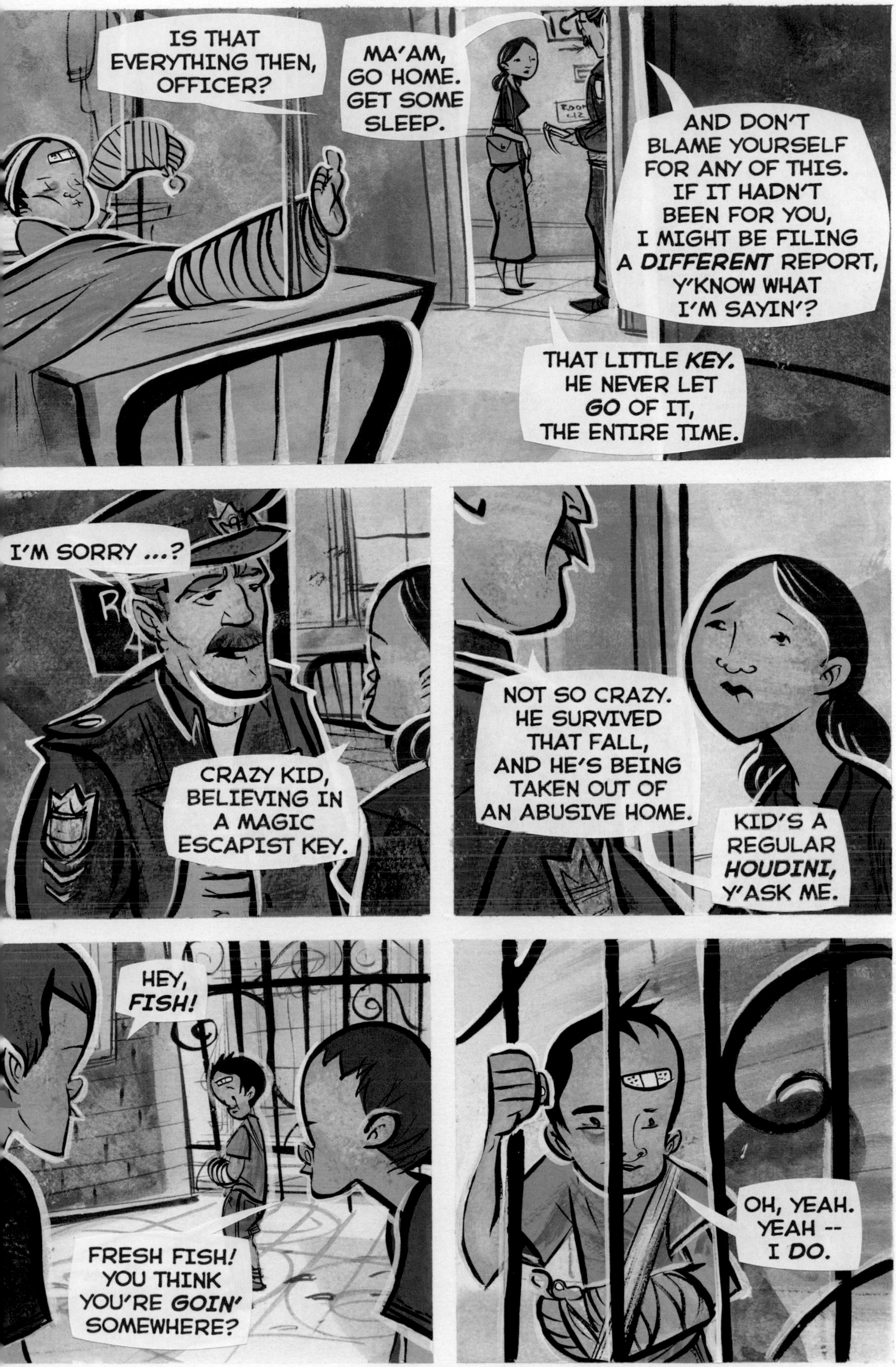
IS THAT EVERYTHING THEN, OFFICER?
MA'AM, GO HOME. GET SOME SLEEP.
AND DON'T BLAME YOURSELF FOR ANY OF THIS. IF IT HADN'T BEEN FOR YOU, I MIGHT BE FILING A *DIFFERENT* REPORT, Y'KNOW WHAT I'M SAYIN'?
THAT LITTLE *KEY.* HE NEVER LET *GO* OF IT, THE ENTIRE TIME.
I'M SORRY ...?
CRAZY KID, BELIEVING IN A MAGIC ESCAPIST KEY.
NOT SO CRAZY. HE SURVIVED THAT FALL, AND HE'S BEING TAKEN OUT OF AN ABUSIVE HOME.
KID'S A REGULAR *HOUDINI,* Y'ASK ME.
HEY, *FISH!*
FRESH FISH! YOU THINK YOU'RE *GOIN'* SOMEWHERE?
OH, YEAH. YEAH -- I *DO.*

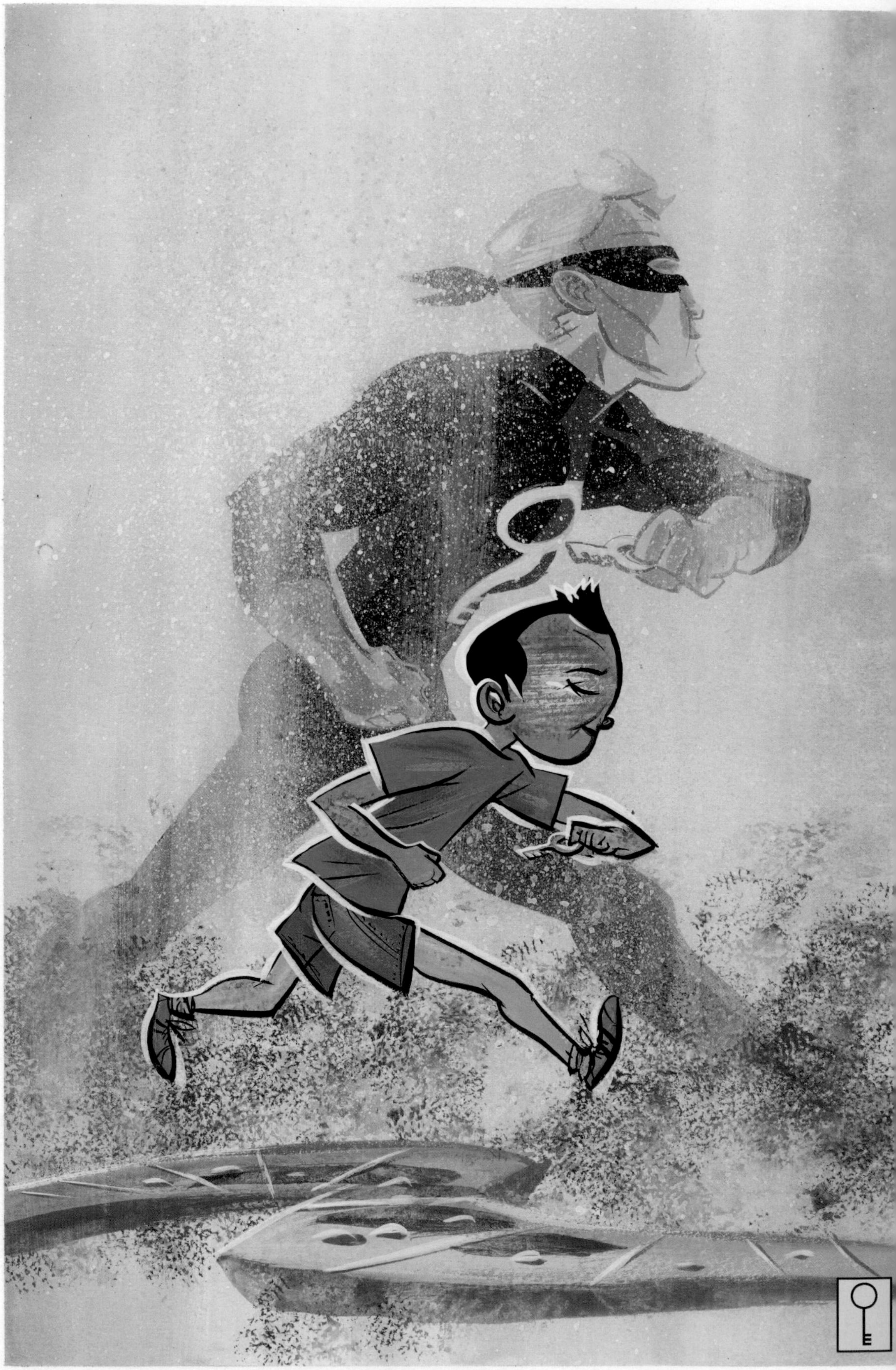

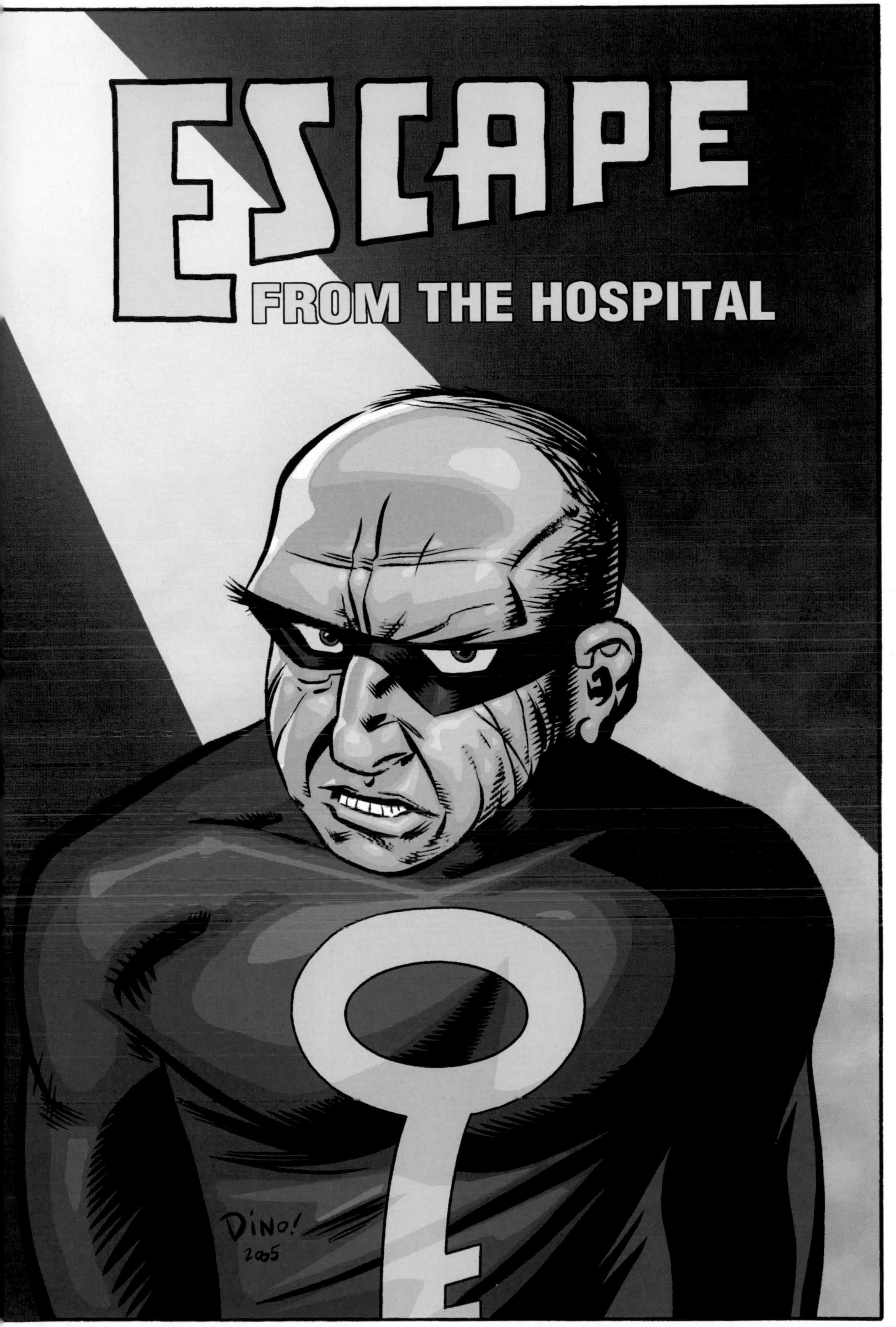
ESCAPE
FROM THE HOSPITAL
DINO!
2005

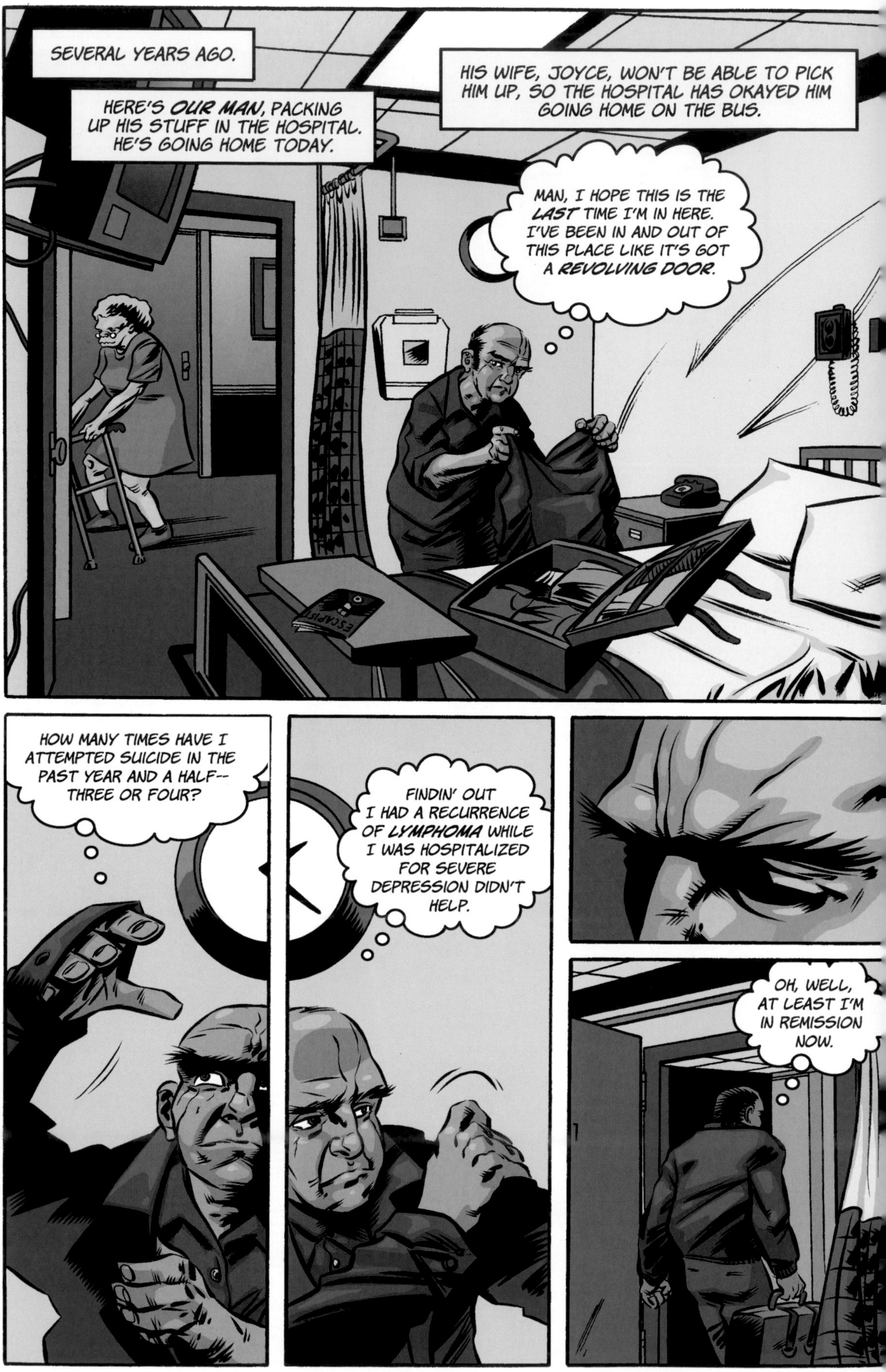
SEVERAL YEARS AGO.
HERE'S OUR MAN, PACKING UP HIS STUFF IN THE HOSPITAL. HE'S GOING HOME TODAY.
HIS WIFE, JOYCE, WON'T BE ABLE TO PICK HIM UP, SO THE HOSPITAL HAS OKAYED HIM GOING HOME ON THE BUS.
MAN, I HOPE THIS IS THE LAST TIME I'M IN HERE. I'VE BEEN IN AND OUT OF THIS PLACE LIKE IT'S GOT A REVOLVING DOOR.
ESCAPIST
HOW MANY TIMES HAVE I ATTEMPTED SUICIDE IN THE PAST YEAR AND A HALF-- THREE OR FOUR?
FINDIN' OUT I HAD A RECURRENCE OF LYMPHOMA WHILE I WAS HOSPITALIZED FOR SEVERE DEPRESSION DIDN'T HELP.
OH, WELL, AT LEAST I'M IN REMISSION NOW.

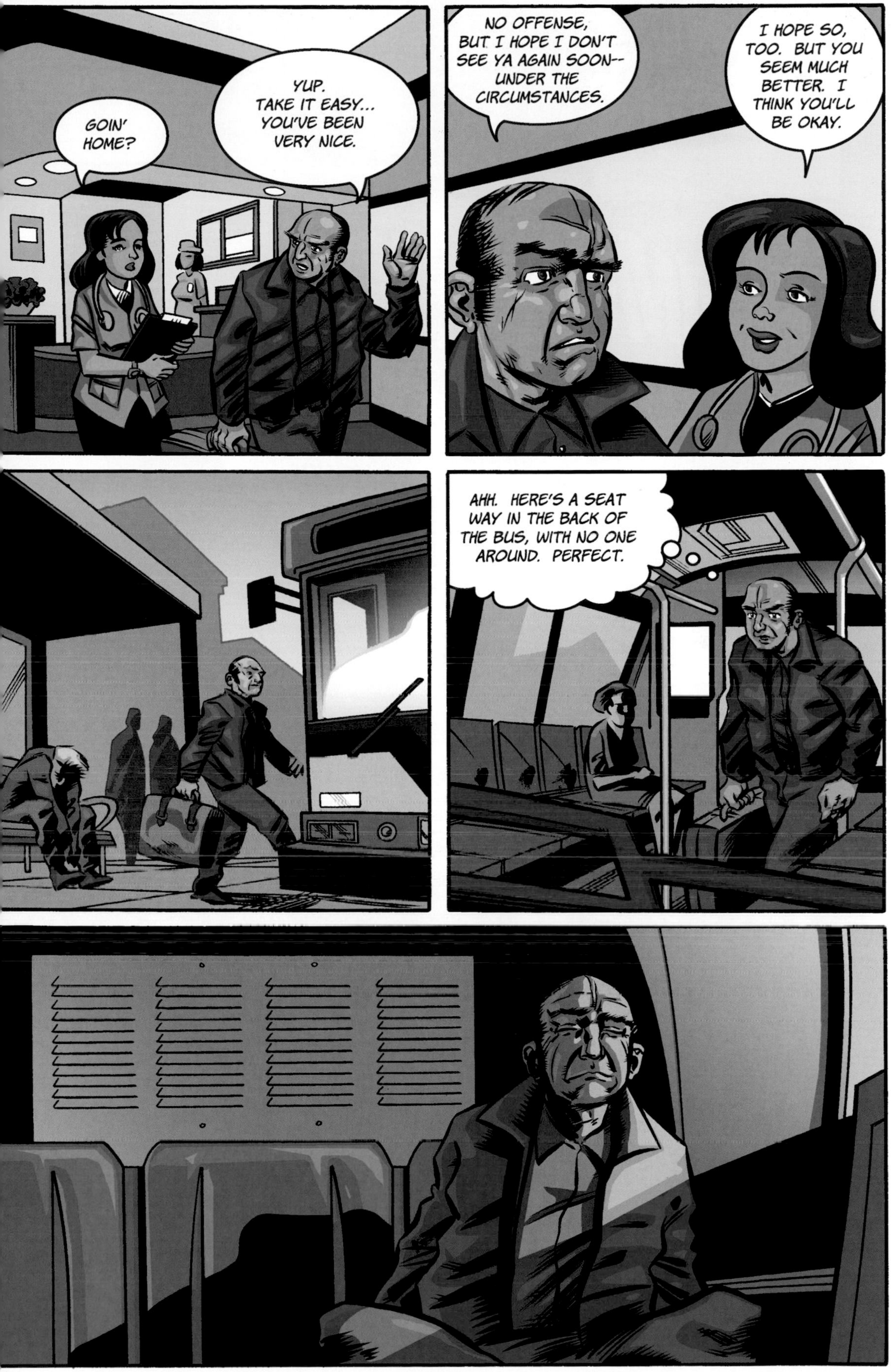
GOIN' HOME?
YUP. TAKE IT EASY... YOU'VE BEEN VERY NICE.
NO OFFENSE, BUT I HOPE I DON'T SEE YA AGAIN SOON-- UNDER THE CIRCUMSTANCES.
I HOPE SO, TOO. BUT YOU SEEM MUCH BETTER. I THINK YOU'LL BE OKAY.
AHH. HERE'S A SEAT WAY IN THE BACK OF THE BUS, WITH NO ONE AROUND. PERFECT.

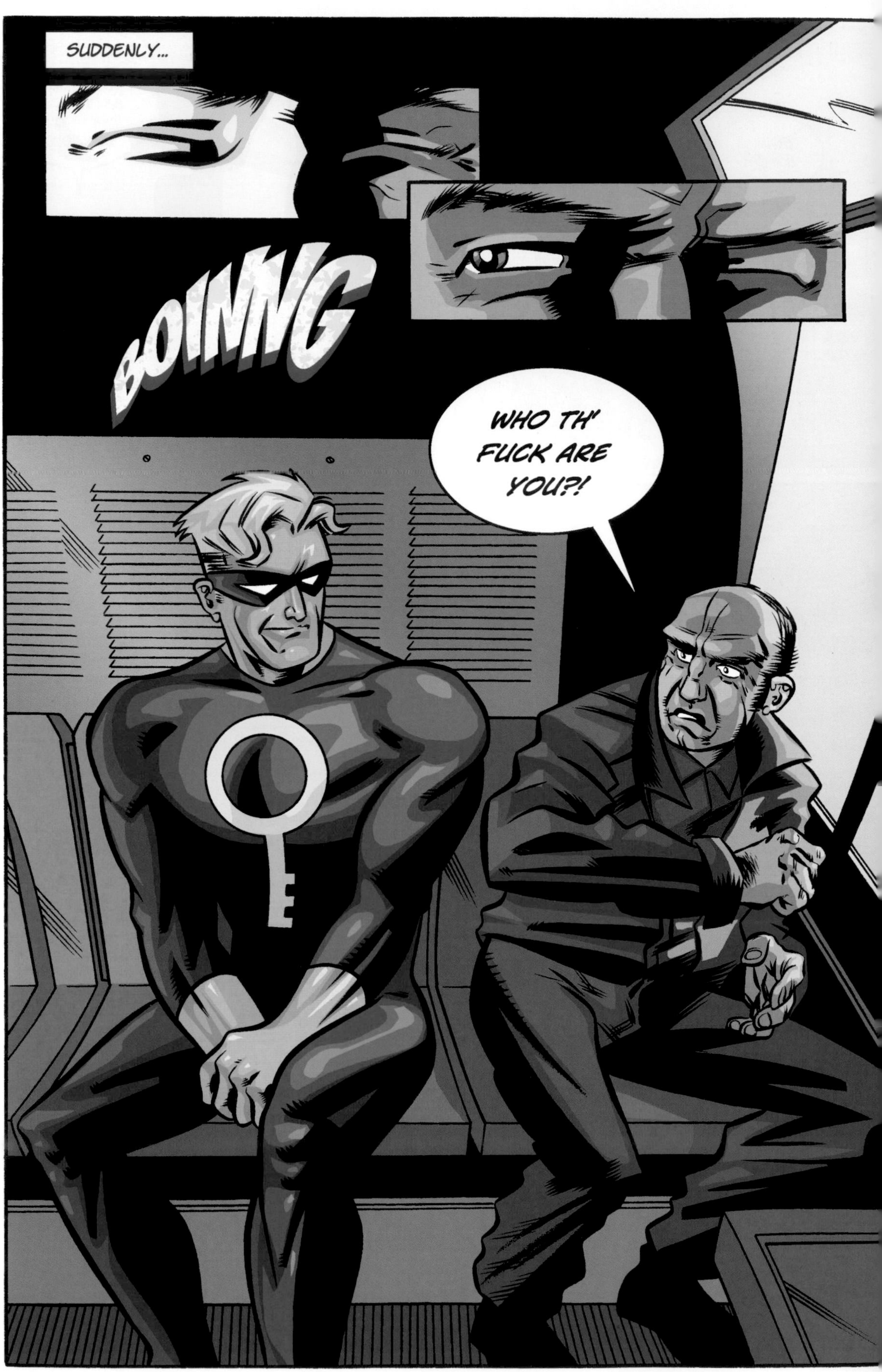
SUDDENLY...
BOING
WHO TH' FUCK ARE YOU?!

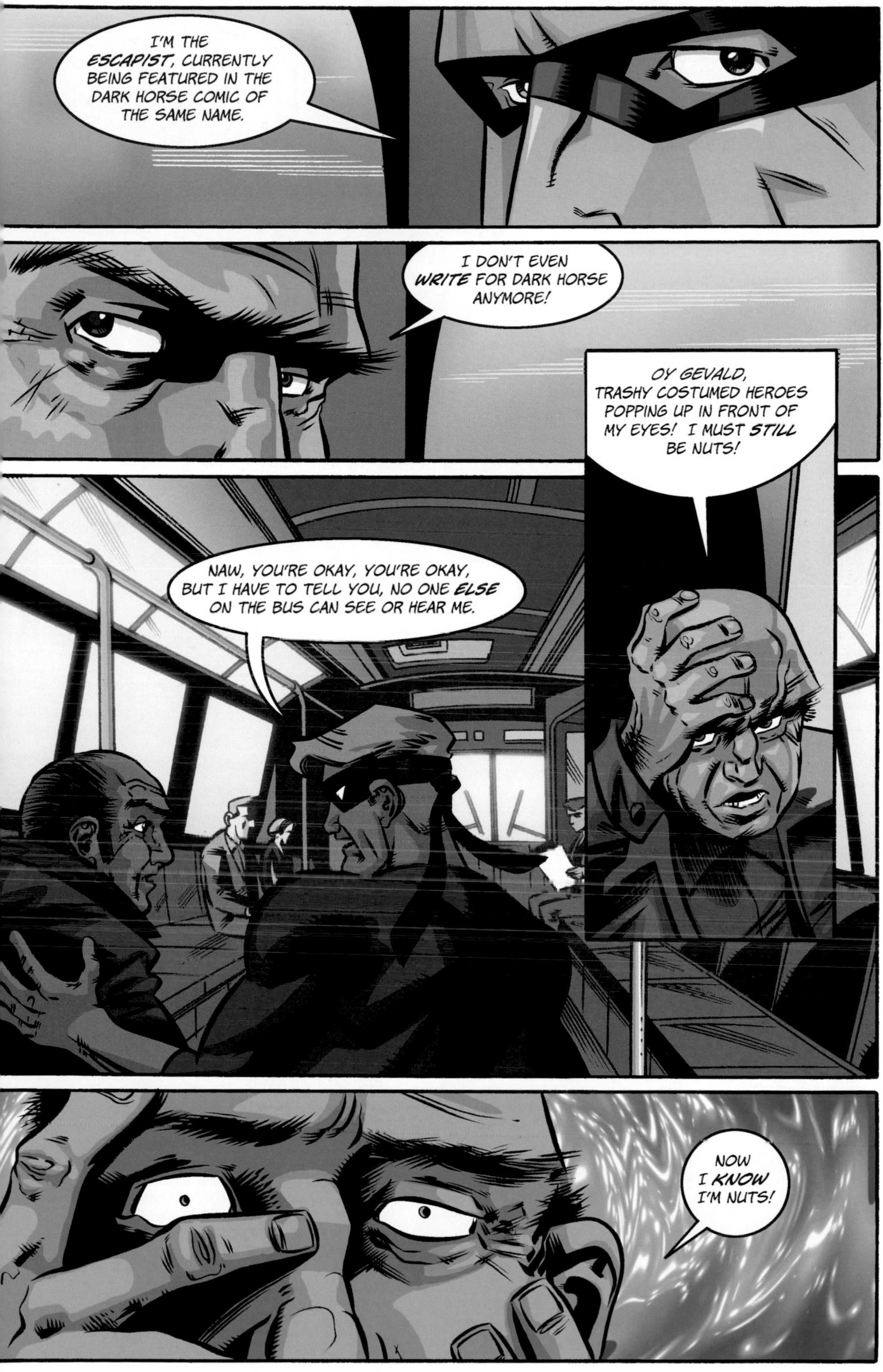
I'M THE ESCAPIST, CURRENTLY BEING FEATURED IN THE DARK HORSE COMIC OF THE SAME NAME.
I DON'T EVEN WRITE FOR DARK HORSE ANYMORE!
NAW, YOU'RE OKAY, YOU'RE OKAY, BUT I HAVE TO TELL YOU, NO ONE ELSE ON THE BUS CAN SEE OR HEAR ME.
OY GEVALD, TRASHY COSTUMED HEROES POPPING UP IN FRONT OF MY EYES! I MUST STILL BE NUTS!
NOW I KNOW I'M NUTS!

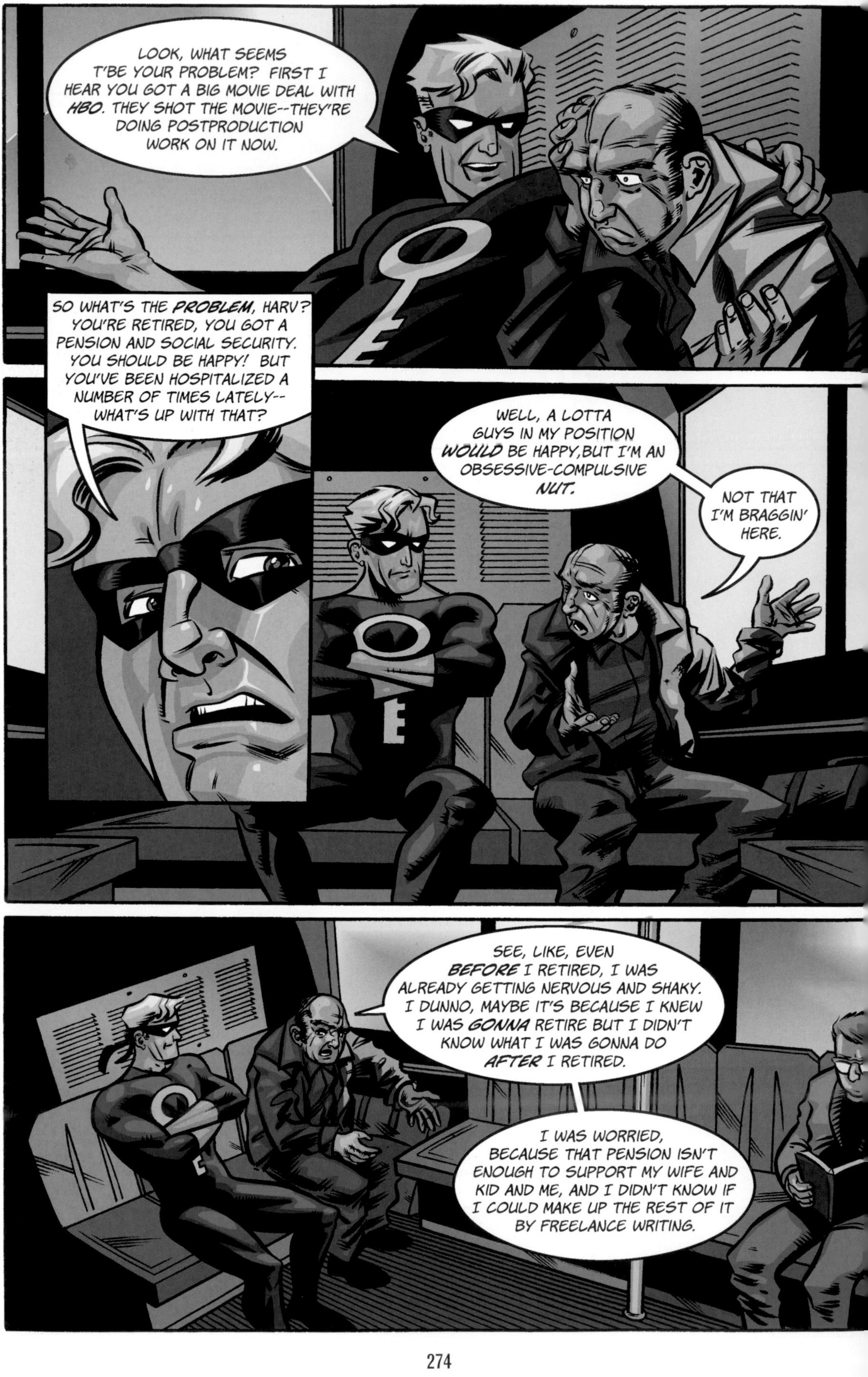
LOOK, WHAT SEEMS T'BE YOUR PROBLEM? FIRST I HEAR YOU GOT A BIG MOVIE DEAL WITH HBO. THEY SHOT THE MOVIE--THEY'RE DOING POSTPRODUCTION WORK ON IT NOW.
SO WHAT'S THE PROBLEM, HARV? YOU'RE RETIRED, YOU GOT A PENSION AND SOCIAL SECURITY. YOU SHOULD BE HAPPY! BUT YOU'VE BEEN HOSPITALIZED A NUMBER OF TIMES LATELY--WHAT'S UP WITH THAT?
WELL, A LOTTA GUYS IN MY POSITION WOULD BE HAPPY,BUT I'M AN OBSESSIVE-COMPULSIVE NUT.
NOT THAT I'M BRAGGIN' HERE.
SEE, LIKE, EVEN BEFORE I RETIRED, I WAS ALREADY GETTING NERVOUS AND SHAKY. I DUNNO, MAYBE IT'S BECAUSE I KNEW I WAS GONNA RETIRE BUT I DIDN'T KNOW WHAT I WAS GONNA DO AFTER I RETIRED.
I WAS WORRIED, BECAUSE THAT PENSION ISN'T ENOUGH TO SUPPORT MY WIFE AND KID AND ME, AND I DIDN'T KNOW IF I COULD MAKE UP THE REST OF IT BY FREELANCE WRITING.

"RIGHT AFTER I RETIRED, THEY SHOT THE *AMERICAN SPLENDOR* MOVIE RIGHT HERE IN CLEVELAND, SO I WENT DOWN TO SEE THAT DONE, AND IT WAS FUN.

"BUT AFTER THE MOVIE CREW LEFT, I DIDN'T KNOW WHAT TO DO WITH MYSELF. I STARTED TO WORRY ALL THE TIME--TO EVEN WORRY ABOUT *WORRYING*.

"IT WAS DRIVIN' ME *NUTS*. I FIGURED MY LIFE WAS OVER, SO I SWALLOWED A WHOLE BUNCHA PILLS AND JOYCE CALLED 9-1-1 AND THEY TOOK ME TO THE HOSPITAL.

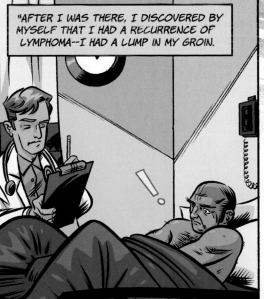

"AFTER I WAS THERE, I DISCOVERED BY MYSELF THAT I HAD A RECURRENCE OF LYMPHOMA--I HAD A LUMP IN MY GROIN.

"THEN I HAD TO GET CHEMOTHERAPY AGAIN, AND I WAS BECOMING EVEN MORE DEPRESSED--TO THE POINT WHERE I COULDN'T GET OUTTA BED.

=MOAN=

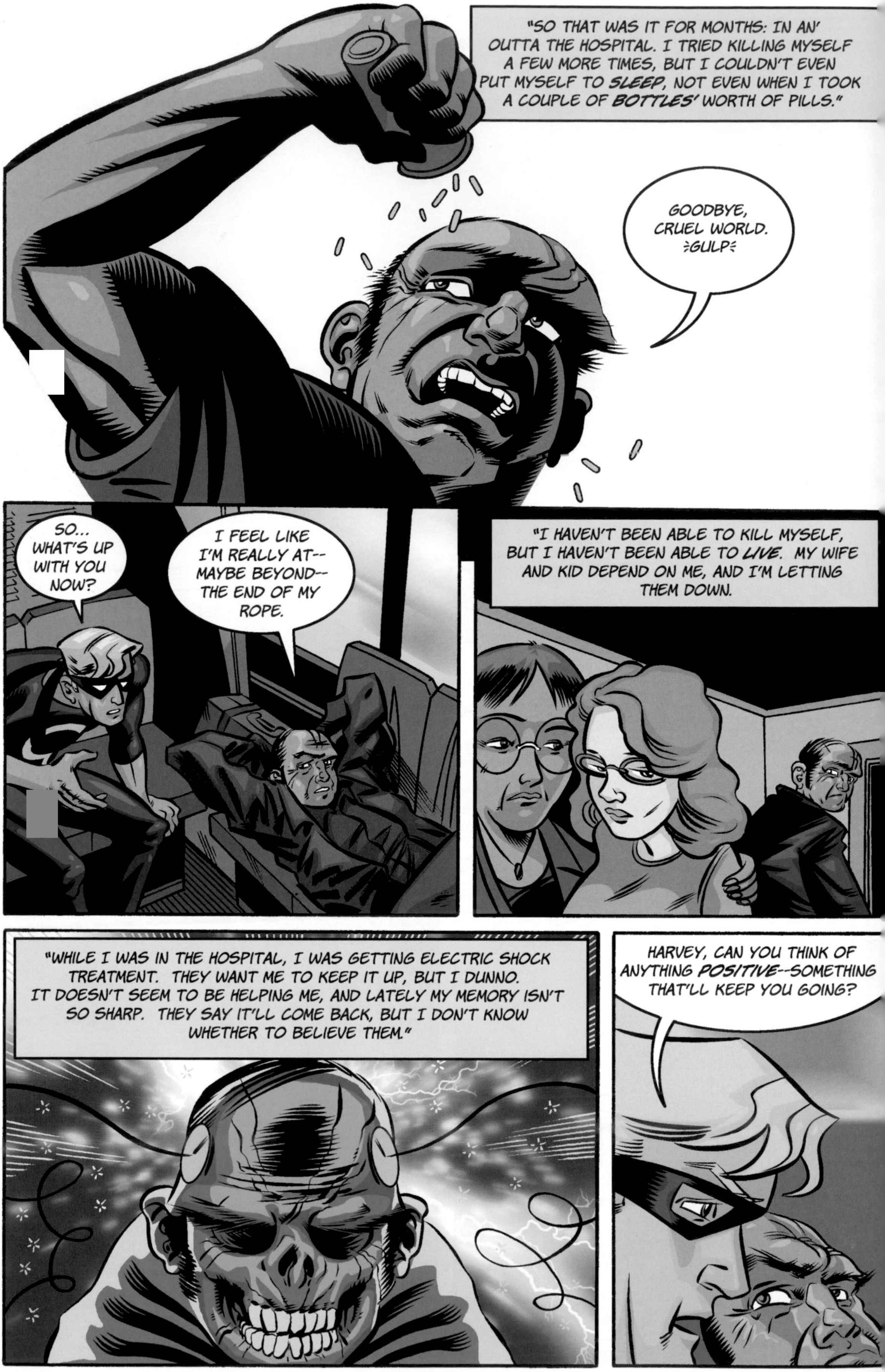
"SO THAT WAS IT FOR MONTHS: IN AN' OUTTA THE HOSPITAL. I TRIED KILLING MYSELF A FEW MORE TIMES, BUT I COULDN'T EVEN PUT MYSELF TO *SLEEP*, NOT EVEN WHEN I TOOK A COUPLE OF *BOTTLES'* WORTH OF PILLS."
GOODBYE, CRUEL WORLD. GULP
SO... WHAT'S UP WITH YOU NOW?
I FEEL LIKE I'M REALLY AT-- MAYBE BEYOND-- THE END OF MY ROPE.
"I HAVEN'T BEEN ABLE TO KILL MYSELF, BUT I HAVEN'T BEEN ABLE TO *LIVE*. MY WIFE AND KID DEPEND ON ME, AND I'M LETTING THEM DOWN.
"WHILE I WAS IN THE HOSPITAL, I WAS GETTING ELECTRIC SHOCK TREATMENT. THEY WANT ME TO KEEP IT UP, BUT I DUNNO. IT DOESN'T SEEM TO BE HELPING ME, AND LATELY MY MEMORY ISN'T SO SHARP. THEY SAY IT'LL COME BACK, BUT I DON'T KNOW WHETHER TO BELIEVE THEM."
HARVEY, CAN YOU THINK OF ANYTHING *POSITIVE*--SOMETHING THAT'LL KEEP YOU GOING?

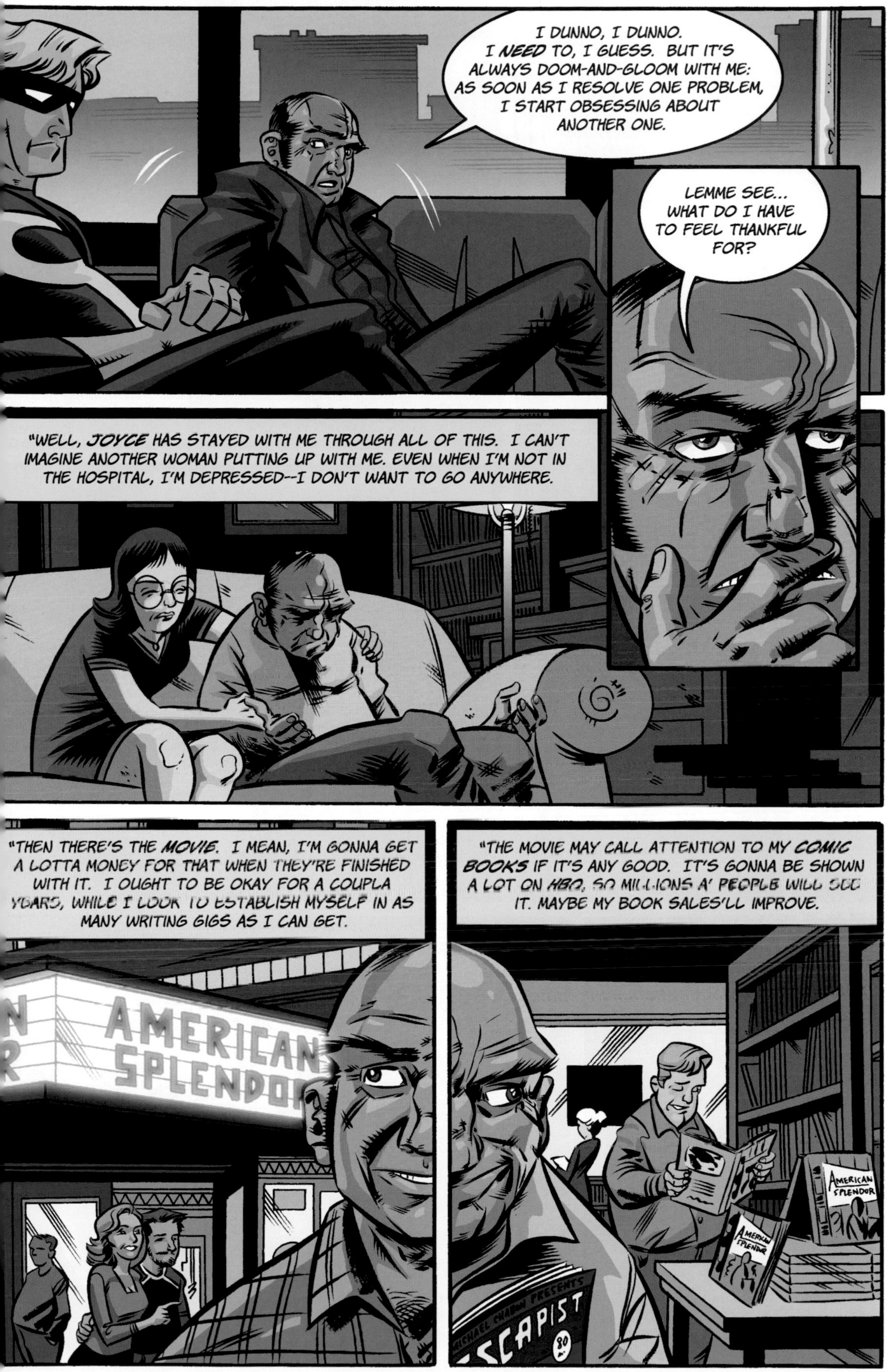
I DUNNO, I DUNNO. I ***NEED*** TO, I GUESS. BUT IT'S ALWAYS DOOM-AND-GLOOM WITH ME: AS SOON AS I RESOLVE ONE PROBLEM, I START OBSESSING ABOUT ANOTHER ONE.
LEMME SEE... WHAT DO I HAVE TO FEEL THANKFUL FOR?
"WELL, ***JOYCE*** HAS STAYED WITH ME THROUGH ALL OF THIS. I CAN'T IMAGINE ANOTHER WOMAN PUTTING UP WITH ME. EVEN WHEN I'M NOT IN THE HOSPITAL, I'M DEPRESSED--I DON'T WANT TO GO ANYWHERE.
"THEN THERE'S THE ***MOVIE***. I MEAN, I'M GONNA GET A LOTTA MONEY FOR THAT WHEN THEY'RE FINISHED WITH IT. I OUGHT TO BE OKAY FOR A COUPLA YEARS, WHILE I LOOK TO ESTABLISH MYSELF IN AS MANY WRITING GIGS AS I CAN GET.
AMERICAN SPLENDOR
"THE MOVIE MAY CALL ATTENTION TO MY ***COMIC BOOKS*** IF IT'S ANY GOOD. IT'S GONNA BE SHOWN A LOT ON ***HBO***, SO MILLIONS A' PEOPLE WILL SEE IT. MAYBE MY BOOK SALES'LL IMPROVE.
AMERICAN SPLENDOR
AMERICAN SPLENDOR

"LOOK, I'VE GOT **SOME** RESOURCES, SOME THINGS GOING FOR ME, I'LL ADMIT THAT. BUT I'VE NEVER BEEN ABLE TO TAKE COMFORT FROM THE POSITIVE ASPECTS OF MY LIFE.

"LIKE I SAID, WHEN I GET ONE PROBLEM WORKED OUT, MY MIND AUTOMATICALLY FOCUSES ON THE NEXT ONE IN LINE. IT'S GOTTEN SO BAD I CAN'T REALLY ENJOY **ANYTHING** THAT USED TO GIVE ME PLEASURE."

WHEW, THAT'S TOUGH. YOU'RE ALMOST ANHEDONIC.* GOING THROUGH LIFE LIKE THAT IS **TORTURE**. CAN YOU THINK OF SOME WAY TO COMBAT IT?

*Incapable of experiencing happiness.
--Bubbles La Webster

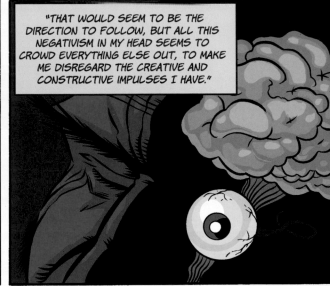

"THAT WOULD SEEM TO BE THE DIRECTION TO FOLLOW, BUT ALL THIS NEGATIVISM IN MY HEAD SEEMS TO CROWD EVERYTHING ELSE OUT, TO MAKE ME DISREGARD THE CREATIVE AND CONSTRUCTIVE IMPULSES I HAVE."

WELL, WHAT WILL YOU DO WHEN YOU GET HOME? YOU DON'T WANT TO ROLL UP IN A BALL AND JUST LIE IN BED.

"FOR SURE I DON'T. I'VE GOT TO **STOP** THIS DOWNWARD SLIDE. MY FAMILY HAS PUT UP WITH HORRIBLE INSECURITY FOR AT LEAST A YEAR AND A HALF. I'VE GOT TO FIND A WAY TO SHOW THEM I'M AT LEAST TAKING POSITIVE STEPS TO SHOULDER MY RESPONSIBILITY TO **THEM**."

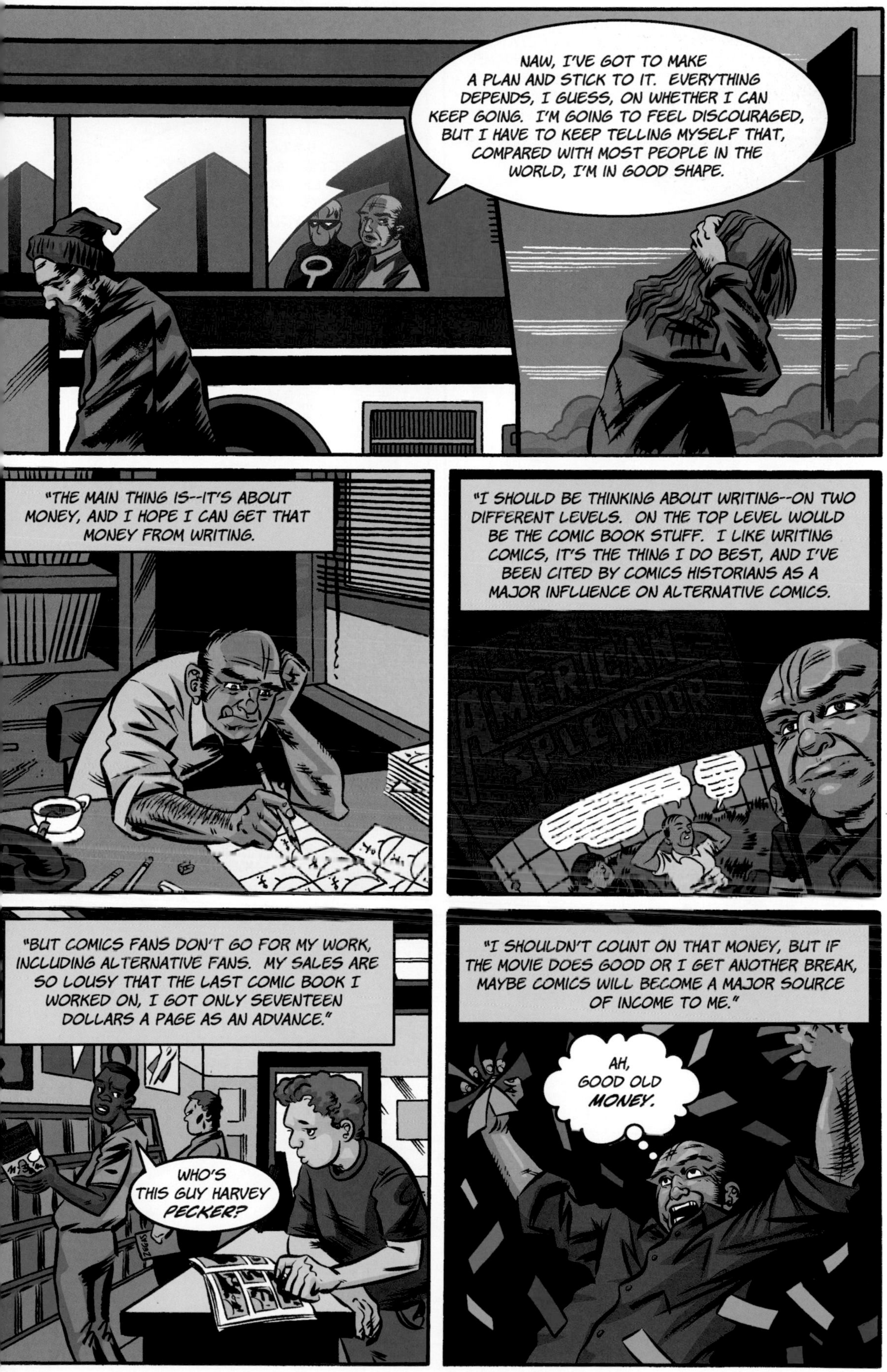

NAW, I'VE GOT TO MAKE A PLAN AND STICK TO IT. EVERYTHING DEPENDS, I GUESS, ON WHETHER I CAN KEEP GOING. I'M GOING TO FEEL DISCOURAGED, BUT I HAVE TO KEEP TELLING MYSELF THAT, COMPARED WITH MOST PEOPLE IN THE WORLD, I'M IN GOOD SHAPE.
"THE MAIN THING IS--IT'S ABOUT MONEY, AND I HOPE I CAN GET THAT MONEY FROM WRITING.
"I SHOULD BE THINKING ABOUT WRITING--ON TWO DIFFERENT LEVELS. ON THE TOP LEVEL WOULD BE THE COMIC BOOK STUFF. I LIKE WRITING COMICS, IT'S THE THING I DO BEST, AND I'VE BEEN CITED BY COMICS HISTORIANS AS A MAJOR INFLUENCE ON ALTERNATIVE COMICS.
AMERICAN SPLENDOR
"BUT COMICS FANS DON'T GO FOR MY WORK, INCLUDING ALTERNATIVE FANS. MY SALES ARE SO LOUSY THAT THE LAST COMIC BOOK I WORKED ON, I GOT ONLY SEVENTEEN DOLLARS A PAGE AS AN ADVANCE."
WHO'S THIS GUY HARVEY *PECKER?*
"I SHOULDN'T COUNT ON THAT MONEY, BUT IF THE MOVIE DOES GOOD OR I GET ANOTHER BREAK, MAYBE COMICS WILL BECOME A MAJOR SOURCE OF INCOME TO ME."
AH, GOOD OLD *MONEY.*

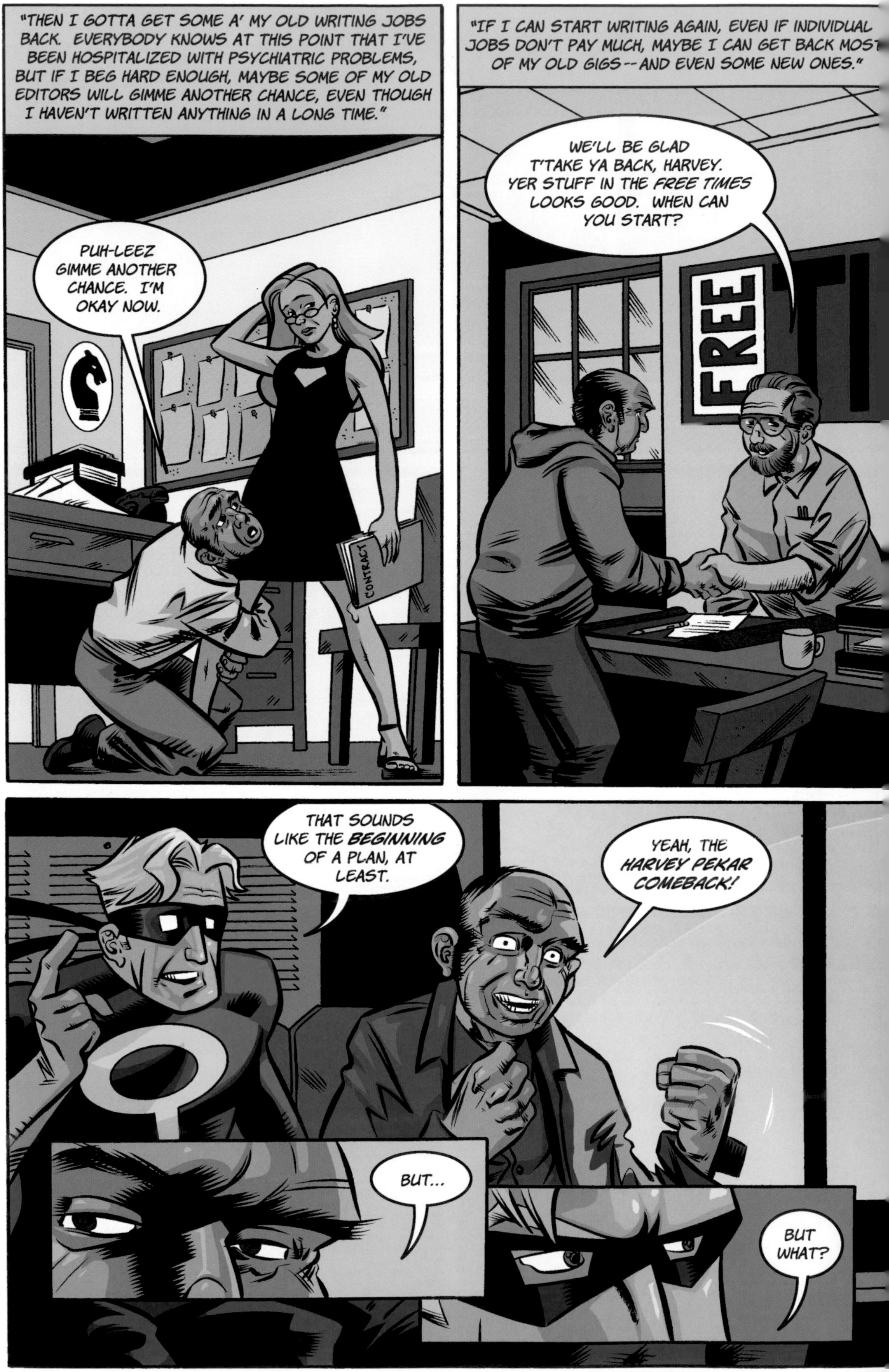
"THEN I GOTTA GET SOME A' MY OLD WRITING JOBS BACK. EVERYBODY KNOWS AT THIS POINT THAT I'VE BEEN HOSPITALIZED WITH PSYCHIATRIC PROBLEMS, BUT IF I BEG HARD ENOUGH, MAYBE SOME OF MY OLD EDITORS WILL GIMME ANOTHER CHANCE, EVEN THOUGH I HAVEN'T WRITTEN ANYTHING IN A LONG TIME."
PUH-LEEZ GIMME ANOTHER CHANCE. I'M OKAY NOW.
CONTRACT
"IF I CAN START WRITING AGAIN, EVEN IF INDIVIDUAL JOBS DON'T PAY MUCH, MAYBE I CAN GET BACK MOST OF MY OLD GIGS--AND EVEN SOME NEW ONES."
WE'LL BE GLAD T'TAKE YA BACK, HARVEY. YER STUFF IN THE *FREE TIMES* LOOKS GOOD. WHEN CAN YOU START?
FREE
THAT SOUNDS LIKE THE *BEGINNING* OF A PLAN, AT LEAST.
YEAH, THE *HARVEY PEKAR COMEBACK!*
BUT...
BUT WHAT?

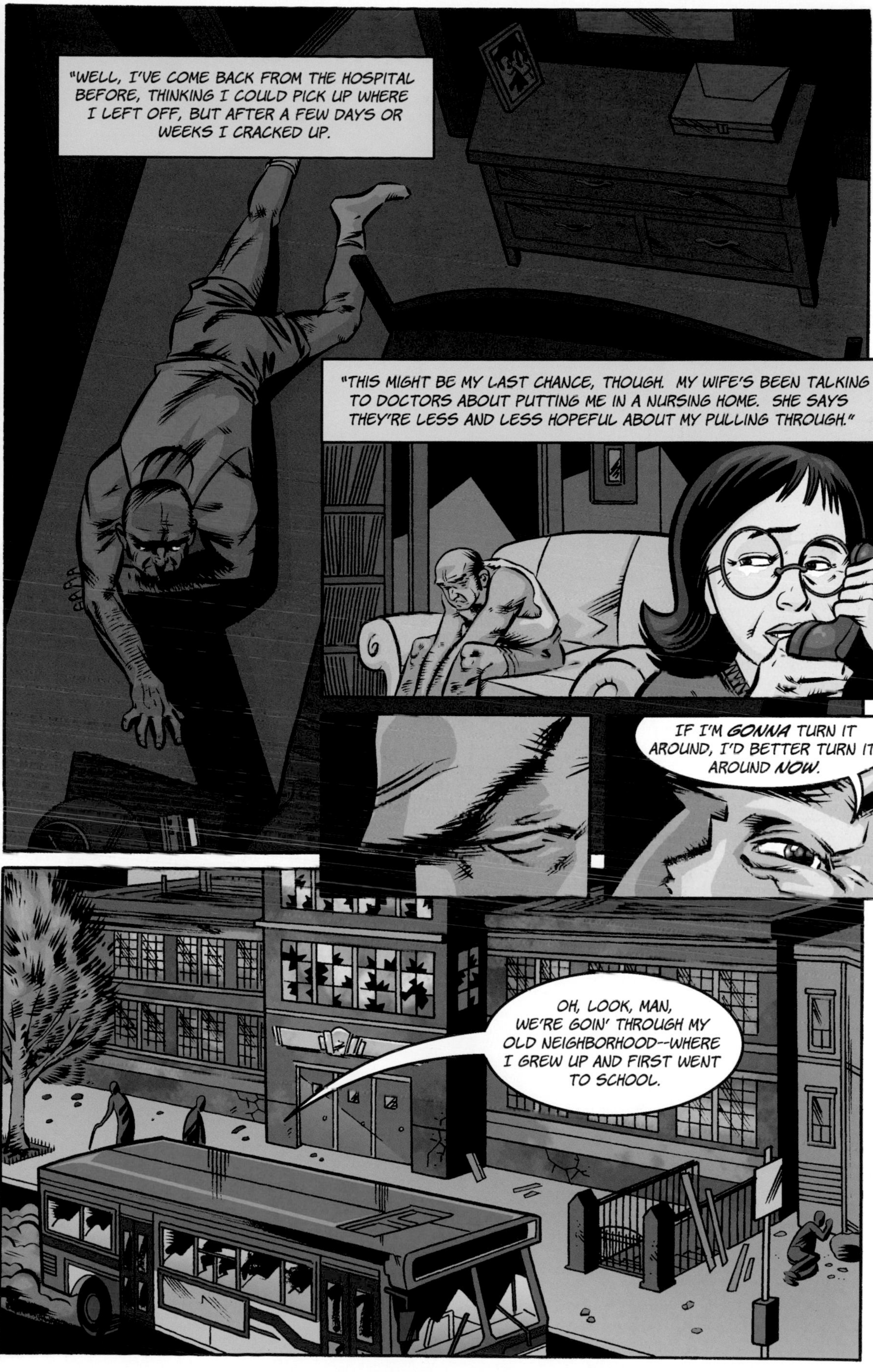
"WELL, I'VE COME BACK FROM THE HOSPITAL BEFORE, THINKING I COULD PICK UP WHERE I LEFT OFF, BUT AFTER A FEW DAYS OR WEEKS I CRACKED UP.
"THIS MIGHT BE MY LAST CHANCE, THOUGH. MY WIFE'S BEEN TALKING TO DOCTORS ABOUT PUTTING ME IN A NURSING HOME. SHE SAYS THEY'RE LESS AND LESS HOPEFUL ABOUT MY PULLING THROUGH."
IF I'M *GONNA* TURN IT AROUND, I'D BETTER TURN IT AROUND *NOW*.
OH, LOOK, MAN, WE'RE GOIN' THROUGH MY OLD NEIGHBORHOOD--WHERE I GREW UP AND FIRST WENT TO SCHOOL.

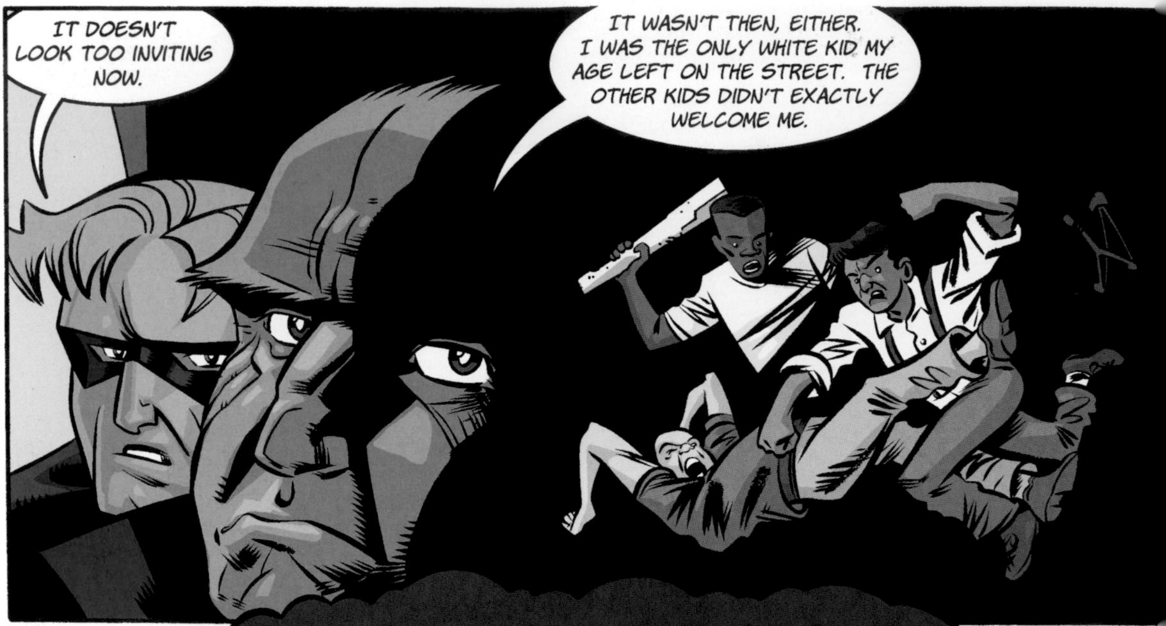
IT DOESN'T LOOK TOO INVITING NOW.
IT WASN'T THEN, EITHER. I WAS THE ONLY WHITE KID MY AGE LEFT ON THE STREET. THE OTHER KIDS DIDN'T EXACTLY WELCOME ME.
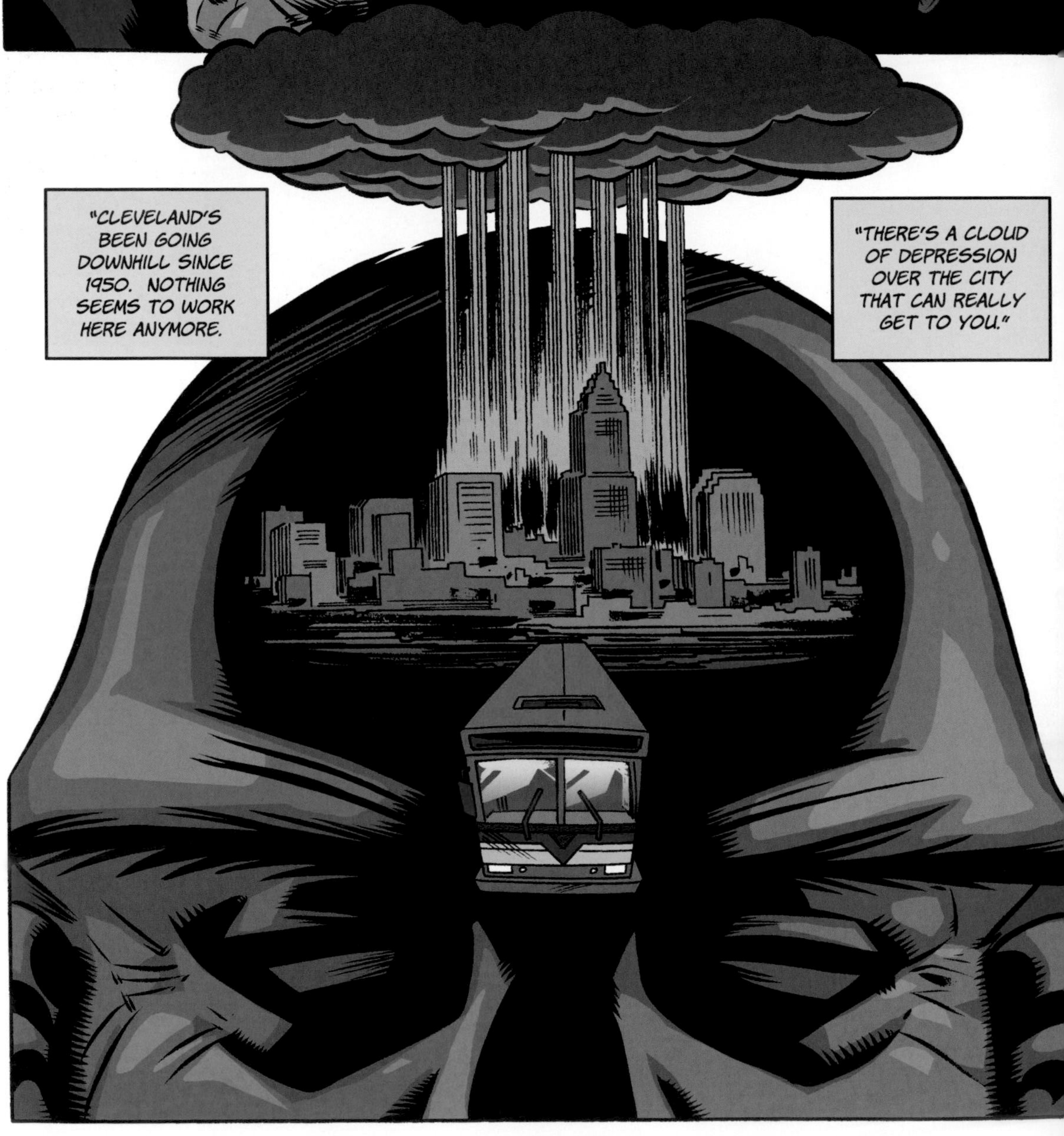
"CLEVELAND'S BEEN GOING DOWNHILL SINCE 1950. NOTHING SEEMS TO WORK HERE ANYMORE.
"THERE'S A CLOUD OF DEPRESSION OVER THE CITY THAT CAN REALLY GET TO YOU."

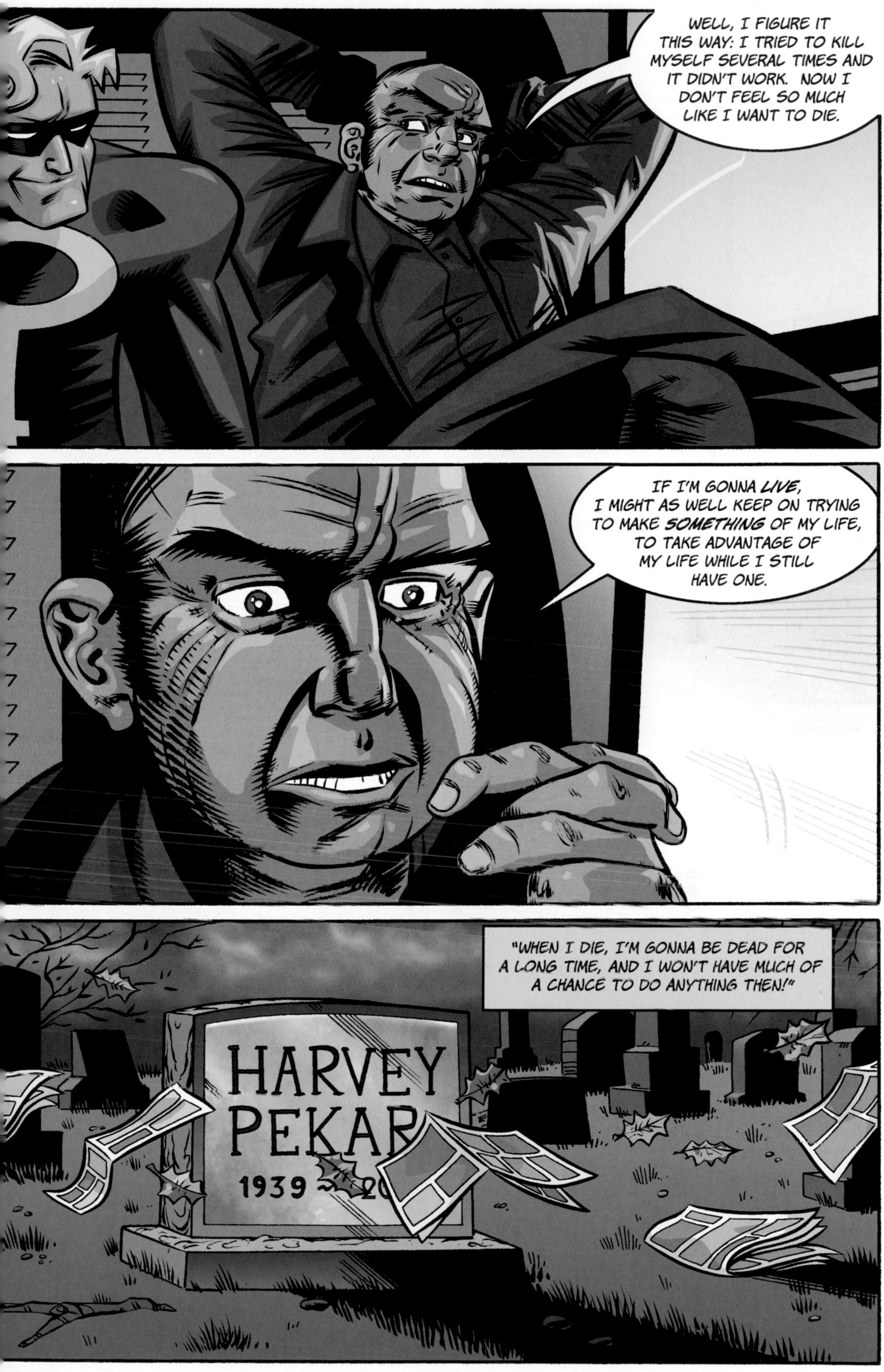
WELL, I FIGURE IT THIS WAY: I TRIED TO KILL MYSELF SEVERAL TIMES AND IT DIDN'T WORK. NOW I DON'T FEEL SO MUCH LIKE I WANT TO DIE.
IF I'M GONNA LIVE, I MIGHT AS WELL KEEP ON TRYING TO MAKE SOMETHING OF MY LIFE, TO TAKE ADVANTAGE OF MY LIFE WHILE I STILL HAVE ONE.
"WHEN I DIE, I'M GONNA BE DEAD FOR A LONG TIME, AND I WON'T HAVE MUCH OF A CHANCE TO DO ANYTHING THEN!"
HARVEY
PEKAR
1939

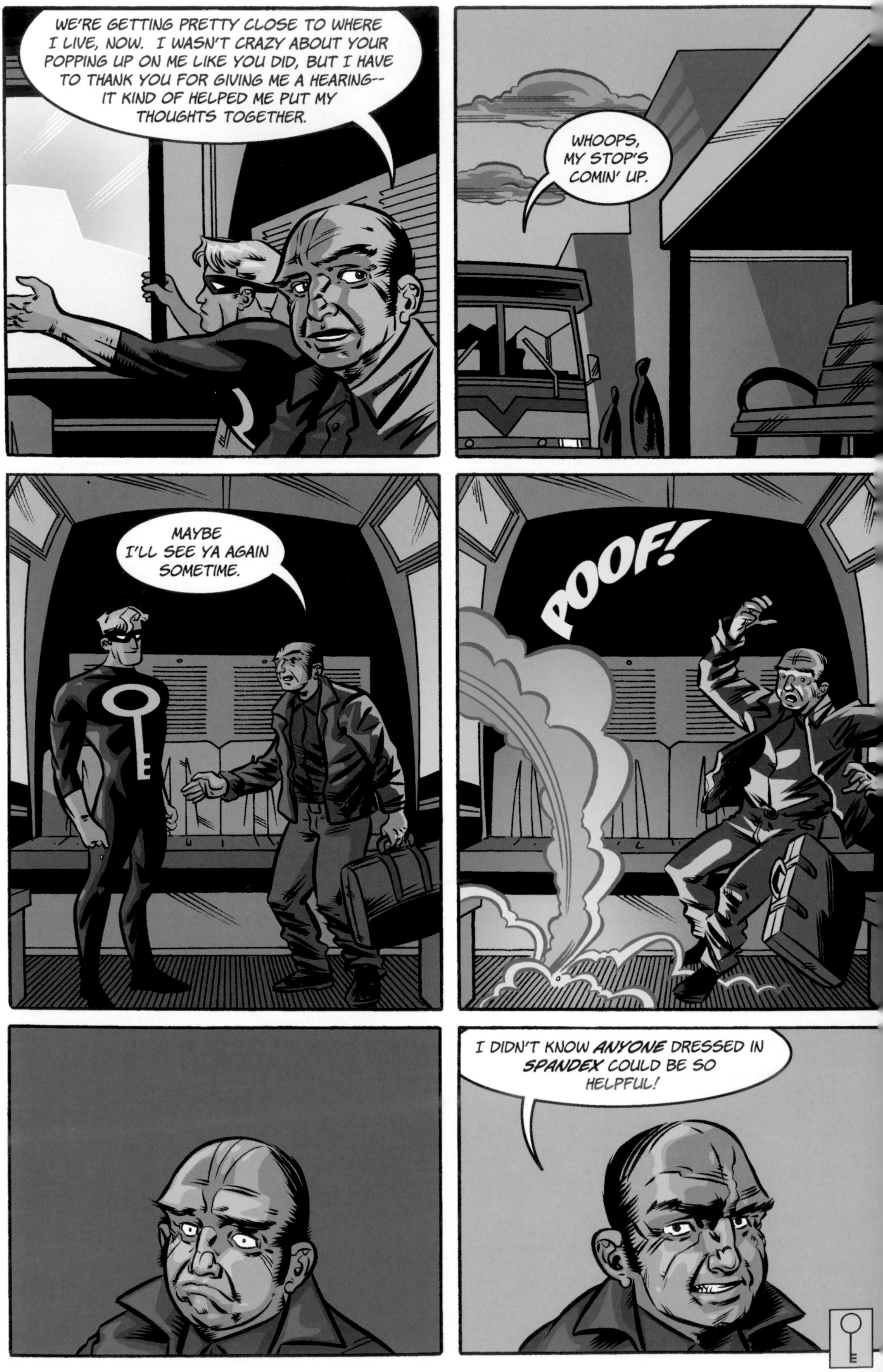
WE'RE GETTING PRETTY CLOSE TO WHERE I LIVE, NOW. I WASN'T CRAZY ABOUT YOUR POPPING UP ON ME LIKE YOU DID, BUT I HAVE TO THANK YOU FOR GIVING ME A HEARING-- IT KIND OF HELPED ME PUT MY THOUGHTS TOGETHER.
WHOOPS, MY STOP'S COMIN' UP.
MAYBE I'LL SEE YA AGAIN SOMETIME.
POOF!
I DIDN'T KNOW ANYONE DRESSED IN SPANDEX COULD BE SO HELPFUL!

# LUNA MOTH

*An Introduction*

## BY BUBBLES LaTOUR

WHILE THE ESCAPIST WAS SURELY THE MOST SUCCESSFUL OF ALL Kavalier & Clay comic book characters, no serious scholar of the medium can deny the impact that Luna Moth had on the readership at large. Legend has it that the mysterious Mistress of the Night was based, in fact, on Rosa Luxemburg Saks, who, as Rose Saxon, wound up chronicling many of the winged woman's adventures herself. [It is also interesting to note that Miss Saks was married to Sam Clay for several years, after having first dated Joe Kavalier prior to his enlistment in the armed forces during World War II.]

The first issue of the (mostly) quarterly *All Doll* series introduced Luna Moth in early 1941. At that time, as Michael Chabon notes in *The Amazing Adventures of Kavalier & Clay*, "the addition of sex to the costumed-hero concept was a natural and, apart from a few minor efforts at other companies — the Sorceress of Zoom, the Woman in Red— yet to be attempted." Bear in mind that National Periodical Publications' Wonder Woman did not debut until *All-Star* #8, cover-dated December 1941–January 1942.

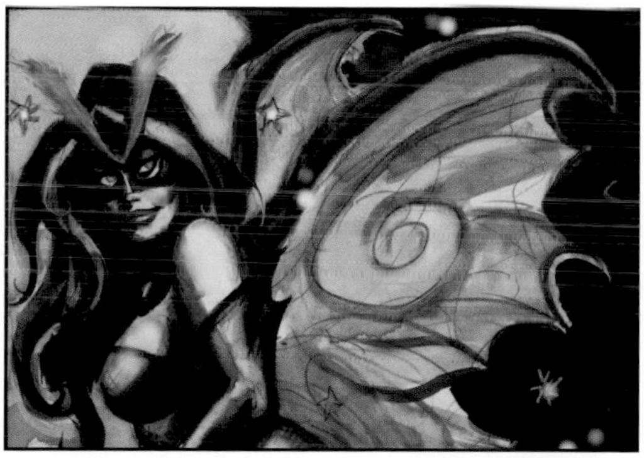

A painterly approach to Luna Moth. Courtesy of the Dan Brereton Collection.

Though initially resistant to the moth-like attributes of the character, Empire Comics publishers Sheldon Anapol and Jack Ashkenazy were won over by her sales potential—specifically by Kavalier's pulchritudinous pinup design: again, according to Chabon, "a woman with the legs of Dolores Del Rio, black witchy hair, and breasts each the size of her head."

Like the Escapist, Luna Moth would undergo a variety of costume and other changes through the years, reflecting the evolving tastes of the comic book industry. One of the more dramatic transformations occurred in 1974, at the height of the Sunshine Comics years, when comics luminary Jim Starlin took a short break from *Captain Marvel* to write and draw a Luna Moth story, re-presented herein with newly remastered digital color effects by Christie Scheele and Krista Ward.

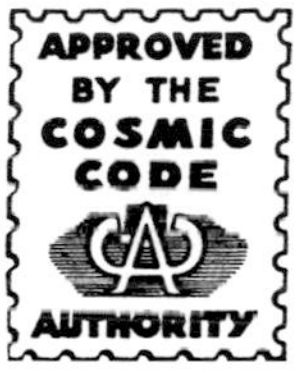
APPROVED
BY THE
COSMIC
CODE
AUTHORITY

["Reckonings" was completed during Starlin's "cosmic" period, and in fact, letterer Tom Orzechowski altered the Comics Code Authority sticker on the cover of that particular issue of *All Doll* (#123) to read "approved by the Cosmic Code Authority"! The joke caught publisher Danny Sonnenschein's eye, however, and he immediately had it corrected. It's worth noting, as do Steve Duin and Mike Richardson in their massive tome, *Comics: Between the Panels*, that Orzechowski was eventually able to slip the anagram past a not-so-eagle-eyed editor at Marvel Comics, on issue #179 of *Strange Tales*.]

In the character's formative years, however, Rose Saxon eschewed the pen-and-ink medium prevalent in comics of the time in favor of rather lush (and one might even argue wanton) watercolors—no doubt a direct result of the many romance comics covers Miss Saxon was also painting during the late '40s and early '50s. Both "The Mechanist" and "Old Flame" reflect the more painterly approach to Luna Moth pioneered by the character's lady chronicler.

---

Bubbles LaTour was resident historian at Dark Horse Comics for twenty-five years before retiring in 2015. Rumored to be penning a *Comics Babylon*-style tell-all, Dr. LaTour continues to dabble in her chosen field, albeit under a German pseudonym. Her current whereabouts are unknown.

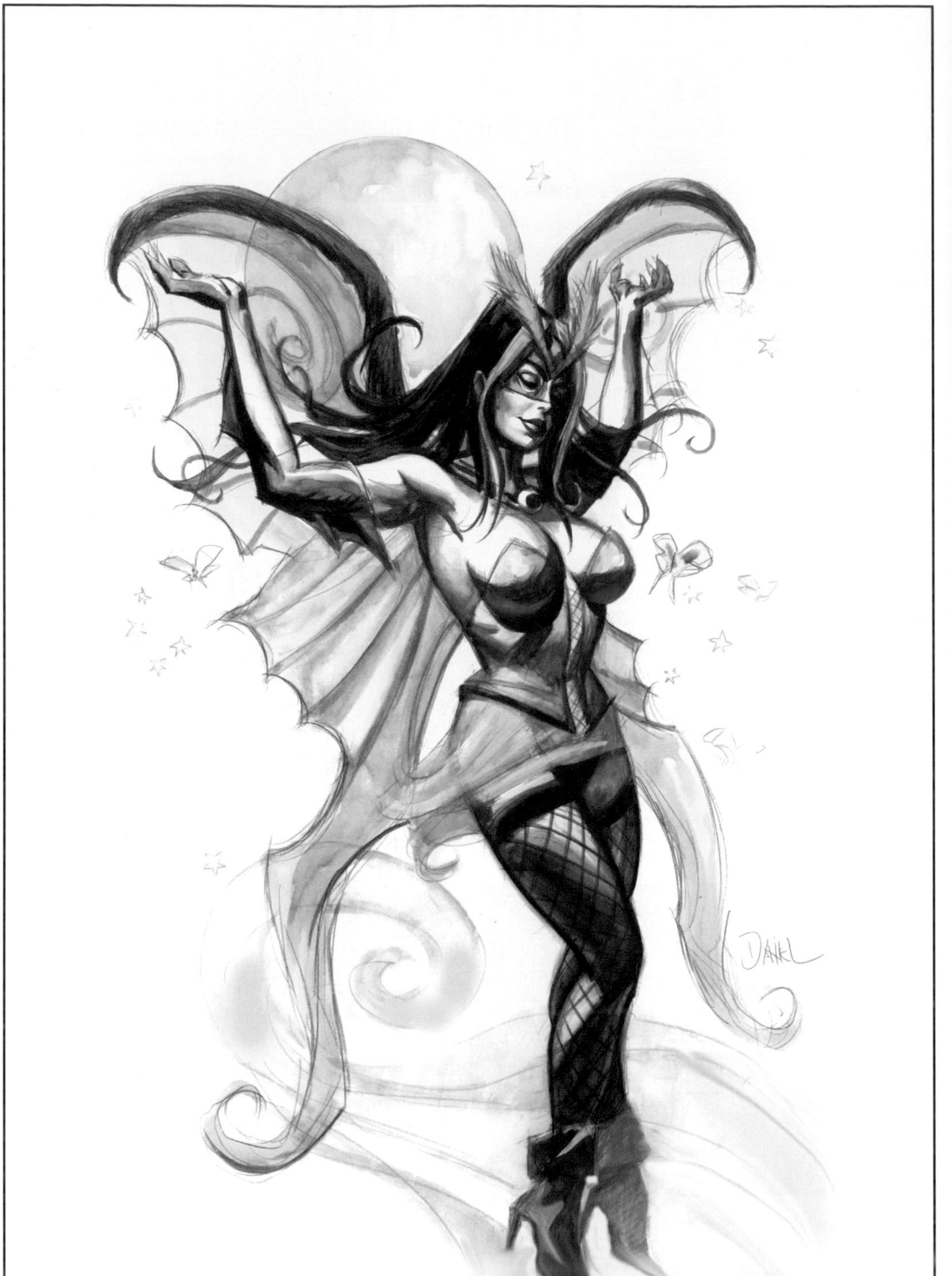

Another look at the captivating Luna Moth. Courtesy of the Dan Brereton collection.

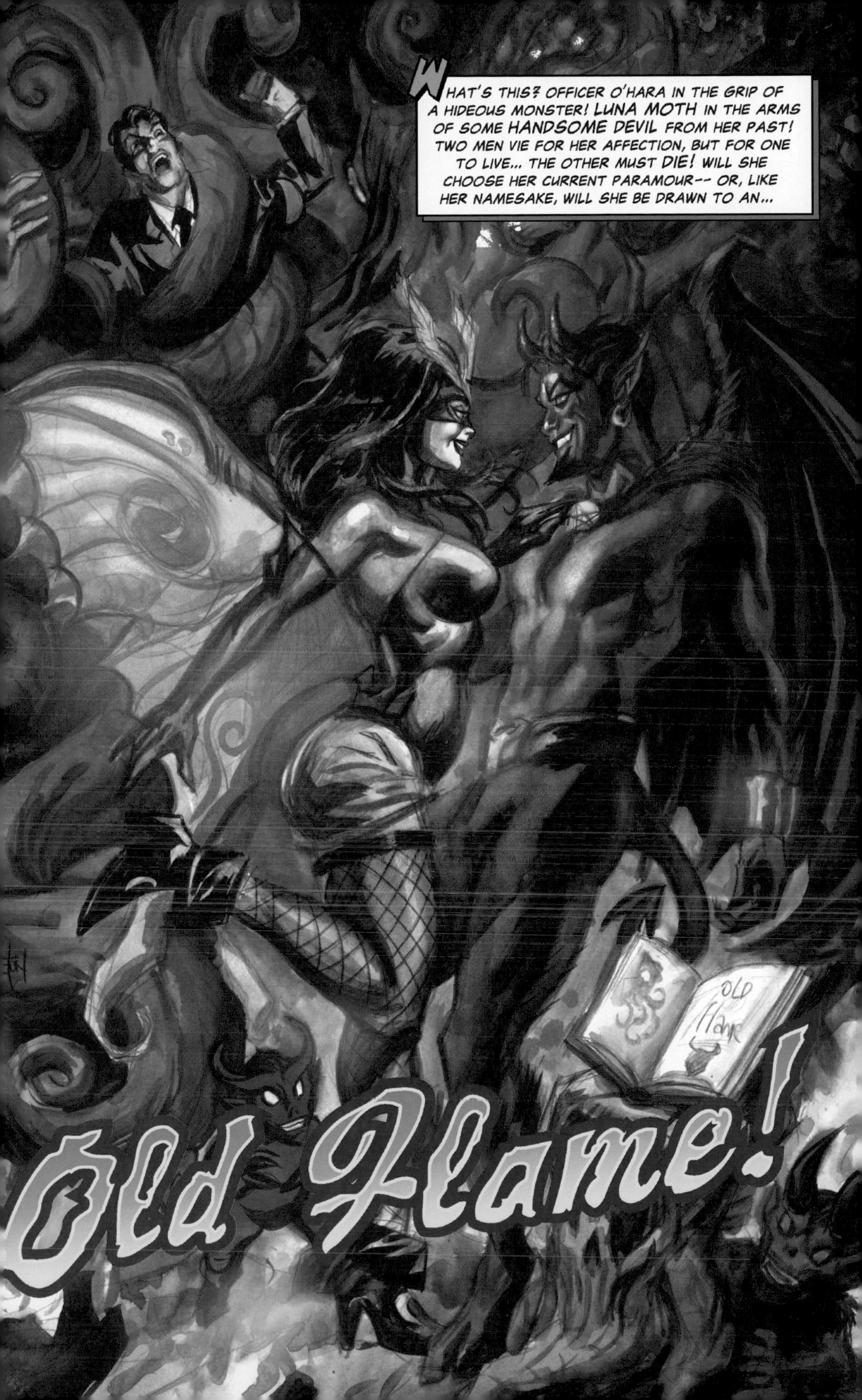
WHAT'S THIS? OFFICER O'HARA IN THE GRIP OF A HIDEOUS MONSTER! LUNA MOTH IN THE ARMS OF SOME HANDSOME DEVIL FROM HER PAST! TWO MEN VIE FOR HER AFFECTION, BUT FOR ONE TO LIVE... THE OTHER MUST DIE! WILL SHE CHOOSE HER CURRENT PARAMOUR-- OR, LIKE HER NAMESAKE, WILL SHE BE DRAWN TO AN...
OLD FLAME
Old Flame!

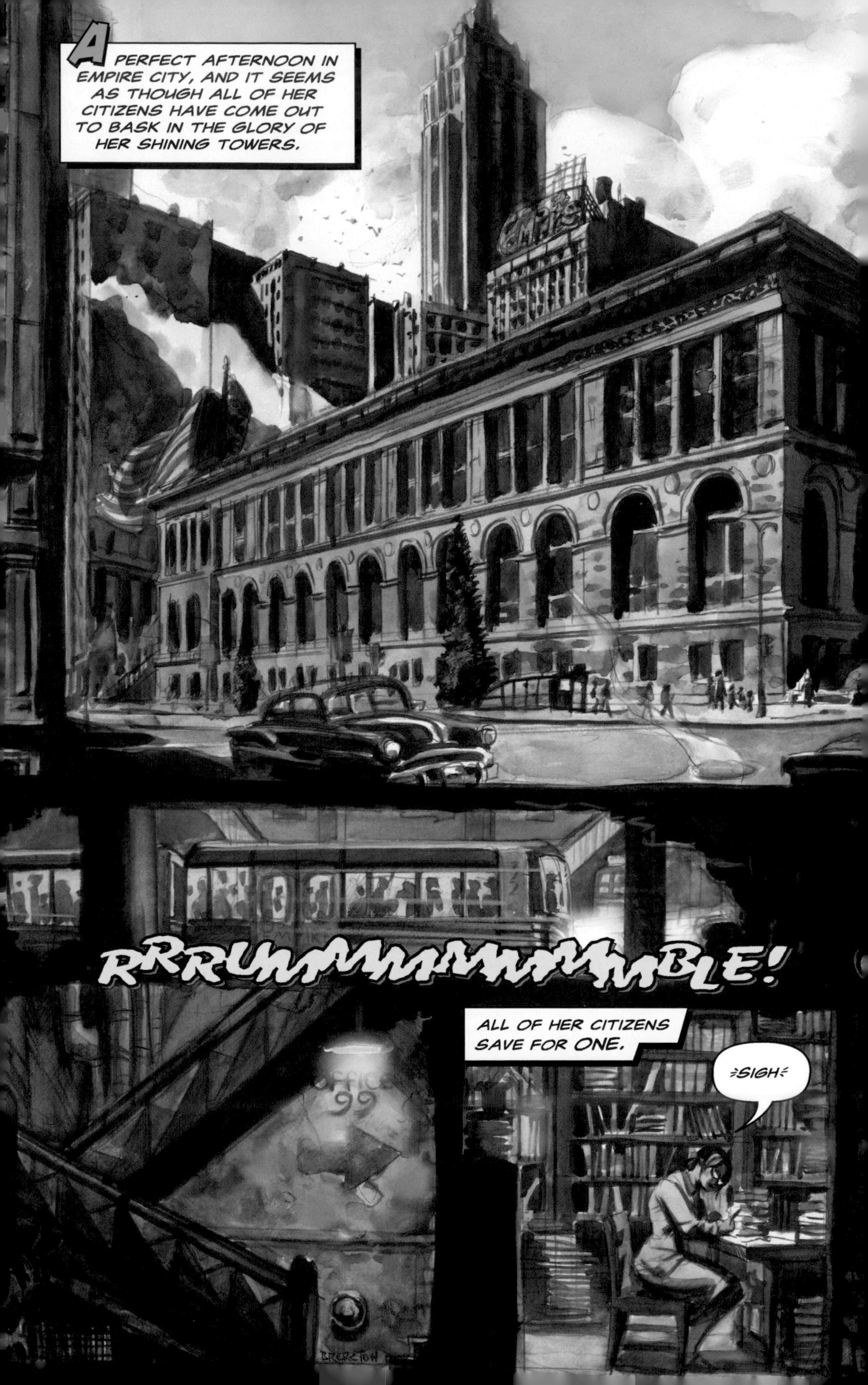
A PERFECT AFTERNOON IN EMPIRE CITY, AND IT SEEMS AS THOUGH ALL OF HER CITIZENS HAVE COME OUT TO BASK IN THE GLORY OF HER SHINING TOWERS.
RRRUMMMMMMMMBLE!
ALL OF HER CITIZENS SAVE FOR ONE.
≈SIGH≈

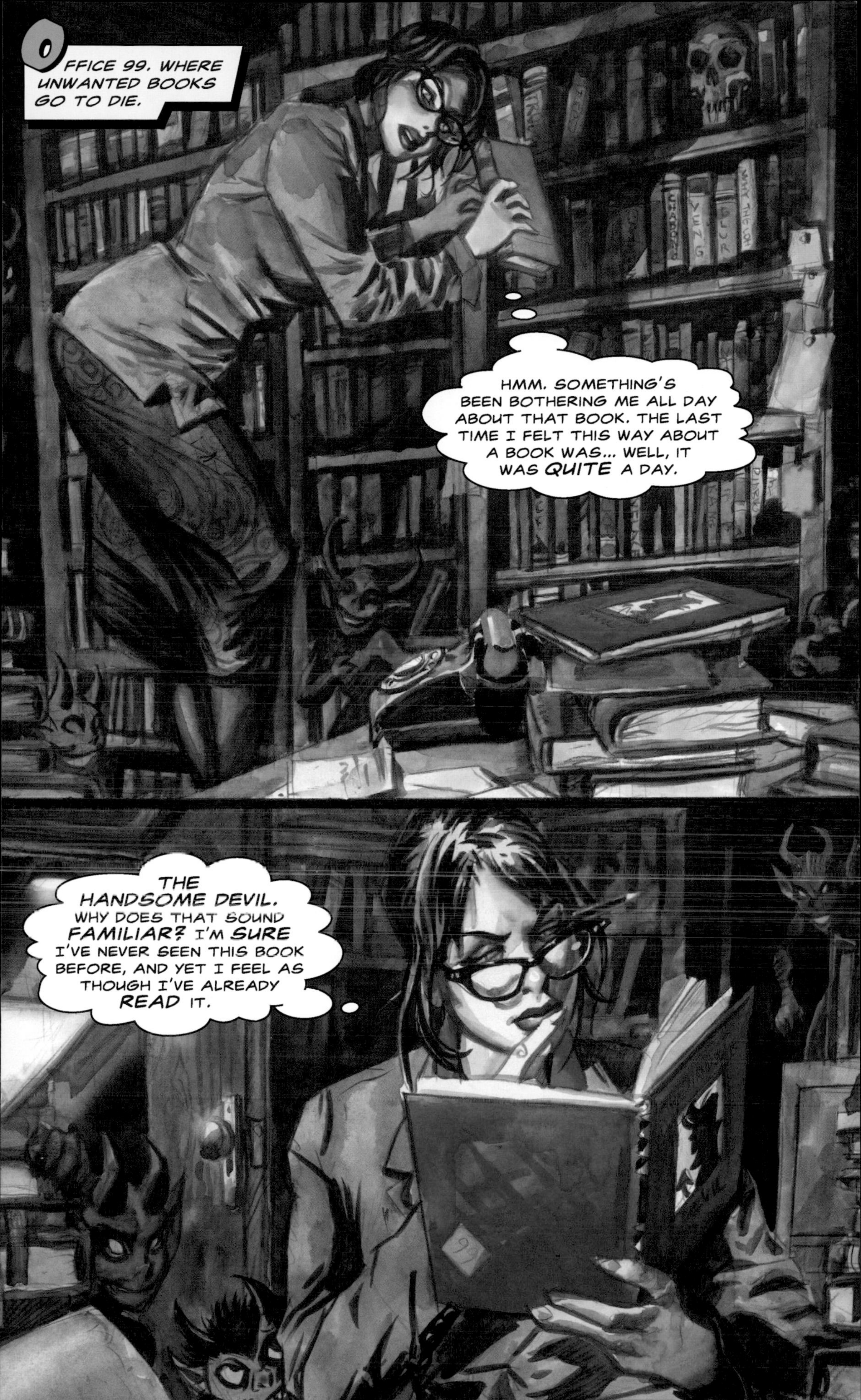
OFFICE 99. WHERE UNWANTED BOOKS GO TO DIE.
HMM. SOMETHING'S BEEN BOTHERING ME ALL DAY ABOUT THAT BOOK. THE LAST TIME I FELT THIS WAY ABOUT A BOOK WAS... WELL, IT WAS QUITE A DAY.
THE HANDSOME DEVIL. WHY DOES THAT SOUND FAMILIAR? I'M SURE I'VE NEVER SEEN THIS BOOK BEFORE, AND YET I FEEL AS THOUGH I'VE ALREADY READ IT.

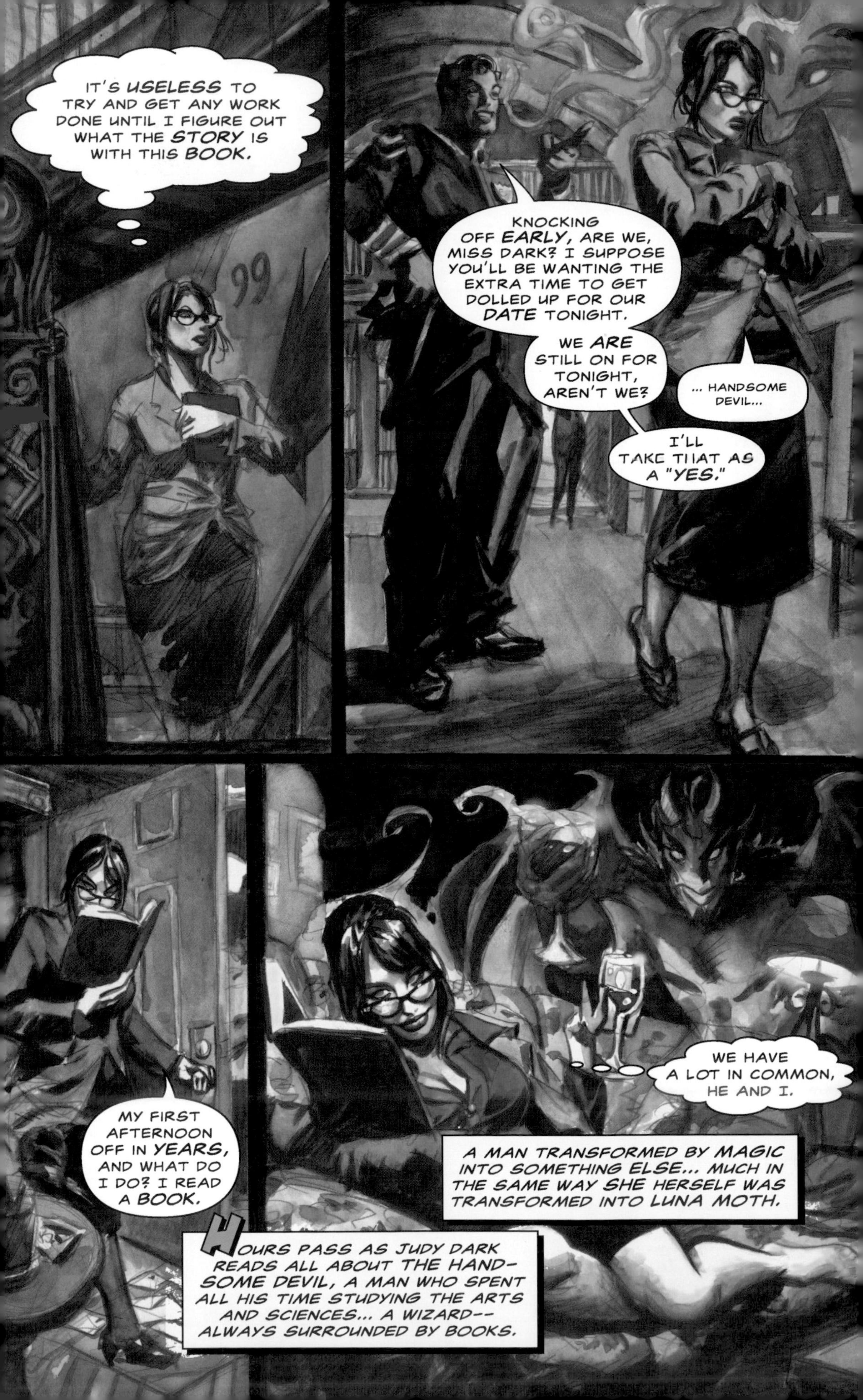
IT'S USELESS TO TRY AND GET ANY WORK DONE UNTIL I FIGURE OUT WHAT THE STORY IS WITH THIS BOOK.
99
KNOCKING OFF EARLY, ARE WE, MISS DARK? I SUPPOSE YOU'LL BE WANTING THE EXTRA TIME TO GET DOLLED UP FOR OUR DATE TONIGHT.
WE ARE STILL ON FOR TONIGHT, AREN'T WE?
... HANDSOME DEVIL...
I'LL TAKE THAT AS A "YES."
MY FIRST AFTERNOON OFF IN YEARS, AND WHAT DO I DO? I READ A BOOK.
WE HAVE A LOT IN COMMON, HE AND I.
A MAN TRANSFORMED BY MAGIC INTO SOMETHING ELSE... MUCH IN THE SAME WAY SHE HERSELF WAS TRANSFORMED INTO LUNA MOTH.
HOURS PASS AS JUDY DARK READS ALL ABOUT THE HANDSOME DEVIL, A MAN WHO SPENT ALL HIS TIME STUDYING THE ARTS AND SCIENCES... A WIZARD-- ALWAYS SURROUNDED BY BOOKS.

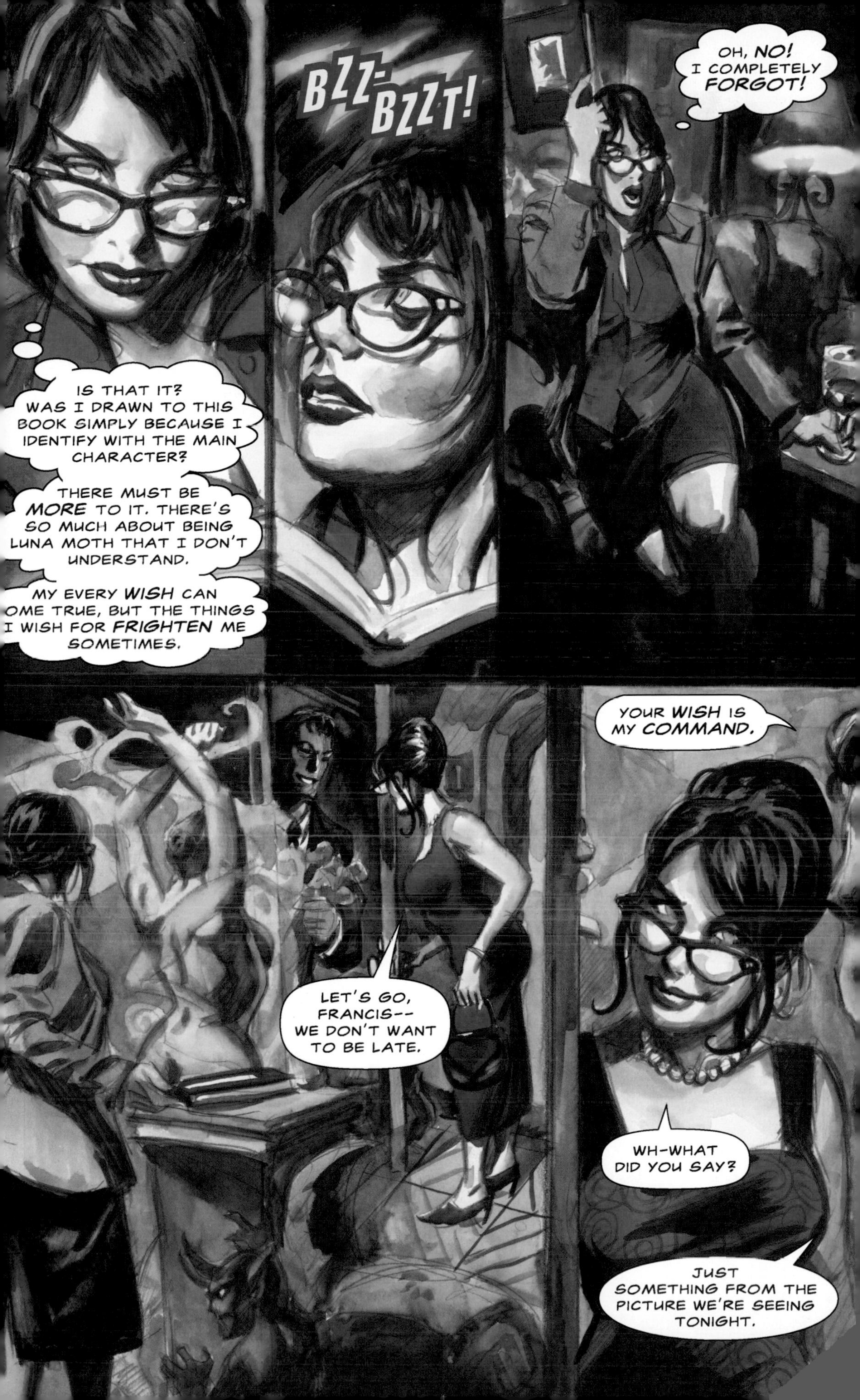
IS THAT IT? WAS I DRAWN TO THIS BOOK SIMPLY BECAUSE I IDENTIFY WITH THE MAIN CHARACTER?
THERE MUST BE MORE TO IT. THERE'S SO MUCH ABOUT BEING LUNA MOTH THAT I DON'T UNDERSTAND.
MY EVERY WISH CAN OME TRUE, BUT THE THINGS I WISH FOR FRIGHTEN ME SOMETIMES.
BZZ-BZZT!
OH, NO! I COMPLETELY FORGOT!
LET'S GO, FRANCIS-- WE DON'T WANT TO BE LATE.
YOUR WISH IS MY COMMAND.
WH-WHAT DID YOU SAY?
JUST SOMETHING FROM THE PICTURE WE'RE SEEING TONIGHT.

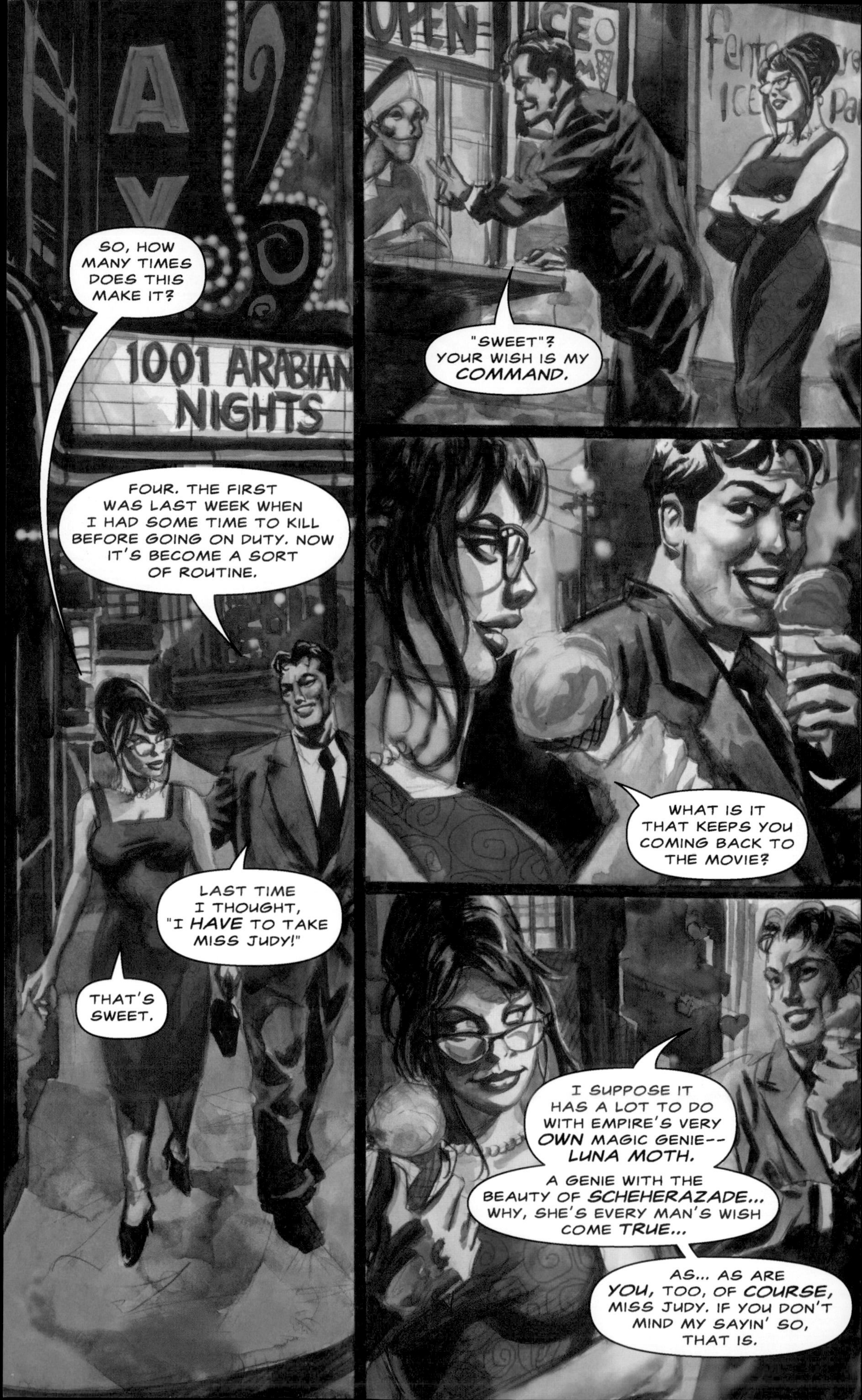
SO, HOW MANY TIMES DOES THIS MAKE IT?
1001 ARABIAN NIGHTS
FOUR. THE FIRST WAS LAST WEEK WHEN I HAD SOME TIME TO KILL BEFORE GOING ON DUTY. NOW IT'S BECOME A SORT OF ROUTINE.
LAST TIME I THOUGHT, "I *HAVE* TO TAKE MISS JUDY!"
THAT'S SWEET.
OPEN
ICE
"SWEET"? YOUR WISH IS MY *COMMAND.*
WHAT IS IT THAT KEEPS YOU COMING BACK TO THE MOVIE?
I SUPPOSE IT HAS A LOT TO DO WITH EMPIRE'S VERY *OWN* MAGIC GENIE-- *LUNA MOTH.*
A GENIE WITH THE BEAUTY OF *SCHEHERAZADE*... WHY, SHE'S EVERY MAN'S WISH COME *TRUE*...
AS... AS ARE *YOU*, TOO, OF *COURSE*, MISS JUDY. IF YOU DON'T MIND MY SAYIN' SO, THAT IS.

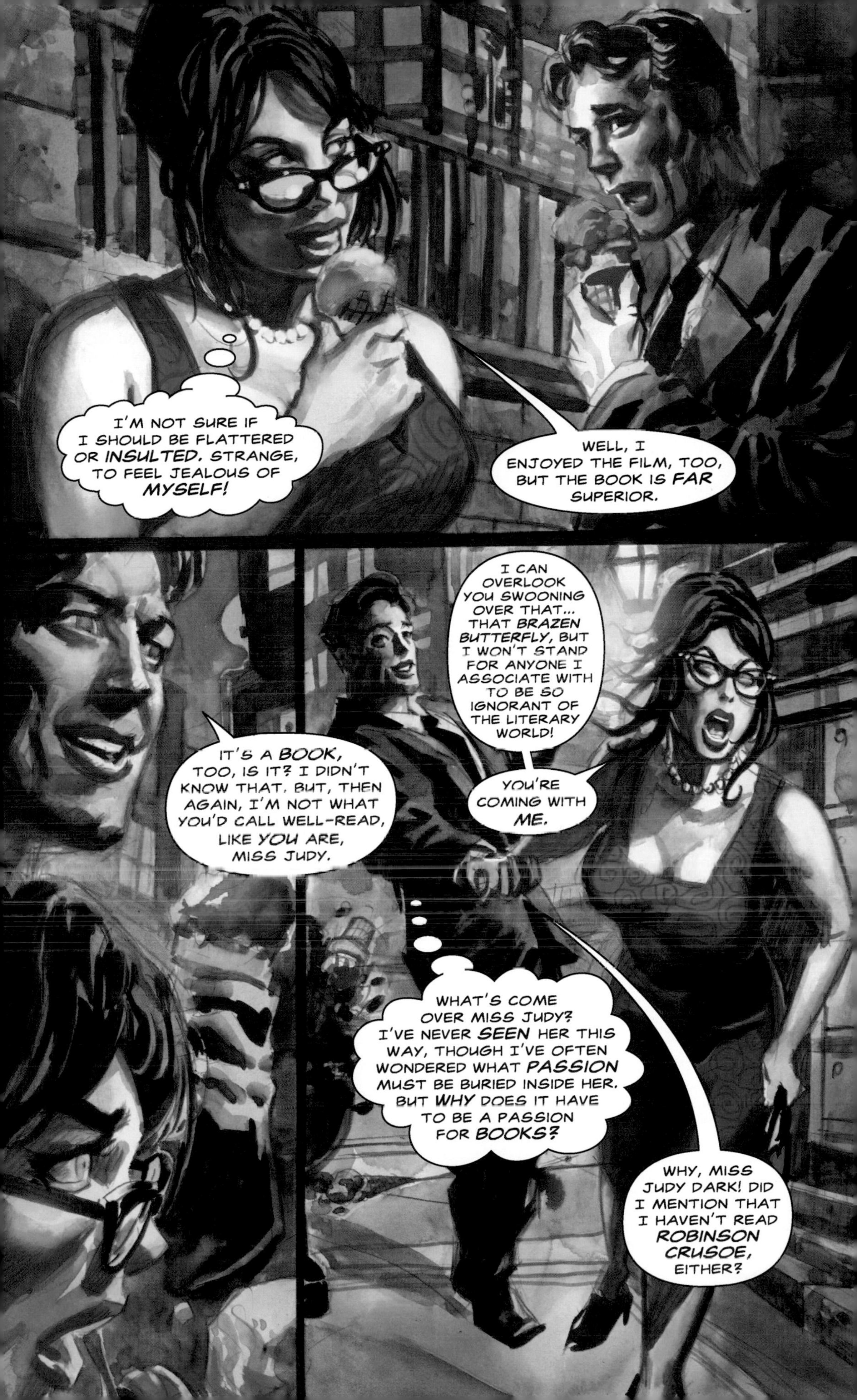
I'M NOT SURE IF I SHOULD BE FLATTERED OR INSULTED. STRANGE, TO FEEL JEALOUS OF MYSELF!
WELL, I ENJOYED THE FILM, TOO, BUT THE BOOK IS FAR SUPERIOR.
IT'S A BOOK, TOO, IS IT? I DIDN'T KNOW THAT. BUT, THEN AGAIN, I'M NOT WHAT YOU'D CALL WELL-READ, LIKE YOU ARE, MISS JUDY.
I CAN OVERLOOK YOU SWOONING OVER THAT... THAT BRAZEN BUTTERFLY, BUT I WON'T STAND FOR ANYONE I ASSOCIATE WITH TO BE SO IGNORANT OF THE LITERARY WORLD!
YOU'RE COMING WITH ME.
WHAT'S COME OVER MISS JUDY? I'VE NEVER SEEN HER THIS WAY, THOUGH I'VE OFTEN WONDERED WHAT PASSION MUST BE BURIED INSIDE HER. BUT WHY DOES IT HAVE TO BE A PASSION FOR BOOKS?
WHY, MISS JUDY DARK! DID I MENTION THAT I HAVEN'T READ ROBINSON CRUSOE, EITHER?

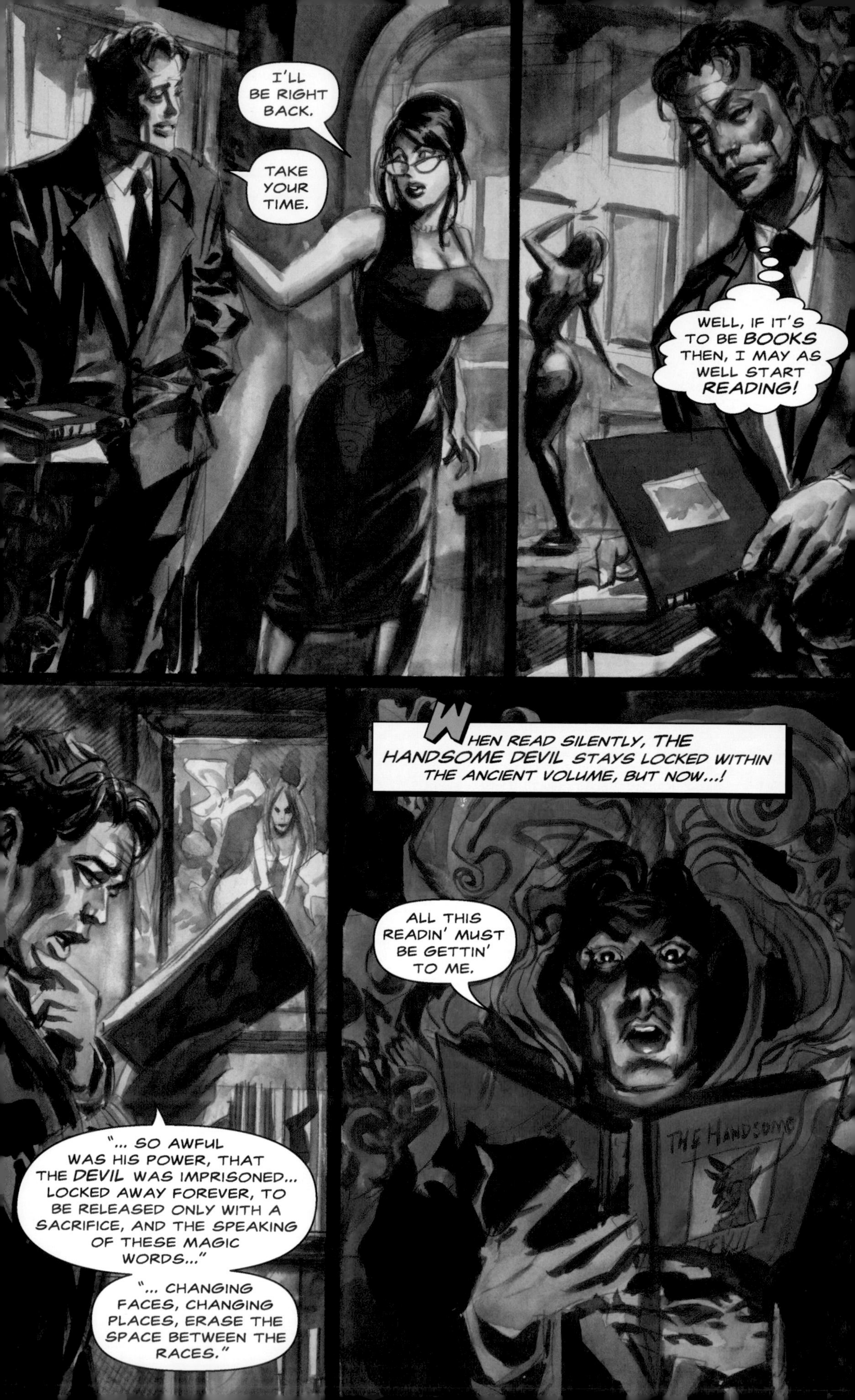
I'LL BE RIGHT BACK.
TAKE YOUR TIME.
WELL, IF IT'S TO BE *BOOKS* THEN, I MAY AS WELL START *READING!*
"... SO AWFUL WAS HIS POWER, THAT THE *DEVIL* WAS IMPRISONED... LOCKED AWAY FOREVER, TO BE RELEASED ONLY WITH A SACRIFICE, AND THE SPEAKING OF THESE MAGIC WORDS..."
"... CHANGING FACES, CHANGING PLACES, ERASE THE SPACE BETWEEN THE RACES."
WHEN READ SILENTLY, THE *HANDSOME DEVIL* STAYS LOCKED WITHIN THE ANCIENT VOLUME, BUT NOW...!
ALL THIS READIN' MUST BE GETTIN' TO ME.
THE HANDSOME

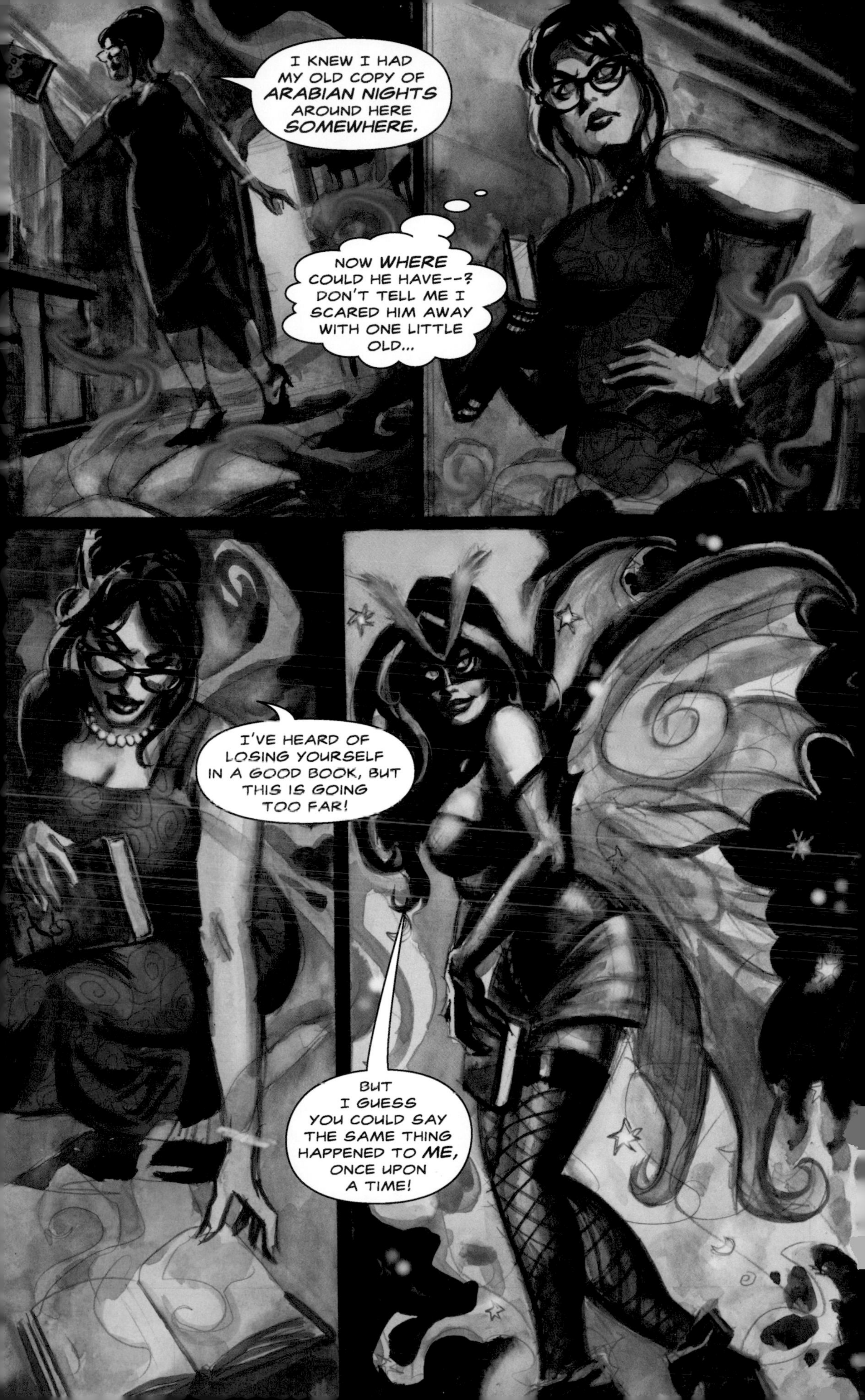
I KNEW I HAD MY OLD COPY OF ARABIAN NIGHTS AROUND HERE SOMEWHERE.
NOW WHERE COULD HE HAVE--? DON'T TELL ME I SCARED HIM AWAY WITH ONE LITTLE OLD...
I'VE HEARD OF LOSING YOURSELF IN A GOOD BOOK, BUT THIS IS GOING TOO FAR!
BUT I GUESS YOU COULD SAY THE SAME THING HAPPENED TO ME, ONCE UPON A TIME!

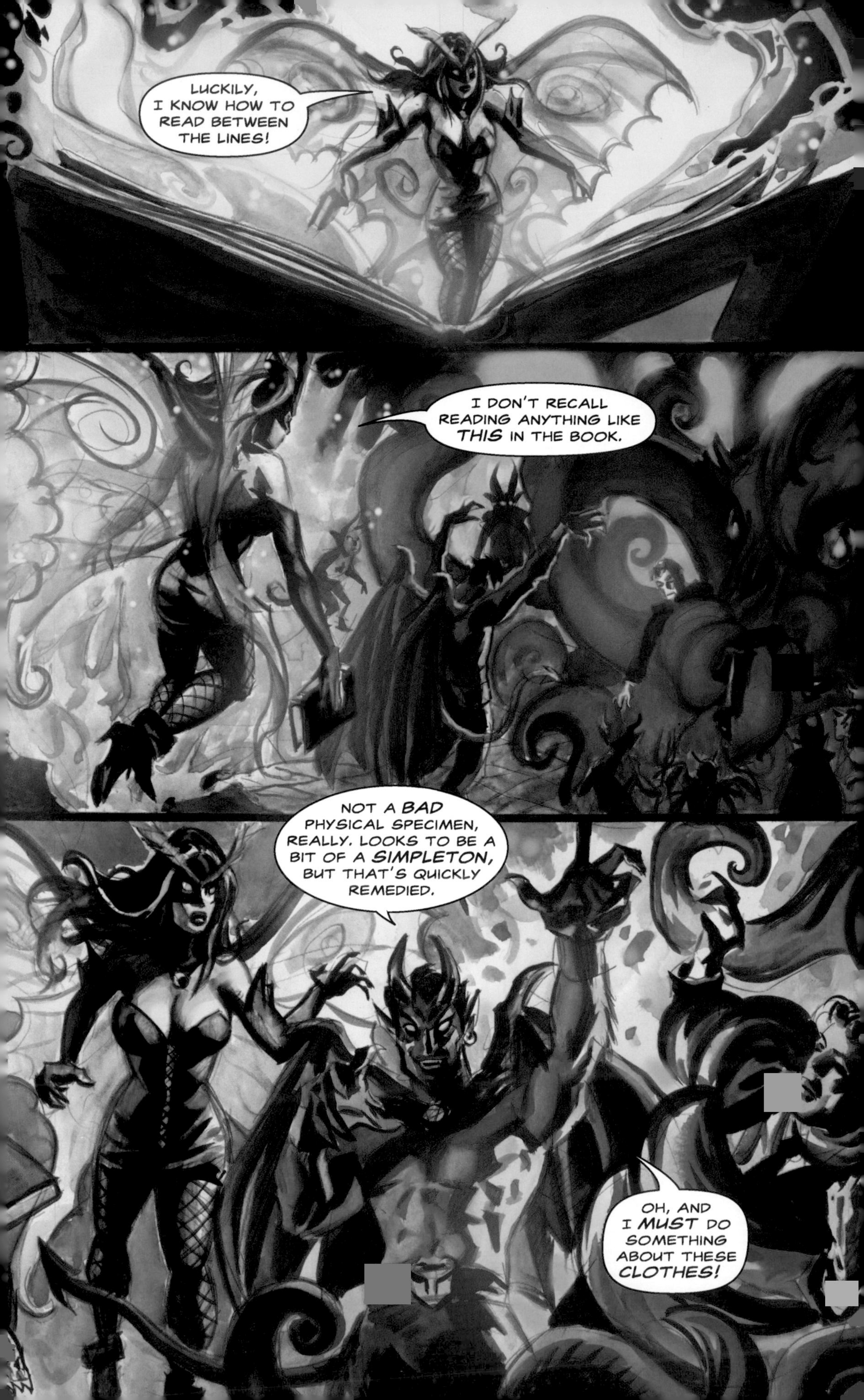
LUCKILY, I KNOW HOW TO READ BETWEEN THE LINES!
I DON'T RECALL READING ANYTHING LIKE *THIS* IN THE BOOK.
NOT A *BAD* PHYSICAL SPECIMEN, REALLY. LOOKS TO BE A BIT OF A *SIMPLETON*, BUT THAT'S QUICKLY REMEDIED.
OH, AND I *MUST* DO SOMETHING ABOUT THESE *CLOTHES!*

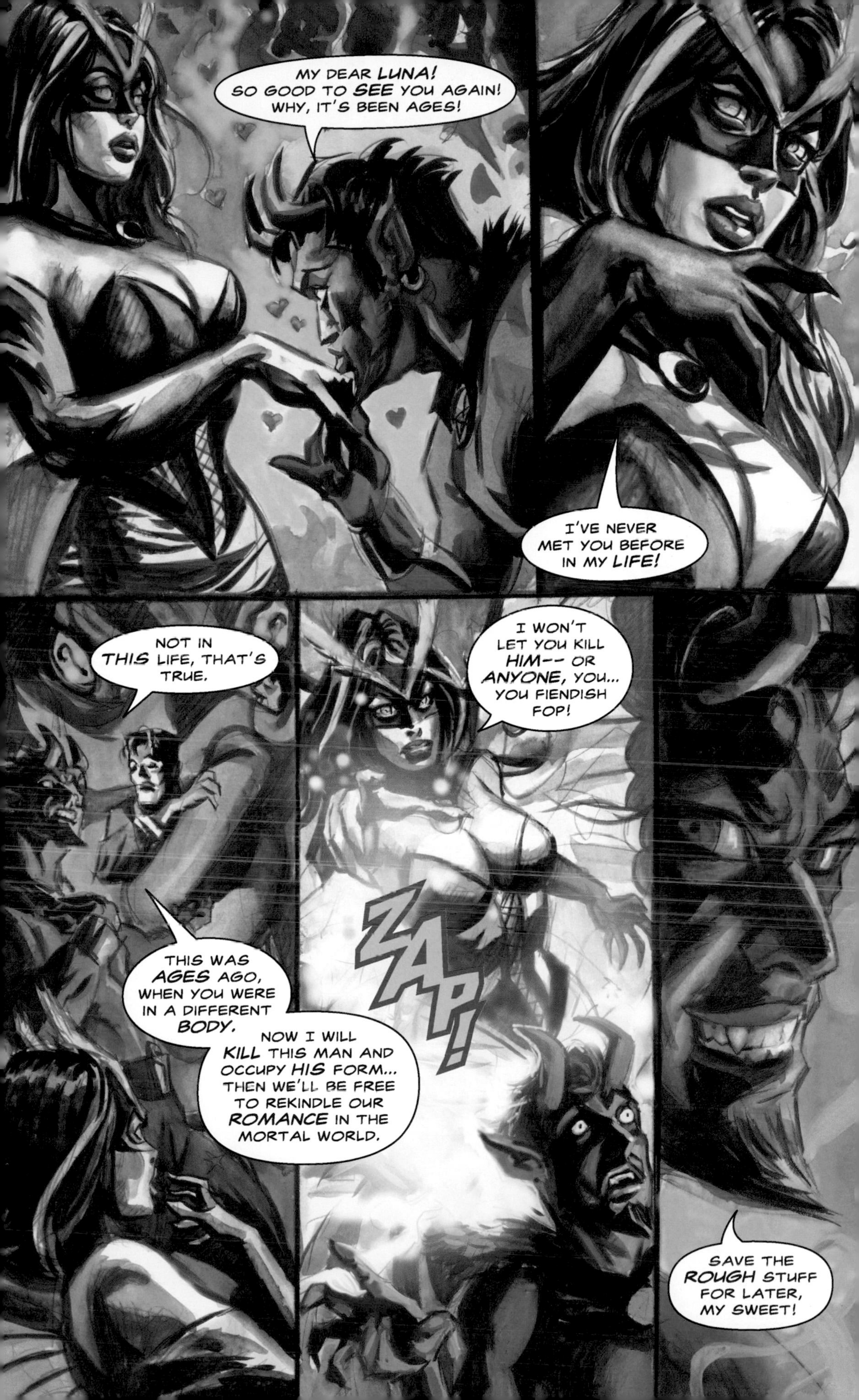
MY DEAR LUNA! SO GOOD TO SEE YOU AGAIN! WHY, IT'S BEEN AGES!
I'VE NEVER MET YOU BEFORE IN MY LIFE!
NOT IN THIS LIFE, THAT'S TRUE.
THIS WAS AGES AGO, WHEN YOU WERE IN A DIFFERENT BODY.
NOW I WILL KILL THIS MAN AND OCCUPY HIS FORM... THEN WE'LL BE FREE TO REKINDLE OUR ROMANCE IN THE MORTAL WORLD.
I WON'T LET YOU KILL HIM-- OR ANYONE, YOU... YOU FIENDISH FOP!
ZAP!
SAVE THE ROUGH STUFF FOR LATER, MY SWEET!

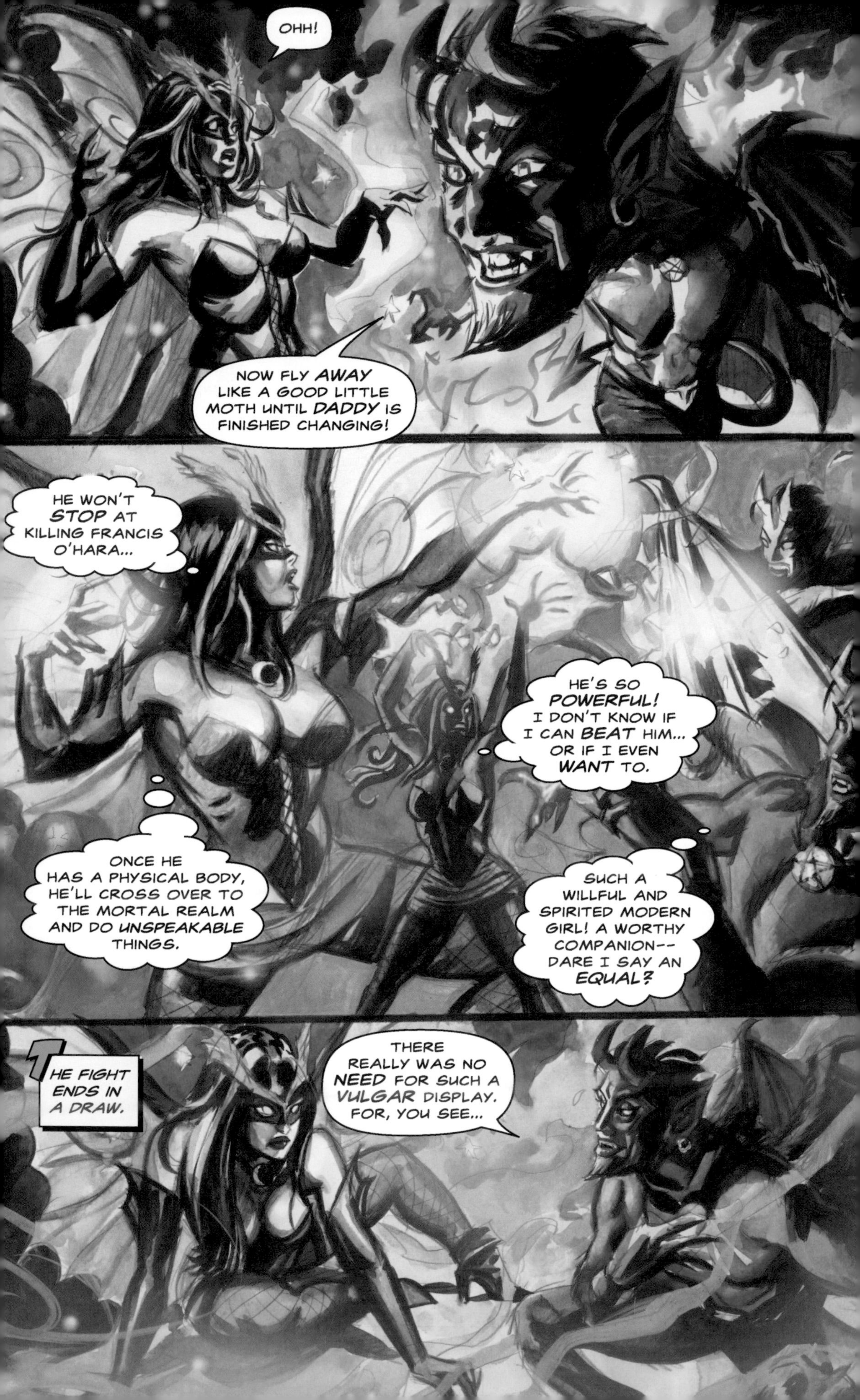
OHH!
NOW FLY AWAY LIKE A GOOD LITTLE MOTH UNTIL DADDY IS FINISHED CHANGING!
HE WON'T STOP AT KILLING FRANCIS O'HARA...
HE'S SO POWERFUL! I DON'T KNOW IF I CAN BEAT HIM... OR IF I EVEN WANT TO.
ONCE HE HAS A PHYSICAL BODY, HE'LL CROSS OVER TO THE MORTAL REALM AND DO UNSPEAKABLE THINGS.
SUCH A WILLFUL AND SPIRITED MODERN GIRL! A WORTHY COMPANION-- DARE I SAY AN EQUAL?
THE FIGHT ENDS IN A DRAW.
THERE REALLY WAS NO NEED FOR SUCH A VULGAR DISPLAY. FOR, YOU SEE...

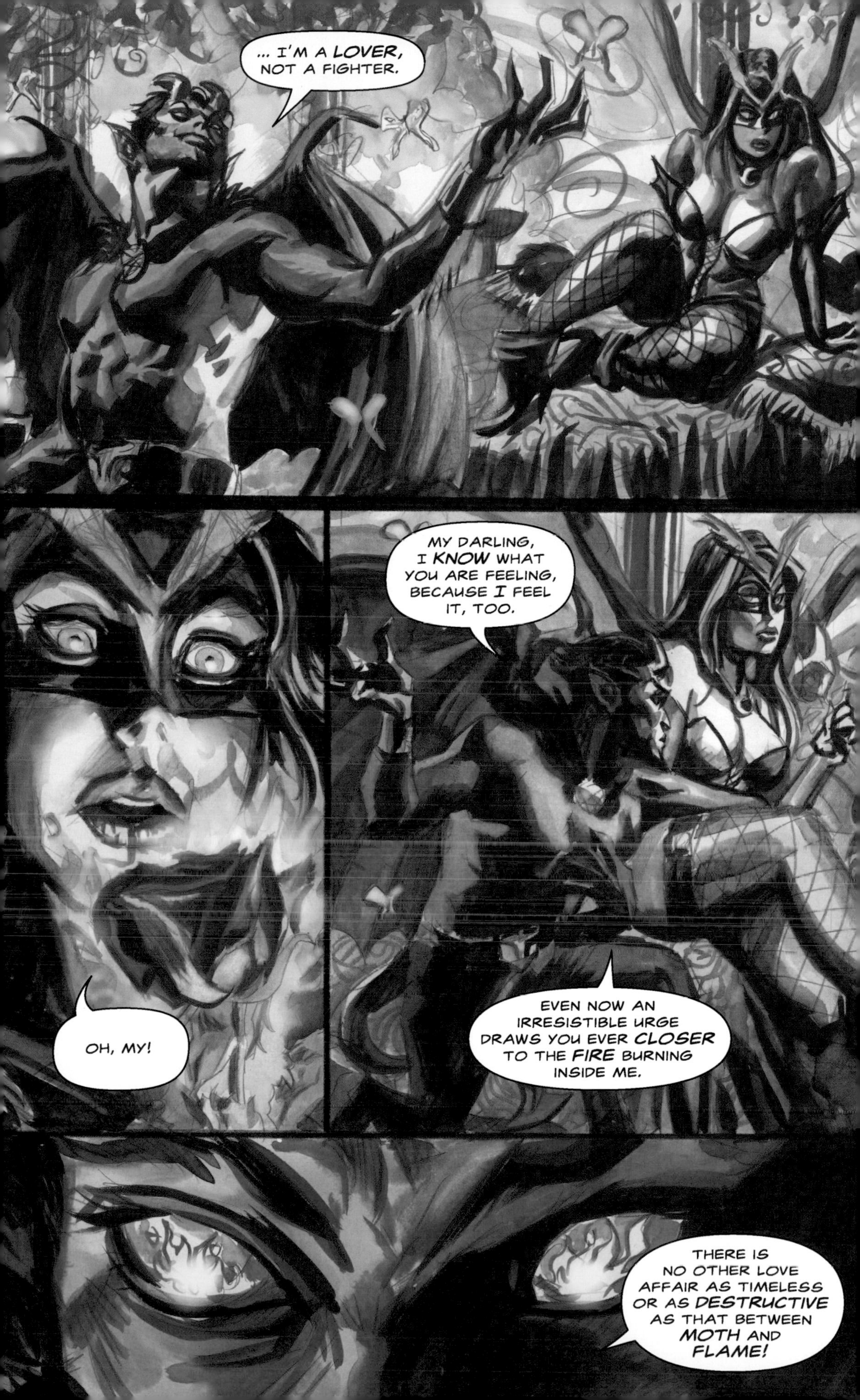
... I'M A LOVER, NOT A FIGHTER.
OH, MY!
MY DARLING, I KNOW WHAT YOU ARE FEELING, BECAUSE I FEEL IT, TOO.
EVEN NOW AN IRRESISTIBLE URGE DRAWS YOU EVER CLOSER TO THE FIRE BURNING INSIDE ME.
THERE IS NO OTHER LOVE AFFAIR AS TIMELESS OR AS DESTRUCTIVE AS THAT BETWEEN MOTH AND FLAME!

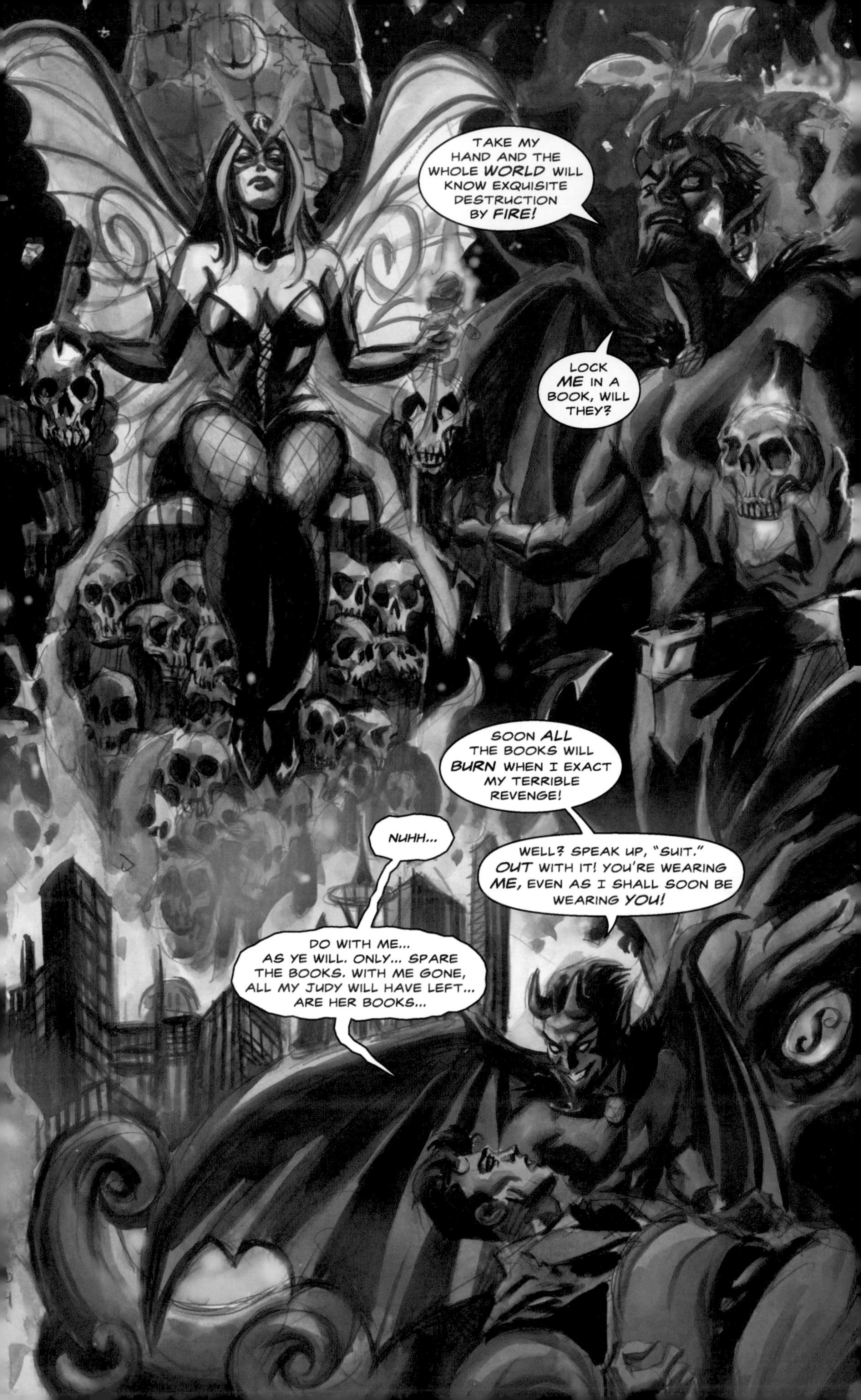
TAKE MY HAND AND THE WHOLE WORLD WILL KNOW EXQUISITE DESTRUCTION BY FIRE!
LOCK ME IN A BOOK, WILL THEY?
SOON ALL THE BOOKS WILL BURN WHEN I EXACT MY TERRIBLE REVENGE!
NUHH...
WELL? SPEAK UP, "SUIT." OUT WITH IT! YOU'RE WEARING ME, EVEN AS I SHALL SOON BE WEARING YOU!
DO WITH ME... AS YE WILL. ONLY... SPARE THE BOOKS. WITH ME GONE, ALL MY JUDY WILL HAVE LEFT... ARE HER BOOKS...

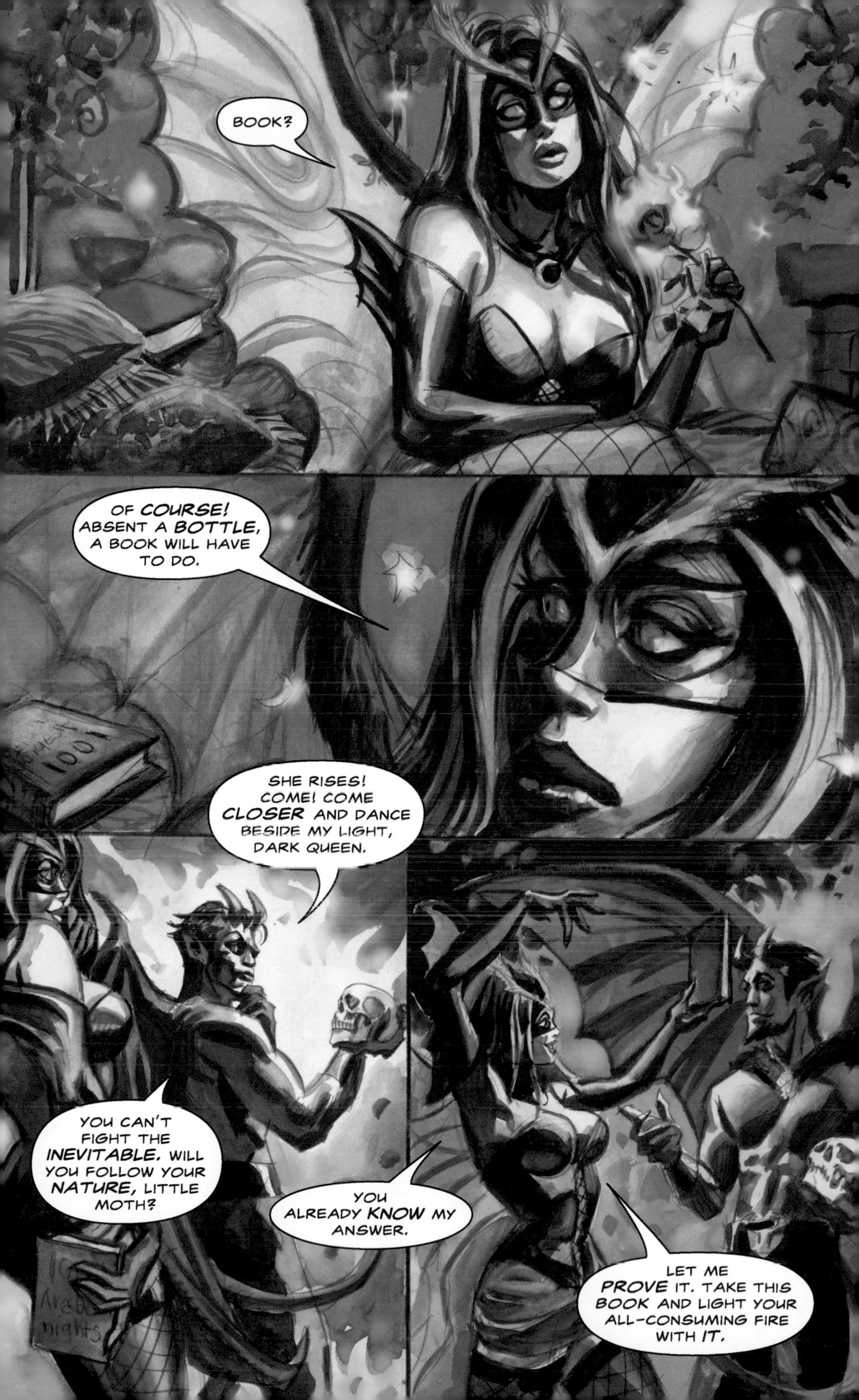
BOOK?
OF COURSE! ABSENT A BOTTLE, A BOOK WILL HAVE TO DO.
SHE RISES! COME! COME CLOSER AND DANCE BESIDE MY LIGHT, DARK QUEEN.
YOU CAN'T FIGHT THE INEVITABLE. WILL YOU FOLLOW YOUR NATURE, LITTLE MOTH?
YOU ALREADY KNOW MY ANSWER.
LET ME PROVE IT. TAKE THIS BOOK AND LIGHT YOUR ALL-CONSUMING FIRE WITH IT.

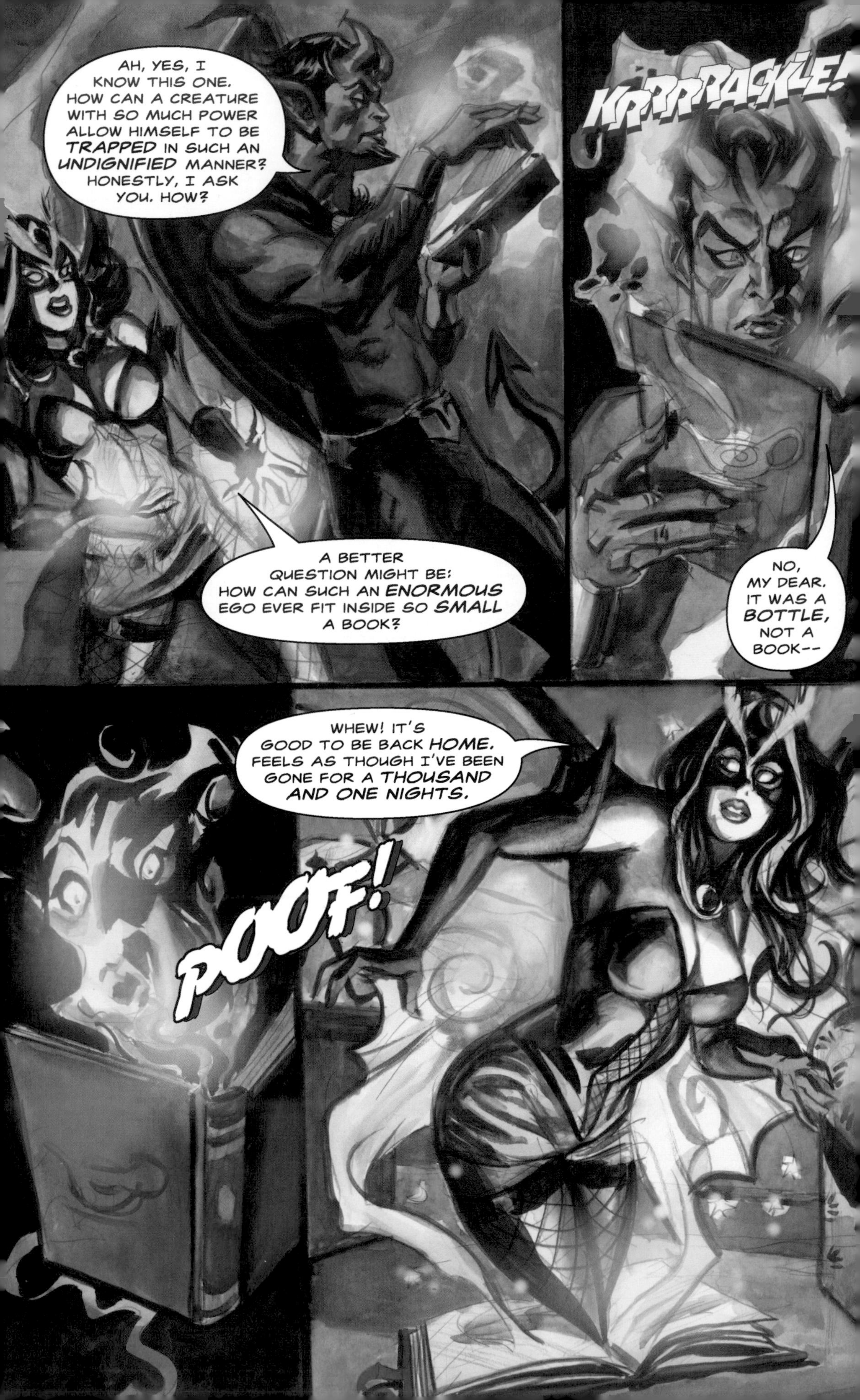
AH, YES, I KNOW THIS ONE. HOW CAN A CREATURE WITH SO MUCH POWER ALLOW HIMSELF TO BE TRAPPED IN SUCH AN UNDIGNIFIED MANNER? HONESTLY, I ASK YOU. HOW?
A BETTER QUESTION MIGHT BE: HOW CAN SUCH AN ENORMOUS EGO EVER FIT INSIDE SO SMALL A BOOK?
KRRRRACKLE!
NO, MY DEAR. IT WAS A BOTTLE, NOT A BOOK--
WHEW! IT'S GOOD TO BE BACK HOME. FEELS AS THOUGH I'VE BEEN GONE FOR A THOUSAND AND ONE NIGHTS.
POOF!

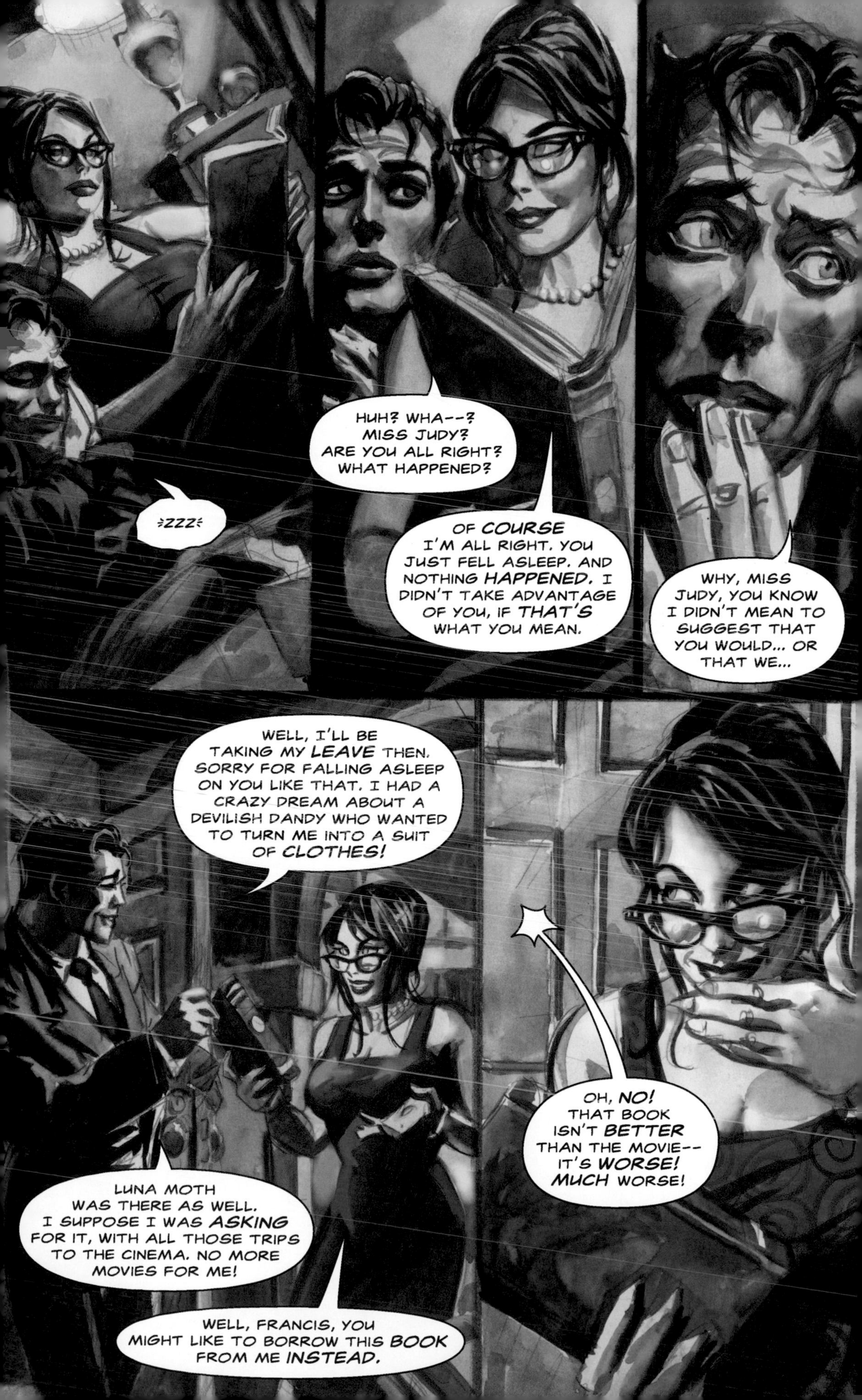

HUH? WHA--? MISS JUDY? ARE YOU ALL RIGHT? WHAT HAPPENED?
ZZZ
OF COURSE I'M ALL RIGHT. YOU JUST FELL ASLEEP. AND NOTHING HAPPENED. I DIDN'T TAKE ADVANTAGE OF YOU, IF THAT'S WHAT YOU MEAN.
WHY, MISS JUDY, YOU KNOW I DIDN'T MEAN TO SUGGEST THAT YOU WOULD... OR THAT WE...
WELL, I'LL BE TAKING MY LEAVE THEN. SORRY FOR FALLING ASLEEP ON YOU LIKE THAT. I HAD A CRAZY DREAM ABOUT A DEVILISH DANDY WHO WANTED TO TURN ME INTO A SUIT OF CLOTHES!
LUNA MOTH WAS THERE AS WELL. I SUPPOSE I WAS ASKING FOR IT, WITH ALL THOSE TRIPS TO THE CINEMA. NO MORE MOVIES FOR ME!
WELL, FRANCIS, YOU MIGHT LIKE TO BORROW THIS BOOK FROM ME INSTEAD.
OH, NO! THAT BOOK ISN'T BETTER THAN THE MOVIE-- IT'S WORSE! MUCH WORSE!

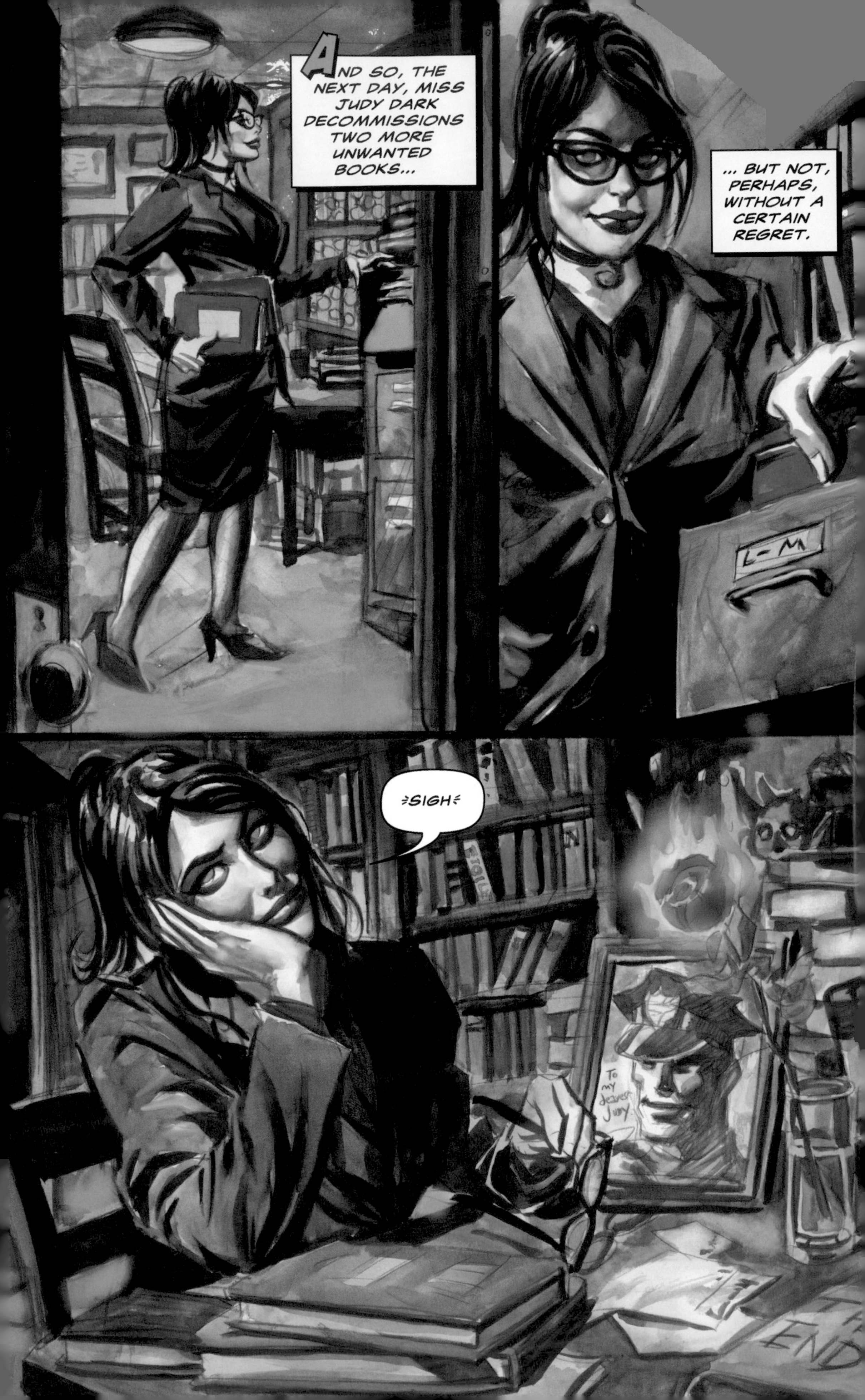
AND SO, THE NEXT DAY, MISS JUDY DARK DECOMMISSIONS TWO MORE UNWANTED BOOKS...
... BUT NOT, PERHAPS, WITHOUT A CERTAIN REGRET.
L-M
SIGH
To my dearest Judy

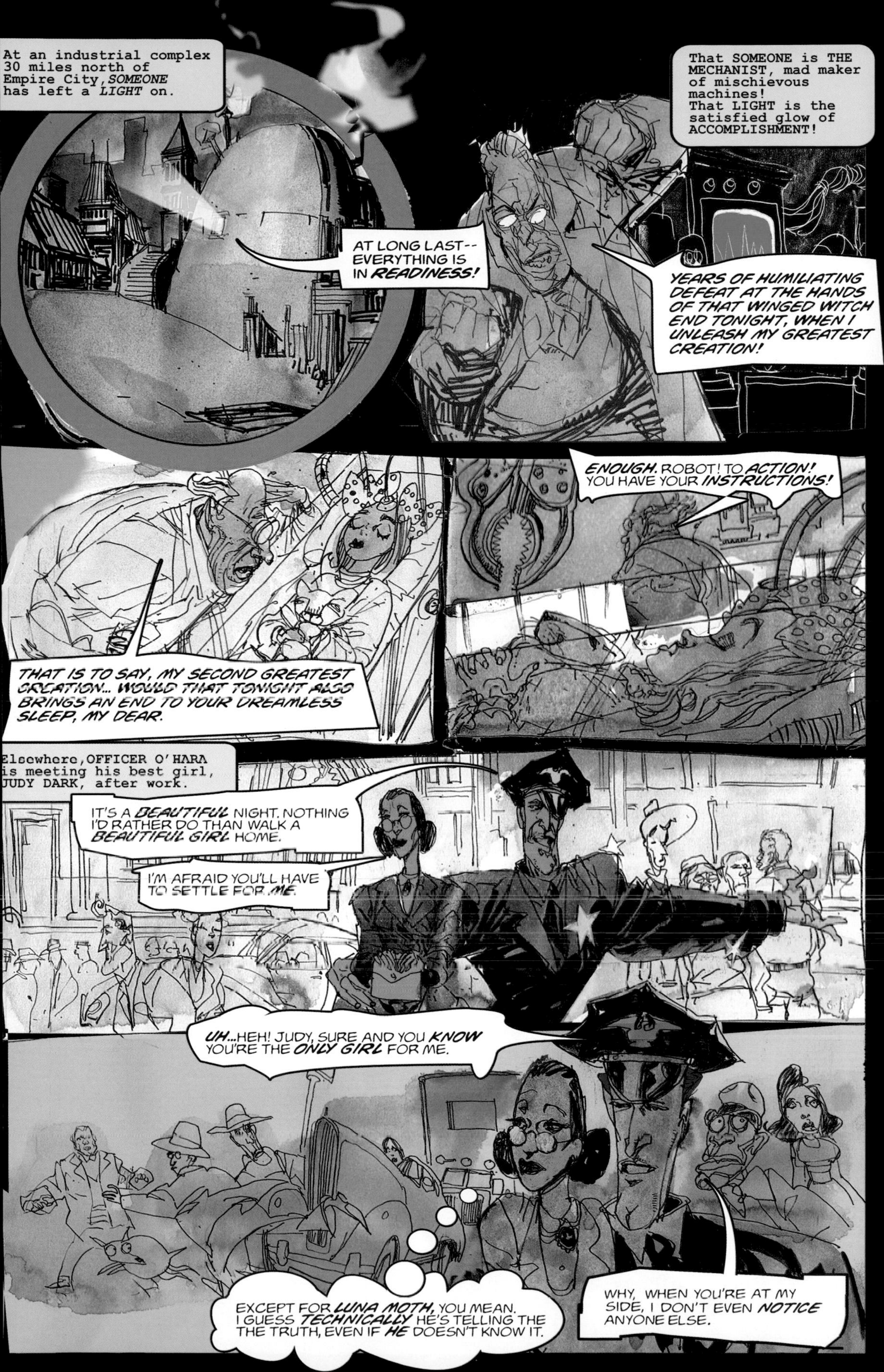

At an industrial complex 30 miles north of Empire City, SOMEONE has left a LIGHT on.
AT LONG LAST-- EVERYTHING IS IN READINESS!
That SOMEONE is THE MECHANIST, mad maker of mischievous machines! That LIGHT is the satisfied glow of ACCOMPLISHMENT!
YEARS OF HUMILIATING DEFEAT AT THE HANDS OF THAT WINGED WITCH END TONIGHT, WHEN I UNLEASH MY GREATEST CREATION!
THAT IS TO SAY, MY SECOND GREATEST CREATION... WOULD THAT TONIGHT ALSO BRINGS AN END TO YOUR DREAMLESS SLEEP, MY DEAR.
ENOUGH. ROBOT! TO ACTION! YOU HAVE YOUR INSTRUCTIONS!
Elsewhere, OFFICER O'HARA is meeting his best girl, JUDY DARK, after work.
IT'S A BEAUTIFUL NIGHT. NOTHING I'D RATHER DO THAN WALK A BEAUTIFUL GIRL HOME.
I'M AFRAID YOU'LL HAVE TO SETTLE FOR ME.
UH...HEH! JUDY, SURE AND YOU KNOW YOU'RE THE ONLY GIRL FOR ME.
EXCEPT FOR LUNA MOTH, YOU MEAN. I GUESS TECHNICALLY HE'S TELLING THE THE TRUTH, EVEN IF HE DOESN'T KNOW IT.
WHY, WHEN YOU'RE AT MY SIDE, I DON'T EVEN NOTICE ANYONE ELSE.

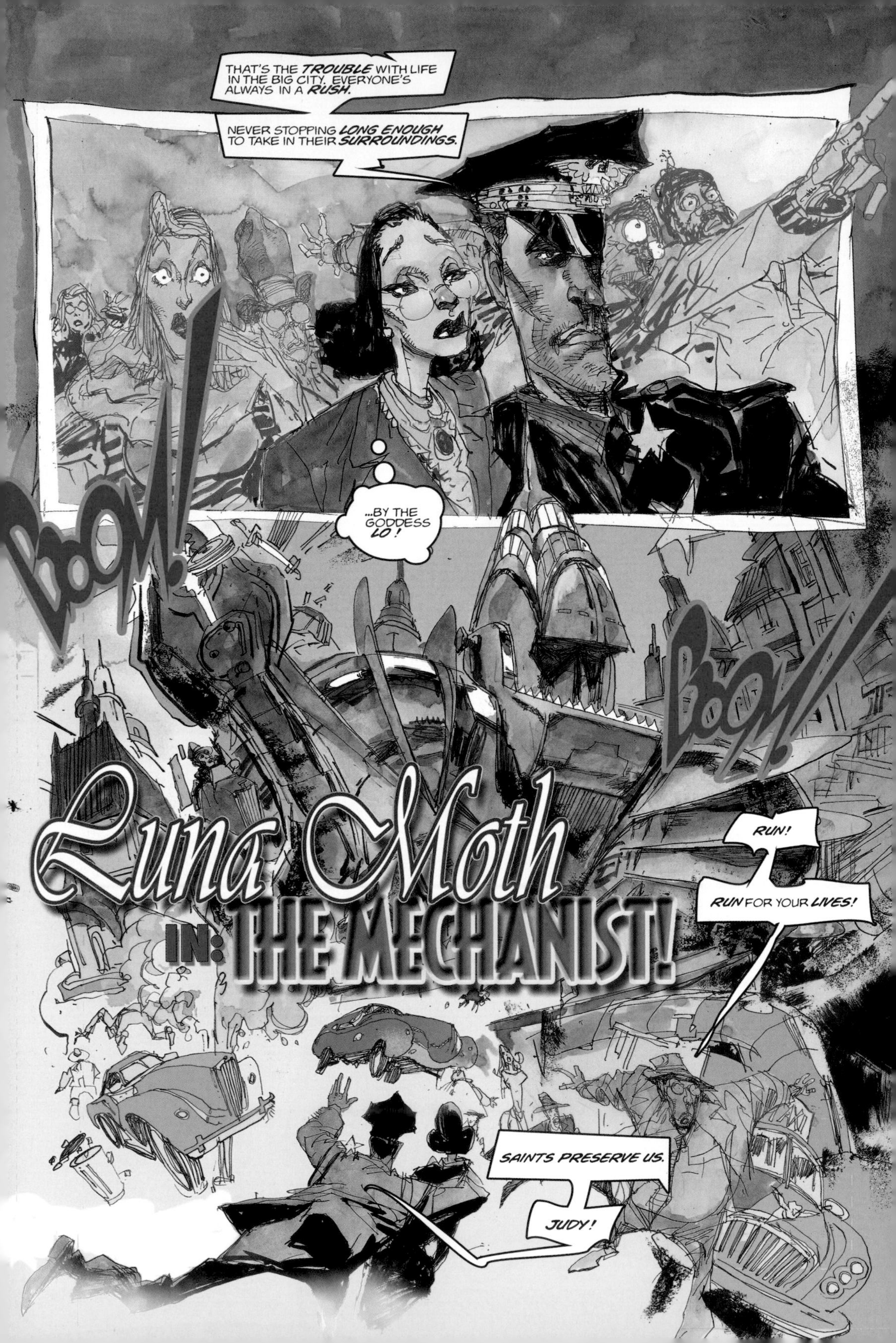

THAT'S THE TROUBLE WITH LIFE IN THE BIG CITY. EVERYONE'S ALWAYS IN A RUSH.
NEVER STOPPING LONG ENOUGH TO TAKE IN THEIR SURROUNDINGS.
...BY THE GODDESS LO!
BOOM!
BOOM!
Luna Moth
IN: THE MECHANIST!
RUN!
RUN FOR YOUR LIVES!
SAINTS PRESERVE US.
JUDY!

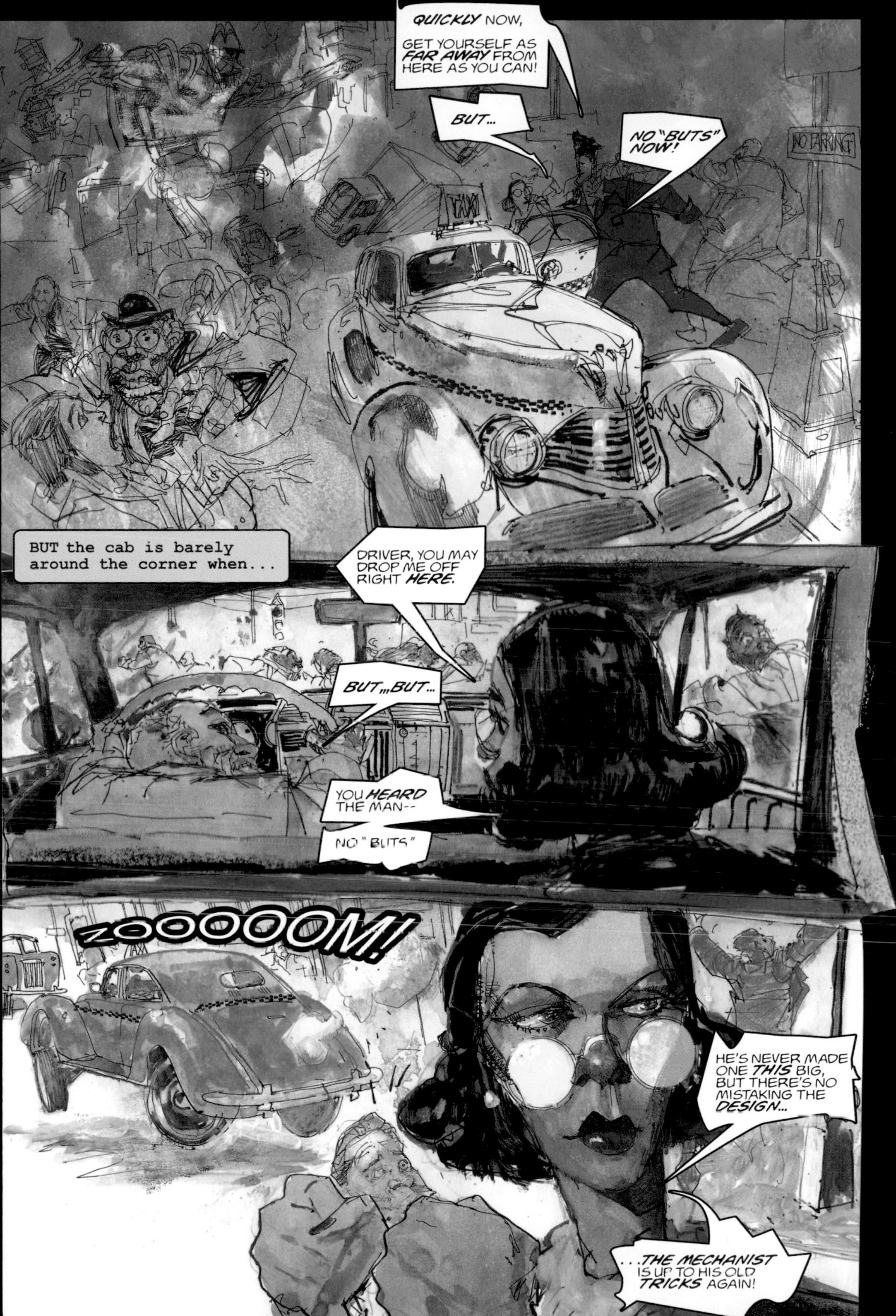
QUICKLY NOW, GET YOURSELF AS FAR AWAY FROM HERE AS YOU CAN!
BUT...
NO "BUTS" NOW!
NO PARKING
TAXI
BUT the cab is barely around the corner when...
DRIVER, YOU MAY DROP ME OFF RIGHT HERE.
BUT,,, BUT...
YOU HEARD THE MAN--
NO "BUTS"
ZOOOOOOM!
HE'S NEVER MADE ONE THIS BIG, BUT THERE'S NO MISTAKING THE DESIGN...
...THE MECHANIST IS UP TO HIS OLD TRICKS AGAIN!

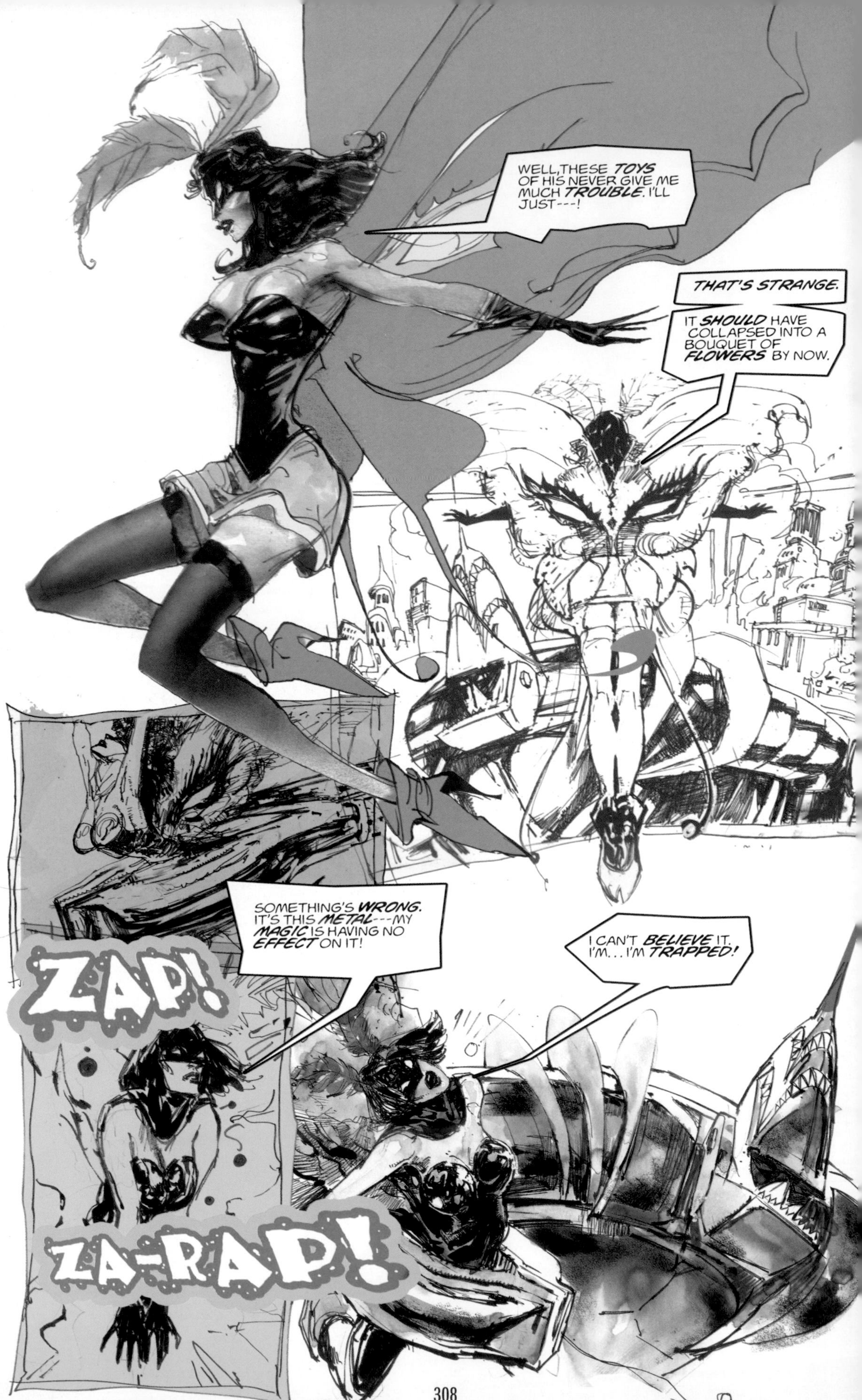
WELL, THESE TOYS OF HIS NEVER GIVE ME MUCH TROUBLE. I'LL JUST---!
THAT'S STRANGE.
IT SHOULD HAVE COLLAPSED INTO A BOUQUET OF FLOWERS BY NOW.
ZAP!
SOMETHING'S WRONG. IT'S THIS METAL---MY MAGIC IS HAVING NO EFFECT ON IT!
ZA-RAP!
I CAN'T BELIEVE IT. I'M... I'M TRAPPED!

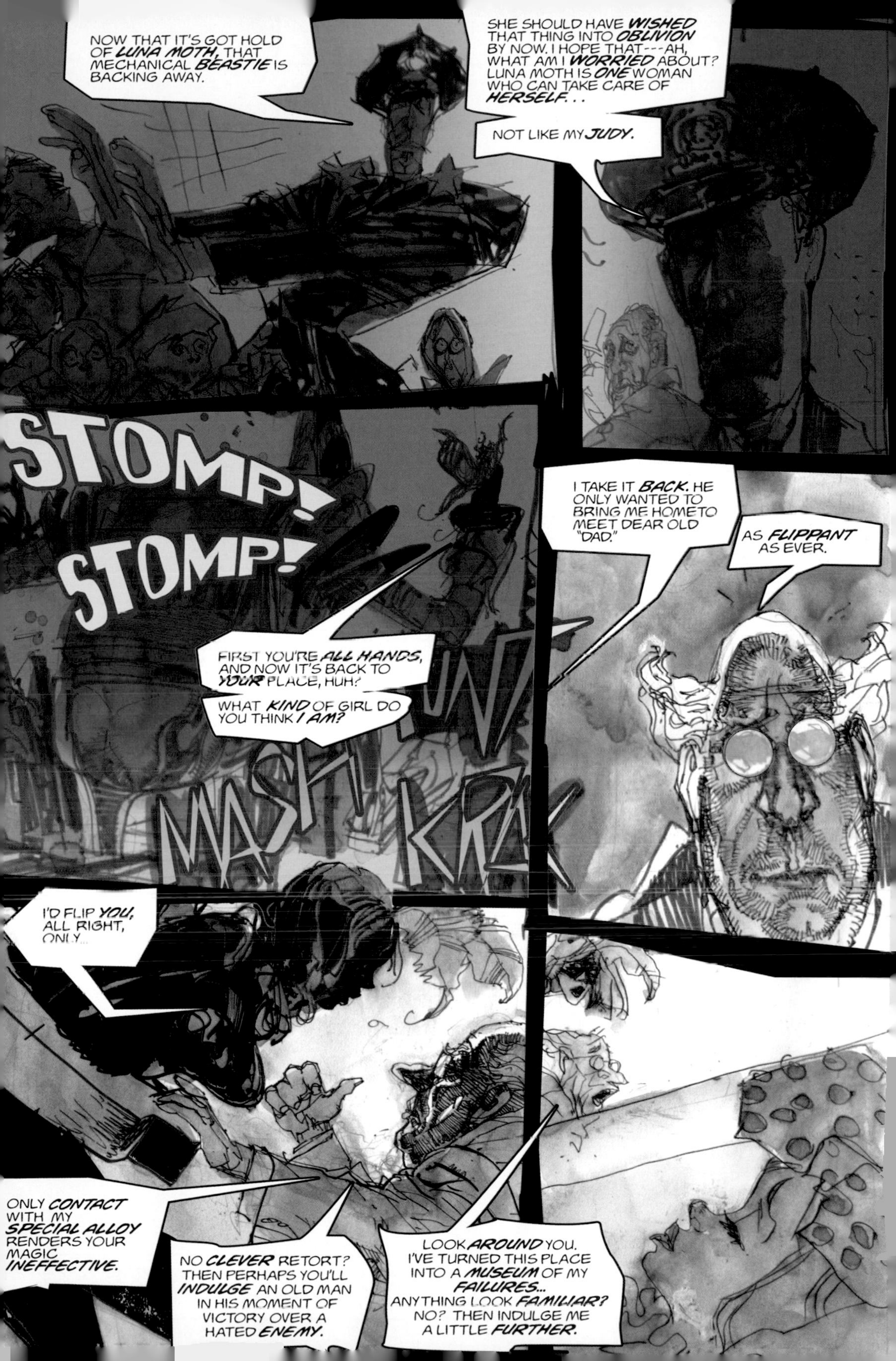

NOW THAT IT'S GOT HOLD OF LUNA MOTH, THAT MECHANICAL BEASTIE IS BACKING AWAY.
SHE SHOULD HAVE WISHED THAT THING INTO OBLIVION BY NOW. I HOPE THAT---AH, WHAT AM I WORRIED ABOUT? LUNA MOTH IS ONE WOMAN WHO CAN TAKE CARE OF HERSELF. . .
NOT LIKE MY JUDY.
STOMP! STOMP!
FIRST YOU'RE ALL HANDS, AND NOW IT'S BACK TO YOUR PLACE, HUH?
WHAT KIND OF GIRL DO YOU THINK I AM?
MASH
KRAK
I TAKE IT BACK. HE ONLY WANTED TO BRING ME HOME TO MEET DEAR OLD "DAD."
AS FLIPPANT AS EVER.
I'D FLIP YOU, ALL RIGHT, ONLY...
ONLY CONTACT WITH MY SPECIAL ALLOY RENDERS YOUR MAGIC INEFFECTIVE.
NO CLEVER RETORT? THEN PERHAPS YOU'LL INDULGE AN OLD MAN IN HIS MOMENT OF VICTORY OVER A HATED ENEMY.
LOOK AROUND YOU. I'VE TURNED THIS PLACE INTO A MUSEUM OF MY FAILURES... ANYTHING LOOK FAMILIAR? NO? THEN INDULGE ME A LITTLE FURTHER.

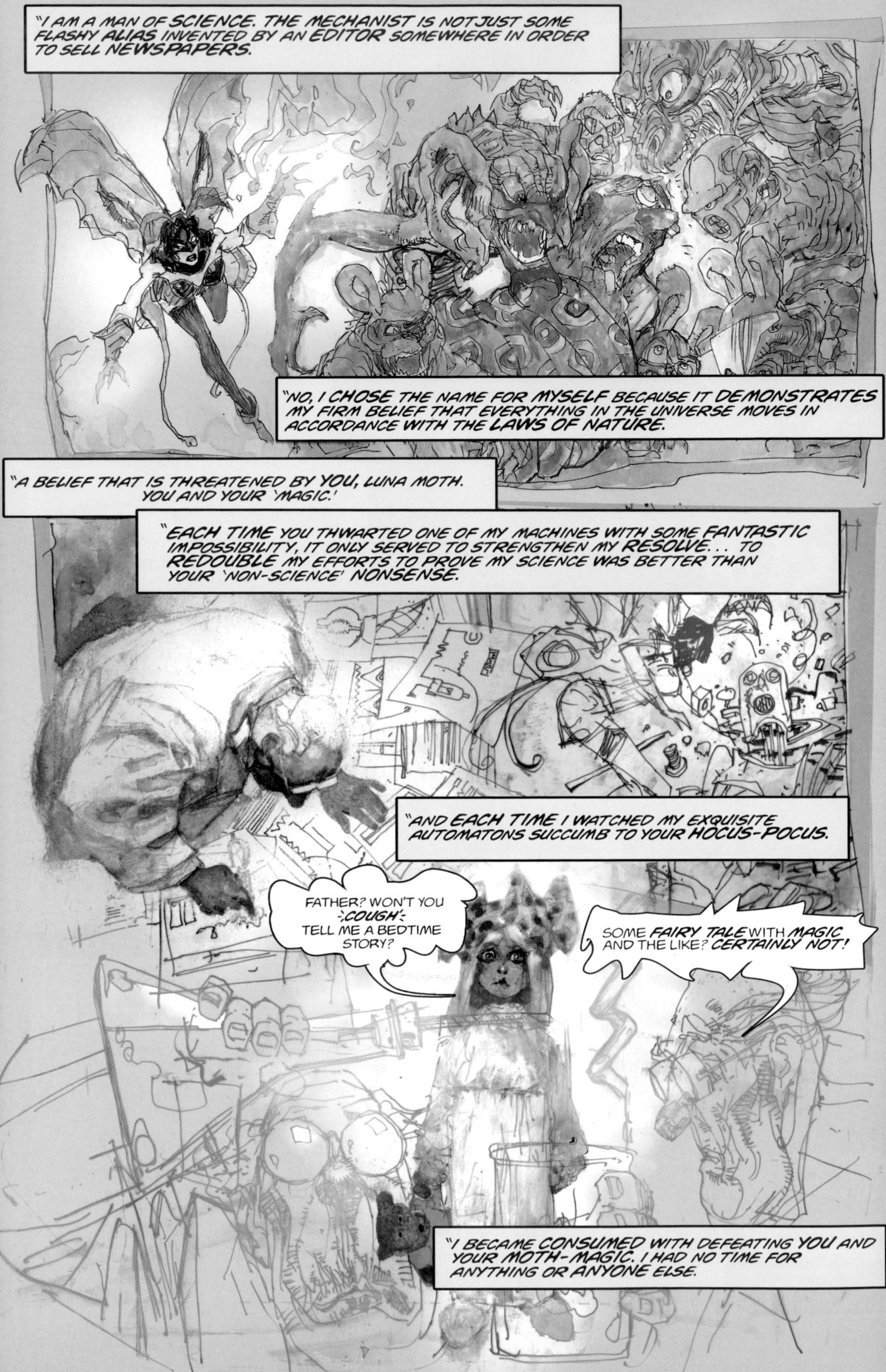
"I AM A MAN OF SCIENCE. THE MECHANIST IS NOT JUST SOME FLASHY ALIAS INVENTED BY AN EDITOR SOMEWHERE IN ORDER TO SELL NEWSPAPERS.
"NO, I CHOSE THE NAME FOR MYSELF BECAUSE IT DEMONSTRATES MY FIRM BELIEF THAT EVERYTHING IN THE UNIVERSE MOVES IN ACCORDANCE WITH THE LAWS OF NATURE.
"A BELIEF THAT IS THREATENED BY YOU, LUNA MOTH. YOU AND YOUR 'MAGIC.'
"EACH TIME YOU THWARTED ONE OF MY MACHINES WITH SOME FANTASTIC IMPOSSIBILITY, IT ONLY SERVED TO STRENGTHEN MY RESOLVE... TO REDOUBLE MY EFFORTS TO PROVE MY SCIENCE WAS BETTER THAN YOUR 'NON-SCIENCE' NONSENSE.
"AND EACH TIME I WATCHED MY EXQUISITE AUTOMATONS SUCCUMB TO YOUR HOCUS-POCUS.
FATHER? WON'T YOU *COUGH* TELL ME A BEDTIME STORY?
SOME FAIRY TALE WITH MAGIC AND THE LIKE? CERTAINLY NOT!
"I BECAME CONSUMED WITH DEFEATING YOU AND YOUR MOTH-MAGIC. I HAD NO TIME FOR ANYTHING OR ANYONE ELSE.

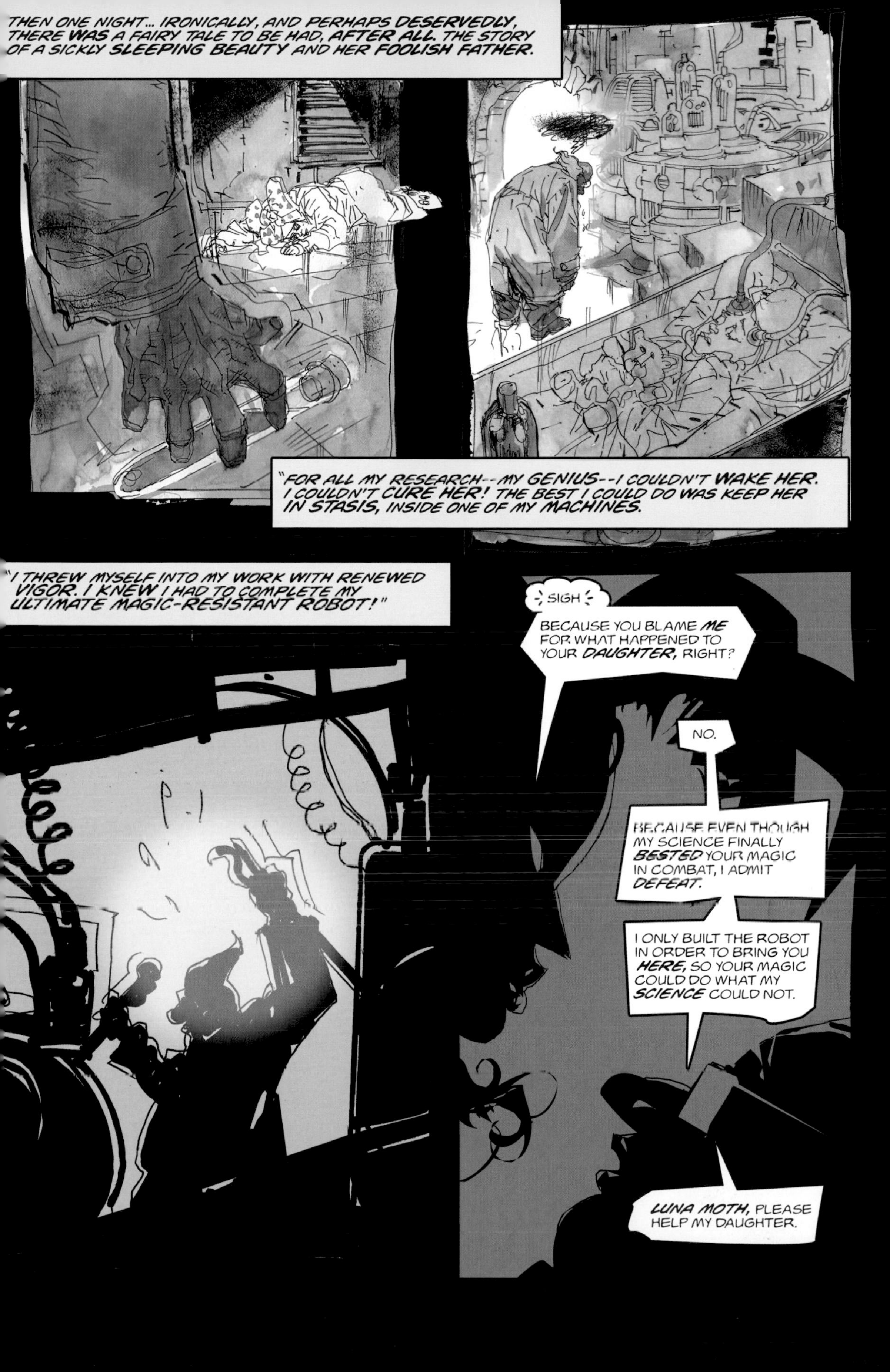
THEN ONE NIGHT... IRONICALLY, AND PERHAPS DESERVEDLY, THERE WAS A FAIRY TALE TO BE HAD, AFTER ALL. THE STORY OF A SICKLY SLEEPING BEAUTY AND HER FOOLISH FATHER.
"FOR ALL MY RESEARCH--MY GENIUS--I COULDN'T WAKE HER. I COULDN'T CURE HER! THE BEST I COULD DO WAS KEEP HER IN STASIS, INSIDE ONE OF MY MACHINES.
"I THREW MYSELF INTO MY WORK WITH RENEWED VIGOR. I KNEW I HAD TO COMPLETE MY ULTIMATE MAGIC-RESISTANT ROBOT!"
SIGH
BECAUSE YOU BLAME ME FOR WHAT HAPPENED TO YOUR DAUGHTER, RIGHT?
NO.
BECAUSE EVEN THOUGH MY SCIENCE FINALLY BESTED YOUR MAGIC IN COMBAT, I ADMIT DEFEAT.
I ONLY BUILT THE ROBOT IN ORDER TO BRING YOU HERE, SO YOUR MAGIC COULD DO WHAT MY SCIENCE COULD NOT.
LUNA MOTH, PLEASE HELP MY DAUGHTER.

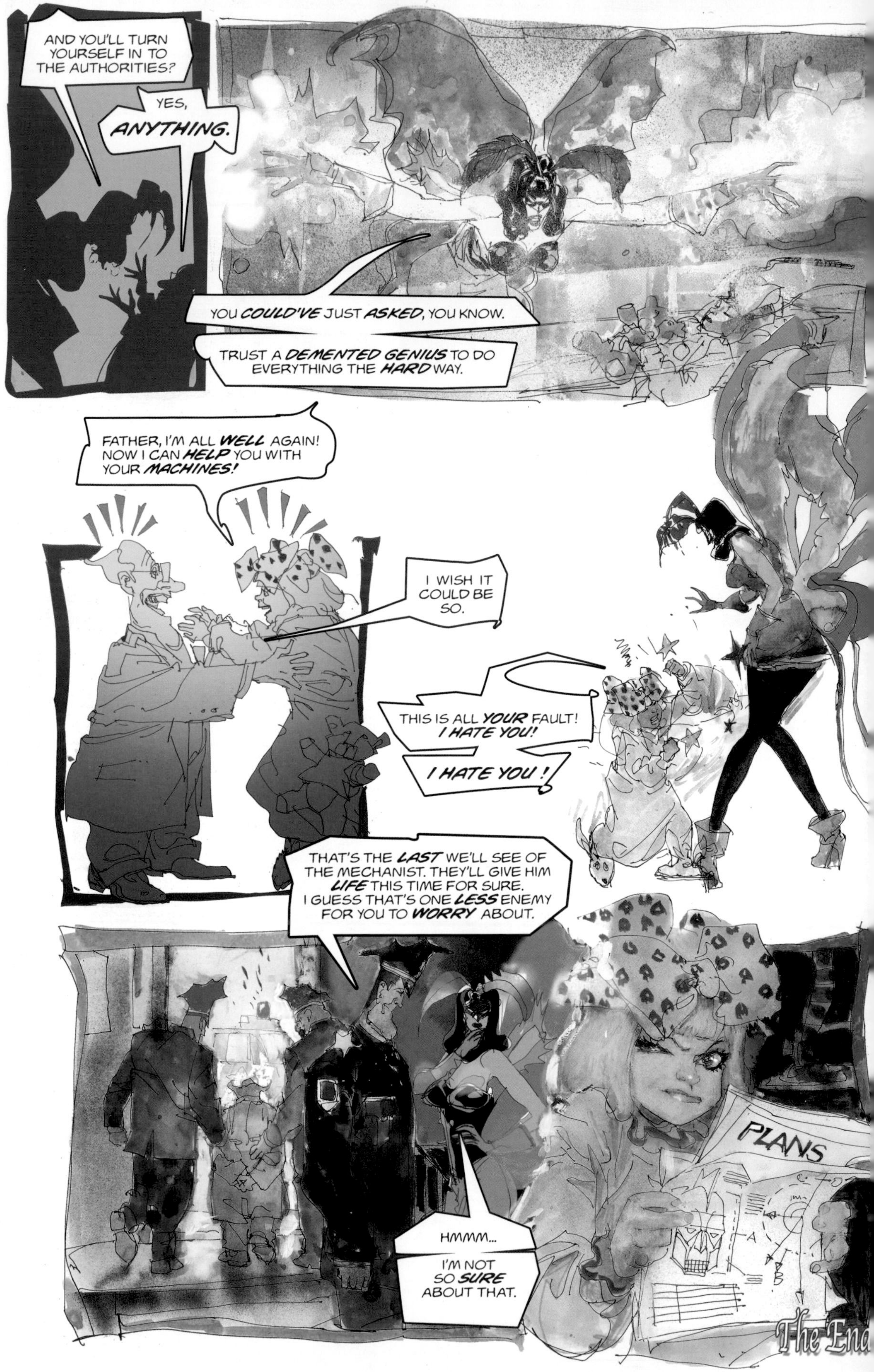
AND YOU'LL TURN YOURSELF IN TO THE AUTHORITIES?
YES, ANYTHING.
YOU COULD'VE JUST ASKED, YOU KNOW.
TRUST A DEMENTED GENIUS TO DO EVERYTHING THE HARD WAY.
FATHER, I'M ALL WELL AGAIN! NOW I CAN HELP YOU WITH YOUR MACHINES!
I WISH IT COULD BE SO.
THIS IS ALL YOUR FAULT! I HATE YOU!
I HATE YOU!
THAT'S THE LAST WE'LL SEE OF THE MECHANIST. THEY'LL GIVE HIM LIFE THIS TIME FOR SURE. I GUESS THAT'S ONE LESS ENEMY FOR YOU TO WORRY ABOUT.
PLANS
HMMM...
I'M NOT SO SURE ABOUT THAT.
The End

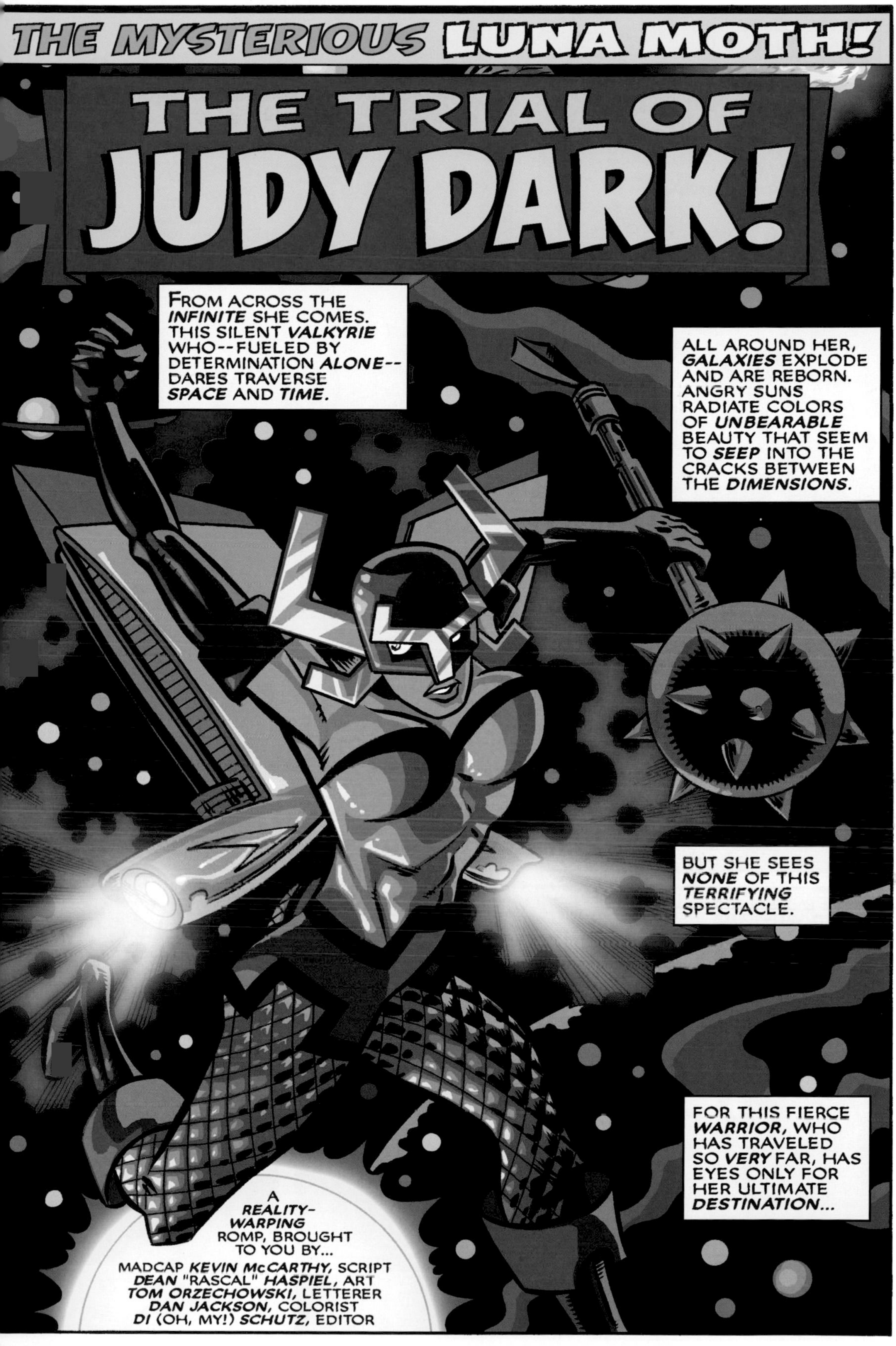
THE MYSTERIOUS LUNA MOTH!
THE TRIAL OF JUDY DARK!
FROM ACROSS THE INFINITE SHE COMES. THIS SILENT VALKYRIE WHO--FUELED BY DETERMINATION ALONE--DARES TRAVERSE SPACE AND TIME.
ALL AROUND HER, GALAXIES EXPLODE AND ARE REBORN. ANGRY SUNS RADIATE COLORS OF UNBEARABLE BEAUTY THAT SEEM TO SEEP INTO THE CRACKS BETWEEN THE DIMENSIONS.
BUT SHE SEES NONE OF THIS TERRIFYING SPECTACLE.
FOR THIS FIERCE WARRIOR, WHO HAS TRAVELED SO VERY FAR, HAS EYES ONLY FOR HER ULTIMATE DESTINATION...
A REALITY-WARPING ROMP, BROUGHT TO YOU BY...
MADCAP KEVIN McCARTHY, SCRIPT
DEAN "RASCAL" HASPIEL, ART
TOM ORZECHOWSKI, LETTERER
DAN JACKSON, COLORIST
DI (OH, MY!) SCHUTZ, EDITOR

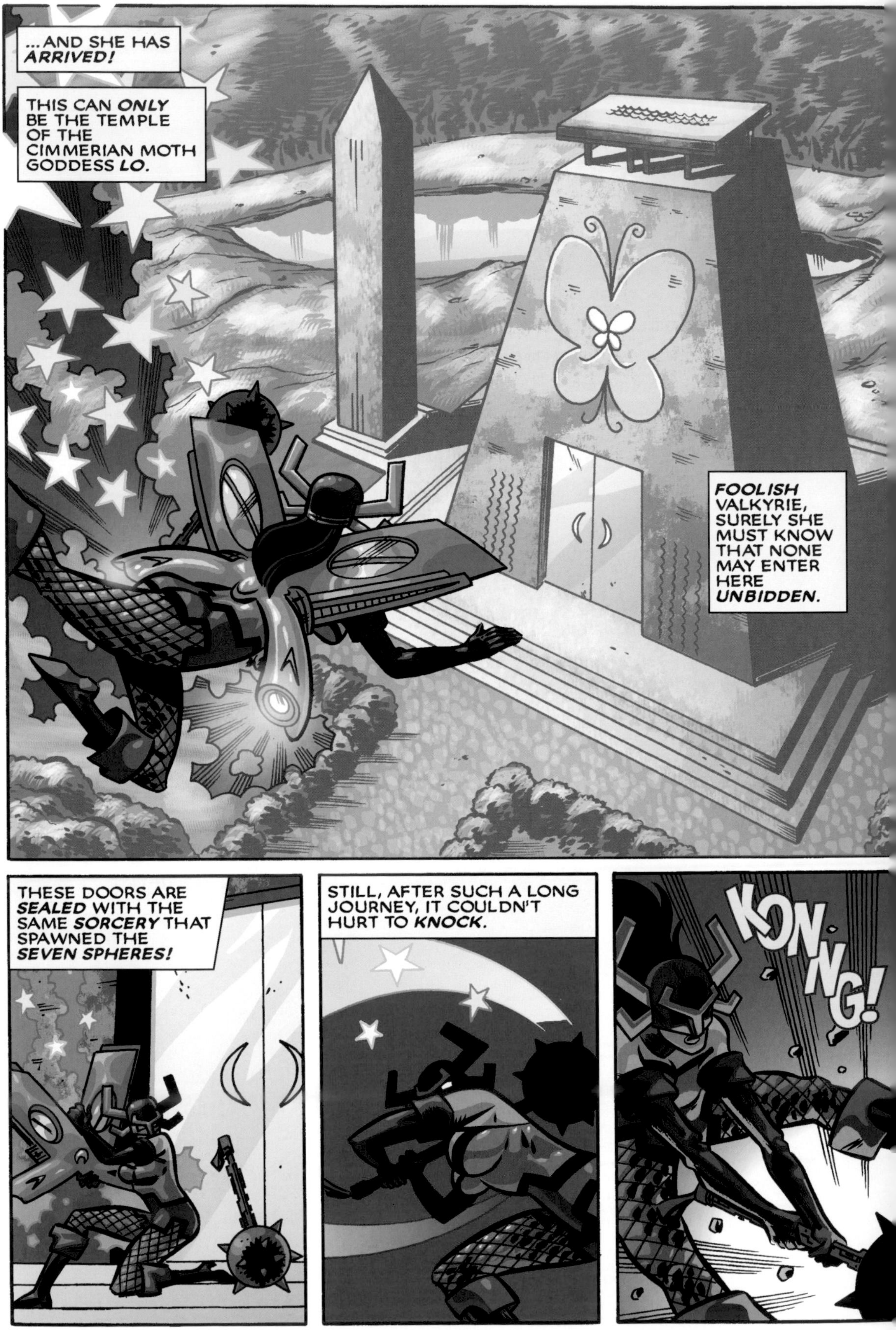
...AND SHE HAS *ARRIVED!*
THIS CAN *ONLY* BE THE TEMPLE OF THE CIMMERIAN MOTH GODDESS *LO.*
*FOOLISH* VALKYRIE, SURELY SHE MUST KNOW THAT NONE MAY ENTER HERE *UNBIDDEN.*
THESE DOORS ARE *SEALED* WITH THE SAME *SORCERY* THAT SPAWNED THE *SEVEN SPHERES!*
STILL, AFTER SUCH A LONG JOURNEY, IT COULDN'T HURT TO *KNOCK.*
KONNG!

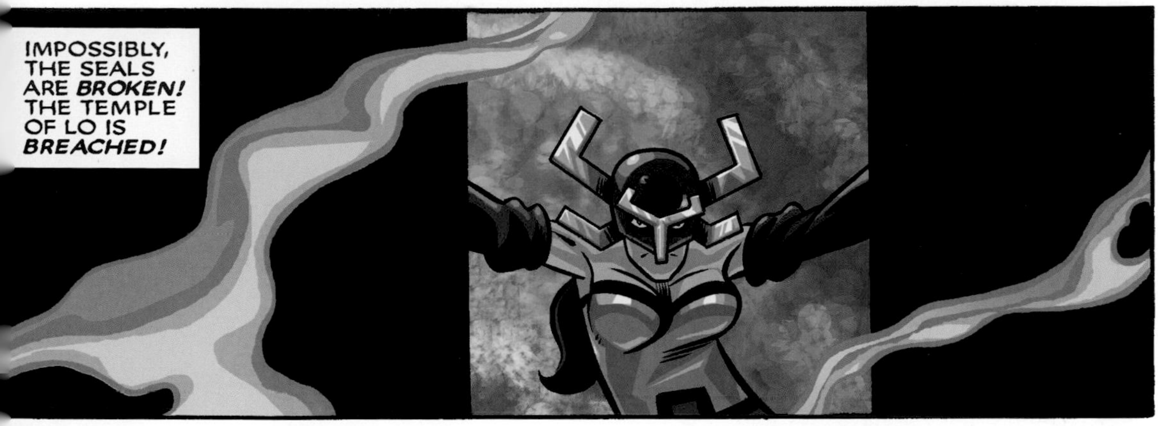
IMPOSSIBLY, THE SEALS ARE BROKEN! THE TEMPLE OF LO IS BREACHED!

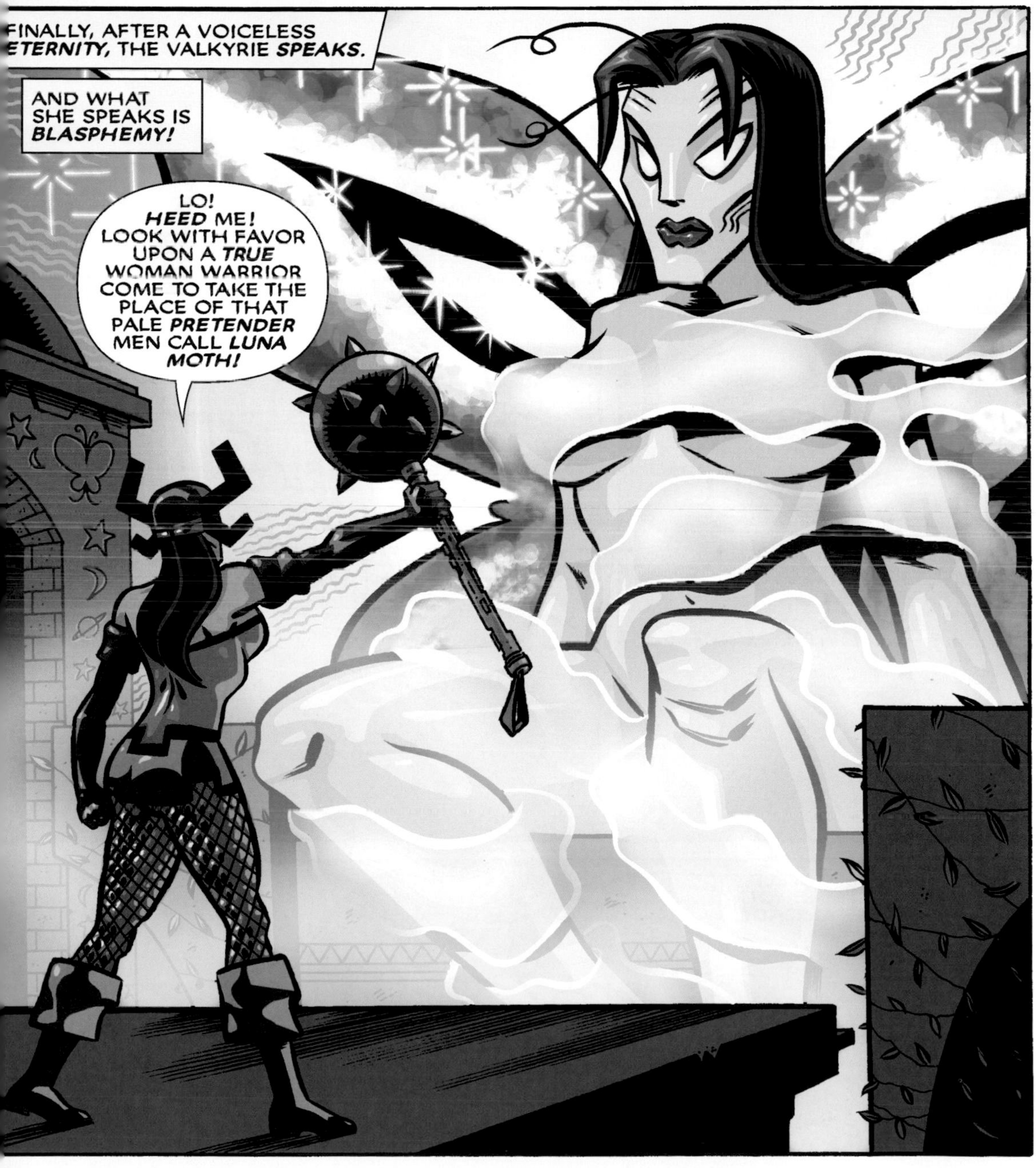
FINALLY, AFTER A VOICELESS ETERNITY, THE VALKYRIE SPEAKS.
AND WHAT SHE SPEAKS IS BLASPHEMY!
LO! HEED ME! LOOK WITH FAVOR UPON A TRUE WOMAN WARRIOR COME TO TAKE THE PLACE OF THAT PALE PRETENDER MEN CALL LUNA MOTH!

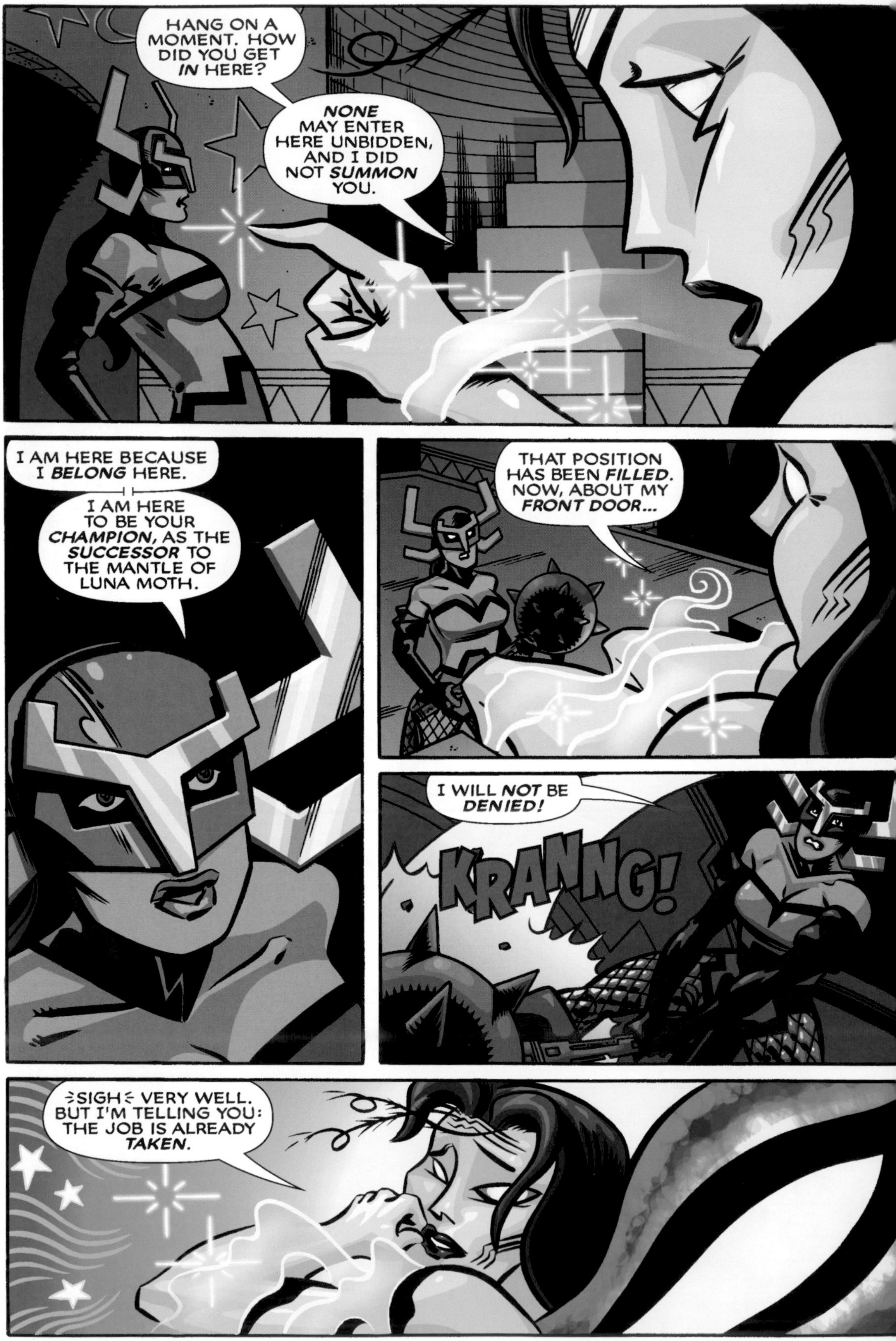
HANG ON A MOMENT. HOW DID YOU GET *IN* HERE?
*NONE* MAY ENTER HERE UNBIDDEN, AND I DID NOT *SUMMON* YOU.
I AM HERE BECAUSE I *BELONG* HERE.
I AM HERE TO BE YOUR *CHAMPION*, AS THE *SUCCESSOR* TO THE MANTLE OF LUNA MOTH.
THAT POSITION HAS BEEN *FILLED*. NOW, ABOUT MY *FRONT DOOR*...
I WILL *NOT* BE *DENIED!*
KRANNG!
⋟SIGH⋞ VERY WELL. BUT I'M TELLING YOU: THE JOB IS ALREADY *TAKEN*.

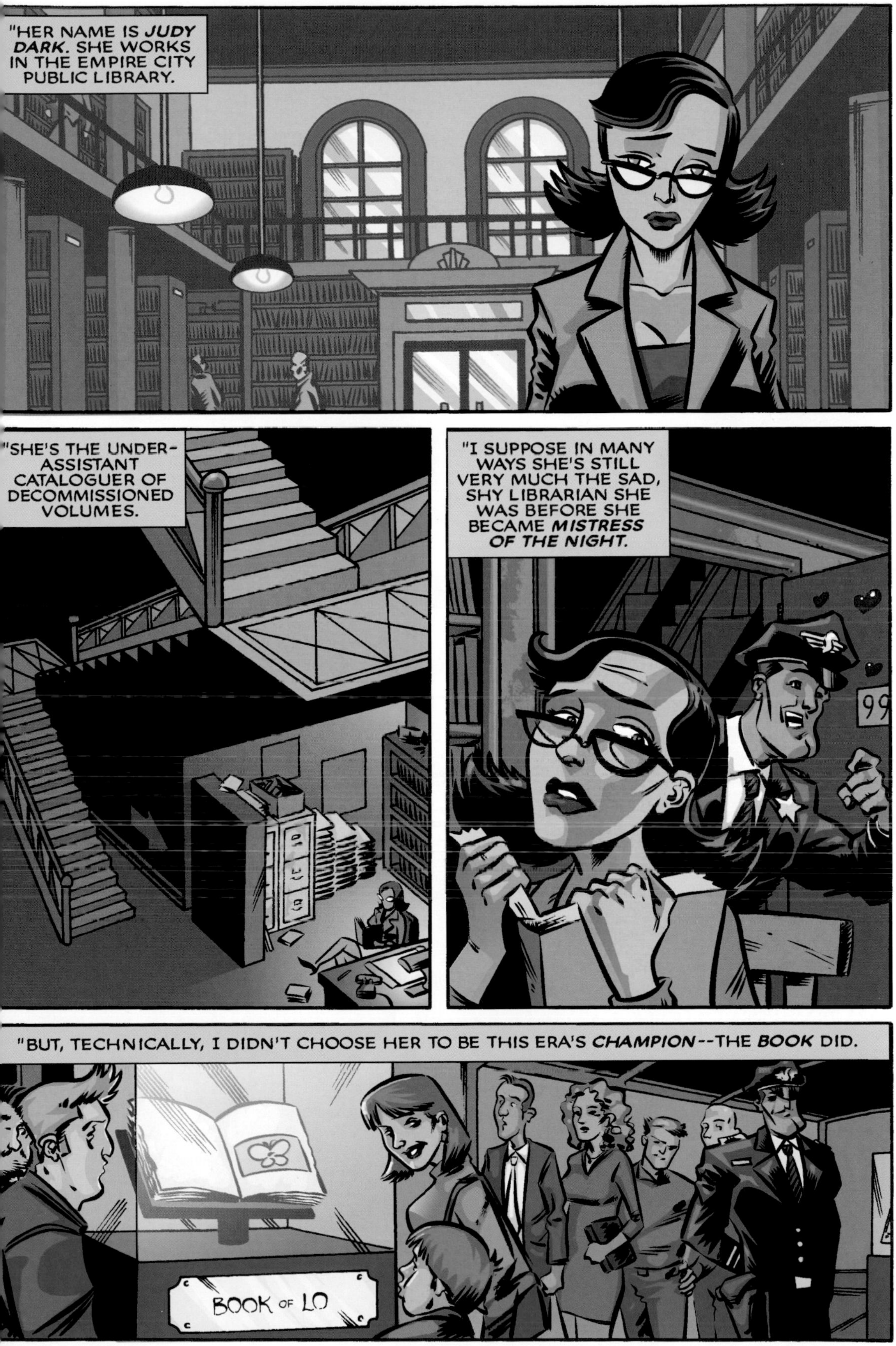
"HER NAME IS *JUDY DARK*. SHE WORKS IN THE EMPIRE CITY PUBLIC LIBRARY.
"SHE'S THE UNDER-ASSISTANT CATALOGUER OF DECOMMISSIONED VOLUMES.
"I SUPPOSE IN MANY WAYS SHE'S STILL VERY MUCH THE SAD, SHY LIBRARIAN SHE WAS BEFORE SHE BECAME *MISTRESS OF THE NIGHT*.
99
"BUT, TECHNICALLY, I DIDN'T CHOOSE HER TO BE THIS ERA'S *CHAMPION*--THE *BOOK* DID.
BOOK OF LO

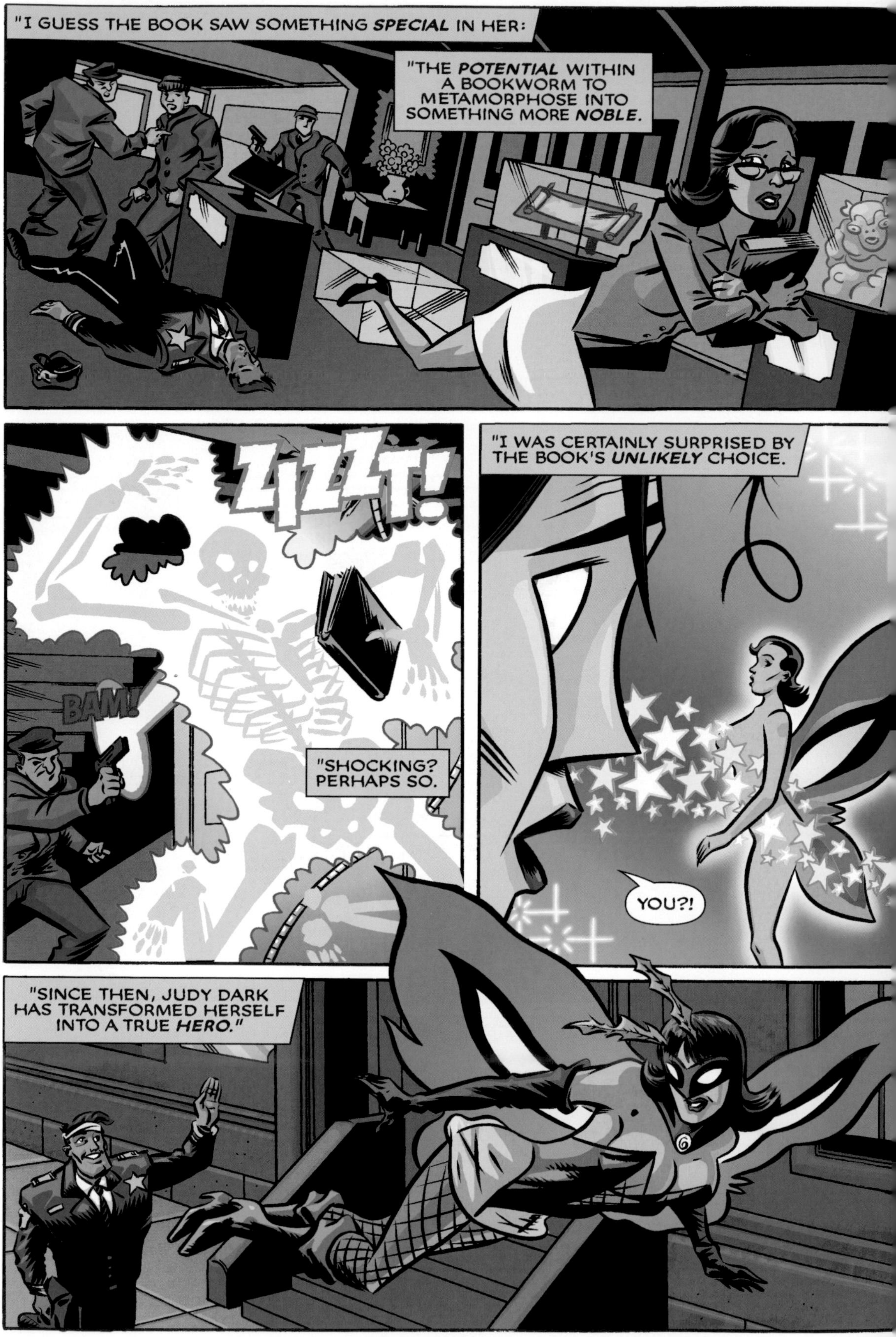
"I GUESS THE BOOK SAW SOMETHING SPECIAL IN HER:
"THE POTENTIAL WITHIN A BOOKWORM TO METAMORPHOSE INTO SOMETHING MORE NOBLE.
ZIZZT!
BAM!
"SHOCKING? PERHAPS SO.
"I WAS CERTAINLY SURPRISED BY THE BOOK'S UNLIKELY CHOICE.
YOU?!
"SINCE THEN, JUDY DARK HAS TRANSFORMED HERSELF INTO A TRUE HERO."

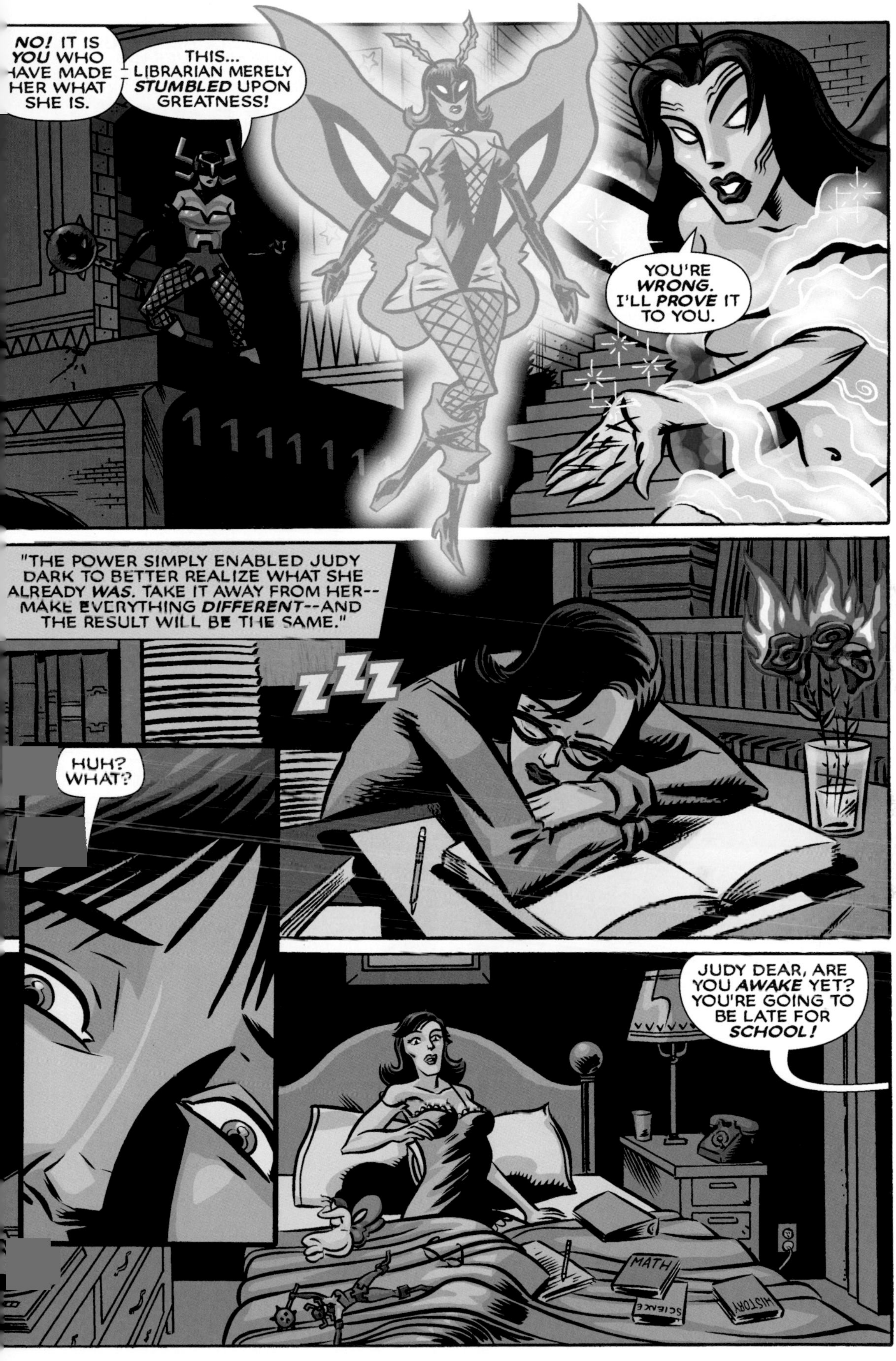
NO! IT IS YOU WHO HAVE MADE HER WHAT SHE IS.
THIS... LIBRARIAN MERELY STUMBLED UPON GREATNESS!
YOU'RE WRONG. I'LL PROVE IT TO YOU.
"THE POWER SIMPLY ENABLED JUDY DARK TO BETTER REALIZE WHAT SHE ALREADY WAS. TAKE IT AWAY FROM HER--MAKE EVERYTHING DIFFERENT--AND THE RESULT WILL BE THE SAME."
ZZZ
HUH? WHAT?
JUDY DEAR, ARE YOU AWAKE YET? YOU'RE GOING TO BE LATE FOR SCHOOL!
MATH
SCIENCE
HISTORY

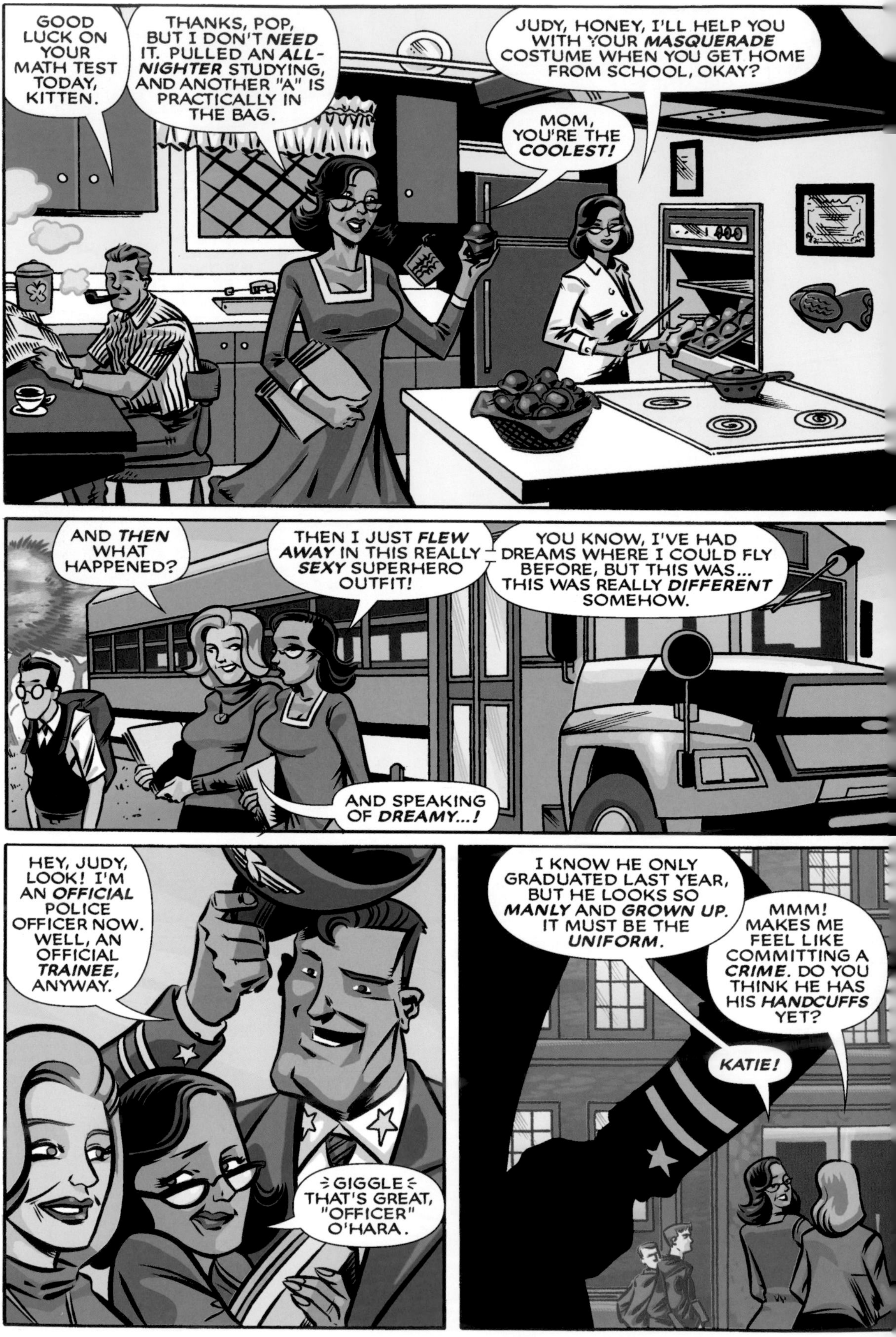
GOOD LUCK ON YOUR MATH TEST TODAY, KITTEN.
THANKS, POP, BUT I DON'T *NEED* IT. PULLED AN *ALL-NIGHTER* STUDYING, AND ANOTHER "A" IS PRACTICALLY IN THE BAG.
JUDY, HONEY, I'LL HELP YOU WITH YOUR *MASQUERADE* COSTUME WHEN YOU GET HOME FROM SCHOOL, OKAY?
MOM, YOU'RE THE *COOLEST!*
AND *THEN* WHAT HAPPENED?
THEN I JUST *FLEW AWAY* IN THIS REALLY *SEXY* SUPERHERO OUTFIT!
YOU KNOW, I'VE HAD DREAMS WHERE I COULD FLY BEFORE, BUT THIS WAS... THIS WAS REALLY *DIFFERENT* SOMEHOW.
AND SPEAKING OF *DREAMY...!*
HEY, JUDY, LOOK! I'M AN *OFFICIAL* POLICE OFFICER NOW. WELL, AN OFFICIAL *TRAINEE,* ANYWAY.
GIGGLE THAT'S GREAT, "OFFICER" O'HARA.
I KNOW HE ONLY GRADUATED LAST YEAR, BUT HE LOOKS SO *MANLY* AND *GROWN UP.* IT MUST BE THE *UNIFORM*.
MMM! MAKES ME FEEL LIKE COMMITTING A *CRIME.* DO YOU THINK HE HAS HIS *HANDCUFFS* YET?
*KATIE!*

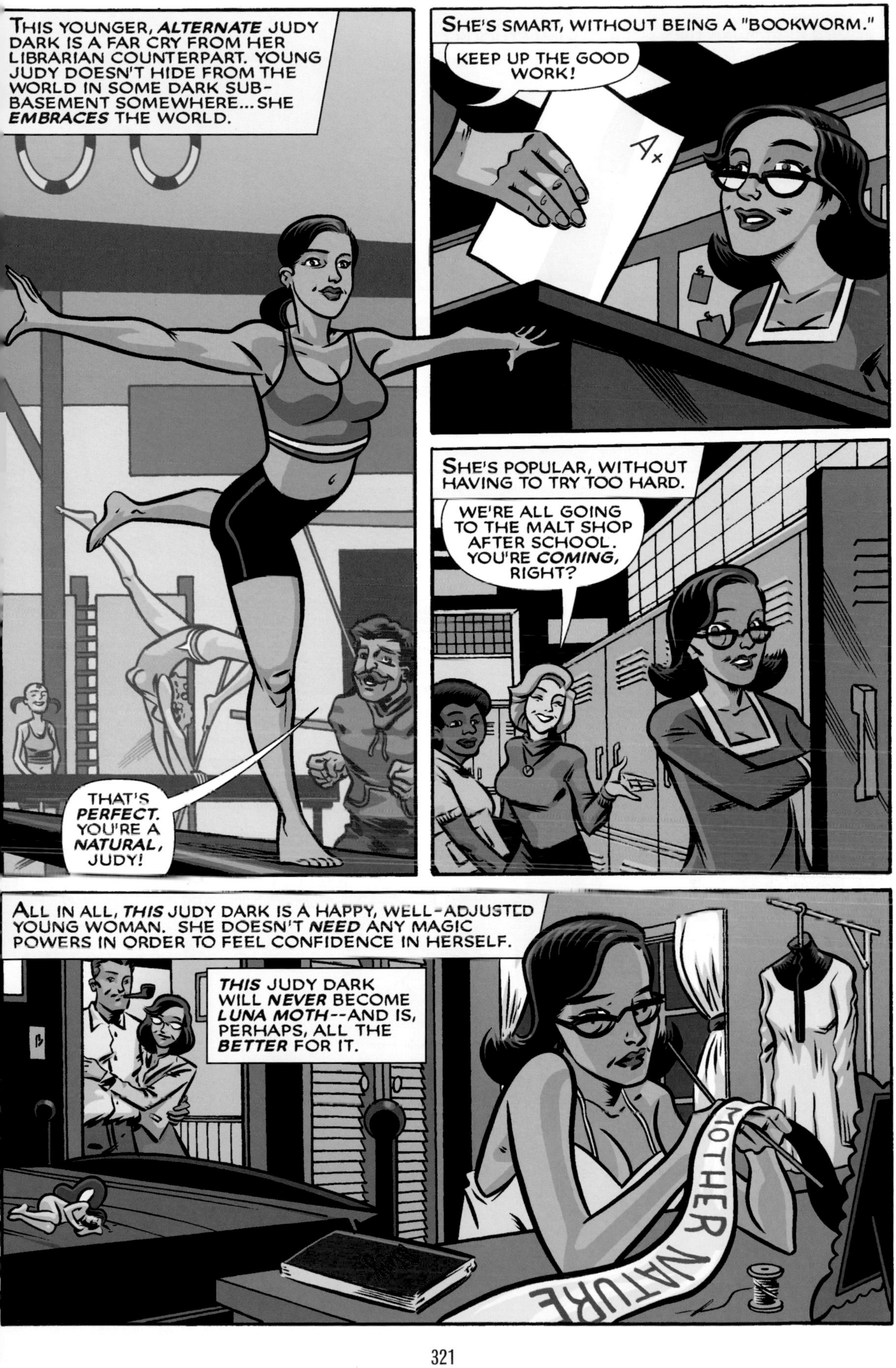
THIS YOUNGER, ALTERNATE JUDY DARK IS A FAR CRY FROM HER LIBRARIAN COUNTERPART. YOUNG JUDY DOESN'T HIDE FROM THE WORLD IN SOME DARK SUB-BASEMENT SOMEWHERE... SHE EMBRACES THE WORLD.
THAT'S PERFECT. YOU'RE A NATURAL, JUDY!
SHE'S SMART, WITHOUT BEING A "BOOKWORM."
KEEP UP THE GOOD WORK!
A+
SHE'S POPULAR, WITHOUT HAVING TO TRY TOO HARD.
WE'RE ALL GOING TO THE MALT SHOP AFTER SCHOOL. YOU'RE COMING, RIGHT?
ALL IN ALL, THIS JUDY DARK IS A HAPPY, WELL-ADJUSTED YOUNG WOMAN. SHE DOESN'T NEED ANY MAGIC POWERS IN ORDER TO FEEL CONFIDENCE IN HERSELF.
THIS JUDY DARK WILL NEVER BECOME LUNA MOTH--AND IS, PERHAPS, ALL THE BETTER FOR IT.
MOTHER NATURE

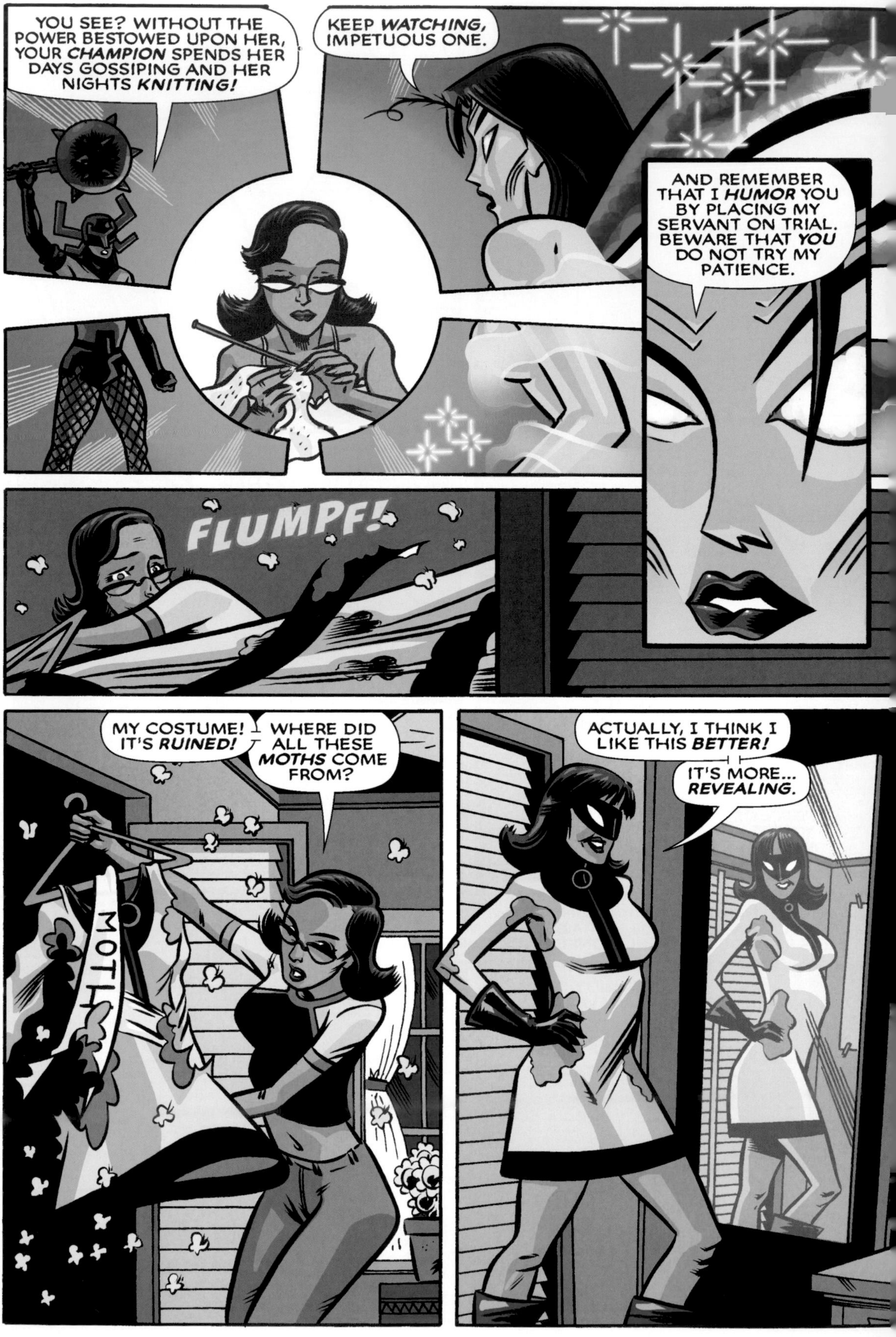
YOU SEE? WITHOUT THE POWER BESTOWED UPON HER, YOUR *CHAMPION* SPENDS HER DAYS GOSSIPING AND HER NIGHTS *KNITTING!*
KEEP *WATCHING,* IMPETUOUS ONE.
AND REMEMBER THAT I *HUMOR* YOU BY PLACING MY SERVANT ON TRIAL. BEWARE THAT *YOU* DO NOT TRY MY PATIENCE.
FLUMPF!
MY COSTUME! IT'S *RUINED!*
WHERE DID ALL THESE *MOTHS* COME FROM?
MOTH
ACTUALLY, I THINK I LIKE THIS *BETTER!*
IT'S MORE... *REVEALING.*

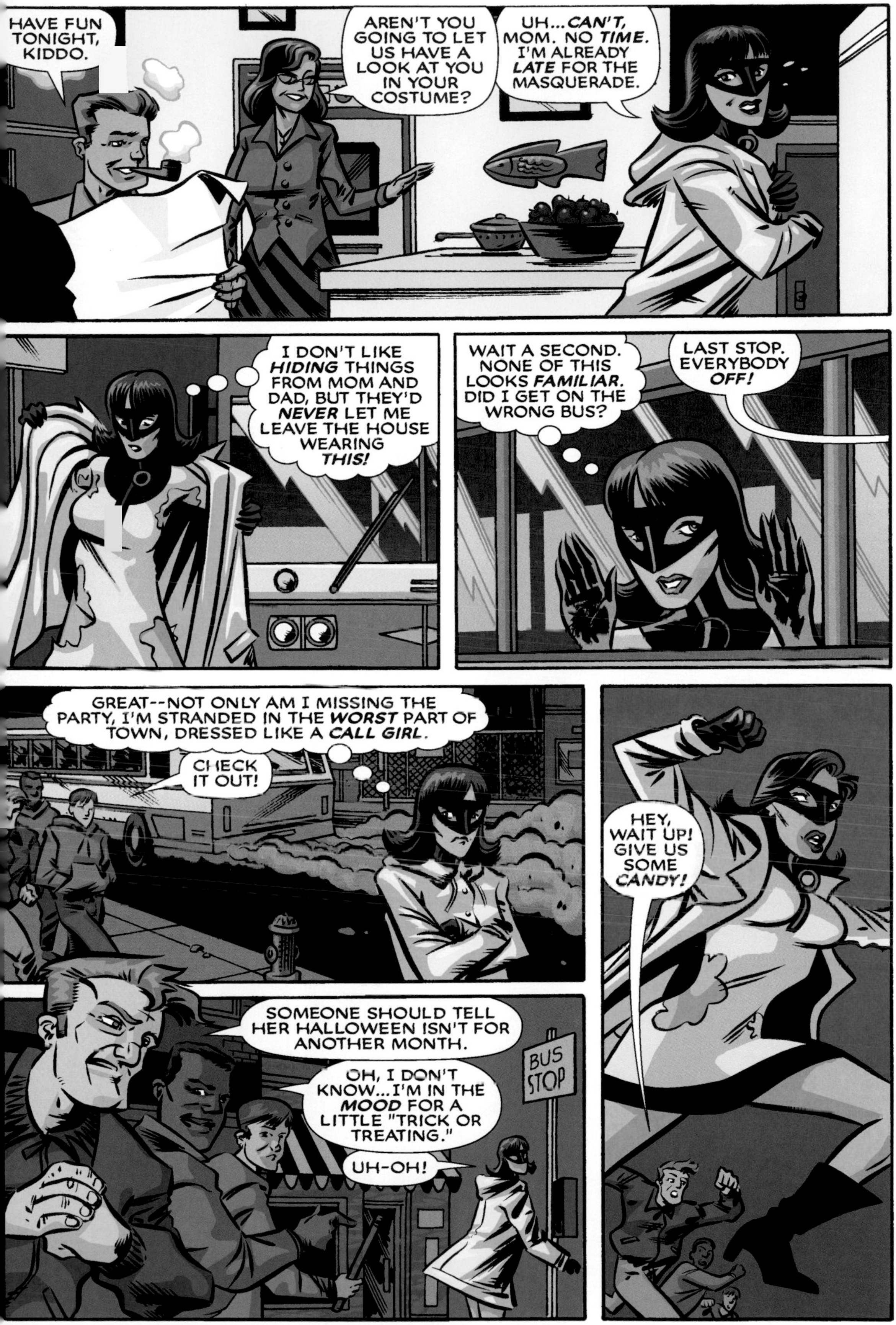
HAVE FUN TONIGHT, KIDDO.
AREN'T YOU GOING TO LET US HAVE A LOOK AT YOU IN YOUR COSTUME?
UH...CAN'T, MOM. NO TIME. I'M ALREADY LATE FOR THE MASQUERADE.
I DON'T LIKE HIDING THINGS FROM MOM AND DAD, BUT THEY'D NEVER LET ME LEAVE THE HOUSE WEARING THIS!
WAIT A SECOND. NONE OF THIS LOOKS FAMILIAR. DID I GET ON THE WRONG BUS?
LAST STOP. EVERYBODY OFF!
GREAT--NOT ONLY AM I MISSING THE PARTY, I'M STRANDED IN THE WORST PART OF TOWN, DRESSED LIKE A CALL GIRL.
CHECK IT OUT!
SOMEONE SHOULD TELL HER HALLOWEEN ISN'T FOR ANOTHER MONTH.
OH, I DON'T KNOW...I'M IN THE MOOD FOR A LITTLE "TRICK OR TREATING."
BUS STOP
UH-OH!
HEY, WAIT UP! GIVE US SOME CANDY!

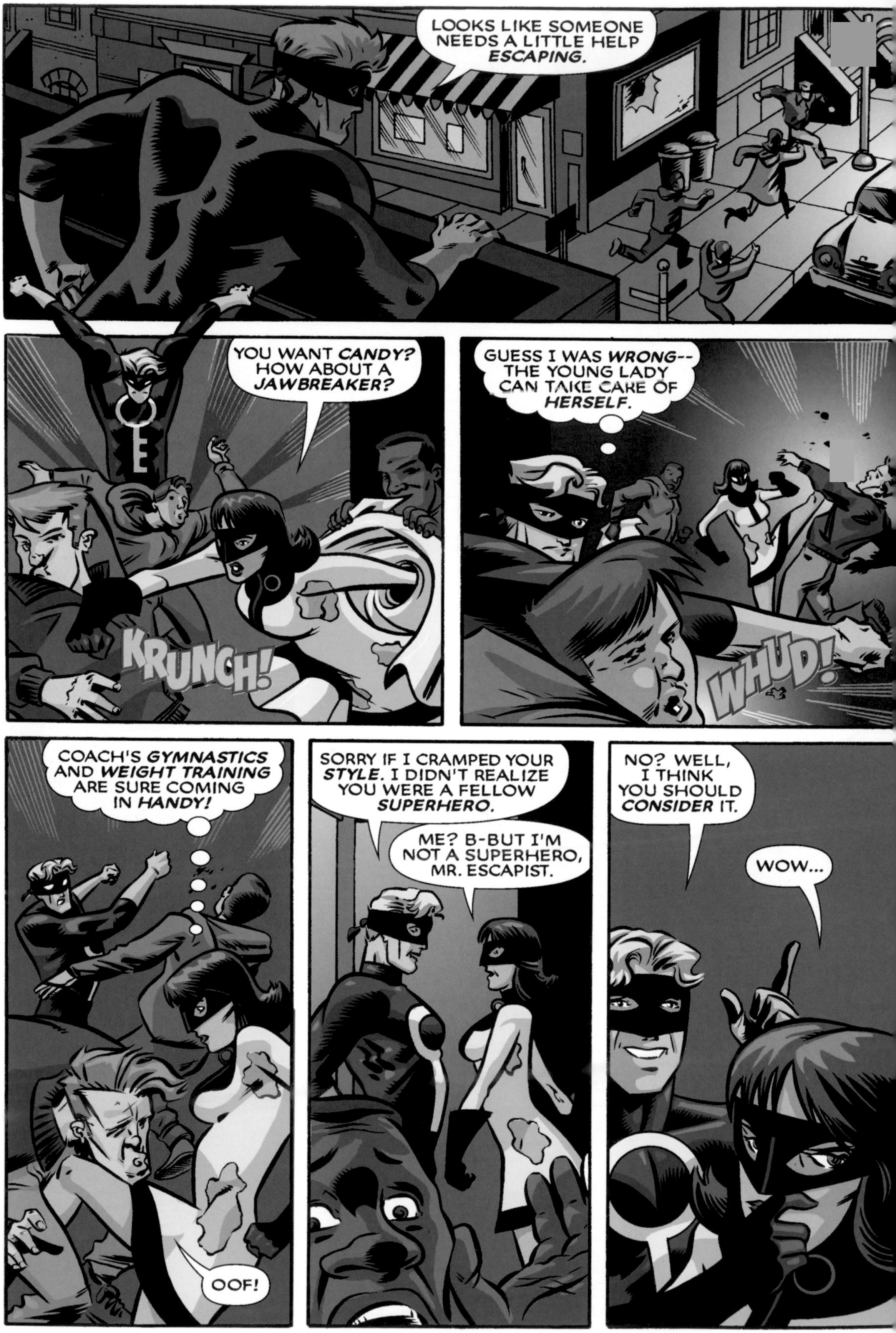
LOOKS LIKE SOMEONE NEEDS A LITTLE HELP *ESCAPING*.
YOU WANT *CANDY?* HOW ABOUT A *JAWBREAKER?*
KRUNCH!
GUESS I WAS *WRONG*-- THE YOUNG LADY CAN TAKE CARE OF *HERSELF*.
WHUD!
COACH'S *GYMNASTICS* AND *WEIGHT TRAINING* ARE SURE COMING IN *HANDY!*
OOF!
SORRY IF I CRAMPED YOUR *STYLE*. I DIDN'T REALIZE YOU WERE A FELLOW *SUPERHERO*.
ME? B-BUT I'M NOT A SUPERHERO, MR. ESCAPIST.
NO? WELL, I THINK YOU SHOULD *CONSIDER* IT.
WOW...

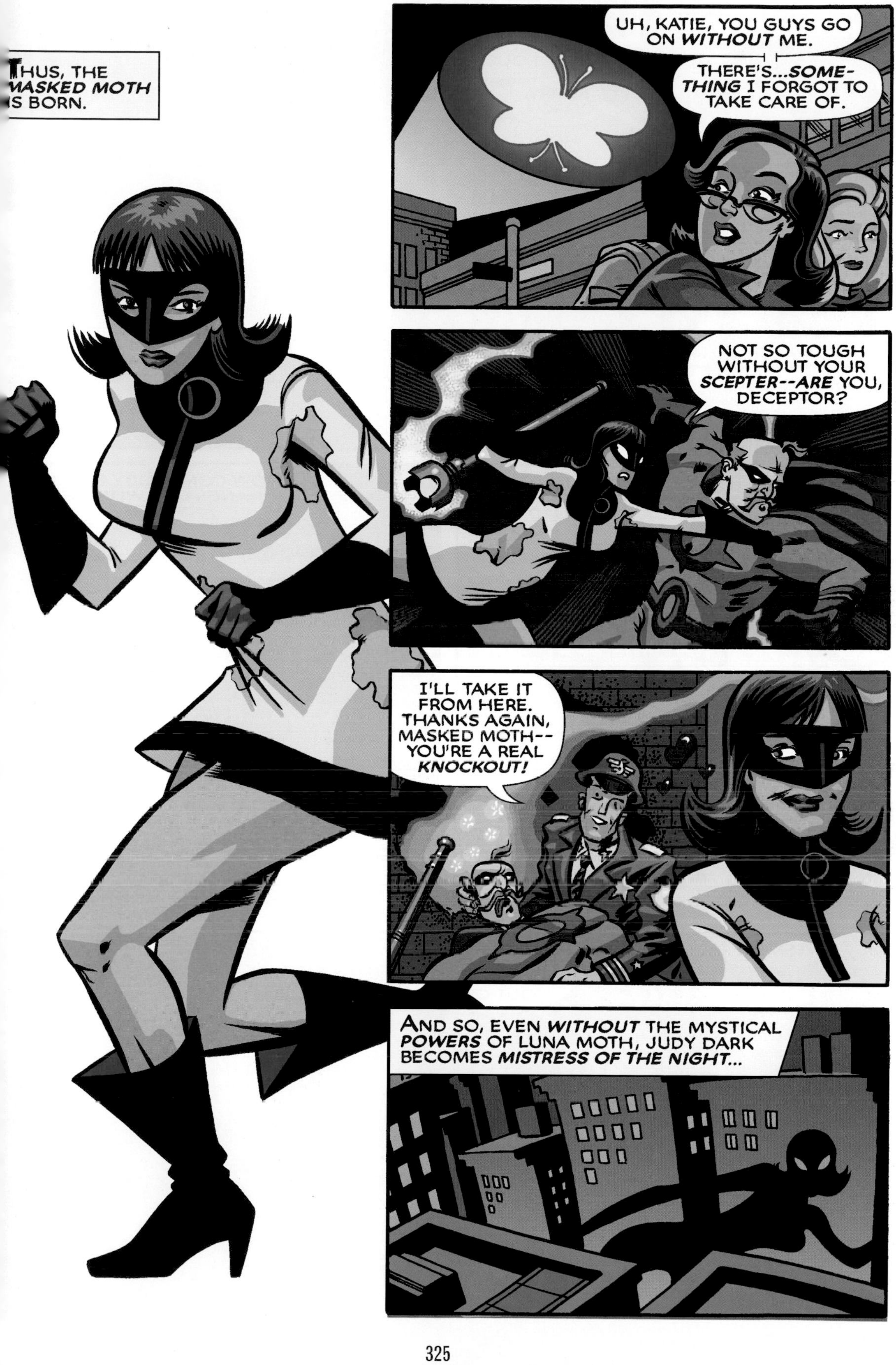
THUS, THE MASKED MOTH IS BORN.
UH, KATIE, YOU GUYS GO ON WITHOUT ME.
THERE'S...SOMETHING I FORGOT TO TAKE CARE OF.
NOT SO TOUGH WITHOUT YOUR SCEPTER--ARE YOU, DECEPTOR?
I'LL TAKE IT FROM HERE. THANKS AGAIN, MASKED MOTH--YOU'RE A REAL KNOCKOUT!
AND SO, EVEN WITHOUT THE MYSTICAL POWERS OF LUNA MOTH, JUDY DARK BECOMES MISTRESS OF THE NIGHT...

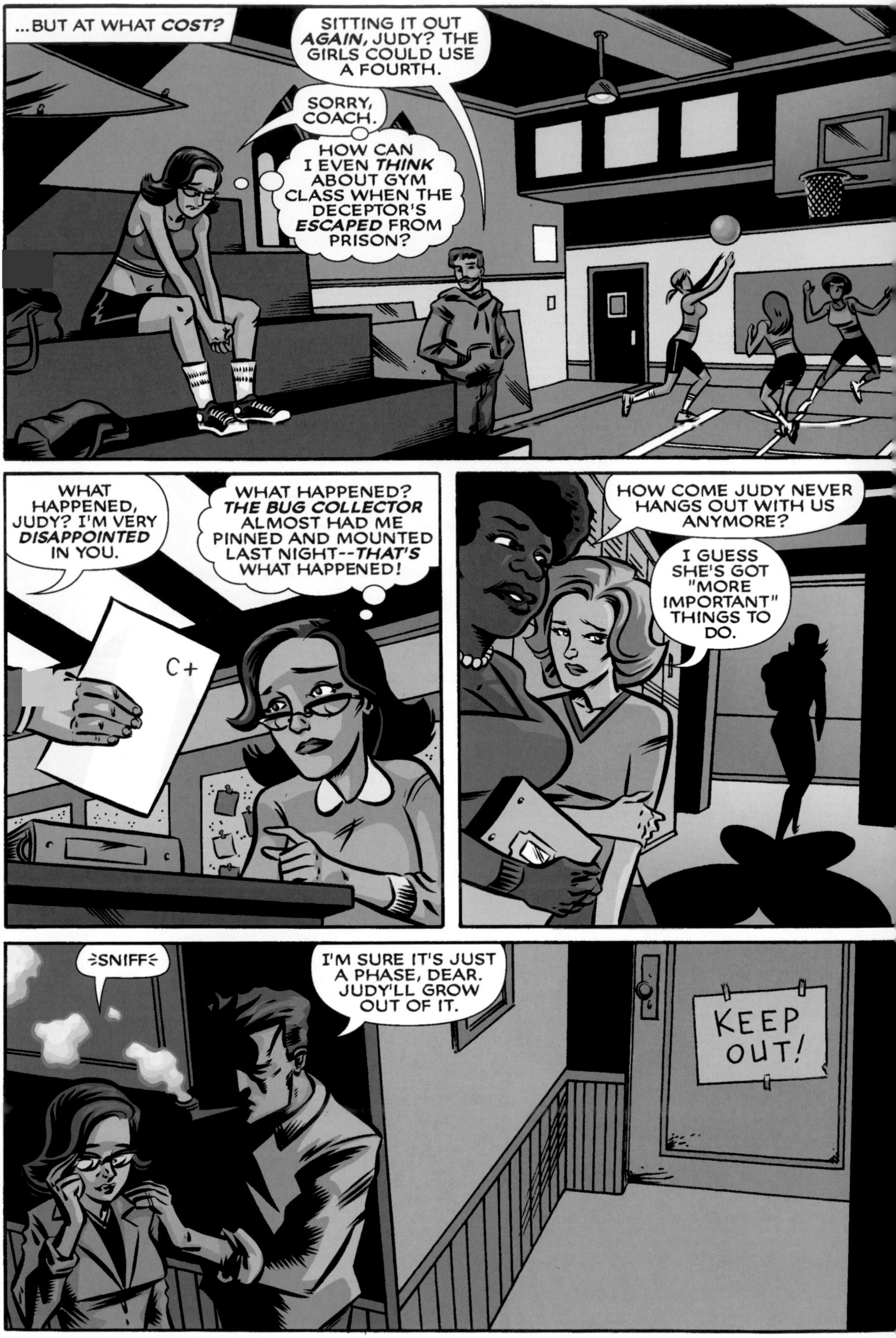
...BUT AT WHAT COST?
SITTING IT OUT AGAIN, JUDY? THE GIRLS COULD USE A FOURTH.
SORRY, COACH.
HOW CAN I EVEN THINK ABOUT GYM CLASS WHEN THE DECEPTOR'S ESCAPED FROM PRISON?
WHAT HAPPENED, JUDY? I'M VERY DISAPPOINTED IN YOU.
WHAT HAPPENED? THE BUG COLLECTOR ALMOST HAD ME PINNED AND MOUNTED LAST NIGHT--THAT'S WHAT HAPPENED!
C+
HOW COME JUDY NEVER HANGS OUT WITH US ANYMORE?
I GUESS SHE'S GOT "MORE IMPORTANT" THINGS TO DO.
SNIFF
I'M SURE IT'S JUST A PHASE, DEAR. JUDY'LL GROW OUT OF IT.
KEEP OUT!

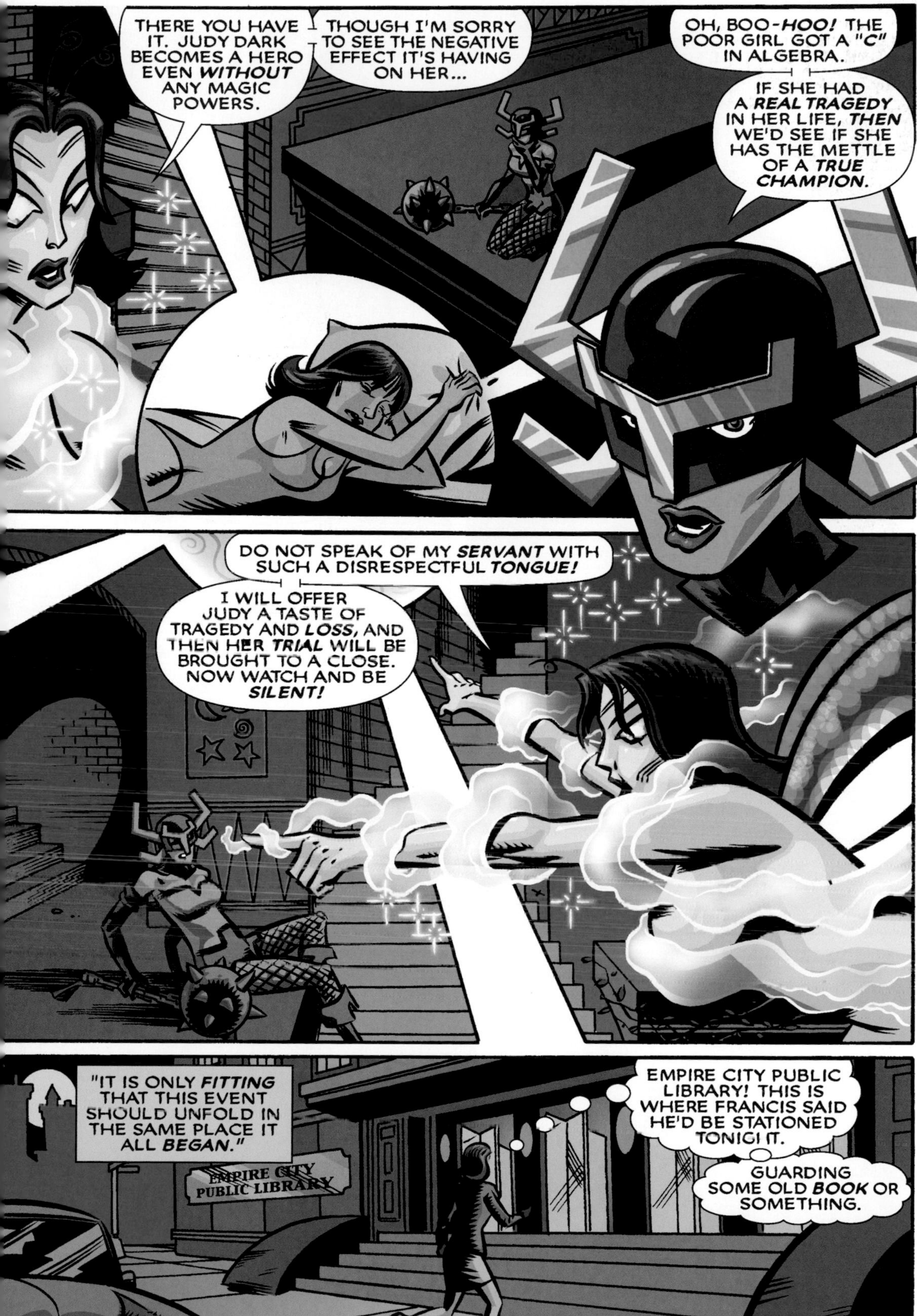
THERE YOU HAVE IT. JUDY DARK BECOMES A HERO EVEN *WITHOUT* ANY MAGIC POWERS.
THOUGH I'M SORRY TO SEE THE NEGATIVE EFFECT IT'S HAVING ON HER...
OH, BOO-*HOO!* THE POOR GIRL GOT A *"C"* IN ALGEBRA.
IF SHE HAD A *REAL TRAGEDY* IN HER LIFE, *THEN* WE'D SEE IF SHE HAS THE METTLE OF A *TRUE CHAMPION.*
DO NOT SPEAK OF MY *SERVANT* WITH SUCH A DISRESPECTFUL *TONGUE!*
I WILL OFFER JUDY A TASTE OF TRAGEDY AND *LOSS,* AND THEN HER *TRIAL* WILL BE BROUGHT TO A CLOSE. NOW WATCH AND BE *SILENT!*
"IT IS ONLY *FITTING* THAT THIS EVENT SHOULD UNFOLD IN THE SAME PLACE IT ALL *BEGAN.*"
EMPIRE CITY PUBLIC LIBRARY
EMPIRE CITY PUBLIC LIBRARY! THIS IS WHERE FRANCIS SAID HE'D BE STATIONED TONIGHT.
GUARDING SOME OLD *BOOK* OR SOMETHING.

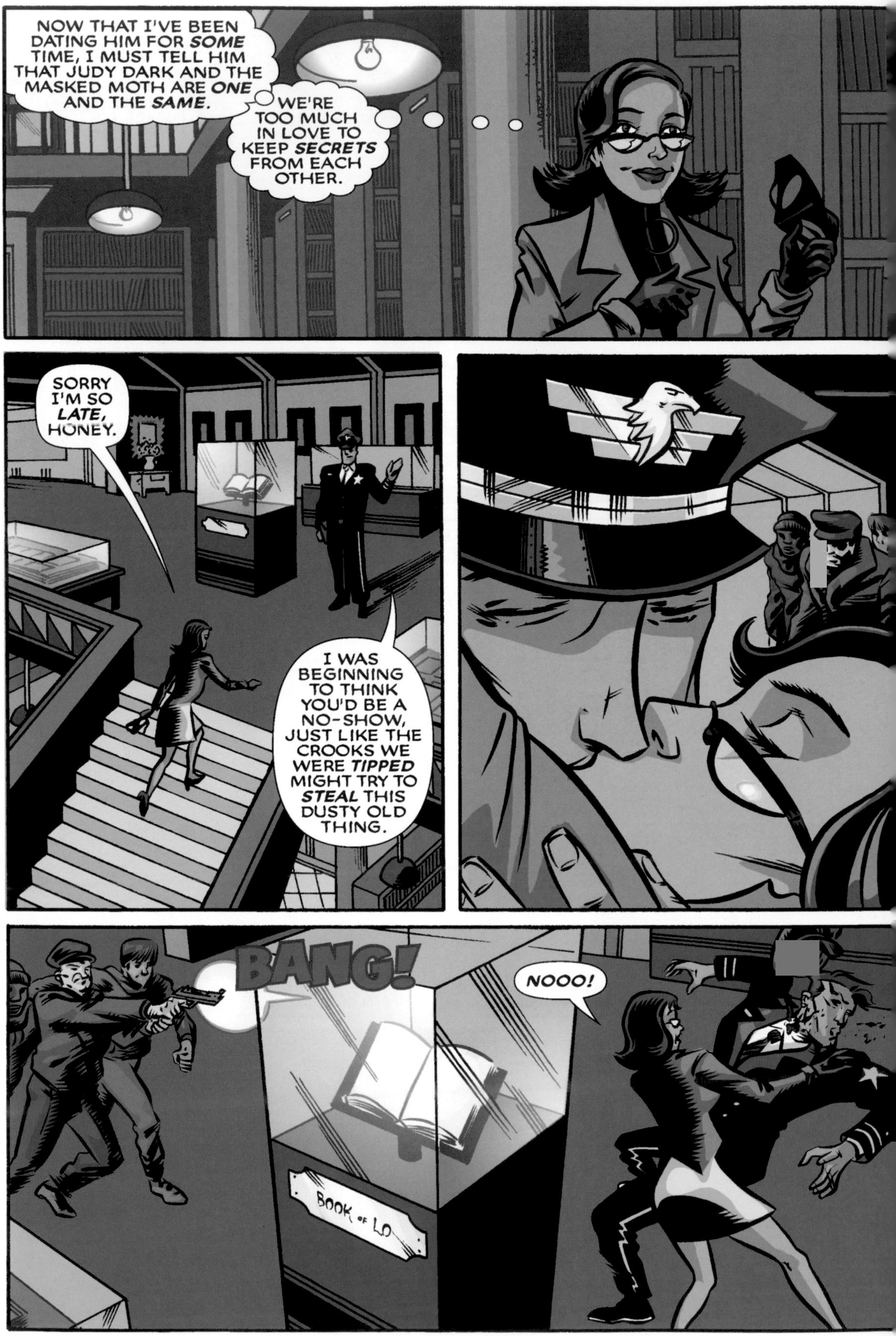
NOW THAT I'VE BEEN DATING HIM FOR SOME TIME, I MUST TELL HIM THAT JUDY DARK AND THE MASKED MOTH ARE ONE AND THE SAME.
WE'RE TOO MUCH IN LOVE TO KEEP SECRETS FROM EACH OTHER.
SORRY I'M SO LATE, HONEY.
I WAS BEGINNING TO THINK YOU'D BE A NO-SHOW, JUST LIKE THE CROOKS WE WERE TIPPED MIGHT TRY TO STEAL THIS DUSTY OLD THING.
BANG!
NOOO!
BOOK OF LO

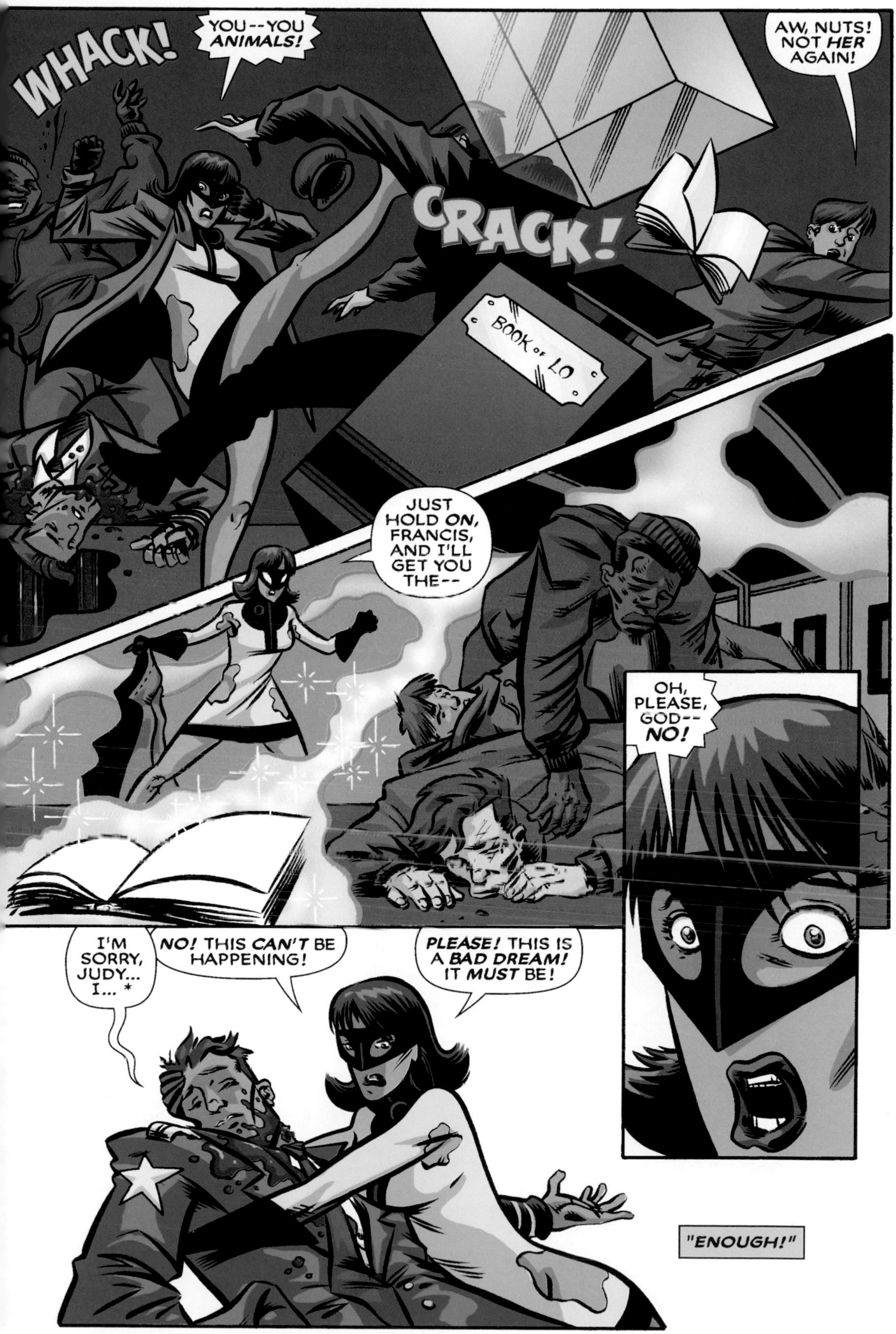
WHACK!
YOU--YOU ANIMALS!
CRACK!
AW, NUTS! NOT HER AGAIN!
BOOK OF LO
JUST HOLD ON, FRANCIS, AND I'LL GET YOU THE--
OH, PLEASE, GOD-- NO!
I'M SORRY, JUDY... I... *
NO! THIS CAN'T BE HAPPENING!
PLEASE! THIS IS A BAD DREAM! IT MUST BE!
"ENOUGH!"

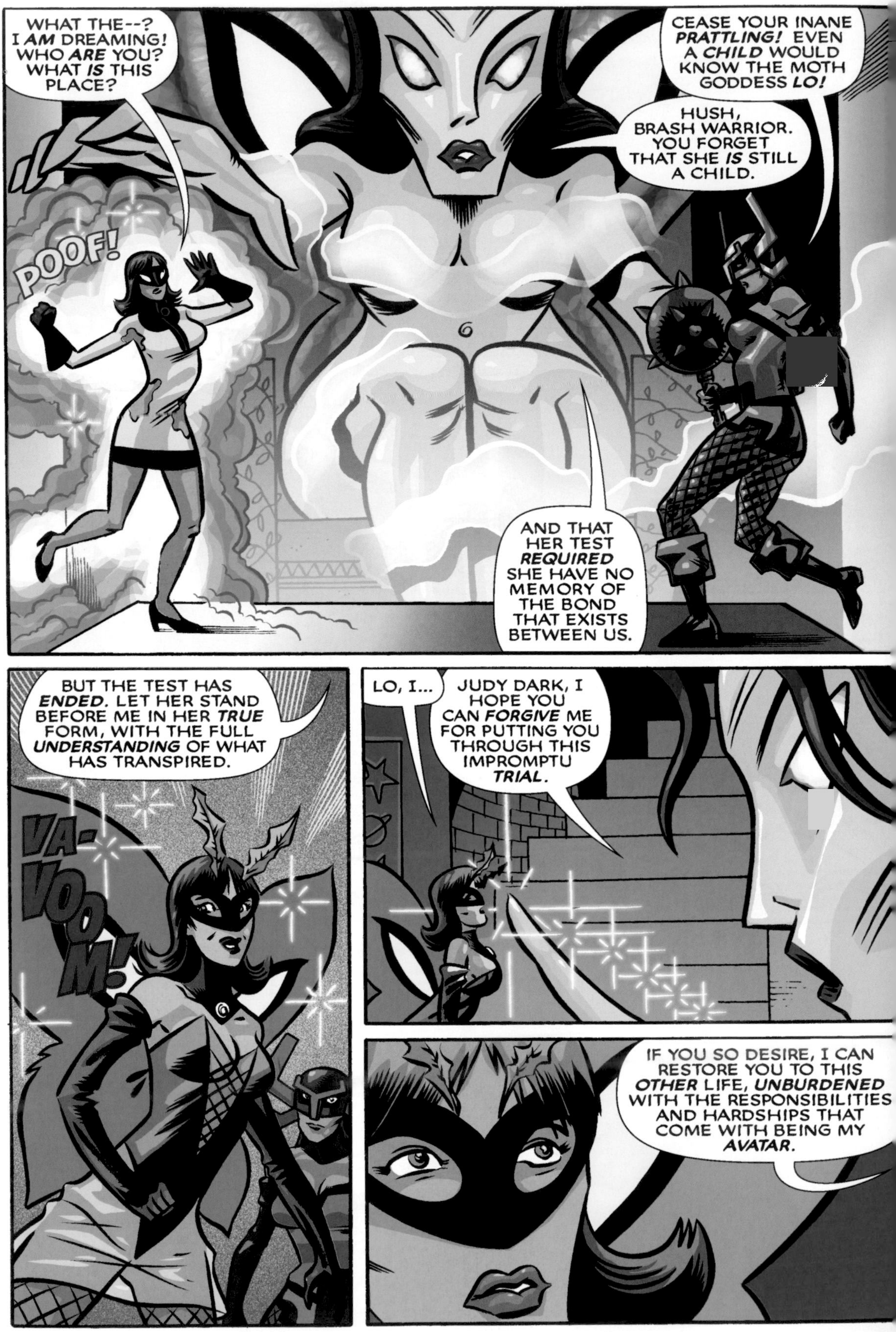
WHAT THE--? I *AM* DREAMING! WHO *ARE* YOU? WHAT *IS* THIS PLACE?
POOF!
CEASE YOUR INANE *PRATTLING!* EVEN A *CHILD* WOULD KNOW THE MOTH GODDESS *LO!*
HUSH, BRASH WARRIOR. YOU FORGET THAT SHE *IS* STILL A CHILD.
AND THAT HER TEST *REQUIRED* SHE HAVE NO MEMORY OF THE BOND THAT EXISTS BETWEEN US.
BUT THE TEST HAS *ENDED*. LET HER STAND BEFORE ME IN HER *TRUE* FORM, WITH THE FULL *UNDERSTANDING* OF WHAT HAS TRANSPIRED.
VA-VOOM!
LO, I...
JUDY DARK, I HOPE YOU CAN *FORGIVE* ME FOR PUTTING YOU THROUGH THIS IMPROMPTU *TRIAL*.
IF YOU SO DESIRE, I CAN RESTORE YOU TO THIS *OTHER* LIFE, *UNBURDENED* WITH THE RESPONSIBILITIES AND HARDSHIPS THAT COME WITH BEING MY *AVATAR*.

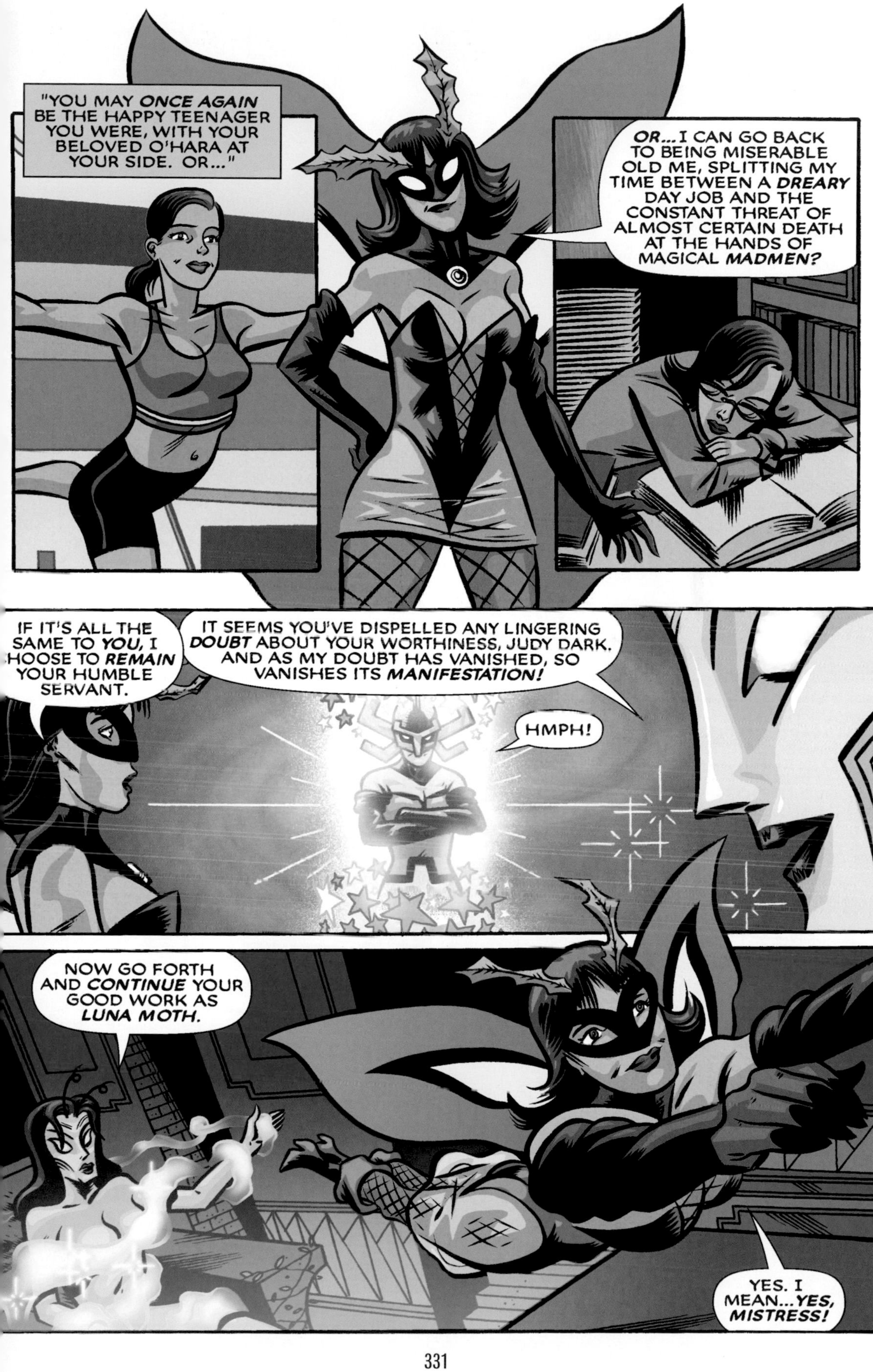

"YOU MAY *ONCE AGAIN* BE THE HAPPY TEENAGER YOU WERE, WITH YOUR BELOVED O'HARA AT YOUR SIDE. OR..."
*OR...* I CAN GO BACK TO BEING MISERABLE OLD ME, SPLITTING MY TIME BETWEEN A *DREARY* DAY JOB AND THE CONSTANT THREAT OF ALMOST CERTAIN DEATH AT THE HANDS OF MAGICAL *MADMEN?*
IF IT'S ALL THE SAME TO *YOU,* I CHOOSE TO *REMAIN* YOUR HUMBLE SERVANT.
IT SEEMS YOU'VE DISPELLED ANY LINGERING *DOUBT* ABOUT YOUR WORTHINESS, JUDY DARK. AND AS MY DOUBT HAS VANISHED, SO VANISHES ITS *MANIFESTATION!*
HMPH!
NOW GO FORTH AND *CONTINUE* YOUR GOOD WORK AS *LUNA MOTH.*
YES. I MEAN...*YES, MISTRESS!*

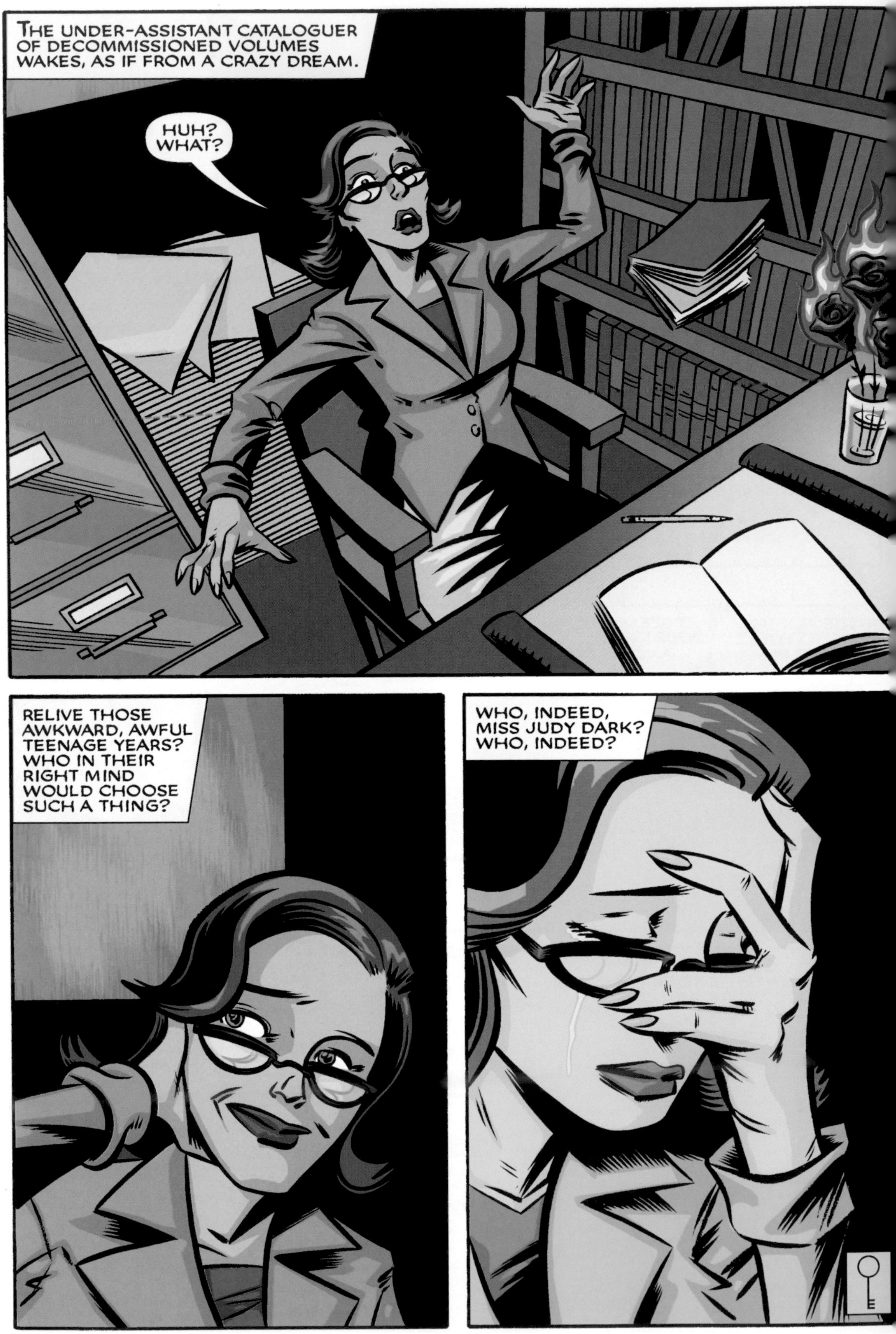
THE UNDER-ASSISTANT CATALOGUER OF DECOMMISSIONED VOLUMES WAKES, AS IF FROM A CRAZY DREAM.
HUH? WHAT?
RELIVE THOSE AWKWARD, AWFUL TEENAGE YEARS? WHO IN THEIR RIGHT MIND WOULD CHOOSE SUCH A THING?
WHO, INDEED, MISS JUDY DARK? WHO, INDEED?

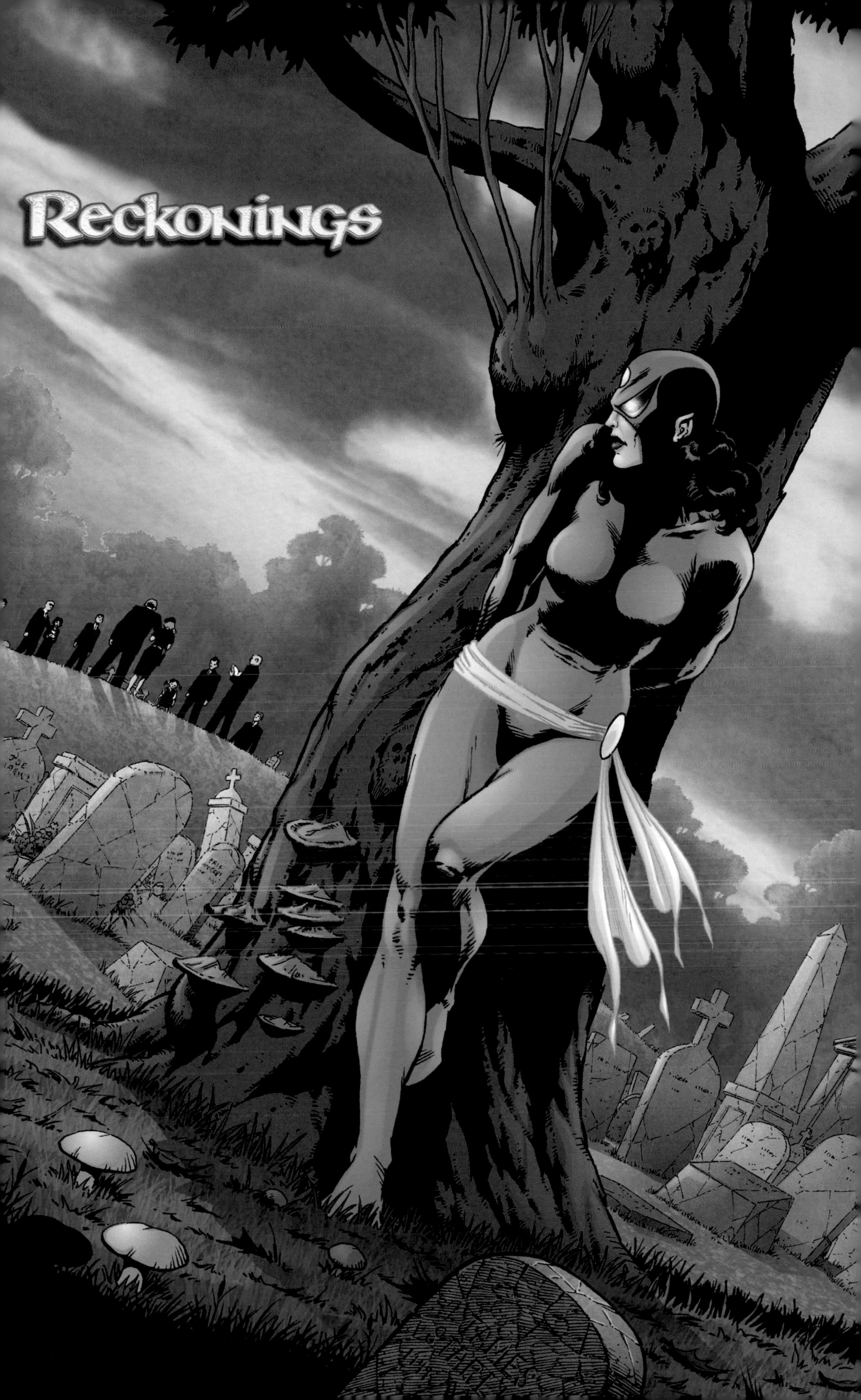
Reckonings

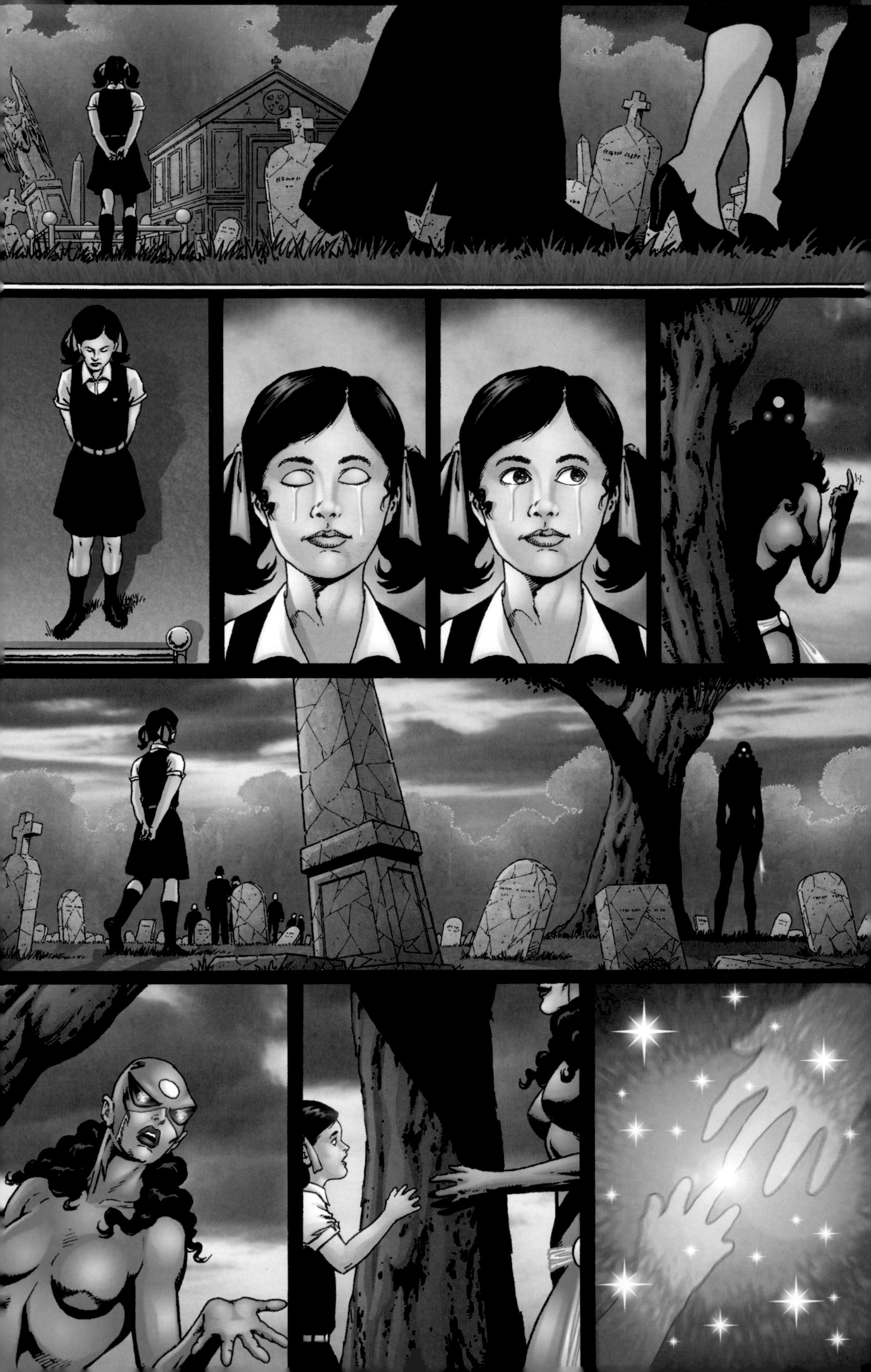

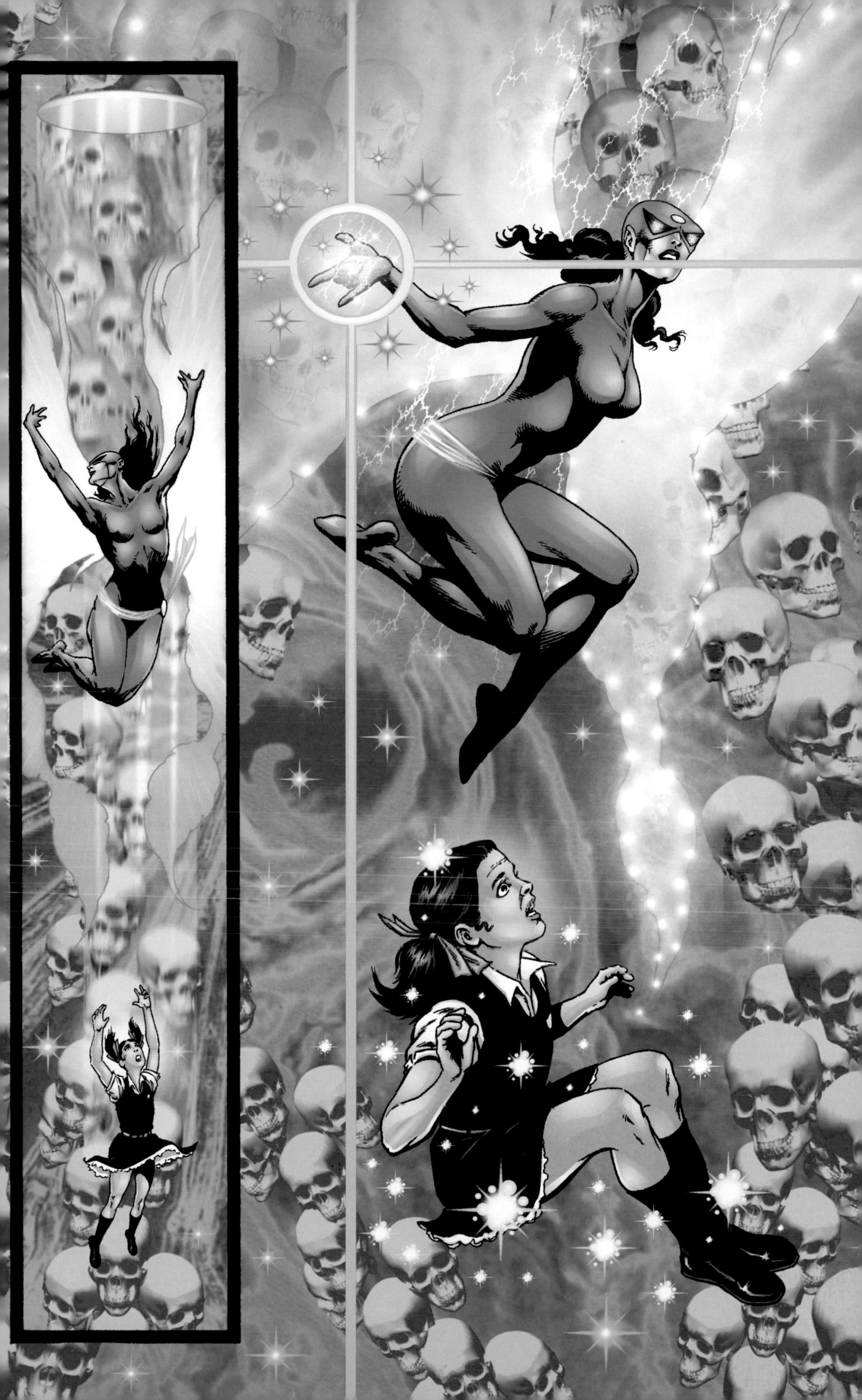

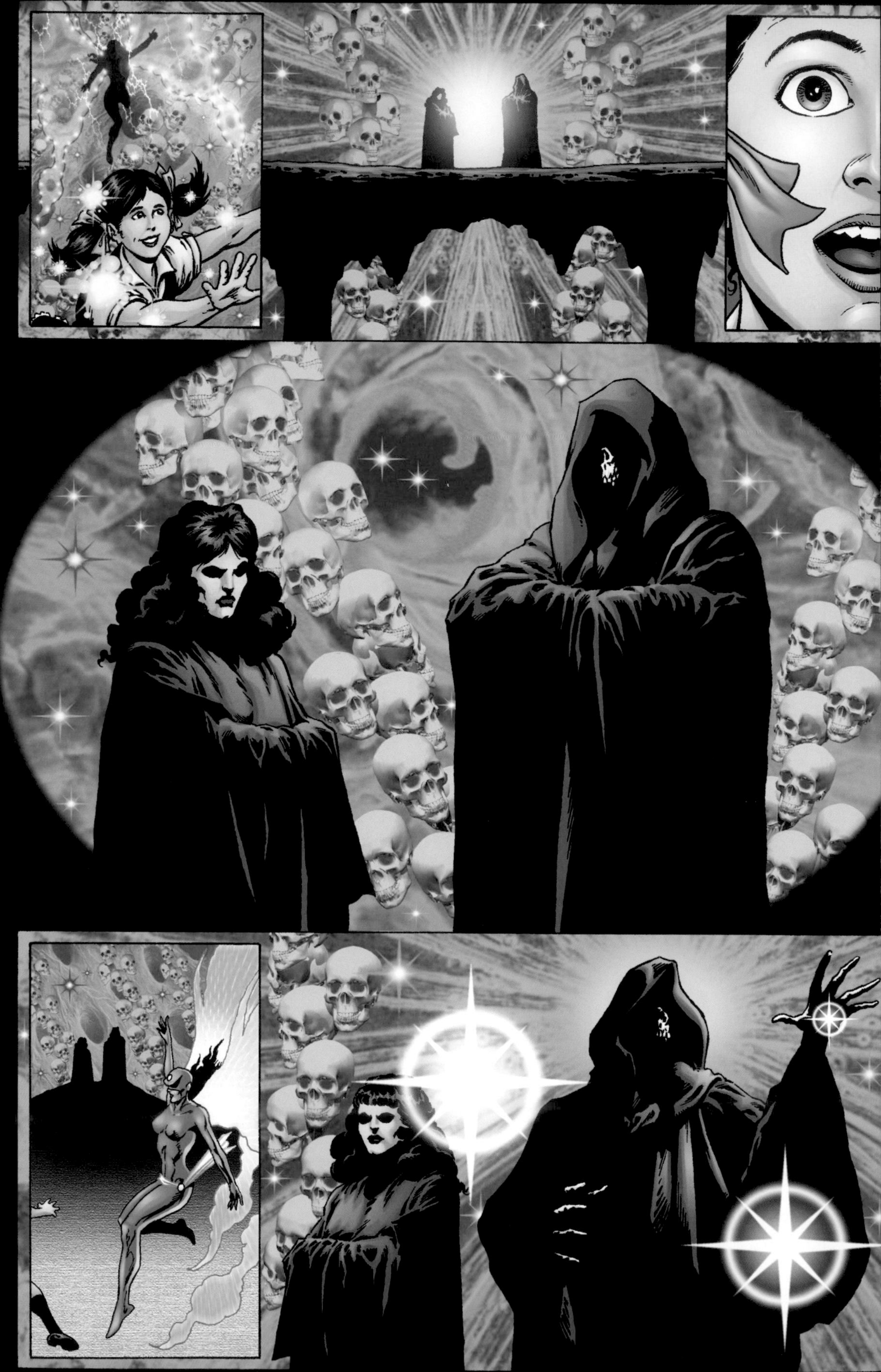

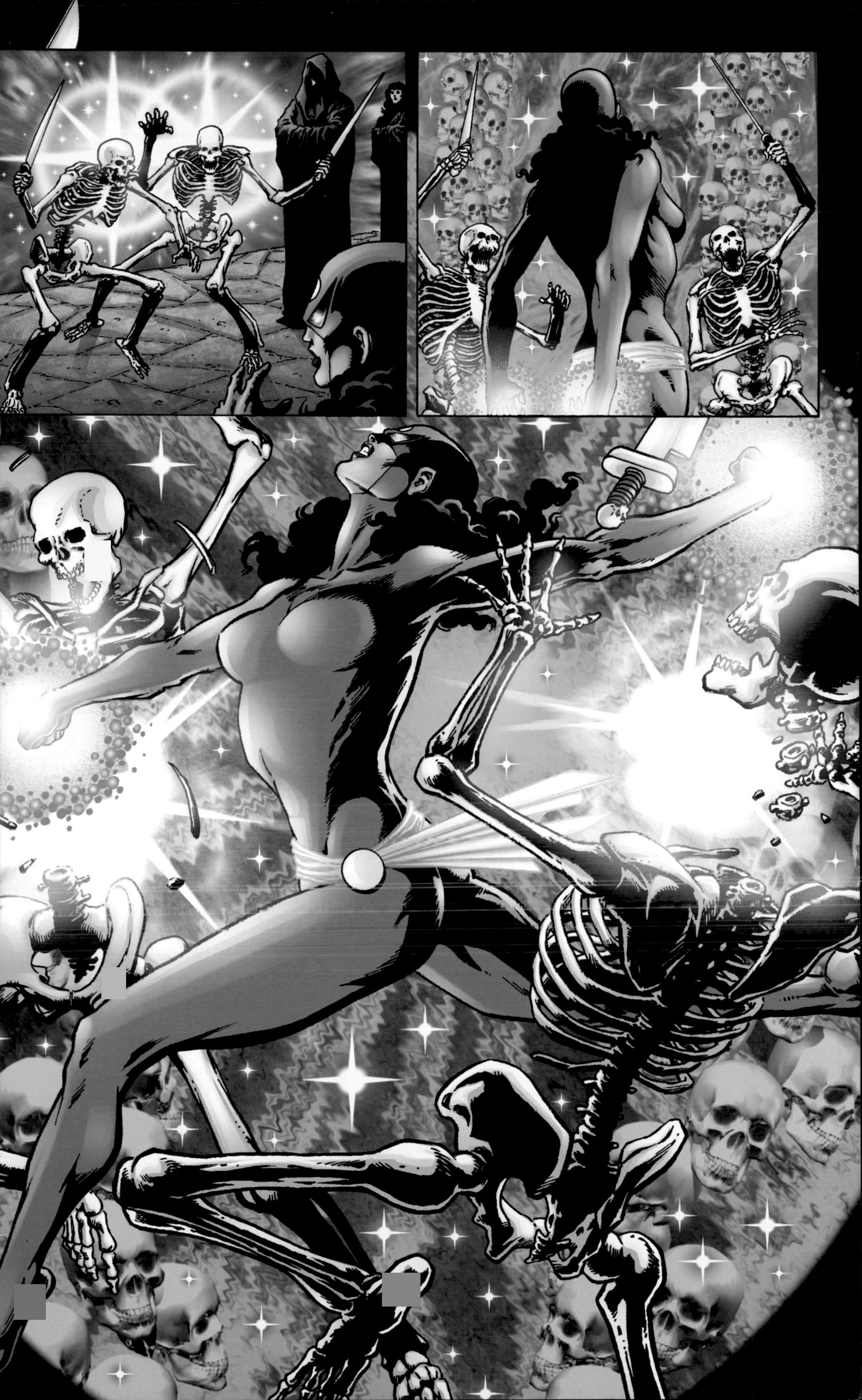

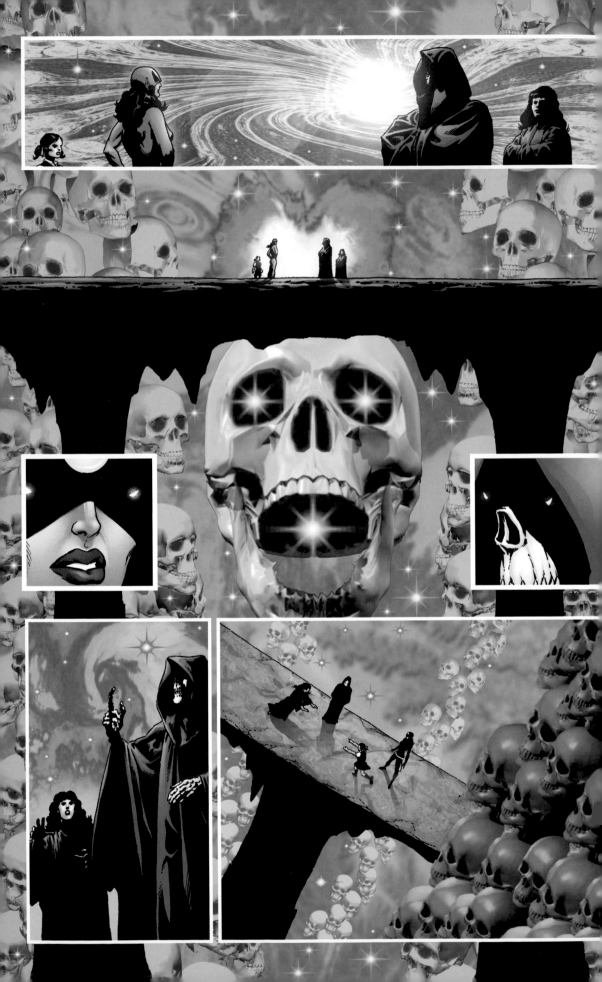

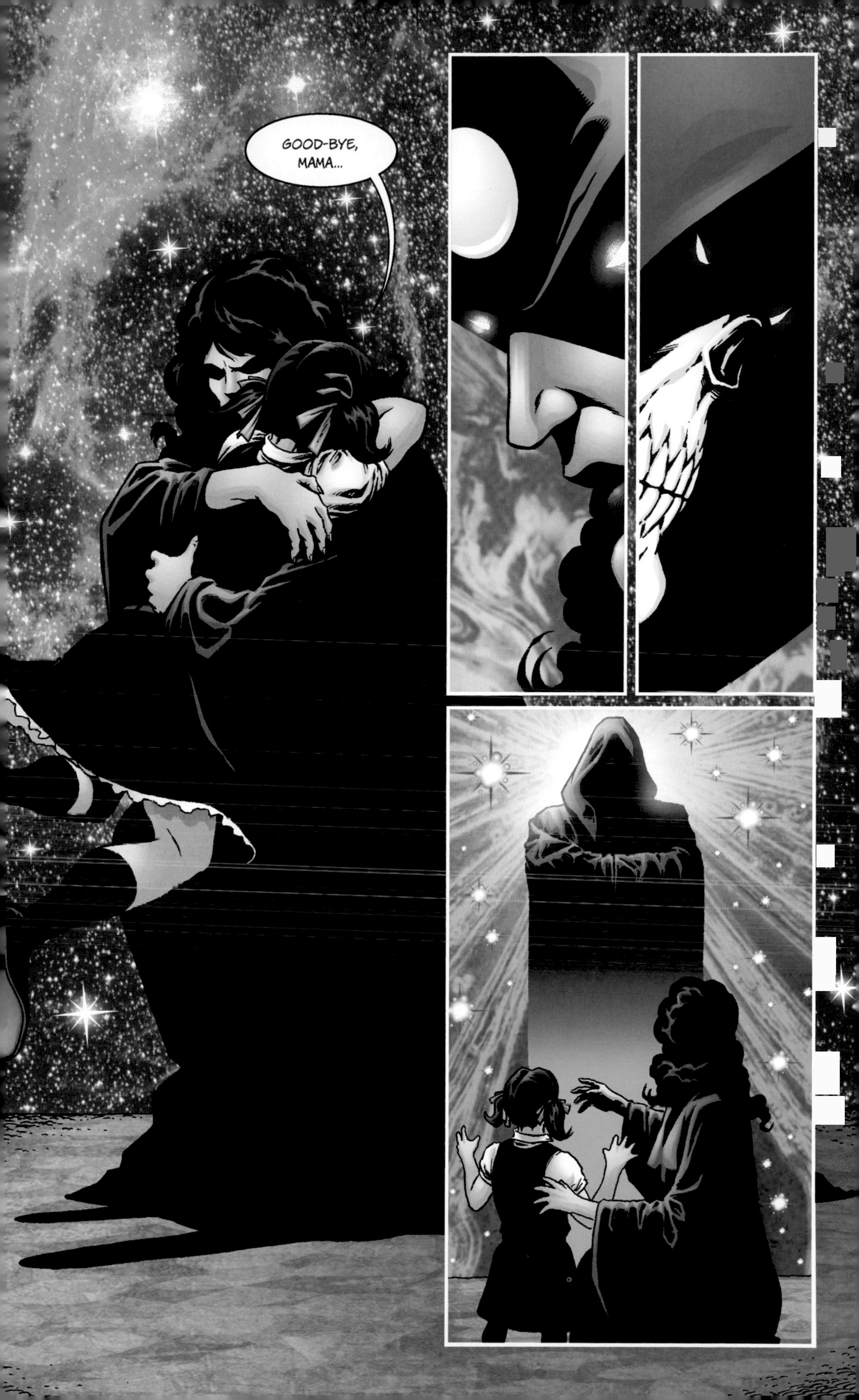
GOOD-BYE, MAMA...

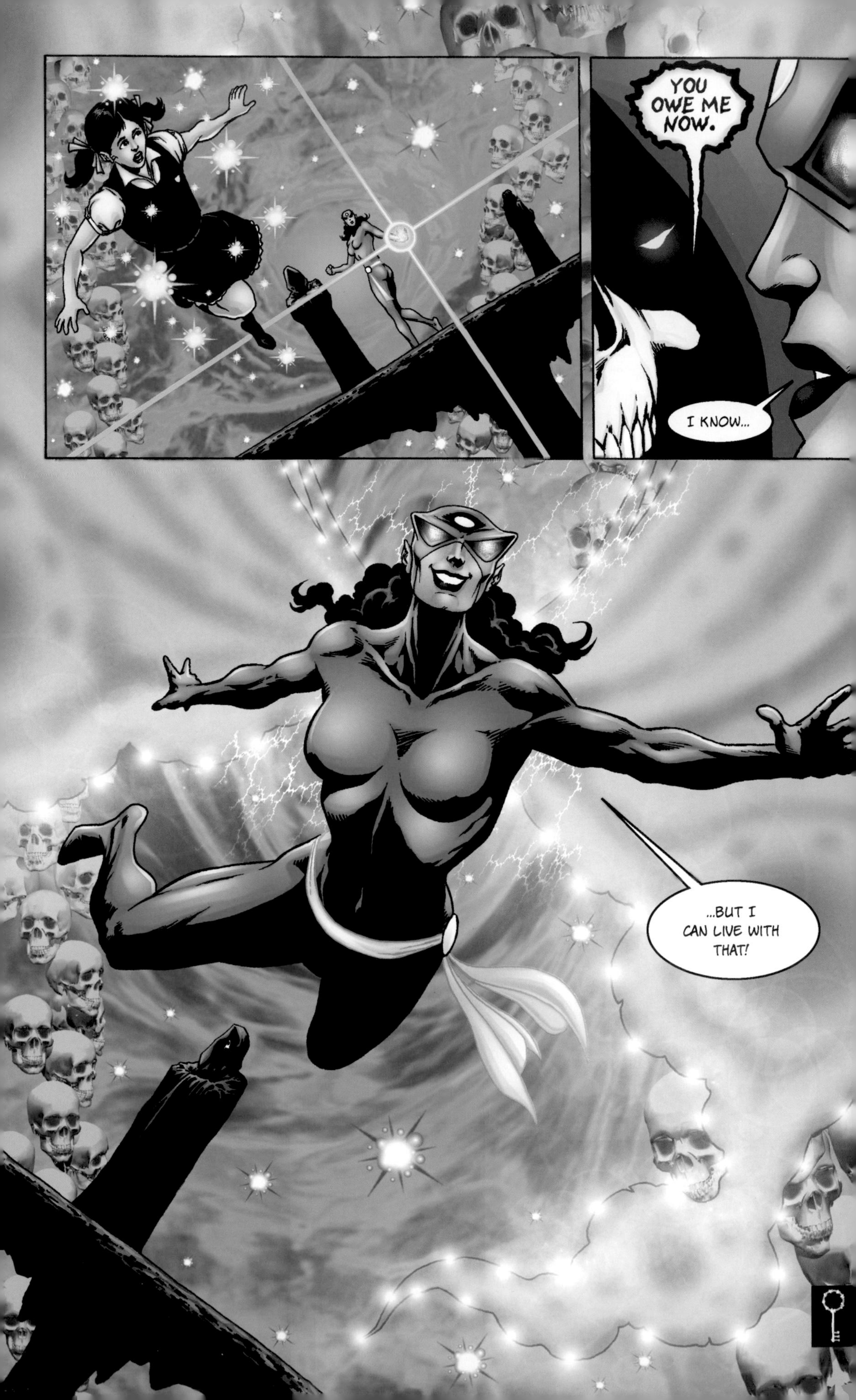
YOU OWE ME NOW.
I KNOW...
...BUT I CAN LIVE WITH THAT!

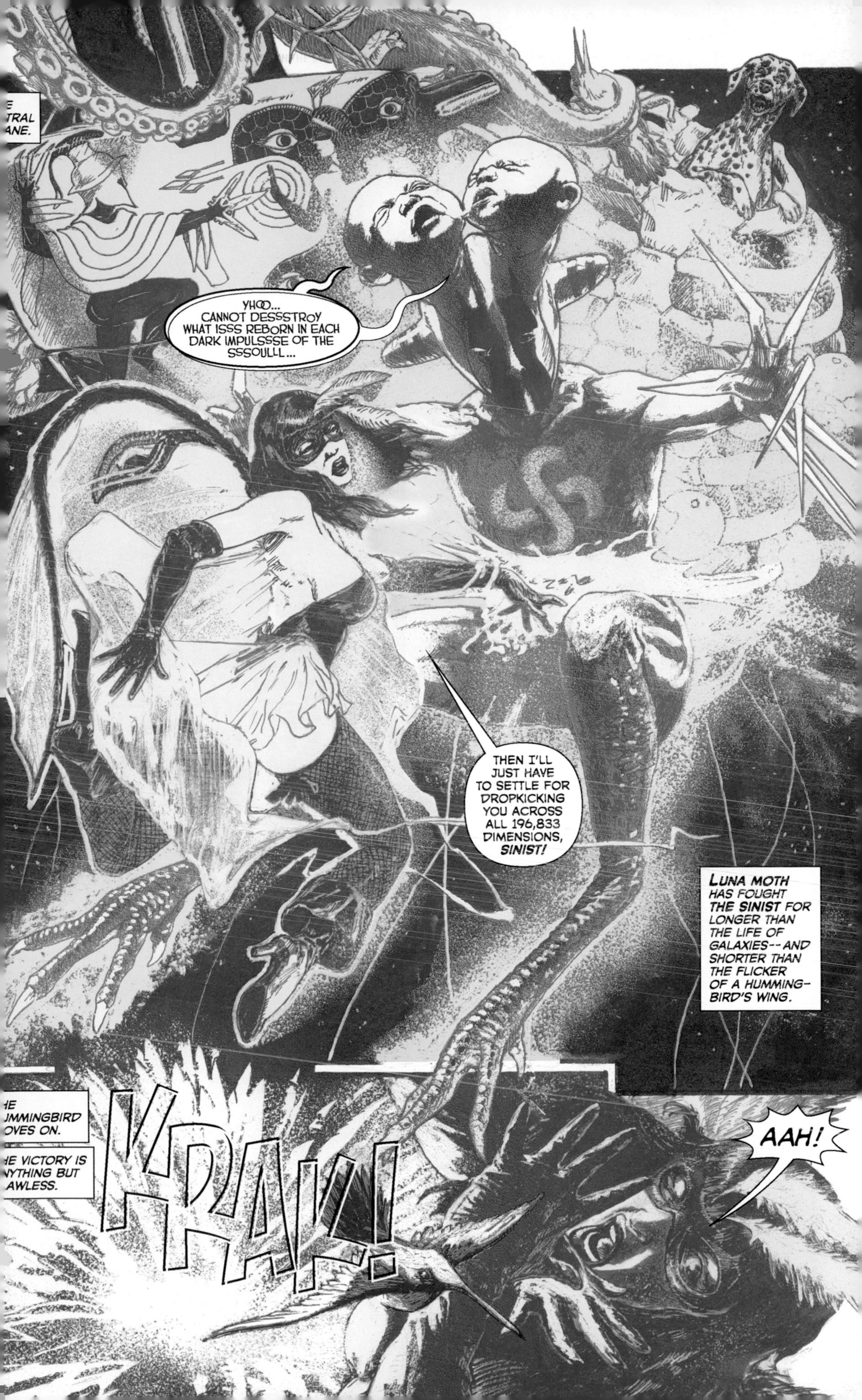

HE
TRAL
ANE.
YHOO... CANNOT DESSSTROY WHAT ISSS REBORN IN EACH DARK IMPULSSSE OF THE SSSOULLL...
THEN I'LL JUST HAVE TO SETTLE FOR DROPKICKING YOU ACROSS ALL 196,833 DIMENSIONS, SINIST!
LUNA MOTH HAS FOUGHT THE SINIST FOR LONGER THAN THE LIFE OF GALAXIES--AND SHORTER THAN THE FLICKER OF A HUMMING-BIRD'S WING.
HE
UMMINGBIRD
OVES ON.
HE VICTORY IS
NYTHING BUT
AWLESS.
KRAK!
AAH!

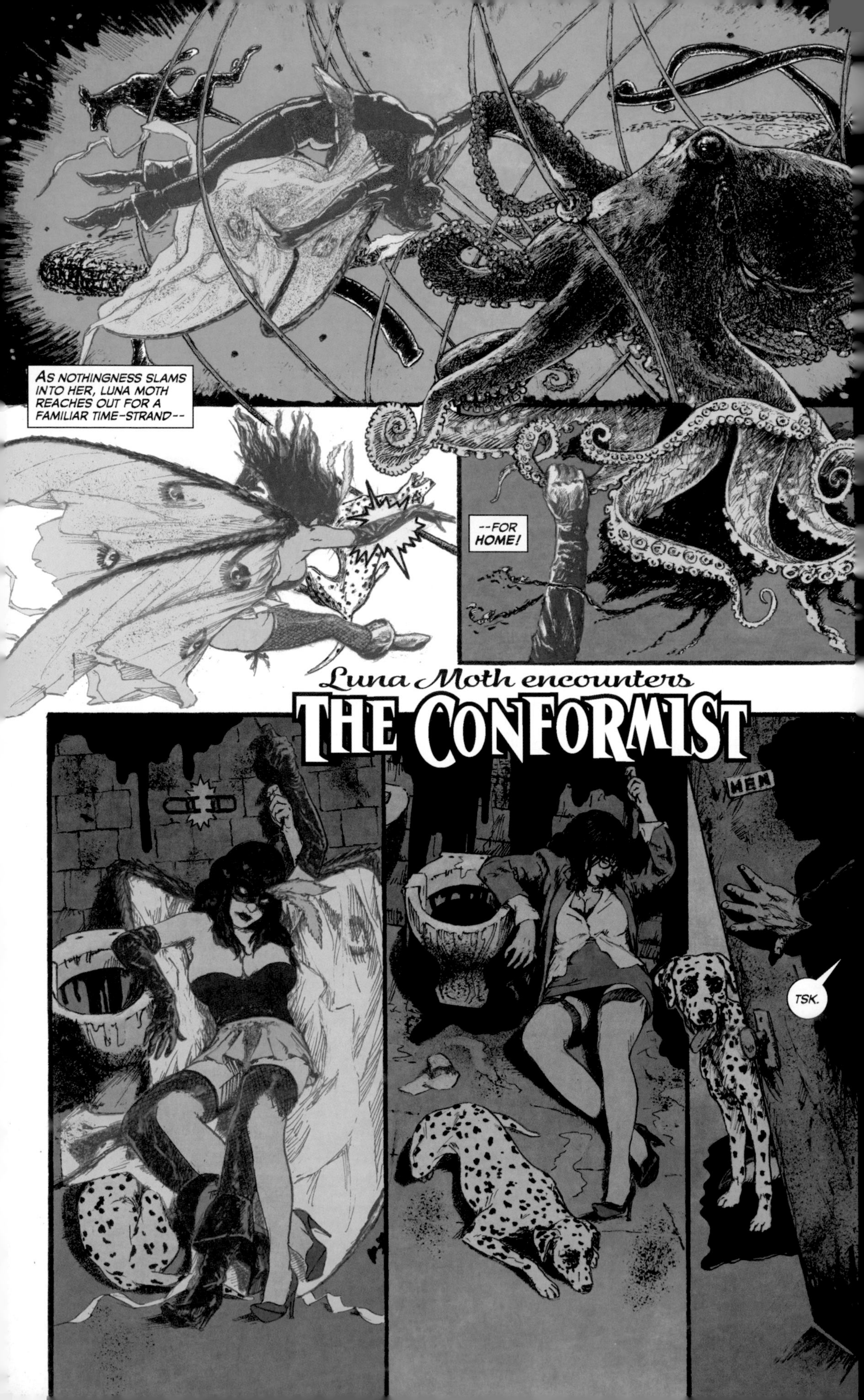
AS NOTHINGNESS SLAMS INTO HER, LUNA MOTH REACHES OUT FOR A FAMILIAR TIME-STRAND--
--FOR HOME!
Luna Moth encounters
THE CONFORMIST
MEN
TSK.

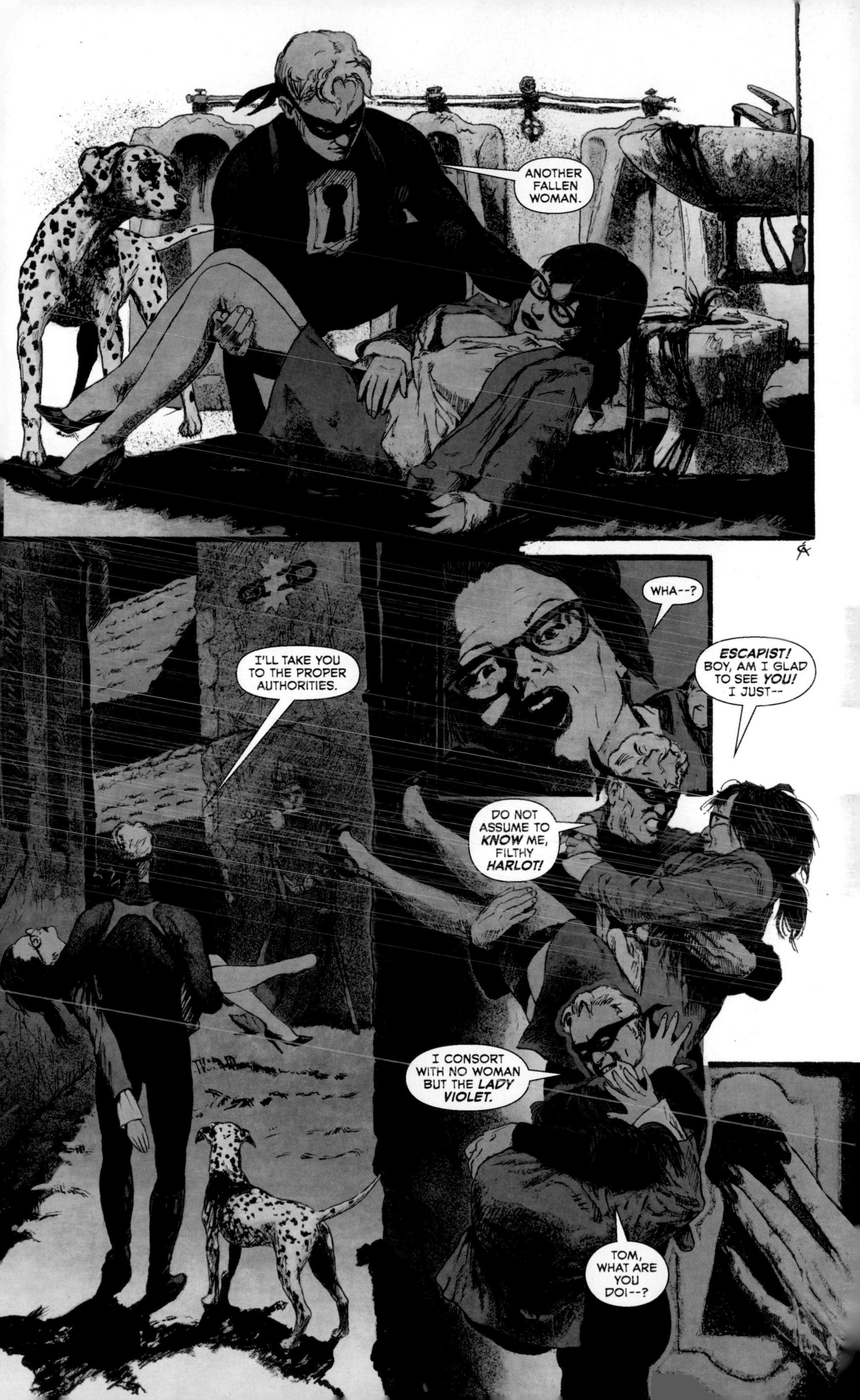
ANOTHER FALLEN WOMAN.
I'LL TAKE YOU TO THE PROPER AUTHORITIES.
WHA--?
ESCAPIST! BOY, AM I GLAD TO SEE YOU! I JUST--
DO NOT ASSUME TO KNOW ME, FILTHY HARLOT!
I CONSORT WITH NO WOMAN BUT THE LADY VIOLET.
TOM, WHAT ARE YOU DOI--?

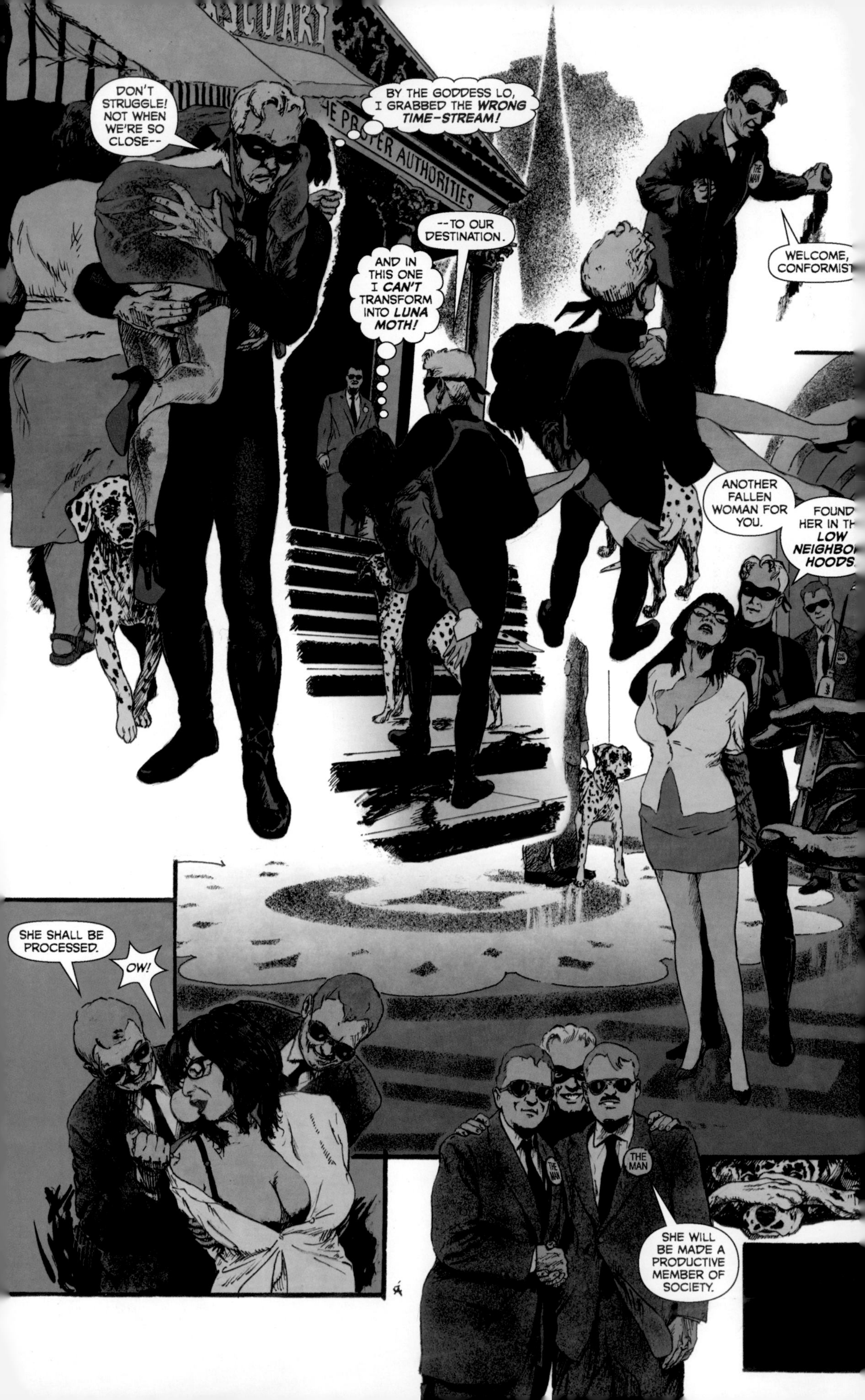
DON'T STRUGGLE! NOT WHEN WE'RE SO CLOSE--
BY THE GODDESS LO, I GRABBED THE ***WRONG TIME-STREAM!***
--TO OUR DESTINATION.
AND IN THIS ONE I ***CAN'T*** TRANSFORM INTO ***LUNA MOTH!***
THE MAN
WELCOME, CONFORMIST
ANOTHER FALLEN WOMAN FOR YOU.
FOUND HER IN TH ***LOW NEIGHBO HOODS***
SHE SHALL BE PROCESSED.
OW!
THE MAN
THE MAN
SHE WILL BE MADE A PRODUCTIVE MEMBER OF SOCIETY.

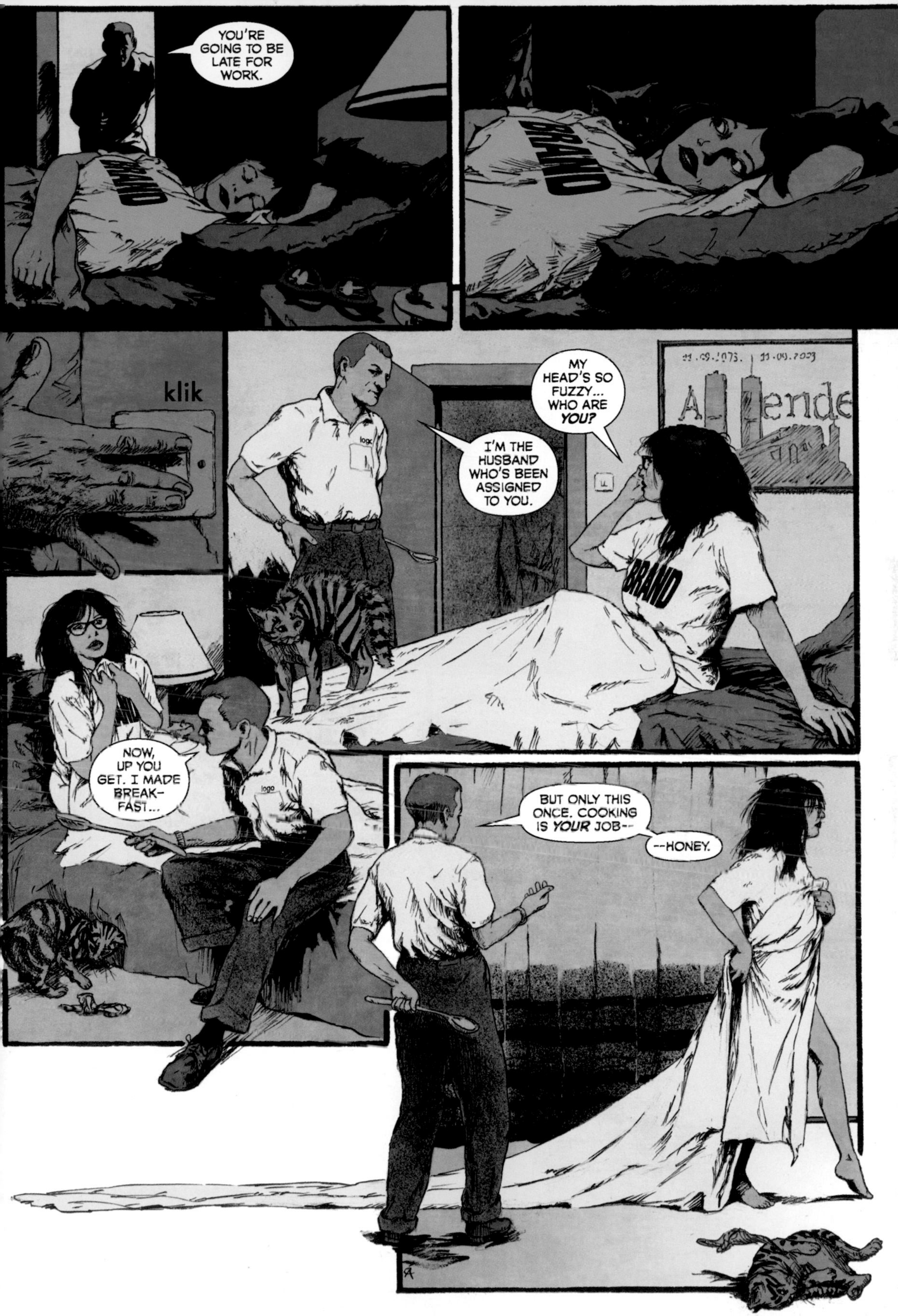
YOU'RE GOING TO BE LATE FOR WORK.
klik
MY HEAD'S SO FUZZY... WHO ARE *YOU?*
I'M THE HUSBAND WHO'S BEEN ASSIGNED TO YOU.
NOW, UP YOU GET. I MADE BREAK-FAST...
BUT ONLY THIS ONCE. COOKING IS *YOUR* JOB--
--HONEY.

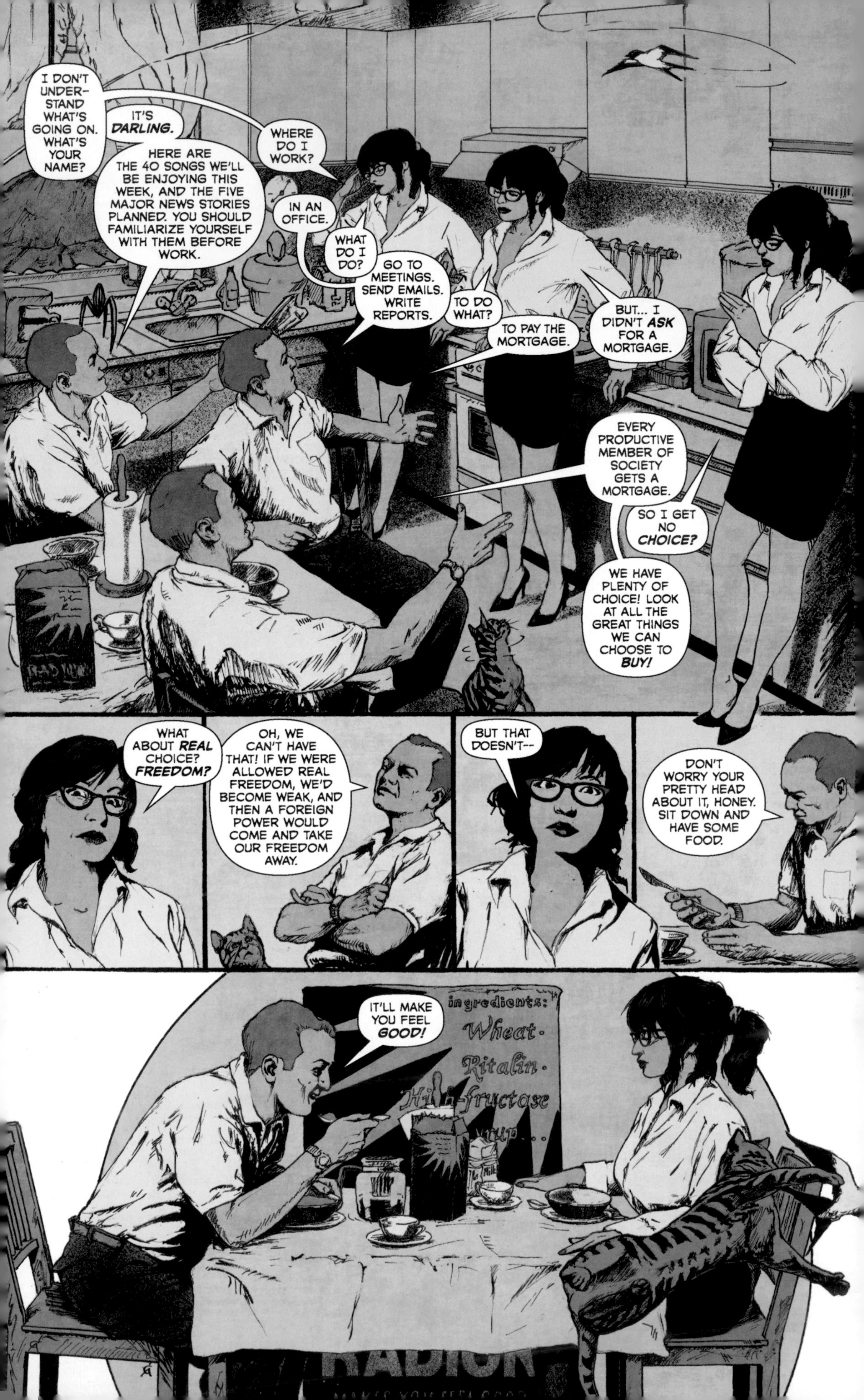
I DON'T UNDER-STAND WHAT'S GOING ON. WHAT'S YOUR NAME?
IT'S *DARLING.*
HERE ARE THE 40 SONGS WE'LL BE ENJOYING THIS WEEK, AND THE FIVE MAJOR NEWS STORIES PLANNED. YOU SHOULD FAMILIARIZE YOURSELF WITH THEM BEFORE WORK.
WHERE DO I WORK?
IN AN OFFICE.
WHAT DO I DO?
GO TO MEETINGS. SEND EMAILS. WRITE REPORTS.
TO DO WHAT?
TO PAY THE MORTGAGE.
BUT... I DIDN'T **ASK** FOR A MORTGAGE.
EVERY PRODUCTIVE MEMBER OF SOCIETY GETS A MORTGAGE.
SO I GET NO ***CHOICE?***
WE HAVE PLENTY OF CHOICE! LOOK AT ALL THE GREAT THINGS WE CAN CHOOSE TO ***BUY!***
WHAT ABOUT **REAL** CHOICE? ***FREEDOM?***
OH, WE CAN'T HAVE THAT! IF WE WERE ALLOWED REAL FREEDOM, WE'D BECOME WEAK, AND THEN A FOREIGN POWER WOULD COME AND TAKE OUR FREEDOM AWAY.
BUT THAT DOESN'T--
DON'T WORRY YOUR PRETTY HEAD ABOUT IT, HONEY. SIT DOWN AND HAVE SOME FOOD.
IT'LL MAKE YOU FEEL ***GOOD!***
ingredients:
Wheat.
Ritalin.

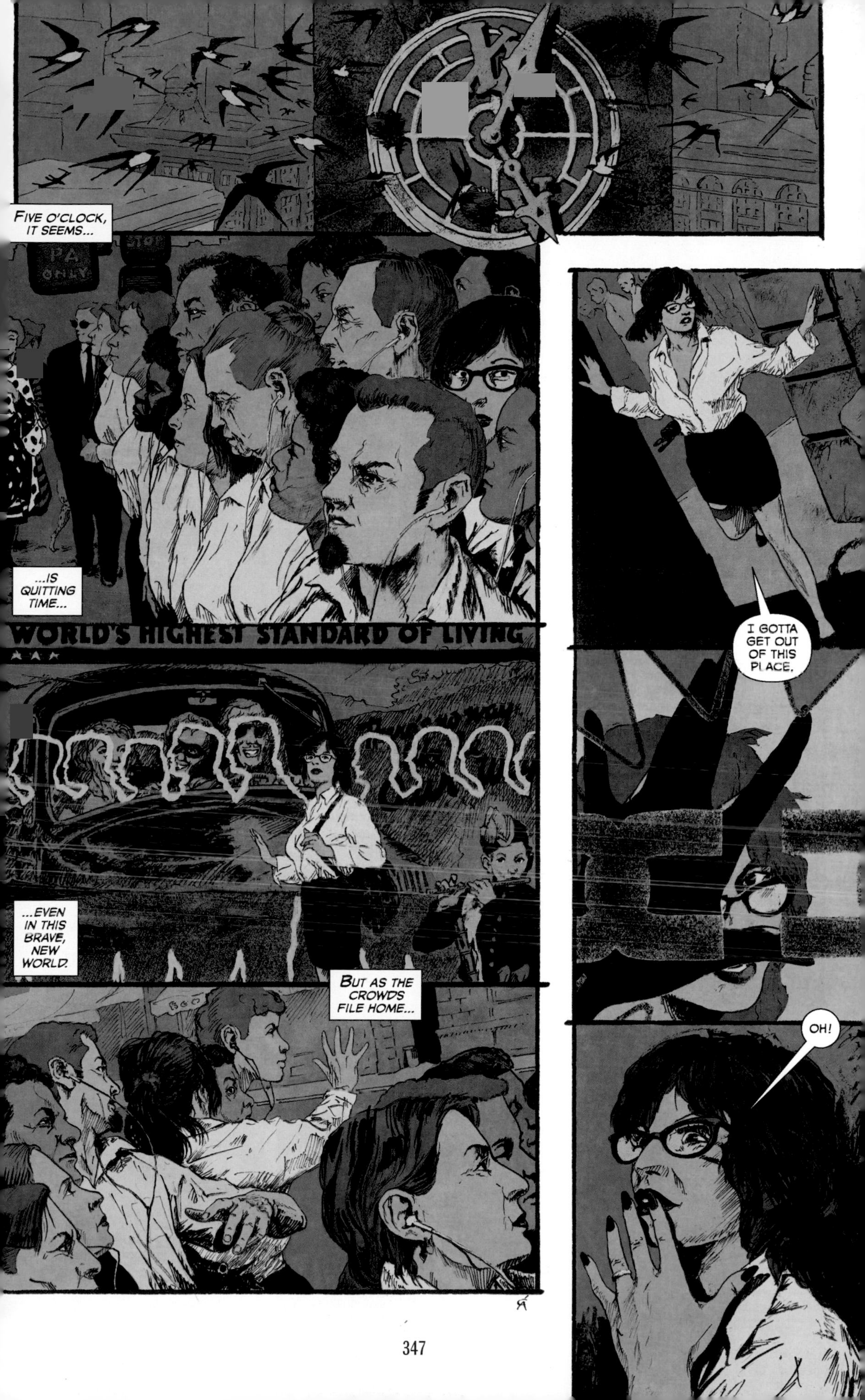
FIVE O'CLOCK, IT SEEMS...
...IS QUITTING TIME...
WORLD'S HIGHEST STANDARD OF LIVING
...EVEN IN THIS BRAVE, NEW WORLD.
BUT AS THE CROWDS FILE HOME...
I GOTTA GET OUT OF THIS PLACE.
OH!

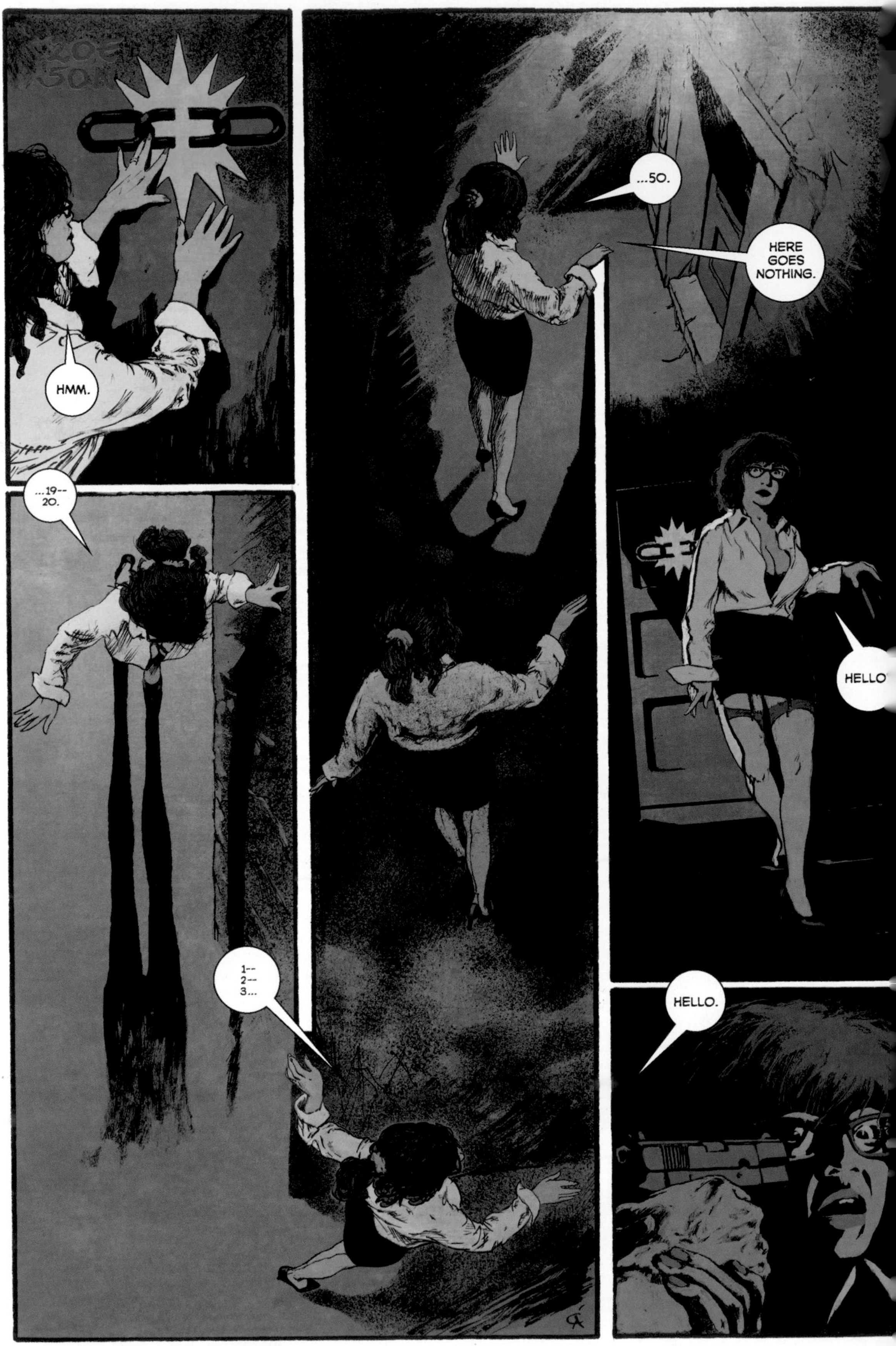
HMM.
...19--
20.
...50.
HERE GOES NOTHING.
1--
2--
3...
HELLO
HELLO.

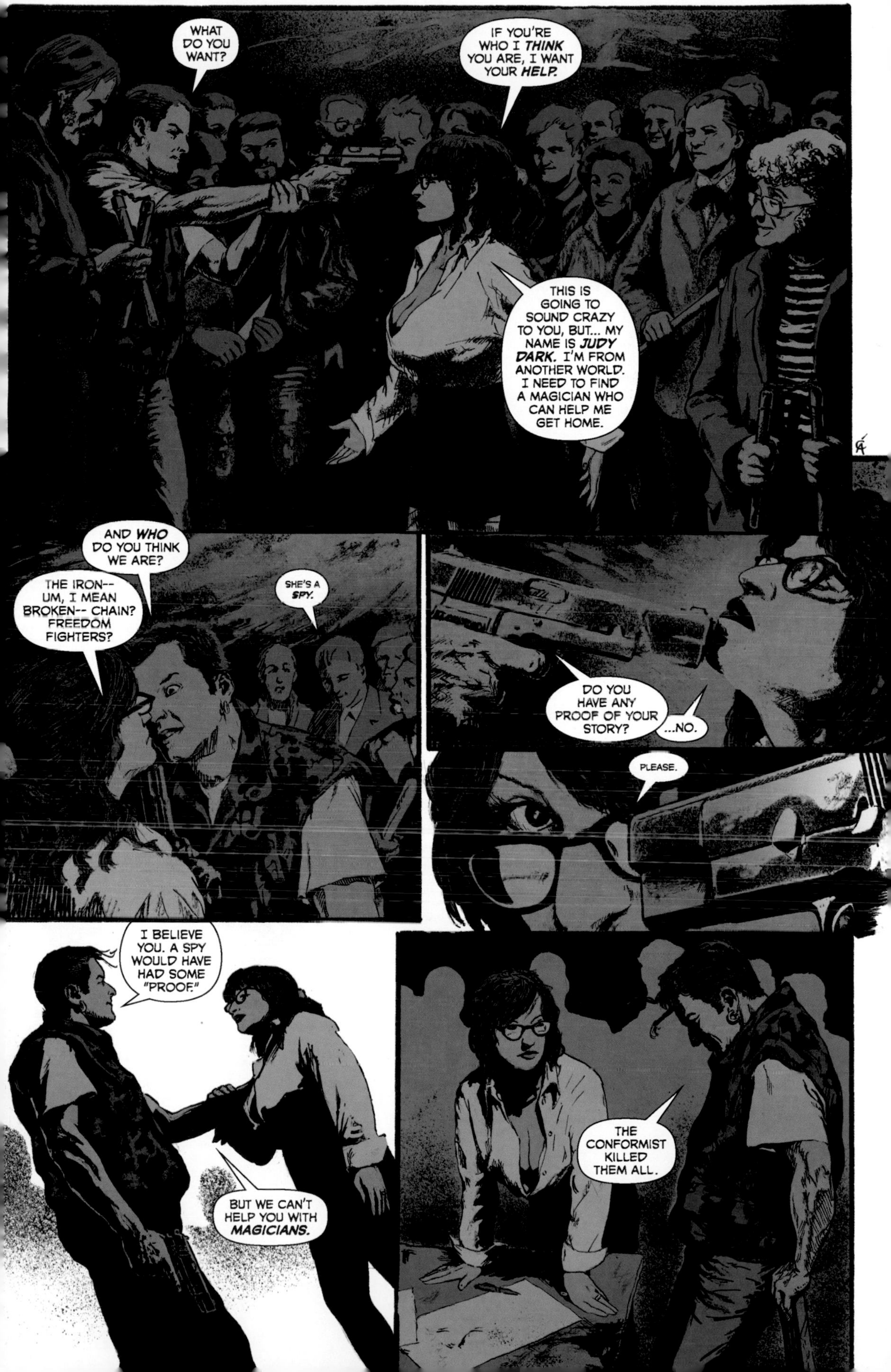
WHAT DO YOU WANT?
IF YOU'RE WHO I *THINK* YOU ARE, I WANT YOUR *HELP.*
THIS IS GOING TO SOUND CRAZY TO YOU, BUT... MY NAME IS *JUDY DARK.* I'M FROM ANOTHER WORLD. I NEED TO FIND A MAGICIAN WHO CAN HELP ME GET HOME.
AND *WHO* DO YOU THINK WE ARE?
THE IRON-- UM, I MEAN BROKEN-- CHAIN? FREEDOM FIGHTERS?
SHE'S A *SPY.*
DO YOU HAVE ANY PROOF OF YOUR STORY?
...NO.
PLEASE.
I BELIEVE YOU. A SPY WOULD HAVE HAD SOME "PROOF."
BUT WE CAN'T HELP YOU WITH *MAGICIANS.*
THE CONFORMIST KILLED THEM ALL.

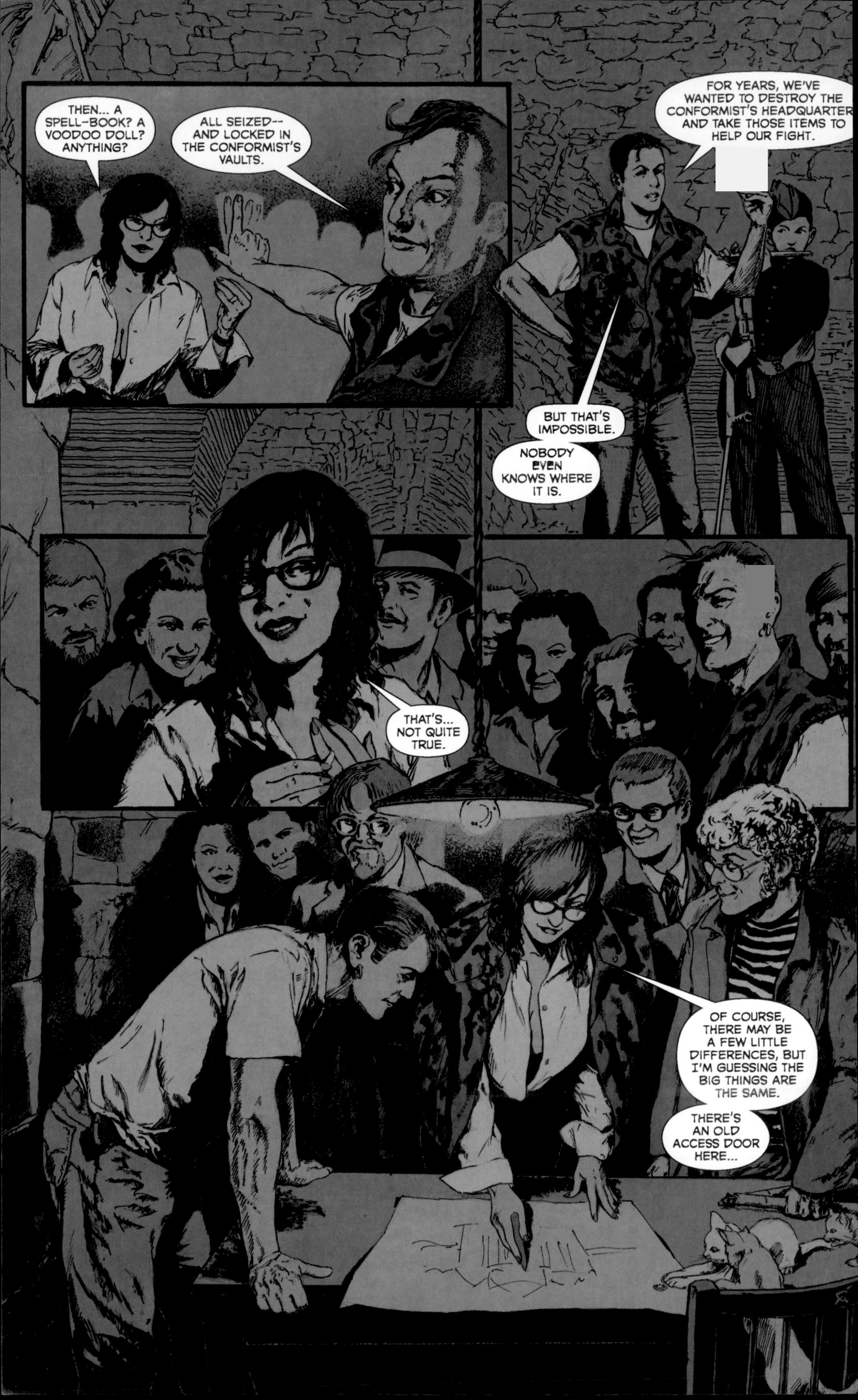
THEN... A SPELL-BOOK? A VOODOO DOLL? ANYTHING?
ALL SEIZED-- AND LOCKED IN THE CONFORMIST'S VAULTS.
FOR YEARS, WE'VE WANTED TO DESTROY THE CONFORMIST'S HEADQUARTER AND TAKE THOSE ITEMS TO HELP OUR FIGHT.
BUT THAT'S IMPOSSIBLE.
NOBODY EVEN KNOWS WHERE IT IS.
THAT'S... NOT QUITE TRUE.
OF COURSE, THERE MAY BE A FEW LITTLE DIFFERENCES, BUT I'M GUESSING THE BIG THINGS ARE THE SAME.
THERE'S AN OLD ACCESS DOOR HERE...

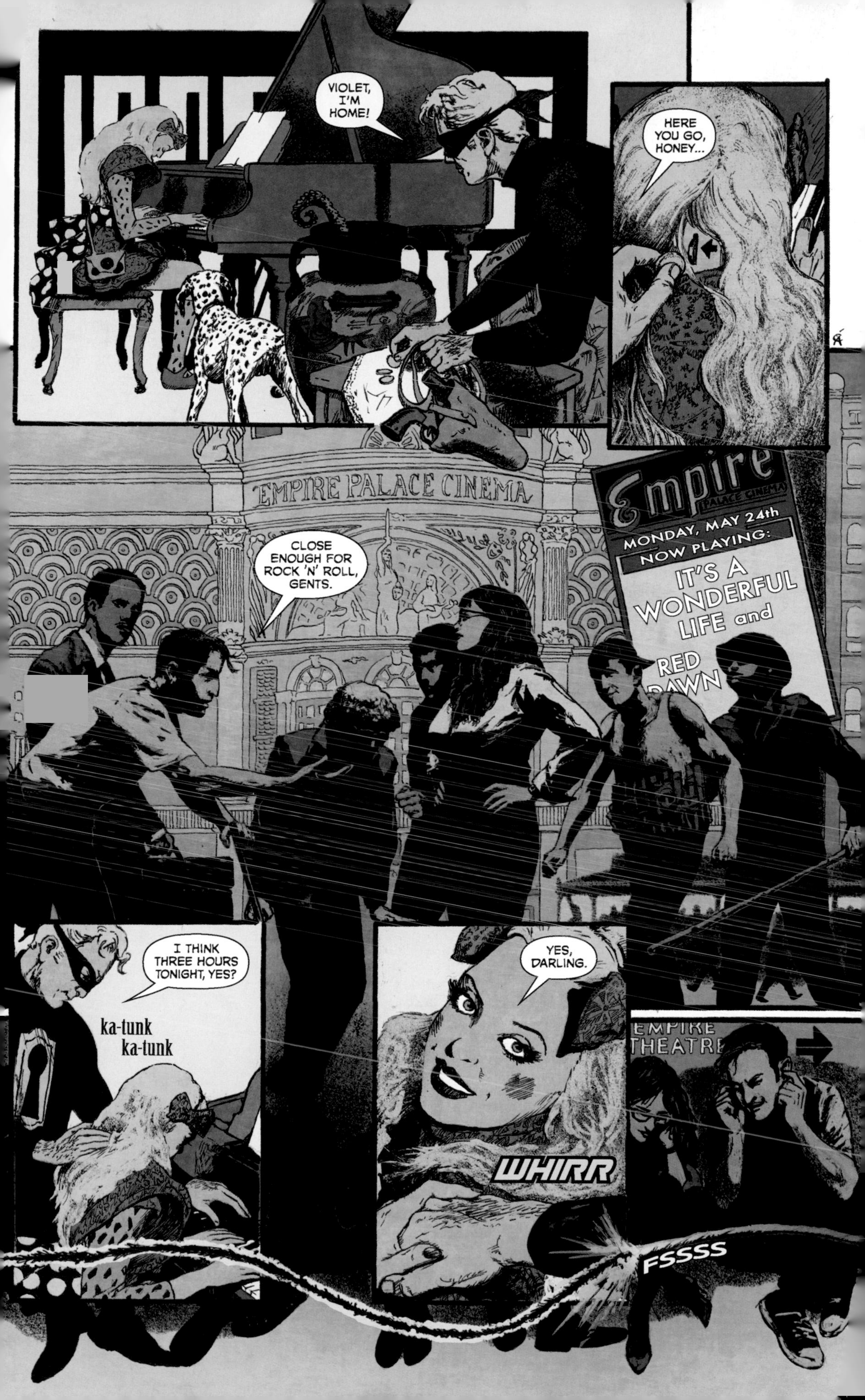
VIOLET, I'M HOME!
HERE YOU GO, HONEY...
EMPIRE PALACE CINEMA
CLOSE ENOUGH FOR ROCK 'N' ROLL, GENTS.
Empire
PALACE CINEMA
MONDAY, MAY 24th
NOW PLAYING:
IT'S A WONDERFUL LIFE and
RED
I THINK THREE HOURS TONIGHT, YES?
ka-tunk
ka-tunk
YES, DARLING.
WHIRR
EMPIRE THEATRE
FSSSS

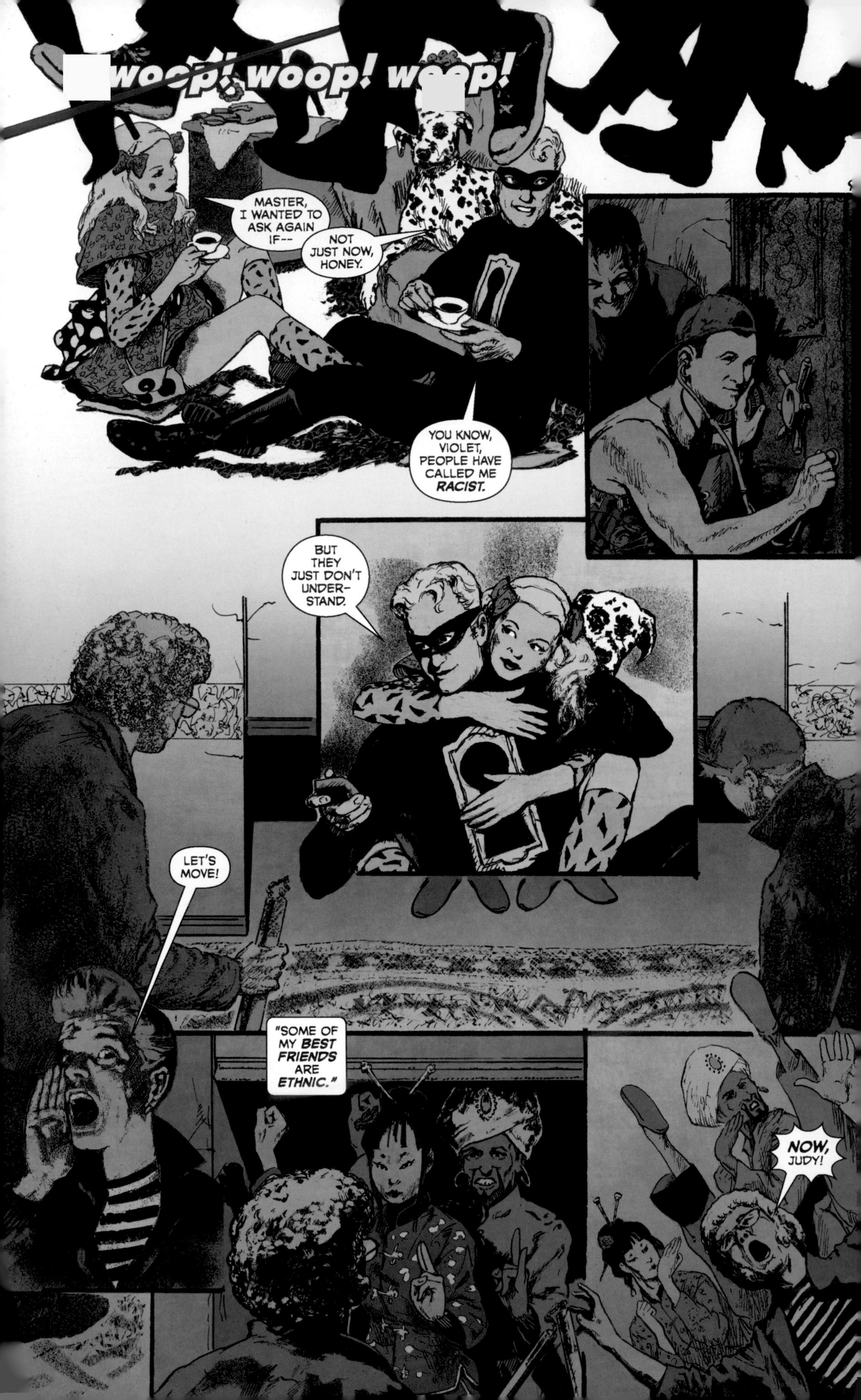
woop! woop! woop!
MASTER, I WANTED TO ASK AGAIN IF--
NOT JUST NOW, HONEY.
YOU KNOW, VIOLET, PEOPLE HAVE CALLED ME *RACIST.*
BUT THEY JUST DON'T UNDER-STAND.
LET'S MOVE!
"SOME OF MY *BEST FRIENDS* ARE *ETHNIC.*"
*NOW,* JUDY!

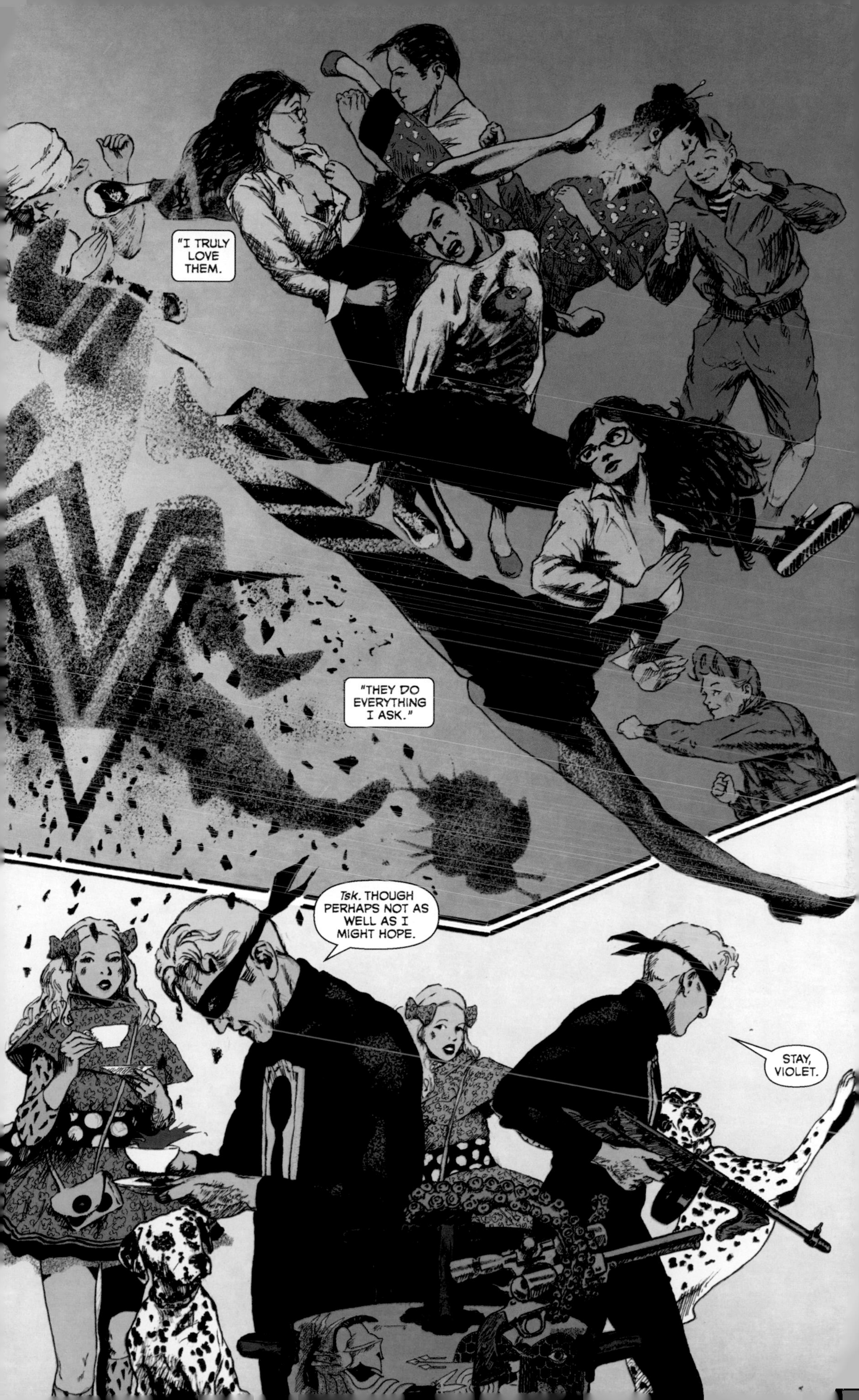
"I TRULY LOVE THEM.
"THEY DO EVERYTHING I ASK."
*Tsk.* THOUGH PERHAPS NOT AS WELL AS I MIGHT HOPE.
STAY, VIOLET.

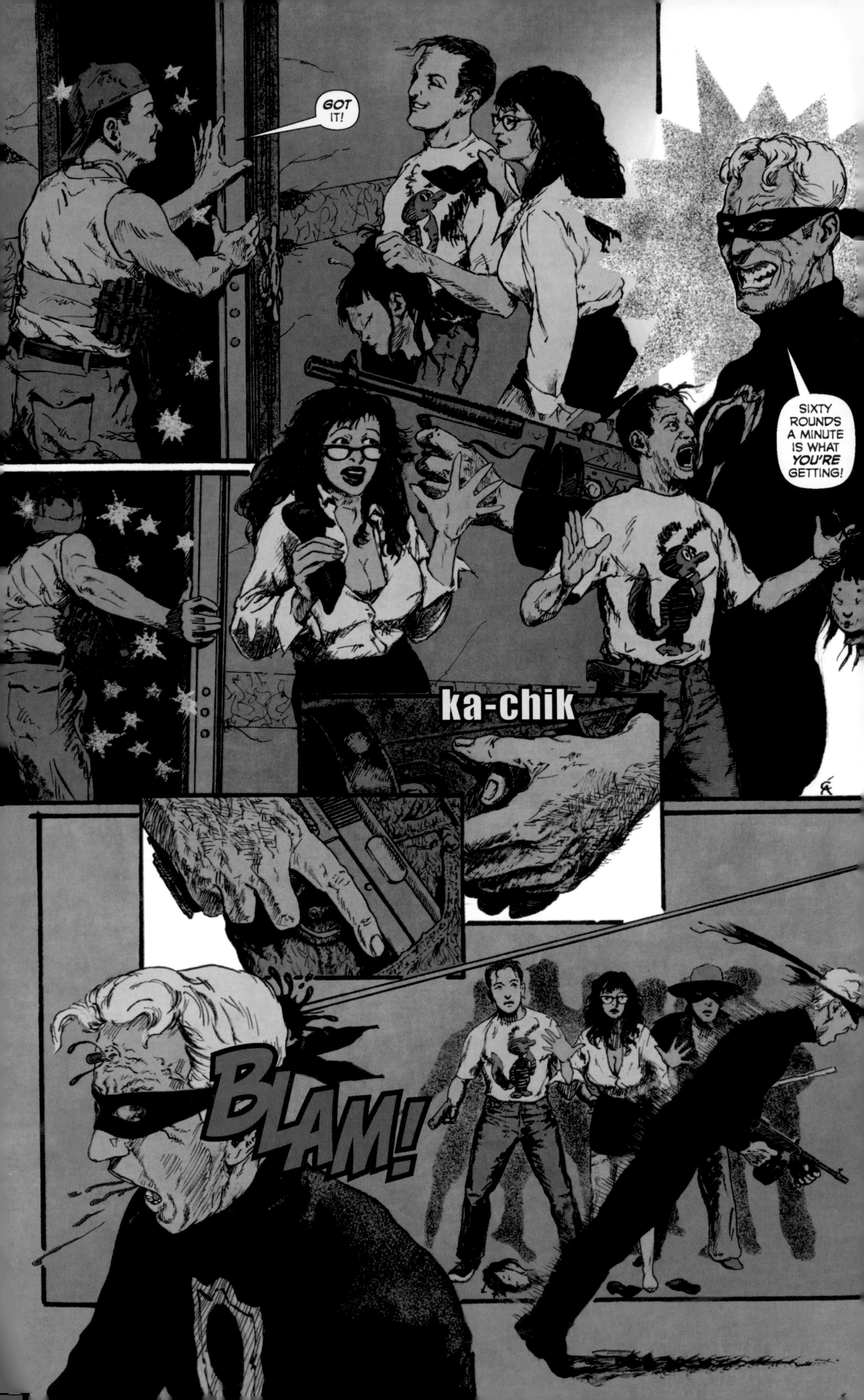
GOT IT!
SIXTY ROUNDS A MINUTE IS WHAT *YOU'RE* GETTING!
ka-chik
BLAM!

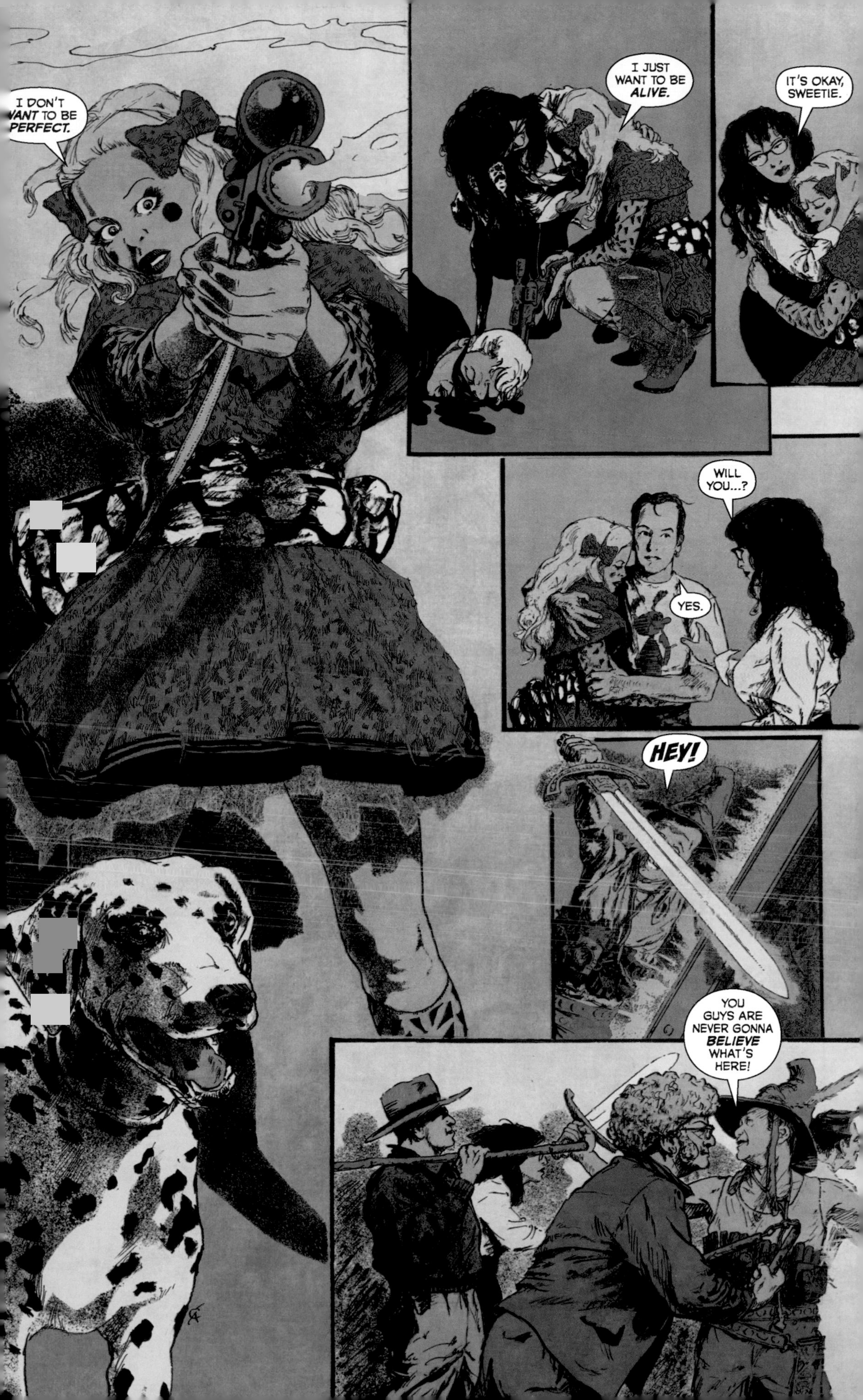
I DON'T WANT TO BE PERFECT.
I JUST WANT TO BE ALIVE.
IT'S OKAY, SWEETIE.
WILL YOU...?
YES.
HEY!
YOU GUYS ARE NEVER GONNA BELIEVE WHAT'S HERE!

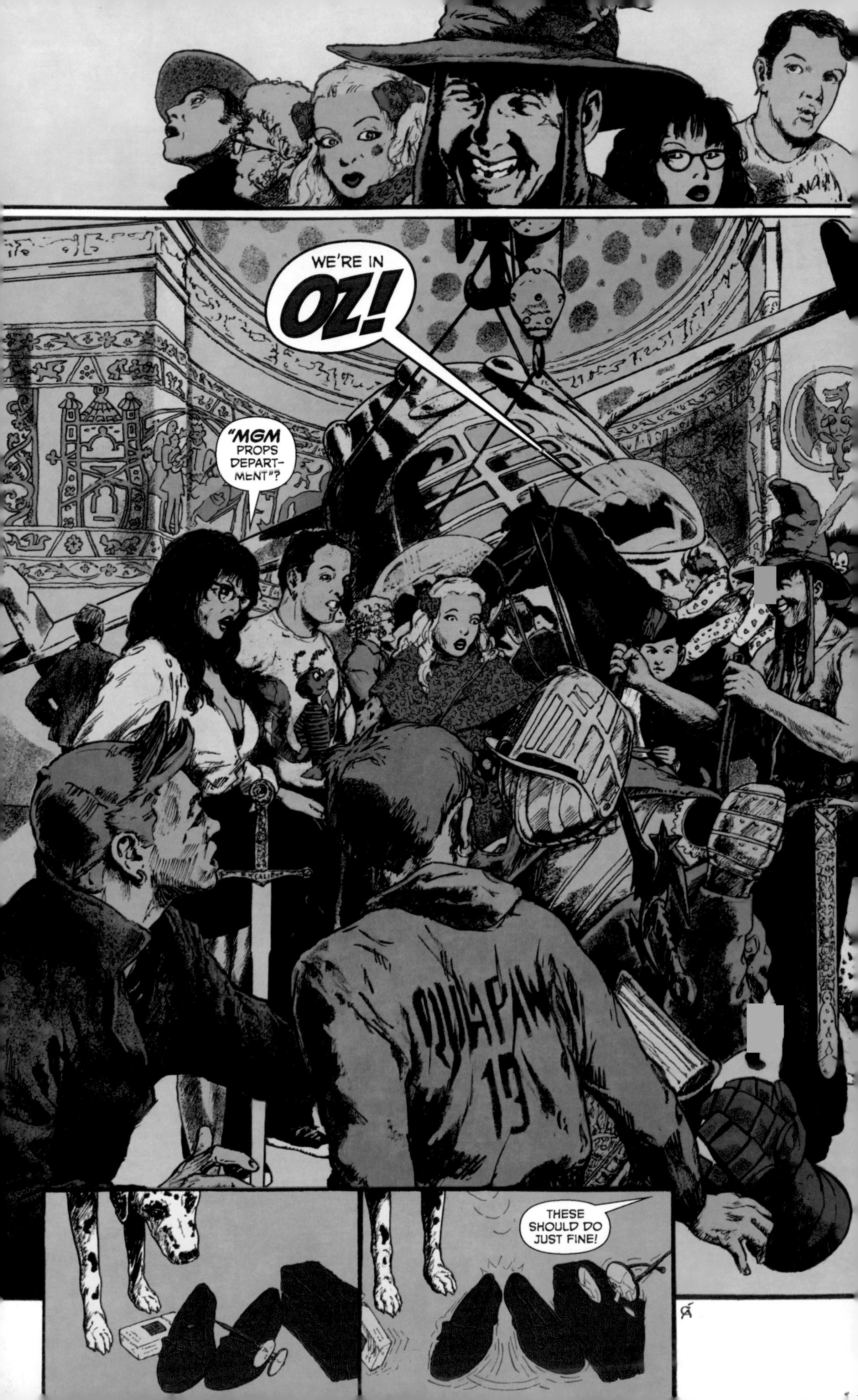
WE'RE IN OZ!
"MGM PROPS DEPARTMENT"?
THESE SHOULD DO JUST FINE!

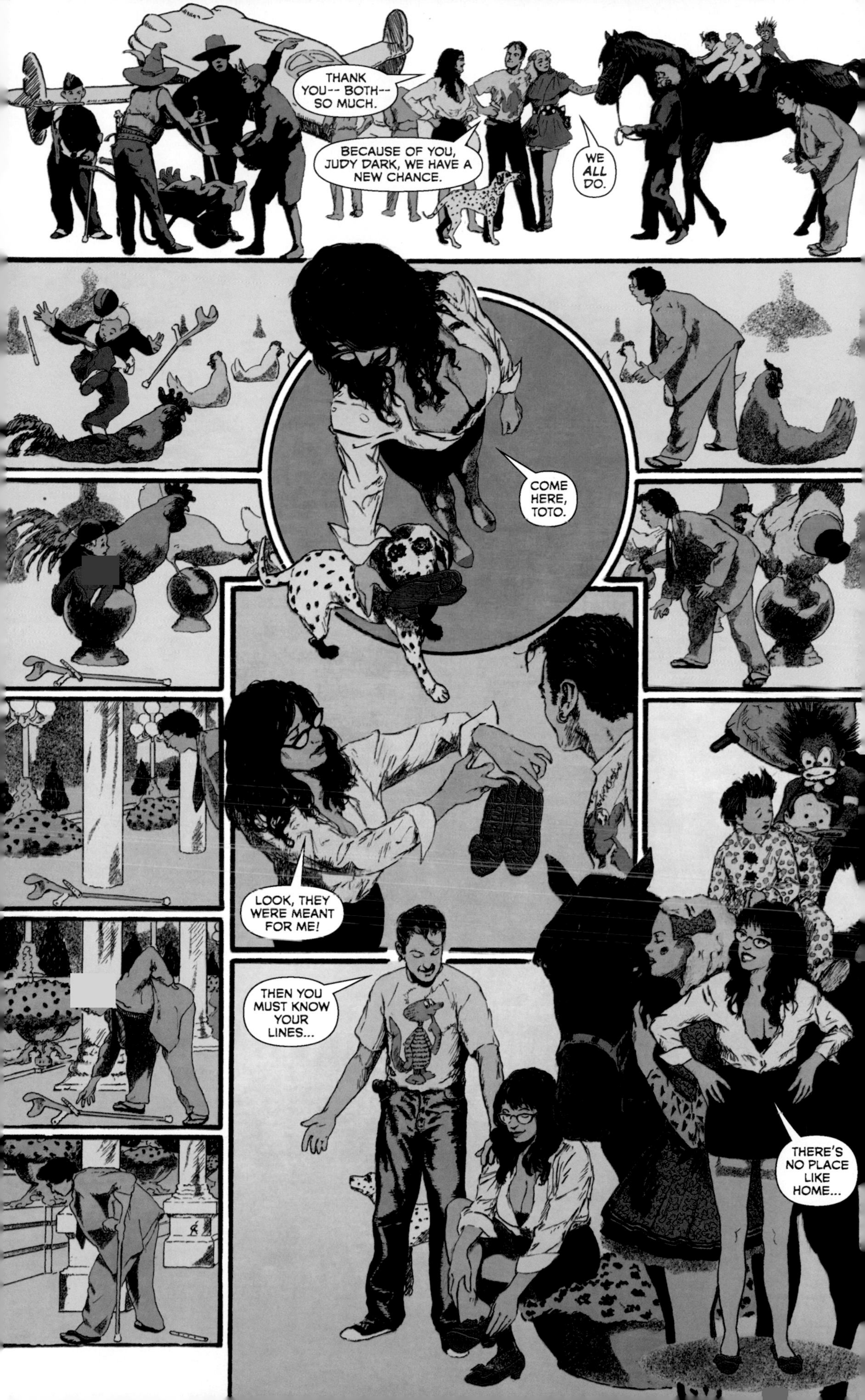
THANK YOU-- BOTH-- SO MUCH.
BECAUSE OF YOU, JUDY DARK, WE HAVE A NEW CHANCE.
WE *ALL* DO.
COME HERE, TOTO.
LOOK, THEY WERE MEANT FOR ME!
THEN YOU MUST KNOW YOUR LINES...
THERE'S NO PLACE LIKE HOME...

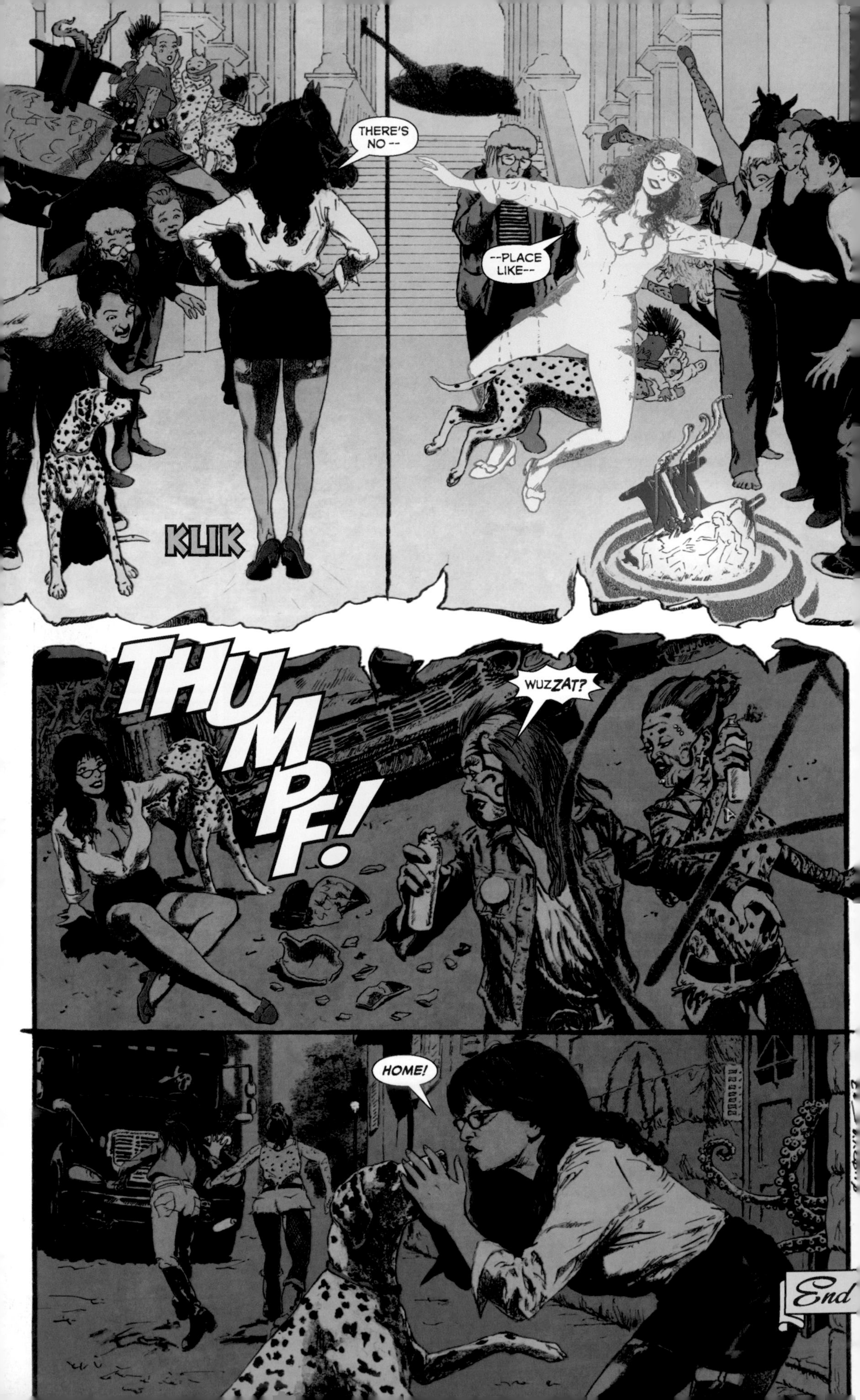
THERE'S NO --
KLIK
--PLACE LIKE--
THUMPF!
WUZZAT?
HOME!
End

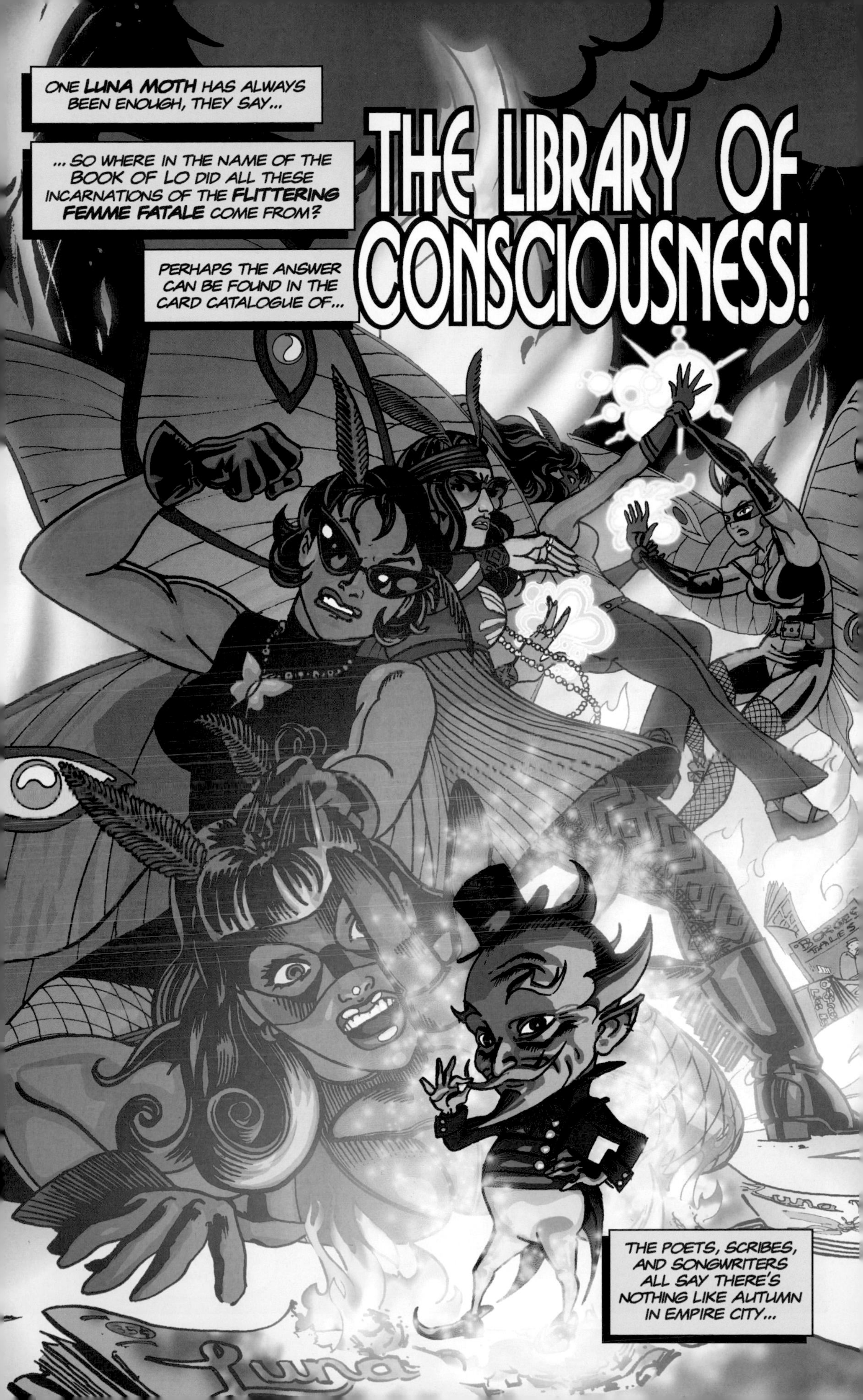
ONE LUNA MOTH HAS ALWAYS BEEN ENOUGH, THEY SAY...
... SO WHERE IN THE NAME OF THE BOOK OF LO DID ALL THESE INCARNATIONS OF THE FLITTERING FEMME FATALE COME FROM?
PERHAPS THE ANSWER CAN BE FOUND IN THE CARD CATALOGUE OF...
THE LIBRARY OF CONSCIOUSNESS!
THE POETS, SCRIBES, AND SONGWRITERS ALL SAY THERE'S NOTHING LIKE AUTUMN IN EMPIRE CITY...

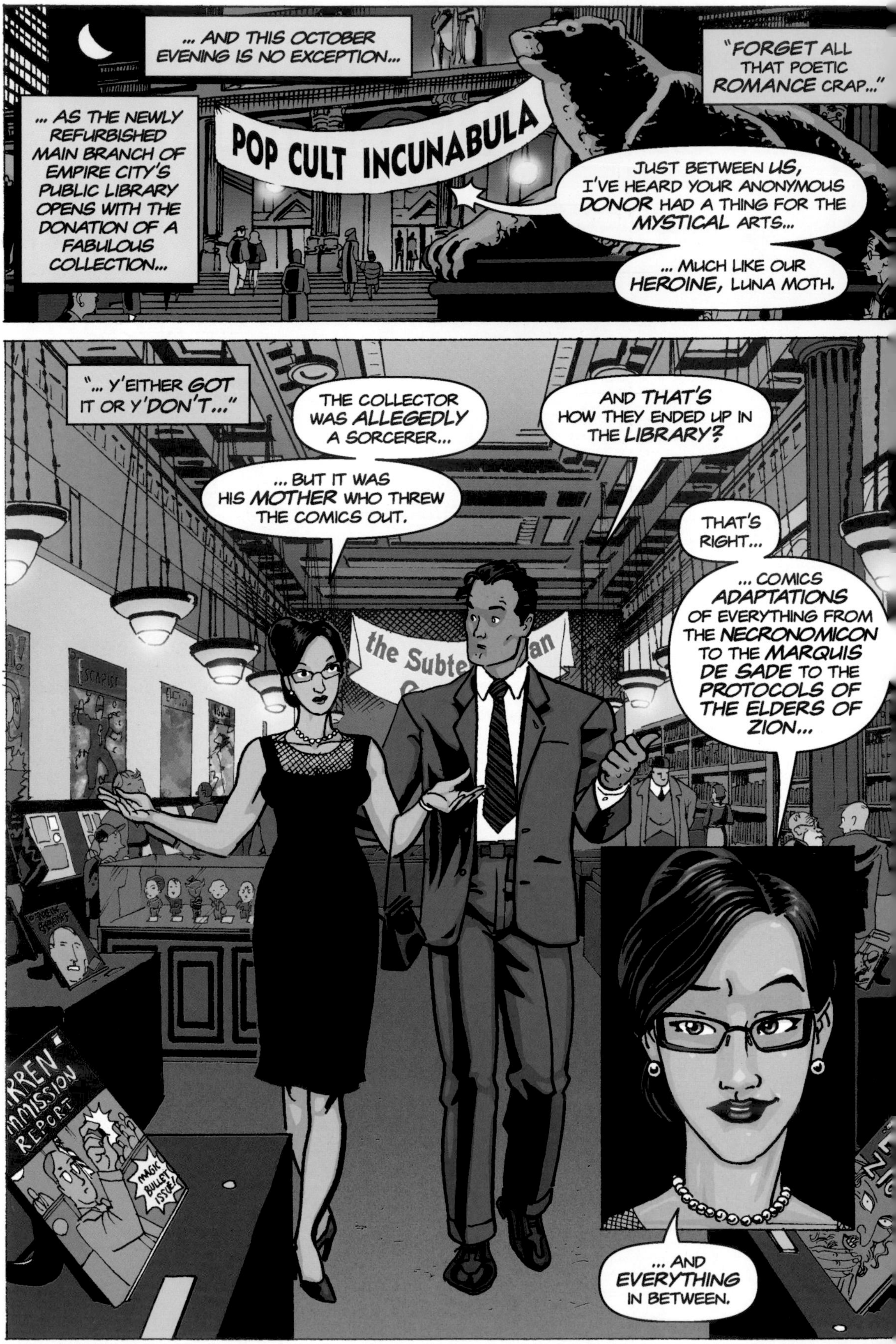
... AND THIS OCTOBER EVENING IS NO EXCEPTION...
... AS THE NEWLY REFURBISHED MAIN BRANCH OF EMPIRE CITY'S PUBLIC LIBRARY OPENS WITH THE DONATION OF A FABULOUS COLLECTION...
POP CULT INCUNABULA
"FORGET ALL THAT POETIC ROMANCE CRAP..."
JUST BETWEEN US, I'VE HEARD YOUR ANONYMOUS DONOR HAD A THING FOR THE MYSTICAL ARTS...
... MUCH LIKE OUR HEROINE, LUNA MOTH.
"... Y'EITHER GOT IT OR Y'DON'T..."
THE COLLECTOR WAS ALLEGEDLY A SORCERER...
... BUT IT WAS HIS MOTHER WHO THREW THE COMICS OUT.
AND THAT'S HOW THEY ENDED UP IN THE LIBRARY?
THAT'S RIGHT...
... COMICS ADAPTATIONS OF EVERYTHING FROM THE NECRONOMICON TO THE MARQUIS DE SADE TO THE PROTOCOLS OF THE ELDERS OF ZION...
... AND EVERYTHING IN BETWEEN.
MAGIC BULLET ISSUE!
REPORT

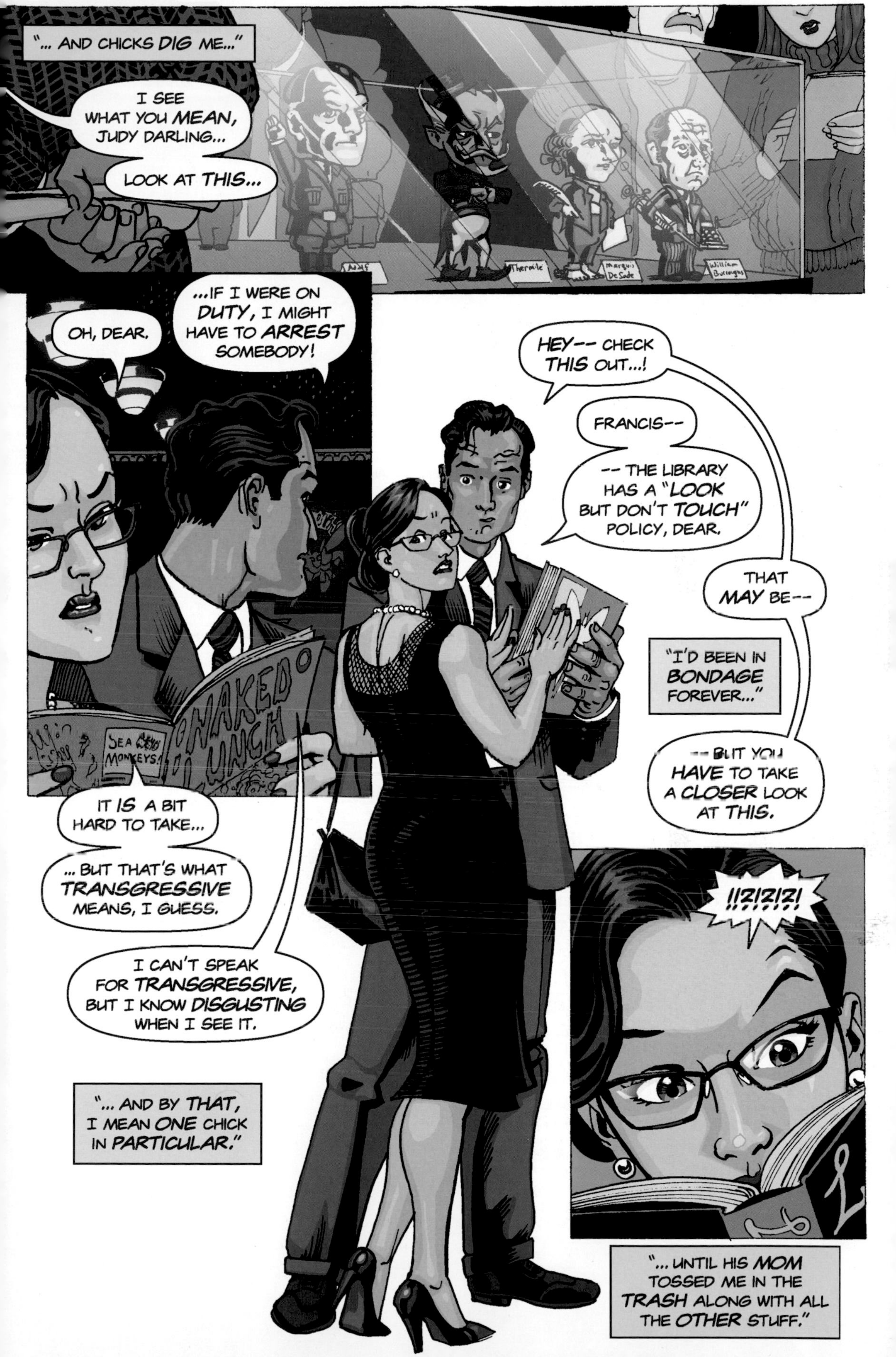
"... AND CHICKS DIG ME..."
I SEE WHAT YOU MEAN, JUDY DARLING...
LOOK AT THIS...
Adolf
Marquis De Sade
William Burroughs
OH, DEAR.
...IF I WERE ON DUTY, I MIGHT HAVE TO ARREST SOMEBODY!
NAKED LUNCH
SEA MONKEYS!
IT IS A BIT HARD TO TAKE...
... BUT THAT'S WHAT TRANSGRESSIVE MEANS, I GUESS.
I CAN'T SPEAK FOR TRANSGRESSIVE, BUT I KNOW DISGUSTING WHEN I SEE IT.
HEY-- CHECK THIS OUT...!
FRANCIS--
-- THE LIBRARY HAS A "LOOK BUT DON'T TOUCH" POLICY, DEAR.
THAT MAY BE--
"I'D BEEN IN BONDAGE FOREVER..."
-- BUT YOU HAVE TO TAKE A CLOSER LOOK AT THIS.
"... AND BY THAT, I MEAN ONE CHICK IN PARTICULAR."
!!?!?!?!
"... UNTIL HIS MOM TOSSED ME IN THE TRASH ALONG WITH ALL THE OTHER STUFF."

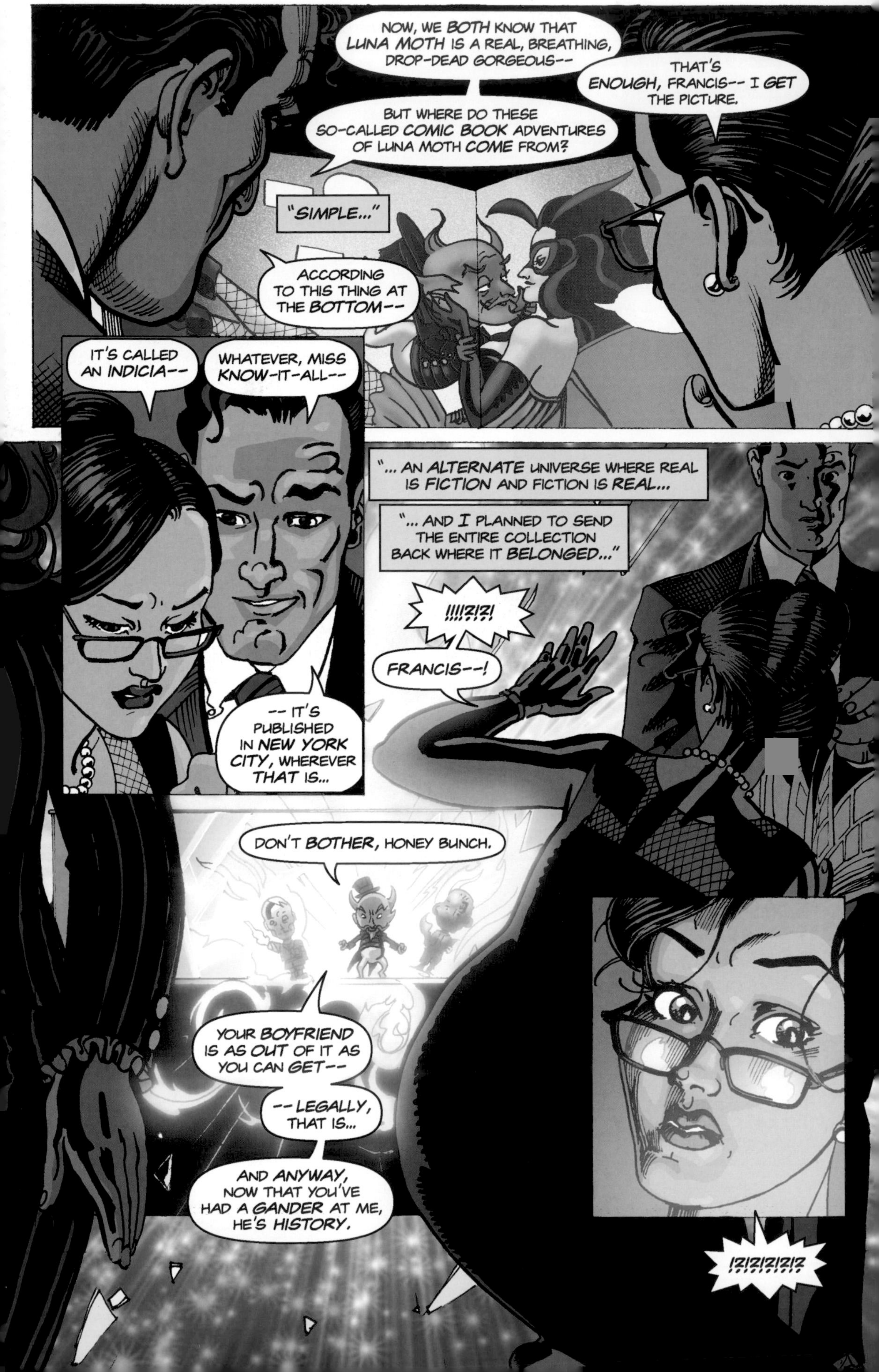

NOW, WE BOTH KNOW THAT LUNA MOTH IS A REAL, BREATHING, DROP-DEAD GORGEOUS--
THAT'S ENOUGH, FRANCIS-- I GET THE PICTURE.
BUT WHERE DO THESE SO-CALLED COMIC BOOK ADVENTURES OF LUNA MOTH COME FROM?
"SIMPLE..."
ACCORDING TO THIS THING AT THE BOTTOM--
IT'S CALLED AN INDICIA--
WHATEVER, MISS KNOW-IT-ALL--
-- IT'S PUBLISHED IN NEW YORK CITY, WHEREVER THAT IS...
"... AN ALTERNATE UNIVERSE WHERE REAL IS FICTION AND FICTION IS REAL...
"... AND I PLANNED TO SEND THE ENTIRE COLLECTION BACK WHERE IT BELONGED..."
!!!!?!?!
FRANCIS--!
DON'T BOTHER, HONEY BUNCH.
YOUR BOYFRIEND IS AS OUT OF IT AS YOU CAN GET--
--LEGALLY, THAT IS...
AND ANYWAY, NOW THAT YOU'VE HAD A GANDER AT ME, HE'S HISTORY.
!?!?!?!?!?

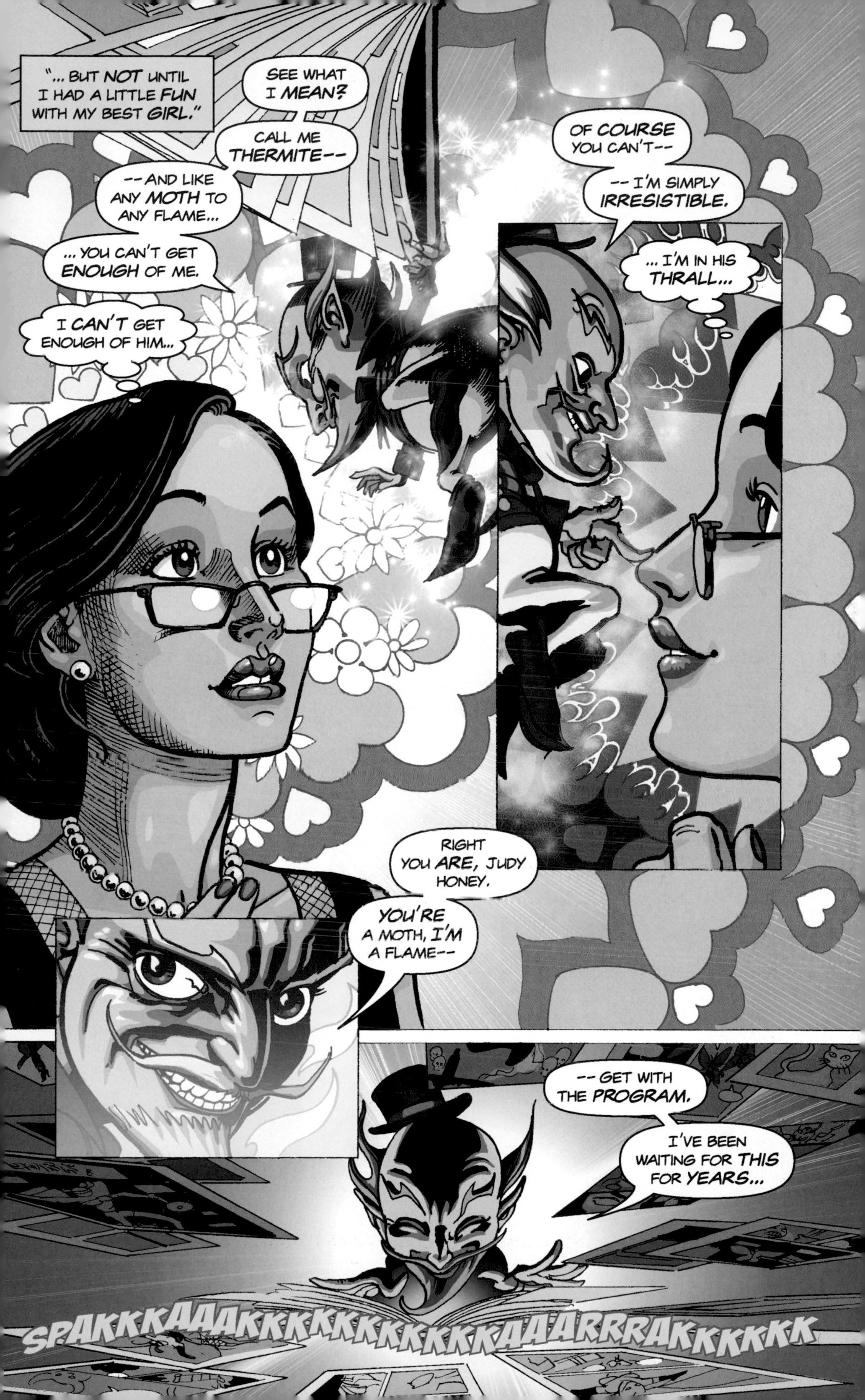
"... BUT NOT UNTIL I HAD A LITTLE FUN WITH MY BEST GIRL."
SEE WHAT I MEAN?
CALL ME THERMITE--
--AND LIKE ANY MOTH TO ANY FLAME...
... YOU CAN'T GET ENOUGH OF ME.
I CAN'T GET ENOUGH OF HIM...
OF COURSE YOU CAN'T--
-- I'M SIMPLY IRRESISTIBLE.
... I'M IN HIS THRALL...
RIGHT YOU ARE, JUDY HONEY.
YOU'RE A MOTH, I'M A FLAME--
-- GET WITH THE PROGRAM.
I'VE BEEN WAITING FOR THIS FOR YEARS...
SPAKKKAAAAKKKKKKKKKKKKAAAARRRAKKKKKK

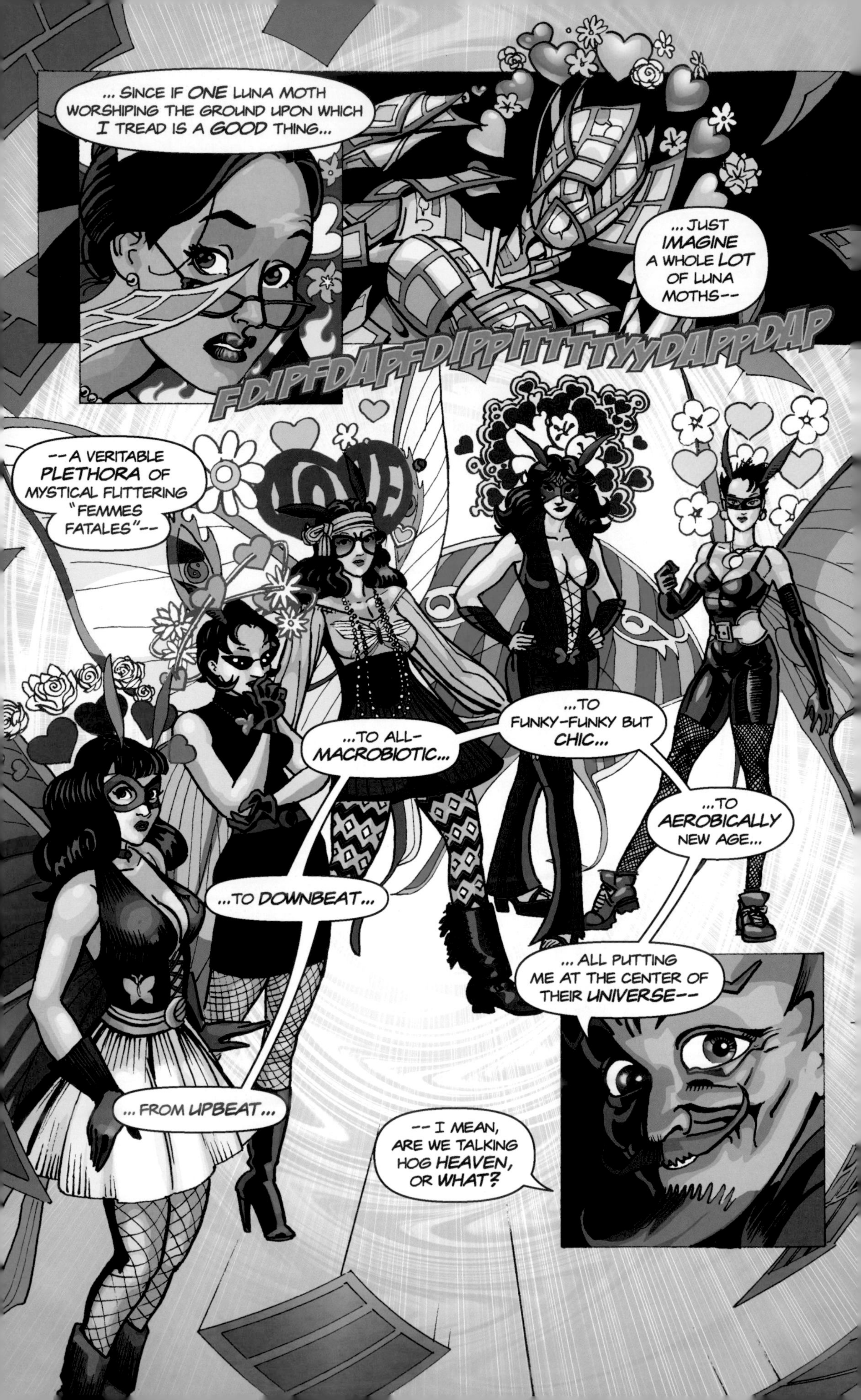
... SINCE IF ONE LUNA MOTH WORSHIPING THE GROUND UPON WHICH I TREAD IS A GOOD THING...
... JUST IMAGINE A WHOLE LOT OF LUNA MOTHS--
FDIPFDAPFDIPPITTTTTYYDAPPDAP
--A VERITABLE PLETHORA OF MYSTICAL FLUTTERING "FEMMES FATALES"--
...TO FUNKY-FUNKY BUT CHIC...
...TO ALL-MACROBIOTIC...
...TO AEROBICALLY NEW AGE...
...TO DOWNBEAT...
... ALL PUTTING ME AT THE CENTER OF THEIR UNIVERSE--
... FROM UPBEAT...
-- I MEAN, ARE WE TALKING HOG HEAVEN, OR WHAT?

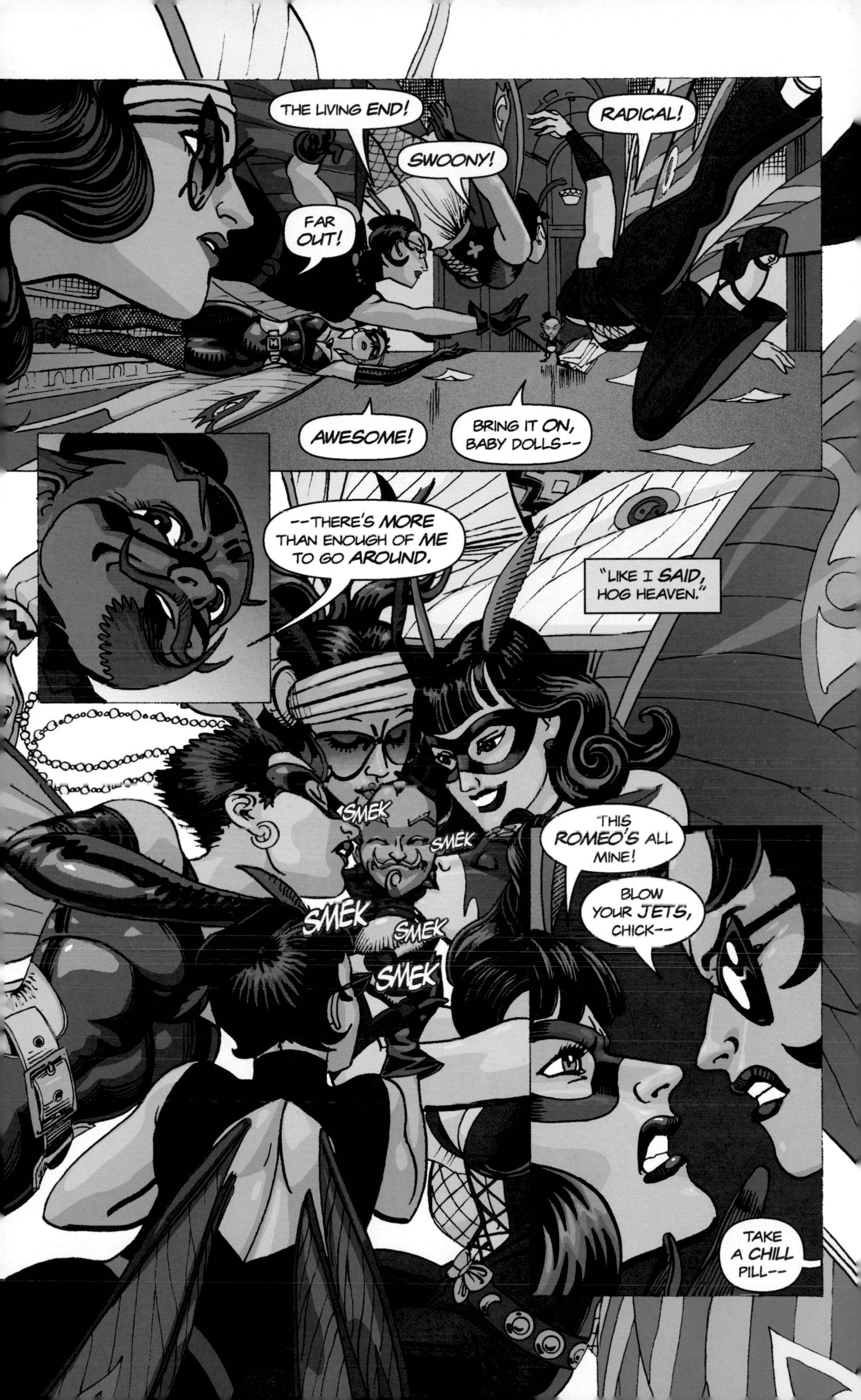
THE LIVING END!
SWOONY!
RADICAL!
FAR OUT!
AWESOME!
BRING IT ON, BABY DOLLS--
--THERE'S MORE THAN ENOUGH OF ME TO GO AROUND.
"LIKE I SAID, HOG HEAVEN."
SMEK
SMEK
SMEK
SMEK
SMEK
THIS ROMEO'S ALL MINE!
BLOW YOUR JETS, CHICK--
TAKE A CHILL PILL--

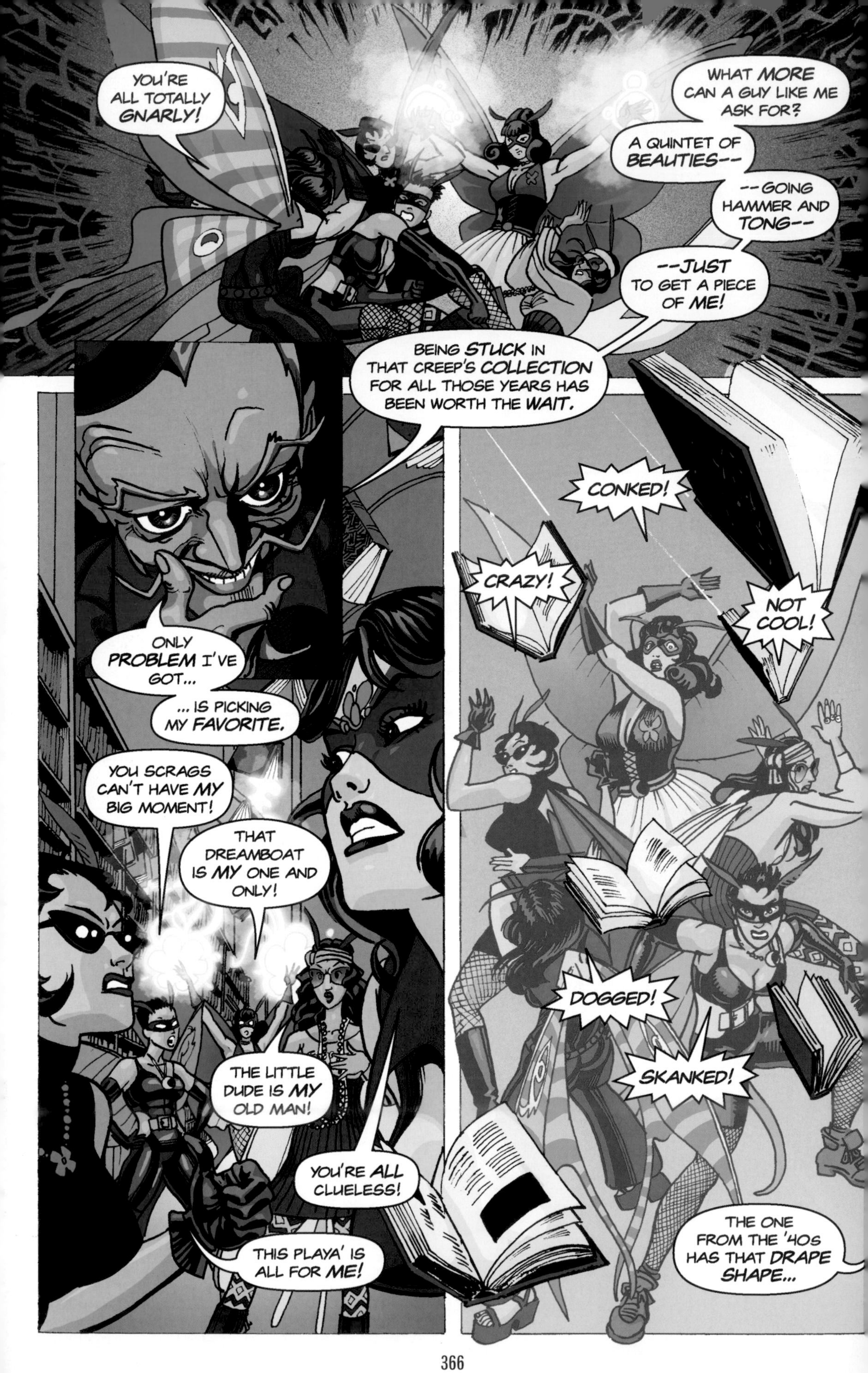
YOU'RE ALL TOTALLY GNARLY!
WHAT MORE CAN A GUY LIKE ME ASK FOR?
A QUINTET OF BEAUTIES--
--GOING HAMMER AND TONG--
--JUST TO GET A PIECE OF ME!
BEING STUCK IN THAT CREEP'S COLLECTION FOR ALL THOSE YEARS HAS BEEN WORTH THE WAIT.
ONLY PROBLEM I'VE GOT...
... IS PICKING MY FAVORITE.
YOU SCRAGS CAN'T HAVE MY BIG MOMENT!
THAT DREAMBOAT IS MY ONE AND ONLY!
THE LITTLE DUDE IS MY OLD MAN!
YOU'RE ALL CLUELESS!
THIS PLAYA' IS ALL FOR ME!
CONKED!
CRAZY!
NOT COOL!
DOGGED!
SKANKED!
THE ONE FROM THE '40s HAS THAT DRAPE SHAPE...

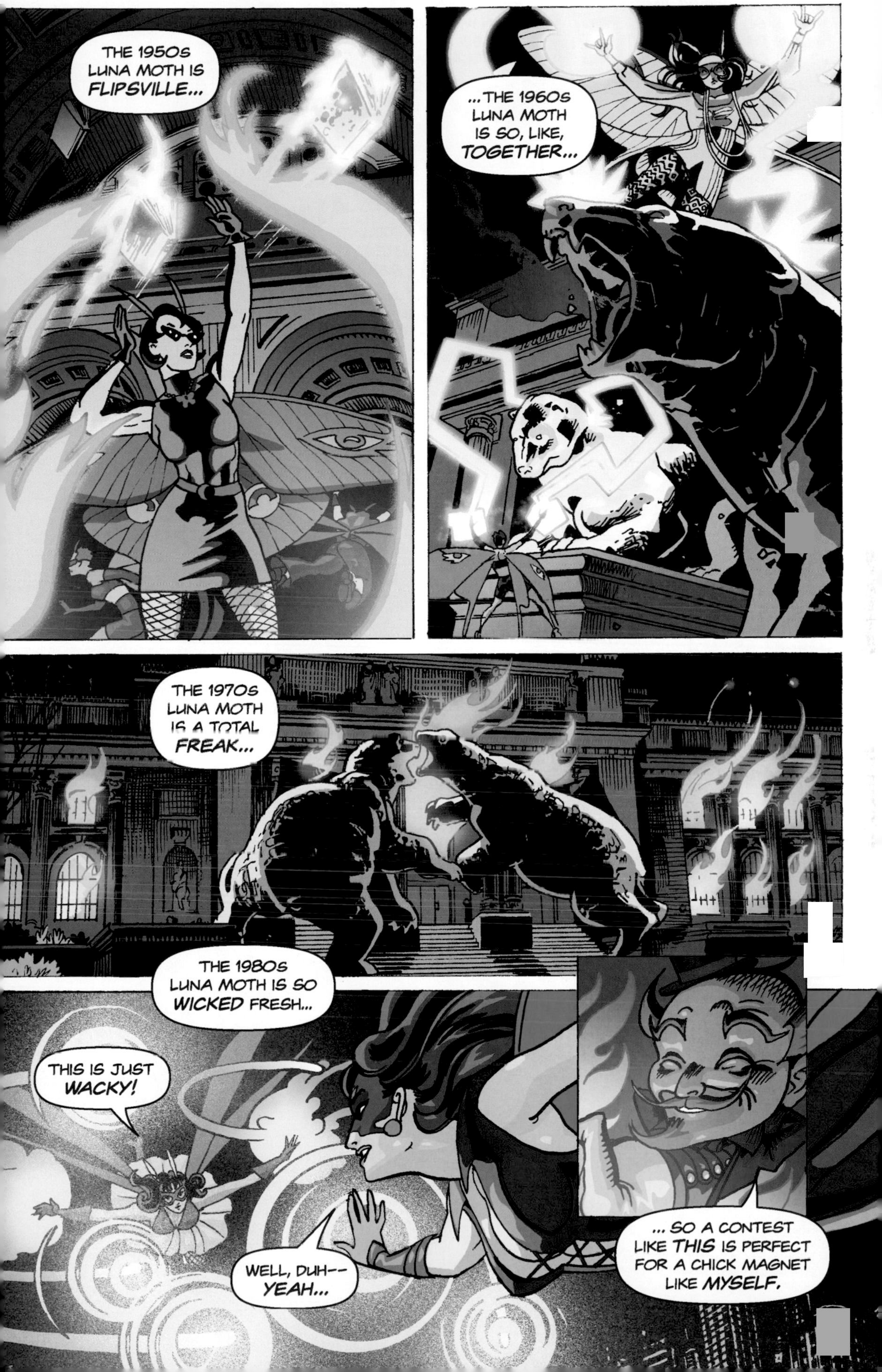
THE 1950s LUNA MOTH IS FLIPSVILLE...
...THE 1960s LUNA MOTH IS SO, LIKE, TOGETHER...
THE 1970s LUNA MOTH IS A TOTAL FREAK...
THE 1980s LUNA MOTH IS SO WICKED FRESH...
THIS IS JUST WACKY!
WELL, DUH-- YEAH...
... SO A CONTEST LIKE THIS IS PERFECT FOR A CHICK MAGNET LIKE MYSELF.

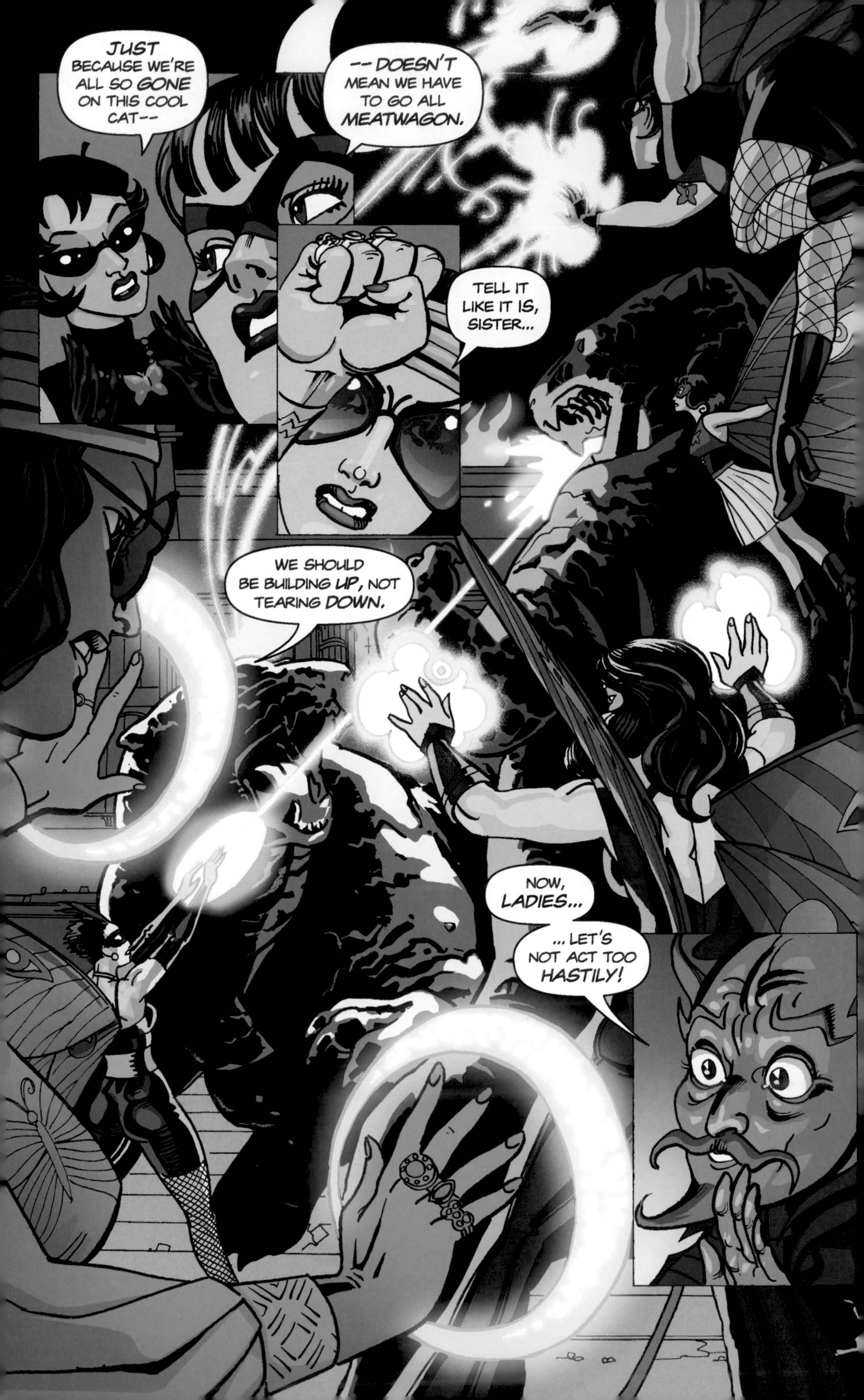
JUST BECAUSE WE'RE ALL SO GONE ON THIS COOL CAT--
--DOESN'T MEAN WE HAVE TO GO ALL MEATWAGON.
TELL IT LIKE IT IS, SISTER...
WE SHOULD BE BUILDING UP, NOT TEARING DOWN.
NOW, LADIES...
...LET'S NOT ACT TOO HASTILY!

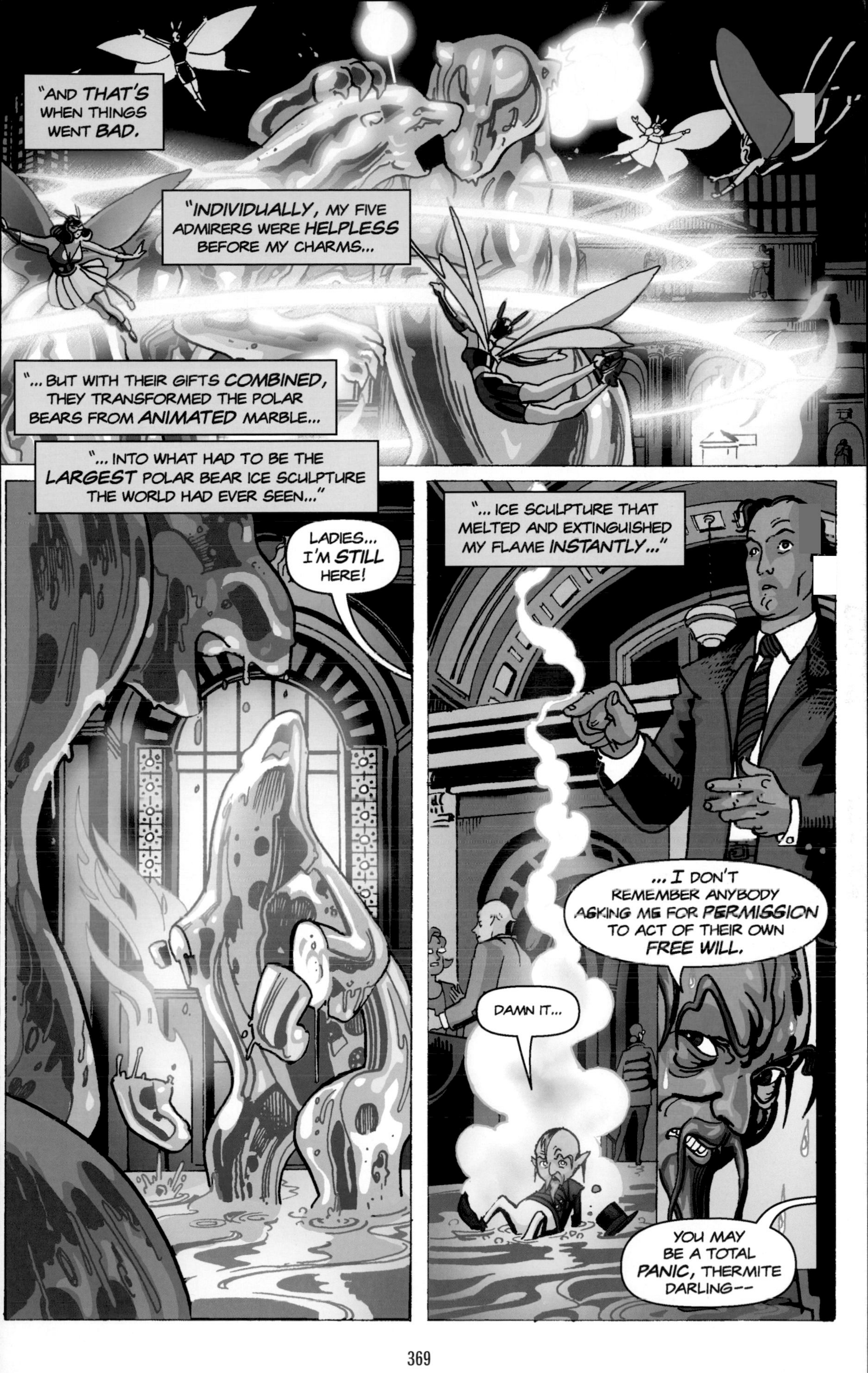
"AND THAT'S WHEN THINGS WENT BAD.
"INDIVIDUALLY, MY FIVE ADMIRERS WERE HELPLESS BEFORE MY CHARMS...
"... BUT WITH THEIR GIFTS COMBINED, THEY TRANSFORMED THE POLAR BEARS FROM ANIMATED MARBLE...
"... INTO WHAT HAD TO BE THE LARGEST POLAR BEAR ICE SCULPTURE THE WORLD HAD EVER SEEN..."
LADIES... I'M STILL HERE!
"... ICE SCULPTURE THAT MELTED AND EXTINGUISHED MY FLAME INSTANTLY..."
... I DON'T REMEMBER ANYBODY ASKING ME FOR PERMISSION TO ACT OF THEIR OWN FREE WILL.
DAMN IT...
YOU MAY BE A TOTAL PANIC, THERMITE DARLING--

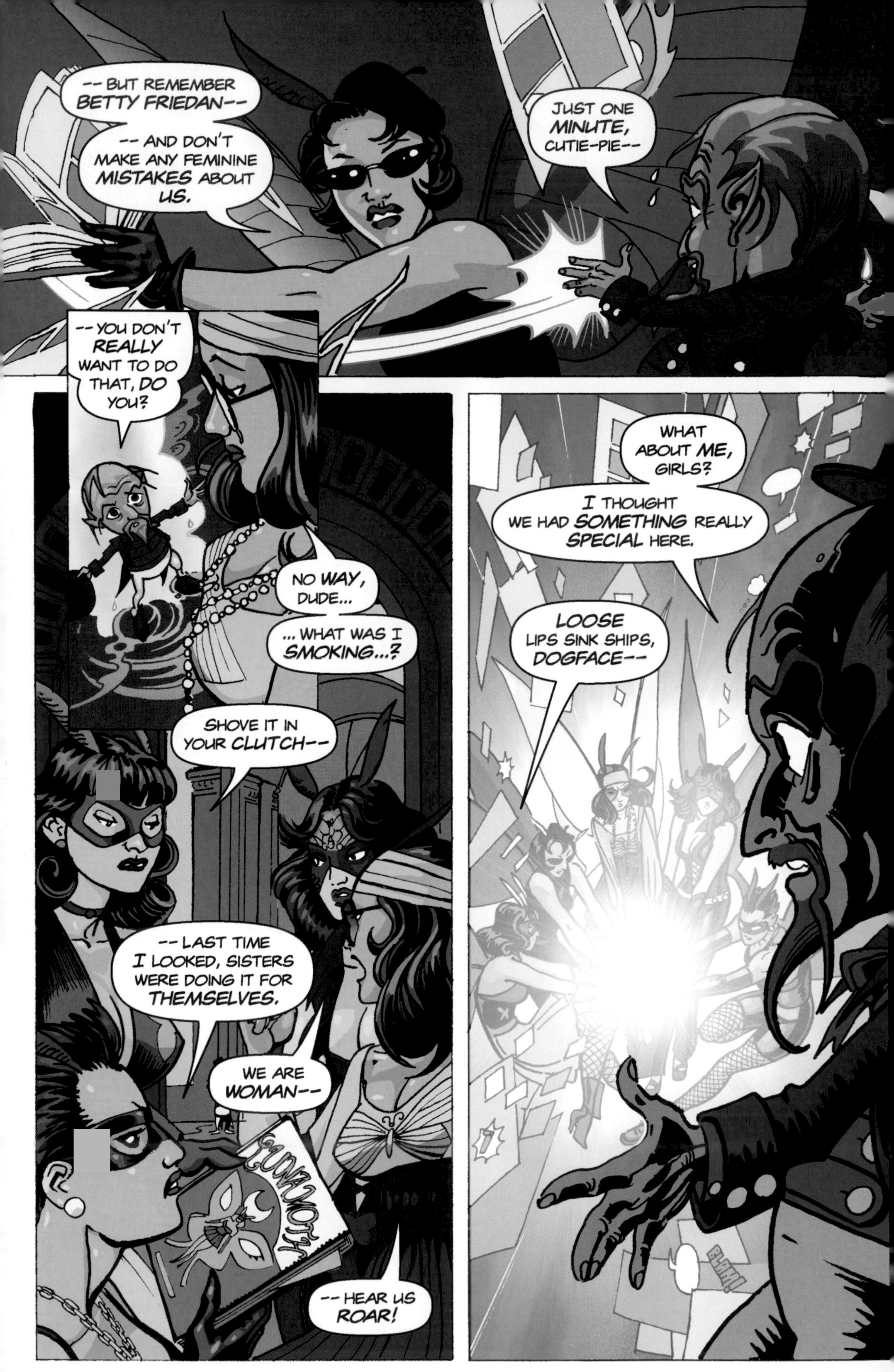
-- BUT REMEMBER BETTY FRIEDAN--
-- AND DON'T MAKE ANY FEMININE MISTAKES ABOUT US.
JUST ONE MINUTE, CUTIE-PIE--
-- YOU DON'T REALLY WANT TO DO THAT, DO YOU?
NO WAY, DUDE...
... WHAT WAS I SMOKING...?
SHOVE IT IN YOUR CLUTCH--
-- LAST TIME I LOOKED, SISTERS WERE DOING IT FOR THEMSELVES.
WE ARE WOMAN--
-- HEAR US ROAR!
WHAT ABOUT ME, GIRLS?
I THOUGHT WE HAD SOMETHING REALLY SPECIAL HERE.
LOOSE LIPS SINK SHIPS, DOGFACE--

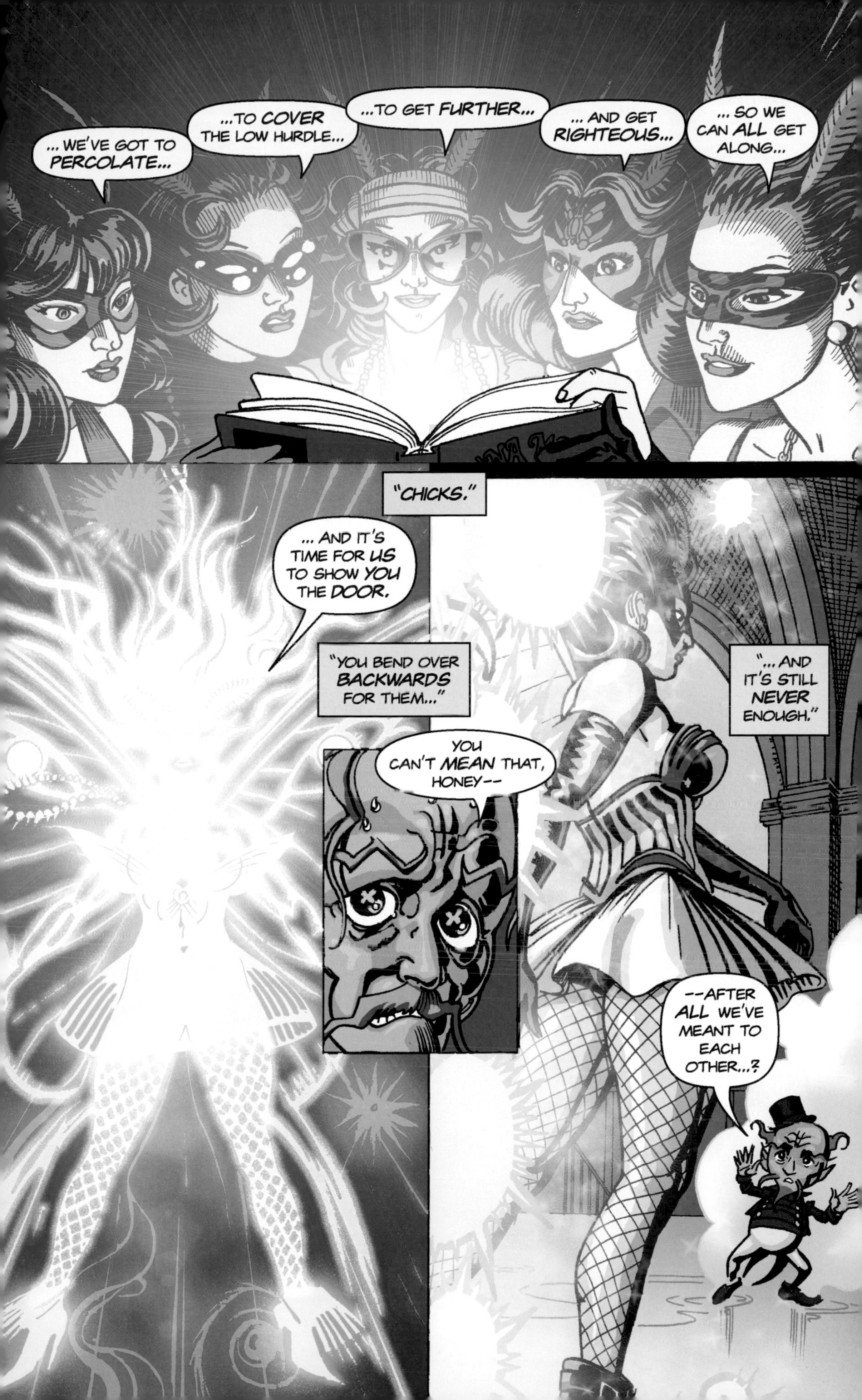
... WE'VE GOT TO PERCOLATE...
...TO COVER THE LOW HURDLE...
...TO GET FURTHER...
... AND GET RIGHTEOUS...
... SO WE CAN ALL GET ALONG...
"CHICKS."
... AND IT'S TIME FOR US TO SHOW YOU THE DOOR.
"YOU BEND OVER BACKWARDS FOR THEM..."
YOU CAN'T MEAN THAT, HONEY--
"... AND IT'S STILL NEVER ENOUGH."
--AFTER ALL WE'VE MEANT TO EACH OTHER...?

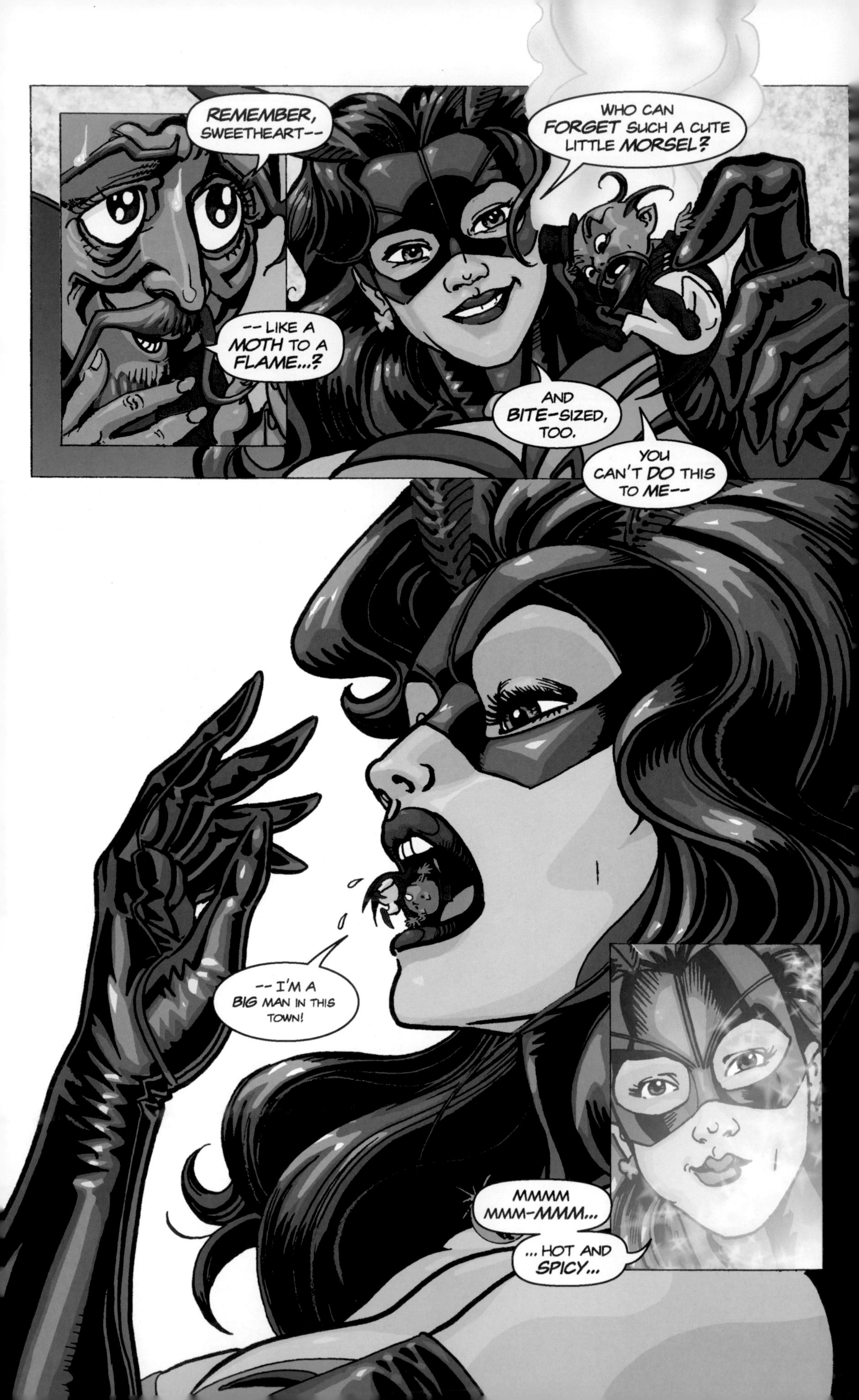
REMEMBER, SWEETHEART--
--LIKE A MOTH TO A FLAME...?
WHO CAN FORGET SUCH A CUTE LITTLE MORSEL?
AND BITE-SIZED, TOO.
YOU CAN'T DO THIS TO ME--
--I'M A BIG MAN IN THIS TOWN!
MMMM MMM-MMM...
...HOT AND SPICY...

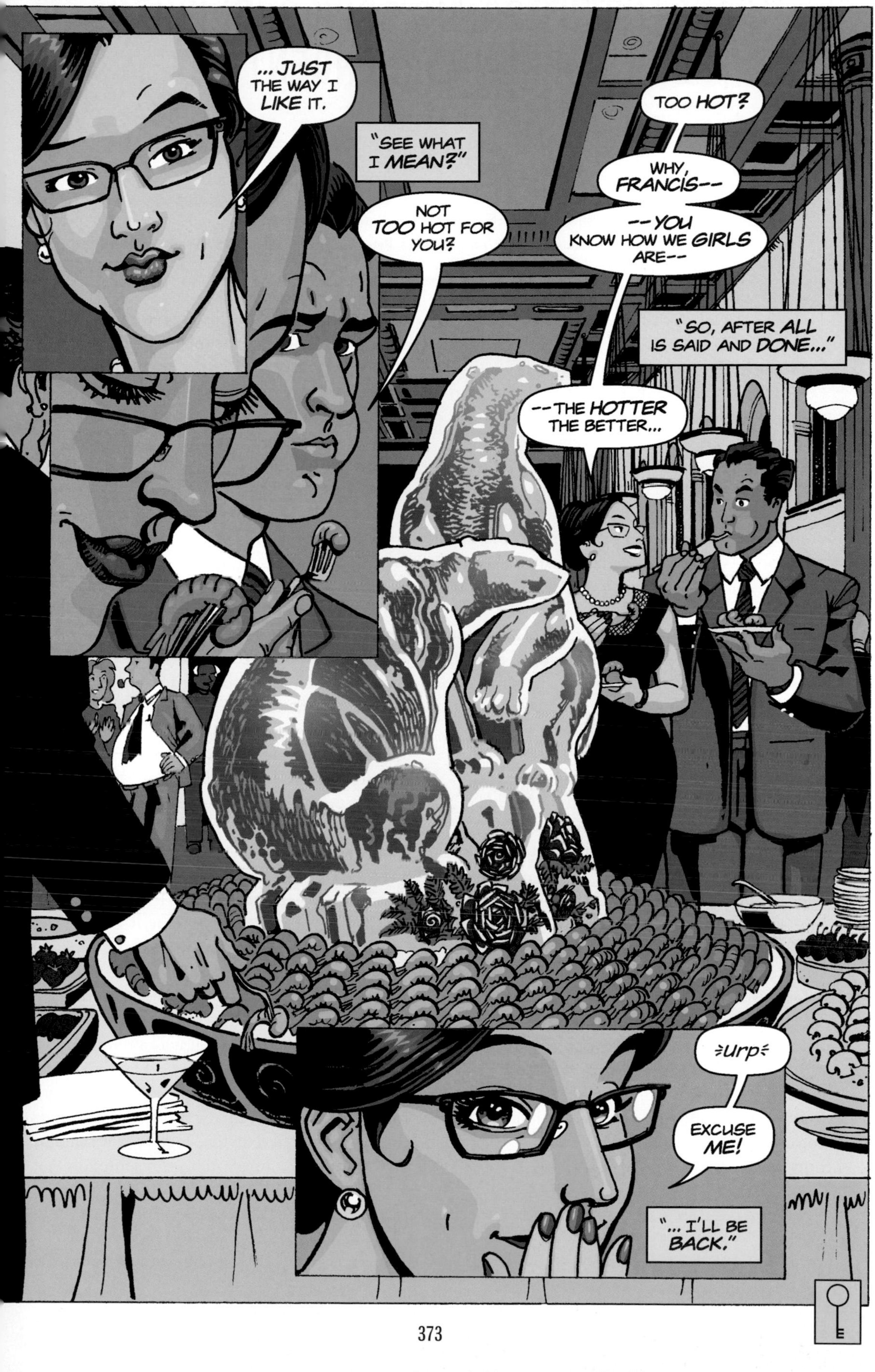

...JUST THE WAY I LIKE IT.
"SEE WHAT I MEAN?"
NOT TOO HOT FOR YOU?
TOO HOT?
WHY, FRANCIS--
--YOU KNOW HOW WE GIRLS ARE--
"SO, AFTER ALL IS SAID AND DONE..."
--THE HOTTER THE BETTER...
urp
EXCUSE ME!
"...I'LL BE BACK."

# INDEPENDENT COMIC BOOK PUBLISHERS OF THE PRE-INDEPENDENT ERA

*Number 113 in a Continuing Series*

## BY MALACHI B. COHEN

**NOVA COMICS (Columbia, Maryland, 1974–1976)**

Publishers: Tony McNeill, Peter Megginson, Michael Chabon
Principal artists and/or writers: Tony McNeill, Peter Megginson, Michael Chabon

THE INITIAL DISCUSSIONS THAT LED TO THE CREATION OF NOVA began at the bottom of Newgrange Garth, where it meets Phelps' Luck Drive. Chabon and Megginson were on their way, on foot, to the neighborhood swimming pool. They had tied their towels around their necks. Megginson was wearing a pair of dark blue bathing trunks; Chabon, a pair of mixed coloration including but not limited to pink, orange, gold, and brown in an abstract pattern that, for reasons which remain obscure, struck both Chabon and Megginson as "Aztec." Bathing trunks of the era, it should be mentioned, were an entirely different type of garment from their modern incarnation. They were made of a thick, slow-drying stretchy knit material resembling that of the uniforms worn by the crew of the starship *Enterprise*. They stopped at mid-upper thigh, and, significantly, tended (as did Megginson's and Chabon's) to feature a built-in belt, of stretchy webbing, that buckled at the front with a heavy metal clasp. "They would get all nubbly," Chabon says now, "from being scraped against the concrete of the pool deck. Especially in the seat." In short, they resembled the trunks typically worn by costumed superheroes (Batman, Captain America, et al). Combined with their knotted, flapping towel capes (Megginson's white, Chabon's gold), the trunks set the minds of Megginson and Chabon—neither of them in any way otherwise resembling a costumed superhero except, perhaps, in his essential loneliness and dawning awareness that his only hope for companionship lay in the company of other freaks like himself—soaring into the dizzying blue halftone sky.

The cicadas throbbed. The trees seemed to move without moving, as if the intense Maryland heat were so powerful as to force them to oscillate, minutely, between parallel dimensions. The blacktop of the street had not yet begun to melt but by two in the afternoon would have done so. Megginson and Chabon took no notice of any of this. They were too busy transforming themselves, with each step, into the characters that would prove to be cornerstones of the short-lived Nova empire: Darklord and Aztec; transforming themselves, at the same time, into the chroniclers of those characters, artist and writer; and finally transforming themselves—with a pair of bath towels and fifteen minutes' conversation!—into the joint proprietors of a still largely fictitious but potentially huge and successful multi-million-dollar publishing enterprise[1] that one day might rival the giants, Marvel and DC. Talking, retying the knots of their capes, flip flops steadily slap-slapping against the bottoms of their feet, Megginson and Chabon were busy transforming not only themselves, however, in the space of that fifteen minute walk to the pool—they were also transforming the world, shaping it, as the trees shimmered in the interdimensional blast of Maryland summer heat, into a place in which such things were possible: a reincarnated Arthurian knight, complete with wonder sword, whose best friend and companion was a reincarnated Aztec knight, knowledgable in the ancient Meso-American martial arts; an empire founded by a couple of boys; a pair of broken childhoods redeemed through accepting, together, the standing invitation that comic books represented. It was

---

[1] At first they called it Star Comics, before the double meaning implicit in the word "nova" struck them, the new stars of the comics world.

an invitation to enter into the game, to join in the fun, to move beyond studying and reproducing the received catalog of acts of self-reinvention, reaching back to Siegel and Shuster's seminal act of 1936, and to begin, with the crash of a rocketship or the knotting of a magical towel, to reinvent oneself.

When they got home from the pool, Megginson and Chabon set to work and in short order had written and illustrated origin tales for the flagship pair of superpowered knights. In due course, Darklord and Aztec were joined by others: the Bullet, who had a pointy hat and propelled himself through the air, doubtless not without some nausea, spiraling wildly on his long axis; the White Shark, with his dorsal-finned jersey but few other obvious sharklike characteristics beyond a fondness for water; the White Shark's natural arch-nemesis, the Fisherman; and a Chabon female creation, Therma, whose ability to make things really, really hot was matched only by the Kirbyesque oomph of her frame.

It was in the fall of that year that Chabon and Megginson got to know McNeill, already respected in the halls of Ellicott City Middle School for his artistic ability, in particular with regard to drawing the ponderous feminine armament required for accurate depiction of heroines of Therma's zaftig ilk. McNeill was African-American, gifted not only with artistic ability but with solemn, pop-eyed good looks and the delectable penumbra of a mustache. He was established if not entirely at home in the black milieu, and it is doubtful if, in the absence of their shared passion for comic books, Chabon and Megginson would ever otherwise have been able to befriend him. He had recently developed several characters of his own, including Voodoo Hunter, Thunderbird, and the startlingly buxom Tigra, each of whose breasts was much, much larger, as McNeill drew her, than her head. McNeill's mother worked as a clerk of the county court, and many of his finest drawings were executed on the blank reverse of court summonses.

Sensing by now the hostile business climate in which they had determined to produce their loose-leaf

and tagboard, stapled, eraser-crumb-haunted epics, the three creators decided to pool their strength, and McNeill's line[2] was merged with the burgeoning Nova group.

There followed a period of intense activity. Several vinyl notebooks were filled with sketches, scripts, and panel breakdowns, and like people who have witnessed or feel they may be about to witness a miracle, the three found themselves, when together, unable to talk about anything else. They struggled with the accurate depiction of plumage (Thunderbird), sword thrusts (Darklord), the depiction of convincing human behavior (particularly in Chabon's ballpoint scripts), and above all with those perpetual nemeses of the comic book artist, hands, feet and noses. McNeill in particular had a tendency to leave faces entirely blank, populating his comics with a series of surreal human blanks. There were the inevitable crossover appearances, sidekick introductions, and gatherings of teams (the Revengers chief among them).

In time, however, the inevitable production problems, as well as creative and business differences among the collaborators, led to strains. Limited access to Xerox machines—or the limited patience, in Chabon's case, of his father's secretary— prevented them from being able to produce more than a dozen or so copies of any Nova title. Ultimately, however, Nova was killed by the bane of all independents, distribution problems. Local retailers proved unwilling to put the Nova product in their racks—where, admittedly, it had a disheartening tendency to look like something that had fallen out of some crazy lady's purse— and local consumers consistently, if not mockingly, declined to shell out for the Nova titles in the places where they could be sold, such as on the blacktop at Ellicott City Middle School, even at half the going price (at that time 20 or 25 cents) of the majors.

When Megginson left to attend a different school, in the fall of 1976, the already tottering company collapsed. By this time Nova Comics had been subjected to public mockery, chronic shortages of paper stock, and the scandal that attended McNeill's and Chabon's discovery that Megginson

---

[2]Of which the author's research has proven sadly unable to recover the name—*MBC*.

had clandestinely produced several "Tijuana bible" versions of the Nova characters, depicting them engaged in a number of energetically if anatomically unlikely acts. Chabon began to concentrate on prose fiction, thereafter, while McNeill moved on to other endeavors, among them a consuming fixation, puzzling to his former collaborators, on the character of Dracula. He has since vanished, leaving fans to mourn the loss of an artist who might one day have proven a second Matt Baker. Megginson continued to pursue art for many years, visited Thailand, and is now employed as a nursery school teacher in the Washington, D.C., area.

As for Nova Comics, born too soon, none mourn it, and neither Marvel nor DC realizes how very close they both came, in the middle 1970s, to seeing the end of their hegemony over the comic book superhero, over that standing invitation, issued in four colors and a pattern of overlapping dots or in the ashy gray smudges of an overworked Xerox machine, to enter through the door of the splash page—the door that is always left open—and, wildly erasing, to reinvent oneself. And, maybe, in so doing, possibly, impossibly, to open up a door or two for somebody else to one day do the same.

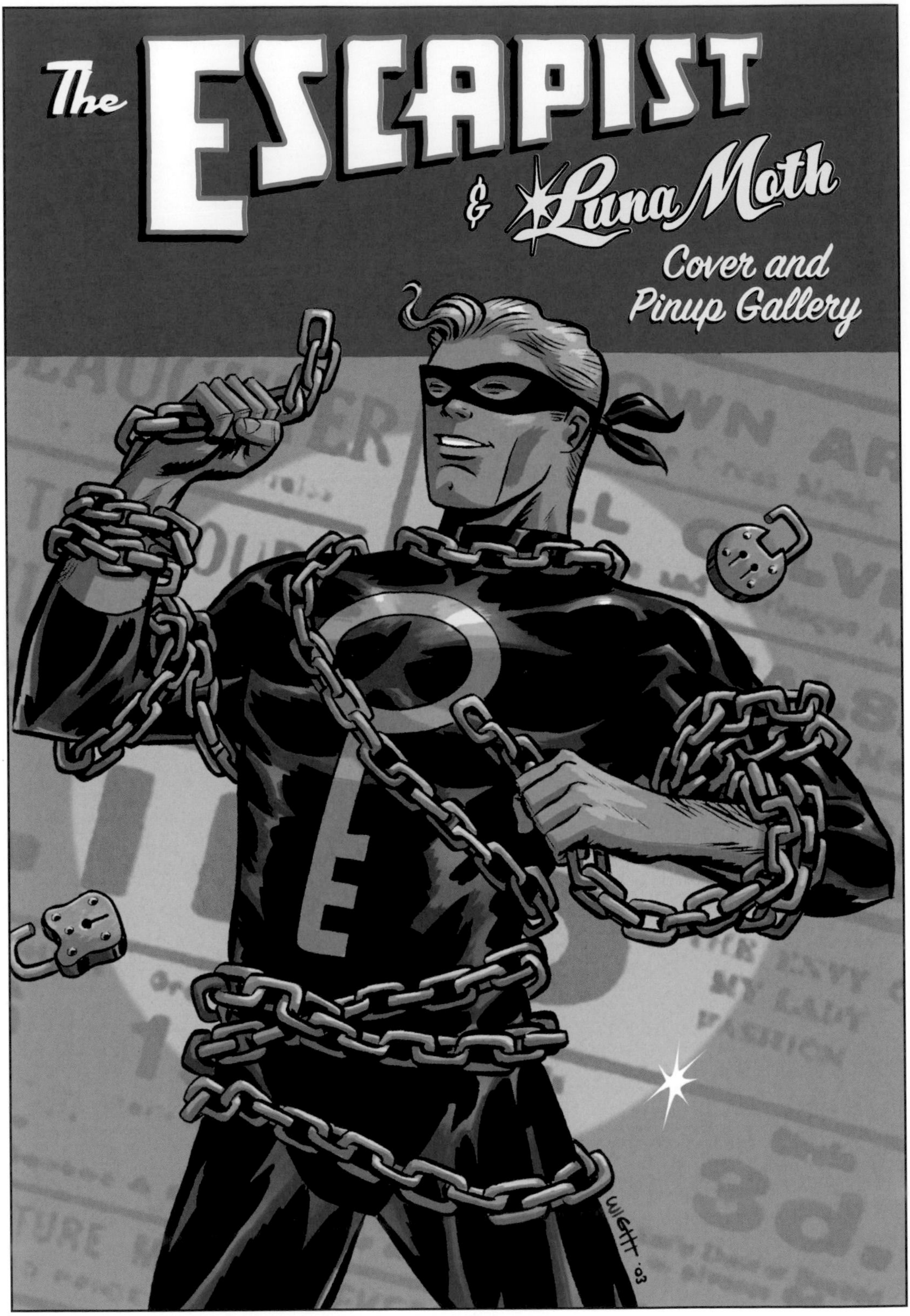
The
ESCAPIST
& Luna Moth
Cover and
Pinup Gallery
WIGHT '03

The following pages feature a variety of the cover artwork from *The Amazing Adventures of The Escapist* comic book series and collections, as well as several just-for-fun pinups of The Escapist and his associate Luna Moth.

ERIC WIGHT, Color by DAVE STEWART

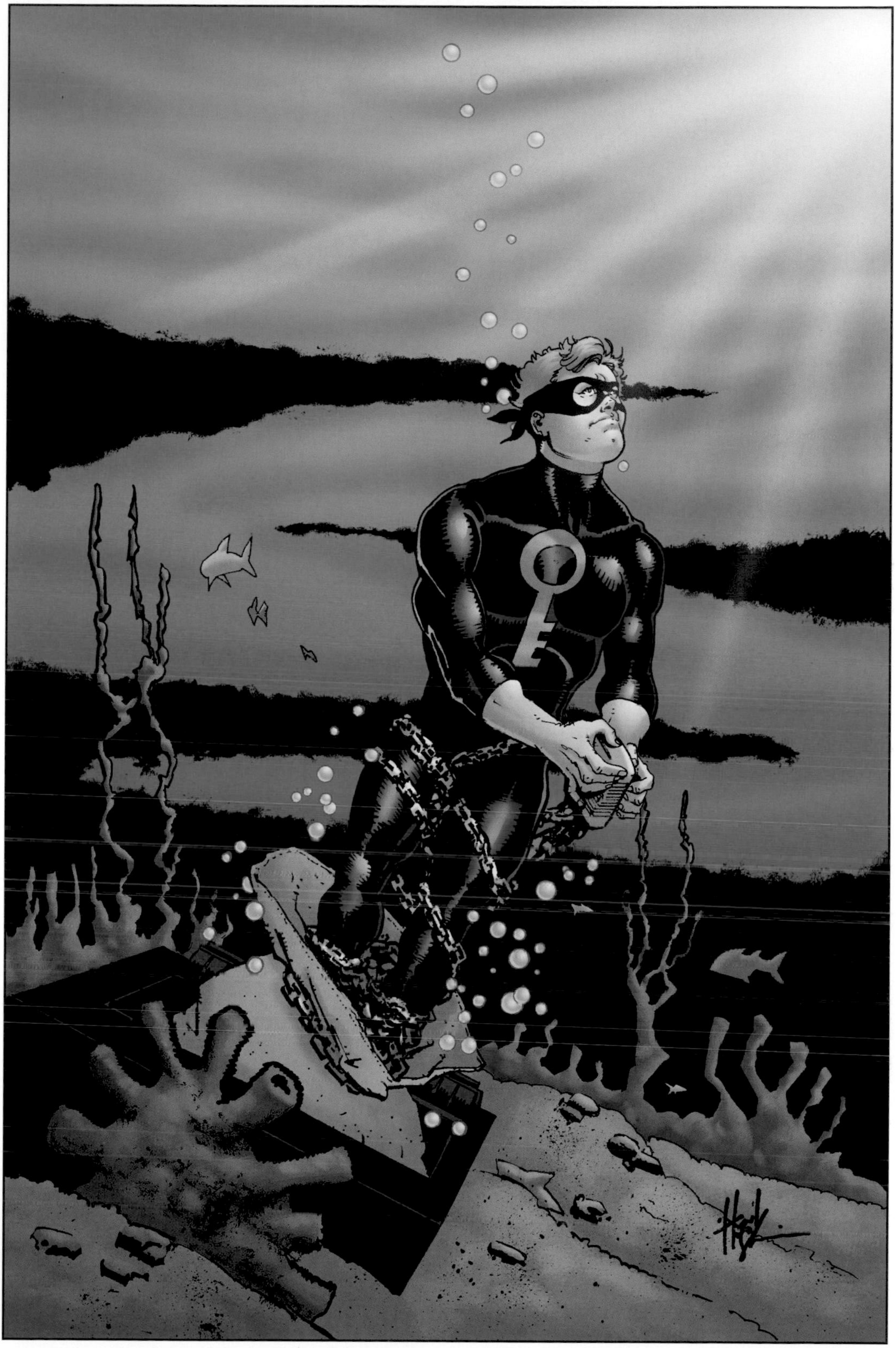

HOWARD CHAYKIN, Color by MICHELLE MADSEN

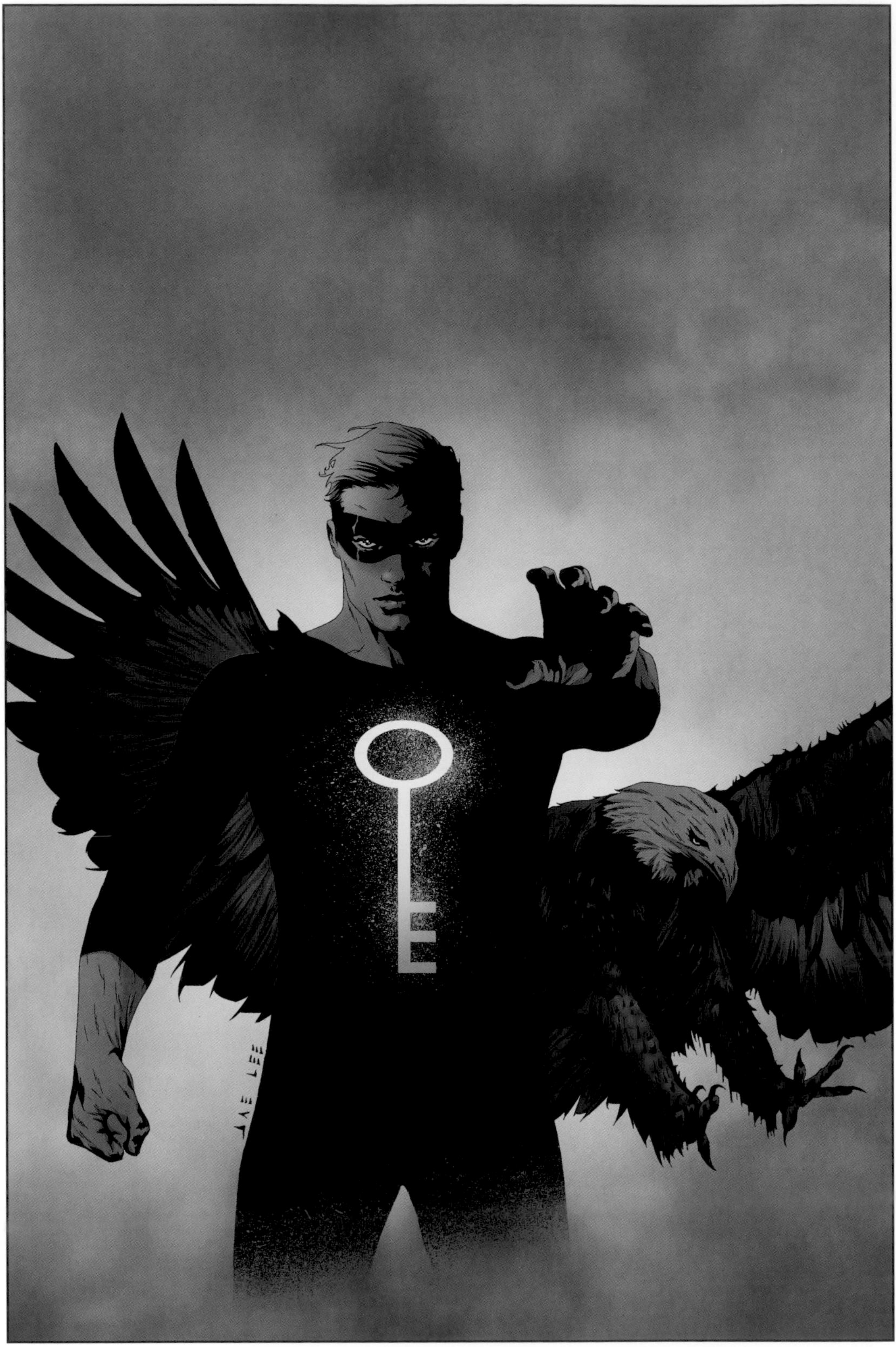
JAE LEE

JAE LEE

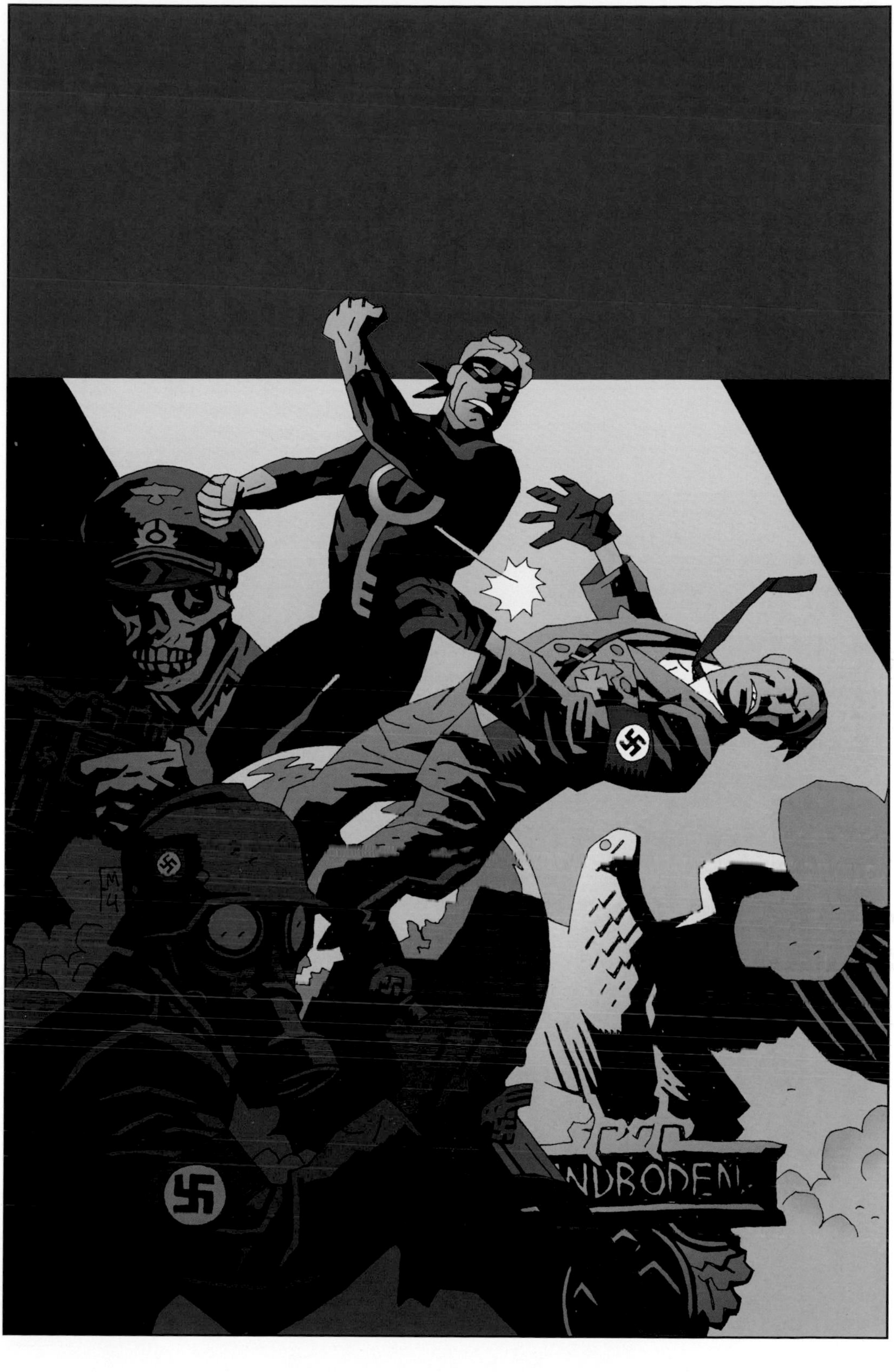
NDRODEN.

MIKE MIGNOLA, Color by DAVE STEWART

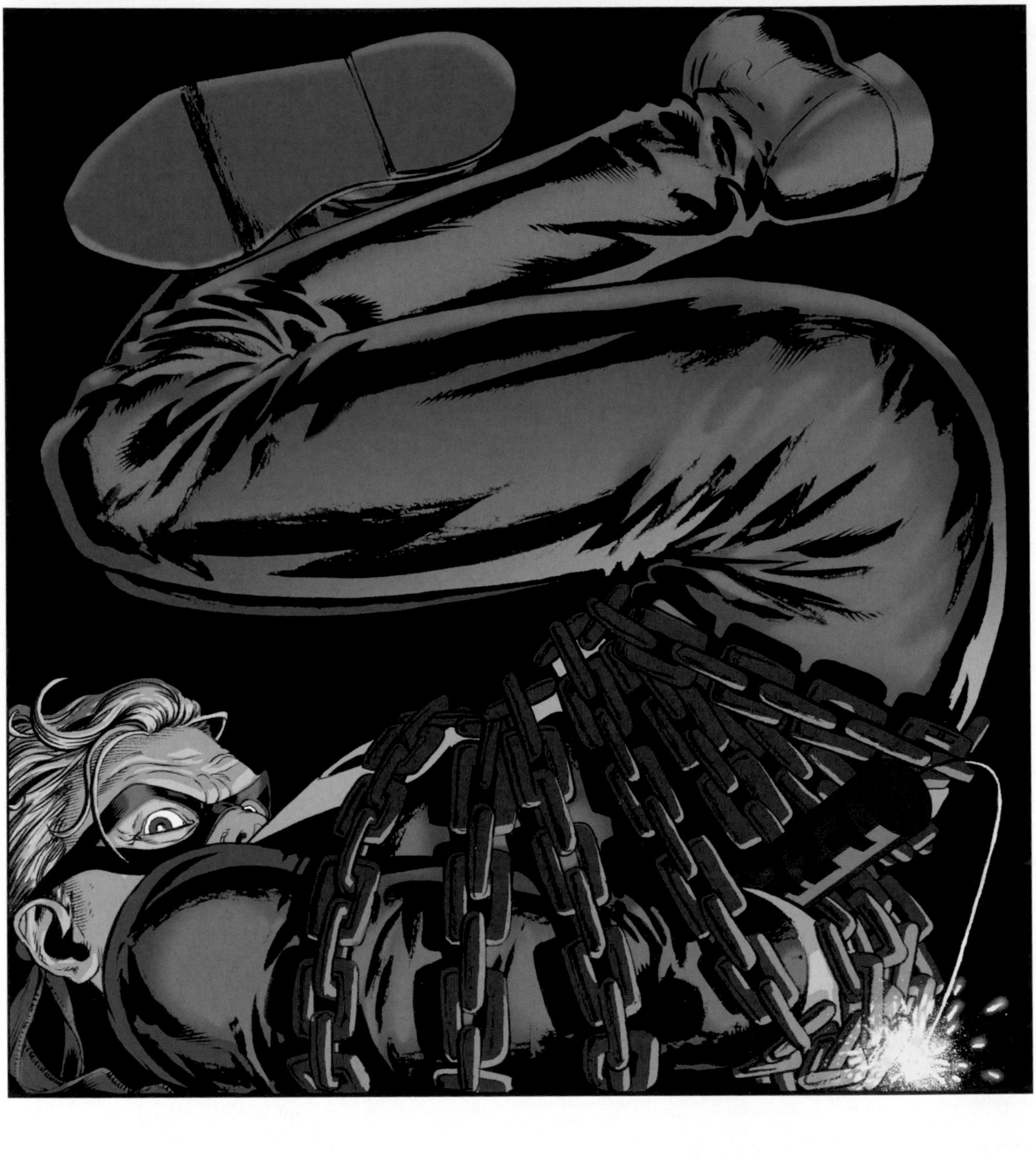

JOHN CASSADAY, Color by NICK DERINGTON with DAN JACKSON

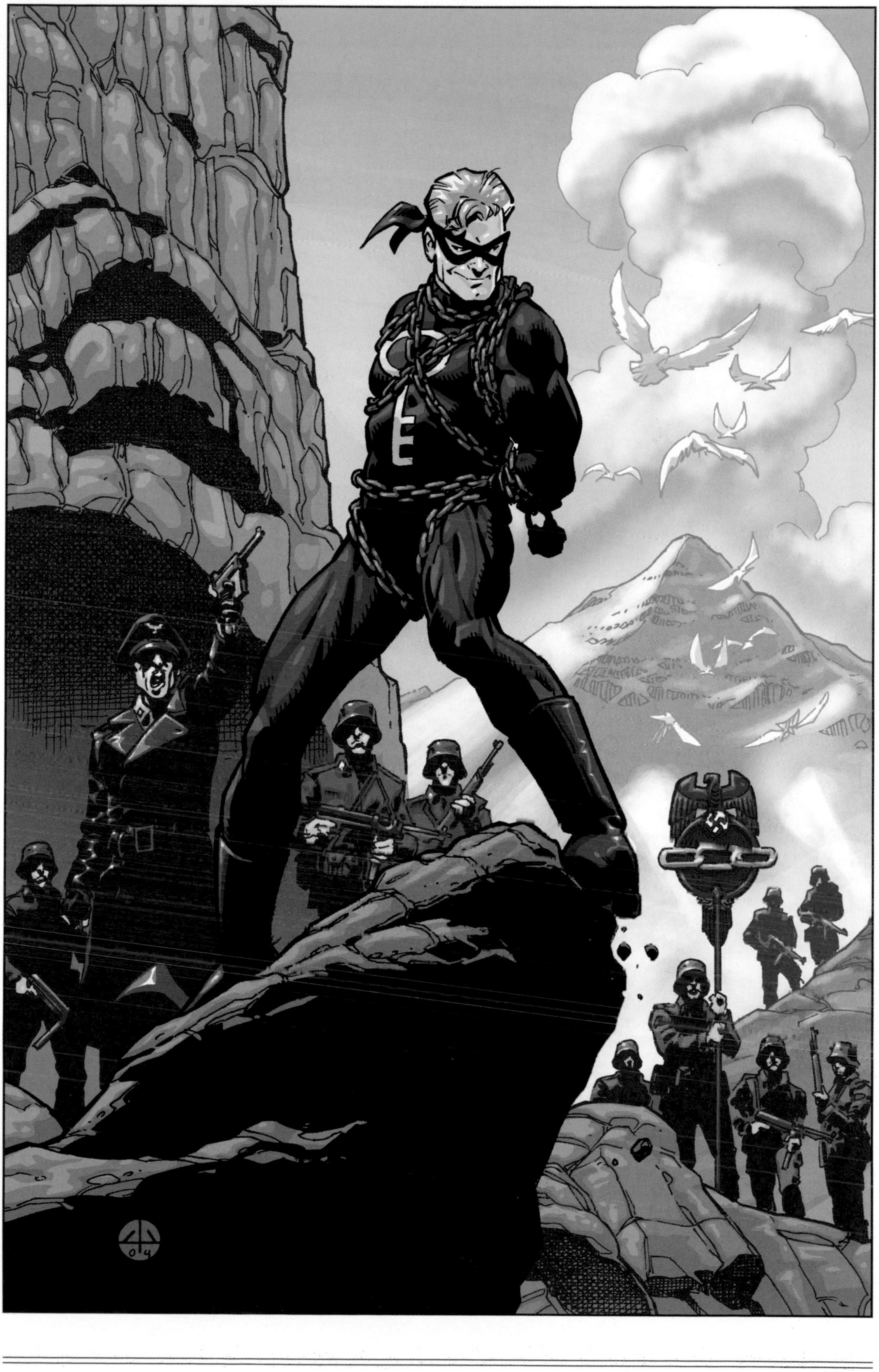

CHRIS WARNER, Color by DAN JACKSON

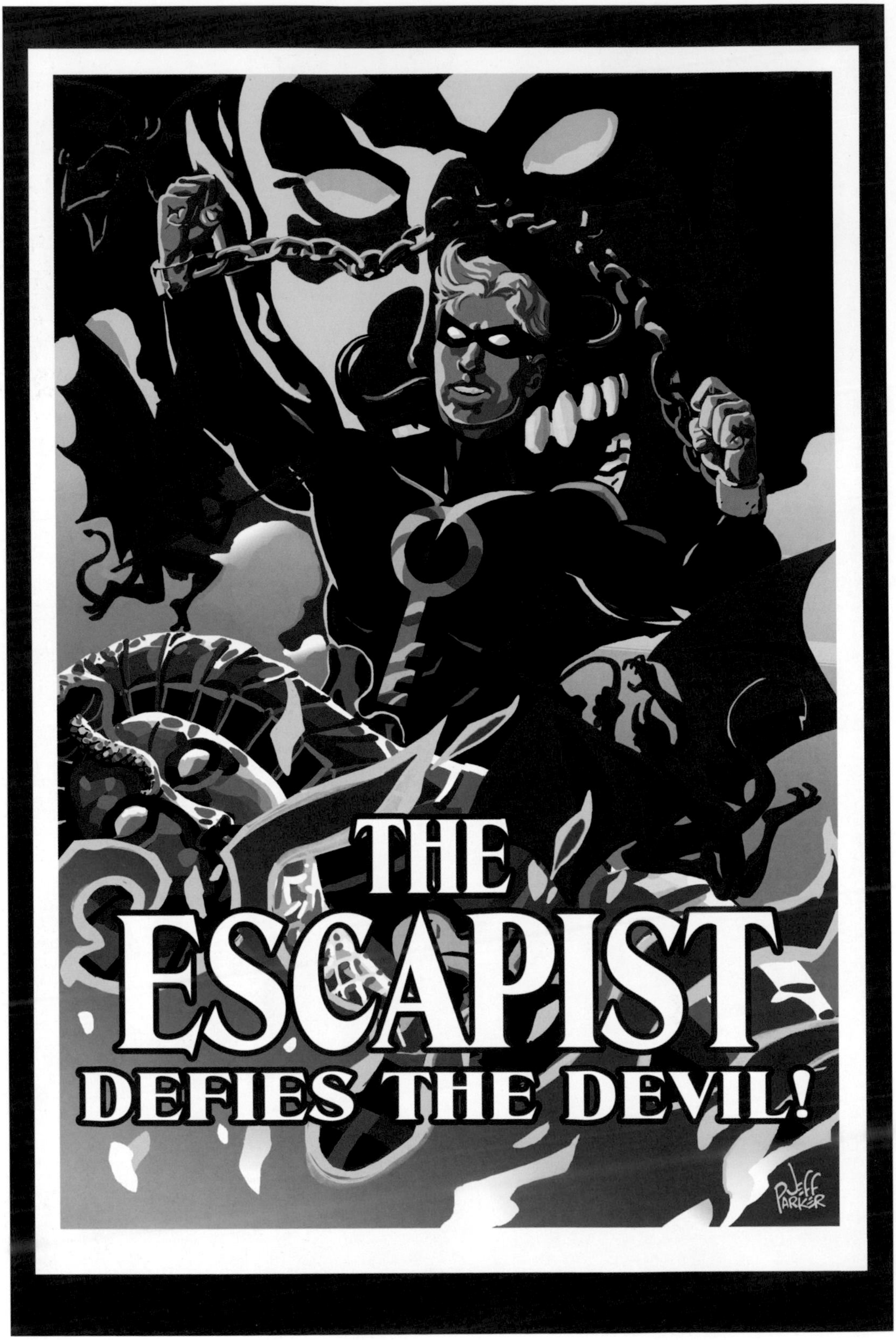
THE ESCAPIST
DEFIES THE DEVIL!
JEFF PARKER

JEFF PARKER

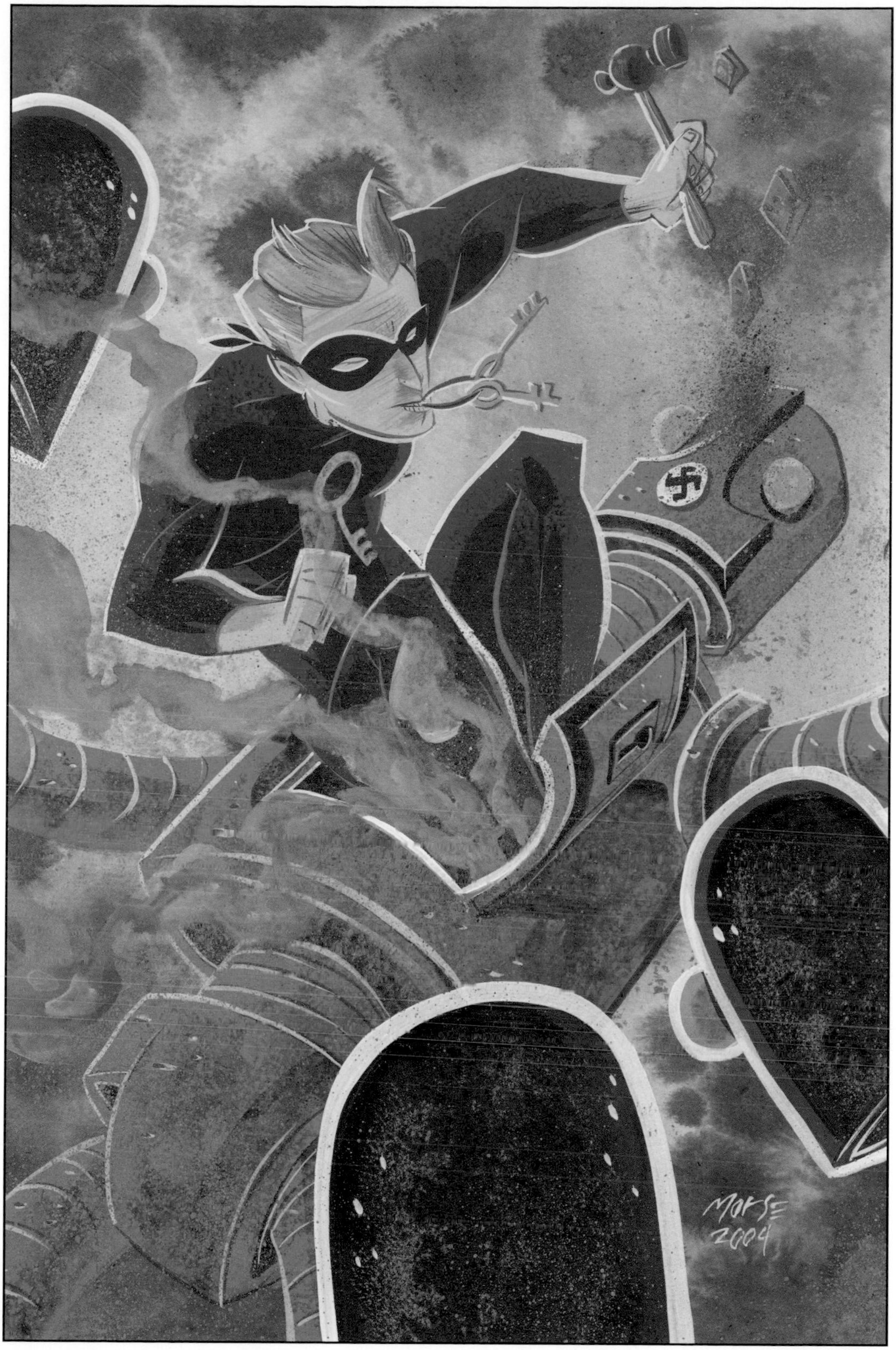
MORSE
2004

C. SCOTT MORSE

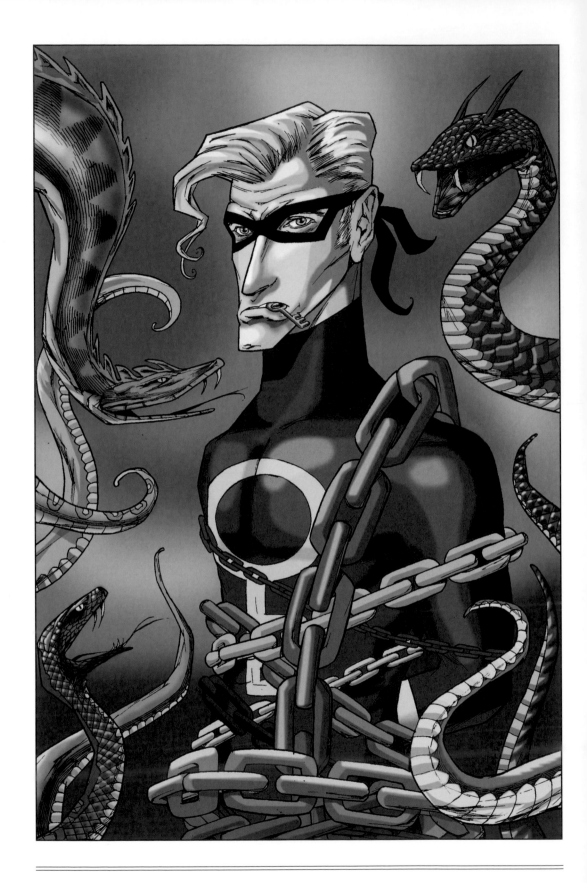

M.K. PERKER

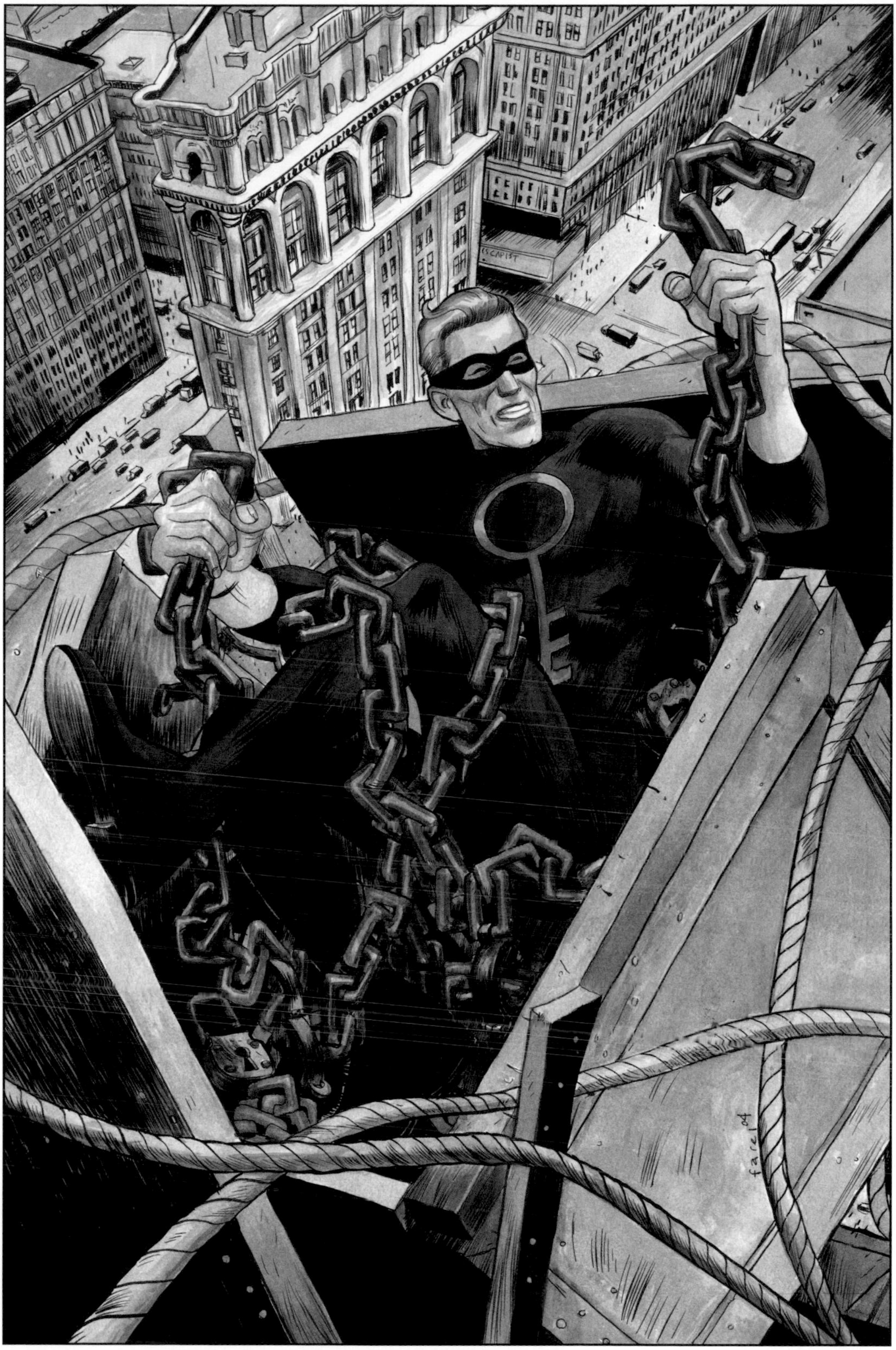

FAREL DALRYMPLE

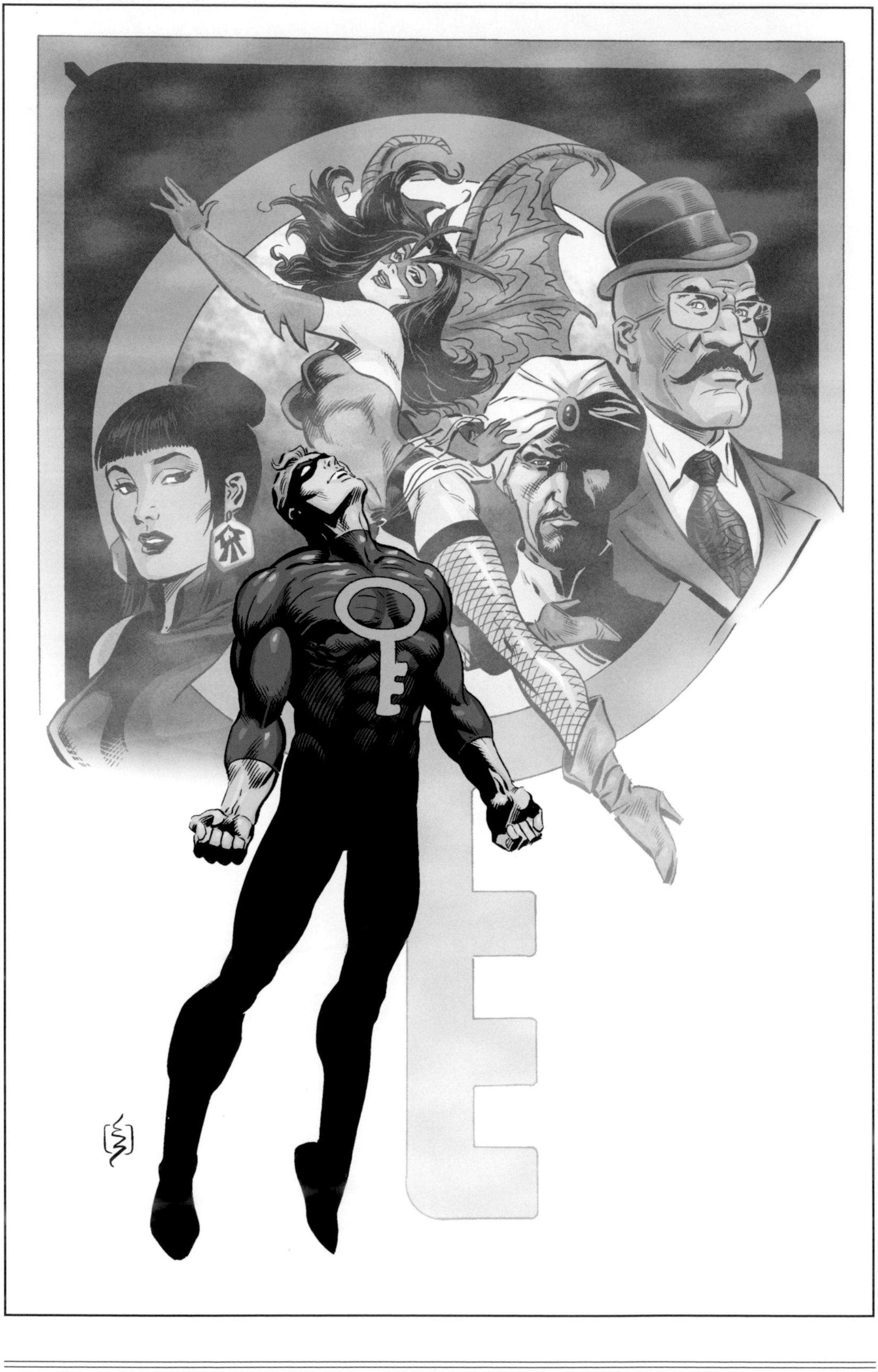

EDUARDO BARRETO, Color by DAN JACKSON

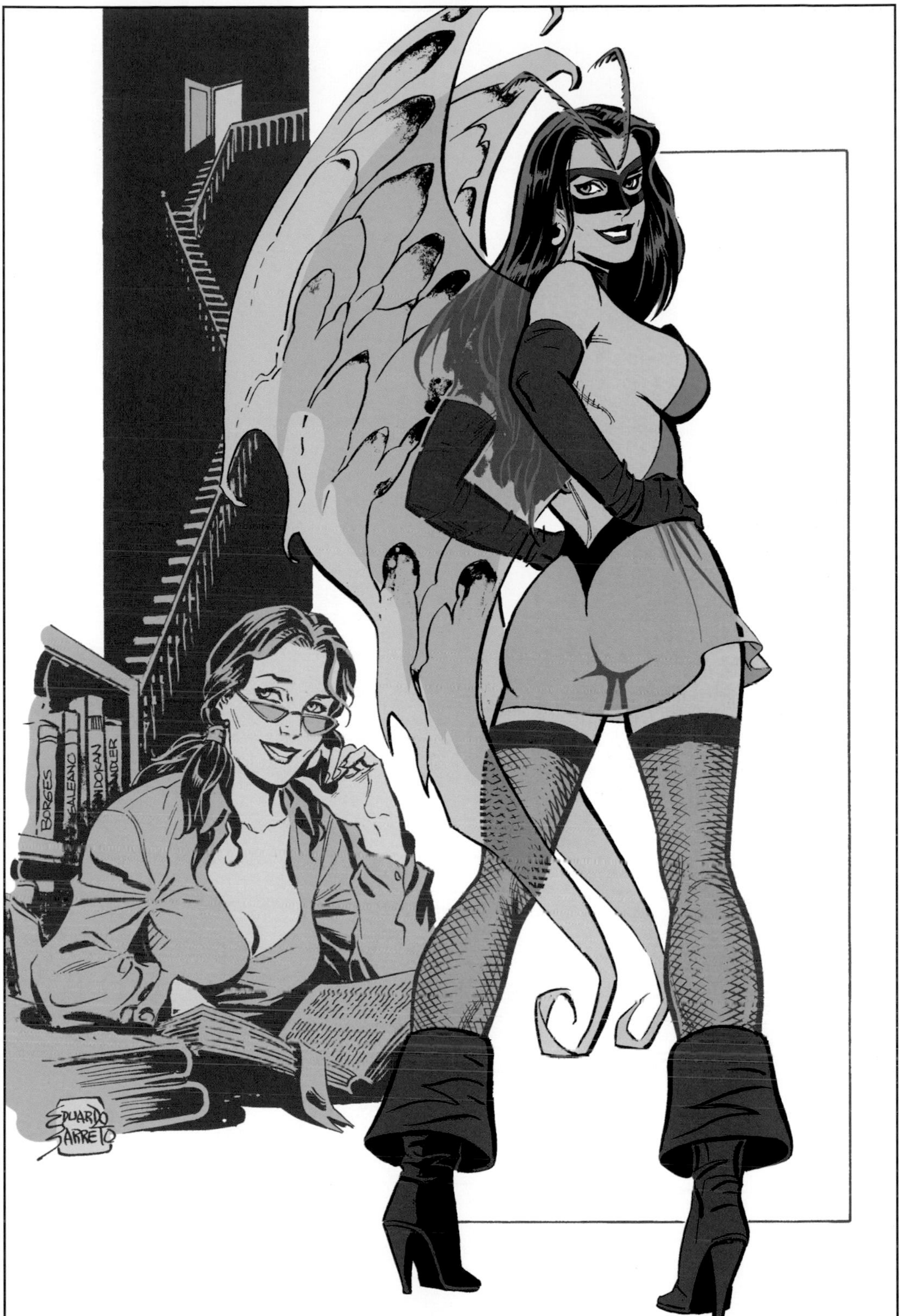
BORGES
GALEANO
DOKAN
NDLER
EDUARDO BARRETO

EDUARDO BARRETO, Color by PAUL HORNSCHEMEIER

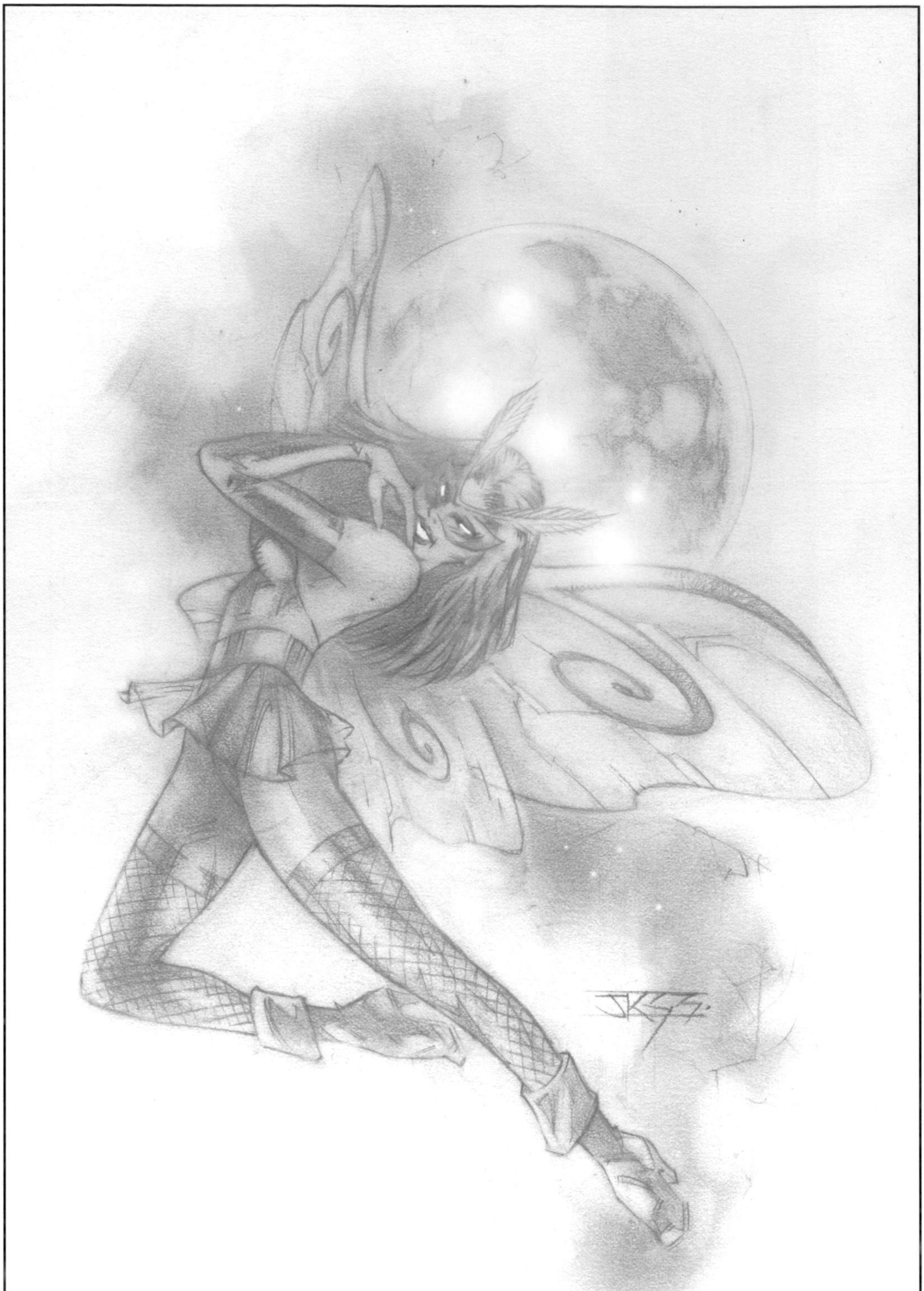

JOHN K. SNYDER III

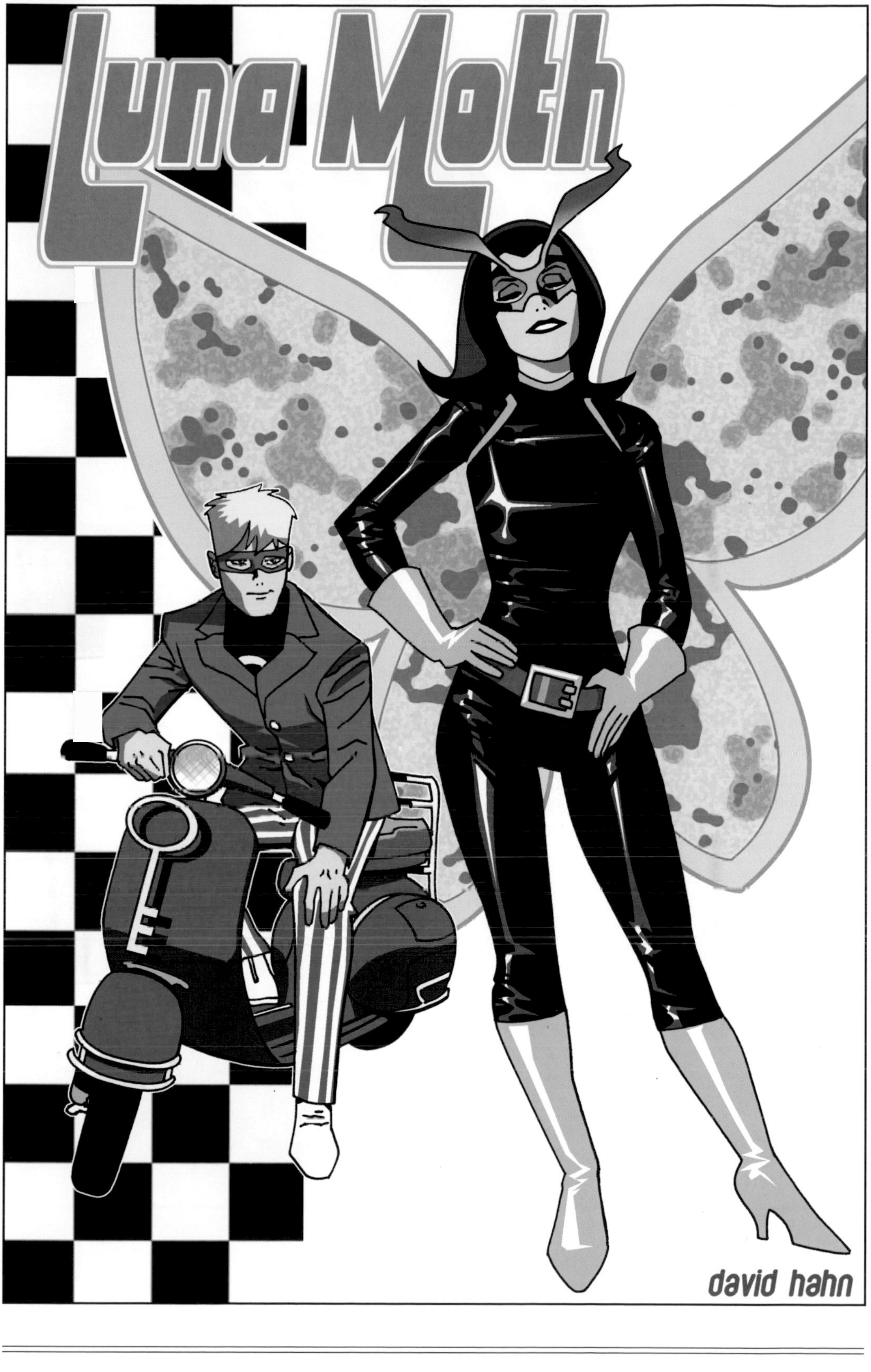
Luna Moth
david hahn

DAVID HAHN

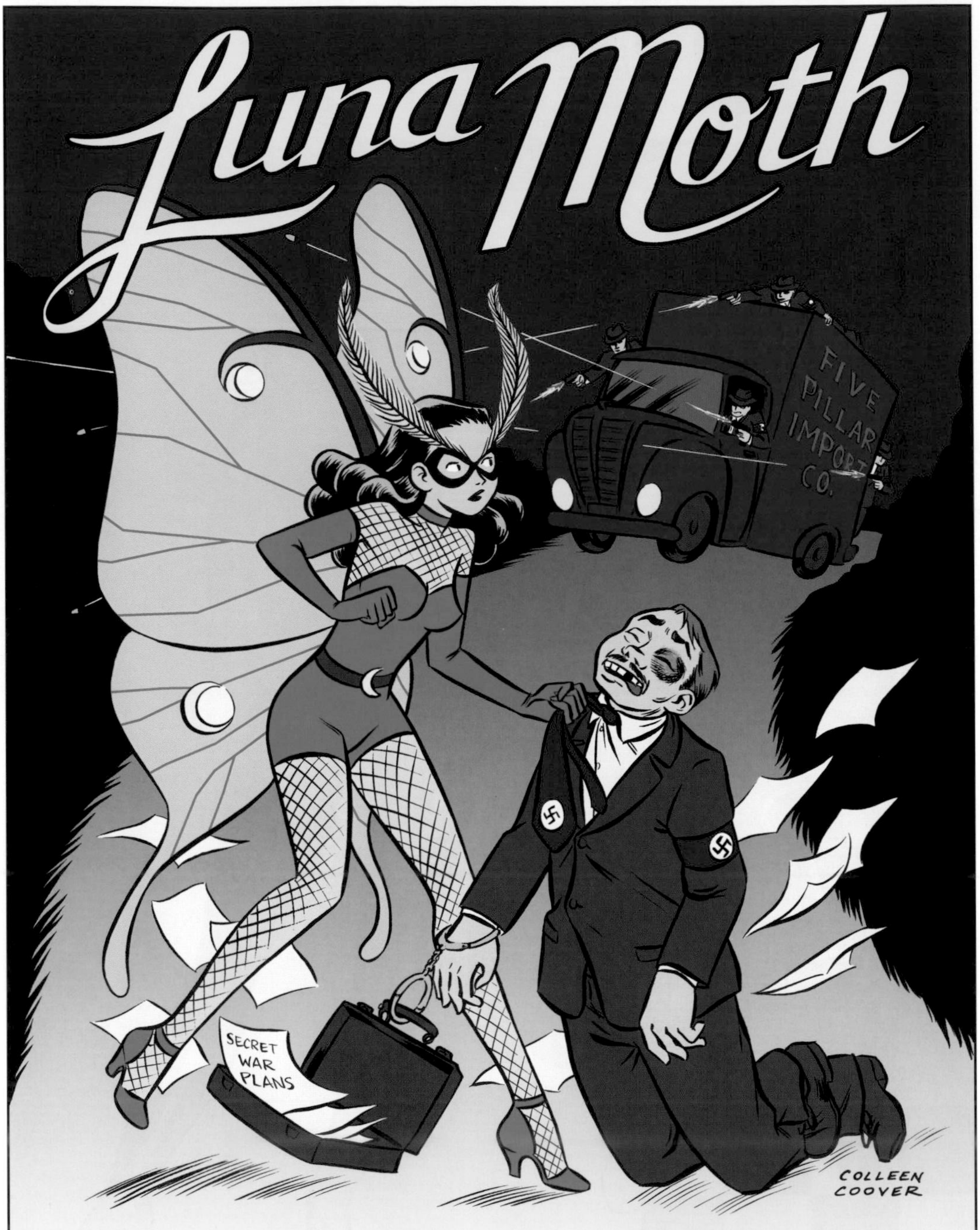
Luna Moth
FIVE PILLAR IMPORT CO.
SECRET WAR PLANS
COLLEEN COOVER

COLLEEN COOVER

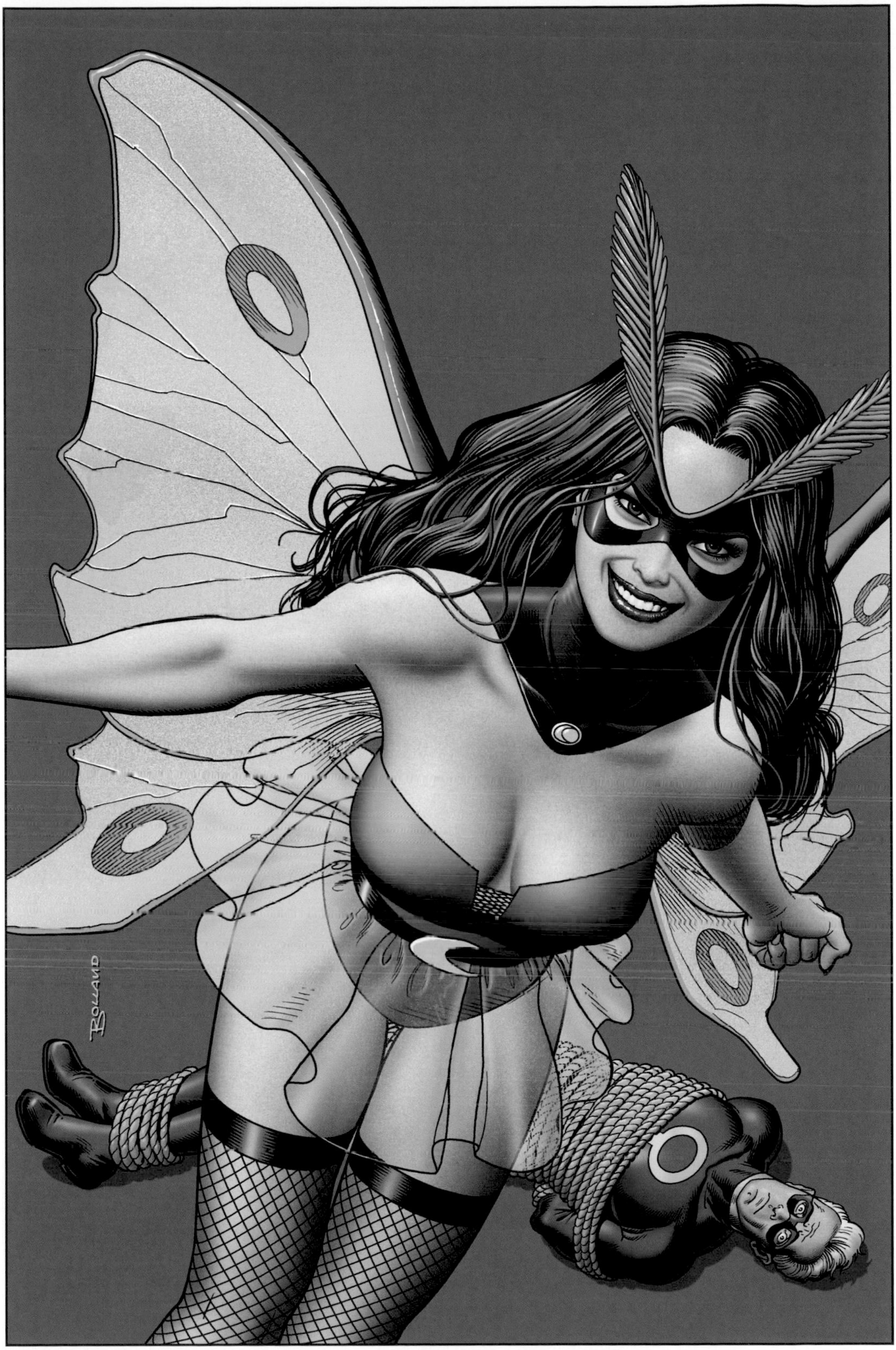
BOLLAND

BRIAN BOLLAND

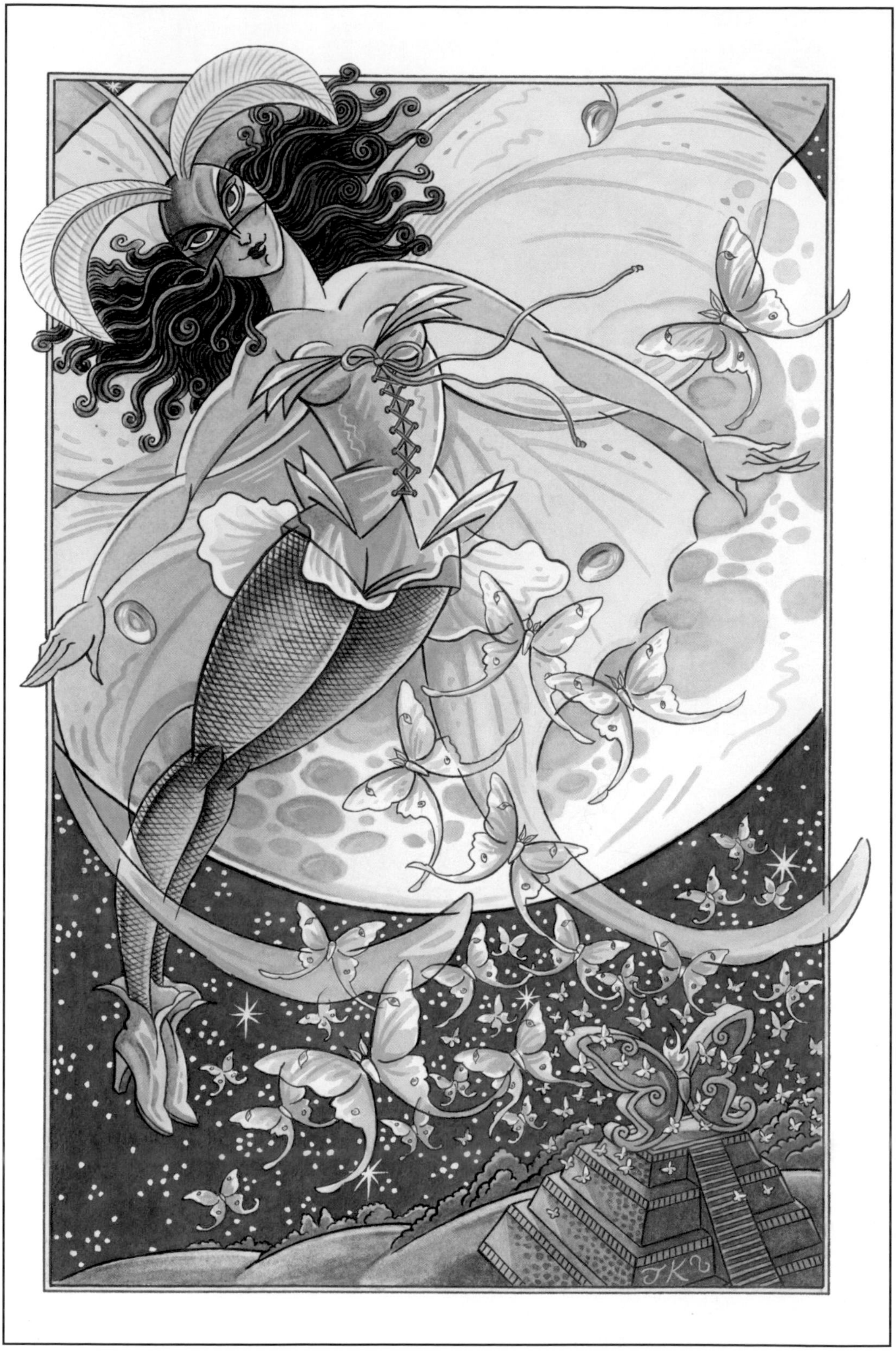
JK

JILL KARLA SCHWARTZ

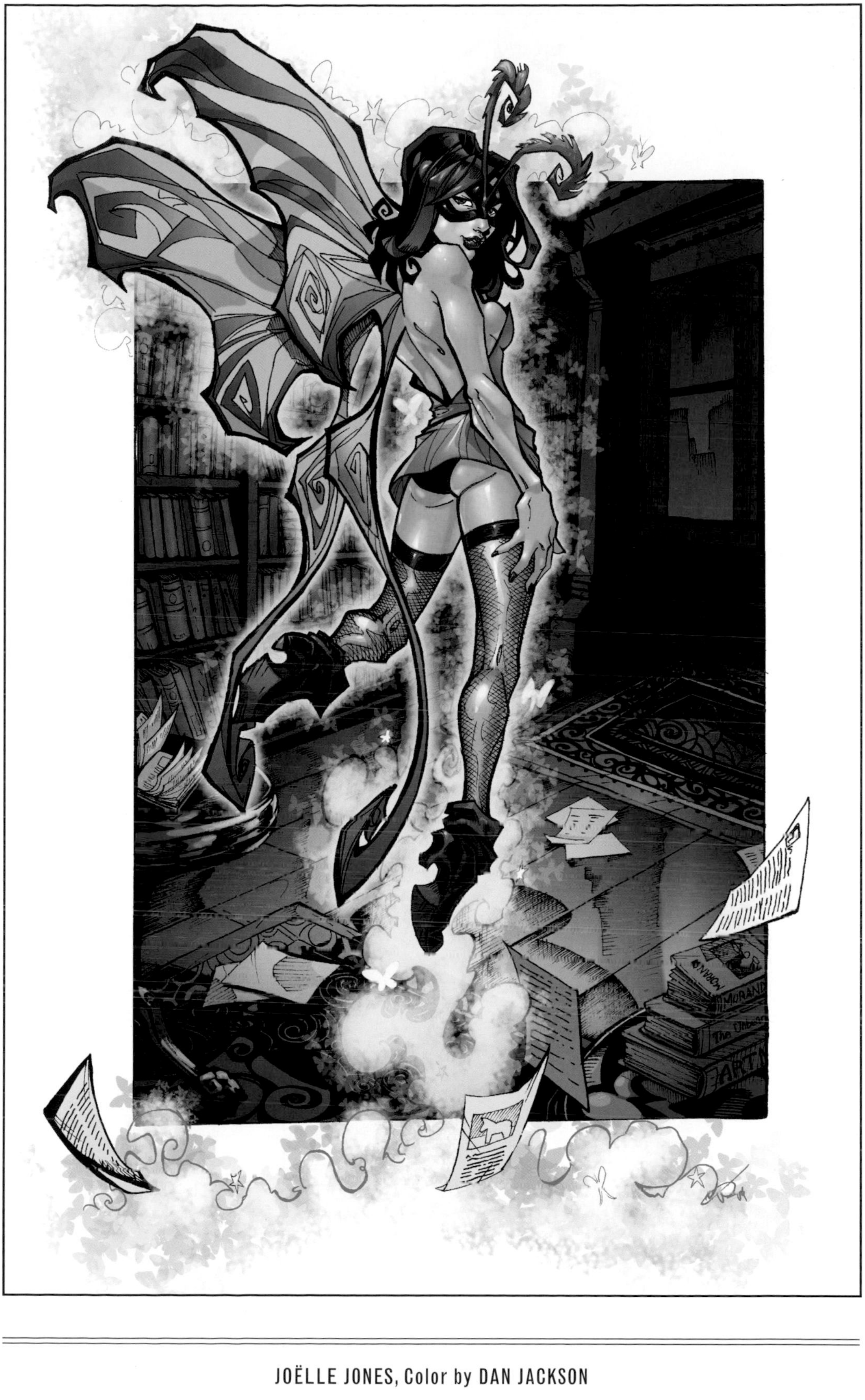

JOËLLE JONES, Color by DAN JACKSON

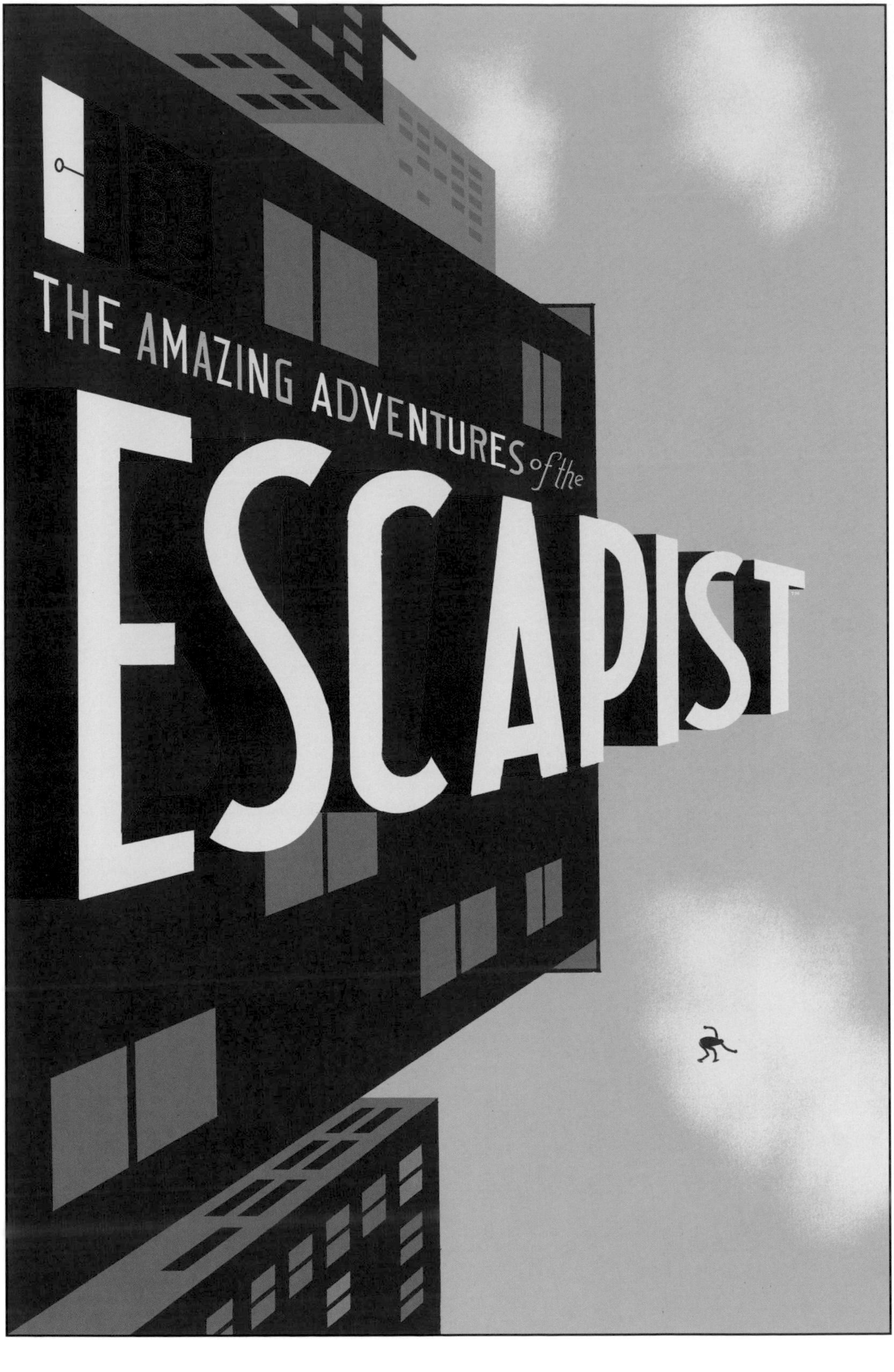
THE AMAZING ADVENTURES of the
ESCAPIST™

*On this page and the following*: front and back covers to *The Amazing Adventures of the Escapist* Volume 1 trade paperback, by Chris Ware.

# An Empire of NOVELTY

WITHIN THESE PAGES!

**Look out, Boys, it's HERE!**

**THE FIRST BOOK COLLECTION EVER** of the original **Amazing Adventures of The Escapist,** the legendary yet seldom-seen comic book feature that **riveted** generations of readers for **decades**—and served as the **secret inspiration** for Michael Chabon's Pulitzer-Prize winning **The Amazing Adventures of Kavalier and Clay.** Thrill to over **sixty years'** worth of carefully selected stories from the **classic days** of comic book industry production, when **men** were **men**—and there was still **money** to be made. Including **rare** art and stories by Howard Chaykin, Jim Starlin, Gene Colan, Michael Chabon, Glen David Gold, and Kevin McCarthy, this is no collection to miss by any **serious student** of **comic book history** or **fan** of **contemporary literature.** Buy it **now!**

**No. 617B7. The Amazing Adventures of the Escapist** (paperbound, 152 full-color pages) **$17.95**

**ALSO INCLUDED, COMPLETELY FREE, TO ALL PURCHASERS OF THIS BOOK (ISBN 1-59307-171-X):**

## MIDGET RADIO

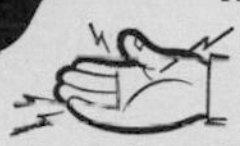

Made of actual, revolutionary pressed paper and discarded cigar excelsior, this **Amazingly Tiny Real Miniature Midget Radio** fits in the palm of any **standard-sized** hand, and then is easily and promptly lost. Search on ground for it in vain. Just **imagine** trying to receive overseas broadcasts and distress calls of ships at sea—if only you could find it.

**No. 3214. Miniature Midget Radio ....... FREE**

## DELUDED SENSE OF EFFICACY

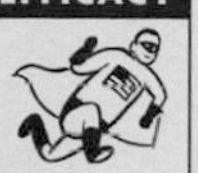

**PERFECT** for any adult who still views the world as a competition between simplistic polarities of "good and evil." Great for cartoonists, moviegoers, presidents. All the rage this season. Everything would be so much better if only someone could just come along and **fix it all.** Hey, why **won't** somebody, anyway?

**No. 632. Time to Grow Up .............. FREE**

## ABSENTEE FATHER

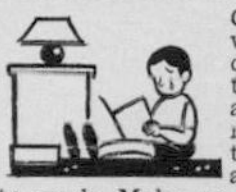

Completely invisible man which acts just like a real dad. Won't ever respond or take a passing interest in anything you do, at all, no matter how hard you try to get him to. Keep him in a closet, or just send him to work. Make up stories to keep yourself occupied. Dress up in a cape. Wish for muscles.

**No. 730. Go Away I'm Busy .......... FREE**

## Our BEST ASSORTMENT of MASQUERADE COSTUMES Available ANYWHERE!

Sizes: Small, 4 to 6 yrs., Medium, 8 to 10 yrs, Large, 12 to 45 yrs. Also available in XL and XXL "convention" sizes; please inquire.

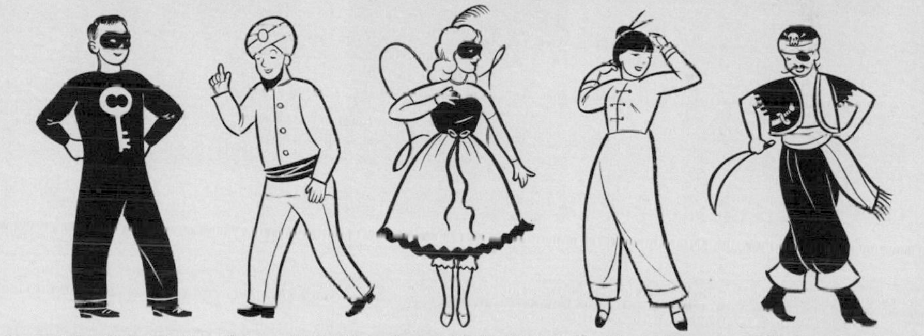

**Escapist** Thick dark blue Russian wool and snazzy gold thread embroidery combine to make this THE hit of the costume parade. Our most popular setup, so please list second and third choices, pending availability. **No. 632. ............ FREE**

**Omar** Small, delicate, and refined, our impassive worldly fellow is just the thing for today's Eastern-curious culture. Includes turban and jewel encrusted amulet pin. **No. 633... FREE**

**Luna Moth** Hotcha! Classy, girly, and mysterious, this little number keeps all the super men guessing. Pantalettes and gossamer wings complete the effect. **No. 634. ..... FREE**

**Ms Plum Blossom** Mandarin jacket, Capri pants, and chopsticks serve to outfit this thin but shapely look of indeterminately received cultural ideas. Slippers, too. **No. 635. .................... FREE**

**Pirate Man** Hotcha! Classy, girly, and mysterious, this little number keeps all the super men guessing. Pantalettes and gossamer sash complete the effect. **No. 636. ..... FREE**

## CLAY LUMP

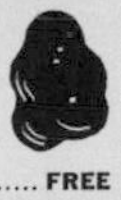

**SILTY EARTH** of a fine, compact texture and consistency, allowing for formation into any shape or figure. Make your own collectibles, imaginary friends, heroes, idols, or just let dry into a hard rock. Specify grey, red, brown, tan, or black.

**No. 74. Metaphor............................ FREE**

## PEN AND INK

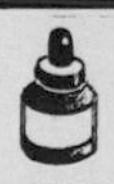

**THE STUFF** of religious doctrine, government charter, poetry, literature, love letters, **and** superhero comics. Particles of carbon and lampblack suspended in a solution of gum arabic and solvent will dry into a permanent time-tested tracing of any trembling hand or restless mind's search for meaning in cosmos. May also cause cancer.

**No.75. Spencerian Swish.................. FREE**

**Empire Comics and Novelties. New York, N. Y.**


9 781593 071714 51795

ISBN 1-59307-171-X


## BAR CODE

Inexplicable language of little thick and thin lines which has redefined commerce and menial labor since first instituted in 1975. **Amazingly** tells a central computer what you're buying, and where. **Allows** teenagers to work stoned or drunk while still enabling almost error-free collection of funds. Wow! **No. 1-559307-171-X. Irritating Little Lines. $17.95**

## MAIL FREE TRIAL COUPON NOW!

**EMPIRE COMICS, c/o Dark Horse Books,**
**10956 South East Main Street**
**Milwaukie, Oregon. 97222.**

Dear Sirs, please include all of the above items in my copy of "The Amazing Adventures of the Escapist." I realize that if I am not completely satisfied, I have absolutely no recourse whatsoever. I've paid $17.95.

Name ..........................................................................................

Address .............City ........... State ........ Age ... Sex .... Mother's Name .....

Annual income ..... Name of girl you were in love with in fourth grade.........

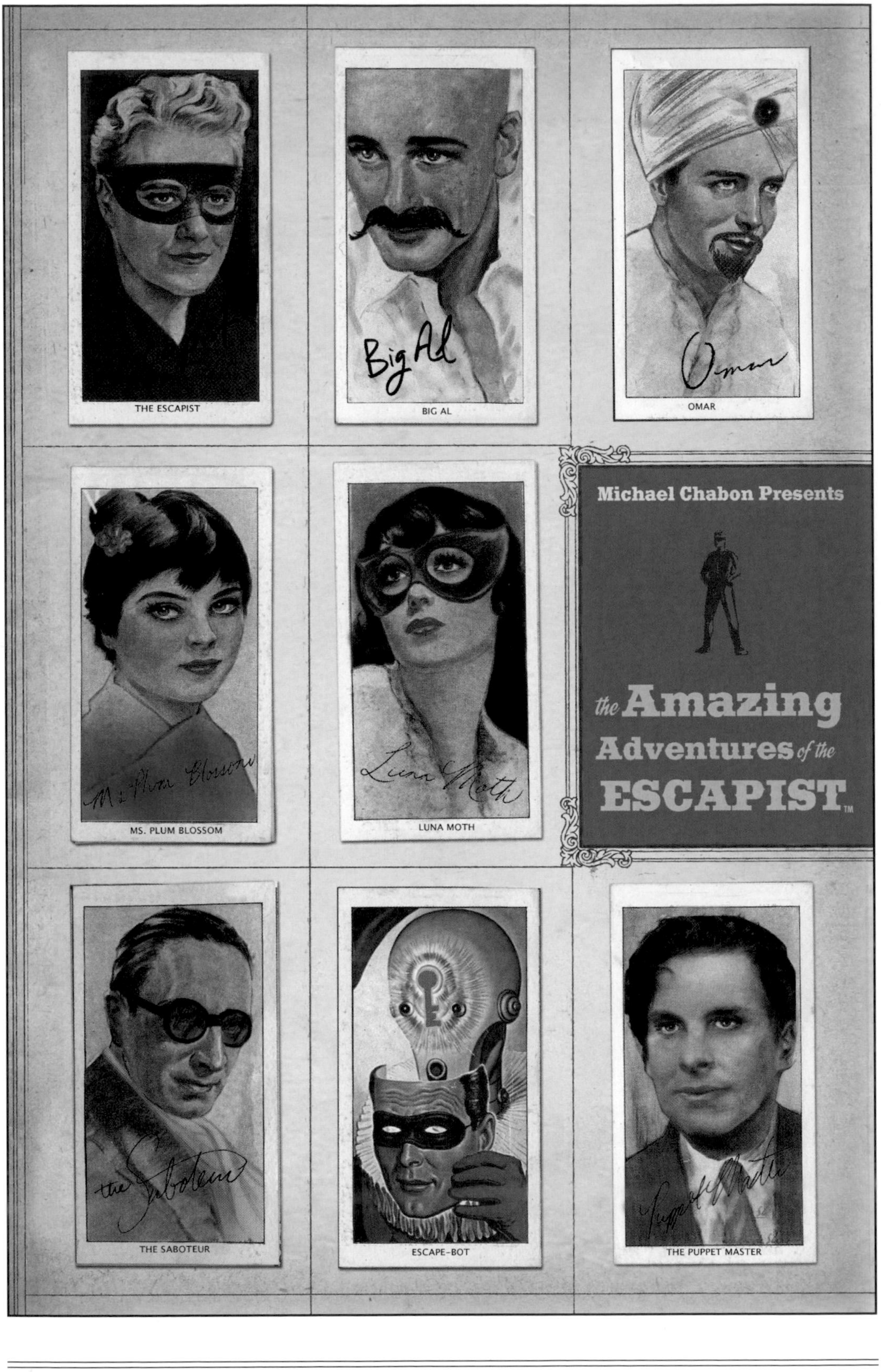
Big Al
Omar
THE ESCAPIST
BIG AL
OMAR
Michael Chabon Presents
the Amazing Adventures of the ESCAPIST™
MS. PLUM BLOSSOM
LUNA MOTH
THE SABOTEUR
ESCAPE-BOT
THE PUPPET MASTER

*On this page and the following*: front and back covers to *The Amazing Adventures of the Escapist* Volume 2 trade paperback, by Matt Kindt.

## STARS OF THE SCREEN

SERIES OF 8     Nº 3

**B**arry Lockwood (Metro-Goldwyn-Mayer). Lockwood grew up on a farm in Neath, Glamorgan, and was given his first film role at the age of six. As he grew into maturity, his roles became more limited due to audience expectations of him to be the tap-dancing, singing, curly-locked youth of the 1920s. However, since his role in "The Escapist and the Forty Thieves" he has made the character "Omar" his own.

ISSUED BY
**DARK HORSE L**ᵀᴰ
NEW YORK, ST. LOUIS, LOS ANGELES, MILWAUKIE

## STARS OF THE SCREEN

SERIES OF 8     Nº 2

**C**harles Massey (United Artists). Born in Racine, Wisconsin, Massey had his heart set on a musical career. His brutish good looks, however, would push him into stardom on the silver screen, playing a lovable brute in such film classics as "He Stalks at Night," "Meat-Hooks," and of course the fan-favorite "Big Al vs. Frankenstein's Monster." He enjoys playing the harp and violin.

ISSUED BY
**DARK HORSE L**ᵀᴰ
NEW YORK, ST. LOUIS, LOS ANGELES, MILWAUKIE

## STARS OF THE SCREEN

SERIES OF 8     Nº 1

**N**elson Mackay (London). Born in Karachi, India, in 1916, Nelson first gained fame in the stage production "The Escapist Melody" and has since starred as the voice of the Escapist in the popular radio plays and cinema serials. His latest films are "The Baby Vanishes," "Devil with a Halo," and "The Hotel Dick." His hobby is collecting antique furniture, and he enjoys sunning on the beach.

ISSUED BY
**DARK HORSE L**ᵀᴰ
NEW YORK, ST. LOUIS, LOS ANGELES, MILWAUKIE

---

$17.95

ISBN 1-59307-172-8

9 781593 071721

51795>

## STARS OF THE SCREEN

SERIES OF 8     Nº 5

**D**eana Hobson (London), the daughter of a Naval officer, was born in Larne, Ireland, in 1917 With aspirations to become a dancer, she moved to Hollywood, only to be discovered by the director of "The Escapist vs. the Mind-Bots." Her ethereal good looks have assured her a place in the pantheon of Luna Moth stars even as she moves on to other roles. Her next feature is "Scarface Justice."

ISSUED BY
**DARK HORSE L**ᵀᴰ
NEW YORK, ST. LOUIS, LOS ANGELES, MILWAUKIE

## STARS OF THE SCREEN

SERIES OF 8     Nº 4

**D**iana Fields. Born in 1927, Fields was presented with the Order of St. John of Jerusalem for her service to hospitals. This attention brought her the debut role as "Miss Plum Blossom" in the smash hit film "The Escapist vs. The Red and Yellow Menace." She has shattered all of the negative Asian stereotypes with her sympathetic turn in the Escapist films and is starring in her own feature this fall, "The Shanghai Traitor."

ISSUED BY
**DARK HORSE L**ᵀᴰ
NEW YORK, ST. LOUIS, LOS ANGELES, MILWAUKIE

---

## STARS OF THE SCREEN

SERIES OF 8     Nº 8

**M**alachi B. Cohen has long been known as a premier "comic book" historian. He has also worked silently behind the scenes as a script-doctor, quietly lending his talents to such Escapist classics as "Escapist vs. The Barbarians," "Who Escapes the Escapist?" and "The Prisoner of Zembla." Cohen made one small appearance as "The Puppet Master" in the classic film "Like a Moth to the Chains."

ISSUED BY
**DARK HORSE L**ᵀᴰ
NEW YORK, ST. LOUIS, LOS ANGELES, MILWAUKIE

## STARS OF THE SCREEN

SERIES OF 8     Nº 7

**A**nton Duprez (London). Born in London in 1903, he is a Shakespearean actor who has won countless stage awards. He is also an accomplished opera star and can be seen nightly at the Orpheum in London. But the role cinema fans worldwide most adore him for is "Escape-Bot," the lovable but misguided technological marvel from the future, as seen in "The Escapist: The Lady or the Robot?"

ISSUED BY
**DARK HORSE L**ᵀᴰ
NEW YORK, ST. LOUIS, LOS ANGELES, MILWAUKIE

## STARS OF THE SCREEN

SERIES OF 8     Nº 6

**G**eorge Wallbrook has a historied career in the cinema. Well known for his role as the cantankerous but lovable neighbor in the hit film "Boy Next Door," he is perhaps better known for his unforgettable turn as "The Saboteur." In a unique twist of fate he discovered Nelson Mackay, who would go on to co-star with him as the "Escapist." They have been best friends ever since and were even roommates at one time.

ISSUED BY
**DARK HORSE L**ᵀᴰ
NEW YORK, ST. LOUIS, LOS ANGELES, MILWAUKIE

# CREATOR BIOGRAPHIES

**MICHAEL CHABON** is the bestselling and Pulitzer Prize–winning author of *The Mysteries of Pittsburgh, A Model World, Wonder Boys, Werewolves in their Youth, The Amazing Adventures of Kavalier & Clay, Summerland, The Final Solution, The Yiddish Policemen's Union, Maps & Legends, Gentlemen of the Road, Telegraph Avenue, Moonglow,* and the picture book *The Astonishing Secret of Awesome Man.* He lives in Berkeley, California with his wife, the novelist Ayelet Waldman, and their children.

**KYLE BAKER** is an award-winning cartoonist, comic book writer/artist, and animator. He is known for his graphic novels, including *Why I Hate Saturn,* Nat Turner, and also contributions to *The Fifth Beatle: The Brian Epstein Story,* and for a revival of the classic series *Plastic Man.* He has won numerous Eisner and Harvey Awards for his work in the comics field. Baker has worked for such companies as Disney, Warner Bros. Animation, HBO, DreamWorks, Cartoon Network, Marvel Comics, DC Entertainment, RCA Records, Random House, Scholastic, and others.

**EDUARDO BARRETO** (1954–2011) began his career working on newspaper strips in his native Uruguay. An artist who enjoys international notoriety, Barreto rose to prominence in the US comic market in the 1980s. He is known for his work on such high-profile titles as *Batman, Superman, The New Teen Titans, Star Wars, Green Arrow, Daredevil,* and *Aliens/Predator.* Over the course of his career he worked for DC, Marvel, Archie Comics, Western Publishing, Dark Horse Comics, Oni Press, and a variety of newspaper and advertising companies.

**DAN BRERETON** burst into the comics scene just barely out of art school in 1989 with the award-winning miniseries *Black Terror* from Eclipse Comics. In the last twenty-five-plus years he's produced a prolific body of work, including his creation, *The Nocturnals,* and a run on DC's *Legends of the Dark Knight.* Brereton has been nominated many times for a variety of different industry and fan awards, and is an Inkpot Award winner. He lives in the California with his family and his many pets.

**HOWARD CHAYKIN** is responsible for some of the most innovative and influential comics of nearly the last half century, including *American Flagg!, Time(Squared), Black Kiss, Power & Glory,* and seminal work on books like *Star Wars* and *The Shadow.* In recent years Chaykin has created *Satellite Sam* with Matt Fraction, as well as *Midnight of the Soul,* both at Image Comics.

Bronx native **GENE COLAN** (1926–2011) has been a pillar of the comics industry since 1946, long associated with such popular characters as Dracula, Daredevil, Batman, Howard the Duck, Captain America, Wonder Woman, Sub-Mariner, Dr. Strange, Silver Surfer, and many others. Colan was comfortable illustrating numerous genres. He was a teacher at both the School of Visual Arts in Manhattan and the Fashion Institute of Technology.

**STEVE CONLEY** is an award-winning cartoonist and designer with a wide range of projects, both comics and otherwise. His comics work includes *Adventure Time, Star Trek: Year Four,* and the Eagle Award–winning *Astounding Space Thrills.* He has also developed websites and content for online publications *USA TODAY* and *The Washington Post,* and also *Comicon.com.* Steve has also worked in convention management, as the former Executive Director of Small Press Expo, and as a member of the Baltimore Comic-Con Advisory Board. His most recent project, *The Middle Age,* appears weekly online and was nominated for an Eisner Award in 2017.

Born in Split, Croatia, **ALEM ĆURIN** spent time at the Croatian National Theatre as a designer before moving into graphic design. Notably, he worked for newpapers *Nedjeljna Dalmacija*, as art director and illustrator, and *Feral Tribune*, as illustrator, in his native Split. Ćurin is also co-founder of the cultural newspaper *Torpedo*. He has continually worked in comics throughout his career; for his 2011 book *Egostriper* he worked both as illustrator and essayist.

**ALEX DE CAMPI** is a comics writer, columnist, and music video director. Notably, her first comics work, the 2005 miniseries *Smoke*, was nominated for a Best New Series Eisner Award. Other credits for De Campi include *Archie vs. Predator*, *Kat & Mouse*, and most recently, *Bankshot*. Her science fiction series, *Grindhouse*, has been described as "groundbreaking" by The British Science Fiction Association's Journal.

An artist who started his illustration career in the Xerox jungle of zines and minicomics, **JED DOUGHERTY** currently works as a painter of Amazonian women and as one of Howard Chaykin's studio assistants. The Luna Moth story in this collection was his first mainstream comics work. Other comics credits include *Batman Eternal*, *Glory*, and *Harley Quinn*.

**MICHAEL T. GILBERT** began his work in comics in the early 1970s with his self-published work *New Paltz Comix*, and quickly began to work for independent publishers Kitchen Sink Press and Star Reach, among others. Gilbert has worked on titles such as *American Splendor* with Harvey Pekar, *Elric* with P. Craig Russell, *Harlan Ellison's Dream Corridor*, and his own *Doc Stearn . . . Mr. Monster* title, and has written or drawn a diverse list of characters including, Batman, Superman, Donald Duck, Mickey Mouse, and Bart Simpson. In 2014 Gilbert was presented with an Inkpot Award for his work in the comics industry.

**GLEN DAVID GOLD** is an American author of screenplays, memoirs, news articles, and short stories. He is known for his novels, *Carter Beats the Devil* and *Sunnyside*. Gold's short stories and essays have appeared in *McSweeney's*, *Playboy*, and *The New York Times*.

Emmy Award-winning artist **DEAN HASPIEL** has worked on a variety of comics in both print and web formats. A regular contributor to Harvey Pekar's *American Splendor*, his credits include *The Alcoholic*, *Cuba, My Revolution*, *The Quitter*, and his webcomic *The Red Hook*. He won his Emmy for his main title design for the HBO series *Bored to Death*. Haspiel can be found in Brooklyn, New York.

The Ignatz, Eisner, and Harvey Award–nominated creator of *Forlorn Funnies*, **PAUL HORNSCHEMEIR** began to have an interest in comics in college. Hornschemeier is an artist, author and director. He has created illustration and prose that has appeared in publications such as *Life Magazine*, *The Wall Street Journal*, and *McSweeney's*; and he has worked in film and television writing, animation, and direction. Currently he is working on writing, directing, producing, and animating his own short film, *Giant Sloth*.

**KEN KRISTENSEN** is a Los Angeles-based writer and producer. His screenwriting credits include the series *The Punisher* for Marvel/Netflix, and *Happy!* for SyFy. A lifelong comic book junkie, Kristensen has also written numerous comics, such as *Todd, The Ugliest Kid on Earth* with Image Comics, *Indestructible* with IDW, and recently, *Fairy Godbrothers* from Adaptive Studios.

Graphic designer and illustrator **TONY LEONARD** has been drawing comics since his teens, having been weaned at an early age on cult films, Eurocomics, and hardboiled Japanese manga. He also worked on a comic adaption of Shakespeare's *Macbeth* with writer Kevin McCarthy.

**STEVE LIEBER** a comic book illustrator and storyboard artist in Portland, Oregon. His work has been been published by DC, Marvel, Dark Horse, Image, Oni, and many others. He has worked on numerous characters, including Batman, Spider-Man, and Hellboy. Lieber is known for his Oni Press series *Whiteout* and its sequel *Melt*, the two of which were made into a major motion picture. He is also a founding member of Helioscope Studio, the largest studio of freelance comics and storyboard artists in North America. His most recent work can be seen in *The Fix* from Image Comics.

Ohio native **VAL MAYERIK** broke into comics in 1972 and has worked alongside the likes of P. Craig Russell, Howard Chaykin, Walt Simonson, Jim Starlin, and Neal Adams. He is the co-creator of Howard the Duck with Steve Gerber. Mayerik has concentrated most of his career in the advertising industry, but he also is a painter of western art, and, as well, continues to work in comics—most recently his original graphic novel titled *Of Dust and Blood*.

**KEVIN MCCARTHY** began working as a comic book writer and artist in 1995 when he created *Casual Heroes*. Since then, in addition to several tales of The Escapist and Luna Moth, his work can be found in Marvel's *Spider-Man Team-Up*, DC's *Orion*, Top Cow's *Laura Croft: Tomb Raider*, and most recently his creation with Kyle Baker, *Circuit-Breaker*, at Image Comics.

**STUART MOORE** is a writer and comics and book editor. He was the founding editor of DC's Vertigo imprint. Recent comics writing includes *Deadpool the Duck*, *Dominion the Last Sacrifice*, and *EGOs*. In his career he has worked with such characters and titles as The X-Men, Batman, Spider-Man, Star Trek, and Transformers. Moore is also a writer of prose for publishers including Disney and Marvel, and currently is freelance editor for Marvel Comics' prose novel line. He lives in Brooklyn, New York, with his wife, author Liz Sonneborn.

A California native, **C. SCOTT MORSE** is an Eisner and Ignatz Award–nominated comics writer, artist, filmmaker, and animator. He has contributed to the animation industry as a character designer, storyboard artist, and art director for studios including Disney, PIXAR, Universal, and Cartoon Network. His graphic novels include *Soulwind*, *Ancient Joe*, *Spaghetti Western*, *Southpaw*, *Visitations*, *The Barefoot Serpent*, and the Magic Pickle series.

**JAMES PEATY** is a United Kingdom-based writer / director who has contributed to various comics titles, such as *2000 AD*, *Doctor Who*, *Green Arrow*, and *Supergirl*. He also wrote and directed the short film, *The Appraisal*, in 2012.

Comic book writer, music critic, media personality, and file clerk, **HARVEY PEKAR** (1939–2010) is most well known for the autobiographical comic book series, *American Splendor*, which was later adapted to film in 2003. Other works from Pekar include more autobiographical and biographical works such as *The Quitter*, *Ego & Hubris: The Michael Malice Story*, *Macedonia*, *The Beats*, and *The Pekar Project*.

Turkish-born cartoonist **M.K. PERKER** has worked extensively in both comics and illustration. He was nominated for an Eisner Award for his work on the series *Air*, as well as contributing art for such books as *The Unwritten*, *Insomnia Café*, and *Cairo*. Perker has produced illustrations for publications such as *The New York Times*, *The Wall Street Journal*, *The Washington Post*, and others, including numerous magazines in his native Turkey.

The grandson of EC Comics great George Evans, **ROGER PETERSEN** was raised on *Tintin*, *Johnny Hazard*, and Bob Hope movies, he has worked in advertising and illustration for all kinds of clients. In addition to The Escapist story in this issue, Peterson has drawn covers and cards for Marvel, *Swamp Thing* for DC, and *Predator: Kindered* and *SubHuman* for Dark Horse Comics.

**BILL SIENKIEWICZ** has earned many awards for his innovative methods of collage and illustration, including a Kirby Award for Best Artist for *Elektra: Assassin*, a collaboration with Frank Miller, and an Eisner Award for his contributions to the anthology *The Sandman: Endless Nights*. He wrote and illustrated the critically acclaimed *Stray Toasters*, and has been exhibited throughout the world. Sienkiewicz has also produced work for magazines, CD and book covers, television, trading cards, and the US Olympics.

**JIM STARLIN**, a luminary in the comics industry for many years, has created dozens of characters and has written or drawn almost every classic hero from DC and Marvel. Working off and on with comics since 1972, Starlin's credits include *The Amazing Spider-Man*, *Batman*, *Captain Marvel*, *Daredevil/Black Widow: Abattoir*, *Doctor Strange*, *Iron Man*, *Silver Surfer*, *The Infinity Gauntlet*, *Warlock*, and *The End* of the Marvel Universe. In 2017, Starlin was inducted into the Eisner Award Hall of Fame.

**BRIAN K. VAUGHAN** is a multi-award-winning comics and television writer and producer. He has written for several of Marvel's and DC's premier titles, including *Ultimate X-Men* and *Runaways*, and Dark Horse Comics's *Buffy the Vampire Slayer* Season 8; and he has created many of his own titles including *Ex Machina*, *Y: The Last Man*, *Saga* with Fiona Staples, and *Paper Girls*. Vaughan continues to write *Saga* and *Paper Girls*, both released through Image Comics, and most recently he released *Barrier* with Panel Syndicate.

Before venturing into comics, **ERIC WIGHT** worked as a professional animator on such projects as *Superman*, *Batman Beyond*, and the proposed *Buffy the Vampire Slayer* cartoon. In addition, his art has been featured on *The O.C.* and *Six Feet Under*. His comics work includes the manga *My Dead Girlfriend*, as well as the series *Frankie Pickle*. He is based in Bucks County, Pennsylvania.

Eisner Award–nominated artist **PHIL WINSLADE** studied art at Birmingham Polytechnic. His comics resume includes *Crisis*, *Revolver*, *Car Warriors*, *Skin Tight Orbit*, *The Red Seas*, all from Epic Comics, *Goddess* with Garth Ennis from Vertigo, and a variety of DC titles like *Howard the Duck*, *The Flush*, *Daredevil/Spider-Man*, *Legends of the Dark Knight*, *Wonder Woman*, and many others.

# Look for these other titles to complete your collection of Michael Chabon's The Escapist!

## MICHAEL CHABON'S
## THE ESCAPIST: PULSE-POUNDING THRILLS

Collected in this comic book anthology are a multitude of the Escapist's amazing exploits, and details on the history of the character—and it includes and encounter with Will Eisner's *The Spirit*!

ISBN 978-1-50670-406-7 | $24.99 US

## MICHAEL CHABON'S
## THE ESCAPISTS

The story of three aspiring comics creators with big dreams, small cash, and publishing rights to once forgotten Golden Age hero—The Escapist—is writer Brian K. Vaughan's love letter to his chosen medium. The lives of Max, Denny, and Case—latter day versions of Joe Kavalier and Sam Clay—are brilliantly woven together with the world of their creations.

ISBN 978-1-50670-403-6 | $19.99 US

Available at your local comics shop or bookstore
To find a comics shop in your area, visit comicshoplocator.com.

 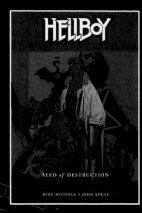  

# CREATIVE GIANTS!

**GET YOUR FIX OF DARK HORSE BOOKS FROM THESE INSPIRED CREATORS!**

## MESMO DELIVERY SECOND EDITION - Rafael Grampá

Eisner Award–winning artist Rafael Grampá (*5*, *Hellblazer*) makes his full-length comics debut with the critically acclaimed graphic novel *Mesmo Delivery*—a kinetic, bloody romp starring Rufo, an ex-boxer; Sangrecco, an Elvis impersonator; and a ragtag crew of overly confident drunks who pick the wrong delivery men to mess with.

ISBN 978-1-61655-457-6 | $14.99

## SIN TITULO - Cameron Stewart

Following the death of his grandfather, Alex Mackay discovers a mysterious photograph in the old man's belongings that sets him on an adventure like no other—where dreams and reality merge, family secrets are laid bare, and lives are irrevocably altered.

ISBN 978-1-61655-248-0 | $19.99

## DE:TALES - Fábio Moon and Gabriel Bá

Brazilian twins Fábio Moon and Gabriel Bá's (*Daytripper*, *Pixu*) most personal work to date. Brimming with all the details of human life, their charming tales move from the urban reality of their home in São Paulo to the magical realism of their Latin American background.

ISBN 978-1-59582-557-5 | $19.99

## THE TRUE LIVES OF THE FABULOUS KILLJOYS - Gerard Way, Shaun Simon, and Becky Cloonan

Years ago, the Killjoys fought against the tyrannical megacorporation Better Living Industries. Today, the followers of the original Killjoys languish in the desert and the fight for freedom fades. It's left to the Girl to take down BLI!

ISBN 978-1-59582-462-2 | $19.99

## DEMO - Brian Wood and Becky Cloonan

It's hard enough being a teenager. Now try being a teenager with *powers*. A chronicle of the lives of young people on separate journeys to self-discovery in a world—just like our own—where being different is feared.

ISBN 078 1 61655 682 2 | $24.00

## SABERTOOTH SWORDSMAN - Damon Gentry and Aaron Conley

When his village is enslaved and his wife kidnapped by the malevolent Mastodon Mathematician, a simple farmer must find his inner warrior—the Sabertooth Swordsman!

ISBN 078 1 61655 176 6 | $17.99

## JAYBIRD - Jaakko and Lauri Ahonen

Disney meets Kafka in this beautiful, intense, original tale! A very small, very scared little bird lives an isolated life in a great big house with his infirm mother. He's never been outside the house, and he never will if his mother has anything to say about it.

ISBN 978-1-61655-469-9 | $19.99

## MONSTERS! & OTHER STORIES - Gustavo Duarte

Newcomer Gustavo Duarte spins wordless tales inspired by Godzilla, King Kong, and Pixar, brimming with humor, charm, and delightfully twisted horror!

ISBN 978-1-61655-309-8 | $12.99

## SACRIFICE - Sam Humphries and Dalton Rose

What happens when a troubled youth is plucked from modern society and thrust though time and space into the heart of the Aztec civilization—one of the most bloodthirsty times in human history?

ISBN 978-1-59582-985-6 | $19.99

COMICS & GRAPHIC NOVELS / LITERARY

**Withdrawn**

# MICHAEL CHABON'S The ESCAPIST™

## AMAZING ADVENTURES

In the fictional world of the Pulitzer Prize–winning novel, *The Amazing Adventures of Kavalier & Clay*, The Escapist—master of elusion, foe of tyranny, and epitome of Golden-Age superhero—was conceived. This comic book anthology is a collection of the hero's exploits and his history, created by an all-star cast of comic book luminaries.

The Escapist and his associates are heroes to all who languish in oppression's chains. They roam the globe, performing amazing feats to foil diabolical evildoers. From preventing a prison break and attack on Empire City, to facing a demonic horde in Japan, to crushing a galactic takeover in the year 2966, and to surfacing a sunken submarine from three hundred fathoms, The Escapist brings hope and liberation. As the history of his creators, Joe Kavalier and Sam Clay, was chronicled in *The Amazing Adventures of Kavalier & Clay*, now a multitude of The Escapist's adventures are collected here, along with the patchwork publishing history of the character. This volume also contains the adventures of The Escapist's colleague, Luna Moth.

Collecting a total of twenty-six tales, along with two never-before-collected stories, this volume also includes six never-before-published stories, as well as a robust gallery of pinups celebrating the world of The Escapist!

*All-star creators within this amazing volume:*

KYLE BAKER   EDUARDO BARRETO   BRIAN BOLLAND   DAN BRERETON   JOHN CASSADAY
MICHAEL CHABON   HOWARD CHAYKIN   GENE COLAN   STEVE CONLEY   COLLEEN COOVER
ALEM ĆURIN   ALEX DE CAMPI   FAREL DALRYMPLE   JED DOUGHERTY   MICHAEL T. GILBERT
GLEN DAVID GOLD   DAVID HAHN   DEAN HASPIEL   PAUL HORNSCHEMEIER   JOËLLE JONES
MATT KINDT   KEN KRISTENSEN   JAE LEE   TONY LEONARD   STEVE LIEBER   VAL MAYERIK
KEVIN MCCARTHY   MIKE MIGNOLA   STUART MOORE   C. SCOTT MORSE   JEFF PARKER
JAMES PEATY   HARVEY PEKAR   M.K. PERKER   ROGER PETERSON   JILL KARLA SCHWARTZ
BILL SIENKIEWICZ   JOHN K. SNYDER III   JIM STARLIN   BRIAN K. VAUGHAN   CHRIS WARE
CHRIS WARNER   ERIC WIGHT   PHIL WINSLADE

$24.99 US
$33.99 CAN
DarkHorse.com

DARK HORSE BOOKS®

ISBN 978-1-50670-405-0

9 781506 704050   52499>